THE REAL STORY
&
FORBIDDEN KNOWLEDGE

D0920452

The Gap Into Conflict and The Gap Into Vision

THE REAL STORY
&
FORBIDDEN KNOWLEDGE

STEPHEN
DONALDSON

Copyright © Stephen R. Donaldson 1991
All rights reserved

The right of Stephen R. Donaldson to
be identified as the author of this work has
been asserted by him in accordance with
the Copyright, Designs and Patents Act 1988.

This edition published in Great Britain in 2008 by
Gollancz
An imprint of the Orion Publishing Group
Orion House, 5 Upper St Martin's Lane,
London WC2H 9EA
An Hachette Livre UK Company

1 3 5 7 9 10 8 6 4 2

A CIP catalogue record for this book is
available from the British Library

ISBN 978 0 575 08334 9

Typeset by Input Data Services Ltd
Bridgwater, Somerset

Printed in Great Britain by
CPI Mackays, Chatham ME5 8TD

www.orionbooks.co.uk

The Orion Publishing Group's policy is to use
papers that are natural, renewable and recyclable
products and made from wood grown in sustainable
forests. The logging and manufacturing processes
are expected to conform to the environmental
regulations of the country of origin.

LUTON LIBRARIES	
939006739	
F	24/11/2008
	07 FEB 2009

To my best editors:
Anne Lesley Groell
Jennifer Hershey
Susan Allison
Jo Fletcher

and

To Colin Baker:
Who knows how much good he's done me?

THE REAL STORY

CHAPTER 1

Most of the crowd at Mallorys Bar & Sleep over in Delta Sector had no idea what was really going on. As far as they were concerned, it was just another example of animal passion, men and women driven together by lust – the kind of thing everybody understood, or at least dreamed about. The only uncommon feature was that in this case the passion included some common sense. Only a few people knew there was more to it.

Curiosity wasn't a survival trait in DelSec; it certainly wasn't the pleasure it might have been in Alpha, Com-Mine Station's alternative entertainment/lodging Sector. Laidover miners, discredited asteroid pilots, drunks and dreamers, and a number of men who never admitted to being ore pirates – the people who either didn't fit or weren't welcome in Alpha – all had learned incuriosity the hard way. They considered themselves too smart to ask the wrong questions in the wrong places, to notice the wrong things at the wrong times. None of them wanted trouble.

For them, the story was basically simple.

It began when Morn Hyland came into Mallorys with Angus Thermopyle.

Those two called attention to themselves because they obviously didn't belong together. Except for her ill-fitting and outdated shipsuit, which she must have scrounged from someone else's locker, she was gorgeous, with a body that made drunks groan in lost yearning and a pale, delicate beauty of face that twisted dreamers' hearts. In contrast, he was dark and disreputable, probably the most disreputable man who still had docking-rights at the Station. His swarthy features were broad and stretched, a frog-face with stiff whiskers and streaks of grease. Between his powerful arms and scrawny legs, his middle bulged like a tire, inflated with bile and malice.

In fact, no one knew how he had been able to keep his docking-rights – or his tincan freighter, for that matter – as long as he had. According to his reputation, anyone who ever became his companion, crew, or enemy ended up either dead or in lockup. Most people who knew him predicted he would end up that way himself – dead, or in lockup until he rotted.

He and Morn looked so grotesque together – she staying with him despite the clear disgust on her face, he ordering her around like a slavey with his yellowish eyes gleaming – that none of the men nearby could resist a little harmless scheming, a bit of gap-eyed speculation. If I could get her away from him— If she were mine— But the story was just beginning. No one was surprised by the nearly tangible current which sparked across the crowd when she and Nick Succorso spotted each other for the first time.

In a number of ways, Nick Succorso was the most desirable man in DelSec. He had his own ship, a sleek little frigate with a gap drive and an experienced crew. He had the kind of piratical reputation that allowed him to seem bold rather than bloodthirsty. His personal magnetism made men do what he asked and women offer what he wanted. And the only flaws in his cavalier handsomeness were the scars under his eyes, the cuts which underlined everything he saw and grew dark whenever he saw something he intended to have. Some people said he'd inflicted those cuts himself, just for effect – but that was merely envy and spite. No one could be as desirable as Nick without inspiring a few snide remarks.

The truth was that he'd received those scars years ago, the only time he'd ever been bested. They'd been put on him to mar him, a sign of contempt for his upstart arrogance: the woman who gave them to him hadn't considered him worth killing.

But he'd learned from them. He'd learned never to be beaten again; learned to make sure that all his contests were unequal, in his favor. He'd learned to wait until he was in control of what happened. Common sense.

Members of his crew later admitted that they'd never seen his scars go as dark as when he spotted Morn Hyland. And her pale beauty ached toward him instantly – passion or desperation – bringing brightness to eyes which were dull in Angus Thermopyle's company. The only surprise was that neither of them did anything about it. The electricity between them was so strong that the spectators wouldn't have been taken aback if Morn and Nick had thrown off their clothes and jumped for each other right there in the bar.

Most of the crowd had no idea what restrained them. She was a mystery, of course. But he certainly didn't have a reputation for restraint.

Nearly two weeks later, however, they did what everyone was waiting for. When Com-Mine Security broke into Mallorys and charged Angus Thermopyle with a crime serious enough to make an arrest succeed even in DelSec, Morn Hyland was suddenly at Nick's side. And just as suddenly they were gone. Lust and common sense. Their charged flesh drew them together; and she got away from Angus at just the right moment. They left to become the kind of story drunks and dreamers told each other early in the Station's standard morning, when Mallorys was quiet and the thin alloy walls seemed safe against the hard vacuum of space and the luring madness of the gap.

The last anyone heard, Angus was rotting as predicted under a life sentence in the Station lockup.

That, of course, was not the real story.

CHAPTER 2

Some of the people who lurked in the dim light knew better. They were the ones in the corners who drank less than they appeared to, smoked less, talked less. Pushing their mugs around in the condensation which oozed off the plastic because the air processing in DelSec was never as good as it should be and nobody could sit in Mallorys without sweating, these men knew how to listen, how to ask questions, how to interpret what they saw – and when to go somewhere else for information.

Most of them were a bit older, a bit less self-absorbed; perhaps a bit more profound in their cynicism. If they were pilots, they were here because this was the life they could afford and understand, not because drink or drugs, incompetence or misjudgment, had cost them their careers. If they were miners who couldn't get or no longer wanted work, they were here to stay near the taste and dreams of prospecting, the vision of a strike so vast and pure that it was better than being rich. If they were born or naturalized inhabitants of the Station, they were here to keep company with the clientele for their particular goods or services – or perhaps to keep tabs on the market for the whispers and hints they purveyed.

Such people looked at what they saw with more discerning eyes.

When Morn Hyland and Angus Thermopyle came into Mallorys, the men in the corners noticed the way her whole body seemed to twist away even when she sat close beside him. They heard the dull, almost lifeless sound of her voice when she spoke – a tone of suppression unexpected from someone who had presumably spent weeks or months away from people and drink. And they observed that he kept one hand constantly fisted in the pocket of his grease-stained shipsuit.

After Angus took her out, some of these men also left – but not to follow. Instead, they went to have unassuming, apparently casual conversations with people who had access to the id files in Com-Mine Station's computers.

The story they gleaned concerned something more interesting than animal passion and common sense.

By one means or another, they learned that there was a perfectly reasonable explanation for the fact that Morn Hyland wasn't known in DelSec. She'd never been there before. During her one previous layover on Com-Mine, she'd stayed in AlSec.

She'd come out from Earth on one of the really wealthy independent oreliners, a family operation so successful that she and all her relatives did everything first class because they could afford it. Crossing the gap, the Hylands had docked at Com-Mine Station, not to pick up company ore for the orbiting smelters around Earth, but to buy supplies: they were headed for the belt themselves. And since they weren't experienced miners and had never been out to the belt before, there could only be one explanation for what they were doing. Somewhere they had bought or stolen the location of an asteroid rich enough to tempt them away from their usual runs. They had caught the dream themselves and were on their way to test it against the bitter rock of the belt.

A common tale, as far as it went. Back on Earth, civilization and political power required ore. Without the resources which Stations like Com-Mine supplied, no government could maintain itself in office. By some standards, the United Mining Companies, Com-Mine's corporate founder, was the only effective government in human space. As a natural consequence, every city or Station of any size spawned at least one earnest, spurious, or reprobate dealer in belt charts, the treasure maps of space. Men and women with some kind of hunger in their bellies were forever buying 'accurate,' 'secret' charts and then risking everything to cross the gap and go prospecting.

But not a successful outfit like the Hyland family. If they left a profitable ore-transportation business and converted their liner for mining, two things were certain.

They had a chart.

The chart was good.

AlSec must have been on fire with that kind of news. Otherwise DelSec would never have heard about it. Specifically, Angus would never have heard about it. As a general rule, the snobs, corporate barons, government officials, intellectuals, and high-class illegals who frequented AlSec didn't share information with the denizens of Delta Sector. And Angus Thermopyle had probably never been in AlSec in his life.

Human nature being what it was, greed and a casual indifference to scruple would have inspired any number of mine jumpers or pirates to follow the Hyland ship, *Starmaster*, when she left Com-Mine Station. But jumpers and pirates had harried Com-Mine's legitimate prospectors and liners for so long – and the battles which took place as outgoing ships fought to keep from being followed had become so fierce – that now the Station itself as a matter of policy fired on any ship which tried to pursue any other ship out of dock. To all appearances, the Hylands got away safely.

Appearances must have deceived them, however. Or else they were simply outsmarted. They had no experience with the belt, or mining, or jumpers, or pirates. And Angus Thermopyle had become as rich as the stars without ever doing a lick of honest work – and without ever having to share his wealth with any partners, backers, or crew. The Hyland ship never came back.

But Morn Hyland came back.

She came back with Angus. With a dull, almost lifeless tone to her voice, and an air of being repulsed by his physical closeness.

And he kept one fist knotted like a threat in the pocket of his shipsuit.

The men who observed these things had no other way to account for them, so they jumped to the one conclusion which made sense to them; a conclusion which suited both Angus' reputation and their own cynicism.

Without any viable external evidence, they chose to believe that he'd given her a zone-implant. He had the control in his pocket.

Zone implants were illegal, of course. They were so illegal that unauthorized use carried the death penalty. But – also of course – mere questions of legality didn't stop people who worked the belt from having them on hand for emergencies.

In essence, a zone-implant was a radio electrode which could be slipped between one of the skull sutures and installed in the brain, where its emissions were remarkably effective. It had been invented by a doctor trying to control grand mal epileptic seizures: its emissions blanked out the neural storm of the seizure. People thought that was where the name

nothing personal, of course. He hated everything. He hated
ly. The people who watched for such things could smell it on
s life was a stew of hate, destructive and unpredictable. Now his
fixed on her, and he desired the thing he hated. He wanted her
at only a zone-implant could make her.
iful and revolted. Capable of any degradation his filthy appetites
nceive – and able to be hurt by it.

ew men in Mallorys who realized what they considered the
out her were sickened by it. Being of various moral characters
es, some of them probably considered it evil. The rest no doubt
ed it evil that the control to her implant was in Angus Ther-
pocket.

s subject, Nick Succorso kept his opinion to himself. Perhaps
tion to Morn was so strong that he didn't think about anything

e his attraction, however, and his reputation for success, he was
restrained from immediate action by the prospect of what
ght do if he were challenged. To Morn Hyland, of course. But
oever challenged him. He had a history of getting rid of his
So instead of leaping to her rescue, Nick waited and plotted.
ave been a criminal or a rogue hero, an operative or a mer-
t he certainly wasn't stupid. And he had no taste at all for

e wanted – so the discerning cynics assumed – was to have
sted by Security with the control to Morn's zone-implant in
. Angus would get the death penalty; the implant would be
nd then Morn Hyland would be free to give Nick Succorso
ward he could possibly want.

part to arrange for Angus to be arrested. He wasn't an
. Piracy, treachery, and murder were what he did best.
less Nick arranged it.
in, the only explanations available were purely speculative.
on lockup, Angus wasn't talking to anybody. And Nick Suc-
s crew were gone, taking Morn Hyland with them. But here
was on fairly solid ground. Knowing Nick, it was possible to
onsiderable confidence what he would do.

'zone' came from: an active implant gave an epileptic the look of being
'completely zoned.' But in fact medical research had quickly discovered
that a variety of results could be obtained by varying the implant's
emissions – by tuning the implant to different zones of the brain. Violent
insanities could be tamed. Manic behaviors could be moderated. Catatonia could be relieved – or induced. Recalcitrance could be turned into
cooperation. Pain could be reinterpreted as pleasure.

Volition could be suppressed. Without interrupting consciousness or
coordination.

Given a broad-spectrum zone-implant, which employed several electrodes, and an unscrupulous control operator, independent human beings
could be transformed into intelligent, effective, and loyal slaves. Even the
more common, narrower-spectrum implants could achieve comparable
results by turning people into physical puppets, or by applying intense
neural punishments and rewards.

Unauthorized use of a zone-implant carried the death penalty automatically, inevitably; without appeal.

But despite the law – and the possibilities of abuse – even otherwise
reputable miners and pilots, orehaulers and -handlers, considered zone-
implants necessary medical equipment.

The reason was simple. Medical science had developed ways for complete idiots to diagnose and treat complex diseases; ways for lost or vision-
struck belt pilots to repair the damage done to their bodies by faulty or
inadequate equipment; ways for crushed limbs and even crushed organs to
be prosthetically restored. Unfortunately, however, no amount of research
had discovered a cure for gap-sickness, that strange breakdown of the mind
which took perhaps one out of every hundred people who crossed the
dimensional gap and reduced him or her to a psychotic killer or a null-
wave transmitter, a raving bulimic or a gleeful self-flagellant, a pedophiliac
or a pill-junkie. Apparently, one out of every hundred people had some
kind of undetectable vulnerability in the tissue of the brain; and when
that vulnerability was translated across light-years of space through the
imponderable physics of the gap, something happened to it. Otherwise
healthy individuals lost command of their lives in invariably startling, often
grotesque, and sometimes murderous fashions.

There was no cure for gap-sickness. But there was a way to cope with
it.

The zone-implant.

Ships and prospecting and mining operations were too fragile: every individual's life depended on everybody else. For that reason, perfectly sane and law-abiding people considered it an unacceptable risk to cross the gap or ride dark space without access to zone implants. Just in case the person standing right over there suddenly picked up a hose and started to spray mineral acid in all directions.

'Authorized use' of a zone-implant occurred when the whole crew of a ship or the entire population of a mining camp testified that they would all have died if they hadn't used the implant to control a case of gap-sickness – and when the person with the implant confirmed that he or she hadn't been deprived of volition in any other situations.

The UMC Police enforced the principle of 'authorized use' with almost gleeful impartiality.

In part for that reason, actual, proven cases of abuse were rare. But there were always stories. So-and-so hit a rich strike on an asteroid so far away that it was off the charts, so far away that he and his crew didn't have enough provisions to stay and mine it – a problem he solved by giving everyone else zone-implants and making them work without food or water or sleep until they died. Such-and-such was prospecting alone and contrived to smash his leg with his ship's cargo boom; in pain and delirious, he neglected normal medical treatment and instead supplied himself with a zone-implant in order to change the pain into pleasure – with the result that he became so happy he lost his mind and bled to death.

What the men in the bars and sleeps of DelSec talked about most often, however, was women. Women were rare on mining Stations. Single women were even rarer. And available women were so rare that they were prohibitively expensive; which meant that most of them lived in AlSec. Men with nothing better to do rarely thought about anything else. Gorgeous women. Astonishing women. Women with zone-implants, who did everything a drink-fuddled or cynical mind could imagine. Because they didn't have any choice, no matter how much they may have hated what was happening to them.

Women like Morn Hyland.

So what must have happened was that Angus Thermopyle found a way to follow the Hyland ship when it left Com-Mine Station.

After all, who knew how much sophisticate
had hidden away aboard his scruffy, rattletra
mines he was said to have jumped, all the or
pirated, all the ships he was reputed to ha
resources must have been enormous. He coul
which even a successful swashbuckler like N
drool. Obviously, he wasn't spending the mo
who had to sit near him in Mallorys would hav
his shipsuit since the invention of the gap driv
sive drinks – or more than a few cheap ones
bought expensive women. As for his ship, w
inapt name, *Bright Beauty*, no one ever saw i
plate and ports and antennae and scanners
driven through a meteor shower and then l
only discernible care he took of her – the on
any interest in her at all – was to keep her n
black letters on either side of her command

What was he doing with all that money?

What else? He must be investing it in hi
the kind of vacuum sniffers and particle sift
most pilots who frequented Com-Mine S
rumor; the kind of equipment which wou
Hyland ship without making either her or
There were still questions unanswered.
size of *Bright Beauty* needed at least two pe
her. Assuming that Morn Hyland worked
must still have had a crew of some kind wh
Who was it? Presumably, it must have bee
to get on and off Com-Mine Station with
Beauty had no crew of record in the co
him? Or them?

What happened to the Hyland ship an

No one knew. But Angus Thermopy
their strike. He must have jumped then
marooned or murdered the family. And
persuasion of the zone-implant she was

Because – so speculation ran – he hat

It wa
everybo
him. Hi
hate wa
to be wl

Beaut
could co

The
truth al
themsel
consider
mopyle

On tl
his attra
else.

Despi
probably

Angus r
also to w
enemies.

He may
cenary; l
defeat.

What
Angus ar
his pocke
removed;
the only r

Herself
The ha
easy victin
Neverth
Once ag
In the Stat
corso and
speculatior
guess with

His background was vague. His id files managed to look both perfectly legitimate and plainly spurious, revealing nothing. All most people knew was that one day he docked his pretty frigate, *Captain's Fancy*, in Com-Mine Station, passed inspection, led his crew into DelSec, selected Mallorys Bar & Sleep apparently at random, and became a regular whenever he was on station. Only the men in the corners, the men who pried below the surface, heard how he had passed inspection.

Being neither asleep nor blind, the Station inspectors had noticed almost immediately that *Captain's Fancy* had a hole the size of a gaming table in her side.

You've been hit, they said. That looks like matter cannon fire.

It is, he replied.

Why were you being shot at?

I wasn't.

No? The inspectors suggested intense skepticism.

No. I was trying to get inside one of those awkward asteroids – too small for heavy equipment, too big to be chewed up by hand-cutters. So I decided to try blasting it apart. Somehow, the beam dispersion hit a glazed surface and reflected back. Nick grinned amiably. I shot myself.

That doesn't sound very plausible, Captain Succorso. Hand over your computer's datacore, and we'll verify your story.

No, he said again. Now his grin didn't look so amiable. I'm not required to let you look at my datacore unless you have evidence of a crime. That's the law. Has there been a crime?

In the end, Nick passed. The ship that shot him must have been burned out of space in return, so it was never able to report that a crime had been committed.

Smiling to make DelSec's women's hearts flutter, basking in the devotion of his crew, and spending money as if he had a UMC credit line, he settled into Mallorys and concentrated on enjoying himself while *Captain's Fancy* was repaired. He seemed to have a talent for enjoying himself, and his good humor – like his unmistakable virility – was infectious. Only people who watched the scars under his eyes could tell that he was engaged in anything more serious than a continuous carouse. And in Mallorys that 'anything' could be only one thing: he was listening, sifting, sorting, evaluating; making contact with sources of information.

Whenever he left Com-Mine Station, he left suddenly. And when he came back, he celebrated.

By some coincidence, unfamiliar ships had a tendency to go 'overdue' while he was away.

Even a null-wave transmitter could have predicted that everything inside Nick would leap up at the sight of Morn Hyland. If he was a pirate, he was the glamorous kind, the kind who slashed and burned his way to virtue in romantic videos. And she was beautiful and pathetic – a maiden in distress if ever there was one, abused and helpless. Not to mention the fact that she belonged to someone else, a pirate rumored to be even more successful than Nick Succorso himself. But only the people who didn't know any better were surprised that he didn't try to rescue her right away. The men in the corners could guess what he would do.

He wouldn't try to steal her directly. He was too smart for that. In other words, he had too much respect for Angus Thermopyle's defenses. And Angus kept his vulnerabilities – as well as his debaucheries – private by sealing them safely aboard *Bright Beauty*. Station Security itself would have come to his assistance if Nick had tried to get past his alarms.

No, Nick would sit and listen, watching Morn Hyland until his scars turned black and waiting for his chance; waiting for Angus Thermopyle to make a move.

He wanted to see that move coming and know what it would be. He wanted to do what Security had never been able to do – penetrate Angus' secrecy. And when he knew what Angus' move would be, he would follow it so that he could betray it. The moment in which Angus was arrested might be Nick's only realistic opportunity to carry Morn away.

He wanted her.

He also wanted to prove himself against Angus Thermopyle.

If he had other reasons, he never gave a hint of them to DelSec.

As it happened, his chance came sooner than he may have expected. Maybe Angus felt cocky with Morn beside him and wanted to show off. Or maybe he was getting greedy – if in fact he could conceivably be any greedier than he was already. Or maybe the bait was just too attractive to be ignored. Whatever the reason, he made his move scarcely two weeks after he first brought Morn into Mallorys.

The incoming supply ship from Earth – arriving several weeks early for some reason – was in trouble. Every receiver in or around the Station picked up the distress call before it went dead. Apparently one of the crew had been taken by gap-sickness. As the ship reentered normal space, this unfortunate individual had become entranced by the idea of installing a crowbar in the memory bank of the navigational computer. By the time his shipmates got him under control, the ship could no longer steer and had no idea where she was. The fact that the distress call went dead seemed to imply that the damage to the computer – perhaps a fire – had spread to the communication gear.

In other words, a full standard year's worth of food, equipment, and medicine was floating out there somewhere against the background of the stars, ripe to be rescued, salvaged, or gutted.

Of course, as soon as the emergency was understood, Com-Mine Center slapped a curfew onto the docks, forbidding any ship to leave until she could be sworn in as part of the official search; until Security personnel could be put aboard to watch the actions of the crew. That was standard procedure. And it was generally respected, even by pirates and jumpers. Ships that shared in the search also shared in the reward, regardless of which vessel actually performed the rescue, while ships that violated curfew, refused to cooperate, or went off on their own became targets by law and could be fired on with impunity.

This time, only *Bright Beauty* and *Captain's Fancy* took that chance. Somehow, both Angus Thermopyle and Nick Succorso managed to uncouple from their berths seconds before the injunction of the curfew, thus preserving at least the illusion of authorized departure.

Center wasn't impressed by illusions, however. Commands to return and redock were broadcast: warning shots were fired.

With contemptuous ease, *Captain's Fancy* winked off the scanners of the Station.

Nick Succorso disappeared by performing a delicate maneuver called a 'blink crossing.' No one in Mallorys doubted his ability to do this. In essence, he engaged his gap drive – and then disengaged it a fraction of a second later, thereby forcing his ship to 'blink' past fifty or a hundred thousand kilometers. It was risky: there was always the chance that dimensional stress would tear the ship apart, or that he would come out of the gap in a gravity well he couldn't escape. But it worked. He got away.

From the look of her, *Bright Beauty* would never have withstood that much pressure. In any case, she had no gap drive. Angus Thermopyle took a completely different approach. As soon as the first warning shots were fired, he started transmitting a distress call of his own.

Every receiver in or around the Station picked that one up, too. *There's a short somewhere. Smoke. Controls are locked – I can't navigate. Don't shoot. I'm trying to come around.*

No one believed him, of course. But Center couldn't afford to ignore the possibility that he might be telling the truth. That idea had to be considered, at least for a few seconds. And during those few seconds Angus cut in thrust boosters no one knew he had. No one thought he had them because no one believed *Bright Beauty* could survive that kind of acceleration.

Like Nick, he got away.

After that, there were no more answers for a while. The people who were following the story could speculate, but for two days they had nothing to base their speculations on.

Then *Bright Beauty* came limping back. Her sides were scarred with matter cannon fire, and her thrust drive stuttered badly. Nevertheless she passed inspection. Angus Thermopyle faced down a board of inquiry. After a few hours, he brought Morn Hyland back to Mallorys. Neither of them gave anything away.

Captain's Fancy coasted into dock later the same day. She also had been hurt, but Nick Succorso didn't seem to care. He talked her past inspection. He laughed circles around a board of inquiry. He and his crew also returned to Mallorys free and eager, ready to enjoy themselves.

The official search was still going on. So far, no trace of the supply ship had been found. After this much time, there was little chance that any trace would ever be found.

But that night Station Security broke into Mallorys to arrest Angus.

They had evidence that a crime had been committed. So they said. That gave them the right to board *Bright Beauty* without permission and take the ship's datacore. The datacore enabled them to find her secret holds. And in the secret holds were food, equipment, and medicine which could only have come from the missing supply ship.

Arrests in DelSec were few. The people who frequented places like Mallorys Bar & Sleep were prone to resent the intrusion of overt law and order into their lives. Even in groups, Security couldn't always pass through DelSec without harassment.

But a supply ship had been robbed – presumably gutted. Com-Mine Station needed those supplies to live. DelSec needed those supplies. Every man and woman in Mallorys would have suffered for this particular crime. And every one of them disliked or feared or even hated Angus Thermopyle.

At first, the arrest didn't go smoothly. Before Angus was taken, he and Morn Hyland began to scuffle: he was apparently trying to hold her back. Nevertheless she managed to break away just as Security closed on him. At once, the crowd opened for her, pried apart by Nick Succorso's crew. And then she and Nick were gone; they disappeared as effectively as a blink crossing.

Captain's Fancy was allowed to slip out of dock unmolested; but that wasn't hard to explain. Nick must have done a certain amount of bargaining with Security before he handed over his evidence against Angus. Obviously, his right to leave was part of the bargain.

So the fair maiden was rescued. The swashbuckling pirate bore her away with all her beauty. For weeks, the sots and relics in Mallorys could hardly talk about anything except what the maiden and the pirate were doing with each other. People who were accessible to romantic emotions contemplated what had happened with a lump in their throats. And even the cynics sitting in the corners were gratified by the outcome. Nick Succorso had done exactly what they expected of him.

There were only two flaws in this story.

One was that the supply ship from Earth arrived on schedule. It hadn't had any trouble along the way. And it reported that there hadn't been any other ship.

The other was that the control to Morn Hyland's zone-implant was never found. Angus Thermopyle didn't have it on him when he was arrested. That was why he was rotting in lockup instead of facing execution.

The first matter was easily explained. Nick Succorso must have arranged the whole thing – faked the distress call, stolen Station supplies himself, planted them on *Bright Beauty*. That was the kind of thing he did. It made the people in Mallorys admire him even more.

The second issue was more disconcerting, however. It didn't make sense. Angus could not have gotten rid of the control earlier: if he had done that, she would have been able to escape him – or, more likely, to butcher him with her bare hands for the things he had done to her. And yet he must have gotten rid of it earlier. Otherwise he would have been caught with it.

The only other explanation was less satisfying. After all, the zone-implant and its control were hypothetical, not proven. Perhaps they had never existed.

But in that case the entire sequence of events degenerated into incomprehensibility. Why did she stay with him, if he had no power over her? And if his power was of some other kind, why did he give it up? What warned him that he was in danger?

No one knew the answers. However, the people who asked them were only interested out of curiosity. The main thrust of the action was clear enough. Details that didn't make sense could eventually be forgotten.

The crowd at Mallorys would have found the real story much harder to live with.

CHAPTER 3

There were parts of the story that would always remain obscure, unless Angus Thermopyle explained them; and he refused.

By the end of his trial, *Bright Beauty* didn't have any secrets left. Despite her pretense of being a prospector's ship, she was indeed equipped with sophisticated particle sifters and doppler sensors, tools that no legitimate prospector would ever need. She was too heavily shielded, too heavily armed. Under boost, her thrust drive could have shifted the orbit of a planetoid. She had cargo holds hidden in places the Station inspectors never imagined. And she had so many relays and servos, compensations and overrides, that it was actually possible for one man to run her alone – although the experts who examined her agreed it would be suicide for any individual to take on that kind of complex strain for more than a few hours at a time.

In addition, the datacore revealed the extent of Angus' 'wealth.'

To the surprise of his prosecutors, his resources turned out to be trivial; almost nonexistent. Regardless of his reputation, he was operating only a few steps ahead of his expenses.

That unexpected detail didn't help him, of course. He hadn't been arrested for his 'wealth.' And in other ways the exposure of his secrets was sufficiently damning. Enough evidence was found to convict him of several acts of piracy – although everyone in Security agreed that the evidence was disappointing, since it wasn't adequate to procure the death penalty. Certainly it wasn't adequate to explain the more tantalizing aspects of Morn's story.

Confronted with this inadequacy – which presumably gave him the opportunity to cast his actions in the most favorable possible light – Angus surprised his prosecutors further by refusing to defend himself, testify on his own behalf. Indeed, he declined to answer any questions at all. With a zone-implant, of course, he could have been inspired to talk; but the law – and the UMCP – didn't consider confession an 'authorized use.' Consequently, Com-Mine Security never found out where or how *Bright Beauty* had been outfitted, or how she'd been damaged. No explanation was obtained for the fact that his reputation so far exceeded the evidence against him. He was unwilling either to account for or to defend the presence of stolen Station food, equipment, and medicine aboard his ship. And no new illumination was shed on his strange relationship with Morn Hyland. In the first weeks of his incarceration, he opened his mouth only when he wanted to complain about the food or the facilities or the treatment in the Station lockup.

And when he was informed that *Bright Beauty* was being sent to the Station shipyard to be dismantled for spare parts. Then he pounded on the walls of his cell and started to howl with such fury that eventually he had to be sedated.

No one knew what had warned him when the Hyland ship had come into Com-Mine Station – or how hard he had tried to get away from her.

Probably he would have been unable to explain that warning. It was a matter of instinct. He had good instincts, and they started to burn as he watched the sleek oreliner nudge its way into dock.

It looked like a prize, the kind of treasure ship *Bright Beauty* could peel apart weld by weld, exposing to theft or destruction the things that made other people think they were superior beings: the money, the possessions, the luck. He had tackled ships like that in the past, had tackled them often, tracking them to their destinations, learning their secrets, then blasting them open in the black void, leaving them ruined, lost forever – had tackled them and raged to himself fiercely as he did so, destroying what other men would have captured as riches because his need for money had limits while his desire to see what matter cannon fire could do was immense. Alone in his ship, or wandering around DelSec, or sitting in Mallorys – Angus Thermopyle was always alone, even when he happened to find some stow- or castaway piece of human garbage to crew for him – he relived the ships he had tackled and hated them.

But not this time.

This time, his instincts burned – and he always trusted his instincts.

As far as he knew, he had no particular reason to be wary. His crimes left little evidence behind; there was no better place than deep space to hide the remains of his plundering. Only his datacore could damage him, and he had long ago taken steps to alleviate that danger – steps which no one would detect because they were theoretically impossible. But because he was a hunter, he had also been hunted. He had the intuitions of prey.

So he did something that would never have occurred to anyone else on or around Com-Mine Station: he turned his field-mining probes toward the Hyland ship.

One of those probes was designed to measure the nuclear weight of thin cross sections of solid rock. It informed him that *Starmaster*'s hull was formed of an alloy he'd only heard about, never seen – an alloy so heavy it could endure matter cannon fire the way stone endured water.

An alloy so expensive no oreliner could afford it. There were no haulers or handlers in space rich enough to afford it.

When he saw the readings, Angus Thermopyle fled.

He didn't take the time to buy supplies. He didn't try to find out what the Station scuttlebutt concerning the Hyland ship was. He didn't even bother to repaint *Bright Beauty*'s name – something he always did before risking the malign vagaries of space. A ship as rich as *Starmaster* would have friends, muscle. Escorts? Fighters hanging off Station to watch for trouble? He took that into account, but it didn't stop him. Sealing his hatches, he called up Station Center, filed a purely fictitious destination report, and received formal permission to undock. Then, because his instincts were still on fire, he meticulously followed the departure trajectory he was assigned. Cursing like a slavey all the way, he left Com-Mine along a route that would attract as little attention as possible. And he didn't risk cutting in boost and shifting his course toward the belt until he was absolutely alone at least fifty thousand kilometers past the known range of any scan from the vicinity of Station.

He was hoping that the belt was far enough away to hide him. The Station had been built at a considerable distance to avoid the meteor storms and other debris which always accompanied asteroid belts through space, the residue of planets that time and gravity had reduced to rubble.

By the time he changed course, the exertion of manning the whole ship himself had begun to make his hands shake and his eyes fill with sweat. He had too many instruments to read, too many systems to monitor, too much data to absorb. And his computer couldn't help him. It had extravagant fail-safes: the very mechanisms which enabled him to run *Bright Beauty* alone would shut the ship down in alarm if he gave the computer control of them. Nevertheless he kept going. His instincts had warned him, and he always obeyed them.

Angus Thermopyle was a pirate and a mine jumper. He hated everybody, and there was enough old blood on his hands to convict a whole prison full of illegals. He was alone now because the decrepit drunk he'd hired to crew for him had made the mistake of asking the wrong question at the wrong time; so he'd flattened the man's head with a spanner and left the body in one of the thruster tubes to be ashed the next time the drive cut in. He may not have been rich, but he was probably everything else the people in Mallorys believed him to be.

He was also a coward.

So he ran from the Hyland ship under as much g as his body could stand and remain conscious. The muscles of his shoulders began to twitch, and he couldn't keep the sweat out of his eyes; but he kept running. When he knew that he had pushed himself too far, he didn't stop: instead, he started pumping drugs into his veins, stim to keep him awake, cat to keep him steady.

He was afraid, and he ran.

Before he was close enough to the belt to begin deceleration, he had been driving under heavy g for half a standard day. Now the drugs were giving him psychotic episodes with increasing regularity, and he no longer knew clearly what he was doing. However, he was familiar with those drugs; before starting them, he'd understood what they would do to him. So he'd taken the precaution of locking *Bright Beauty*'s course. When he was finally forced to surrender control of his ship's systems to her command computer, the course-lock and her fail-safes managed the hard braking for him. As a result, he arrived without crashing – and without pulling his ship away into madness – at a part of the belt which everyone knew had been mined out years ago; a long stretch of sailing rock where other ships were unlikely to come.

There he picked a particularly dead asteroid, parked *Bright Beauty* in a mining crater, shut down everything except life-support, and went to sleep in his g-seat, catted out of his mind.

If the Hyland ship could find him there, then he was lost anyway. He had never really had a chance to escape.

He still had no reason to believe the people on that ship even knew he existed.

Hours later, he awoke screaming because there were skinworms all over him, crawling, gnawing, starting to burrow in—

The sensation was terrible. It was also normal; a predictable consequence of the drugs. However, for him so much of what was terrible was also familiar that he knew exactly what to do. Although he couldn't swallow the bright terror rising in his throat or unknot the red pain closing around his heart, his hands were almost steady as he injected more drugs into his veins – analgesics to flush the now-poisonous stimulants and cataleptics away, antihistamines and steroids to soften his body's reactions. As soon as these new drugs took hold, he slept again.

The next time he awakened, he had trouble breathing because the air in *Bright Beauty* was going bad. He'd left Com-Mine Station without supplies. That meant he now had only a little water, less food – and no clean pads for the scrubbers which were supposed to keep his air breathable. Checking the computer's maintenance log, he confirmed that his present pads were long overdue for a change.

This development made him rage as if he were on the verge of a breakdown. But that, too, was normal. He still knew exactly what to do. Risking anoxia because he didn't have the strength to put on an EVA suit, he shut down circulation and took the pads out of the scrubbers. While his head throbbed with CO_2 overload and his vision blurred in and out of focus, he used half his water to make a chemical bath for the pads. He left the pads in the bath as long as he could – until he was close to unconsciousness. Then he refitted them in the scrubbers and restarted the circulation.

Unfortunately, his problems were just beginning.

He was probably safe where he was; but he couldn't stay there. His food would last for only two or three more days. He could reuse all his water – but only if he had his purifiers serviced. And the superficial cleaning he'd given the pads might not hold up even that long. He had only two choices.

Return to Com-Mine Station.

Or find some other source of supply.

He never considered returning to the Station. He wasn't deterred by the prospect of humiliation. If anyone ever found out that he'd panicked and run, only to return limping because he'd run out of food, water, and air, he would be sneered at everywhere in DelSec; but he could live with that. The world had been sneering at him from the first. He took revenge when he got the chance. However, there was still the Hyland ship—

That ship was to blame, of course. She'd scared him, and he hated everything that scared him. As he lifted *Bright Beauty* out of the mining crater and eased back from the belt to give his scanning equipment range, he began to plot ways to make *Starmaster* pay for what was happening to him.

Ways to wreck a ship with *that* hull? The bare concept was nonsense – and Angus Thermopyle wasn't prone to nonsense. Nevertheless thinking about it helped him do what he had to. In a state of cold rage which served as calm, he spent the next two days searching the belt with his sniffers and sifters, prospecting not for ore but for miners.

Toward the end of that time, he came close to panic again. The pads were starting to give out; his brain was being squeezed in a vise of bad air. His tongue was thick from drinking bad water, and he was urgently hungry. Still his cold, black rage kept him going. And a judicious application of drugs kept him steady.

At last he found what he needed – a mine on a craggy and pockmarked asteroid with a look of depletion about it, as if it had already had all its riches cut out. Yet the people working there had a ship. It stood on its struts a short distance from their camp, which was in turn a short distance from the hole they'd cut into the asteroid. The ship was cold: it had been shut down a considerable time ago, when the miners had settled in to work this hunk of rock.

Under other circumstances, Angus Thermopyle would have ignored those miners. He could tell their whole story with a glance at their ship, their camp, and his field-mining probes. This asteroid had once been rich, but it had in fact already been mined; played out. The people on it now – probably a family, people who had to spend long periods of time on ships or in mines tended to do things by families – were essentially scavengers. Too timid or defeated or poor to go prospecting for an original strike, they sweated their bare survival out of the rock by gleaning what little had been missed by previous miners. A pirate or jumper wouldn't waste his time on them.

On the other hand, they had food and fresh water and scrubber pads. Angus was having trouble keeping his anger and distress from choking him, and he didn't hesitate. He went in hard.

The miners saw him coming. His board picked up shouts of warning and protest, appeal and outrage: he ignored them. As he approached, he used torpedoes to collapse the mouth of the mine, blocking it with dead rock. Then he set *Bright Beauty* straight down on the camp so that his braking blast incinerated the habitation domes, charred the suited figures outside.

The radio shouts died in a gabble of static. Got you, you bastards. The camp had been large enough to support perhaps twenty people. With luck, he'd killed them all. He didn't want any witnesses.

A quick scan for life readings, distress calls, suit-tosuit communications. None. Good. That left him with a clear path to the other ship. As soon as he put on a suit himself, he could go over there and get everything he needed. Then he would be able to hide out in the belt as long as necessary. Until he got a chance to repay some of his fear.

He was on his way to the EVA locker when *Bright Beauty*'s klaxons went off like several dozen screams of pain.

The asteroid's tiny gravity didn't hold him back: with a powerful kick, he sent himself diving for the command module. One hand caught the back of his g-seat; the other slapped instructions at the computer, demanding an explanation. He was already in the seat, strapped down, and keying thrust for takeoff by the time the computer told him what was going on.

His sifters and sniffers and sensors had detected the approach of another ship. And not just any other ship: a ship the same size and configuration as *Starmaster*.

In fact, it was *Starmaster*. His probes weren't likely to be mistaken about that alloy. He'd programmed the computer to watch for her. And to make enough noise to wake him from his grave if it spotted her.

She was coming at him fast.

How the fucking hell did she *get* here? How did she *find* me? No time for that. Coming fast. But not fast enough to catch him. *Bright Beauty* was bound to be more agile than any oreliner, no matter how much cash that bitch cost. And this was the belt, where agility was worth more than matter cannon fire. He was terrified – but he also knew what he could do. What his ship could do. Let that fornicating hunk of money try to chase him and see what happened.

The only problem was that he didn't have enough food. Or water. Or air.

No time for that either. Survival was the highest priority Angus Thermopyle understood: it took precedence over everything. And he was sure from the core of his bloated belly to the sweat rolling down his jowls that the Hyland ship didn't intend him to survive. As if he really were calm, he hit thrust and began lift-off. At the same time, he primed his cannon, diverting precious boost to build up charge. And he made sure his communications board was clear, set to receive everything and transmit nothing.

Starmaster was still a considerable distance away, but her first transmission reached him before he was a hundred meters off the asteroid.

'Set down.' The voice sounded crisp and commanding above the hull-roar of thrust. '*Bright Beauty*, you are ordered to set down.'

Despite the intensity of his concentration on his instruments and controls, Angus was able to mutter a few obscenities under his breath.

'Angus Thermopyle, you are ordered to set down.' The voice was sure of itself. 'This is Captain Davies Hyland, commanding officer, United Mining Companies Police destroyer *Starmaster*. You have committed murder. If you do not set down to be boarded, you will be fired upon.'

UMCP. That got his attention. For a second, he actually stopped swearing and took his hands off his console. The cops. It made sense; so much sense that he should have figured it out earlier. Who else was there anywhere who could pool enough money to hull an entire ship with that alloy? Who else thought they owned the fucking universe? No one. Only the United Mining Companies – and their private cops, the muscle which enforced or invented the law that kept Earth and its huge appetites fed.

And this was why they were here: to hunt the pirates and jumpers and scavengers who fed off all the mining operations in vast space. In just a few seconds, they would be close enough to ash him.

'Message repeats,' the radio announced, stupidly unafraid. 'Angus Thermopyle, you are ordered to set down. This is Captain Davies Hyland, commanding officer, United Mining—'

'No,' Angus coughed in desperation. With one heavy finger he stabbed at his console, cut off reception. At once, the noise of his thrusters through the hull seemed to get louder, more frantic. 'I don't care if you come from fucking *God*. You can't have my *ship*.'

Holding his breath against the stress, he wrenched *Bright Beauty* around scarcely two hundred meters off the asteroid and slammed on full boost, piling up more g than he ought to be able to stand in order to put the asteroid between him and *Starmaster*. Then he drove away toward the heart of the belt.

He didn't cut thrust, reduce acceleration, until the simple weight of his body under so much g pushed him to the edge of blackout.

Klaxons howled at him, proximity sensors squalling with overload. Light-headed in physical relief as g eased – relief that didn't touch his essential terror – Angus skimmed past a small meteor, then deflected *Bright Beauty* between two larger rocks. At the same time, he rigged his ship for battle.

Under normal operating conditions, she required two people to run her. In combat situations, she could have used six. But Angus Thermopyle handled everything himself.

He made no effort to turn his cannon on the UMCP ship. Instead, as fast as his targeting computer could track, he started blazing away at every meteor and asteroid in range, filling the space behind him with chunks of all sizes caroming in all directions; covering his tail with debris. He wasn't trying to lure *Starmaster* into a crash; not yet: she was still too far away to be threatened by a little rubble. But she was closing fast – and a destroyer as expensive as she was probably had artillery which would make his cannon look like popguns. He was doing his best to confuse her targ.

It worked for a while. Out of the black, light came in bright flares, matter fire hitting rock; the rock went incandescent as it burst into its component particles; static sizzled across *Bright Beauty*'s scan; light collapsed to black again. Angus rode a meson torrent deeper into the belt and snatched his ship past obstacles that could have crushed her, and went on firing himself, madly throwing up scree like a screen against *Starmaster*'s guns.

But the destroyer learned fast. She turned his own tactics against him. There was a lull in the fire – fifteen seconds, twenty, twenty-five – during which no attempt was made to hit him. Then a dead stone lump the size of a small space Station hardly a thousand kilometers ahead took a shaft of incandescence through its center and broke apart so violently that chunks as big as ejection pods came at him like thunderbolts.

His proximity alarms went wild, then dead as their circuits overloaded.

In the sudden silence, Angus ducked, squirmed, twisted – and almost made it. *Bright Beauty* was agile, and he was desperate. At the last instant, however, one rock slapped her in the side and sent her tumbling like a derelict through the belt.

The next collision was gentler, just a kiss that flattened out some of the gyration. He didn't feel it. G and anoxia had stretched him too thin. He was unconscious. As far as he knew, he was still trying to scream.

CHAPTER 4

Moments later, he came back to himself. Just in time: *Bright Beauty* was plunging toward the kind of collision that would crumple her like an empty can. Hardly aware yet of what he was doing, reacting by plain instinct and fear, he punched at his console, fought the spin, got his thrusters aimed for braking. Only a few hundred meters off an asteroid almost large enough for colonization, he wrestled his ship under control.

Running on automatic pilot himself, still gasping for air and barely able to focus his eyes, he checked for damage. *Bright Beauty* had a cabin-size dent in her side; but her shields held, interior bulkheads held, preserving a fragile integrity. One part of her nose looked like it'd been hit by an impact-ram, and a number of sensors and sniffers were dead; but no structural harm had been done. She would still function. She could go someplace and get help – at the moment, he had no idea where, his brain was too fuzzy from oxygen starvation, but *someplace*, it was still possible, she could do it somehow.

Entirely by accident, one of the cameras which had been scanning *Bright Beauty*'s hull gave him a glimpse of the UMCP ship.

She was coming for him, coming fast.

She had a straight shot at him. As soon as she fired, his whole life would be reduced to light and electrons.

And there was nothing he could do about it. He couldn't even play dead. That wouldn't fool her. She'd seen him brake: she knew he was alive.

The thought turned his guts to water. He didn't want to die. Almost without realizing it, he hit his distress beacon. Don't shoot, don't shoot, you fornicating filthy bastards, *don't kill me*, I surrender.

Starmaster came ahead as if she wanted to eviscerate him at point-blank range; as if Captain Davies Hyland wanted to see Angus Thermopyle die with his own eyes.

The terrible injustice of it made Angus burn to shoot first, to key targ and at least go out fighting, even though matter cannon fire couldn't hurt the UMCP ship. But he didn't do that. Fear was more imperative than hate. Raging like a maniac, he fed his transmitter all the gain it could handle and sent his distress call into the dark like a wail.

His cameras gave him a perfect view as *Starmaster* altered course, turned in the direction of the asteroid – and broke in half.

Broke in half.

A blast like that: one of the drives must have blown up. Fire and metal sprayed without a sound into the belt. Out of the center of the explosion, *Starmaster* toppled as if she were falling toward the surface of the asteroid.

Angus watched in complete astonishment as the ship crashed and died.

Instead of gutting *Starmaster*, the fire went out almost immediately. That implied— He was too stupefied to realize what it implied. On automatic again, his hands fumbled across the console, activating short-range scanners, focusing cameras. He was trying to think. He should already be dead, fried in his g-seat. The UMCP ship had a straight shot at him. But he was still alive. *Starmaster* broke in half. The fire went out almost immediately.

That implied—

Oxygen.

The fire went out because it didn't get oxygen. But the ship was full of air. Angus understood fires in space: he knew *Starmaster* should have burned longer than that. Some of her interior bulkheads must be holding. Parts of her retained structural integrity.

That, too, had significant implications. They eluded him, however. Bad air and the fundamental shock of his survival muddled his head. Ideas that should have been clear to him refused to come into focus.

Then he got it.

If parts of *Starmaster* retained integrity, then some of her people might have been protected or shielded. There might be survivors.

There were survivors. When he pulled his eyes down from the screen where his cameras reported what they could see, down to his scan displays and readouts, he discovered that his instruments registered life. Three or four people were still alive.

No, not three. Definitely four.

Still stunned by what had happened, and hardly able to breathe because *Bright Beauty*'s atmosphere had deteriorated considerably during the past few minutes, Angus struggled to think.

He never considered trying to rescue the survivors. Even with all his wits about him, he would have dismissed that idea. Those people were cops; his enemies. And he didn't bother to wonder what had happened, how *Starmaster* had died. He would probably never know the answer to that question. He would probably never care. His thoughts were more basic:

Air.

Water.

Food.

And he thought, Bastards! If he went down there, one of the survivors might shoot him. He would have to wait here until they were dead.

But he didn't know how badly they were hurt. If they were hurt at all. They might be able to outlast him. Without adequate air or water or food, he might collapse long before they did.

Caught between need and cowardice, he was paralyzed. Sucking sweat off his upper lip, he stared at *Starmaster*'s image on his screen and wrestled with his fear.

Then he thought about what had been done to him.

His heart began to swell with old rage, familiar and malign. The strength which had kept him alive so long, against such odds, came back to him. Snarling curses as fiercely as he could with the little oxygen the rank atmosphere provided, he shifted *Bright Beauty* into landing attitude and started her moving.

While he was still negotiating a touchdown, scan informed him that one set of life-signs had stopped. Good. Only three left.

Gently he set *Bright Beauty* on her struts beside the UMCP ship. Leaving his g-seat, he bobbed like a balloon against the asteroid's gravity toward her lockers.

Once he'd donned his EVA suit and clamped the faceplate shut, he spent a minute simply breathing the sweet air from the tanks. But he couldn't afford to delay. The remaining survivors might be aware of him. They might be trying to train *Starmaster*'s guns on him right now.

He took an impact rifle with him, a miner's weapon because it could clear rockfalls and powder stone; in a pinch it could be used to buckle steel plate. He was no longer swearing: he was too scared to swear. The UMCP ship terrified him. The survivors terrified him. And EVA always terrified him. But he thought about air and revenge, and went to get them.

Cycling through the airlocks, he eased himself onto the surface of the asteroid.

Out here, the only light was the distant glitter of the starfield. Without the enhanced sensitivity of his cameras to help him, he could only see *Starmaster* as a silhouette, blacker than space. She looked huge and treacherous, riddled with secrets. Playing a beam along her sides helped put her in perspective; but that small light couldn't muffle the way his air tanks hissed in his ears, sounding so loud against the impenetrable silence of the belt that it seemed to mark him like a beacon for all his enemies. He loathed EVA because the sound of his own breathing made him feel puny and vulnerable. Now air and food and water didn't matter to him anymore. He thought he could live without them somehow. It was only rage that kept him going.

Bright Beauty had been hurt. She would never be the same again.

Starmaster's survivors were going to pay for that. The people who had sent her out against him were going to pay.

Sweating hate, he crossed to the UMCP ship.

Without much trouble, he found an airlock in the intact part of the ship. As soon as he'd entered the lock and closed it behind him, he began to recover. The ship's air pumping into the lock muted the hiss of his tanks. Her survivors might be waiting to ambush him as soon as he came out of the lock – but now at least he was no longer outside, exposed. And inside his rifle would be a devastating weapon.

As the lock cycled open, he ducked to the side, pressed himself against the wall: an instinctive precaution.

His instincts were good. A man stood waiting for him.

At first glance, the man looked all right. His silver hair was rumpled, but that only increased his appearance of eagle authority. Captain's bars marked the shoulders of his tunic. In one fist he held a beam gun.

Angus nearly cried out, 'Don't shoot!' even though his suit's transmitter was switched off and his voice would have been inaudible.

'I'm Captain Davies Hyland,' the man said. 'Angus Thermopyle, you're under arrest.' Through the suit's receiver, his confidence sounded insane, detached from reality. 'We're going to commandeer your ship.'

His eyes hadn't reacted to Angus' movement. He wasn't looking at Angus now. His gun was aimed at the back of the lock.

The parbroiled skin around his eyes betrayed what had happened to him.

Flash-blinded in the crash.

In spite of that, he was trying to bluff—

Commandeer my ship? My SHIP?

Cackling hideously behind his faceplate, Angus fired. The impact rifle spattered a fine spray of blood thirty meters down the corridor.

Then he hastened to apologize. I'm sorry, Captain Davies Hyland, he said in gleeful courtesy. You can't have my *ship*.

There were a few pieces of the Captain's body left on the floor. Angus kicked them out of his way and went looking for the other two survivors. He was starting to feel much better.

The bridge was in this part of *Starmaster*. He went there first – carefully, surveying each corner and passage with his rifle before he risked it, because he had no way to find those two people except by hunting them down. His caution was wasted, however: he didn't see anyone until he reached the bridge. And there the man hunched over the helm console was in no condition to threaten anyone. He was dying where he sat – internal bleeding, Angus guessed. Nothing to worry about.

Angus pushed the man out of his g-seat. New pain made the man cry out; but it also brought his eyes into focus, which was what Angus wanted. Laughing inside his suit, he blasted the man to pulp and splinters, a splash and smear of blood on the floor.

One more to go. Then air filters. Food lockers. A line to the water tanks. And everything else worth taking.

The ship's datacore would have been worth taking, of course. But one look at the bridge computer told him the datacore had already been destructed. Staunch Captain Davies Hyland had probably taken care of that automatically, while his ship was still falling toward the asteroid. So that his precious codes and contacts and orders and even specs wouldn't survive to be used against his masters.

Fuck Captain Davies Hyland, Angus thought. Fuck him everywhere. He's got enough holes in him for that.

Cheered by this observation, Angus pushed a body out of his way and sat down at the scan Station. The secondary systems which ran the locks were still operating; that implied parts of the ship still had a bit of juice. This console was one of them. Refocusing short-range scan inward, he used it to locate the last survivor.

There: in a room the scan computer identified as the auxiliary bridge.

That made him snarl under his breath. From the auxiliary bridge, it might still be possible to fire on *Bright Beauty*.

Hurrying now because he knew where his prey was and didn't need caution, he went to finish off the last of *Starmaster*'s crew.

Under the circumstances, his concern for his ship was greater than his desire to inflict pain. He broke into the auxiliary bridge fast with his rifle ready, intending to shoot first and think later.

Morn Hyland stopped him without lifting a finger; without threatening *Bright Beauty*; without so much as reacting to his entrance. Instead, she stared through him with stark, blank horror on her face, as if she could see something so ghastly that it blinded her, making him invisible to her.

In the first few minutes, he didn't even notice his own surprise at finding a woman when he was expecting a man.

Although he knew there was no one else alive on the ship, her fixed stare had the power to turn him around in an effort to see what had appalled her.

Nothing. Of course. She was the only one here. There weren't even any bodies. She'd come through the explosion and the crash without having to watch any of her crewmates die.

Something like a worm of suspicion crawled through Angus Thermopyle's belly. He tightened his grip on his rifle as he confronted her again.

Apparently she still couldn't see him. Her eyes remained nailed to her personal horror, ignoring his movements as if he were too insubstantial to impinge on her vision. She was in shock. If he didn't do anything to help her, she might stay that way for hours. Until something inside her started to heal. Or until she slipped over into madness.

He had no intention whatsoever of helping her.

But then she spoke. In a sore whisper, as if her voice were worn out from screaming, she said, 'Let me die.'

Inside his suit, Angus had begun to sweat again.

'I don't want help. Let me die. Go away.'

He stared at her, studied her. He didn't know it, but his expression resembled hers. Despite its distress, her face had lines that reminded him of Captain Davies Hyland. And the badge on her shipsuit said 'Ensign M. Hyland.' The Captain's daughter? That was quite possible. Ships were often crewed by families. Especially in organizations like the UMCP. Where loyalty was the only thing more important than power and order, muscle and stability, the two essentials of civilization and money. But she looked too young to be a veteran. Her first mission?

'Go away.'

What did she see that made her want to die?

Abruptly he keyed his suit's mike. 'Why?' Through the speaker, his voice was harsh, like the demanding metal noise of ships in collision. 'What did you do to them?'

Without warning, she gripped the sides of her head and began to wail; a thin, weak keening.

'Stop that,' he barked. 'Tell me what you did to them. If you don't, I'll be glad to beat it out of you.'

Her wail cracked, hurt her throat, and scaled higher.

'Shut up!' He brandished his rifle. 'They're all dead. Nobody can hear you. I shot your father myself. *Shut up.*'

That made her look at him. Some kind of recognition ate into her like acid. For part of a second, she gave him a flare of straight, absolute anguish.

'He survived? He was alive?'

Angus nodded. 'Until I blew him apart.'

During the space between one heartbeat and the next, she seemed to collapse inward like the core of a fusion reactor, compressing herself for an explosion. Then she flung herself out of her g-seat, clawing at his faceplate.

With her bare hands, she ripped and beat at him, trying to reach him through the suit. Her wail became a screech, as wild as the cry of a mad thing.

At that moment, for no clear or even conscious reason, he took his first step away from himself, his first step along the course which led to his real doom.

He didn't pity her. He didn't pity anybody: any man or woman weak enough to be pitied was weak enough to be taken advantage of. He wasn't ashamed of having killed her father. Captain Davies fornicating Hyland had damaged *Bright Beauty;* he deserved worse than he got. And Angus Thermopyle certainly had no intention of rescuing the Captain's daughter. What use could he possibly get out of a madwoman? Never mind the fact that she was UMCP, muscle for all the worlds which had ever despised him, in addition to being a witness to what he had done to that mining camp – a danger to him as long as she lived.

And yet he didn't shoot her.

Maybe he was simply tired of being alone. Maybe on some level he'd begun to notice that behind her fierce distress she was obviously a woman. Maybe his desire to know what had happened to *Starmaster* was stronger than he realized. Or maybe she presented possibilities of revenge which he hadn't yet had a chance to appreciate.

Whatever the reason, when she attacked him he actually dropped his rifle.

For a moment, he grappled with her, fought to pin her arms. But she was too crazy and frantic for that; so he drew back one heavy fist and clubbed her to the floor.

She whimpered, twisted, tried to squirm away from the pain – and then lay still, breathing in a graceless rasp like the sound of his own respiration inside his suit.

Hitting her – that kind of violence – was so seductive that he wanted to do it again. He wanted to give her ribs a kick and see what would happen. He restrained himself, however. Unexpectedly, he found he had one too many things to worry about. Filters. Supplies. Loot. And her.

And there was always the chance that some other ship was near enough to respond to the distress call he had sent out. *Starmaster* herself may have sent out a distress call. If he were caught here, with a broken UMCP ship to explain, and dead miners not very far away —

Better to forget about her. Forget about looting the ship. Take all the filters and supplies he could get, and leave fast.

Suddenly he was profoundly tired. His suit still had plenty of fresh air; but he'd been hungry and thirsty for several days, and *Starmaster* had nearly killed him. Muttering obscenities at Morn Hyland, hating her because it was all her fault, because she was the only one left of the ship and crew that had made him panic and run as if he were a coward, he slung her over his shoulders and went looking for an EVA locker.

Ominous and slow, like a capped volcano, he suited her, checked her tanks, and carried her against the asteroid's small gravity back to *Bright Beauty.* There he took her into the cubicle of his sickbay. Roughly he strapped her down, so that she couldn't move, and left her, still in her suit because *Bright Beauty*'s air was so foul. Let her come to consciousness alone and not know where she was and be terrified: she deserved it. After pausing to find out what his sniffers and sensors could tell him, he returned to the UMCP ship.

Forcing himself to work long past the point where he wanted to lie down in exhaustion, Angus retrieved his rifle and then set about taking everything that could conceivably be of any value out of *Starmaster.* Enough filters to keep his air clean for years. Food stores of a much higher quality than he would have been willing to pay for. Expensive liquor. Clothes. Spare parts. Medicines. And guns. And tools. Finally he ran a line which allowed him to pump water across to his ship. When he was done, *Bright Beauty* was better supplied than she'd been since the day when he'd first stolen her.

He was wild for rest; but even then he didn't stop. Morn Hyland was awake now. Stripping off his suit, he climbed into his g-seat and tuned a receiver to her transmitter so that he could listen to her fear. That kept him going while he lifted off the asteroid and went hunting with glazed eyes and unsteady hands for a place to hide.

He took the first place he found. By then, Morn's voice was stretched and frayed, barely audible; she sounded like she'd lost her mind. He made sure her straps were still secure, shot her full of cat so she wouldn't disturb him. Then he climbed into his bunk and collapsed.

CHAPTER 5

When he woke up, the air in *Bright Beauty* was so fresh that he could smell himself stink. Too much work. Too much sweat. Too many days in the same shipsuit. Angus Thermopyle wasn't particularly interested in personal cleanliness, but occasionally he felt good enough to take a shower. For some reason, he felt good now. He felt a sense of anticipation.

Munching some of *Starmaster*'s rations, he checked his scan and the computer log to verify that there were no ships anywhere near his hiding place. Then he went to the sickbay to look at Morn Hyland.

She was awake too; the cat had run out of her. When he took off her faceplate, she made a small whimpering noise. 'Please.' She could hardly force her throat to produce words. 'What are you doing? What are you going to do to me?'

He smiled, waved the food bar he was eating, and moved away.

Nearly humming, he stripped, entered the san cubicle, and sprayed himself clean.

Because he was clean – and wearing a fresh shipsuit – when he returned to the sickbay, he was able to tell that Morn herself stank. She'd fouled her suit. Fouled it rather dramatically. Her eyes were raw and dark, full of fear; but he could see in her face that she was still capable of self-disgust.

'You stink,' he announced happily.

His tone made her flinch. Apparently the desire to die had been scared out of her.

He looked at her features closely. Just to see what she would do, he ran the tips of his fingers along her cheek. She closed her eyes as if she were fighting a need to vomit.

Grinning, he stepped back. 'You hungry?'

She opened her eyes and stared dismay at him.

'Want to get up and move around?'

No answer except dismay.

'Want to get clean?'

That reached her. A tiny hope twisted her mouth, and her eyes filled with tears.

'Good.' He folded his arms, rested them on his belly. He was going to enjoy this. 'Tell me what you did to them.'

She surprised him. Something that looked like anger shone out through her tears; the muscles of her jaw knotted. In a voice so cracked and worn he could hardly hear it, she said, 'You bastard. If you're going to kill me, do it. Don't make me lie here like this.'

He wanted to hit her. That also would have been enjoyable. But he refrained because he wasn't ready to go that far yet. She was still wearing a suit.

Grinning again, he leaned closer to her and rasped, 'You're right. I'm a bastard. The worst bastard you'll ever meet. And I'm going to let you lie there and *stink* until you tell me what you did to them. You had your guns all lined up. You were going to blast me apart. Then you crashed.

'I want to know why. What did you do?'

The memory hurt her. He was glad to see that. She turned her head as far away as she could inside the EVA suit. Tears dripped past her nose.

Angus sucked his upper lip for a moment, then asked, 'What's your name?'

She still didn't speak. Probably trying to be tough. Or maybe she assumed he already knew the answer. After all, he must have seen the badge on her shipsuit.

Roughly he reached one hand to her neck and jerked up her id tag. His computer could have read her entire public file from that tag, but all he wanted was the name.

'Morn Hyland. Captain Davies motherfucking Hyland was your father. That right?'

Now she was crying with her mouth as well as her eyes.

'I shot him. But he was dead anyway.' Angus bent over her, whispered in her ear. 'His ship crashed. He was going to die no matter what happened. I didn't cause that. I didn't have anything to do with it. It was your doing.

'What did you do to them?'

And she still didn't speak. For the second time, he wanted to hit her. But that could wait. Instead he did something out of character. Without realizing it – entirely without realizing it – he took another small step along the course of his doom. He tried to explain himself.

Almost softly, he said, 'You know who I am. What I've got to lose. You know I can't afford to let you loose until I know what I'm up against. I can't do anything for you until I know what kind of danger you represent.'

Almost gently, he returned her tag, then put a hand on her chin and turned her face toward him.

The stark horror was back in her eyes.

Her whisper was faraway and forlorn, lost in darkness. 'I initiated self-destruct. From the auxiliary bridge.'

His fingers clamped onto her jaw as if he could force her to tell the truth. He thrust his face close to hers.

'You did *what*?'

'We were chasing you.' Her gaze didn't react to his proximity: the things that appalled her were so bright she couldn't register anything else. 'Dodging asteroids. G was awful. I thought we were going to break up. I was at my Station. Auxiliary bridge. I thought the straps on my seat were going to tear. Or I was going to rupture.

'Then it stopped.

'I could see you on the screens. But I didn't care. You destroyed that mining camp. I'd already seen you kill all those miners. I didn't care. I should have cared, but I didn't. The whole inside of my head was different.

'I was floating, and everything was clear. Like a vision. It was like the universe spoke to me. I got the message, the truth.' Her stare remained fixed; but now she had to fight to keep her sobs down. 'The truth.

'I knew exactly what to do. What I had to do. I didn't question it.

'I keyed the self-destruct sequence into the computer. That was supposed to blow up both drives. We would have been turned to powder.'

'You aren't an officer,' Angus objected. 'You're practically a kid. How did you know the self-destruct codes?'

'We all knew the codes. Any one of us could do it. So *Starmaster* wouldn't be captured. That was our first priority. Not be captured. Under any circumstances. If forbidden space got us – a ship like that— We can all be trusted. We're all reliable. Most of us are family. They wouldn't let anybody who wasn't reliable on a ship like that.

'But fa— Captain Hyland caught what I was doing. He tried to abort. Only the thrusters exploded. I could hear him yelling at me over the intercom – yelling at me because I was his daughter and I was destroying his ship, I was destroying him. His sister and brothers. My cousins. Destroying them.

'And then it wasn't clear anymore. There wasn't any vision. We weren't in any danger. It was all a lie. I killed my whole family for no reason.'

Fighting to contain her grief, she did her desperate best to shout, '*Get me out of this suit!*'

He ignored the demand. 'Stop whining. Let me think.' Suddenly he was sure of his suspicions. He'd taken a maniac aboard *Bright Beauty*, a human time bomb. And yet it didn't make sense.

'How many times have you crossed the gap?'

'Twice,' she answered, cowed not by his irritation but by her own despair.

'Twice,' he echoed viciously. 'Of course. Cops like you have to be deep-space certified. So they test you in the Academy. To weed out the crazies who get gap-sickness. And then you had to reach Com-Mine Station. You've only crossed the gap twice because this is your first deep-space assignment. It doesn't make *sense.*'

But while he was still speaking, he guessed the truth. Gap-sickness came in every conceivable shape and disguise. He had heard of people who crossed the gap once – or even several times – and then lived perfectly normal lives until the right stimuli came along, until the right combination of circumstances occurred to trigger their personal vulnerability, their peculiar flaw.

Combat? G-stress?

'How many times' – he took hold of her face again, forced her gaze toward him – 'have you been under heavy g since the first time you crossed the gap?'

She gaped at him, anguish changing into comprehension in her eyes.

'*Answer* me. You did all kinds of g work in the Academy. They trained you for everything they could think of. Did you do that before or after your first gap crossing? When was the last time you were under heavy g?'

39

'Before,' she husked weakly. Her voice seemed to stick in her teeth. 'The gap comes last. Only if you want to crew in deep space. Earth can't afford to risk people who want to work in-system. Can't risk wasting all that training and expense for people who aren't going to be in any danger.'

She must have understood what he was getting at, because she concluded with thin, cracked lucidity, 'Chasing you was the first time I've been under heavy g since before my first crossing.'

'Great. Wonderful.' Angus tried a few obscenities, but they seemed inadequate. 'Bitch. I never should have rescued you. I must have been out of my mind. It's not bad enough you're a fucking cop. And a witness. It's not bad enough you're going to turn me in the first chance you get. On top of that, you're going to go crazy and try to kill me as soon as we hit heavy g.' He gouged his fingers into the sides of her face, then released her. 'I should have left you to die.'

Again she surprised him. Her gaze steadied, and her voice gave an improbable suggestion of strength, of sarcasm. 'It's not too late. You can still kill me. No one will ever know.'

A smile stretched his features, making him look more than ever like a malign frog. He wasn't accustomed to the way he felt: happy; eager. She might turn out to be exactly what he needed.

'If I did that,' he replied, 'I wouldn't have a crew.'

'*Crew*?' The idea seemed to focus her stubbornness. 'I'm not going to crew for you. I'm not—'

Yet in spite of what she felt, her voice trailed away. He wasn't paying any attention to her refusal.

Deliberately, obviously, so that she could watch everything, he instructed the sickbay computer to prepare an anesthetic and pump it into her. While the needle probed her veins, he savored her dismay.

As she lost consciousness, she breathed in appeal, 'Get me out of this—'

'Oh, I will,' he promised. 'I will.'

If he'd been that kind of man, he would have chuckled.

Thanks to the advances of medical technology, even *Bright Beauty*'s tiny sickbay was sufficiently well-equipped to administer a zone-implant.

He had to unstrap her in order to get her head and shoulders out of the suit. That was the hard part, hampered as he was by her dead weight and the confines of the cubicle. The rest was simple. All he had to do was tell the sickbay computer what he wanted and then get out of the way. Cybernetic systems took care of the rest.

Long ago, he'd disconnected the sickbay computer from his ship's datacore. Law-abiding ships had that right, to protect the privacy of their passengers and crew: as long as the sickbay computer didn't feed directly to the datacore, no permanent record was kept of who needed treatment and why; so private citizens didn't need to worry that their medical records would be used against them. After all, crucial information – such as the presence of gap-sickness – was recorded on id tags. And any Captain could add data to anyone's id file as necessary. However, Angus' intentions had nothing to do with abiding by the law. He simply wanted to neutralize his sickbay computer as a source of evidence against him.

In fact, he'd carried his precautions to the extent of programming the computer with an automatic erase, so that it immediately 'forgot' every treatment it dispensed, every procedure it performed. According to his official sickbay log, he was the only person who had ever been aboard *Bright Beauty* – and he had never used his sickbay.

Confident of his own security, he left the cybernetic systems alone while they worked on Morn Hyland, preparing her for his use.

Instead of watching what was done to her, he lifted *Bright Beauty* gently out of hiding and went in search of a better covert, a place where he could feel safe for the time it would take to train his crew. Before long he found the kind of asteroid he liked: played-out and deserted, riddled with abandoned tunnels and workings which would attract nobody. Deep in one of the old mine shafts, out of reach of any ordinary scan, he parked his ship. Just in case he lost control of what he was doing, he shut down her drive and locked everything in the command module with priority codes. Then he went to check on his patient.

The sickbay computer was done with her: in fact, it had already washed the anesthetic out of her body, and she was starting to wake up. He just had time to pick up the implant control and make sure it was functioning properly before she began to stir, moving her arms groggily and blinking her eyes.

'You stink,' he said before she was altogether able to understand him. 'Go get clean.'

With an effort, she got her eyes into focus. At the same time, she seemed to realize that her limbs were free – that he had undone the straps. She frowned at him, struggling to think. Reflexively, she pulled her legs up, stretched her arms.

'What're you doing?' Her voice sounded rusty, as if she hadn't used it for a long time. 'Why did you put me to sleep?'

Watching her closely, he rasped, 'I said, you stink. Go get clean.'

'Yes, sir.' She was fresh from the Academy: assent to authority still came naturally. Her gaze blurred, and her nose wrinkled as she smelled the mess she had made in the suit. Carefully she swung her legs over the edge of the surgery berth, eased herself into a sitting position. Just for a second, he thought she was actually going to thank him for the opportunity to use the sanitary cubicle.

But movement helped clear her head. Her frown sharpened. Gripping the edge of the berth to steady herself, she looked at him again. 'Why am I free? Why did you put me to sleep?'

He bared his teeth. 'I told you. You're my crew now. You're mine. You've been *impressed*.' He relished the word. 'When I tell you to do something, I expect it done.'

He could see suspicion mounting to panic in her face. 'You bastard,' she breathed for the second time. 'I'm not your crew. I'm UMCP. I'm going to leave you rotting in lockup if it's the last thing I do. *What have you done to me?*'

Angus didn't answer directly: he was having too much fun. Instead, he showed her the control in his hand.

The shock when she recognized the small box was everything he could have wanted. It was like her horror of the way she had murdered her family, like that in helplessness and extremity; and yet profoundly different in other, crucial respects. Terror and loathing burned across her face. Her hands sprang to her mouth; she made an attempt to cry out.

Then she hurled herself at him.

Unhindered by the asteroid's negligible gravity, she came at him like a crazy. In her frenzy, she was so wild that she looked rabid – frantic enough to tear him apart.

But he had good reflexes. They'd often saved his life. And as a matter of instinct he was already braced against the bulkhead, ready. He shoved himself to the side, moving almost as fast as she did.

At the same time, he pushed one of the main function buttons on the zone-implant control.

That one was for emergencies: it was intended to save the people around her from her fits of gap-sickness after everything else failed. When he pushed it, she went instantly catatonic.

Limp as an empty shipsuit, she collided with the bulkhead and flopped backward. The asteroid's small tug pulled her down slowly, so that she fell like a grotesque feather against the edge of the surgery berth and settled toward the floor.

'You *stink*!' Angus raged at her, squeezing the control triumphantly. 'Go get clean. When I tell you to do something, *I expect it done.*'

She could hear him: he knew she could hear him. Her eyes retained the color of consciousness. That was the blessing – or the curse – of the zone-implant's cataleptic function. It didn't affect her mind: it only short-circuited the connection between what her mind wanted and what her body did. She could hear him; yet she lay on the floor in a heap of flaccid limbs. If he'd taken a welding torch to her belly, she wouldn't have reacted in any way.

Her state wasn't particularly rewarding for him, however. After a moment, he keyed off the control. At once, a spasm ran through all her muscles, making her twitch like an epileptic.

Helpless to do anything else, she burst into a fury of tears.

Once again, she seemed to find a chink in his character, a small way in which he was unlike himself. He let her cry for a little while, gave her a chance to understand his power over her. Then, almost without gloating, he said, 'You had enough? Go get clean. Down there.' He pointed along the passage toward the san and the head.

She flinched as if he'd tried to put a hand on her. Hugging herself against the bulkhead, she looked up at him. So thinly that he could hardly hear her, she asked, 'What do you want from me? You'll get the death penalty for this. You might be able to get off with life imprisonment for what you did to those miners. You might be able to convince a court you had some kind of reason – or you were just crazy. But you can't get away with this. Nobody ever gets away with "unauthorized use of a zone-implant." Why are you doing it?'

Without warning, he felt vulnerable to her – violent and angry. But he still didn't hit her. Because of the chink she'd found in him, his answer was simple. 'I need a crew. How else can I get a gap-sick cop to crew for me?'

Eventually she nodded, as if what he said made sense.

With misery in her eyes, struggling visibly against her fear, she got to her feet and did what he told her. She went past him down the corridor.

For no reason he could explain – no reason he knew – he handed her a clean shipsuit before she entered the san.

By the time she emerged, however, the inexplicable inconsistency of his own behavior had made him savage. He was a coward; and when he did things he didn't understand, things that weren't what he'd intended, things that weren't what he wanted, he scared himself. When he was scared, he took action.

He was being weak. He should have forced her to live in that fouled suit in order to humiliate her properly, teach her what his power meant. What was he doing? Was he feeling sorry for her? The idea made him want to break her arms. He would see her dead – he would *crush* her – before he would allow her to do anything that might make him weak.

And yet he contained himself until she came out of the san of her own volition. Fuming, fretting, swelling into a fury, he still waited, storing up violence, until she opened the door herself and came out to face him.

Then he lost his self-possession.

He was already on the edge of his restraint: the sight of her pushed him past his limits. She was clean – and being clean brought back her fundamental beauty. She was probably the most beautiful woman he'd ever seen this close. And she showed a kind of courage simply by leaving the san; she had the capacity to face her fate. Her eyes shone with a heart-wrenching combination of fright and defiance, with a dread of what he could do to her mixed with a refusal to be cowed. And he could do anything he wanted. She was his: he had the control to her zone-implant clenched in his sweating fingers.

For that reason, he pushed the button which took away her ability to move. Then he put down the control and beat her bloody with his bare fists, marring her beauty so that it wouldn't terrify him anymore.

44

Several hours passed before he came to the realization that he'd hurt himself as well as her.

With the zone-implant control, of course, he could have overridden the damage to some extent. As soon as she regained any measure of consciousness, he could have forced her into motion, made her serve him in any number of ways. Certainly he could have muffled the sensations of damage for her. But she would still have been useless as crew: he had left her in no condition to learn the things he needed to teach her about *Bright Beauty*. He would have to give her time to recover before he could get any real use out of her.

In other words, he'd increased the amount of time he would have to spend in hiding. He'd delayed the moment when he would be able – if not safe – to travel with Morn's help instead of hindrance. And no matter how well hidden he was, the fact remained that a stationary target was easier to find and hit than a moving one.

He'd increased the risk to himself for the satisfaction of beating her.

And he'd hurt himself in another, subtler way as well. She was *his*. Wasn't she? Like his ship, she was in his command. With the zone-implant, he could make her do anything he wanted; perhaps by taking control of her body and directing it as he wished; perhaps by exerting neural pressure – pain and pleasure strong enough to coerce her. He could make her (now that she was unconscious and out of sight, his imagination began to tease him) do *that*. He could do *that* to her. So why was he afraid of her looks? Beauty only made it better – only increased her humiliation, demonstrated his power more completely. Anything that marred her took something away from him.

He was so surprised – in a sense, so shaken – by this perception that

45

he went to her without thinking, carried her back into the sickbay, and instructed the computer to treat her injuries.

Another step.

Soon his surprise became a visceral trembling, an ague in the core of his distended gut. New ideas were working on him. He wasn't thinking about revenge now – about having a UMC cop as his crew, about making her suffer for what *Starmaster* had done to *Bright Beauty*. Now his thoughts were more visceral. He'd never had much to do with women. In the course of his piracies, he'd captured or kidnapped a few, used them hard, then gotten rid of them. But none of them had had Morn Hyland's capacity to make him shiver, make him do things he didn't expect. None of them had been so entirely in his possession – or so desirable.

She was still unconscious, perhaps because of his beating, perhaps because of the drugs the sickbay computer gave her. She had no idea what was happening as he undid her shipsuit and peeled it off her limbs.

He couldn't stop trembling. After all, it was a good thing that he'd hit her. The darkness and swelling of her bruises made her bearable: if she'd remained perfect, he would have had no choice but to kill her. So he paid no attention to the firm lift of her breasts or the velvet curve of her hips. He concentrated exclusively on the livid hurt of her bruises as he climbed on top of her.

His orgasm was so intense that he thought for a moment he'd broken something.

Before he rolled off her, he had the satisfaction of seeing her eyes flutter open, seeing her begin to realize what he'd done. He filled her with revulsion, even though there was nothing she could do about it. That was good.

Nevertheless he continued trembling.

He could no longer tell whether he was excited or afraid.

'Does that make you feel like a man?' She sounded bitter and miserable – and faraway, as though the after-effects of his blows muffled her distress. 'Do you have to destroy me to feel good yourself? Are you that sick?'

'Shut up,' he replied amiably. 'You'll get used to it. You'll have to. He was grinning; but he still had to brace his hands on his hips to conceal the way they shook.

As if she hadn't heard him – as if she were still on the same subject –

she muttered, 'It's because of men like you I became a cop.'

It occurred to him that what he was doing to her might make her come apart. Maybe she had already begun. At the idea, he bared his teeth.

'Is that so?' he drawled. 'I thought it was because you like guns. Muscle. They make you feel like a man.'

Maybe she was still stupefied by blows and rape and medication: maybe she didn't hear him. Or maybe she really was trying to threaten him. 'Forbidden space is bad enough. We don't need any worse threats than that. But men like you are worse. You betray your own kind. You prey on human beings – on human survival – and get rich.' She didn't look at him. Perhaps if she had looked at him she would have lost the courage for what she was saying. 'I'll do anything I can to stop you,' she recited like an article of faith. 'No price is too high for stopping a man like you.'

Angus had to respond. Involuntarily he remembered the insane bravado with which blind Captain Davies Hyland had tried to outface him. He couldn't let the captain's daughter think he cared about her threats.

'Me?' he retorted, gathering anger or pleasure as he spoke. 'I'm a danger to human space? What about you? I wasn't the one who blew up your ship. I didn't make you gap-sick. I didn't hunt you down. I didn't even fire on you. You killed all those cops yourself, you.' This was fun. He was going to teach her what her threats were good for. 'I'm just a freighter Captain. You're a traitor.'

He could see his words hit her: she winced and turned her head away. As if he'd switched her off – or as if she were trying to find some hidden place where she could still believe in herself – she seemed to sink out of awareness.

Where she went, he couldn't follow. For him, fear was a source of inspiration: it enabled him to make the sort of intuitive leap which had brought him to an understanding of her gap-sickness. But the same inspiration or intuition also blinded him to perceptions which involved emotions other than fear.

The place where Morn went would have made no sense to him. He would have assumed it was a cynical lie – the kind of falsehood which conceals itself in order to sting more effectively.

She was sinking down to her basic memories, to the place where she had become who she was; to her home and parents.

Like a little girl, unselfconsciously, she appealed to her mother and father for help.

In a sense, their power to help or hinder her, like their power to shape her life, came from the fact that they'd been so much absent. They were both cops; and the UMCP policy of crewing ships with families stopped short of children. In consequence, Morn was left with her grandparents (themselves retired veterans of Space Mines Inc. Security) while Davies and Bryony Hyland served missions in the deep void, risking their lives to protect humankind from violence and forbidden space.

Morn kept the weight of this abandonment to herself. Of course, she grieved when they went away; she thrilled with joy when they returned. But the deeper impact she concealed. Perhaps she herself didn't know there was any deeper impact. After all, her parents left her in a home where she was loved and attended to; a home where a strict affirmation of law and citizenship was complemented by warmth and affection. For her grandparents, as for her parents, children were the future which the UMCP labored and bled to secure.

Virtually everyone Morn knew as a child either was or had been a cop. And they were *believers:* they esteemed their own work in the same way that they esteemed her, and for the same reason. They spoke of her parents with a fundamental respect, an unquestioning validation, which taught her that what her mother and father did was the most necessary and valuable job imaginable. Life beyond the hegemony of the UMCP thronged with profound perils, threats to the human species itself, which Davies and Bryony Hyland had the courage and the conviction to oppose. Vast space was deadly: it called for valor, determination, and idealism.

How could a child question all this? Whom could she tell that she felt abandoned – or punished? By the time she was old enough to know the right words, they were no longer credible. Abandonment? Punishment? No. She'd been taught to see her father as an eagle, scouring the skies for predators. And her mother was a panther, sleek and soft for her kittens, but ready with fangs and claws to fight her kittens' enemies.

In addition, her grandparents, aunts, uncles – and her parents when they were on leave – conveyed the perfect assumption that Morn herself would eventually become a cop. Precisely because she was bright, capable, and loved, she would naturally choose to follow in her parents' footsteps.

Morn nodded solemnly, as if she were accepting her mission. Nevertheless she knew it was false. She would never be a cop. When the pain of her abandonment or punishment lost credibility, she learned resentment. But there was no place for that in her life, so it remained hidden. Instead of aspiring to be like her parents, she learned to hold a grudge.

Even at that age, she was able to hold a grudge steadily – and give no sign of it.

However, her resentment turned to shame – her whole emotional makeup changed – when she heard of her mother's death.

Of course her grandparents were the first to tell her that Bryony had been killed. But in her core, where her image of her mother's invincibility resided, she didn't believe the news until she heard it from her father. He came home on leave after the ship which he had served as first officer, the UMCP cruiser *Intransigent*, limped to the haven of Orion's Reach. As soon as his debriefing at UMCPHQ permitted, he sat down with Morn and told her the story.

She saved us all, he said. She'll be given the Medal of Valor for it. He must have assumed that Morn would want to know this. If she hadn't sacrificed herself, we would all have been lost.

He held his daughter on his lap with his arms around her as he talked. Under the circumstances, she wasn't too old for this. His voice was steady and clear – the voice of a man who valued what his wife had done too much to protest against it. Yet tears ran from his eyes, collected along the certainty of his jaw, and dropped like stains onto Morn's small breast.

We picked up a distress call from the ore transfer dump off Orion's Reach. The dump was raided. An illegal came in on them hard, blasted most of the habitation and control centers, then took all the ore that was ready for shipping and headed away. They would probably have been safe if the illegal had known we were in the vicinity. But no one knew. We were hunting. We didn't advertise our movements.

We left medical supplies and personnel at the dump and took off after the illegal.

She called herself *Gutbuster*. She wasn't fast, and she didn't show gap capability. But she was heavily armed – as heavily armed as a battlewagon.

We'd never heard of her before. We didn't know there were any illegal ships that powerful. We were only a day of hard g away from Orion's Reach when we engaged her. But by the time we drove her off, we were so badly damaged that we couldn't get back for a week.

Of course, we ordered her to come about. We told her she was under arrest. And we didn't charge in recklessly. We could tell by her particle trace that she was something we hadn't seen before, so we were cautious. But she kept on running, ignoring us. Finally we had to attack.

We were careful – but we should have been more careful. We were too sure of ourselves. And too angry at what *Gutbuster* did to the dump. And we're cops, Morn. We're the police. We can't simply destroy illegals without giving them every conceivable chance to surrender. If we did that, we wouldn't be any better than the people we're fighting.

Because we weren't careful enough, and because we gave her too much chance to surrender, her first blast ripped one whole side of *Intransigent* open as if we had no shielding, and had never heard of evasive maneuvers.

A pure super-light proton beam. It was no wonder she was slow. Every bit of energy she could produce must have been necessary to power that cannon. Captain Davies Hyland couldn't resist lecturing for a moment. That's why UMCP cruisers don't use them. We need mobility and speed. We can't afford the kind of energy-utilization priorities those cannon require.

I was on the bridge. The bridge wasn't hit. But that blast did us so much damage that we immediately lost targ. The cables were cut. We still had power, but we couldn't aim our guns. Another beam like that would have finished us. As it was, the only reason we survived was that *Gutbuster* needed time to recharge her cannon.

Your mother was on Station in targeting control. And targeting control was in the part of *Intransigent* that *Gutbuster* hit. All the control spaces were close to the core, of course. But that whole side of *Intransigent* had been ripped open to vacuum. Even your mother's Station lost structural integrity. A bulkhead cracked, welds parted. Targeting control began to lose atmosphere.

She could have saved herself – for a minute or two, anyway. The leak was slow enough. She could have left her Station, sealed it behind her. The automatic systems that locked the doors had enough override tolerance for that. But she didn't. Instead, she stayed at her board. While her Station depressurized and her air ran out, she worked to reroute targ function so that we could use our guns.

She succeeded, Morn. That's why *Intransigent* survived, why I'm here talking to you. She restored targ in time. We hit *Gutbuster* with everything we had. And because *Gutbuster* needed power to maneuver, she couldn't use her proton beam again. We fought until she couldn't stand any more damage. Then she pulled away.

But your mother was lost. By the time she finished saving us, the automatic locks wouldn't let her out of targeting control. Depressurization exceeded their tolerances.

You know how people die in vacuum, Morn. It isn't pretty. But it's beautiful to me, as beautiful as your mother herself. She gave her life for her shipmates. If I die that way myself someday, I'll die proud.

And I promise you this. Now the look of an eagle shone through Davies Hyland's tears, as familiar as his certainty and his strong arms. No one in the UMCP will ever rest until your mother has been avenged. We will stop *Gutbuster* and every ship like her. We will stop every illegal who sells out humanity.

By the time his story ended, Morn had decided that she, too, would be a cop. She was too ashamed of herself to make any other choice. She already felt – an emotion which lost credibility as soon as it was put into words – that she'd killed her mother with her secret grudge. So she told herself that she owed it to human space, to her father, to the image of her mother, and to herself to join those who opposed the betrayal of humankind. But those were only words. The truth was that she was trying to recant.

However, it was a matter of historical record that *Gutbuster* was never stopped. Morn learned this during her years in the UMCP Academy. Indeed, that ship was never encountered again. She died of her wounds in the void; or found the problematic safety of forbidden space and never returned; or transformed herself in some way (perhaps by replacing her datacore), changed her registration and codes so that she couldn't be recognized. The promise Morn received from her father was never kept.

At the time, in the Academy, she took that failure as a reason to rededicate herself to her calling. If *Gutbuster* and similar ships still existed, perhaps flourished, then people like Morn were needed more than ever; people who had both reason for passion and experience to give their passion focus. She made herself one of the best cadets in her class – an honor to her father, and to her mother's memory. If she had any questions about what she was doing – if she felt any uncertainty about her father, or the UMCP, or about her own courage – she kept that hidden, even from herself.

By the time she joined *Starmaster* and Captain Davies Hyland in their quest to preserve the integrity of human space, any doubts she might have retained were hidden so deep that only a man like Angus Thermopyle could have dredged them up.

But she'd killed her father. She'd brought what was left of her family to ruin.

That struck her in the deepest part of her shame – in the part which believed she'd deserved to be abandoned; the part which believed her resentment had killed her mother.

When she needed them most – helpless in *Bright Beauty*'s sickbay, with a zone-implant in her head and Angus leering over her – her parents didn't answer her appeal.

How could they? Nothing they'd ever given her or done for her had prepared her for the crisis of gap-sickness; for the knowledge that the destructive flaw which endangered those she loved existed, not in illegals and forbidden space, but in herself.

The look in her eyes as she came back from her search for courage was one of unmitigated and irremediable anguish.

'Even if I can't do it,' she said as if her heart were hollow, 'somebody else will. It doesn't matter what you think of me. Maybe you're right. Maybe I'm as bad as a traitor. But there are better cops than me – stronger— They'll stop you. They'll make you pay for this.'

Her throat closed. The glaze across her eyes was fading. She began to look sharper, more dangerous; her nipples were poised on her breasts as if they could do damage.

Instinctively, Angus put his hand in his pocket, closed his fingers around the control. His grip was damp with sweat.

But she was wrong. He had no doubt that she was wrong. Oh, the fucking cops would stop him if they could. They would gut his ship and kill him gladly. But not because of what he did to her – or to those miners. Reasons like that were only excuses, as empty as her tone. The UMCP didn't protect people. Why should it? It protected money. It protected itself. It protected the power to despise people like Angus himself.

The cops would try to stop and kill him, not because he shed blood, but because he cut into UMC profits.

Under the circumstances, he had no idea why he'd left her alone so long; why he'd given her time to go looking for courage. He didn't have any reason for it. Nevertheless he was either excited or angry; and that confusion held him. And he had the control to her zone-implant in his pocket: he was secure. Let her find courage, if she could. The braver she was, the more pleasure he would get out of breaking her.

When he thought about breaking her, he grew erect again.

Instead of arguing with her, he removed his hand from his pocket. A twitch of his fists parted the seals on his shipsuit, allowing him to jut out.

'They'll never get the chance,' he rasped, showing his yellow teeth. 'I told you. I'm a bastard. The worst bastard you'll ever meet. And I'm good at what I do. I've been dancing circles around the fucking cops all my life. If they ever catch me, it'll be long after you're dead.

'In the meantime, I'm going to have some fun with you. You're my crew now. You're going to learn to take orders. And I've got old scores to settle. A lot of them. I'm going to settle them on you. By the time I'm done, you're going to want to run away so bad it'll damn near kill you, but I won't even let you scream.'

She glanced down at his crotch. Her mouth betrayed an unmistakable desire to wail. And yet she fought not to let him appall her. Her withdrawal may not have brought her courage; nevertheless she possessed a strength of her own which had never been tested before. Her voice shook as she said, 'If nobody else stops you, I'll have to do it. I'll get the chance somehow. I can't fight a zone-implant. You've got that on your side. But I can't crew for you while you're keeping me passive. You'll have to let me move on my own – think on my own. I'll get the chance.'

Her defiance was secretly disturbing – and secretly stimulating. He wanted to hit her again; but he knew that would be an inferior pleasure. To crush her spirit would give him a positive joy. Furthermore, it was necessary. She was right: she wouldn't be able to crew for him under the control of the zone-implant. The requirements of the job were too complex – and the functions of her implant were too crude. If he had to tell her what to do all the time, she would be useless. If he needed her help with *Bright Beauty*, he would be vulnerable. He wouldn't be able to leave his hiding place until he was sure she was broken.

And yet her spirit was part of what made her so desirable.

He didn't hesitate, however. He'd already taken too many steps in a direction he didn't understand. Still jutting from the seam of his shipsuit, he took out the implant control and snapped it on.

Helpless to resist, she lapsed into a pliant state similar to hypnosis; a state in which she could no longer choose her own movements.

He had to swallow several times to moisten his throat. As he tapped buttons on the control, he rasped, 'Sit up.'

Eyes disfocused, features slack, she sat up on the edge of the berth.

He reached into one of the compartments along the bulkhead, selected a scalpel, and handed it toward her. 'Take it.'

Her fingers closed involuntarily. Only the darkness in her gaze hinted that she knew what she was doing.

He had to clench his fists to keep himself still. He was approaching orgasm again. 'Put the edge on your tit.'

The control compelled her. She didn't need to watch what she was doing. Blindly she moved the scalpel until the blade rested against her nipple, intense silver against brown. The nipple was erect and hard, as if it were ready to be cut.

'You can understand me,' he said thickly. 'I know you can, so pay attention. I can make you cut yourself. If I want to, I can make you cut off your whole tit.' He was tempted to have her draw blood, just to demonstrate his power; but he was afraid if he did so he would come right away. 'Remember that when you think about breaking my neck.

'I'm going to break you. I'm going to break you so hard you'll start to love it, need it. Then I'm going to break you some more. I'm going to break you until you don't have anything but me to live for.'

Her eyes were still out of focus; but he could see anguish in their depths, a wail she was unable to utter.

She looked so lost that he almost turned off the zone-implant. It would be an exquisite display of possession to make her do what he wanted by plain fear rather than with the implant – to make her return the scalpel to its compartment, then come to him, kneel in front of him, and open her mouth so that he could thrust himself down her throat. His thumb was on the switch to release her.

But at the last moment, instinct prevailed. He couldn't take the risk of ignoring her threats. She might be stronger than he could predict. If she was— The idea took some of the stiffness out of him.

Angrily, he kept her under control.

Moving like a robot – responsive to nothing but the implant's functions – she replaced the scalpel in its compartment. When he instructed her to smile, she obeyed; but the lift of her lips remained as expressionless as the rest of her face. Obediently she knelt in front of him.

His organ was no longer as intensely eager as it had been a few moments ago. Down in the black bottom of his heart, he was disappointed. His cowardice had cost him something he wanted. But disappointment made him angry – and anger had its uses. Suddenly furious, he forced open her mouth and drove himself into her, gagging her fiercely until he came.

Then a sense of depletion as sudden as his rage took everything else away. Without a glance at her, he pushed the buttons which put her to sleep; he left her naked on the floor of the sickbay. Thinking he was tired, he lumbered away toward his berth to get some rest.

But he wasn't tired. What he felt wasn't fatigue: it was loss. After several restless minutes, he left his berth and went, fuming bitterly, to *Bright Beauty*'s bridge and the command console. There he keyed on the cameras and screens so that he could look at the damage *Starmaster* had done to his ship.

She had a cabin-size dent in her side. Her steel skeleton was no longer true. One part of her nose looked like it'd been hit by an impact-ram.

She could be repaired. He knew where to go to get her patched and welded and sealed: fixed. But she would never be the same again.

As he studied her wounds, Angus Thermopyle's eyes began to spill tears.

CHAPTER 7

From that point on, he no longer hit Morn Hyland. She was his, and he was ready, eager, to use her hard; but he didn't want her damaged.

Driven by anger and grief, and by a vague, inexplicable sense that he was no longer in control of his life, he used her so hard that several days passed before he could begin teaching her how to help him with *Bright Beauty*. He'd never had much to do with women. In fact, he'd never doubted that he could live perfectly well without them altogether. But now his brain teemed with lust. Perversions which had never occurred to him before now seemed exciting, even compulsory. The more he saw of her helpless beauty, and the more he exercised himself on her flesh, the greater her hold on his imagination became – the more power she seemed to have over him.

It was madness to stay where he was: Stationary, hidden, defenseless. He should have been on his way to the nearest bootleg shipyard days ago. It was weeks or months away under hard boost, inside the borders of forbidden space, where cops never went; he should have gotten started immediately. But he kept thinking of things he could do to Morn – of ways to enjoy her imposed compliance – of outlets for his most intimate and personal rage. The firm line of her thighs and the soft pillow of her belly haunted his dreams: he was kept awake by the way her breasts lifted to him despite the intensity of her loathing. For several days, he was simply unable to think about anything else.

Finally, during one of the periods when he released her from the zone-implant's control so that he could take a look at her despair, abhorrence, nausea – look at them and savor them – she asked, 'Why are you doing this? Why do you hate me so much?'

They were in the sickbay because its berth was easier to use than any of the others. She sat on the floor, against the bulkhead, with her legs hugged to her chest in misery and her face hidden between her knees. He'd seen sewer rats on Com-Mine Station and elsewhere, derelicts, nerve-juice addicts, even null-wave transmitters, with more energy and hope than she showed. She was breaking, as he'd promised she would. Already it seemed impossible that she would ever have the courage to threaten him again.

And yet she was still groping – still reaching for something—

'Why are you doing this? Why do you hate me so much?'

She was like *Bright Beauty:* she had surprises in her.

'What difference does it make?' he growled, just for something to say. 'How come you're the one with gap-sickness, instead of me? Who knows? Who cares? I've *got* you. That's all there is.'

She lifted her head a little: her eyes showed, black as rot and ruin, past her kneecaps. Her voice twitched as if she were afraid or crazy. 'You can do better than that.'

He sucked his upper lip, thinking casually. For some reason, he felt expansive, almost magnanimous. It was possible that she was crazy. Possessiveness warmed him as if it were a species of affection.

Abruptly he said, 'All right. I'll tell you something about me. A little story to help you understand.' He was sneering. 'I had a roommate once.'

Morn Hyland stared at him without any reaction at all.

'Back on Earth,' he explained. 'In reform school. I was a snot-nose kid – didn't know enough to keep them from catching me. Fuckers. Caught me helping myself in a foodvend. But of course they didn't care I was doing it because I was *hungry*. All they cared about was reforming me. Make me "a productive member of society." Break me. So they locked me up in school.

'I hated it. One thing I promised. Nobody is ever going to lock me up again—'

That was a digression, however: Angus had no wish to think about being locked up. If he did, he would lose his present sense of indulgence and fall into a fury. Over the years, he'd done some desperate things – reckless things, things that probably made him look brave. But courage had nothing to do with them. He'd done them to escape the danger of being locked up.

'I had a roommate,' he resumed. 'They told me I was lucky I only had one. Crowded three or four into a room was more like it. But it wasn't luck. They put me alone with that shithead because they thought he'd be good for me.

'They were all *cops*.' The taste of their power over him made him want to spit. 'Like you. They talked about protecting and reforming, but what they really liked was muscle. Just like you. Muscle to kill me. Or break me – it's the same thing. I was just a street rat who got caught raiding a foodvend. I couldn't defend myself. They thought they could beat me.

'My roommate was supposed to be a good example. One of their big successes. They got him for lifting paper from his stepfather's wallet, and after only five years in reform school he was on the path of virtue. They wanted him to help reform me.

'His name was Scarl. He was a big fucker – the kind of illegal who eats shit and smiles. Lots of teeth. He wanted to *reform* me, for sure. Anything to make himself look good. He already figured out the way to beat them was be their little darling, make them think he was sugar – make them take care of him. I was his big chance to show off.

'It was pathetic. He sure did want me to believe he was my friend. So he made a big deal out of taking care of me. Taught me how the school worked. Didn't let the big shits pound me. Showed me how to get perks – how to lift treats – how to be on the nice-kid list. After a whole day of him every day, I wanted to puke.

'But I got him.' Angus had arrived at the part of the memory he liked. 'I got him. Good old Scarl never knew what hit him.

'We had lockers. It was supposed to be good for kids to have something private. Everybody hid the keys, like what was in the lockers was precious. But he wasn't good at hiding things. I took his.

'Then I raided some of their rooms, the cops'. Lifted a bunch of small stuff – vials of nerve-juice, fancy pens, whatever I found. And one of them had a really great collection of dirty pictures.' He bared his teeth at Morn. 'That's where I still get most of my ideas.'

She didn't react, however.

'I put it all in Scarl's locker, locked it up. Then I put his key back. He never missed it.

'Next morning they went crazy. They stormed into all our rooms. Made us give up our keys and stand there naked until they got around to searching our lockers.

'When he saw all that stuff in his locker, good old Scarl fainted.'

Angus forced a guffaw, but it wasn't particularly successful. For some reason, the pleasure of what he'd done to Scarl had lost its flavor. There was a bitter taste in his mouth, as if someone had cheated him.

Trying to muster relish for his story, he concluded, 'Those dirty pictures finished him. They were too embarrassing for the school. He got shipped out. Maybe they sent him to the big boys' lockup.' Unfortunately, he felt no relish. 'I got put in a room with a bunch of motherfuckers who liked to cornhole me when they didn't have anything better to do.

'It was like that until I finally got a chance to break out and get away.'

Her stare hadn't shifted. She was still peering at him darkly over her kneecaps, still waiting. When he stopped, she watched him scowl for a while. Then she asked, 'What does that have to do with me?'

'Huh?' He'd forgotten her question.

'You betrayed your roommate.' Her voice was husky with the stress of all the things he'd done to her. 'But he was the one who protected you. Betraying him probably hurt you worse than it did him. What does it have to do with me?'

Cursing the loss of his expansive mood, Angus sealed his shipsuit. 'It felt good. That's what it has to do with you. It felt good.'

He started to leave in disgust; his back was turned when she said softly, thinly, 'Stop this.'

He paused.

'So far you've got "authorized use." For this zone-implant. I'll testify to that. I'll say you had to do it. To save both of us. Just stop this. Just stop.'

Angus turned to look at her, but now she was not looking at him.

'What happened to being a cop? What happened to all those threats? I thought you were going to find some way to do me in.'

'I'm afraid,' she murmured as if she were pleading. 'I want to live.'

The way she clutched her knees and hid her features suddenly gave him the impression she'd come face-to-face with an essential cowardice.

'I'll crew for you back to Com-Mine Station. I'll testify – I'll say you did the right thing. They'll believe me. I'm UMCP. I won't say anything about those miners. 'I'll' – her voice caught, but she forced herself to go on – 'I'll do whatever you want. I'll be your lover. Just so you stop. Stop hurting me.'

For one strange moment, Angus found himself listening to her as if he could be persuaded – as if she had the power to make him pity her. Had he broken her already? Was she really that far gone? Almost immediately, however, the odd emotion she aroused turned to fear and anger.

'No,' he rasped. 'I'm never going to stop. I'm never going to stop hurting you. You're too frightened. That's what I like.'

Before she could upset him anymore, he left her alone so she could use the san or rest, do whatever she wanted to get herself ready for him.

CHAPTER 8

He found, however, that his drive for her flesh had inexplicably soured. Somehow, the memory of his new roommates in the reform school made him think harder about the dangers of his present position. He was risking too much. Granted that his treatment of Morn Hyland felt as good as he said it did, it still wasn't worth the risk of remaining Stationary, hidden, without repairs.

He had no way to assess absolutely the damage which had been done to his ship. Metal fatigue had strange effects. *Bright Beauty*'s bulkheads might have been weakened; they might start to leak soon – might even rupture. And Morn was *his:* he could have her anytime. Therefore it was stupid to remain where he was, risking himself to gain nothing.

While she took an interminable shower – trying, he supposed with a leer, to get clean of his touch – he began turning some of *Bright Beauty*'s systems back on.

First, in self-defense, he programmed a new series of priority codes and alerts, circumscribing what Morn would be able to do when he gave her access to a console; he arranged warnings for himself if she tried to do anything else. When that was done, he started testing his scanners and sifters.

His tests confirmed what he already knew: *Bright Beauty* had a dangerous blind spot where her ports and antennae had been smashed. That meant he would have to run her under spin, rotating constantly so the sweep of functioning sniffers and sensors could compensate for the blindness. A problem in more ways than one: tricky for the pilot; more difficult to analyze incoming data. But there would be one advantage. While *Bright Beauty* was spinning, Morn wouldn't be able to move around: she would have to stay in her g-seat, strapped against the pull. One less detail to worry about.

He was almost ready to summon her for her first lessons when a small blip on his screen began flashing.

His heart nearly failed at the sight. Instinctive alarm poured through him, as if *Bright Beauty* were under attack. But of course she wasn't, he knew that, *knew* that, despite the way his hands shook as he keyed in commands, identified the alert.

Sickbay.

Morn Hyland was no novice. They'd taught her well in the Academy. During the few seconds he spent identifying the alert, she succeeded in reprogramming the sickbay computer.

Her instructions copied across his screen. She was telling the sickbay to give her a lethal injection of nerve-juice.

Morn.

Angus Thermopyle was a coward: he was at his best when he was afraid. Without thinking about it, without time to think about it, he knew that overriding the sickbay computer from his console would be too slow. There were too many steps to go through; the injection might start before he completed them. And he'd long ago eliminated the automatic safeguards from his medical equipment. Sickbay computers were programmed to preserve rather than endanger the lives of their patients – but scalpels and drugs were such convenient ways of getting rid of crew he despised that he'd deliberately deleted all restrictions from the sickbay systems.

Taking advantage of the asteroid's thin gravity, he flung himself out of his g-seat, kicked himself almost floating in the direction of the sickbay.

At the same time, he grabbed in his pocket for the zone-implant control.

He'd had a lot of practice during the past few days: he was adept at finding the right buttons on the control. Hardly more than four seconds after he understood the alert, he squeezed the function button which rendered her catatonic.

But even that took too long. She'd outsmarted him. She'd stretched out on the berth before keying in her instructions: she'd even strapped herself down. The fact that she was now as blank as a disconnected circuit couldn't save her from the cybernetic probe which reached toward her from the sickbay's equipment bank, aiming its needle for the vein in the side of her neck.

As fast as fear, Angus heaved his bulk through the doorway and grappled for the probe. Too quickly to be careful, he snatched at the needle with his fingers, snapped it off.

At once, the probe stopped. A malfunction light signaled at him from the computer panel.

He ignored it. Even though Morn was catatonic, he knotted his fists on her shoulders, shook her. '*What's the matter with* you?' he raged into her empty face. '*Are you out of your* MIND?'

The fact that she couldn't respond made his desire to hit her unbearable. But when he let go of her to brace himself, cock his arm, one of his hands left a small smudge of blood on her shoulder.

Oh, shit.

He jerked up his hand, gaped at it.

Breaking the needle had scratched his fingers.

He thought he could see a clear fluid mingling with his blood around the scratch.

Oh, *shit*. Nerve-juice was a clear fluid: colorless, tasteless, odorless; attractive only to neurons in their synapses; capable of killing.

With difficulty, he resisted a lunatic impulse to put his fingers in his mouth and suck at the wound.

Nevertheless, he knew exactly what to do. Desperation was almost normal for him.

A rapid slap-and-jerk motion unstrapped Morn from the berth. Careless of her condition, he shoved her to the floor and climbed into her place. Then he turned to the computer's control panel.

Emergency.

Cancel injection.

Clear malfunction.

Treat nerve juice poisoning.

Source of poisoning: right hand.

Trying not to hurry, not to speed up the spread of the juice by hurrying, he stretched himself on his back and opened his right hand for the probes.

With mechanical efficiency, the probes cleaned and sealed his scratch. Attaching a new needle, the cybernetic arm gave him an injection which – according to the monitor – contained a small dose of a block that would cause the nerve-juice to be flushed out of him as waste rather than absorbed as poison.

Coincidentally, the shot also contained a significant amount of cat to ease his supercharged pulse and respiration.

The whole treatment took less than a minute.

Feeling a little light-headed, a little giddy, Angus sat up and looked at Morn Hyland's crumpled form.

She was wearing a shipsuit. Even though she intended to kill herself, she'd gotten dressed first. Maybe she could no longer bear the sight of her own body – of the physical frame which had brought the spirit inside so much grief. Despite the shipsuit, however – and despite her contorted posture, arranged for her by the force of his shove and the asteroid's g – she'd never looked so poignant to him, so lost and desirable.

Cat was having a strange effect on him. A sense of eerie calm filled him as he took the zone-implant control out of his pocket and released her.

A twitch ran through her: her eyes jerked open. For a moment she seemed unable to focus her mind on what had happened. Then she saw the way he was looking at her, and her whole face turned to despair.

'Get up,' he said gruffly, but without violence.

As if what she felt were choking her, she remained where she was at first, clamped rigidly about herself and unable to move. Slowly, however, the spasm eased. She unbent her limbs, got her legs under her; finally she stood in front of him. But she refused to lift her eyes to his face.

In his mind, he saw himself hitting her. He felt his arm rise heavily, felt the shock as the back of his fist caught her face. She deserved it. But he didn't do it. His calm was amazing.

Maybe he'd accomplished something wonderful by making her desperate enough to attempt suicide.

'I want you alive,' he said quietly. 'If you ever try that again, I'm going to do things to you that'll make what you've already been through look romantic. Don't think there isn't anything worse. There is. If I want, I can take you to the nearest bootleg shipyard and make you a public screw for every syphilitic illegal in the whole fucking belt.'

Then he shifted himself off the berth. In a state of grace, as if he'd just granted her absolution, he said, 'Come on. I want you to start earning your keep,' and lumbered away toward *Bright Beauty*'s command module.

He still wasn't sure why he hadn't hit her. Must have been the effect of the cat. Or of the possibility that soon she might be desperate enough to fall in love with him.

CHAPTER 9

In fact, he had every intention of taking her to the nearest bootleg shipyard. He also had every intention of castrating the first man who so much as put a finger on her. He discovered, however, he didn't have that choice.

The truth came to him two days later, while Morn was running *Bright Beauty* through a warm-up, getting ready to lift out of hiding. Morn was a fast learner – much faster than he'd expected. And one thing she'd learned was how to obey him in a way he found reassuring, a way which defused his possessive desire to keep all of *Bright Beauty* under his control.

She'd become subdued, pale in her emotions as well as in her looks. Apparently her sheer abhorrence of his lusts had broken down her resistance to him. And at the same time she was reassured, stabilized, by the fact that she now had something to do, a role which involved ships and skill. As if she were actually grateful to him for letting her work, she obeyed him so implicitly and so well that she instilled confidence. Impressed despite himself by the speed, accuracy, and compliance with which she served his ship, he went so far as to disconnect some of his waldos and relays, transferring a number of secondary functions to her console.

As soon as he did that, of course, he worried about it. But a little ingenious programming enabled him to install a parallel control for her zone-implant on his board, so that he could turn her on and off without having to reach into his pocket – a reach which might not be easy in a crisis, under spin and g.

Calm once again, he actually stopped watching what she did and let her get *Bright Beauty* ready for lift-off by herself. While she worked on that, he spent some time analyzing his finances.

Then he spent more time cursing savagely to himself – all the more savagely because he didn't want her to hear him, so he had to keep his mouth shut.

Money was why he couldn't go where he'd intended. No matter how well they knew him – maybe because of how well they knew him – the shipyard just inside forbidden space wouldn't so much as cycle their airlocks for him on spec. Even their hunger for the goods he supplied, the goods they fenced for him, wouldn't inspire them to extend credit. If he were unable to pay in advance for the work *Bright Beauty* needed, the work wouldn't be done. And if he tried to run a bluff, he risked murder or worse; risked having his ship snatched from him.

Of course, repairs were cheaper on Com-Mine Station. And some people were even given credit. But that was out of the question. In order for the Station shipyard to do repairs, the workmen would need access to some of his ship's secrets. And they would never keep what they discovered to themselves: he was sure of that. They would talk; and Security would hear about it; and he might never get out of dock again.

He couldn't get *Bright Beauty* fixed until he had more money.

He chewed on that for a while, until the implications made him feel cornered and murderous – more like his old self than he had felt for days. Then he snapped at Morn, 'Shut down.'

He appreciated the way she obeyed, without hesitation; so he glared at her like a butcher of babies as she quickly and precisely reversed the warm-up, settled *Bright Beauty* to cool, and keyed off her console before turning to face him.

'I'm sorry,' she said dully. 'What did I do wrong?'

Her assumption that she'd made a mistake pleased him, despite his anger. He dismissed it with a snarl. Brutally, trying to startle the truth out of her because for some reason he was reluctant to trust anything she might tell him under the influence of her zone-implant, he demanded, 'How many people back on Com-Mine know you're after me?'

She was startled; he saw that. Several different responses flickered like hints across her face before she spoke.

'We weren't after you.'

'You found me, didn't you?' he rasped. For some reason, it frightened him to realize he was going to believe whatever she told him. 'You can't expect me to think you were looking for those pissed-out miners. Captain Davies fucking Hyland knew my name. Of course you were after me.'

'Yes.' She spoke slowly, as if she had trouble remembering that part of her past. 'Sort of. We didn't know anything about you when we came out from Earth. I mean personally. But Com-Mine Security gave us your name. Just a list of "suspicious characters" – people to watch out for, ships. They didn't do that because we're UMCP. They didn't know. It's standard procedure for them – they give the same list to any legitimate oreliner that asks. And a lot of rumors mentioned you. We correlated that with the way you pulled out so soon after we arrived. Almost like you knew who we were. That made us interested in you. Very interested. How did you know who we were?

'But we weren't *after* you specifically. We were on patrol, that's all. Looking for pirates. Mine jumpers. Bootleg operations. We just happened to find you.'

The effort of memory hurt her: she had to reach back through so much horror. Therefore she was telling the truth.

'"Just happened,"' he snorted. 'Don't try to con me, bitch. I was in a played-out part of the belt. The only people there who need *protecting* are scavengers. Like those miners. You don't patrol places like that. You patrol where the money is.'

Again her expression hinted at horror. She'd killed her whole family. 'You forget. We were covert – pretending to be a new oreliner. If we wanted to lure anybody after us, we had to go somewhere unexpected – somewhere that would surprise people who knew the belt.

'That's the main thing we were trying to do. Lure somebody like you to follow us.

'But I suppose we *were* after you, in a way. Even if we weren't covert, it's standard practice for ships like *Starmaster* to go where they aren't expected. Shake people up a little. And the way you headed out when we came in made us think you were ripe for shaking. We didn't know where to find you, but we thought it made sense to scan the nearest played-out parts of the belt first, just to see what we could stir up. Where would a ship go if she wanted to hide?

'I guess it was a deliberate coincidence. It happened because we were trying to make it happen. We were looking for you. But we weren't doing anything out of the ordinary.' She spoke tonelessly, without expression, holding herself numb to pain. 'Until you blasted those miners, we knew there was always the chance you were innocent.'

'All right. All *right*.' His glare was yellow with malice and fear, but he didn't get out of his g-seat, or make her come to him, or work any of the buttons on her zone-implant control. 'If you fuckers left me alone, none of this would have happened. You haven't answered my question. Who did you tell? Who knew what you were doing?'

For a moment or two she remained silent, staring at her board. Then she sighed. 'Nobody. That's the whole point of going covert. When we come out from Earth, we don't know who we can trust. So we don't tell anybody anything. We do our job and take the rest one step at a time.

'The last mission my fa— Captain Hyland was on, somebody in Station Center turned out to be feeding information to half a dozen pirates. It's better if we don't tell anybody anything.'

Angus believed her. In fact, the only reason he'd doubted her at all was that the intensity of his need to believe her made him suspicious. Everything hinged on it. At the moment, he had no other hope. He couldn't run *Bright Beauty* in this condition indefinitely. Sooner or later, she would fail him if he put that much pressure on her.

But if Morn were telling the truth—

If she were telling the truth, he could get away with it. It might be the riskiest bluff he'd tried in years, but he could get away with it.

If she were telling the truth.

And if he could control her.

If he could break her into small enough pieces.

Abruptly he heaved himself out of his g-seat. 'Come on.' Ignoring the involuntary revulsion that ached across her features before she could suppress it, he headed toward the sickbay. 'You kept your mouth shut for the cops. I'm going to make sure you do the same for me.'

In the sickbay he studied her face, drilled her, dredged the information he needed out of her, and drove himself between her legs in spasms of fear and hope. Eagerly, avidly, he watched her for signs that she was falling in love – that she was growing dependent on her helplessness.

CHAPTER 10

He did his best to believe it was happening. In an odd way, as long as he kept her alive his survival depended on her: he could be truly safe only if he killed her and disposed of her body. And that option was one he no longer considered. He was as likely to destroy *Bright Beauty* as to murder Morn. Therefore he couldn't afford to be wrong. He had to break her and be sure of it; damage her so much that he could trust the results.

Because he was afraid, he was in no danger of trusting them prematurely.

In the end, however, his success was inevitable. After all, what choice did she have? He'd made himself her entire world; he was everything she felt. He knew how this kind of pressure worked: it had been tried on him more than once. His control of her circumstances – as well as of her physical being – was absolute. With the tap of a button, he could reduce her mind to a brute howl of pain. When she satisfied him, he could reward her, not with pleasure – for some reason, he was reluctant to see what she would look like pleased – but with relief from hurt; with sleep; with the occasional opportunity to choose her own movements, take care of herself in her own way.

By degrees, he beat her down until she was like a child toward him: dependent; urgent to please. He taught her that his survival was hers as well; that any peril he met would hit her first, and harder. And he played on the bizarre ethic to which she'd sworn herself when she became a cop. Again and again, he assured her that she deserved what was happening to her. She'd killed her family, hadn't she? She'd betrayed them all. No, it wasn't something she'd done by conscious choice. It was worse: it was something she'd done because of who she was; because of the fundamental flaw which left her vulnerable to gap-sickness.

With all his cunning, he worked to deprive her of her capacity to think in any terms which didn't come to her from him.

And he watched the results, studied them with a coward's intuitive precision. He saw the darkness accumulating in her gaze; the gradual slackening of her skin; the change in the way she moved, so that every action became a limp. When he fucked her, he felt her begin to respond, driven to swallow her revulsion by self-loathing and the need to satisfy him. When she slept, he heard her whimpering for help which never came.

At last even his grubby, suspicious nature believed that she'd been damaged enough to risk.

Still cautious, he prepared his safeguards and coercions. Then, with a UMC cop for crew, he took his ship out of hiding.

Six days later, *Bright Beauty* sputtered into Com-Mine Station's control space and requested permission to dock.

No one asked any awkward questions at that point. No one had reason to: no one knew *Starmaster* was lost. *Bright Beauty* was given permission to dock and instructed to await normal inspection.

The inspector assigned to clear Angus Thermopyle and *Bright Beauty* wasn't particularly interested in his job that day. Even brain-numb on cat, however, he could hardly have failed to notice the anomalous fact that Angus had left Com-Mine Station purportedly alone and now returned with a woman as crew.

He didn't ask Angus to explain this detail. He had no wish to risk making a fool of himself. Instead, he got Morn's name and fed it into the Station's id computer.

After that, the situation got messy.

Bright Beauty was slapped in quarantine, and a whole parade of inspectors trooped through her, asking questions, issuing directives, making demands. As the inspectors went up in rank – therefore in determination to be obeyed – their questions and directives and demands became more aggressive and personal. And all of them were aimed at Morn Hyland.

What happened to *Starmaster*?

How did you survive?

How did you end up with *him*?

Unfortunately, the authorities found themselves in a frustrating position. Center was worried – in fact, outright alarmed – about *Starmaster*. Security practically salivated for the chance to get their hands on Angus. But they had nothing to go on: no formal record of the truth about *Starmaster;* nothing but hints. And Morn refused to answer their questions. She was a cop – and she refused.

Periodically, an inspector tried to appropriate *Bright Beauty*'s datacore. Angus positively declined to release it until he was required to do so by law – until he was formally charged with a crime.

Periodically, attempts were made to get Morn away from him. Each time, she brandished her UMCP id tag and dismissed any superior authority. Although she chose not to speak, she tacitly covered Angus with her police mantle.

The more perceptive Station personnel observed that there was more than a little pain in the way she stood beside Angus. For a cop, she looked unusually vulnerable; almost frightened. If they'd met her alone in the halls of DelSec, they would have assumed she was a derelict. If they were kind, they would have tried to help her.

But here they could do nothing. Her id tag put her beyond challenge. And Angus held his ground with his hands in the pockets of his shipsuit, glowering at everybody and stonewalling expertly.

What happened to *Starmaster*?

Blew up, he answered for her. For no reason. Must have been sabotage. We'll give you the coordinates if you want to search the wreck.

How did you survive?

Freak accident. The auxiliary bridge held. She still would have died eventually, but I rescued her.

Angus could see the terrible hurt behind her eyes, but he relied on the zone-implant to keep her quiet. And he relied on her silence – and her id tag – to baffle the inspectors.

Why are you with him? He's a known pirate. We just haven't been able to prove it yet. You're UMCP. What kind of hold has he got on you? Do you actually expect us to believe he's telling the *truth*?

I don't care what you believe, Angus said with relish. I told you. *Starmaster* blew up. She was sabotaged. That must have been done here. Before she left Com-Mine Station. Morn nodded dully. Angus glowered at everybody and kept his hand in his pocket. She doesn't know who she can trust, but she's damn sure she can't trust you.

The inspectors wheedled and demanded, but they were unable to make Morn speak.

The only question they really wanted Angus to answer was: What happened to your ship? You look like you've been in a dogfight.

Look again. Scan me. That isn't matter fire. I got hit by a rock.

An experienced 'Captain' like you? That must have been some rock.

I was in the belt. I was running *Bright Beauty* by myself. I miscalculated. Is that a crime?

The inspectors were in no mood to give up, however. They tried to trap him.

Starmaster was after you. You crashed trying to run. Isn't that the truth?

No.

Then how did you happen to be the one who came to the rescue – you with a damaged ship?

Coincidence. I was close enough. The blast made my scan go crazy. Radio interference. Particle noise. That kind of static doesn't happen unless there's been a disaster, so I tracked it back and found her. With an effort, Angus refrained from pointing out how virtuous his conduct had been.

The dock manifest says you left without buying supplies. Your air scrubbers should have failed a long time ago. How come you're still breathing?

Rescuer's privilege. I took filters from her ship.

His bluff was working. As long as Morn didn't come apart under the strain, he was going to be safe.

Why is she staying with you? What's your hold on her?

She's going to hire somebody to carry a message back to Earth. We'd do it ourselves, but *Bright Beauty* can't cross the gap. When UMCPHQ sends out instructions, she'll know what to do. Until then, she trusts me more than you.

In the end, the inspectors had no choice. Of course, they didn't believe the story. Under other circumstances, they might have stretched the law far enough to keep *Bright Beauty* quarantined at least until Station techs had a chance to visit and analyze *Starmaster*'s wreckage. But Morn Hyland was UMCP; not under Station jurisdiction. The assumption had to be made that she knew what she was doing, that her actions were reasonable and shouldn't be interfered with.

Bright Beauty was cleared.

Angus Thermopyle took Morn Hyland directly to DelSec.

His bluff had worked.

He had no actual desire to go to Mallorys. He wanted to seal his hatches and fuck Morn until she wept. It was still possible that his hold on her might snap, and he didn't want to risk her in public. But he knew he was going to be watched for a long time – at least until inspectors got back from *Starmaster*. It was important to behave normally. At that moment, 'normal' meant Mallorys, where he could start trying to buy the information he needed to make money.

He'd been walking down the path to his doom for some time. Now his doom started moving toward him.

Even though she was unfamiliar with DelSec, he stayed half a step behind Morn's shoulder so he could keep an eye on her. At once elated and afraid, possessive and angry, he noticed how every man they passed looked at her – noticed it and hated them. In the same way that he'd planned revenge against *Starmaster* for driving him off Com-Mine Station, he now evolved elaborate, impossible schemes which would teach all these bastards to fear him. It was conceivable that he could claim salvage on *Starmaster*. Morn's UMCP id tag might make that possible. With enough money, he would get *Bright Beauty* rebuilt, better than before. Then he would be invulnerable. He could do anything he wanted.

Dreams like that helped him endure the crowds he despised in DelSec and Mallorys.

He hated Mallorys, of course. But it was better than any of the alternatives. As a group, the drunks and ruins and illegals there knew more and cared less than the rest of the people in DelSec. They meant him harm in ways he understood. For that reason, they were less dangerous than they thought.

Station gravity – roughly .9g – made him feel leaden, bloated; he was in no mood for a drink. His bluff had worked! But everybody on Com-Mine was waiting for him to make a mistake and get caught; all the inspectors, everybody in Security, every prospector or miner who'd ever

73

tried the belt, everybody in Mallorys who knew his reputation and didn't trust him. And Morn walked as if the weight meant nothing – as if in spite of the many ways it could be hurt, her body carried its beauty easily. All those men wanted her. They wanted to get her away from him.

He was already feeling frightened and bloodthirsty when he caught sight of Nick Succorso through the heat and din of Mallorys.

At once, he felt like he'd been hit in the chest by an impact-ram – more so because he couldn't show it, didn't dare react in front of all these people, let them see his weakness.

He would have recognized Nick as an enemy immediately in any case: he knew how to interpret that careless grin, that sharp, buccaneering gleam of humor and superiority. He knew Nick's contempt for him was instantaneous. He was ugly and luckless and not very clean, and Nick had already begun to sneer at him.

Under any circumstances, Angus would have gone a long way out of his way to damage Nick Succorso. That was instinctive and fundamental, like his initial panic when he saw *Starmaster*.

But this was worse, much worse: this was like watching someone aim a rifle straight into his face and fire. He saw Nick glance at him, dismiss him – and look at Morn. He saw the scars that underlined Nick's gaze darken, as if his vision had begun to smolder. And he saw Morn's reaction.

Her face betrayed nothing. She said nothing. But he knew her intimately – knew every pulse of her heartbeat, every hue of her skin, every shade of horror and hurt in the depths of her eyes. He knew immediately, in front of all those people, without another second for consideration or effort, that Nick Succorso had more power over her than he did.

Nick had the power to make her want him.

And yet that recognition was only the beginning: the full truth was still worse. Until this moment, when he saw and understood – or thought he understood – the way Morn and Nick looked at each other, Angus Thermopyle hadn't known how weak he really was. He hadn't realized how much power he lacked – and how much he wanted that power, how much he grieved for it. He could make – had made – Morn do anything and everything his lust or loathing conceived. Like a drunk or a derelict, he'd believed that was enough. But it wasn't enough, oh no, never enough, not now. He'd duped himself, blinded and fooled himself.

He'd taught her to cooperate in her own degradation. He'd taught her to act as if he were necessary to her. No matter what he did, however, he could never make her *want* him. The buttons on the zone-implant control which tuned her so that every nerve in her body obeyed his desire were impotent compared to the jaunty burn of Nick's gaze.

It wasn't fair. She belonged to Angus. She was *his*.

He had no way to know he was wrong.

CHAPTER 11

The truth was that Morn Hyland didn't see Nick Succorso as a sexual being at all. On that point, everyone who noticed her situation or gave any thought to her reactions was wrong. She hardly noticed Nick was male. If she had, she would have turned her back on him, would have refused him with the same debased instinct for survival which had caused her to refuse any possibility of hope which the Station inspectors might have represented.

She didn't want a man. Any male touch would have made her ache to scream and puke, just as Angus himself did. She'd been raped and raped until the violation had reached through her flesh to her spirit; pain and abhorrence had soaked into the marrow of her bones. If Nick Succorso had put his hand on her as a man, she would have flinched away, exactly as she did when Angus touched her.

Angus had more power over her than he realized.

Yet he was right when he sensed that something leapt up inside Morn at the sight of Nick Succorso.

That 'something,' however, had nothing whatever to do with Nick's handsomeness, his virility, his physical appeal. Instead it had to do with his look of raffish eagerness, his scarred and buccaneering appearance of bravado. She wanted him, not as a man, but as an effective force. He might be strong and cunning – not to mention unscrupulous – enough to destroy the man who was destroying her.

Did she think Nick might set her free, redeem her from her anguish? No. Angus had come too close to breaking her. She no longer had the imagination – or the courage – to dream so far.

But he'd taught her how to hate. And she had learned that lesson profoundly. Her own hate lived with the pain and abhorrence in the marrow of her bones. The 'something' which had leapt up in her at the sight of Nick Succorso was simply the hope that Angus could be beaten.

As for Nick himself—

Like Angus, the other people in Mallorys were wrong about him as well.

Oh, he noticed her beauty immediately and was attracted to it. His virility was no sham: his taste for lovely female flesh never left him. In part for that reason, he had nurtured a wide reputation as a lover. But he had other reasons also. He liked winning, so he did whatever was necessary to make his women respond to him passionately. And he had a hunger for revenge; especially sexual revenge. He yearned to get even.

The truth – which he kept to himself – was that he didn't actually like women. In secret, he feared and despised them. Their bodies had value only to the extent that his response to them could draw an even greater response from them. Where such satisfactions weren't at issue, he had no interest in them. He preferred seeing them hurt.

The explanation for this was a mystery only in the sense that he never spoke of it.

Once, when he was barely a man in years, and no more than a boy in experience, he'd been bested by a woman. And as she beat him, cheated him, ruined his dreams, she sneered at him. His scars were the marks of her contempt, the visible sign that she hadn't considered him worth killing. Everyone else she *had* killed, every other man on that ship, nearly twenty of them; but him she'd left with only his scars to remember her by. There was nothing he could do that would make her fear him.

That ship had been the original *Captain's Fancy*, the inspiration of the name Nick now used for his pretty frigate. The love he felt for his present ship was an echo of his yearning for that earlier vessel. She'd been his dream from the moment when he'd first become old enough to have such dreams.

Nick Succorso – which, incidentally, wasn't his real name – had been born Station-bound in the same sense that some people were planet-bound, unable or unwilling to leave for one reason or another. He was the son of a family of administrators living on a Station like Com-Mine, but half a hundred parsecs away, a Station that tended one of the official (therefore rich) trading routes between Earth and forbidden space. There he'd begun watching scan at an early age, just as most of the children of administrators did on that Station, to learn the skills they would need for the rest of their lives.

Unlike most of his peers, however, he'd fallen in love with what he watched, with the vast gulf of space and the lure of the gap, with the romance of sailing the imponderable stellar winds, with the mysterious lurch-and-translation which took men and ships across dimensions beyond the reach of their former lives.

Specifically, he'd fallen in love with *Captain's Fancy*.

She seemed to him the bravest of the best, a trim metal sheath of power which pierced the heavens and the gap. Her lines were sleek, yet she bristled with weapons. Her holds were huge, yet she swept across scan and docked and undocked as gracefully as a creature of the great deep. Her crew were exotic men drawn from the strangest parts of the galaxy, men with the strength to pit themselves against the vacuum and forbidden space, and the wealth they traded was fabulous. Young Nick Succorso ached to sign aboard their ship under any imaginable contract or conditions.

Good heavens, no! said his mother.

Are you out of your mind? asked his father.

As for the Captain of *Captain's Fancy*, he simply said, No. Regal as a lord in his braid and authority, he dismissed Nick out of hand. If the command second hadn't taken pity on Nick's crushed look, Nick never would have been given any explanation at all. But the command second, who meant well, had taken the time to say, Forget it, kid. We never take crew from Stationers. Too much trouble. Haven't got the instincts. Only way you'll ever get on a ship is, go to one of the academies. Earth. Aleph Green. Orion's Reach.

Good heavens, no! his mother repeated.

Are you out of your mind? demanded his father. What makes you think we've got that kind of money?

Nick was never stupid. He could see his dreams curdling. He would never be able to earn 'that kind of money' by himself. The only jobs which paid that well were jobs on ships.

But he couldn't bear to see his dreams curdle, so he let something else inside him go sour.

He began to plot crimes.

In those days, piracy was a constant and maddening problem across the shipping lanes. The UMC Police were relatively new; their ability to enforce the laws Earth made didn't reach far. And forbidden space didn't appear to make any reliable distinction between sanctioned and dishonest trade.

With the logic of the young, Nick reasoned that wherever there was piracy, there were pirates. And wherever there were pirates, there was a demand for information.

Destinations. Cargoes. Arrival dates. Departure trajectories. Route clearances.

Nick worked scan. Indirectly, at least, he had access to that kind of information.

Even as a youth, hardly a young man yet, he was someone whose chances came to him when he needed them, when he was ready for them. As soon as he was sour enough, and had made his plans sufficiently concrete, and had developed his access to information, he met the woman who scarred him.

The scars came later, of course. She knew what she was doing and did it well. First came casual conversation. Casual drinks. Casual sex. His first casual mention of *Captain's Fancy* passed as if she hadn't heard it. Only after he'd told her enough about his plans, his information, his needs – only then did she let him see the hunger in her eyes.

She wanted that ship.

And he was really just a kid. He didn't have any trouble convincing himself that she wanted *Captain's Fancy* the same way he did.

So he betrayed the ship he loved. He thought he would end up as part of her new crew. Eventually – so the dream went – he would end up as her new Captain.

For what he later swore was the last time in his life, he was wrong.

The woman took him with her aboard her own ship. He was with her as she ambushed *Captain's Fancy*, crippled the merchanter, forced the vessel to surrender. He accompanied her when she boarded the drifting hulk.

Already reality diverged from his dream. *Captain's Fancy* wasn't supposed to be ruined like this. As for the regal Captain and his crew – Nick wanted them humiliated, of course; but he was a bit young to stomach such frank slaughter.

Nevertheless reality continued to diverge.

The woman didn't take him with her when she left. After killing the crew, emptying the holds, gutting the communication gear, she laughed at Nick and scarred him and abandoned him.

He pleaded, of course. He believed he loved her. He believed she loved him. He was young enough to have persuaded himself of almost anything for the sake of his dreams. But his ideas of love only made her giggle in scorn. Her knife told him what she thought of having him in her bed. When she left, there were tears streaming through the blood into his mouth.

After that, he was alone on a wreck a million kilometers from the Station, with no skills, no knowledge – and no engines. By rights, he should have died.

He didn't. Instead, he became the Nick Succorso he was now. By the time he'd contrived to be rescued – some rather ingenious manipulation of *Captain's Fancy*'s residual emissions produced the effect of a beacon and eventually attracted a passing cruiser – he'd assumed the id files and certifications of the ship's cabin boy, the real Nick Succorso, and had taught himself the skills to back up his new credentials.

Once rescued, of course, he'd given the UMCP everything he knew about the woman who cut him. That enabled them to harry her out of his part of space. He never saw her again.

Naturally, however, he never forgot her. From the time of his first legitimate shipboard post until the day when he snatched the present *Captain's Fancy* for himself, from the moment of his first successful raid until now, she was always with him. His scars grew dark under his eyes whenever he saw something he wanted, something that wasn't his; the slashes on his cheeks turned the color of curdled blood.

Under other circumstances, he wouldn't have lifted a finger to help Morn Hyland. Women in pain were the next best thing to women who loved him. Both pain and love helped him get even.

But under *these* circumstances—

Nick Succorso was drawn to the idea of rescuing Morn for several reasons. Angus Thermopyle himself was one of them. Nick knew Angus' reputation, of course: he knew Angus wasn't just a competitor; he was a dangerous competitor. And Nick was prepared to tolerate competition only as long as it wasn't good enough – wasn't dangerous enough – to get in his way; to cast him in the shade. He saw Morn Hyland immediately as a handle on Angus, a lever to use against the competition.

His other reasons were more complex.

Her relevance – if any – to his concerns as the master of *Captain's Fancy* was unclear. Did he see her as a source of wealth? Did he mean to exact ransom from the Hyland family? From Com-Mine Station? The UMCP itself? He may have had a source of information about her that wasn't generally available. If so, he didn't mention it.

However, her relevance to his personal buccaneering was plain enough.

In some of its details, her condition was obvious at a glance. She was attached to a man she hated, fixed to an illegal who repelled her. What did that imply about her? On this point, his reasoning was unique in Mallorys. For him, her attachment implied, not that she was subject to coercion, but that her capacity to respond was so intense, so over-whelming, that she couldn't control it. She couldn't help herself.

And if she had *that* kind of response to someone like Angus Thermopyle, if her own passions left her *that* abject—

Nick Succorso's scars darkened and his mouth actually went dry at the thought of how Morn's passions might make her respond to him.

So Angus Thermopyle was wrong about Nick – as wrong as he was about Morn herself. But he was also right. The danger was real. Without a word to each other, with no more contact between them than a gaze or two, they had banded together against him.

And he had to face it all, realize it all, and swallow it, show nothing. Instinct was of no use to him here. He was cornered by his situation, trapped with a perception he would have cheerfully committed murder to avoid. He needed money. Therefore he needed Mallorys; needed the people who came to Mallorys and sold secrets. In addition, Security was watching him. Even in DelSec, there were spies. He was being studied for any sign of a mistake, scrutinized for any evidence of weakness. He couldn't afford to give himself away by retreating; by revealing that he recognized his danger.

He stayed where he was, keeping his mask of belligerent disinterest in place, simply because he was afraid of the consequences if he did anything else.

Gruffly he ordered Morn to a seat at one of the condensation-stained tables – a seat with her back to Nick Succorso. He made sure the way he talked to her was loud enough to be overheard, so her obedience would be noticed. Then he sat down beside her and squeezed her against him possessively. Look at us, you bastards, you motherfucking sons of shit. Look at her. She's *mine*. Mine!

He put on a good performance. Nobody in Mallorys knew that he'd witnessed the way Morn and Nick looked at each other, that he'd felt the electricity between them. But his success gave him no satisfaction. It was Morn he wanted, her desire, her willingness – the parts of herself which he'd been unable to extort from her; the parts which she'd just given away.

He was going to have to kill Nick. There was no other answer. There was no other way to hurt her enough, to punish her for doing this to him.

Through a haze of rage and grief, he ordered drinks he didn't want and paid for them. He heard people talking around him. Some of them spoke to him. He spoke to some of them. The ones who mattered knew why he was here, what he wanted; he didn't need to go looking for them, not yet.

By no flicker of attention or shift of expression did Morn betray she knew Nick Succorso was alive. But Angus read the heightened hue of her skin and thought he understood it.

Through sheer force of panic, he stayed in Mallorys for more than an hour: long enough to appear normal; to ensure the word would be passed that Angus Thermopyle was back on Station; long enough so no one would guess he was afraid. Then he took Morn back to *Bright Beauty*.

She expected trouble. He saw it in the covert way she glanced at him, in the concealed alarm and compliance of her posture. She had a secret now, an intention she needed to protect. Well, good for her. He meant trouble. He was perfectly willing to defile and humiliate every inch of her to take the sting out of his heart. His stomach was a knot of black hate, and his brain was so full of violence he could hardly keep his balance.

When they'd boarded the ship, he made a deliberate and meticulous show of sealing the hatches, rigging security alarms, cutting off communication; isolating *Bright Beauty* from the Station, as if he wanted to prolong the suspense for her, give her every chance to be terrified by what was coming.

After that, he engaged her zone-implant control.

He planned only to make her passive. He wanted her to see and feel everything he did. But his fingers seemed to have a mind of their own. His whole body ignored the dark ruin clamoring inside him. Instead of tuning Morn to passivity, or even catatonia, he pushed the buttons which put her to sleep. Then he scooped her up in his arms and carried her to a berth.

He settled her on the thin mattress; adjusted a pillow under her head; tucked a blanket around her, securing it to its g-seals. While his stomach clenched and tore, and his brain reeled, he left her and closed off the passageway to her cabin, locking himself alone in the command module.

Then he started to howl like a grief-stricken beast.

CHAPTER 12

He would have been better off if he had gone to a bootleg shipyard, of course. Perhaps he could have sold Morn's favors for the money he needed to get *Bright Beauty* made whole. Power over her would have brought a much higher price there than on Com-Mine Station. And – assuming Nick Succorso followed him – he could have faced his enemy in a more naked and therefore fairer arena.

He would have been better off if he'd simply undocked from Com-Mine Station, launched a few torpedoes at *Captain's Fancy*, and then fled for his life.

He would have been better off if he'd killed Morn Hyland and ashed her in *Bright Beauty*'s thruster tubes.

In fact, from moment to moment during the next two standard weeks he fully intended to do any one or all of those things. But he didn't.

Instead, he worked on arranging Nick's destruction.

First, of course, he took care of *Bright Beauty*. He had her serviced as thoroughly as possible without major repairs. He paid for X-ray analysis to test her shell and bulkheads for metal fatigue. He bought all the new components he could afford. And he gave her name and id letters a fresh coat of paint.

At the same time, however, he asked questions whenever he could. He paid sums which nearly broke him for information – even for hints. And finally, guided by those hints, for one brief, glorious moment he succeeded at breaking into the Station's main computer. Before the computer's security systems forced him to retreat so that his intrusion wouldn't be traced, he pulled as much data as he could.

By some standards, it wasn't much. Routine files aside, all he gleaned was the codes and routing by which *Captain's Fancy* talked to the Station's computer network.

In theory, this knowledge was useless to him. After all, he couldn't get at the physical lines which carried *Captain's Fancy*'s business to the computers and back again. Anything that tampered with the integrity of those lines would register immediately. And knowledge of the codes and routing was pointless without access to the actual data-stream.

Angus was desperate, however. In his own opinion, he'd lost his mind. In self-defense, he put Morn to sleep, so that she wouldn't know about and couldn't interfere with what he did. Then, hyperventilating so hard that his suit could hardly keep up with it, and sweating like a beast, he went EVA.

He got away with it because it was such an odd thing to do. People who wanted to work outside their ships did so in the shipyard, over on the other side of Com-Mine. And only men as suspicious as Angus himself scanned the ships around them while they were in dock. Apparently Nick Succorso wasn't that suspicious. Or maybe he had too much confidence in his own invulnerability. Nobody noticed what Angus was doing.

Clamped to the metal surface with limpets, and keeping his head turned grimly away from the fathomless starfield, he moved along the staggering curve of Com-Mine's skin from *Bright Beauty* to *Captain's Fancy*. When he got there, he used a current sensor to read each of the lines connecting the ship to the Station until he identified the one that carried the data-stream. Then, with savage care, he wrapped a dummy line tightly around it from output to receptacle and ran the dummy back to his ship.

Aboard *Bright Beauty* again, he didn't give himself time to recover from the ordeal of EVA. He was obsessed. His hands shook in eagerness and fear as he sent power down his line, surrounding *Captain's Fancy*'s data-stream with a delicate magnetic field. Then he put a scope on his line and watched the field for fluctuations.

It worked. Under full boost, his scope began to show a swift series of spikes and scoops, a fluttering progression too quick for the eye to interpret.

His computer had the codes and routing: now it had an echo of the actual data-stream. Soon he could call up a display of everything *Captain's Fancy* and Com-Mine Station said to each other.

Under different circumstances, his interest in this information would have been specific and temporary. He would have used what he knew to plunder Nick's finances, transfer to himself everything Nick owned. It wouldn't have been difficult to make that kind of computer transaction untraceable, using his own codes and routing. Then he would have detached his dummy line and sat back, daring anyone aboard *Captain's Fancy* to guess what had happened.

Now, however, Angus had other plans.

In a sense, the situation was simplified by the fact that Nick didn't have enough money to repair *Bright Beauty*. Despite his successful air, he was no wealthier than Angus. Without that temptation, Angus had an easier time stifling the impulse to touch or alter anything he found. He didn't want to warn his enemy of the danger, didn't want to let Nick know he was being stalked.

Instead of tampering with the data-stream, he programmed his computer to alert him if any one of a long list of key words and names appeared in the ship-Station dialogue. As an afterthought, because he was inherently suspicious, he told the computer to do the same if any unidentifiable codes were used.

Then he left *Bright Beauty* and went about the business of behaving normally.

When he returned to his ship and reviewed what his computer had gleaned, he found no mention of himself or Morn or anything he could recognize. He learned only that Nick Succorso was faithful about logging in and out of *Captain's Fancy*.

And Nick had received two messages in a code Angus' computer didn't recognize and couldn't crack.

Angus had no way to read those messages. But he could trace them because he already knew the routing.

They came from Station Security.

When he discovered that, he wanted to laugh and scream and break something and celebrate all at once. It was the perfect touch – the final reason why his bluff had worked. There was in fact a leak in Security, a traitor. Why else would Nick Succorso be receiving coded messages from that source? The vacuum-based accusation Angus had prepared to protect his hold on Morn had hit Com-Mine's inspectors where they lived: its blind accuracy had given it an almost prescient credibility.

And Nick Succorso's swashbuckling success was based on inside information. He had an ally in Security; a friend in power.

Characteristically, Angus didn't worry about *why*. He didn't even care about *how*. The fact itself was all that interested him.

Nick Succorso had an ally in Security.

That made him more dangerous. But it also diminished him. He didn't stand on his own: he was a good face with nothing behind it; empty bravado. A nerve-juice addict could do everything he did – as long as the junkie had inside information to back him up, a friend in power. Nick could sneer at anybody he wanted; but it only mattered because he had Security on his side.

'You bastard,' Angus muttered through his teeth. 'You shit-eating bastard. I'm going to rip your balls off.'

It was just a question of when and where.

CHAPTER 13

During this period – nearly a week – Morn Hyland spent most of her time either catatonic or asleep. When Angus wanted to use her, he did so without rousing her from the influence of her zone-implant. He didn't want her to know what he was doing: he couldn't take the risk that she might find some way to sabotage him. For that reason, he got her out of bed only for meals, or to go to Mallorys with him.

Every time he used her body, he hardened his resolve against Nick Succorso. And every time he took her out in public, the desire to protect her burned as brightly as terror in him.

But the second week was different. Now Angus timed his trips away from *Bright Beauty* to coincide with Nick's absences from *Captain's Fancy*. And he wore under his shipsuit a nerve beeper, a small electrode taped to the skin and set to tingle whenever *Captain's Fancy* relayed a summons for Nick through Com-Mine communications, requesting his return to his ship. Taking Morn with him now to Mallorys was part of Angus' plan, part of the bait. He wanted to make Nick see her and do something: he wanted to make Nick want her badly enough to take action.

In fact, he almost went so far as to buy her new clothes. She could be ravishing, if he gave her the chance. And he ached to do that, for his own sake as well as hers, so that she would be ravishing and *his*, like *Bright Beauty* with fresh paint.

But in the end he decided to keep her in her rumpled, illfitting shipsuit, not because of the money, but because of the danger. If she looked too good, she might attract trouble he wasn't ready for. And there was always the possibility – he took it seriously only because he was too suspicious to do anything else – that Nick was smart enough to smell a trap when it was smothered in perfume.

He wanted Nick to do something because almost anything he did would give Angus an excuse to kill him – and would provide as well a plea of self-defense against any murder charge. Angus could be ready for almost anything because he knew more about Nick's business and activities than Nick could guess.

And when Nick was gone, Angus would be in an ideal position to make use of what he knew about Station Security. Nick's ally might become his. A little leverage, a little blackmail, might make it possible for Angus to live as well as Nick did now.

So he made sure Nick saw Morn as often as possible. Secretly, cunningly, so that no one grasped what he was doing, he flaunted her in front of Nick, urging him, goading him.

At the same time, darkness swirled around in Angus' head and his hands itched for blood because he knew that behind her blank expression, her wounded and necessary emptiness, Morn was on fire for his enemy.

Each time he put her where she and Nick could see each other, he swore to himself, *promised*, that as soon as he got her back to the ship he was going to rip out her female organs and feed them down the garbage processor, so that no man would ever have any reason to desire her again.

And each time, when they returned to *Bright Beauty*, he couldn't control the gentleness which came over him. He flung obscenities at her with his mouth; but his touch was soft, nearly tentative. The things he made her do were strangely decorous, almost considerate, as if after depriving her of will and hope and humanity he wished her to forgive him.

She tried to hide it, but she couldn't conceal her perplexity. He knew her too well: he could read the color of her eyes, the small muscles in her cheeks. She felt the change in him, the distress, and didn't know what it meant.

Gentleness? From Angus Thermopyle? She knew him too well.

She watched him as if she could see that he was doomed.

Was she gloating? He believed she was. He believed that she already counted on Nick Succorso to rescue her and destroy him. He believed that she was already measuring out his blood in drops of pain. The thought made all his limbs knot with the force of his need to tear her apart.

Yet he didn't hurt her. She was too precious. And too perplexed. Her confusion had implications he couldn't begin to understand. He wasn't the kind of man who could imagine that she might be reconsidering her hate. He could never have understood that his fear and gentleness might have touched her in the very place which his abuse had made vulnerable.

Alone in the command module, he had to grind his teeth to keep from howling.

Damn you completely to hell and horror! What have you done to me?

He told himself he was ready. He'd been a match for men like Nick Succorso since he was twelve. And he knew everything he needed about Nick except the content of those coded messages. He was *ready*. Of course he was ready.

But the clenched ache deep down in his gut told him he wasn't ready. He felt that he was never going to be ready again.

What have you done *to me?*

He spent all the time his enemy allowed him feverishly trying to break that secret code. But whenever Nick left *Captain's Fancy*, Angus also took Morn out of *Bright Beauty* so that no one would know – so that he himself wouldn't know – how fundamental and compulsory his fear had become.

Finally he reached the end of his endurance. He'd waited and plotted and struggled for a week, and still Nick did nothing. Angus never doubted that some harm was being planned against him: he simply couldn't bear the suspense any longer. Any day now, he was going to fall on his knees and beg Morn to pardon him. And if that happened, he was ruined.

Fear and desperation made him do things that looked brave – or at least foolhardy.

With Morn, he spent an inordinately long time in Mallorys, buying drinks that only tightened the knot in his stomach, glowering ferociously at everyone who addressed him, seething under Nick's gaze and ignoring it. But when Nick got up to leave with his crew, his retinue, Angus also heaved upright, snarled Morn to his side.

Without much difficulty, he contrived to arrive in the doorway in time to block Nick's way.

In fact, it seemed a little too easy. Angus' instincts were shrill with alarm. Nick seemed to want this encounter as much as he did.

But he couldn't back down; not now. He was too scared.

'After you, Captain Succorso,' he growled, making no effort to disguise his malice. 'I know you're in a hurry.'

Nick bowed gracefully, but didn't move. 'On the contrary, Captain Thermo-pile.' Except for his scars, his expression was bland. 'I'm in no hurry at all. Please' – he gestured expansively – 'after you.'

His gaze and his bow and his gesture were all aimed at Morn.

'Ther-*mop*-a-lee,' Angus retorted. 'Ther-*mop*-a-lee. Get it right, Succorso.'

'Really?' Nick cocked a self-assured eyebrow. Apparently he liked the situation. Perhaps it was a kind of stim he especially enjoyed, an adrenaline rush. 'Right here in the door? Extraordinary.

'You're plotting, Captain Thermo-pile. You're hatching something. You've got it in your pocket right now. Or are you just playing with yourself?

'Why don't you open up about it? Let someone in to help you.'

In one way, Angus seemed to go blind with rage. Playing? *Playing*? But in another, he'd never been clearer, calmer. I'll show you who's *playing*.

He was at his best when he was terrified.

Nick and his retinue – three men, two women – were unarmed; otherwise they wouldn't have been allowed into Mallorys. But they didn't need needle-lasers or old-fashioned shivs against one man. And they were ready to fight for their Captain, at any time, in any place. What he'd done to deserve that kind of loyalty, Angus couldn't imagine. But he didn't doubt that the six of them would relish beating him into the deck-plates.

Outside Mallorys, the wide public passages of DelSec were deserted. It was the time of day when most people either drank or stayed in their quarters. Assuming that anybody on Com-Mine Station would have been willing to help Angus in a fight, that help wasn't available now.

He let Nick see him swallow, hesitate. Then he said, 'Let's talk about it outside.' Deliberately he copied Nick's gesture. 'After you.'

'No, I insist.' Nick grinned. '*I'm* after *you*.'

'The hell you are,' Angus muttered. 'You don't care about me. You're after her.' Then he shouldered ahead of Nick through the doorway.

In his pocket, one of his fingers tapped Morn's zone-implant control, sending a spasm through her muscles, a neural storm that looked like violence. As a result, she blocked the exit behind Nick as if she was on Angus' side and wanted to fight for him.

At the same time, Angus pivoted on Nick, grabbed him by his shipsuit, and slung him like a duffel bag around and against the wall.

Surprise and strength gave him all the advantage he needed. With the back of his hand, he struck Nick across the side of his head – a blow that cracked and echoed in the passage like a rivet shearing under stress. The blow made Nick crumple; but Angus held him up and struck him again.

Then he was out of time.

Nick's retinue burst out of Mallorys, knocking Morn to the deck. They were hot for blood.

Angus faced them as if he were calm. With his hands, he dangled Nick's unconscious form in front of them. His fingers were wrapped around their Captain's neck.

'Go fucking back inside.' His voice sounded like an amiable mine-hammer. 'Leave me fucking alone. I'm not fucking done with him.'

For a second, Nick's crew faltered, chagrin on their faces.

Then the two women jerked Morn up from the deck and clamped hands to her windpipe.

Morn continued thrashing. Now she looked like she was seriously fighting for her life. Her eyes took in everything; she understood how Angus was using her. But she couldn't stop her struggles.

'Standoff,' a man said. 'You kill him, we kill her.'

The danger wrenched Angus' heart. The need to remain still was so acute it nearly broke him. He wanted to drop Nick and charge at the women, hit and crush everybody who stood in his way, everybody who threatened Morn. But that would be suicide. He couldn't beat all five of them before one of them got him. Or Morn. Somehow, he stood where he was and pretended he didn't care.

'You've got it wrong. You kill her, I kill him. I don't want him dead. I'm just protecting myself. Shits like you like six-to-one odds. I don't.'

Abruptly he roared with all the force of his rage, '*Put her fucking down!*'

They obeyed. They wanted to save Nick. And – Angus guessed – they didn't want the responsibility of killing the woman Nick desired. They let go of Morn and backed away.

She dropped convulsively to the deck.

While he was still wrestling with his wish to attack them all, Angus' nerve-beeper tingled, warning him that *Captain's Fancy* had sent out a call for Nick Succorso.

He didn't hesitate. If what he'd just done didn't provoke some action, nothing would. Carelessly he opened his fists and let Nick fall. With the efficiency of long practice, he keyed the commands on the zone-implant control which brought Morn back to her feet, restored her control of her limbs. Then he released her.

The way her gaze sprang involuntarily to Nick's sprawled form hurt him worse than anything Nick could have done in a fight.

But *Captain's Fancy*'s crew ignored her now. They didn't try to stop Angus from leaving. Surely they had their own beepers. And their Captain needed them.

Without interference, Angus returned Morn to *Bright Beauty* and sealed the hatches.

This time he was determined to do her serious harm. The blows he'd already struck flamed in his arm, burning for repetition. Violence made him hungry for more. He meant to damage her, *needed* to damage her. She deserved it.

But first he checked the computer monitoring *Captain's Fancy*'s Station communications. He wanted to know why Nick was being summoned.

The explanation was in code. *Captain's Fancy* had received one of those messages from Security and immediately requested Nick Succorso's return to his ship.

Cursing as foully as he knew how, Angus Thermopyle abandoned his purpose against Morn Hyland. Something was about to happen. His instincts were shouting at him, yelling at him to *leave*, go at once, escape before Nick could take revenge. But he ignored that warning. There was no way to leave; he was already committed. He ordered Morn to her g-seat, ordered her to strap herself in. Then he keyed his monitor to display current data from *Captain's Fancy*.

He knew it when Nick got aboard.

After that, for some reason *Captain's Fancy* cleared all channels and stopped talking to Station.

Because his instincts clamored like klaxons, Angus snapped at Morn, 'Warm up. Get ready. I think we're going somewhere.'

She obeyed the way he liked: correctly, without question or delay. *Bright Beauty*'s systems came alive. Function lights winked awake on his console. Checklists and verifications flickered across the screens. Scanners started to feed running data into the computers: automatic navigational input from Station; information about the presence and movements of ships in Com-Mine Station's control space.

While Morn worked, Angus concentrated on *Captain's Fancy*.

What was Nick doing?

Getting ready. Of course. Getting ready to leave.

But why?

Because Security had told him something.

What?

Angus sucked his upper lip. What had Security told Nick Succorso?

His boards and screens cleared. *Bright Beauty* was prepared to go. Morn sat still, staring at nothing, her hands resting on her console so they could do whatever he told her quickly.

Indecision paralyzed him. He didn't know how to go against his instincts. They'd saved him too often. If he didn't listen to them, he was lost.

He felt the pain; but until he tasted blood, he didn't realize he'd bitten into his lip.

Muttering obscenities automatically, as if they no longer had any meaning, he disconnected his ship from the dummy line which fed him *Captain's Fancy*'s datastream .

Bright Beauty's communication systems crackled awake. Like every receiver in and around Com-Mine Station, his gear caught the codes and frequencies of a distress call. Immediately his speakers broadcast the call.

It froze him in his seat. One part of his mind went completely blank with surprise and alarm as the incoming supply ship from Earth cried for help. Navigational computer wrecked. Somebody on the crew crazy with gap-sickness. Coordinates lost. Control lost. Crisis urgent. Triangulate and pursue. Distressdistressdis—

But the rest of him was thinking furiously.

Incoming supply ship. The richest treasure this side of an asteroid full of pure cesium. And it was weeks early. Probably a trick to protect it from pirates.

That was what Security was talking to Nick Succorso about. Telling him the ship would be early. So he would have a clear shot at it. The change of schedule would backfire. The ship wouldn't be expecting his attack.

But nobody could have predicted this emergency. Any second now,

Station was going to slap a curfew on the docks, forbidding anyone to leave making it a life offense for anyone to leave – until an official rescue mission could be organized. If he didn't move fast, Nick would lose his chance—

With his heart triphammering and a rush of sweat soaking his shipsuit, Angus snapped into action.

The distress call went dead only a few seconds later. Apparently the damage to the navigational computer had spread to communications. But by that time he'd already dropped all his lines and uncoupled from Station. By some definitions, he was no longer in dock; he still had to obey Center, but he wasn't legally bound by Security.

His scan told him *Captain's Fancy* was doing the same.

Station took a different view of the situation, of course. Center wanted absolute command over every ship in its control space; Security wanted authority over any rescue or salvage. Angus' receivers picked up a burst of static; the orders blared in his ears.

'*Bright Beauty*, this is Station Center. You must re-dock. An emergency has been declared. Emergency procedures are in force. You may not depart.

'If you ignore this instruction' – Angus heard satisfaction in the metallic voice – 'we will be forced to consider you illegal. You will be fired upon.'

Typical authoritarian attitude – arrogant and unjustified. Like the UMC cops and Security, Station Center was in love with muscle. Unfortunately, that didn't change anything. Angus would still die when the Station started shooting.

Captain's Fancy must have received the same orders. Nick ignored them. Blithely, as if she were deaf or invulnerable, his ship pivoted into her normal escape attitude for departure; under easy thrust, she ran out a few dozen kilometers from Station – directly into pointblank range for Com-Mine's cannon.

She waited for the first warning shots to be fired. Then she winked off Angus' screens; disappeared as completely as if she'd ceased to exist.

He watched and swore, helpless to stop her.

At the same time, however, he didn't let anything interfere with his own actions. *Bright Beauty* was already in her escape attitude, and he was pulling her out from the Station with all the thrust she was known to have.

The shit-eaters in Center had that one chance to kill him, but they missed it. As required by law, they sent their first shots across his trajectory, to warn him.

At once, he fed stutter into his drive and started transmitting his own distress call.

There's a short somewhere. Smoke. Controls locked – I can't navigate. Don't shoot. I'm trying to come around.

That froze Center. They didn't have any choice: they had to wait to see whether he was telling the truth.

While his call went out, he growled to Morn, 'Brace yourself. This is going to hurt.'

Steeling himself in his g-seat, he engaged *Bright Beauty*'s power boosters.

After that, Com-Mine's guns couldn't track him. He wasn't literally moving too fast for their capabilities: he was simply moving faster than anyone could believe. Surely his ship wasn't built for that kind of acceleration? By the time Center adjusted its preconceptions – and its targ programming – *Bright Beauty* was out of range.

Angus and Morn were unconscious, of course. The stress was too much to sustain. But the ship's boosters cut off after a preset interval, reducing g to more tolerable levels; and in the meantime, *Bright Beauty*'s automatic helm set her course by tracing the supply ship's distress call back along its transmission vector.

Angus recovered first. He stayed where he was, however, breathing deeply and trying to clear his head. Made it. Once again, his ship had saved him. Hurt as she was, she was *his*. If he had to, he would make the entire Station pay for the damage done to her. No one was allowed to harm anything *his*.

A short time later, Morn twitched, groaned, lifted her head. Unconsciousness and the strain of g took a moment to fade from her eyes. Then, without hesitation, she put her hands on her console and started tapping in instructions.

He was too stunned and relieved; and too much time had passed: he'd forgotten the danger. He wasn't looking at his own console, so he didn't see the blip which began to flash as soon as she set to work.

Luckily, he glanced over at her and saw the look of rapture on her face.

That look was unmistakable.

The whole inside of my head was different. I was floating, and everything was clear. It was like the universe spoke to me.

In sudden panic, he slapped at his console, identified the alert.

She was trying to feed a self-destruct sequence into *Bright Beauty's* engines.

Bitch. Fucking daughter of a fucking whore.

Gap-sickness.

He was too tired to swear at her aloud. The thought of her illness made him weary and slightly nauseous. A strange burning sensation filled his eyes. He should have gone over to her and hit her, of course, should have pounded her back into her right mind. But he was too tired for that. And anyway, *Bright Beauty* was running under spin. Sighing as if he were sad, he activated the zone-implant control.

Morn's hands fell off the console, and she slumped in her g-seat.

That was necessary; he had to do it. When he engaged *Captain's Fancy*, he couldn't take the risk that she might interfere somehow, hamper or weaken him. There was no reason why he shouldn't switch her off like a robot with its power supply cut.

And yet he felt about her gap-sickness the same way he felt about *Bright Beauty's* wounded side.

Somebody was going to pay for it. He would get even with the entire parsec if he had to.

In the meantime, however, he had to take care of himself. He was confident that the place where the supply ship stopped transmitting was at least half a day away under strong thrust: ships crossing the gap were required to reenter normal space that far from any Station, to minimize the chance of an accident. And his scanners would warn him as soon as he crossed the supply ship's particle trail. So he had time for some food and a little rest. If he weren't at his best, he might not be able to beat *Captain's Fancy*.

He was relying on surprise. Nick Succorso couldn't know his data-stream had been tapped. And he couldn't know *Bright Beauty* had been able to get away from Com-Mine Station.

He couldn't know Angus Thermopyle had no interest at all in the supply ship.

Without gap capability, *Bright Beauty* lacked *Captain's Fancy*'s ability to leave Com-Mine and the belt for some other star system or Station, someplace where she wasn't known. For that reason, Angus couldn't risk an attack on the supply ship. If he found her, he would be forced to rescue her crew and salvage her cargo in the legally prescribed manner. DelSec lived on those supplies as much as the rest of Station did. If he pirated them – and DelSec was given any reason of any kind to believe he'd done it – he would be murdered the next time he set foot in Mallorys.

No, Angus was after Nick himself. What he wanted was to catch Nick gutting the lost ship. If he could do that, all his options were good – as long as he destroyed *Captain's Fancy*. He could rescue the crew (if Nick had left any of them alive); keep as much of the cargo as he wanted for himself ('lost in combat'); salvage the rest; go back to Com-Mine like a hero.

His instincts assured him this was the wrong thing to do.

He ignored them.

First he stopped *Bright Beauty*'s spin and went to get himself a quick meal. Then he returned to his g-seat and began testing all his sensors and sifters and sniffers to make sure they were in proper tune.

Whenever he chewed on his upper lip, he tasted blood again.

CHAPTER 14

Three hours sooner than Angus was expecting, the alarm linked to his tracking gear chimed.

He grunted in surprise. It was too soon. The supply ship should never have crossed back into normal space this close to the Station.

And that wasn't all. Ignoring g, he hauled *Bright Beauty* around and dropped spin to improve his scan. The particle trace didn't look right. Big haulers like supply ships had throatier engines: they left a wider track across the dark, more garbage at the fringes and more complete dispersion in the core. Studying his displays and readouts made him so suspicious that he felt like throwing up.

And yet—

The sheer coincidence of another ship having passed directly across the supply ship's transmission vector was staggering.

And if this *was* the supply ship's trace, he was much closer to her than he'd anticipated. She was closer to Com-Mine; therefore her distress call had taken less time to reach Station; therefore she'd had less time to blunder away from this spot; therefore he could catch up with her more easily.

And by rights Nick's departure from Station should have taken him well past this point. It was virtually impossible to cut a blink crossing this short. Which meant he was already out where the ship should be. If the ship was there, Angus might not be able to catch him in time. But if the ship was *here*—

If the ship was here, Angus could get to her first. Nick would have to come back looking for her.

The perfect situation for an ambush.

Angus' dilemma was terrifying. If he guessed wrong, he would lose his only chance to take *Captain's Fancy* by surprise. Then he would have to live with the consequences of his earlier attack on Nick. And Nick had Security on his side. He had a newer ship. He had an entire crew to back him up. Angus might be forced to hide out in the belt for years.

His sweat made him stink like a swine. Nevertheless he knew exactly what to do. Focusing scan back along the trace, he went looking for the characteristic burst of radiation and dimensional emission which accompanied every crossing from the gap into normal space.

Before long, he found it.

There: the supply ship had entered normal space right there. She was too much of everything – too soon, too close, too easily crippled; her trace was too narrow. But she was *there*, where he could get to her hours ahead of his enemy.

Giving *Bright Beauty* as much boost as he could stomach, he reversed course and followed the trace.

When he plotted the ship's speed from the density of the particle trail, he saw she was decelerating slowly. That made sense. Unable to navigate, she would naturally want to reduce her own momentum so she would be easier to catch and board. Instead of pushing ahead, however, he began to cut his own speed correspondingly. He didn't want the supply ship to know he'd found her. She might try to beacon him – and that might betray his position. He intended to sneak up on her, hovering just outside normal scan range and playing dead so he wouldn't show up on *Captain's Fancy's* instruments. He even went so far as to ride straight down the center of the supply ship's trace, confusing it with *Bright Beauty's* to hide himself.

He would wait until Nick came. He would wait until *Captain's Fancy* cut the supply ship's heart out, eliminated embarrassing witnesses, arranged easy access to the cargo. He would wait until Nick docked with the supply ship's carcass.

Then he would rip Nick Succorso and everything that bastard loved down to raw electrons and space dust.

He intended to release Morn Hyland so she could watch. He would let her see the blast and try to guess which piece of incinerated debris represented the man she wanted instead of him.

After that – if she was lucky – he would strip off her shipsuit and make her do things that sickened her. He would teach her who owned her until she was in no danger of ever forgetting it.

If she wasn't lucky, he might do a little surgery on her, rearrange parts of her body somewhat, just for fun.

First, however, he had to find the supply ship.

He didn't understand it: she kept slowing and slowing – and yet she remained out of scan-range, invisible somewhere ahead of him. At her present rate of deceleration, he should be almost on top of her by now. Yet he couldn't locate her.

That was impossible. He knew for a fact that his equipment was capable of tracking down one lost EVA suit in a hundred thousand cubic kilometers of black emptiness. The supply ship couldn't hide from him, even if she had a reason to try, which of course she didn't because she was dead unless somebody came to her rescue, she had to be here *somewhere*, had to be—

When he found the explanation, it stunned him for a few seconds. That much delay nearly killed him.

Ahead of *Bright Beauty*, a sudden powerful roar along the trace showed that the ship he was following had cut in full thrust, enough sheer power to pull away from him at an acceleration of several g.

Which was why he hadn't caught up with her. She'd been piling up speed while he'd been slowing down.

But that was crazy. No crippled supply ship would do something like that. A crippled supply ship with runaway thrusters would jettison her engines rather than let herself race out of reach of help.

Therefore the ship he followed wasn't a crippled supply ship.

He'd been tricked. There was no supply ship. The distress call was a ruse. He'd set out intending to spring an ambush; but the ambush had been sprung on him, he was already caught—

Stunned, he stared at his readouts and displays, and for a moment he didn't move. The extent to which he'd been duped paralyzed him. What chance did he have against people who could do *this*? He'd been so thoroughly outmaneuvered that he was as good as dead.

Gaping dismay, he looked over at Morn.

She hadn't moved, of course. The zone-implant blocked the neural impulses which connected her mind to her body. She was conscious, but helpless. Like his ship. Unless he could find a way to save them, they would both be destroyed.

A howl rose in his throat; but he had no time for it.

Bright Beauty had been running without spin. And all his attention had been focused on the particle trace. He hauled her into a turn, bringing sensors and sniffers to bear on her blind spot.

At once, her klaxons went off, wailing like the damned.

A ship came at him fast. No, worse than that: the ship had already fired, throwing a flight of torpedoes in his direction at terrible speed.

His terror was absolute: it made him superhuman. *Bright Beauty* was still turning, still starting into spin. He gathered boost and unleashed it at an angle, kicked her to the side so hard that she tumbled away as if she were totally out of control, wheeling like a derelict.

Every alarm she had on her seemed to go off simultaneously. She wasn't made for stress like that. Damaged as she was, she was in danger of breaking apart.

But the torpedoes missed.

Under so much g, he should have gone completely blank; crushed unconscious in his seat. It should have been impossible for him to retain any sense of orientation, of the spatial relationship between himself and his attacker.

Nevertheless, while *Bright Beauty* tumbled, he opened fire.

The spray of his matter cannon went miraculously close to the other ship. She was forced to veer off.

He had no way of identifying his attacker, but she was almost certainly the ship he'd been following – almost certainly *Captain's Fancy*. Somehow, Nick Succorso had been able to cut his blink crossing short enough to intersect the transmission vector of the bogus distress call. Or he'd blinked far enough past that point to return with another crossing. He'd lured Angus to follow him. Then, when he'd slowed Angus nearly to a standstill, he'd accelerated and looped back to attack.

None of that mattered, of course. It didn't matter who Angus' enemy was – not now. The only thing that mattered was that he was trapped and had to fight for his life.

For his life and *Bright Beauty*'s. And Morn's.

His ship's tumble was dangerous. It was also much too slow. Under this kind of g, he couldn't read his screens. Still he knew somehow what the other ship was doing, where she was in relation to him.

As his attacker came around and brought her guns to bear, he hit braking thrust, straightened out *Bright Beauty*'s fall, got her tubes behind her, and gave her as much drive as he thought he could stand without losing his mind to the dark.

Matter fire licked her sides, but didn't do any real damage. Then she pulled out of range, surprising her attacker with the fact that she was still under control and could perform maneuvers which should have been impossible.

Angus' head was jammed brutally against his g-seat; but now at least he could look at his displays and screens, his console. Targ plotted the other ship automatically, showing her on a grid even a crazy could have understood.

She was gaining on him. At this rate, she would be in position to open fire in a matter of seconds.

Angus ought to be taking evasive action.

But he already knew *Captain's Fancy* was fast. If he really wanted to outrun her, he would have to give *Bright Beauty* all the power his drive could generate. Then he would black out. He wouldn't know whether he was alive or dead until his ship reached the end of her fuel and stopped accelerating.

He didn't pile on any more boost.

He also didn't take any evasive action. To do that, he would have to slow down; or else the inertial stress might be enough to make him hemorrhage.

Instead he started seeding the space behind him with static-mines.

He didn't know it, but his mouth and chin were covered with blood. Every time he bit his upper lip, it bled more.

Static-mines were tiny: a scan officer with his mind on other things might miss them. Angus released them in clusters of ten or twelve, but they scattered so quickly that they shouldn't create a combined blip for the attacking ship to read.

If she fired at him and hit one—

Or if she simply ran into it—

She fired. His displays showed him the characteristic energy-burst of matter cannon. *Bright Beauty* was struck – another scar along her flank. Yet she was lucky: the hurt was no worse than a slap.

The salvo also caught a few of the static-mines.

He'd keyed them to set each other off. In seconds, his trail was covered by disruptive explosions, a barrage of particle noise, doppler signals, and radio garbage loud enough to randomize every scanner *Captain's Fancy* had.

In effect, *Bright Beauty* – and space itself – disappeared. The attacking ship was left deaf and blind.

She would stay that way for ten or fifteen seconds, until her computers were able to filter the chaos, distinguish between noise and fact.

At that instant, Angus wrenched *Bright Beauty* to the side, away from her former course. He gave her one quick slam of extra boost.

Then he shut her down.

Everything. Even life-support. Thrust; communication; lights; sensors: everything except minimal computer function and passive scan systems which didn't give out signs of life; everything except the faint, almost undetectable nuclear hum of charged matter cannon.

He was trying to make himself invisible.

Trying to compensate for the fact that he was outgunned and out-manned and probably outpowered.

Sweat drenched his shipsuit, but he didn't notice that. He forgot to curse; he almost refused to breathe because in his imagination he could taste his air already starting to go bad. His whole body was focused on the dull screens of his passive scan – sifters which sent out nothing, but only accepted and interpreted what came to them across the void. Where was his attacker? By rights, his sense of space told him, she should be *there*. But his equipment said nothing. He was as blind as *Captain's Fancy*. The only difference, the only hope, was that *Captain's Fancy* was the one in pursuit, that—

The only difference was that she was still moving under power.

His screens flickered. *There.*

Moving cautiously now, hunting, groping – but still using her engines, life-support, internal communications; still sending a shout of data through the residual noise left by the static-mines.

Because she didn't know where he was, she was about to come under his guns.

Come on, you bastards.

He didn't so much as whisper aloud: he was irrationally afraid his attacker might hear him.

Come on, you sons of whores. Let me have just one good shot at you. Just one.

His ship made no sound, gave away nothing except the small hum of her guns. Surely the only way Nick could spot her was by picking out her silhouette against the starfield? And surely they were far enough away from each other to make that difficult, nearly impossible? Surely it would take time for the computers to run that kind of analysis on what they saw?

Time: all Angus needed was time. His attacker was already within range. If he fired now, he wouldn't miss. But he might not kill her. If he waited until she came closer, he would have a chance to catch her with a torpedo.

Just one torpedo would be enough to break her back. He was sure of that. He knew what his torpedoes could do.

He waited.

Come on, you shithead motherfucking cocksuckers.

Waited.

Too late, his equipment registered the sudden blast of power as the other ship fed boost to her thrusters.

She'd spotted him. Just when he was about to gut her, tear her entirely to pieces, she'd spotted him. Or she'd guessed what he was doing.

With all her strength, she accelerated out of his way.

Raging, he jabbed at his guns, sent cannon fire like hate at her, hot and savage, frantic for destruction. One entire barrage got her, skimming open the metal skin of her side, spilling atmosphere and debris into the vacuum. But that wasn't enough to kill her.

He knew it wasn't enough because she kept returning his fire until she pulled out of range.

And she hit him.

He didn't have time to assess the damage: he had to get moving, had to get *Bright Beauty* under thrust before his attacker could turn. Fiercely, he brought her back to life, ignited her engines.

He knew his ship. She was *his*, and he'd taken care of her intimately for years. When his thrusters roared alive, he knew instantly that one of them had been hurt. It stuttered and choked, sending a terrible shudder through the hull.

That last hit had holed one of his thruster tubes.

The side-blast would make *Bright Beauty* almost impossible to control.

He tried: brutally, desperately, he tried. Ignoring the strain on his body, his heart, the strain on Morn, the strain on every suture of *Bright*

Beauty's skin and every weld of her frame, he fought for speed and control, wrestled with the side-blast for his life.

It was no good. He couldn't do it. It would have taken all his skill just to run her in a straight line at a limp. While his attacker turned and scanned him and studied the situation and then started back toward him to finish him off, he accomplished nothing except a wild cartwheel into the dark, an off-center spin that made *Bright Beauty* completely unmanageable. Now if he tried for speed the only thing he would do was rip his own mind away so that he would be unconscious when he died.

He didn't know what to do. He didn't know how to fail and die, but that was his only alternative. While *Bright Beauty* reeled out of control like this, he couldn't so much as fire his guns. They were useless. And he knew his enemy was closing on him, knew it without a glance at scan – which was hopelessly confused in any case. By the time he succeeded at pulling his ship out of her spin, Nick Succorso would be ready to blast him to dust.

Only because *Bright Beauty*'s motion was so painful, he struggled with it. He shut down the engine with the damaged tube, then used braking against the spin. But when her screens cleared, he saw that he'd done nothing except make life easier for his enemy.

The other ship was in position: poised; primed.

For the second time, he found himself staring down the pitiless gullet of enemy cannon.

The sight made him want to weep.

There was nothing he could do. All his anger and inspiration were gone, expended. His attacker was within range now, but it wasn't worth the trouble to fire at her. He might be able to scar her a little, that was all. A few scars wouldn't prevent her from eviscerating him and his ship and everything he'd ever wanted.

Abruptly, a communication channel crackled.

'Captain Thermo-pile.'

Nick Succorso. Of course.

'You're beaten. Remember that. I warned you.'

Angus had the distinct impression Nick was laughing at him.

Without another shot, *Captain's Fancy* shifted course and started to pull away.

He couldn't believe it. He stared at his displays, his readouts. His cameras couldn't see far enough to be sure; but all his sensors agreed with each other. *Captain's Fancy* had turned her back on him. With taunting ease, she ran out of his reach almost immediately. He was left alone and damaged.

He felt like he'd been marooned. For the second time, he had no idea why he was alive.

CHAPTER 15

Bright Beauty's life-support didn't seem to be working well enough. His mouth was full of sand. The whole inside of his head was a desert. *You're beaten.* He wasn't angry anymore. *Remember that.* He didn't have any hope. *I warned you.* Something had been taken away from him – something he needed and couldn't define and didn't know how to live without.

His ship was crippled. He'd been gone from Com-Mine Station for less than twelve hours, but he would be lucky to get back in thirty-six.

Morn Hyland still slumped in her g-seat, deaf and blind to everything. He couldn't afford to have *Bright Beauty* fixed. If he reached Com-Mine in one piece, that would be as far as he went. He couldn't make any money without using her, and she was in no condition to be used. He was trapped; there was no escape. He might as well have been marooned—

It was Morn's fault, of course. None of this would have happened to him – or to his ship – if she hadn't conceived a passion for Nick Succorso.

And yet he wasn't angry.

He wanted to be angry. If he could get angry, maybe he would be able to think of something.

After staring at his screens for a long time, he keyed the parallel control to Morn's zone-implant and let her have her body back.

Trying to be angry, he didn't look at her. Instead, he let his hurt, numb thoughts wander to the question of how much she remembered, how much she knew about what had happened. She'd been in the grip of her gap-sick vision, the message from the universe commanding self-destruction, when he activated her zone-implant. Had she been lost in mad clarity all this time? Was she still sick? Or had she been capable of seeing, absorbing, understanding?

She twisted against her seat, stretched her muscles, studied her console and the displays. Involuntarily he turned to watch her. Her features were pale and concentrated. Then, by degrees, horror crept into her face – the horror he recognized.

In a stark and absolute whisper, she asked, 'Did I do that?'

He should have let her believe she was responsible. That would be worse than anything physical he could do to her. She was horrified by him, of course, revolted to the core and helpless; but to fear herself like that, to be revolted again at herself like that, to be helpless against her own destructiveness – that would be worse. It would be as bad as what he'd been striving for until the moment when she and Nick first saw each other – as bad as finding in herself the knowledge that she needed what he did to her and loved it.

She deserved to believe she was responsible.

He couldn't do it; he had no idea why. Part of his brain was still planning what he would say to pin the blame on her as he replied, 'Succorso got us. A trap – there was no supply ship. You can see the damage.' Her console would give her all the details she needed.

For several moments she didn't say anything. Her relief was so strong that she seemed unable to think. But then, slowly, she began to frown.

Keeping her voice neutral, she asked, 'Why are we still alive?'

Angus shrugged as if he were the one who was helpless. 'He let us go.'

She had to consider that for a while: even in her condition, she could see it didn't make sense. Nick attacked because he wanted to kill Angus. Then why did he leave *Bright Beauty* alive? He set his trap so that he could rescue Morn. Then why didn't he? Why did he risk killing her?

Nevertheless something made sense to her; Angus could read her expression well enough to know it when she reached a conclusion.

Carefully she cleared her throat and said, 'You're beaten.'

Oh, yes.

'He beat you.'

Yes.

'You'll be lucky if you can make this thing crawl back to Station.'

The words were fierce, almost vindictive; she might have been gloating. But she didn't sound that way. Her tone was too flat, too well-controlled. If anything, she sounded a little sad, as if she, too, had been hurt in some way.

Trying to be angry, he growled, 'Proud of him, aren't you? You think that fucker's some kind of hero. *Beat* me. You're counting the minutes until you two' – he had no words strong enough – 'until you can screw him.'

Abruptly, she licked her lips; she appeared to have trouble swallowing. 'Angus.' She'd never used his name before. 'Angus, listen to me.

'I can save you.'

He thought his heart was going to stop beating.

'I'll testify for you. When you go back to Com-Mine, they'll charge you with illegal departure. I'll support you. I'm not much of a cop anymore, but I've still got my id tag. I'll tell them you left on my orders. And I'll tell them there was no supply ship. It was a hoax – that other ship set it up. I'll tell them to arrest Nick Succorso. I can't save your ship, but I can save you.'

Tell them? Turn on Nick Succorso? Give up that piece of meat for me? Impossible. Angus felt sure he was losing his mind. For me?

'Just give me the control.' Her voice was husky, full of need. 'The zone-implant control.'

Then he understood. Shit, how he wished he could be angry! She wanted the control. It wasn't for him. Nothing was for him. She wanted all that power for herself. Power *over* herself – power to be whatever she wanted. No gap-sickness. No fear: immune to fear. And no consequences for all the harm he'd done her. The perfect cop. The perfect lover. As close as human flesh could come to immortality.

He'd broken her in ways he hadn't anticipated. Her damage was as profound as *Bright Beauty*'s.

He had trouble seeing. His eyes ran and wouldn't stop. 'You're crazy,' he rasped as if he were weeping. 'That's as illegal as what I did to you. You're a cop. Your whole family will be discredited, heroic Captain Davies Hyland and his reputation shot to hell.'

She reacted bitterly. 'What does that matter?' she retorted. 'They're *dead*.'

Angus tried a different tack.

'You aren't thinking straight. You're a *cop*. It's worse when a cop breaks the law. They'll crucify you. Mandatory death penalty. They'll find out. They have to find out. And then you'll be finished.'

Behind his tears, he could see her in lockup; see her waiting to be executed, vaporized. As precious as *Bright Beauty*.

'I'll lose my ship.'

'You can't save it,' she shot back, suddenly angry, more than a little desperate. 'I can handle Station Security. And the UMCP. I'll think of a way. But *nothing* can save your ship. It's too badly broken. We'll need a miracle just to get back to Com-Mine alive.

'Please. Give me the control.' Now she was pleading nakedly. 'I'm not going to use it against you. I need it to heal.'

He tried to clear his vision. Softly he said, 'And give up my ship. That's the deal, isn't it? You'll save me. If I let you have the control. But I have to give up my ship.'

My life.

She nodded. After a moment, she replied, 'What else have you got to bargain with?'

At last, something like his old energy came back to him. Roughly he undid the straps and pushed his bulk out of his g-seat. He needed to be angry at her one last time, needed to hate her the way he'd always hated her, the way he hated everyone.

He went toward her.

Clamping one hand on the armrest of her seat, bracing his feet on the deck, he struck her a blow like the one which had felled Nick, a blow with the whole weight of his existence behind it. If her seat hadn't absorbed some of the impact, she might have been knocked unconscious. He might have broken her neck.

'Bitch. I'll never give up my ship.'

Red welled in her cheek; blood trickled from the cuts of her teeth inside her mouth. Pain and shock glazed her eyes: for a moment, she couldn't focus them.

But she made no effort to defend herself. If he wanted to hit her again, she was there.

He couldn't do it. It was like hurting *Bright Beauty*. She was too beautiful. The stark red line of blood across her fine skin wrung his heart. He needed rage and violence, but they were gone.

'Now you listen to *me*,' he panted as if he were groaning. 'It's impossible. You couldn't get away with it.

'Maybe you can get them to believe you ordered me to violate Center's orders so you could come out here after Succorso. But they won't believe anything else unless you file charges. If you don't, your credibility's gone.

Then you're in the same shit I am. Only you'll be suspect for destroying *Starmaster*. If they find evidence of self-destruct, you'll be court-martialed. They'll find the zone-implant *and* the control, and then you're dead.

'You'll have to file charges.

'But if you do that, you'll have to give them my datacore. Otherwise you don't have any evidence.' He could survive that – he could retain his life, if not his freedom – but she didn't know that. And he had a horror of lockup. Imprisonment alone might be enough to ruin him. 'You'll end up killing me.

'And if you do all that, they'll still find the implant and the control.

'*Think* about it. After what you've been through, they're going to give you a physical. They're going to insist on it. If you resist, they'll get suspicious – they'll force it on you. No matter what you do, you're dead.

'You're going to have to play this out the way it is.

'I'm trying to save your life too.'

Now he wasn't able to meet her dull, smoldering gaze. Slowly he pushed back to his seat. He strapped himself in. His movements were abrupt, jerky, as if he didn't have them entirely under control; as if he could have used a zone-implant himself

'We've got a holed thruster tube,' he muttered. 'It'll take everything I can do just to make her run in a straight line. You'll have to handle everything else.'

Glowering like one of the lost, he routed most of his command functions to her console. Then he concentrated all the determination he had left on making *Bright Beauty* go where he wanted.

He knew Morn would do her part. What choice did she have?

But he also knew what he'd done to her. He'd destroyed her last hope. And he'd hit her again, after all his gentleness; after his gentleness had almost persuaded her he could be reached.

He understood the consequences.

Now she had no choice but to help destroy him.

CHAPTER 16

Two days and more after her departure, *Bright Beauty* sputtered back into dock at Com-Mine Station.

The trip was harder and longer than Angus had anticipated. For the first time since Morn started crewing for him, he needed drugs to stay alert.

In fact, she accepted stim herself. The chore of maintaining the ship while he navigated wasn't exhausting, but his refusal to stop for rest wore her down. She had a hot glitter in her eyes and a feverish patch of color on each cheek as he settled *Bright Beauty* into the berth Center assigned; she looked like a woman whose life was on the line.

He noticed that. Despite his own fatigue and the muzzy-headedness of drugs, he noticed everything about her. She needed sleep.

If he could have let her have it, he would have. Unfortunately, there were Station inspectors pounding at his airlock. He'd ignored an order of curfew to go off after *Captain's Fancy*. And the supply ship was still missing. The official search hadn't found anything. And *Captain's Fancy* hadn't returned. A board of inquiry wanted to ask Angus Thermopyle questions. Until he answered them, he was effectively under arrest.

He couldn't afford sleep. And he couldn't afford to let Morn sleep. He needed her to back him up again.

He keyed off his console and got out of his g-seat, swearing uselessly at the force of Station gravity. 'Shut her down,' he told Morn. 'We're going to be here for a while.' Then he added, 'Don't say anything. I'll handle the fucking inspectors. You just sit there and do your best to look like a cop.'

She nodded once, tightly. With her hands on the console, she got to work rigging *Bright Beauty* for rest.

Angus was afraid he would never be able to warm his ship up again. But even that fear was good for something. Relying on it because he had so little anger or strength, he went to let the inspectors aboard.

They had a lot to say to him: they made a number of demands.

For once, what he told them came close to the exact truth.

I don't give a shit about the supply ship. I was after Nick Succorso.

Really? A treasure like that – just waiting to be looted? Do you expect us to believe that, Captain Thermopyle?

Do you think I'm crazy? A supply ship? Angus didn't have to fake his exasperation. If I put one finger on her, the sewage in DelSec would have me for breakfast. And I sure as hell wouldn't come back here. With a treasure like that, I could buy all the repairs I need somewhere else.

Then what were you doing?

I already told you. I was after Succorso.

Why?

Deliberately Angus looked at Morn. That also was the truth, but it had the effect of a lie. Snarling, he said, *Succorso* was after the supply ship.

How do you know?

Shit! Why the fucking hell do you think he broke curfew and blinked out of here? Why do you think he hasn't come back?

All right. What happened?

I never found the supply ship. He attacked me. Holed my thruster tube. The only thing I've done since then is crawl back here.

Why did he attack you?

With difficulty, Angus refrained from yelling. Take a guess.

Are you sure it was him?

No. You got any ideas who else would jump me out in the middle of fucking nowhere for no fucking reason?

The inspectors shrugged as if the list of people who might fit that description were endless.

You broke curfew, Captain Thermopyle. That charge will stick. You weren't docked, but you were in Station control space. You'll have to surrender your datacore.

The hell I will. I told you. I was after Succorso.

That changes nothing. You broke curfew.

I had orders. Again Angus turned his glare on Morn. I couldn't obey them and you too.

Still she didn't say anything. This time, however, she took out her UMCP id tag for the inspectors to worry about.

Faced with the unexplained possibilities she represented – the possibility, for instance, that she'd commandeered Angus Thermopyle's ship to pursue Nick Succorso despite the curfew – the inspectors couldn't shake Angus' story. They searched *Bright Beauty* as well as they could without knowing her secrets, but they didn't find anything. Finally they looked at the damaged thruster tube. It seemed to give them a certain amount of satisfaction.

If Captain Succorso comes in, we'll treat him the same way we did you. If we find anything from that ship – anything at all we'll lock him up for the rest of his natural life. But if he's clean, we're not going to charge him for shooting at you. Not unless you can prove it was him. The inspectors smiled humorlessly. Not unless you hand over your datacore and let us read it.

Thanks so much, Angus rasped. You're all heart. It's a pleasure getting justice and decent treatment from you.

But he was too worn-out to feel much relief – or any hope. The ability to bluff the inspectors didn't solve his problems.

He was forbidden to leave Station, of course, but that was a minor inconvenience under the circumstances. When the board of inquiry granted him temporary permission to disembark and make use of Com-Mine Station's facilities, he escorted the inspectors off *Bright Beauty* and sealed the locks. Then he put Morn to bed asleep and climbed into his bunk because there was nothing else he could do.

A few hours later, he woke up in a sweat of alarm; a knife against his heart told him he'd forgotten something, neglected something. Something deadly. He seemed to be waking up from a dream in which a terrible mistake was made clear to him.

Now, however, what that mistake was drifted out of his grasp while his lungs heaved and his chest pounded. *Bright Beauty*'s air conditioning chilled the sweat on his skin, but didn't do anything to cool off his fright.

Maybe it was just Station gravity weighing him down, making him feel leaden and defeated; maybe he was getting too old to shift easily between the presence and absence of g. He wasn't used to thinking of himself as either old or young. In fact, he didn't often pay much attention to his physical organism. But now he tried to comfort himself with physiological speculations.

He was getting old. He was having trouble adjusting to Station g. That was all.

No.

He'd forgotten something.

Nick's taunts came back to him.

You're beaten. Remember that. I warned you.

He still had no idea why Nick let him live.

Neglected something.

He went back to the beginning to try to reason it out.

The explanation had to do with Morn, of course. Nothing else made sense. Nick let him live because killing him would kill her as well. Nick was willing to risk her during the fight, for the sake of beating Angus Thermopyle, for the sake of repaying what Angus did to him; but after he won, he held back so she wouldn't be hurt.

Really? Did that make sense?

Maybe not; but it was good enough to ease Angus' distress a little. Rolling heavily out of his bunk, he scratched at the itch of sweat and grime inside his ship-suit, used the head, dabbed antiseptic from the sickbay on his swollen lip, and lumbered into the command module.

Almost at once, he saw the blip signaling automatically on his board.

He froze.

It was one of the alerts he'd programmed to warn him if Morn tried anything off-limits at her console.

For a moment – just for a moment – he didn't care what the alert actually was. He was stunned by the impossibility of the situation. He'd never given her a chance to do anything. He watched her all the time. When *Bright Beauty* was shut down, there wasn't any blip. Was that right? He scoured his memory. Yes, that was right. No blip then. And after that he'd put her to sleep. *When* could she have set it off?

No. The recognition hit him harder than the alert itself. He was remembering wrong. He *had* given her a chance.

He'd left her alone in the command module while he went to let the inspectors aboard. And again when they went away. And after that he hadn't so much as glanced at his own controls. He'd been too busy with the inquiry – too tired—

Too beaten—

Oh, shit.

Jerking into motion, he stabbed buttons on his console to identify the alert.

It was so far from what he expected that at first he couldn't believe it. The computer must be making a mistake. Surely she'd done something worse than *that*? Wasn't she trying to kill him, get even with him? Didn't she want to sabotage *Bright Beauty*?

But of course the computer wasn't making a mistake. It showed clearly that Morn had jimmied the locks on one of *Bright Beauty*'s exterior hatches, fixed them so they didn't seal. Then she'd disconnected the automatic signal which warned of an unlocked hatch.

That was ridiculous. His brain reeled, groping. Unselfconsciously he wiped blood off his chin. What had Morn accomplished? The hatch still closed securely. His ship still had integrity against the void.

But now—

— now the hatch could be opened from outside.

Anybody with an EVA suit could sneak aboard.

Anybody with an EVA suit could have sneaked aboard while Angus was sleep.

Shitshitshitshit.

He was so surprised and lost that he jumped to all the wrong conclusions. He checked on Morn first, half-expecting to discover she was already gone. But she still slept where he'd left her under the influence of her zone-implant. So then he tuned *Bright Beauty*'s life-sign scanners to read the whole ship for stowaways, hidden murderers, saboteurs.

There was no one else aboard: just Morn and himself.

You're beaten. Remember that. I warned you.

Finally panic brought him a burst of inspiration. He went to look in his secret holds.

They were full from deck to ceiling with food, equipment, and medicine.

Every crate and carton bore the seal which identified it as the property of Com-Mine Station – the kind of supplies Com-Mine received from Earth. The kind of supplies a supply ship would carry.

When he went back to the command module and scanned around him, he saw *Captain's Fancy* in dock hardly fifty meters away. She'd come in while he was asleep.

He was trapped. Finished. Dead.

The perfection of it astonished him. No wonder Nick had seemed more than willing to encounter him in the doorway of Mallorys. That gave Nick the chance to say the word 'hatch' in front of Morn. And with that slender link between them they found a way to destroy the man they hated.

'Slender' was too strong a word for it. It was slim to the point of nonexistence. Nevertheless Angus believed it instantly.

You're hatching something.

What else had she ever had to hope for?

Why don't you open up about it?

What else did she have left?

Let someone in to help you.

From the moment when she'd heard those words, she must have clung to them, searching them for meaning, chewed them inside and out. In her place, he would have done the same thing. Desperate for rescue, she must have worked like a maniac to find some interpretation which could save her.

And Nick's attack showed her he was serious, showed her she had reason to hope.

That was all she needed. When she got the chance, she did something about it.

No, it wasn't enough. It might have been enough for Morn in her desperation, but it wasn't enough for Nick. He would need to *know* she understood him.

What else had he said?

You've got it in your pocket right now. Or are you playing with yourself?

Angus had assumed that was a reference to the zone-implant control; a lucky guess. But now another possibility occurred to him. Like everything else Nick had said, it was aimed at Morn.

There had been plenty of time during the scuffle for Nick's people to put a note in Morn's pocket. A note she would have found later, read, and then destroyed.

A note which told her what Nick wanted her to do.

That was why Nick had allowed Angus to arrange their encounter so easily. So that his people could give Morn his message.

The rest of the plot was simple.

There never was a supply ship. No, of course not. The distress call was a fake, engineered by Nick Succorso and his ally in Security. If the supply ship had been genuine, Security could have given him advance warning; but the emergency on which the plot depended couldn't have been predicted. Therefore the whole thing hadn't happened. The distress call had been faked to lure Angus away from Com-Mine – to set the stage for his ruin.

With a way to sneak aboard *Bright Beauty*, did Nick have Angus killed? Did he simply kidnap Morn? Of course not. A murder would have caused serious trouble for Nick. Despite Angus Thermopyle's reputation, Security would have done everything possible to nail his killer – if for no other reason than to demonstrate its own integrity. And if Morn disappeared from *Bright Beauty* while Angus was left alive, Nick would never be able to rest for fear of Angus' revenge.

No, the trap was perfect. By filling *Bright Beauty*'s holds with supplies provided – no doubt – by his ally in Security, Nick was able to arrange for Angus' destruction without risking Morn. Or himself.

Now all he had to do was give the inspectors some evidence that a crime had been committed. Then they would have the legal right to appropriate *Bright Beauty*'s datacore. That would enable them to find the secret holds. It would inform them of the murder of those miners. And it might give them a clue about Morn's zone-implant: the sickbay log was blank; but the datacore contained evidence of the parallel control he'd programmed into his board.

A life sentence for the theft of Station supplies. And the death penalty for murder, if not for the use of a zone-implant.

And Morn would go free, of course. Straight to Nick Succorso.

The trap was perfect and horrible. Stark panic rushed through Angus: every instinct he had gibbered for action. Without pausing to think – without really realizing what he did – he strapped himself into his g-seat and began to warm up *Bright Beauty*'s engines.

Get away: escape: run. He was a coward; his instincts were compulsory. Undock and get out of here before Security had time to make a formal arrest. They were going to kill him, *kill* him. Get away *now*.

But he'd been forbidden to leave. If he tried to pull away without permission, Com-Mine would fire on him. With a holed thruster tube, he would never be able to evade the Station's guns.

Bright Beauty would be destroyed.

Morn would be killed.

Get away! You fool, you shithead, *go*, GO!

Morn would be killed.

Dismay twisted a cry out of him. He was willing to risk *Bright Beauty*. He'd done it before, when he had to. But Morn—

The last time he hit her, blood welled in her cheek; blood trickled from the cuts of her teeth inside her mouth. Her beauty was marked red. Thinking about her made his guts heave with terror and desire. She was his, his, his, and if he tried to save himself, she would die.

So what? he demanded of his lonely, forsaken life. She's a bitch, and she did this to me so she can go whore with Nick Succorso. Butcher her now, while she's asleep. She deserves it.

That was what he wanted. Every instinct in him wailed for it. Kill her and *go*! Better to get blasted fighting for your life than sit here and let them give you the death penalty while Nick motherfucking Succorso watches and laughs!

Unfortunately, his body refused to do it.

Shaking wildly, scarcely controllable, his hands discontinued the warm-up, shut *Bright Beauty* down again. For a long time he sat where he was with his palms clamped over his eyes while instinct and terror fired back and forth inside his head like meteors across the dark.

Then, still shaking, he reached out and erased the parallel zone-implant control from his command computer.

He verified that his sickbay log contained nothing incriminating.

He made a few slight adjustments to his datacore, elisions which were theoretically impossible as well as actively illegal, but which he was able to accomplish because his techniques were so subtle.

After that, he woke up Morn Hyland.

She didn't meet his eyes. That wasn't unusual, not in itself; but this time he knew what it meant, oh, he knew what it meant. Briefly she struggled to shake off the effects of sleep.

However, she didn't get out of bed.

With an effort, her mouth produced a crooked smile. If she noticed his stretched and haggard expression, she gave no sign. Instead, she extended her arms toward him as if she'd been dreaming about him.

As if she wanted, actually wanted, to make love to him, despite his power over her; despite the things he'd done to her.

Involuntarily he recoiled. Behind her smile, her face was studiously empty; blank and beautiful; determined to give nothing away. She couldn't know what was going on, of course; not for sure: she could only guess. She had little to pin her hopes on except one short note and the few sentences he and Nick had exchanged in the doorway of Mallorys. And yet she fought for those hopes.

She was trying to distract him, in case he hadn't yet realized what she'd done.

When he saw that, something inside him broke.

For a moment, he hated her. Somewhere, she'd found the one thing he'd always lacked, the courage to meet her doom head-on, to do what she could to control it. And it was Nick she wanted, Nick she did it for; not Angus. Now, however, it made no difference whether he hated her or not; whether he feared her or loved her. He was no longer in command of his own actions. What he said and did came to him like impulses from outside, abject and unpremeditated.

If he tried to get away, he would be killed.

If he didn't try to get away, he would be killed.

'Get up,' he rasped without anger or conviction. 'We're going to Mallorys.'

Somehow she managed to keep her features expressionless; she accepted his rejection and rose from the bed without so much as a flicker of surprise or fright. Watching her, he felt unexpectedly outclassed, as if the things he had done to her had made her greater than he was.

It might be too late. Station Security might already be on the way to arrest him. The control to her zone-implant felt like a grenade in his pocket, primed to destroy him. Nevertheless he went ahead without hurrying.

After she'd used the head, they left *Bright Beauty* for the last time and went to DelSec.

CHAPTER 17

Mallorys was crowded. The time was Station evening; rats and cynics of every description had come out of the bulkheads to cadge drinks or sell secrets, share loneliness or court oblivion. Nevertheless Angus Thermopyle didn't have any trouble finding a table. His reputation was bad enough already: nobody wanted to be near him, not while he was suspected of looting a supply ship. If any shooting started, Mallorys' patrons didn't want to get caught in the cross fire.

Most of the crowd probably desired nothing more complex than companionship or peace; or maybe satisfaction for their guesses about what was going on. That night was a bad one for quiet, however.

Angus and Morn looked much the same as usual, as unsuited to each other as ever. Still they emitted an expectant tension which affected everyone around them, making calm men uneasy and uneasy men nervous. Angus glowered violence at anybody who crossed his gaze; blood from his swollen lip marked his chin. Pale, blank, and unsure, Morn held herself like a coiled spring, restrained only by willpower and circumstance from doing something wild.

The mood in Mallorys thickened steadily around them.

Then Nick Succorso and some of his people came in.

He was in a cheerful humor, laughing and joking, but no one was reassured. The way he ignored Angus and Morn didn't make anybody relax: the scars under his eyes were too dark. Something was going to happen.

The people who didn't wish to know what that was left as inconspicuously as possible. Everyone else got ready for sudden movements.

When Security broke into the bar, some of the observers were surprised. The ones who'd probed a bit below the surface and thought they knew what was going on weren't.

Tables and chairs clattered back hastily: people milled around, jeering, cheering, trying to clear the way: a squad of guards drove into the confusion as fast as they could, determined to get their hands on Angus before he escaped.

So quickly that most people didn't see her do it, Morn Hyland left him and started through the crowd in Nick's direction.

But Angus was braced for her flight. He had good reflexes, and fear made him fast. This was the reason he'd brought her to Mallorys, the moment on which his life depended. He was a coward; and like a coward, he wanted to go on living even though his heart was broken. He hardly saw Security: he took note of the confusion around him only as a screen for his own actions.

Quick as a snake, he caught Morn by the wrist.

She struggled as well as she could. He was too strong. While she thrashed against his grip, she looked at him: the loathing and fright in her face were as loud as screams. Or maybe what she felt was incomprehension; maybe she thought he'd decided on a particularly brutal form of suicide. She'd been hoping, pleading, aching for an escape with every gram of her spirit – and now he'd caught her.

If he didn't release her—

He wanted to say something, but there were no words for it. And no time. His doom gathered against him. Security charged in from the door: Nick and his crew thrust forward from the other side, wedging a path for Morn through the crowd.

Holding her by the wrist, he slipped the control to her zone-implant into her hand.

'I accept. The deal you offered. I'll cover you.

'Remember,' he hissed as if he were pleading with her, *begging* her, 'I could have killed you. I could have killed you anytime.'

Then he let her go.

For a second, her eyes flared, and she stared at him.

During that moment, she seemed to understand him. Recognition passed between them. He had brought her here for this. To let her go. To give her what she wanted. And to ask her to spare his life.

Inside himself, he was stark naked with terror.

She had only a second to make her choice. Then Nick's people reached her, snatched her away.

But by that time she'd already shoved the zone-implant control like a small piece of immortality into one of her pockets, where no one could see it and take it to use against Angus Thermopyle.

Or against Morn herself.

After that, she was gone.

CHAPTER 18

So the fair maiden was rescued. The swashbuckling pirate bore her away with all her beauty, and her tormentor was left to pay the price of his crimes.

Angus was convicted of nothing more than stealing Station supplies. The evidence of *Bright Beauty*'s data-core was curiously imprecise. And the techs who examined *Starmaster* couldn't find any indication that the UMCP ship did anything except blow herself up; whether by sabotage or self-destruct was unclear. Without Morn's testimony, nothing else could be proved against Angus Thermopyle. Nevertheless that was enough to put him in lockup for the rest of his life.

Morn must have had an easier time with Nick than with Angus. Almost certainly he would have treated her better than Angus did – especially if he knew nothing, or could never be sure, about the zone-implant. With the control in her own hands, she was effectively as free as if the implant had been removed. A timer and a little common sense made it possible for her to take care of her own gap-sickness.

The fact that he'd rescued her so cleverly only enhanced Nick Succorso's reputation. The way he'd framed Angus was too perfect to be criticized. After all, the Station recovered its supplies. And the arrival of the real supply ship on schedule revealed just how clever Nick had been.

The real story, however, was that Angus never complained he'd been framed. He never mentioned there was a traitor in Security; he made no effort to defend himself. For the most part, he betrayed no reaction at all to his doom. When he heard *Bright Beauty* was going to be dismantled, he howled as if he were in agony; but he let Morn and Nick go. He had that much courage, anyway.

Despite his horror of imprisonment, he was condemned to stay in lockup until he rotted.

This is the end of
The Real Story.
The story continues in
Forbidden Knowledge.

AFTERWORD

Most writers hate the question, 'Where do you get your ideas?'

This is because the answer tends to be at once ineffably mysterious and excruciatingly mundane. We are all in love with the magic of the imagination – otherwise we wouldn't be able to survive as creative artists – but none of us can explain how it works. In a sense, writers don't get ideas: ideas get writers. They happen to us. If we don't submit to their power, we lose them; so by trying to control or censor them we can make the negative choice of encouraging them to leave us alone. But we can never *force* ourselves to be truly creative. The best we can do is to teach ourselves receptiveness – and trust that ideas will come.

However, once the magic of the imagination has been accepted as given, any specific answer to the question often becomes almost violently anti-creative: for instance, 'Well, I got that particular idea off a can of Lysol disinfectant in the men's room at Circle K.' (I'm not making this up. One of the strongest scenes in *The Power that Preserves* was triggered in my head by a can of Lysol disinfectant in a men's room.) Such an answer may be perfectly accurate, but who wants to say it out loud? In these cases, the concrete source of the idea seems to demean its underlying imaginative magic. Hence the apparently arrogant or dismissive answers which writers have been giving ever since readers began asking the question.

But occasionally one or another of us is able to offer a practical answer without experiencing too much dissonance between what we say and how we feel about what we're saying. This *Afterword* is a case in point. I can discuss the sources and development for the sequence of four novels which follows directly after *The Real Story* while suffering no more severe distress than a blind astonishment that my mind works so *slowly*.

*

For some reason, a fair number of my best stories arise, not from one idea, but from two. In these cases, one idea comes first; it excites me enough to stay with me; yet despite its apparent (to me) potential, it stubbornly refuses to grow. Rather than expanding to take on character, event, and context, it simply sits in my head – often for many years – saying over and over again, '*Look* at me, you idiot. If you just *looked* at me, you would know what to do with me.' Well, I *do* look; but I can't see what I need – until the first idea is intersected by the second. And then: Step back, boys and girls. She's a gusher.

I've heard Brian Aldiss talk about the same phenomenon. For him, a novel often requires two ideas. He describes them as a combination of 'the familiar' and 'the exotic.' He begins with 'the familiar' – usually something germane to his personal life, either thematically or experientially – but he can't write about it until 'the familiar' is impacted by 'the exotic.' In his case, 'the exotic' is usually a science fictional setting in which 'the familiar' can play itself out: 'the exotic' provides him with a stage on which he can dramatize 'the familiar.' Rather like a binary poison – or a magic potion – two inert elements combine to produce something of frightening potency.

The same dynamic works in reverse for me. I start with 'the exotic' (remember that these are Aldiss's terms, not mine), but that idea declines to turn into a story until it is catalysed by 'the familiar.'

For example: *The Chronicles of Thomas Covenant* is squarely – and solely – founded on two ideas: unbelief and leprosy. The notion of writing a fantasy about an 'unbeliever,' a man who rejects the whole concept of fantasy, first came to me near the end of 1969. But the germ was dormant: no matter how I labored over it, I couldn't make it grow. Until I realized, in May of 1972, that my 'unbeliever' should be a leper. As soon as those two ideas came together, my brain took fire. I spent the next three months feverishly taking notes, drawing maps, envisioning characters, studying the implications of unbelief and leprosy. Then I began writing.

This dynamic reverses Aldiss's because leprosy represented 'the familiar' rather than 'the exotic.' I'd never written fantasy before: The whole concept of writing a fantasy about an 'unbeliever' was exotic. However, thanks to the fact that my father was an orthopedic surgeon in India for twenty-one years, I was accustomed to leprosy on a variety of levels.

In the case of the four novels which ensue from *The Real Story*, the two ideas might be labelled 'Angus Thermopyle' and 'Richard Wagner.'

Contrary to what one might expect, Angus represents 'the familiar.'

I wrote the first draft of *The Real Story* in the summer of 1985. At the time, I thought I was simply writing a novella: The idea came to me, so I worked on it at my earliest opportunity.

(Where did *that* idea come from? Well, this is a little embarrassing. It grew entirely out of the names of the characters. Driving through Albuquerque one day, I suddenly found myself chanting like a mantra, 'Angus Thermopyle. Angus Thermopyle.' I couldn't begin to guess why that name had appeared; but I could feel its importance, so I kept on chanting it. For weeks. And then, as if accidentally, another name manifested itself: Morn Hyland. So I chanted, 'Angus Thermopyle,' and, 'Morn Hyland' until they were joined by Nick Succorso. By this time, I liked the names so much that I began consciously trying to pull together a story good enough for them.)

My original intentions were explicitly archetypal. What I had in mind was an aesthetically perfect variation on *the* basic three-sided story: the story in which a Victim (Morn), a Villain (Angus), and a Rescuer (Nick) all change roles. (This, incidentally, is the essential difference between melodrama and drama. Melodrama presents a Victim, a Villain, and a Rescuer. Drama offers the same characters and then studies the process by which they change roles.) Victimized by Angus, Morn is rescued by Nick – but that, of course, is not the *real* story. The *real* story has to do with the way in which Nick becomes Angus' victimizer and Morn becomes Angus' rescuer.

When I'd finished the first draft of the novella, however, I found myself in a state of acute distress, for at least three reasons – only two of which were conscious. First, I realized immediately that what I'd written was by no means 'aesthetically perfect.' My work had fallen below my original intentions rather farther than usual. I'd planned a balanced triangle, with equal attention paid to each character and equal emphasis placed on each shifting role. But in practice I was unable to produce that balance.

Put simply, the problem was that Angus had taken over the story. Vital and malign, he dominated the narrative, reducing Morn to a shadow –

and Nick to a cypher. In some ways, this made sense: as long as the action was viewed from Angus' point of view, Morn's motivations were unknowable, and Nick's were unimportant. But the result was that I'd written an intensive study of Angus's movement from Villain to Victim; but I'd only sketched in Morn's shift from Victim to Rescuer; and I hadn't paid any attention at all to Nick's change from Rescuer to Villain.

(If I weren't so damn *slow*, this would have given me a powerful clue to the third, unconscious reason for my distress.)

I was quite disappointed in myself.

Yet I was also aware of another reason for my distress. Unlike any other character I'd ever created, Angus made me feel *exposed*. It was as if in imagining him I'd tapped directly into the dark side of my own nature; as if I'd found him inside myself instead of inventing him. (In Aldiss's terms, he was 'the familiar.') And that in turn shamed me. I felt irrationally sure that anyone who read *The Real Story* would see the 'real' me, recognize the truth, and be disgusted.

Because I was ashamed of the novella, both artistically and personally, I decided not to publish it. At the time, I believed that I would never publish it.

Well, time works wonders. Among other things, it gives us the chance to think. And after I'd thought for a while, I began trying to do something about my shame.

There was nothing to be done about my personal shame, of course. I could only dismiss it. Time and thought brought me to the realization that I had no reason to feel ashamed. Suppose for a moment that my worst fears were realistic: that I am in fact an Angus Thermopyle thinly disguised by niceness; that this fact is transparent in *The Real Story;* and that all right-thinking readers will be disgusted by the results. So what? None of that impinges on the integrity of *The Real Story* itself. If I drew on some buried part of myself to create Angus, so much the better: at least I'm writing what I know. In any case, the crucial question for any artist is not: What are people going to think of me? It is: Have I given my best to my work? Nothing else matters.

Where *The Real Story* was concerned, I had to answer, 'Yes and no.' Yes, I was doing exactly what I'm supposed to do when I wrote the novella: I accepted the idea of 'Angus' for the simple and sufficient reason that it came to me; I followed the idea where it chose to lead me, rather than trying to make it serve my own purposes. And no, I hadn't given my best to the work: I hadn't done everything in my power to raise the aesthetic level of the novella as high as possible.

So I spent the next two years, off and on, rewriting *The Real Story*. Indeed, I put it through my word processor at least six different times, developing and focusing Morn, enhancing Nick. And eventually I came to the conclusion that I was never going to be able to make it 'aesthetically perfect.' Judged by the standard of my original intentions, this book would always be a failure. For me as a writer, the effort of dealing with Angus was so urgent and compulsory that I couldn't treat Morn and Nick as his equals. What we might call the spatial constraints of the narrative didn't leave enough room for them.

(There it was again: a clue to the third, unconscious reason for my distress. But I still didn't recognize the truth.)

Fortunately, I was saved from the belief that *The Real Story* was doomed to artistic failure by what Dr Who refers to as 'lateral thinking.' If you have an unscalable cliff in front of you and an unbeatable monster behind you, go sideways. Obedient to that dictum, I began to ask myself, not, 'How did I go wrong within the novella?' but, 'Where did I go wrong in my original intentions?'

Where, indeed? Well, where else? *The Real Story* was based on only one idea – and a *fair number of my best stories arise, not from one idea, but from two*. My problems with the book resulted from the need for a second idea.

However, I've told *this* story backward. *The Real Story* was actually the second idea, not the first. When I combined it with another idea which had already been in my head – alive, exciting, and totally static – for twenty years, I had a gusher.

The real story, however, was that Angus never complained he'd been framed. He never mentioned there was a traitor in Security; he made no effort to defend himself. For the most part, he betrayed no reaction at all to his doom. When he heard *Bright Beauty* was going to be dismantled, he howled as if he were in agony; but he let Morn and Nick go. He had that much courage, anyway.

Despite his horror of imprisonment, he was condemned to stay in lockup until he rotted.

So ends *The Real Story*. There's no indication here, certainly, that events will take four more books to run their course – or that the course they run will be epic in the Wagnerian sense; as large-scaled, intense, and ambitious as anything in *The Chronicles of Thomas Covenant*. That's because the original source for this sequence of novels was a recording of Richard Wagner's *Götterdammerung (The Twilight of the Gods)*; the true genesis began in the fall of 1966.

That recording, which I purchased in September of 1966, wasn't my first experience with Wagner; but it was my first taste of Wagner's four-part opera cycle, *Der Ring des Nibelungen (The Ring of the Nibelung)*, and it inspired me to purchase as quickly as my finances permitted (I spent three years saving pennies) recordings of the other three parts of *The Ring: Das Rheingold (The Rhine Gold)*, *Die Walküre (The Valkyrie)*, and *Siegfried* (no translation necessary). In a relatively short time, I knew that I'd discovered my musical alter-ego – a kind of transcendental *Doppelgänger*. Wagner's music inspired me. (Indeed, some of the literary techniques of *The Chronicles of Thomas Covenant* were extrapolated from the way Wagner used musical ideas.) And the story of *The Ring – especially* in the twin climaxes of *The Valkyrie* and *The Twilight of the Gods* – moved me as deeply as any story I've ever encountered.

Soon after I fell in love with *The Ring*, I conceived the ambition of writing a sequence of novels based on Wagner's epic.

My intentions were conceptual rather than literal. I wasn't interested in simply retelling the story of Wotan's doomed struggle to preserve the power of the gods in the face of pressure from giants, dwarves, and humankind. Rather I wanted to create an analogue which would allow me to explore the same themes and exigencies on my own terms. Most particularly, I was fascinated by Wotan himself, who finds that an understanding of his own power leads to the destruction of that power, as well as of himself and everything he represents; even more, that an understanding of his power leads him to *will* his own destruction.

But the idea remained utterly and entirely static – until 1987, when I realized that the world of Angus, Morn, and Nick offered me the perfect setting for the story I had in mind.

(In addition, of course, I realized that using *The Real Story* to launch a larger narrative gave me a perfect opportunity to make constructive use of the ways in which it didn't measure up to my original intentions. The relative imbalance of the roles in the novella becomes a strength rather than a weakness when its implications can be pursued in subsequent books. *This* was the third, unconscious reason for my distress concerning *The Real Story*. My work there disturbed me because it wasn't *complete and* couldn't be completed without the catalysis of a second idea.)

As the ending of *The Real Story* suggests, the relevance of Wagner's epic to Angus's fate may not be readily apparent. That's the only excuse I can offer for my slowness to comprehend that Wagner and Angus needed each other.

Fortunately or unfortunately, depending on whether afterwords are considered a pleasure or an affliction, I can't explain the relevance without discussing *The Ring* in some detail.

Put simply, Wagner's opera cycle tells the story of how the gods were brought down by two things: a bitter curse; and an act of unselfish heroism.

Das Rheingold

In a world where humankind is the weakest and least effective form of life, the gods (Wotan; Fricka, his wife, goddess of family and hearth; Donner, god of storm; Froh, god of light; Loge, god of fire; and Freia, goddess of eternal life) rule proudly – although they are neither the oldest nor the most potent forces or beings in their sphere. However, their power is precarious: It depends on their ability to compel submission from two magical and creative races, the giants (builders of large things) and the dwarves (builders of small things), both of which aspire to supplant the gods. Hungry for supremacy, Wotan has carved a staff from the World Tree; and into his staff he cuts the bargains and treaties he makes to consolidate his dominance, so that his authority becomes part of the natural order. But precisely because his rule is based on authority and law rather than on love or virtue, it inspires resentment. So, to make himself and the gods secure, he cuts a deal with the giants to build an impregnable fortress for him: Valhalla. His idea is to fill Valhalla with heroes to fight for him, so that he can resist any challenge from either giants or dwarves.

Two problems arise immediately, however: one of his own making, one outside his control.

The one he can't control involves three watery females, the Rhine

Maidens, and a dwarf, Alberich, who falls in lust with them. (All right, I admit it: I've never found the Rhine Maidens themselves especially convincing.) The Maidens were fathered by one of the aforementioned older beings, and their purpose in life (or at least in the Rhine) is to guard the Rhine Gold, one of the archetypal sources of power (like the World Tree). Now, the secret of the Rhine Gold is this: Any being who 'foreswears love,' giving up all bonds of passion or commitment, takes the Gold, and forges it into a ring, will gain the power to impose his will on others. This the Maidens gleefully reveal to Alberich, primarily because they think his lust – and loneliness – are funny. (Characters with nothing better to do in a story than sit around being archetypal are often rather insensitive.)

But they underestimate the scale of his loneliness and desire. Taunted past bearing by beauties he cannot have, he does indeed foreswear love, take the Gold, and forge it into a ring. Before anyone notices what he's up to, he gains dominion over all the dwarves, accumulates a vast treasure – and commences to plan his attack on the gods. Thus begins an evil which can only be ended by returning the Gold to the Maidens.

The problem Wotan could have avoided, if he were wiser – i.e., less hungry for power – is that for the sake of getting Valhalla built 'on the cheap' he has made a bargain with the giants which he has no intention of keeping: He has offered them Freia (source of the gods' immortality) in exchange for the fortress. This is manifestly misguided, since his supremacy depends on bargains and agreements; but he is young, strong, and arrogant – and he believes that once Valhalla is built he'll be able to persuade the giants to accept some other payment.

No such luck. The giants want *Freia*, or to hell with Valhalla and the gods. (They realize, of course, that without her the gods can't endure; so their insistence on correct payment is inspired by a desire to bring Wotan down.)

This is a terrible moment for Wotan – he's doomed if he breaks his bargain, and doomed if he keeps it – but he isn't yet wise enough to realize the full implications. Instead of facing up to the consequences of his own actions, he hits upon a solution of convenience. Maybe the giants will accept Alberich's treasure (and ring) as payment in Freia's place. The giants agree: they've heard about the ring.

At this point, Alberich's only weakness is that he isn't yet accustomed to the sheer size of his new power. He doesn't really understand that he stands on the brink of godhood himself: He's too busy enjoying his treasure – and his ability to torture his own people with impunity. In consequence, he's vulnerable, not to force, but to trickery. Helped by the cunning of Loge, Wotan obtains the ring by subterfuge and immediately uses it to master both Alberich and the treasure.

This would be a self-destructive act on Wotan's part in any case: He has no right to the ring, but he is immediately consumed by desire for its power. However, his position deteriorates further when Alberich curses the ring. Only in losing the ring does Alberich grasp its magnitude. In an apotheosis of grief and rage, he cries:

> As its gold gave me power without limit,
> now let its magic bring death to whoever wears it.
> No happy man shall be glad of it,
> no fortunate man know the smile of its bright gleam.
> Whoever possess it shall be seared by anxiety,
> and whoever has it not, shall be nagged by envy.
> Everyone shall hanker for its possession
> but no one enjoy it to advantage.
> Without gain its master shall guard it,
> for it draws him to his assassin.
> Condemned to death the coward will be in fear's grip.
> As long as he lives he shall long for death,
> the ring's master be slave to the ring . . . .

Now Wotan is in *real* trouble. The ring is cursed, but he desires it too much to give it up. Yet it is the only payment the giants will accept in Freia's place. Without her, the gods must die. Wotan can't simply declare war on the giants because the enforcement of his bargains is carved into his staff, the source of his power: to violate his own commitments will undo him. And the natural order of existence can only be restored by returning the Gold to the Rhine Maidens – which will force Freia into the hands of the giants.

At last Wotan begins to understand his plight. With a little help from Erda, the Earth Mother (another of those preexisting beings), he gains enough insight to realize that he must surrender the ring. So the giants take the ring; Freia remains with the gods; and Wotan gets Valhalla.

Alas, this is only a stop-gap resolution. The natural order is still in jeopardy. The ring remains a threat to the gods. And the curse *works:* The giants proceed to slaughter each other until only one remains to hold the ring; and that one sequesters himself (as a dragon), dedicating his entire being to the simple goal of preventing anyone from getting the ring away from him.

Die Walküre

Wotan is now obsessed with understanding his dilemma. After some intensive study with Erda (study which just happens to produce eight daughters – the Valkyries), he learns that the only cure for the evil of the ring is to return the Gold to the Maidens. Unfortunately, he can't do that: He can't get the ring away from the dragon without breaking his bargain with the giants. However, in due course he hits on the only apparent solution to the problem: He decides to use an agent to obtain the ring for him.

First, on a human woman he gets himself a son, Siegmund (and, not coincidentally, a daughter as well, Sieglinde, Siegmund's twin). Then he trains his son to be strong, brave, and *desperate* enough to tackle a dragon. Sadly, this training involves separating Siegmund and Sieglinde and abandoning them both to lives of extreme loneliness, abuse, and danger. Neither of them has any idea that their father loves them – and needs them. All they know of life is bitter survival against cruel odds.

Too bad. Wotan's plan was flawed from the beginning – a fact that becomes transparent when Siegmund and Sieglinde find each other and fall in love (she gets pregnant). This attracts the attention of Fricka: As goddess of matrimony, she's responsible for punishing sins like incest. She forces Wotan to recognize that any agent of his is no different from him; that for Siegmund to get the ring will be the same as if Wotan himself took it. Therefore Wotan can't use Siegmund to solve his problems for him; and so he has no defense against Fricka's argument that Siegmund and Sieglinde must die for their crime. Broken-hearted – and aware of his own doom – Wotan commands his favorite Valkyrie, Brünnhilde, to make sure that Siegmund and Sieglinde are killed by Hunding, Sieglinde's rapist/husband.

It is Brünnhilde's act of unselfish heroism which changes the nature of the dilemma.

As Wotan's favorite, she thinks of herself as his will incarnate. However, his pain when he condemns Siegmund and Sieglinde moves her deeply. And she is further distraught by Siegmund's passionate and fatal loyalty to Sieglinde. At the last, the Valkyrie chooses not to help Hunding execute Siegmund. Instead, she fights for Siegmund against Hunding, directly defying Wotan, the All-Father.

Outraged, Wotan intervenes personally, killing both Siegmund and Hunding. In the confusion, however, Brünnhilde escapes with Sieglinde. If Siegmund cannot be saved, perhaps his son can be preserved. She helps Sieglinde flee into a trackless forest (the same forest, incidentally, where the dragon guards his treasure), then turns to face Wotan's wrath (thereby buying Sieglinde time to run).

Because she has opposed him, Wotan condemns Brünnhilde to an enchanted sleep, from which she can only be awakened by the shame of being 'taken' as a mortal's lover. And because he loves her, he guards her sleep with a fire which will prevent any man who isn't utterly fearless from approaching her.

Siegfried

Sieglinde, meanwhile, struggles on into the forest. Close to death, she comes upon a cave where Mime, Alberich's brother, has been living ever since Alberich's hold over the dwarves was broken. Mime keeps her alive until her son, Siegfried, is born; after she dies in childbirth, he raises young Siegfried with one goal in mind: to make Siegfried utterly fearless so that he'll be brave enough to fight the the dragon and get the ring for his foster father.

Like most plans in this story, Mime's proves flawed. For one thing, both Wotan and Alberich know what he's doing – and Alberich has plans of his own. For another, Mime succeeds only too well: He teaches Siegfried to be *so* fearless that Siegfried can't stand the sight of his craven foster father and won't do anything for the dwarf. Trying to trick him, Mime tells Siegfried he'll learn something wonderful – fear – if he meets the dragon; so Siegfried decides to accept the adventure, despite his loathing for Mime. But this, too, doesn't work out well for poor Mime.

Instead of learning fear, Siegfried kills the dragon (laughing all the way) and gets the ring; in addition, he captures a magic talisman, the tarnhelm, which makes him a shape-changer, and gains from the dragon's blood the ability to understand birds. At once, a bird tells him that Mime is about to poison him. In righteous indignation, Siegfried kills Mime. Then the bird tells him about Brünnhilde. Hungry for more adventures, he goes off to rescue her.

Along the way, he encounters Wotan, who forbids him to approach the magic fire. But Siegfried is nothing if not self-willed: Oblivious to symbolism, he breaks Wotan's spear and continues his quest to rescue the enchanted woman.

(Without his spear, of course, Wotan is finished. In fact, he had reason to believe that his spear wouldn't stop the boy. His decision to challenge Siegfried regardless is complex. On the one hand, he knows that if his spear can't stop Siegfried the gods are doomed anyway: They'll never be able to control whatever use is made of the ring. On the other, he understands that unless his spear – his rule – is shattered, the world will never be free of the destructive effects of his bargains. He challenges Siegfried in an attempt to simultaneously save and destroy himself.)

Götterdammerung

In a manner of speaking, Siegfried is a dream come true for Brünnhilde – a mortal so heroic that he might as well be a god. She gives him her heart, as well as a spell to protect him from any danger as long as he doesn't turn his back on it; and he goes out into the world to have more adventures so that she'll be proud of him. (I should perhaps have mentioned earlier that Siegfried isn't very bright.)

Almost immediately, he finds himself in the domain of the Gibichungs, a human tribe with failed ambitions and an imprecise moral sense. They are led by Gunther, unwed; his spinster sister, Gutrune; and his half-brother, Hagan (Alberich's son and agent). The Gibichungs want glory through Siegfried; Hagan wants the ring. Toward those ends, they conspire to give Siegfried a potion which causes him to forget Brünnhilde. Then they send him to obtain Brünnhilde for Gunther (using the tarnhelm to appear as Gunther), for which his reward will be Gutrune's hand in marriage. (This only works because Siegfried can't remember ever meeting another woman, so to him Gutrune looks good.)

When Brünnhilde is brought from the safety of her magic fire and given to Gunther, she is quite understandably outraged by Siegfried's apparent betrayal. She denounces him furiously. Hagan promptly gives Siegfried another potion which causes him to remember Brünnhilde and forget Gutrune; and as soon as Siegfried unselfconsciously admits the substantial accuracy of Brünnhilde's denunciation, Hagan claims that revelation as an excuse to spear Siegfried in the back.

Even in death, however, Siegfried is so strong that no one can get the ring away from him. And Brünnhilde is at last able to see the truth of his behavior. To honor him, she commands a funeral pyre and joins him on it. As soon as fire melts the ring, the Rhine Maidens are able to reclaim their gold. The story ends with the natural order restored – and Valhalla burning in the background. So the gods are brought to an end, and humankind is freed from arbitrary external dominance to work out its own destiny.

(The logic here is profound, yet difficult to explain. Once Wotan's spear was broken, the gods were, in effect, kept alive by the force of Alberich's curse. They couldn't die: The holder of the ring could be murdered, but everyone else who fell under the curse was compelled to yearn and suffer helplessly, as long as the ring – and therefore the curse – endured.)

So what, one might well ask, does all this have to do with ore piracy and space Stations?

The answer is simple enough, as long as another, more concrete question is answered first. If Angus Thermopyle is a pirate who preys on human miners and shipping, to whom does he sell his booty? Ore isn't cash, after all: It's relatively useless unless it can be processed. And ore processing is capital intensive. Pirates like Angus and Nick would never exist – and the UMCP in turn would have no mandate to combat them – unless they had a market for their ill-gotten gains. So what kind of world lies behind *The Real Story*? Is humankind publicly divided against itself? Or is it in conflict with something else; something anti-human? Doesn't the UMCP mandate against piracy derive its moral authority from the fact that the pirates are, in effect, selling out humankind?

Once such questions have been asked (in the context of *Der Ring des Nibelungen*), the step from *The Real Story* to the next book, *Forbidden Knowledge*, is a small one. As soon as I began to think of the UMCP as legal gods threatened by the science fiction equivalent of shape-changing dwarves, I could hardly stop before I reached the wonderfully perverse notion of Angus and Morn as Siegmund and Sieglinde. And after that, as I've already indicated, my story became a gusher.

However, imagining Angus and Morn as Siegmund and Sieglinde suggests just how fundamentally non-literal my use of *The Ring* is. *The Ring* is not my story: It is one of the seeds from which my story grew. In several ways, I've moved a considerable distance from my source.

For one thing, there are themes in Wagner that I don't want to pursue. His work contains a kind of structural sexism which leaves me cold. (The Rhine Maidens make me think of the scene in *Monty Python and the Holy Grail* where a peasant shouts at Arthur, 'You can't wield supreme executive power just because some watery tart pitched a sword at you!') And I don't respond to characters whose power derives from their innocence: To my mind, Siegfried is untrammeled by fear, not because of his innocence, but because he's too stupid to live. Wagner's idea that knowledge paralyzes power seems inadequate to me – witness the entire *Chronicles of Thomas Covenant*.

For another, 'Angus Thermopyle' alters the essential terms and possibilities of 'Richard Wagner.' In a sense, setting *is* story – and the setting of *The Real Story* is science fictional rather than mythopoeic. Almost by definition, the conflicts of the story now become political rather than archetypal. Of necessity, every valence of *The Ring* is transformed. The most obvious result is that the onus of the story shifts from gods and dwarves to human beings. If human life in space is to be preserved, it must be preserved, not by All-Fathers and Valkyries, but by the descendants of the Gibichungs.

The consequences of this transformation are everywhere. Just to mention a few examples, My 'gods' derive their ability to endure, not from immortality, but from their control over information. As a crime against the order which the UMCP is pledged to protect, incest would have no meaning; so there's no reason for Angus and Morn to be siblings. And I use no direct analogues to either Wotan's staff or Alberich's ring – although Angus' ability to edit datacores has interesting implications.

Yet *The Ring* is present in each of the four novels which follows *The Real Story*. When characters like Warden Dios, Min Donner, Godsen

Frik, and Hashi Lebwohl take the stage, they come, as one might say, 'trailing clouds of glory' – the ether of their Wagnerian avatars. And who better to represent the dwarves than the Amnion, who desire nothing less than the destruction of the natural existence of humanity?

Whether Angus and Morn can preserve their own humanity (not to mention their entire species) is a question which could only have arisen from the intersection of *The Real Story* and *Der Ring des Nibelungen*.

FORBIDDEN KNOWLEDGE

ANGUS

Milos Taverner sighed, ran his hand back across his mottled scalp as if to verify that what remained of his hair was still present, and lit another nic. Then he glared again at the transcript hardcopy on his desk and tried to imagine an approach that might work – without getting himself into so much trouble that the people he was paid to please would turn against him.

He was responsible for the ongoing interrogation of Angus Thermopyle.

It wasn't going well.

That pleased some people and infuriated others.

Angus' trial had been a simple enough affair, as such things went. Com-Mine Security had recovered the pirated supplies. The search which located the supplies aboard Angus' ship, *Bright Beauty*, had adequate legal justification. With a number of vague, troubling exceptions, the evidence of the ship's datacore supported the charges against him – the less damning ones. He mounted no defense, apparently because he knew it was futile. Everything was correct and in order; Angus Thermopyle was guilty as charged.

On the other hand, despite provocative rumors concerning zone-implants, rape, murder, and the wrecked UMCP destroyer *Starmaster*, no evidence had turned up to convict him of anything more serious than the burglary of Station supplies. He was sentenced to life imprisonment in Com-Mine Station's lockup; but the law simply could not be stretched to include his execution.

Case closed.

Station Security had no intention whatsoever of letting matters rest there.

Milos Taverner had mixed feelings about that. He had too many conflicting priorities to juggle.

As Deputy Chief of Com-Mine Station Security, interrogation was his responsibility. True, the present charges against Angus Thermopyle had been adequately proven – and true, the evidence didn't justify any other charges. But Security knew Angus of old. His piracies were a moral, if not a provable, certainty; his dealings with illegals of every description, from druggers and psychotics to the bootleg ore industry in all its guises, were unquestionable, if indemonstrable. His crew had a distressing tendency to disappear. Additionally the unexplained chain of circumstances which brought him back to Com-Mine accompanied by a UMC cop who should have died aboard *Starmaster* was profoundly intriguing – not to mention disturbing.

All things considered, Milos couldn't question the decision to keep after Angus Thermopyle until he broke or died.

Nevertheless the Deputy Chief didn't really want the job. For a number of reasons.

Because he was personally fastidious, he found Angus repulsive. As far as anyone knew, an addiction to nic was Milos' only vice. Even people he made no effort to please would have admitted that he was clean, circumspect, and correct in all his dealings. And no sane observer would have ascribed those virtues to Angus.

More than anything, Angus looked like a toad bloated by malice. His bodily habits were offensive: he only took a shower when the guards forced him into the san cubicle, only put on a clean prisonsuit at stun-point. That and the way he sweated made him smell like a pig. The color of his skin was like ground-in grime. His mere existence made Milos feel vaguely ill: his presence inspired a sense of active nausea.

In addition his eyes glared yellow with a belligerent wisdom that made Milos feel exposed, dangerously known.

Angus was cunning, crafty; as insidious as disorder. And people like that were risky to work with. They lied in ways which confirmed their interrogators' illusions. They learned from the questions they were asked, they gained as much knowledge as they gave – as much or more, in Angus' case – and they used that knowledge to perfect their lies; to work for the ruin of their interrogators even when they had nothing tangible to work with and had themselves been worked over regularly by

146

experts to encourage cooperation. When they should have been at their weakest, they became most malignant.

Angus caused the Deputy Chief to feel that he himself was the one being tested, the one whose secrets might be laid bare; the one put to the question.

And, as if all that weren't enough to contend with, Milos had to wrestle daily with the fact that his interrogation was potentially explosive. Angus Thermopyle was an ore pirate. Therefore he had buyers. He had obtained *Bright Beauty* by illegal – if unproven – means; had outfitted her illegally. Therefore he had access to bootleg shipyards. Some of his technology smelled alien, and his records were patently too clean, even though they were unimpeachably recorded in his ship's datacore. And all those conclusions, all those strands of inference, ran in only one direction.

Forbidden space.

Angus Thermopyle had dealings – direct or indirect – with secrets destructive enough to shift the balances of power everywhere in the United Mining Companies' vast commercial empire. Those secrets could threaten the security of every Station; perhaps they could threaten the security of Earth.

Milos Taverner wasn't sure he wanted those secrets to come out. In fact, as time passed he became more and more convinced that he needed them to remain hidden. Angus' silence infuriated some of the people Milos was paid to please: his secrets, if they were revealed, would infuriate others. But the people who hated Angus' silence were less immediately dangerous.

On the other hand, every moment Milos spent with Angus Thermopyle was recorded. Transcripts were regularly reviewed on-Station. Copies were routinely forwarded to the UMCP. The Deputy Chief of Com-Mine Station Security couldn't tackle this assignment with anything less than complete diligence and expect to get away with it.

No wonder he couldn't give up nic. He found the habit disgusting in other people – and yet he couldn't quit himself. Sometimes he thought nic was the only thing that enabled his nerves to bear the stress.

Fortunately Angus Thermopyle refused to participate in his own interrogation.

He faced down questions with unflagging hostility and silence. He absorbed stun until he puked his guts out, and his entire cell stank with ineradicable bile; but he didn't talk. He suffered hunger, thirst, and sensory deprivation relentlessly. The one time he cracked was when Milos informed him that *Bright Beauty* was being dismantled for scrap and spare parts. But then he only howled like a beast and did his best to wreck the interrogation room; he didn't say anything.

In Milos' opinion, telling Angus about *Bright Beauty*'s fate had been a mistake. He'd said so openly to his superiors – after taking considerable pains to plant the suggestion in their minds. It would reinforce Angus' intransigence. They'd insisted on the ploy, however. After all, nothing else seemed to work. The outcome was about what Milos had expected. That was one small victory, anyway.

In other ways, most of the interrogation sessions were unenlightening.

How did you meet Morn Hyland?

No answer.

What were you doing together?

No answer.

Why would a UMC cop agree to crew for a murdering illegal like you?

No answer.

What did you do to her?

Angus' glare never wavered.

How did you get those supplies? How did you get into the holds? Computer security wasn't tampered with. Nothing happened to the guards. There's no sign you cut your way in. The ventilation ducts aren't big enough for those crates. How did you do it?

No answer.

How did *Starmaster* die?

No answer.

How did Morn Hyland survive?

No answer.

She said she didn't trust Station Security. She said *Starmaster* must have been sabotaged – she said it must have been done here. Why did she trust you instead of us?

No answer.

Why were you there? How did you just happen to be in the vicinity when *Starmaster*'s thrust drive destructed? No answer.

You said – Milos consulted his hardcopy – you were close enough to pick up the blast on scan. You implied you knew a disaster had occurred, and you wanted to help. Is that true?

No answer.

Isn't it true that *Starmaster* was after you? Isn't it true she caught you in the act of some crime? Isn't it true you crashed when she chased you? Isn't that how *Bright Beauty* got hurt?

No answer.

Sucking nic so he wouldn't start to shake, Milos Taverner studied the ceiling, the stacks of hardcopy in front of him; he studied Angus' stained face. Angus' cheeks used to be fat, bloated like his belly; not anymore. Now his jowls hung from his jaw, and his prisonsuit sagged down his frame. The punishment he'd received had cost him weight. Nevertheless his physical deterioration hadn't weakened the way his eyes fixed, yellow and threatening, on his tormentor.

'Take him outside,' Milos sighed to the guards. 'Soften him up. Again.'

Shit, the Deputy Chief thought when he was alone. He didn't like foul language: 'shit' was the strongest expletive he used.

You shit. I shit. He shits. We all shit.

Now who am I supposed to be loyal to?

He went back to his office and made his usual reports, dealt with his usual duties. After that, he rode the lift down to Communications and used Security's dedicated channels to tight-beam several transmissions in his private code, none of them recorded. Just to reassure himself, he put through a data req which – when an answer came – would tell him the balance of the bank account he held on Sagittarius Unlimited under an alternative name. Then he resumed Angus Thermopyle's interrogation.

What else could he do?

His one and only definite opportunity to break his prisoner came when Angus attempted to escape.

In spite of his personal intransigence, his plain sociopathy, Angus was hit hard by what Milos told him about *Bright Beauty*. When his burst of grief or fury was over, he didn't crumble in any obvious sense. He was failing, of course, worn down by the physical stress of interrogation and stun; but in front of Milos Taverner, at least, he preserved his uncooperative demeanor. Nevertheless his behavior when he was alone in his cell changed. He began eating less; he spent hours sitting on his lean bunk, staring at the wall. Observers reported that his manner was listless, almost unreactive; that when he stared at the wall his eyes didn't shift, didn't appear to focus on anything. As a matter of course, Milos ran this information through Security's psy-profile computer. The program paradigms suggested that Angus Thermopyle was losing, or had already lost, his will to live. In the absence of that will, the use of stun as an aid to questioning was contraindicated. Angus could die.

Milos thought Angus was faking his loss of will in an effort to get his punishment eased. The Deputy Chief decided to ignore the computer.

That was another small victory. His judgment was confirmed when Angus contrived to beat up his guard and break out of his cell. He got as far as the service shaft which led into the labyrinth of the waste processing plant before he was recaptured.

Shit, Milos said to himself over and over again. He was using the word much too often, but he didn't have any other way to express his visceral disgust. He didn't *want* Angus' interrogation to succeed – but now he had a lever he could use, and he would never get away with not using it.

When he'd issued certain very explicit instructions, so that his own plans wouldn't be compromised, he let the guards have Angus for a while to vent their frustrations. Then he had Angus brought in front of him again.

In a sense, stun wasn't a very satisfying outlet for frustration. Its effects were strong, but it felt impersonal; the convulsions it produced were caused by mere neuromuscular reaction to an electric charge. So this time the guards hadn't used stun: they'd used their fists, their boots, perhaps a sap or two. As a result, when Angus reached the interrogation room he could hardly walk. He sat like a man with cracked ribs; his face and ears oozed blood; he'd lost a tooth or two; his left eye was swollen shut in a grotesque parody of Warden Dios.

Milos found Angus' condition distasteful. Also it scared him because it increased his chances of success. Nevertheless he gave it his approval before he dismissed the guards.

He and Angus were alone.

Smoking so hard that the air-conditioning couldn't keep up with it, he left Angus to sit and sweat while he keyed a number of commands into his computer console. Let Angus' resolve erode under the pressure of silence. Alternatively, let him use the respite to recover his determination.

Milos didn't care. He needed the time to take the risk on which he'd decided to stake his own safety, even though the dangers made his fingers tremble and his guts feel like water.

He was preparing the computer to provide two recordings of this session. One would be the actual recording; the other would be a dummy designed to protect him in an emergency.

When the session was over, he could use whichever recording he needed. He was the Deputy Chief of Security: he knew how to take all trace of the other recording out of the computer.

But if he were caught before then—

The rather imprecise nature of his loyalties would be exposed. He would be ruined.

Deep in his guts, he hated Angus for putting him in this position.

He couldn't afford to falter, however. Once his preparations were complete, he hid his hands behind the console and faced Angus across the table. Covering his anxiety with assertiveness, he didn't waste any time coming to the point.

'That guard died.' This was a lie, but Milos had made certain no one would betray the truth to Angus. 'We've got you for murder. Now you're going to talk. I won't even try to bargain with you. You're going to talk, you're going to tell me everything I want to know, everything you can think of, and you're going to *hope* we consider what you're saying valuable enough so that we won't have you executed.'

Angus didn't reply. For once, he didn't look at his interrogator. His head hung down; it seemed to dangle from his neck as if his spine had been broken.

'Do you understand me?' Milos demanded. 'Have you got the brains left to know what I'm saying? You are going to *die* if you don't give me what I want. We're going to strap you down and stick a needle in your veins. After that, you'll just be *dead*, you won't even feel it happen, and nobody will ever care what happens to you again.'

That last sentence was a mistake: Milos felt it as soon as he said it. For a moment, Angus' shoulders twitched. He should have been crying – any other prisoner with a scrap of human frailty would have been crying – but he wasn't. As soon as Angus raised his head, Milos saw that he was trying to laugh.

'Care what happens to me?' Angus' voice sounded like his face, bloody and beaten. 'You motherfucker.'

Unfortunately 'motherfucker' was a word Milos particularly disliked. Helpless to stop himself, he flushed. He tried to conceal his reaction behind another nic, but he knew Angus had seen him. He couldn't control the tremor in his hands.

The damage to Angus' features made him look maniacal. Glaring at Milos, he said, 'I'll talk, all right. As soon as you file your murder charge, I'll talk. I'll talk to everybody.'

Milos stared back at Angus. Angus was the only one sweating, but Milos felt that he himself was the only one afraid.

'I'll tell them,' Angus said, 'there's a traitor in Security.' He said the words as if he could prove them whenever he wanted. 'I'll even tell them who it is. I'll tell them how I know. I'll tell them how to be sure I'm telling the truth. As soon as you file your charge.

'I'll trade his name for immunity. Or maybe' – Angus was sneering – 'I'll try for a pardon.'

Tensing against the distress in his bowels, Milos asked, 'Who is it?'

Angus' glare didn't waver. 'When you file your charge.'

Milos did the best he could to face down the danger. 'You're bluffing.'

'*You're* bluffing,' Angus retorted. 'You aren't going to file that charge. You don't want to find out what I know. You never have.' Then he concluded happily, 'Motherfucker.'

Milos bit down on his nic. Because he was fastidious, he felt no desire to assault his prisoner physically. He didn't want the sensations of Angus' sweat and pain on his hands. Instead he keyed a command that brought the guards back. When they arrived, he instructed them to take Angus away. Then, abruptly, he became calm.

The trembling was gone from his fingers as he dumped the actual recording from the computer and substituted his dummy. After that he stubbed out his nic, thinking, Filthy habit. I'm going to quit. Remembering that he'd made similar commitments in the past, he added, I mean it. Really.

At the same time, in a part of his mind which had suddenly become a separate compartment, like a computer file that couldn't be accessed without a secret command, he was thinking, Shit. Shitshit. Shitshit*shit*.

He appeared quite normal and perfectly correct as he went down to

Communications to make two or three tight-beam transmissions which weren't recorded, couldn't be traced, and might have been impossible to decipher if they were intercepted. Then he returned to his office and continued working.

The recording of his session with Angus attracted no particular attention, and deserved none.

Angus resumed his yellow-eyed and irreducible silence.

On Com-Mine Station, nothing changed.

Milos Taverner might as well have been safe.

Nevertheless when the order came through to have Angus Thermopyle frozen, Milos heaved a sigh of entirely private and malicious relief.

CHAPTER 1

Morn Hyland didn't open her mouth from the moment when Nick Succorso grabbed her arm and steered her through the chaos in Mallorys to the time when he and his people brought her to the docks where his frigate, *Captain's Fancy*, was berthed. His grip was hard, so hard it made her forearm numb and her fingers tingle, and the trip was a form of flight; frightened, almost desperate. She was running with all her courage away from Angus even though Nick never moved faster than a brisk walk. Nevertheless she clung to the zone-implant control in her pocket, kept both fists buried in the pockets of her shipsuit to mask the fact that she was concealing something, and let Nick's grasp guide her.

The passages and corridors were strangely empty. Security had cleared them in case Angus' arrest turned into a fight. The boots of Nick's crew struck echoes off the decking: the knot of men and women protecting Morn from Station intervention moved as if they were followed by a suggestion of thunder, metallic and ominous; as if Angus and the crowd in Mallorys were after her. Her heart strained against her lungs, filling her with pressure. If anybody stopped her now, she would have no defense against a charge which carried the death penalty. But she fixed her gaze straight ahead of her, kept her mouth shut, clenched her fists in her pockets; let Nick's people sweep her along.

Then they reached the docks. Beyond the clutter of tracks and cables between the gantries lay Nick's ship. She missed her footing on a power line and couldn't use her hands to catch herself; but Nick hauled her up again, kept her going. Here the danger of being stopped was gravest. Station Security was everywhere, guarding the docks as well as the cargo inspectors, dock-engine drivers, stevedores, and crane operators. If Nick's deal with Security fell apart—

But nobody made any move to stop her, or the people protecting her. The Station-side lock stood open; *Captain's Fancy* remained shut until one of Nick's crew keyed it.

Nick took Morn inside, nearly drove her through the airlocks with the force of his grip.

After the expanse of the docks, she had the sensation that she was entering a small space – almost that she was being cornered. The frigate's lighting seemed dim and cloying compared to the arc lamps outside. She'd done everything she could think of to get away from Angus: she'd committed herself to this when she accepted the zone-implant control. But now she caught her first glimpse of the place she was escaping *to*, the constricted passages of an unknown ship, and she nearly balked.

Captain's Fancy was a trap: she recognized that. For a moment the knowledge that she was going aboard another ship, *another ship*, where there was little hope and certainly no help, came close to seizing her muscles, paralyzing her like a spasm.

Then all Nick's people were aboard; and she had no time for paralysis. The airlock cycled closed. Nick Succorso took hold of her by the shoulders: he was about to put his arms around her. This was what he'd rescued her for – to possess her. The first crisis of her new life was upon her, when she was so full of alarm that she wanted to strike at him, drive his touch away.

Nevertheless she had the presence of mind to stop him by saying, 'No heavy g.'

Morally more than physically, Morn Hyland was exhausted to the core of her bones. Under the circumstances, perhaps the best that could be said about her was that she was half insane from rape and gap-sickness, from horror and panic and Angus' manipulation of her zone-implant. During her weeks with him, she'd done and experienced things which would have sent her into caterwauling nightmares if she'd had the strength to dream. And then, despite everything, she'd saved his life. To all appearances, she'd been conquered by the desperate vulnerability which made the victims of terrorists fall in love with them.

Appearances were deceptive, however. She hadn't fallen in love: she'd made a deal. The price was that she was *here*, aboard Nick's ship, at his mercy. The recompense was that she had the control to her zone-implant in her pocket.

Saving Angus may have been the only cold-bloodedly crazy act of her relatively young life.

But if she'd lost her mind, she was still only half insane. No one who was totally mad could have come through that ordeal with the presence of mind to protest to Nick Succorso, 'Please. No heavy g. Not without warning me.'

She may have been cornered, but she wasn't beaten.

Her gambit succeeded. He stopped, stared at her oddly. She could see that he was suspicious. He wanted her. He also wanted to know what was going on. And he needed to get his ship away from Com-Mine.

'What's the matter?' he demanded. 'You sick or something?'

'I'm too weak. He –' She managed a shrug as eloquent as Angus' name. 'I need time to recover.'

Then she forced her mind blank, as she'd done so often with Angus, so that her visceral abhorrence of any male contact wouldn't make her do anything foolish – like kneeing Nick in the groin when he embraced her.

He was accustomed to women who dropped dead with pleasure when he took them. He wouldn't have been amused by the truth of how she felt about him.

He also wouldn't have been amused by the real reason she dreaded heavy g.

That was the key to her gap-sickness, the trigger which made her truly and helplessly insane. It had caused her to wreck *Starmaster*, to attempt a total self-destruct, even though *Starmaster*'s Captain was her father and much of the crew was family; even though *Starmaster* was a UMCP destroyer which had just watched Angus Thermopyle slaughter an entire mining camp.

Gap-sickness was the sole justification of any kind for the zone-implant Angus had placed in her brain – or for the zone-implant control she now held. And that control was her only secret; her only defense when she went aboard *Captain's Fancy*. She would have tried to kill anybody who took it away from her.

To deflect his suspicions, she was prepared to tell Nick as much about *Starmaster* as he wished, even though the ship was entirely classified and Morn herself was a cop. As a last resort, she would tell him how *Starmaster* died. But she would never tell him that Angus had given her a zone-implant – and then let her have the control.

Never.

She was a cop: that was the problem. She was a cop – and 'unauthorized use' of a zone-implant was the single worst crime she could commit, short of treason. The fact that she was helping Angus Thermopyle by hiding the control to her own zone-implant only made matters worse. She'd dedicated her life to fighting men like him and Nick Succorso, to fighting evils like piracy and the unauthorized use of zone-implants.

But she knew what the control could do for her. Angus had taught her that, inadvertently but well. It had become more important than her oath as a UMC cop, more precious than her honor. She would never give it up.

Rather than betray the truth about herself, she did her best to go blank so that she wouldn't react as if Nick were Angus when he kissed her.

Fortunately her ploy worked. He had more immediate exigencies to consider. And, after all, the idea that Angus had left her sick and damaged was plausible. Nick released her suddenly and wheeled away.

Over his shoulder, he told his second, 'Assign her a cabin. Get her food. Cat if she wants it. God knows what that bastard did to her.'

As Nick strode away, Morn heard him say, 'We're leaving. Now.' He had hunger in his voice and a livid flush in the scars under his eyes. 'Security doesn't want us to hang around. That's part of the deal.'

Morn knew what his hunger meant. But now she would have a little time to get ready for it.

Inside her shipsuit she was sweating so fearfully that she reeked of it.

Nick's second, a woman named Mikka Vasaczk, was in a hurry. Maybe she was eager to get to the bridge herself. Or maybe she knew she was being supplanted and didn't like it. Whatever the reason, she was brusque and quick.

That suited Morn.

Riding the soft pressure of hydraulics, they took the lift down – 'down' would become 'up' as soon as *Captain's Fancy* undocked and engaged her own internal-g spin – to the cabin deck which wrapped around the ship's holds, engines, data banks, and scan- and armament-drivers. *Captain's Fancy* was luxurious by any standards, and she had more than one cabin for passengers. Mikka Vasaczk guided Morn to the nearest of these, ushered her inside, showed her how to code the lock and key the intercom. Then the second demanded, not quite politely, 'You want anything?'

Morn wanted so many things that her desire left her weak. With an effort, she replied, 'I'm all right. I just need sleep. And safety.'

Mikka had assertive hips; she moved like she knew how to use them in a variety of ways. The way she cocked them now suggested a threat.

'Don't count on it.' She grunted sardonically. 'None of us is safe while you're aboard.

'You'd better be careful. Nick has better sense than you think.'

Without waiting for a reply, she left. The door swept shut behind her automatically.

Morn felt like weeping. She felt like curling herself into a ball and cowering in the corner. But she had no time for tears and cowardice. Her bare survival was in doubt. If she couldn't find a way to defend herself now, she would never get another chance.

First she tapped a code into the keypad of the lock, not because that would keep people out – the ship's computer could override her instructions whenever Nick wished – but because it would slow them down; it would warn her when somebody was about to enter.

Then she took out the control to her zone-implant.

That small black box was her doom. It showed how much Angus had cost her, how deep the damage he'd done her ran. Her ruin was so profound that she was willing to turn her back on her father and the UMCP and every ideal she'd held worthy – and turn her back, too, on rescue by Com-Mine Security, which would have led to every form of help and comfort the UMCP had at its command, as well as to Angus' execution – for the sake of control over her own zone-implant.

But she also knew the control was her last hope. That was true no matter where she went: it was only more obvious aboard *Captain's Fancy*, not more true. With the zone-implant, Angus Thermopyle had made her less than she could bear to be. He'd taught her that her physical and moral being were despicable; mere things to be used or abused with impunity, and then discarded if they failed to satisfy him; ill-made objects with no claim on respect. By the same logic, however, the zone-implant was the only means by which she could become more than she was. It was her only way past her smallness, past the contemptibility of her own resources. It was power – and she'd been powerless too long. Without it she would never recover from the harm she'd suffered. Nothing else could counteract the lessons Angus had taught her.

Therefore she was dependent on it – and therefore she had to avoid any kind of external help. Com-Mine Station and the UMCP would have done everything they could think of for her; but they would have taken the control away. In effect they would have abandoned her to her unworth.

Once she'd said to Angus, *Give me the control. I need it to heal.* But he'd refused her then, and now her needs were altogether more compelling.

At the moment, however, they were simply more immediate.

If Nick knew – or guessed – that she had a zone implant, how long would she be able to keep the control itself secret? More than anything, she needed energy. Energy to force down her fear; energy to face him. Energy to distract him.

The zone-implant could give her that. It could suppress her brain's necessary ability to acknowledge fatigue. Unfortunately she only knew what the implant could do: she didn't know how to use it. Of course, she could read the labels imprinted above the buttons; but she didn't know how to tune them, how to combine them to produce specialized effects. She could only make her implant function at its crudest.

That had to change. She would be fatally vulnerable until she gained complete mastery over the control, over herself; until she could play her own nerves and synapses the way Angus Thermopyle had played them.

To learn that kind of mastery she needed time. A lot of time.

Right now, the best she could hope for was a few hours.

None of us is safe while you're aboard. She ignored that. *You'd better be careful. Nick has better sense than you think.* She dismissed everything except her immediate problem. Her cabin had a private san cubicle and head – and one of the cabinets beside the head held a guest supply of toiletries and personal items; even a small mending kit for torn shipsuits. She took tweezers and used them to open the cover of her zone-implant control. Then, with a needle from the kit, she scraped a gap in a tiny section of the control's circuitry – the section which enabled the control to render her helpless by blocking the link between her brain and body. Angus had used that function often: it allowed him to do what he wanted to her flesh while her mind could only watch and wail.

As well as she could, she made sure that nobody would ever again have the power to simply turn her off. Her electronics training in the Academy was good for that, anyway.

Her fingers were trembling by the time she was done, and she was terrified that she'd made a mistake. But she couldn't afford to be terrified. *None of us is safe while you're aboard.* She also couldn't afford mistakes. Nick wanted her. But to her 'wanting' meant Angus; it meant brutality and rape. *Nick has better sense than you think.* Fighting the shakes, she closed the control cover. Deliberately circumspect, she returned the evidence of what she'd done – the tweezers and needle – to the san. Then she sat down on the berth with her back braced against the bulkhead, raised the control, and touched a button.

At once a wonderful lassitude washed through her. Her body seemed to fill up with rest as though she had a syringe of cat plugged into her veins. Drowsiness spread balm along her limbs, soothed ravaged nerve endings, denatured old and essential anxieties. She relaxed slowly down the bulkhead; her head nodded over her chest.

Healing. Safety. Peace.

She was nearly asleep before the desperation she'd learned from Angus came to her rescue.

That sting of panic gave her the strength to turn off the control.

When reality flooded back into her muscles and neurons, sheer visceral disappointment brought tears to her eyes.

But she already knew that living with a zone-implant wasn't easy. She didn't expect it to be easy: she expected to be in command of it.

She had a nagging sense that she was asking too much of herself, that no human being could do what she intended and get away with it; that the law against 'unauthorized use' was absolutely reasonable. In order to make the zone-implant serve her effectively, she needed something akin to prescience – a kind of crystal ball. The control included a timer, and that would help. But suppose she decided to risk the rest her body craved. How could she know how long it was safe to sleep? Suppose she turned on energy by suppressing fatigue in an attempt to get through heavy g without going mad. How could she know how much was necessary, or how long her flesh could stand the strain? For that matter, how could she know which centers of her brain were involved in her gap-sickness, which parts of herself she should stifle in order to avoid that state of lunatic calm when the universe spoke to her and told her what to destroy?

She would be guessing every step of the way. And every guess was dangerous. Any mistake, any miscalculation, any accident might betray her to Nick.

But the problem went deeper. Angus' use of her had left her half insane and profoundly weary, even though he'd frequently imposed rest on her. How could she know that madness and exhaustion weren't endemic to the use of a zone-implant? How could she know that her efforts to save herself weren't about to damn her?

She couldn't know. She wasn't wise enough to tamper with herself this way.

On the other hand, she was here because Angus had driven her half insane. There was no escape that didn't also involve insanity.

A small thunk carried through the ship's hull – the characteristic jolt of undocking. When the grapples and cables snapped clear, everyone aboard always knew it.

Morn was running out of time.

As *Captain's Fancy* floated free, g disappeared. The involuntary contraction of her muscles, bracing herself against undock, sent her adrift in the cabin.

In moments, however, the intercom piped a warning, and the bridge crew engaged the spin that produced internal g. The berth reoriented itself; Morn settled to the new floor.

Such maneuvers were familiar to her. Instead of distress, she felt simple gratitude that Nick engaged g so soon. Most Captains liked to run a considerable distance out from dock – to be sure they were clear, and to refresh their recollection of zero g – before they took on the inertial inflexibility of spin.

Grimly she pushed another button.

Wrong one, wrong one, this button brought *pain*, the entire surface of her skin seemed to catch flame. Angus had told her that her father was flash-blinded when he blew up *Starmaster*'s thrust drive. His face must have felt like *this*, all fire and agony, every nerve excoriated beyond bearing.

Her muscles convulsed in a spasm of fire and remembrance. She stabbed wildly at the control, trying to hit CANCEL.

She missed. Instead she got the button she'd already tried, the one that made her rest.

The effect astonished her. In an instant she was transformed.

It was magic, a kind of neural alchemy. Out of absolute pain, it created something she needed more than energy, something which would enable her to deal with Nick – something which Angus had never tried on her, either because he didn't know what it would do or because he didn't want it.

In a sense, the combination she'd keyed didn't ease the pain, not entirely. Instead the hurt was translated almost miraculously into something quite different – a sensual ache which focused itself in the most sensitive parts of her body, so that the tips of her breasts burned as if they could be quenched by kisses, and her mouth and loins became hot and damp, hungry for penetration.

For several moments she was so overwhelmed by the sensations of desire that she couldn't stop them. She didn't realize she was writhing hungrily on the berth until thrust ran through *Captain's Fancy* and caught her off balance, toppled her to the floor.

Not much thrust: just enough to get the ship under way. Nevertheless the fall restored Morn's self-awareness; she grabbed the control and canceled it.

Then she clung to the berth and breathed hard, trying to absorb the shock of sensation and discovery.

She'd found it, the answer to her immediate problem: a way of responding to Nick that wasn't predicated on revulsion. For the time being, she now had the means to endure his touch.

And if, like Angus', Nick's lust included the desire to inflict pain, she would be able to experience it as pleasure. She would be protected—

No wonder Angus had never used this particular function. It would have made her paradoxically invulnerable: accessible to everything his hate required; inaccessible to terror.

Now she could rest. At the moment, the only guess she had to make was, when would Nick come? How much time did she have? Thrust complicated the direction of *Captain's Fancy*'s g; it made movement around the cabin awkward. All the more reason to roll into the berth, velcro herself secure, and let her exhaustion take her away. When he arrived, she would have to face his suspicions. Whatever they were. Until then—

She didn't do it. Angus Thermopyle had taught her more things than either of them had realized. There were still precautions she could take, ways to camouflage the truth.

She went back to work on her door lock.

This time she keyed the door to open on request – after a five-second delay, and a chime to warn her that someone wanted in.

Then, bracing herself against the tug of complex g, she moved into the san, peeled off the ill-fitting shipsuit Angus had given her, consigned it to the disposal chute, and took a long shower. She didn't emerge until her arms felt leaden from scrubbing herself, and the san's suction had dried her pristine. She couldn't wash away her crime, but the shower made her skin more comfortable.

After that, she stretched out naked on the berth and hid her zone-implant control under the head of the mattress; she pulled the blanket up to her chin and sealed the velcro strips.

While thrust took the ship away from Com-Mine Station – away from sanity and any conceivable help – she settled her clean body in the clean berth and began doing what she could to evolve contingency plans. Under the influence of the zone-implant, she wouldn't be able to think effectively. She had to prepare herself now for whatever might happen.

Maybe it was a good thing Angus had given her so much enforced rest. No matter how her head – or her soul – felt, her body really didn't need sleep.

Captain's Fancy would do a certain amount of maneuvering when she left dock, getting clear of Com-Mine's gear and grapples, the antennae and ports and gantries, the tugs and other ships; assuming attitude and trajectory for departure. That, presumably, would occupy Nick's attention for a while. Of course, he wouldn't be obliged to oversee any of this personally: his bridge crew could handle it. Mikka Vasaczk looked like she could handle almost anything. But most Captains enjoyed the business of running out from Station. All that communication with center and all those routine decisions could be made by habit; but it was good to refresh the habits, good to renew the priorities and necessities of command. In fact, most Captains wouldn't consider leaving the bridge until they were well outside Station control space, beyond the likelihood of encountering other ships. Morn didn't expect that much diligence from Nick Succorso; but she did expect him to make sure *Captain's Fancy* got away clean before he turned over the bridge to anyone else.

She would have that much time before he put her to the test.

*

She was right. Whether he intended to or not, he gave her that time.

When he came for her, she was as ready as possible, under the circumstances.

She had to compartmentalize her mind to do it. Angus Thermopyle in one box; everything he'd done to her in another. The harsh death of *Starmaster*. Her gap-sickness. Revulsion. Fear of discovery. Everything dangerous, everything that could paralyze or appall her, had to be separated and locked away, so that she could be at least approximately intelligent in her decisions.

Willpower was like the zone-implant: it dissociated mind and body, action and consequence.

Angus had taught her that, too, without knowing it.

When the door chimed, she felt a new shock wave run through her, the brisance of panic. Nevertheless by her own choice she'd entered a world of absolute risk, where nothing could save her except herself. Before her door opened, she reached under the mattress and hit the combination of buttons her life depended on. Then she rolled over to face the man who'd rescued her.

Nick Succorso looked like he belonged in the romantic stories people told about him back on Com-Mine; like the stories were true. He had smoldering eyes and a buccaneer's grin, and he carried himself with the kind of virile assurance that made every movement seem like an enticement. His hands knew how to be gentle; his voice conveyed a caress. Those things alone might have made him desirable. But in addition he was dangerous – notoriously dangerous. The scars under his eyes hinted at fierceness: they showed that he was a man who played for blood. When his passions made those scars turn dark, they promised that he was a man who played for blood, and won.

He entered her room as if he were already sure that she could never say no to him.

Morn Hyland knew virtually nothing about him. He was a pirate, a competitor of Angus Thermopyle's; as illegal as hell. And, like Angus, he was male. In fact, the differences between him and Angus were cosmetic, not substantive. He'd only been able to trap Angus by making use of a traitor in Com-Mine Security. That was all she had to go on.

Nevertheless she was in no danger of seeing him in romantic terms. She knew too much about what piracy – and maleness – cost their victims.

But instead of nausea, or panic, or the deep black horror which had lurked in the back of her mind, waking or sleeping, since the destruction of *Starmaster*, she felt a yearning heat arise. Her blood became a kind of liquid need, and the nerves of her skin seemed to leap into focus like a vid scan. That sensation helped her raise her arms as if she wanted Nick to come straight into her embrace.

He replied with a smile, and his scars intensified his eyes; but when he'd stepped into the cabin and locked the door behind him, he didn't approach closer. He studied her hard, although his manner was relaxed. After a moment he said easily, 'We don't have any choice about heavy g. That bastard did us damage. My engineer says we've got a gap flutter. We might go into tach and never come out. If we want to get anywhere, we'll have to use all the thrust we've got.'

He paused; he seemed to want Morn to say something. *Better sense than you think*. But she didn't respond. The problem of g could wait: it didn't scare her now, not with this warm ache surging through her veins and every inch of her skin alive. As long as Nick was in her cabin, she was safe from gap-sickness. *Captain's Fancy* wouldn't increase thrust now: his hunger wasn't something he could satisfy under hard acceleration.

She held out her arms and waited. She couldn't see her own face; but the way she felt must have been plain to him.

He came nearer, balancing against the ship's movement effortlessly. With one hand, he unsealed the blanket's velcro and flipped it aside. In one of the compartments of her mind, she flinched and tried to cover herself again. But that compartment was closed, shut off. All of her body aspired to his caress. She arched her back, lifting her breasts for him.

Still he didn't touch her; he didn't come into her embrace. Instead he reached for the id tag on its fine chain around her neck.

He couldn't read the codes, of course, not without plugging the tag into a computer. And he couldn't access any of her confidential files without plugging her tag into a Security or UMCP computer. However, like virtually everyone in human space, he knew what the embossed insignia meant.

'You're a cop,' he said.

He didn't sound surprised.

Didn't sound surprised.

Through the pressure mounting inside her, she thought, He should be surprised. Then she realized: No. He had an ally in Com-Mine Security. He could have known from the day he first saw her that she was a cop.

That possibility might help protect her. It would encourage him to think about her in terms of covert operations and betrayal, not helplessness and zone-implants.

'You rescued me.' Her voice was husky, crowded with desires which transcended reason or fear. 'I'll be anything you want me to be.'

For the moment that was true. The zone-implant made it true. She took hold of his hand, drew it to her mouth, kissed his fingers. They left a trace of salt on her tongue – the sweat of his concentration when he ran *Captain's Fancy* out from Station; the sweat of his hunger.

And yet, despite the way her whole body urged him, he still held back. The demands of the zone-implant mounted in her; synapses she couldn't control fired out messages of need. She didn't want him to talk; she wanted him to come to her, come into her, quench himself in the center of her.

'Is this the approach you used on Captain Thermo-pile? Is that why he kept you alive?'

'No,' she said automatically, 'no,' without thinking. But she needed to think, *had* to think, because the next words she would say without thinking were, *He didn't use this combination.*

Her own hunger seemed like a roar in her ears. Swallowing hard to muffle it, to equalize the pressure, she offered the cheapest answer Nick might accept. 'You've seen him. I left him for you. I couldn't feel this way about him.'

She knew nothing about him. Maybe he would be vain enough to accept that.

He wasn't. Or his vanity was too profound to be satisfied cheaply. He didn't move; his smile was crooked and bloodthirsty. 'Try again.'

Try again. Try again. She couldn't think. She wasn't supposed to think, not while the zone-implant did *this* to her. What could she tell Nick that would be true enough to be believed and false enough to protect her?

'Please, Nick,' she said, almost whimpering with urgency, 'can't we talk about this later? I want you now.'

He smiled and smiled, but he didn't relent. Instead, he ran his hand down her chest and circled her breast with his fingertips. Involuntarily this time, she arched her back again. His smile and his eyes gave her no warning as he flicked her nipple hard with one of his fingernails.

Just for an instant the balance of the zone-implant shifted toward pain. She gasped; she nearly screamed.

'Your name is Morn Hyland,' he said almost kindly. 'You're UMCP. And Angus Thermo-pile is the slimiest illegal between forbidden space and Earth. He's sewage – and you're one of the elite, you work for Min Donner. He should have obliterated you. He should have taken you apart atom by atom and never risked coming back to Com-Mine. Tell me why he kept you alive.'

Fortunately the functions of the control recovered their poise almost immediately. Her scream evaporated as if it had never existed.

'Because he needed crew,' she answered. True enough to be believed. 'He was alone on *Bright Beauty*. And I was alone on *Starmaster* – I was the only survivor.' False enough to protect her. 'There was nothing I could do to threaten him. So I made a deal with him. He could have left me to die.' She couldn't think – but she'd made herself ready to answer him. 'He kept me alive to crew for him.'

Perhaps because she burned for him so hotly, she seemed to see Nick struggling with himself. His scars were black with blood; everything he looked at was underlined by primal and acquisitive passion. His fingers stroked her nipple as if to wipe away the hurt. She felt a tremor in his muscles as he bent over her and lightly kissed her breast.

'That's not good enough.' His voice seemed to stick far back in his throat; it came out in a rasp. 'But it's a start. Right now, I want you. You can tell us all the rest later.'

When Morn heard him unfasten his shipsuit, what was left of her mind went blank with anticipation.

Now at last she had a chance to learn what she needed most to know about him.

She had no conception of the romantic way her escape from Angus Thermopyle to Nick Succorso was viewed back on Com-Mine. The idea that anything about her situation was romantic might have made her hysterical.

CHAPTER 2

The first thing she learned was that Nick Succorso had limits. He could be exhausted.

During the hours they spent wrapped around each other in her berth, their roles were ones he set for them: artist and instrument. He played her nerves as though they were alive to his will, responsive to nothing except his private touch. In her turn, she replied with a kind of blind, willing ecstasy that bore no resemblance to anything she'd ever felt with Angus Thermopyle – an abandonment so complete that she seemed transported into a realm of pure sex.

For a while that terrified her: in one of her locked compartments, she dreaded his effect on her. If he could do *this* to her, if he could make her feel *this* and *this*, then she was lost, useless; she had no hope.

But then she discovered that 'artist' and 'instrument' were only roles. She and Nick were acting out an illusion. She was the one with the zone-implant: she could have kept going no matter how absolutely she responded to his desires, how completely she abandoned herself. Until the moment when her brain or body burned out, and her synapses consumed themselves in an endorphin conflagration, she could do everything Nick required and more.

He, on the other hand—

In a final burst, his intensity expended itself. Groaning with pleasure, he collapsed suddenly into sleep.

As his passion drained out of them, his scars lost their fierceness. Without hunger behind them, they became only pale and aging tissue, old wounds; the marks of defeat.

The artist ended, but the instrument endured.

A little while passed before she understood what had happened. When he slumped beside her, her first reaction wasn't satisfaction or even triumph: it was disappointment. The need which drove her couldn't be satisfied by anything less than a kind of neural apotheosis. She wanted to ride the zone-implant's emissions until she went nova.

But short of suicide he was the one who had limits. She didn't.

Because of that, the entire experience was an illusion.

And the illusion was aimed squarely at him. She performed it for his benefit: he was its victim. The appearance that she abandoned herself, that she was wholly his, was false.

She had that much power.

It might be enough to protect her. The thing she'd dreamed and prayed and suffered for when she accepted the zone-implant control from Angus was starting to come true.

Then she felt a touch of satisfaction – and then a hint of feral and necessary rage. In its concealed compartment, her fury received its first taste of the food it craved. When she'd betrayed Angus – when she'd enabled Nick's people to plant Station supplies aboard Angus' ship by disabling the blip which would have warned him *Bright Beauty*'s holds were unlocked – she hadn't felt any rage.

She'd been too caught up in the risk of what she did: the danger of Angus' response, and her helplessness against it.

But now she felt that anger. One of her compartments cracked open, and a passion hotter than the zone-implant's enforced yearning leaked out.

It guided her hand as she reached under the mattress and switched off the control.

The transition was hideous. She was going to have to learn how to manage transitions, or else the shock of them would ruin her. They hadn't been this bad when Angus held the control. Whatever he'd imposed on her, she'd always been eager for it to end, frantic to regain some sense of herself. But now the functions of the zone-implant were hers to choose. That made a profound difference.

Earlier, waiting for Nick, she'd tried to prepare herself for the flood of weariness which poured through her when the implant was switched off. To some extent, she was ready for that. But she wasn't prepared for the grief she felt now, for the keen pain of resuming her ordinary mortality. She'd lost something precious and vital by ending her abandonment.

However, the transition was swift. Or else it was more complex than she realized. Faced with the knowledge that she was only human after all, she started to cry – biting her lip for silence, so that she wouldn't wake Nick. But then, almost immediately, her rage came back to her. And it was followed by her revulsion. If she was only human, then Nick Succorso was only another version of Angus Thermopyle: male; therefore ultimately interested in sex only as a masque of rape and degradation.

Now she had to bite her lip *hard* to keep herself from crying out or flinching; to master the electric jolt of her reaction against what Nick had just done to her. She had to think, and think quickly—

Not Angus. Not like Angus. Even if Nick was essentially the same, he was effectively different. His passions were less naked than Angus': he was caught up in the masque. No, more than that: he liked the illusion that his personal virility and magnetism were capable of making her respond so utterly.

And if he remained caught up in the masque, if she could keep him there – if he liked the illusion enough—

He would be blinded to the truth.

Without realizing it, she'd stopped biting her lip. Her need for that small hurt was over: her need to fling herself away from Nick was receding. He looked vulnerable now, asleep, and that had never been true of Angus. Despite the long, clean line of his muscles, despite his unmistakable grace and strength, he looked like he could be killed before he woke up. That eased her revulsion.

Now, perhaps, she could have rested. Most of the immediate intensity of transition had declined: the weariness remained. The external reality of her body, as opposed to the internal reality of the zone-implant, was that Nick had used her extravagantly. She was acutely sore in some places, and there was a price to be paid for all those endorphins. Sleep would be good for her, if she could sleep without dreaming about Angus. If she could sleep without waking up back aboard *Bright Beauty*.

But she didn't trust sleep. Nick had said, *That's not good enough.* She had that threat hanging over her. *You can tell us all the rest later.*

She had more getting ready to do.

Of course, the 'getting ready' she needed most involved further experimentation with the zone-implant control. That was too dangerous, however. If Nick caught her at it, she was finished. She left the zone-implant control where it was.

Instead she tried to guess what 'tell us all the rest' meant. Did he mean, 'tell us all,' the whole crew? or 'all the rest'?

None of us is safe while you're aboard.

There were too many unknowns. She only knew one thing about Nick, had only that one lever. Everything else was blank. How much had he learned about her through his contact in Com-Mine Security? What had the UMCP told Com-Mine? How many of his secrets did he share with his crew? What was their loyalty to him based on: personal gain? success? reciprocity?

Who *was* he, that he could get Com-Mine Security to help him betray Angus Thermopyle?

Since she had no way to approach any of her other questions, she concentrated on that one.

Angus Thermopyle was guilty of almost any illegal act imaginable – and yet he was innocent of the specific crime for which he'd been arrested. She knew the truth: she'd been there when he was framed. That was disturbing enough. But even more disturbing to her – considering that she was UMCP born and trained – was Security's complicity.

Why would Security risk vital Station supplies to help one known pirate betray another?

No, worse than that: what on earth possessed Security to *trust* Nick Succorso against Angus Thermopyle?

And here was another question, now that she thought about it: Why did Security let Nick take her?

It was one thing to leave her alone with Angus. After all, she'd used her UMCP authority to demand that Com-Mine keep its hands off her. But it was something else entirely to risk Station supplies to help one pirate betray another, with a UMC cop in the middle, and then to simply let that cop depart unquestioned. Why had Security allowed her to leave its jurisdiction?

Yet the issue was even more complex than that. Under any circumstances, Com-Mine Security must have sent a message to UMCPHQ when she first appeared with Angus. Security would have relayed everything she said and did to UMCPHQ as a matter of course. Why hadn't Enforcement Division replied? Granted, communication across interstellar distances was no instantaneous business. Nevertheless gap courier drones could have carried messages to UMCPHQ and back in a few days. Ordinary ship traffic could have done the job in a couple of weeks. Surely her time with Angus hadn't been too short to permit a reply? And surely, if ED had replied, Security wouldn't have let Nick take her?

She was lost in it. If Min Donner, the Director of Enforcement Division, had instructed Com-Mine Security to let Nick Succorso take her – Morn couldn't get past that point. There were too many levels involved, too many implications of treachery. And she'd trusted the UMCP from the day she was born: it was the same thing as trusting her father.

She had to stick with what she knew, or else she would paralyze herself. She had to focus on the present; on survival and the zone-implant.

She had to concentrate on Nick Succorso.

Before she could get any further, the cabin intercom chimed. A voice that sounded like Mikka Vasaczk's said neutrally, 'Nick.'

As if he'd never been asleep, Nick sat up and swung his legs over the edge of the berth. Ignoring Morn, he scrubbed his hands up and down his face for a second or two: that was all the time he needed to collect himself. While Morn was still trying to decide how to react, how to play her role now, he stood up and keyed the intercom.

'Here.'

'Nick, you're wanted on the bridge.' The intercom flattened the voice, made it sound impersonal; untouched.

Nick didn't reply. Instead he keyed off the intercom and reached for his shipsuit and boots.

He still hadn't glanced at Morn.

She was too vulnerable, too much at risk: she had to say something. Swallowing weariness and old fright, she asked with as much naturalness as she could summon, 'What is it?'

He finished sealing his shipsuit and pulling on his boots before he turned to her.

His eyes were bright; they focused on her with a keenness, an inner intensity, which she might have loved, or at least desired, if she'd met him before she met Angus – if she'd never met Angus. Despite the easy way he carried himself, he conveyed a tense, coiled quality, as if his physical relaxation were a part of what made him dangerous.

He was smiling – even his tone of voice smiled – as he said, 'We're pretty casual here. Not like the UMCP.' And yet she knew she was being warned; perhaps threatened. 'We've only got a few simple rules. But they aren't negotiable. Here's one of them.

'When you hear the word "want", you don't ask. It isn't up for discussion. You just do.

'Understand?'

Morn was definitely being threatened. Keeping her face as blank as a mask, she nodded once, firmly.

'Good,' he said.

The door hissed open, and he was gone.

When the door shut itself after him, she stayed where she was and stared at his departure as if he'd turned her off – as if he'd taken away her reasons for doing anything.

Nick was 'wanted' on the bridge. And *want* had a special meaning aboard his ship. It was the command that couldn't be questioned, the absolute imperative, like the coded order her father might have given her if he'd decided *Starmaster* had to self-destruct; if she'd let him live, and the occasion to issue such an order had ever arisen.

Something had happened.

Captain's Fancy was on a routine departure trajectory out from Com-Mine Station. Presumably. What could have happened? What was conceivable? What kind of danger or exigency could have come up after only a few thousand kilometers; still within Station's control space?

Almost certainly, the explanation involved Com-Mine in some way. It involved Security and Angus.

Morn couldn't stop staring at the door, at the spot where Nick had left her; she couldn't move. What was she going to do now? She was losing control of her compartments: pieces of doubt and black horror bled together, combining like elements of a binary poison. She wanted to flee, but she had nowhere to go. There was nothing around her except panic.

Riding a visceral tremble, as if she were caught at the epicenter of a quake and needed to get away from it, she decided to leave the cabin.

Half expecting a shift in *Captain's Fancy*'s g which would indicate a change of direction – to return to dock, or to meet interceptors from

Com-Mine – she left the berth and began hunting through the built-in lockers for a clean shipsuit.

She found one easily: *Captain's Fancy* was equipped for guests. Female guests, judging by the cut of the shipsuits. But Morn hardly noticed the comfort of wearing clothes that fit. She was in a hurry, and the only thing she cared about was the tremors driving through her – or the danger that they might make her do something foolish.

She sealed the shipsuit; located her boots in the san. Because of the nature of her panic, she went back to the berth and retrieved the zone-implant control. She didn't want to be separated from it.

But then she stopped herself. The part of her which had been shaped by Angus Thermopyle responded to fear in ways which were new to her. Mere physical possession of the control was dangerous. If she carried it with her, anybody who searched her or simply bumped against her could find it.

Her cabin was the only simulacrum of privacy available to her. She had to conceal the control somewhere here.

Under the mattress was convenient, but too easy. With the right tools, she would have preferred to open either the door's panel or the intercom and bury the black box among their circuit boards and wiring. Unfortunately she only had the mending kit to work with.

Inside her the tremble built so that every movement felt unsteady as she went back to the san, to the mending kit. She tossed some of the patches and velcro into the disposal to make room; then she put the control in the bottom of the kit and covered it with the remaining supplies.

That would have to do. If she stood where she was and tried to imagine the perfect hiding place, the trembling would break down her defenses, and she would panic.

Almost in a rush, she left the cabin.

Exploring, that's what she would do, she would go exploring. Nick hadn't told her to stay where she was. And anybody would understand her desire to familiarize herself with a new ship. As long as she didn't accidentally gain the bridge.

In part to keep her hands from shaking, and in part to make the action habitual, so that no one would consider it unusual, she shoved her fists deep into her pockets. Then she started hurrying along the passage in the opposite direction from the lift Vasaczk had used to take her to her cabin.

No, she shouldn't hurry. She couldn't afford to be caught hurrying. That would lead to questions.

She could feel her willpower fraying under the strain, but she forced herself to slow down, attempt a more casual stride.

She passed four or five doors, all of them identical to hers; presumably *Captain's Fancy* had that much accommodation for passengers. Then she reached another lift.

There was no way to leave this section of the ship without using a lift. Bulkheads sealed both ends of the passage. And the movement of all the lifts would be monitored and controlled by *Captain's Fancy*'s maintenance computer. She couldn't use one without the risk of attracting attention.

She didn't want to be noticed.

Her shaking grew more violent. Without realizing it, she pulled her hands out of her pockets and covered her face. For several moments she stood frozen in front of the lift with her palms clamped over her eyes while her shoulders quivered.

She couldn't do it. Angus hadn't left her enough courage. Nothing was safe enough. She should have stayed in her cabin and worked with the zone-implant control until she found a cure for her fear.

But in this state she might not have been able to make her fingers hit the buttons she chose. And, in any case, the computers could watch her door as easily as the lifts. She'd already put herself in jeopardy by leaving her cabin.

Slowly she pulled her hands down from her face. When she'd succeeded at pushing one of them back into a pocket, she used the other to key the lift.

If the different levels served by the lift had been labeled, she might have been able to make a neutral choice. If she'd been able to think clearly, she might have been able to reason out some of the ship's internal structure. Since she didn't have anything else to go by, she took the lift down one level and got out to look around.

Almost at once she smelled coffee. By good fortune she'd arrived near the galley. At a guess, this level was the crew's: it contained the galley and mess, wardrooms and cabins, used by Nick's people. It might also hold the sickbay – a possibility she set aside for future exploration. As soon as she smelled the coffee, she realized that something as simple and ordinary as hot, black caffeine might be what she needed to steady her.

She followed the smell away from the lift without pausing to consider the likelihood that the galley was already in use.

She could smell coffee because the galley had no door: it was essentially a large niche in one of the interior bulkheads, with equipment built into the three walls and a round, easily reached table. She noticed a particularly luxurious foodvend, quite a few storage cabinets for staples and special supplies, and, of course, a coffee maker. The pot steamed richly in the ship's dry atmosphere.

She also noticed a man sitting at the table.

At the sight, she froze again. She didn't know whether to retreat or move forward. Everything was dangerous, and she didn't know which risk was preferable.

But she remembered to keep her fists in her pockets.

The man had his hands wrapped around a hot mug as if he wanted the warmth. His fingers looked fat because they were stubby, and his face looked fat because it was almost perfectly round; nevertheless he was only compact, not overweight. Like his face, his eyes were circles. They were a gentle shade of blue Morn had never seen before. Combined with his fine, sandy hair and steady smile, they made him look friendly.

He glanced up as soon as she appeared. When he saw her, his eyes and his smile showed mild surprise. She obviously didn't disconcert him, however. He gave her a moment to move if she could. Then he said, 'You look like what you need most is sleep, but you're too scared to get it.' His voice was mild, too. 'Come have a cup of coffee. It's fresh. Maybe I can give you a reason or two to be less scared.'

Morn stared at him. She wasn't prepared to trust anything aboard *Captain's Fancy* – especially not mildness from a total stranger. It might be camouflage, like Nick's air of relaxation. She stood where she was, with her elbows locked and her hands buried.

Controlling her voice as well as she could, she said, 'You know who I am.'

The man's smile held. 'I should,' he replied without sarcasm. 'I saw you in Mallorys often enough. And you're the only passenger Nick invited to go with us this time.'

'That's one reason you're scared. We all know who you are – we know that much about you. You don't know any of us. You only know Nick, and that may seem like it's not much help.'

He paused, giving her a chance to say something or move. When she didn't do either, he resumed.

'Well, let me introduce myself, at any rate. I'm Vector Shaheed. Ship's engineer. Off duty at the moment. My second is a pup off Valdor Industrial, where they don't teach you anything, but he's competent to keep us going under this much thrust. So I've got time to exercise my only real talent, which is making coffee.'

Morn continued staring at him. Her hands were damp with sweat, but she kept them curled in her pockets.

Stiffly, as if all his joints hurt – but still smiling – Vector Shaheed stood up to get a mug from one of the cabinets. He filled it at the steaming pot and set it on the table for her. Then he seated himself again.

'That's not a reason to trust me, of course,' he continued. 'We're all illegals, and you're UMCP. You would have to be crazy to trust any of us. But we're alone here, and I'm willing to talk. You really can't afford to miss an opportunity like this.'

That made sense. Morn shook her head – not rejecting what he said, just trying to break herself out of her paralysis. She felt a visceral desire to pull away from him. His mildness was seductive: he was a trap. But she was trapped anyway; and whatever he chose to reveal might be useful.

With a stiffness of her own, she entered the galley.

She didn't take her fists out of her pockets until she was sitting at the table. Then, abruptly, she pulled up both hands and cupped them around the coffee mug. She needed something to steady her so that she could think. The coffee was seductive, too, but she was prepared to trust it.

He was right about one thing, anyway: he had a talent for coffee. A couple of hot sips made her feel almost instantly stronger. In simple gratitude, she said through the steam, 'Thanks.' Then she sipped again.

'That's better.' To all appearances, Vector Shaheed's approval was genuine. 'I don't like to see anybody scared – especially not a woman like you. Out here, there's many an old spacer who thinks women are worth dying for. I myself' – his smile became rueful for a moment – 'am gratified just to have you sit here and drink my coffee.

'What would you like to know about us?'

Without thinking, Morn asked, 'Where are we going?'

Vector's smile lost none of its soft ease, but the muscles around his eyes tightened. He drank some of his coffee before he replied, 'You can probably guess that that's not one of the subjects I'm prepared to talk about.'

She shook her head again, chagrined by her own weakness. She shouldn't have asked that question: it exposed too much. And she certainly couldn't ask what exigency had called Nick to the bridge. Groping for some sense of poise, of being in control of herself, she tried again.

'How bad is the gap drive?'

His eyes relaxed. 'Bad enough. Bad enough so I can't fix it myself, anyway. If I had to stake my reputation on it, I would say we can get into tach and out again one more time. If I had to stake my *life* on it' – he chuckled gently – 'I would say it's too dangerous.'

'How long can you last without it?'

'At least a year. We've got that much food and stores. Not to mention plenty of fuel. At the rate we're traveling, we'll starve before we run out of fuel.'

Vector's manner didn't give the words any special importance. Nevertheless Morn knew they were important. As long as *Captain's Fancy* used only this gentle thrust, there was only one destination Nick could reach in a year: the belt. And of course there was no place in the belt to get a gap drive repaired. But even at much higher velocities, *Captain's Fancy* had nowhere else to go in human space.

Forbidden space was another matter. Its proximity to the belt and Com-Mine Station was a large part of what made them so crucial to the UMC – and to all humankind. Running hard, the ship could probably get there in a few months. But then what? The possibility that Nick might be headed for forbidden space was too complex for Morn to evaluate. In any case, Com-Mine Center would never have authorized a departure trajectory in that direction.

Vector watched her think for a while. Then he started talking again. 'I offered you a reason or two to be less scared. I can see that wasn't one of them. Let me try again.

'There are twenty of us aboard, and from your point of view we probably all look like reasons to be scared. But that isn't true. I don't mean you can trust us. I mean you don't need to worry about whether you can trust us. The only one of us you need to worry about is Nick.

You see' – Vector spread his hands – 'he isn't just the Captain here. He's the center, the law. None of us is a threat to you, as long as he's happy.

'And I'll tell you something else about him. He never gives away his castoffs. You don't need to worry that he'll get tired of you and pass you off to one of us. You're his. On this ship, you're either his or you're nothing.

'That's why it doesn't matter whether you can trust any of us. We're no danger to you. We never will be. All you have to worry about is Nick. Everything else will take care of itself.'

Morn was stunned. Hearing her dilemma stated so nakedly made her brain go blank. *He's the law. He never gives away his castoffs. It doesn't matter whether you can trust any of us.* But because Vector was smiling at her, and she knew she couldn't afford to be paralyzed, she forced herself to ask, 'Is that supposed to help me feel better?'

'It should,' he replied promptly. 'It simplifies your situation.'

Her mind was practically useless. 'I guess you're right,' she said slowly, struggling to think, to articulate her incomprehension in some way. 'But it would help me more if I understood it. Why —' Why are you so loyal to him? 'Why is he my only problem? You're all illegals, you said that yourself. I don't know why you do it, but you all want to get away from law somehow. That's got to be true.' The only pirate she knew personally, Angus Thermopyle, would have committed any conceivable atrocity to make sure nobody else had power over him. 'You don't want rules, you want opportunities. So why is he the law? Why do you let him do that? Why does what he want take precedence over what the rest of you want?'

Vector Shaheed seemed to consider that a good question. His eyes appeared inordinately blue and clear as he answered, 'Because he never loses.'

Then he grinned like a man with a secret joke. 'Besides, it's axiomatic that nobody likes law more than us illegals do. It's a love-hate relationship. The more we hate the UMCP, the more we love Nick Succorso.'

Morn blinked at him. 'That doesn't make sense.'

Vector lifted his shoulders in a mild, humorous shrug.

A moment passed before she noticed just how smoothly he'd distracted her from his idea that Nick never lost.

While she was still trying to collect her thoughts, however, the intercom in the galley chimed. The same neutral voice she'd heard earlier said, 'Morn Hyland, come to the bridge.'

A moment later Vasaczk added, 'Acknowledge.' Morn didn't move. She was frozen again; taken by surprise and snared in fright.

Vector's stiffness seemed constant. His movements gave such an impression of resistance in his joints that Morn expected him to wince as he got up from his chair and went over to the intercom. Nevertheless his expression remained as calm as blue water: any pain he may have felt remained far below the surface.

Keying the intercom, he responded, 'She's with me. I'll make sure she doesn't get lost.' Then he clicked off the pickup.

By way of explanation, he told Morn, 'This will give me an excuse to be on the bridge. I want to know what's going on myself.'

She hardly heard him. No, she insisted to herself, no, don't panic, not now. Any risk she failed to face might kill her: she could only hope to survive if she met each danger as it came. Don't panic now.

Nevertheless she was suddenly afraid right to the bottom of her belly. And the zone-implant control was back in her cabin; she had no defense. She could feel what remained of her will crumbling. Her reserves drained out of her as if she were a broken vessel. Without her black box, she was only the woman Angus had raped and tormented, nothing more. If Vector Shaheed had left her alone, she would have put her arms down on the table and hidden her face against them.

He didn't do it. Instead he touched her shoulder gently, urging her to her feet.

She stood as though she were under his control. 'Come on,' he said. 'You don't want to miss this. It might be interesting. You can be scared later.'

His hand on her shoulder guided her out of the galley.

'I told you that you don't need to worry about whether you can trust us. That's true. But there are a couple of people you should watch out for. Mikka Vasaczk is one. She can't hurt you – but she would if she could.'

A moment later, in the same tone of secret humor he'd used earlier, he added, 'Hell, we all would.'

CHAPTER 3

Hell, *we all would.*

For several minutes nothing else penetrated Morn Hyland's distress, although Vector kept talking while he led her through *Captain's Fancy*. Retailing information and descriptions like a tour guide, he steered her to the nearest lift and down to one of the outer levels; he may have thought that the sound of his voice would steady her.

But she only heard, *We all would.*

She was sure she'd guessed the truth. Nick had been summoned from her cabin to deal with some urgent development which involved her. It involved Com-Mine Security and Angus. Something had gone wrong with the deal Nick had made for his departure – with the deal Security's traitor had arranged for him.

Or some hint or rumor about her zone-implant had been passed to Nick, and now he meant to expose her; ruin her.

Surely there were other, less fatal possibilities? If there were, she couldn't imagine them. Angus had burned that capacity out of her. She had to brace herself for the worst and face it.

Somehow.

All would.

Her training in the Academy must have been good for something. Hadn't it taught her enough toughness to pull her brain into focus? Hadn't Angus taught her enough desperation? She needed the zone-implant control, wanted it so badly that she almost begged Vector to let her detour to her cabin; but she knew the risk was too great, she couldn't hazard having the proof of her falseness in her possession. And she couldn't go to her cabin, switch on the control, and then leave it behind. It wouldn't work if she moved out of its range, and its transmitter wasn't powerful enough to reach more than ten or twenty meters.

She had to face the bridge with nothing but the tattered and unreliable resources she had left.

It wasn't far from the lift. *Captain's Fancy* was a frigate, not a disguised destroyer like *Starmaster* – or even a masquerading orehauler like *Bright Beauty*, with much more space for cargo than crew. Except for her luxuries, Nick's ship was built to a more compact scale. The outer levels converged on an opening like an aperture in the structural bulkhead; through the aperture was the command module.

At need this command module could be sealed, even detached, from the main body of the frigate. In fact, the module could almost certainly function as a separate craft while the rest of the ship was operated from the auxiliary bridge.

Urged gently ahead by Vector Shaheed, Morn crossed the aperture and entered the compact circle of the bridge.

The perspective would have disoriented her if she hadn't been familiar with it. She stood in a space like the cross-section of a cylinder, with her feet on the inner curve and her head toward the axis. In that respect, the bridge was no different than the rest of *Captain's Fancy*: it was simply smaller. The floor swept up and arced over her head on both sides. Some of the bridge crew sat at their Stations beside her, almost level with her; others appeared to hang upside down above her. But, of course, wherever she or anyone else stood, the floor was 'down' and the axis of the cross-section was 'up.' The big display screens for scan, video, data, and targ were built into the concave wall opposite the aperture. Their status lights winked green, but the screens themselves were blank. In all likelihood, Nick didn't want Morn to have the information she could have gleaned from the displays.

Vector and Morn gained the bridge beside Nick's command Station. Like everyone else on the bridge, Nick was in his g-seat; his hands rested on his board, tapping buttons occasionally with accustomed ease. Nevertheless Morn noticed at once – even before she tried to take an inventory of the people arrayed against her – that he hadn't strapped himself in.

Mikka Vasaczk stood near him, defenseless against any change in g.

Which meant *Captain's Fancy* was in no immediate physical danger. Otherwise Nick would have been preparing for maneuvers of some kind.

'Nick,' Vector said with a nod like a little bow. Apparently nobody aboard called Nick 'Captain.' 'I was trying to seduce her with coffee. If you hadn't interrupted me, I might have succeeded.' His smile remained mild, almost impassive.

Nick's was altogether different. It was fiercely happy; it gave the impression that he was baring his teeth.

'That doesn't worry me,' he said like a cheerful tiger. 'If I didn't do it, you would find some way to interrupt yourself. You like the process of seduction too much. You never actually want to succeed at it.'

Vector didn't attempt a rejoinder; he seemed absorbed by the implications of Nick's insight. Still smiling, he walked up the curve to an empty seat and sat down in front of what was probably the engineer's console.

Morn was left alone beside Nick and Mikka.

Belatedly she tried to take in the rest of the bridge.

Apart from Nick, Mikka, and Vector, she counted five other crewmembers. Vector's presence wasn't necessary to the normal operations of the ship. That left six essential bridge positions: command, scan, communication, targeting and weapons, helm, and data and damage control. First, second, and third for each position: eighteen people altogether. Vector and his second brought the crew total to twenty. Vector's 'pup' was probably on duty in the drive space, monitoring the thrusters directly.

None of the bridge crew had anything urgent to do. They were all staring at Morn.

'Carmel.' Nick continued to focus on Morn while he addressed other people. 'What's scan got from Com-Mine?'

Carmel was a gray-haired, chunky woman who looked old enough to be Morn's mother. 'No change,' she reported. 'Routine traffic. They haven't sent anything after us yet.'

'Lind?' Nick asked. As he watched Morn, the hue of his scars deepened.

'We're getting regular demands for acknowledgment,' replied a pale, wispy, nearly walleyed man with a communications receiver jacked into his ear. 'They want to know if we hear them. And what we're going to do. But they aren't making threats.'

'All right.' Nick slapped his hands on the arms of his seat and pivoted his chair away from Morn. 'We've got a decision to make, but we have time. They know we took damage. The longer we put on velocity this slowly, the more they're likely to figure we can't trust tach. And if we can't go into tach, they probably figure they can chase us down. If it's that important to them. Which might encourage them to postpone their own decision for a while.'

That, Morn thought, might be the real reason Nick had acceded to her request for no heavy g.

'But whichever way they jump,' he went on, 'we need to be ready to jump ahead of them.'

Abruptly he swung around to face Morn again. 'We've got a problem.' But his tone wasn't abrupt: he spoke laconically, as if all he wanted was to engage her in conversation. 'Our deal with Com-Mine Security isn't holding – the deal we made to get you out. They want us to come back. If we don't, they may decide to come after us.'

'Why?' she asked neutrally. The crisis was upon her, but it didn't surprise her: it was just what she'd feared. To that extent, she was ready for it. Yet hearing Nick state it caught her in a new way, despite her alarm. Was it possible he'd made a mistake? Was it possible that he could lose?

She already knew he had limits—

He replied casually, but there was nothing casual about his scrutiny as he said, 'They think you've got something they want.'

She couldn't help it: her whole body flushed with panic and remembered passion. Shame burned on her skin, as if he'd stripped her naked and offered to sell her to the highest bidder. The entire bridge crew was staring at her; even Vector watched her. Mikka Vasaczk's animosity was palpable at her back, even though she was held by Nick's gaze and couldn't look away.

The zone-implant control, of course; that's what Com-Mine wanted. Angus didn't have it on him when he was arrested. By now, Security had had time to search *Bright Beauty*; they knew the control wasn't there. They must have figured out she had it.

They wanted to arrest her. And they wanted an excuse to execute Angus.

As if in confirmation, Nick concluded, 'They want us to return you.'

In a small voice, like a bird horrified by a snake, she asked, 'What are you going to do?'

'That's easy.' The darker Nick's scars became, the more he smiled. 'We're going to get the truth out of you. Then we'll be able to decide.'

'What "truth"?' Suddenly she hated the way she flushed, the way her body betrayed her. She hated Nick's bold hunger and Mikka's hostility. She had rage in her, and it began to leak past her defenses. 'You already know I'm UMCP. You knew that before you picked me up.' She gathered strength as she went on. 'What other secrets do you think I've got? What "truth" are we talking about here?'

Nick's manner remained perfectly nonchalant; only his eyes revealed the intensity of his focus on her. 'We'll take it one "truth" at a time. What makes you think we knew you were a cop when we rescued you? If we'd known that, we would have known you didn't need rescuing.'

'Because,' she retorted, 'you've got a connection in Com-Mine Security. There's no other way you could have framed him.' Angus' name wouldn't pass her lips; she couldn't force it out of her throat. 'I helped you plant those supplies, but you couldn't have stolen them in the first place without inside help – without somebody in Security who was willing to take risks to help you.

'Maybe that's what's going on now. Maybe your connection is feeling the heat – maybe he needs to get me back to distract the rest of Security from the way those supplies were stolen.

'But that's beside the point. Whoever he is – whatever reasons he's got for helping you – he would have told you everything Security knows about me. He would have told you who I am.'

Nick didn't contradict her. He may or may not have liked intelligence in women, but he accepted hers. He spread his hands expressively. 'So you see our problem.'

'No,' she began, 'I don't. I've got a problem of my own to worry about. I don't understand why—'

'I'll spell it out for you,' Mikka interrupted, as harsh as mineral acid. 'You're a cop. Maybe that's why you let us take you. Security got Thermopyle. Now you want to make sure the UMC Police get us.'

Morn allowed her mouth to fall open. Anybody who believed her capable of making decisions like that knew nothing about the experience of being Angus Thermopyle's victim.

Which was of course true for everyone aboard *Captain's Fancy*.

Which in turn meant that they had no reason to guess the existence of her zone-implant. Their preconceptions and anxieties ran in an entirely different direction. They were misled by the knowledge that she was a cop; by the assumption that she had a cop's reasons for what she did.

Keeping her back to Mikka, facing only Nick, she replied scornfully, 'I'm not suicidal. If I wanted to betray you, I wouldn't put myself in this position. As soon as Security arrested him' – despite her anger, she still couldn't say Angus' name aloud – 'I would have flagged a guard and told him not to let you leave Station. Then I would have had all the time I needed to talk to Security. Safely. You *and* Security's traitor would have been arrested.'

Her answer silenced the command second, but it didn't shift Nick's study of her. Again he said, 'So you see our problem.'

'No.' Her fear and fury continued to grow; she could barely refrain from shouting. 'I'm not a mind reader. I don't know what problems you've got unless you tell me.

'*My* problem is figuring out what you want a cop for.'

When Morn said that, Lind let out a satirical chuckle, and the woman at the targ board snorted 'Crap.'

Nick threw back his head and laughed.

'Morn,' Vector remarked like a man discussing routine traffic trajectories, 'if you think about it, you'll understand why we need to know what made you stay with Captain Thermopyle.'

'You're a cop.' Mikka's tone was soft and vicious. 'He's a pirate and a butcher – he's slime.' She might have been quoting Nick. 'But you crewed for him. You stayed with him when he got to Station. You backed him against Security. The only thing you did against him was unseal his hatches.

'If you don't tell us why, we're going to put you in an ejection pod and jettison you back toward Com-Mine. Let them have you, and good riddance.'

Morn could feel the hostility on the bridge building against her. In an unexpected way, it reassured her. Mikka and the others wanted to uncover her secrets: therefore her secrets were still hidden. She couldn't imagine why that might be true, but she staked herself on it.

'I told you,' she said, speaking to Nick, always speaking to Nick. '*Starmaster* was wrecked. I was going to die out there. He found me – and he needed crew. So I made a deal with him. To save my life. I gave him immunity – as much immunity as I had. *Starmaster*'s Captain was my father. Half the crew was my family. I didn't want to die in their tomb.'

'If that were true,' Mikka countered harshly, 'you would have left him as soon as you reached Com-Mine.'

'Jettison her,' Carmel pronounced. 'We don't need this.'

The large, misshapen man at the data console spoke for the first time. In an unexpectedly timid voice, as if he were asking a question, he said, 'I agree. If she stays, she's going to cause trouble.'

Nick glanced around the bridge, then returned his gaze to Morn. As if he were still laughing inside, he said, 'You see? You're simply going to have to do better.

'And don't tell me' – she heard the threat in his tone – 'you did it because of your passion for me. I've heard that before. Women like that are fun to play with on Station. I don't take them into space with me.'

Morn was cornered. But nobody had mentioned the zone-implant control yet. And she'd spent hours trying to prepare herself for this. She went on fighting.

'You're right,' she said, not weakly, not as if she were defeated, but angrily, exposing as much of her outrage as she dared. 'He knew something about me you don't.

'He knew I wrecked *Starmaster*.'

Except for the faint hum of air-scrubbers and the low pressure of thrust through the hull, the bridge was silent.

She didn't say any more until Nick drawled, 'Now why in hell would you do a thing like that?'

Morn glared straight at him. 'Because I've got gap-sickness.'

That startled him. She could see the blood drain from his scars: he turned as still and ominous as a ready gun. Someone she didn't know muttered a curse. Mikka Vasaczk drew a hissing breath; Vector watched her solemnly.

'It comes on under heavy g.' The memory – and the fact that she was forced to admit it – filled her with bitterness; but she used gall and self-loathing to focus her anger. 'It's like a commandment, I don't seem to have any choice about it. It makes me engage self-destruct. I would be dead myself, but my father managed to abort part of the sequence. Only thrust blew – the gap drive didn't. The auxiliary bridge held. I was the only one there.

'I did the same thing when *Bright Beauty* went after you. But he knew about the problem – he stopped me in time.

'That's why I stayed with him. I didn't have anywhere else to go. If I can't do heavy g, I'm finished as a cop. Until I destructed *Starmaster*, I could have hoped for a Station job, UMCPHQ maybe. Now the only thing I can hope for is that they'll give me a zone-implant to keep me under control.

'Do *you* want a zone-implant?' she demanded. 'Do you want somebody to hit buttons that turn you on and off? I don't. So I let him rescue me. I stayed with him. I promised not to turn him in. I backed him up when he needed it. And I came to you when I got the chance because' – she nearly choked on the recollection – 'because he is what he is. And you'd already beaten him. I didn't have anywhere else to go.'

'You bitch!' Lind was practically frothing; his walleye rolled. 'What makes you think we want a gap-sick crazy here?

'Jettison her!' he shouted at Nick. 'Blast her back at Com-Mine. Let them have her – let her try her sickness on them. She's a time bomb.'

'She'll paralyze us,' Mikka put in. 'We can't trust the gap drive. With her aboard, we can't trust thrust, either. We won't be able to maneuver at all – we'll be a sitting target for anybody with ambitions against us.'

'Mikka's right,' asserted Carmel. 'Com-Mine wants her. If she's gap-sick, that's all the excuse we need to give them what they want.'

'That's enough,' Nick said before anyone else could object. He didn't raise his voice, but his tone demanded compliance. 'You aren't thinking. You're crazy yourself, Lind – that's why you hate crazies so much. Carmel, you've argued against every risky decision we've ever made. Sometimes you're so cautious you blind yourself. And *you* —' He flicked his attention like the end of a whip at Mikka. 'You're just jealous.

'There are a couple of interesting points here you seem to have missed,' he went on more nonchalantly. 'The first is that Captain Thermo-pile must have known how to handle her problem, or else he wouldn't have kept her. She would have been too dangerous. If he could do it, we might find it worth our while to try the same thing.

'The other is that she must have a reason for telling us all this.

'Personally,' he concluded, studying Morn with his scars pale as if he'd never been hungry for her, and never would be, 'I would like to know what it is.'

Morn tasted bile and triumph. No one had mentioned the zone-implant control. That meant Com-Mine Security hadn't mentioned it when they demanded her return – and nobody aboard *Captain's Fancy* had guessed the truth. Not even Nick.

As long as her fundamental secret remained safe, she could answer the challenges thrown at her.

'Actually,' she replied with more steadiness than she'd felt for days, 'I'm not hard to handle. As far as I can determine' – she tried to sound as clinical as she could – 'my gap-sickness is specific to self-destruct sequences. I don't feel driven to hurt myself or attack anyone else. And it passes pretty quickly when g eases. You can lock me in my cabin. Or you can do what he did – you can dope me up with cat until the ship is safe. The rest of the time, there's nothing to worry about. I might even be useful.

'I told you about it' – she tightened her grip on herself and concealed her triumph with bitterness – 'because I think I can trust you. You weren't planning to send me back when you called me to the bridge, and you aren't going to send me back now. Unless I do something to make you change your mind – like hiding a problem that could be a danger to you.

'I think there's a reason you took me away from Security, and it doesn't have anything to do with' – she fumbled because she couldn't say the right words – 'with me.' With sex or hunger. 'It has to do with the fact that I'm UMCP.'

'Go on,' Nick remarked. His smile had recovered its fierceness. 'Crazy or not, you're as entertaining as hell.'

'You're a pirate,' she answered boldly. 'Your reputation is better than his, and after the things he did to me I'm sure the difference is justified – but you're still a pirate. And you knew I was a cop. You knew that before you rescued me.

'So what kind of pirate deliberately takes a cop on board? As long as I'm here, I'm a danger to you. I can testify to any crime you commit. Eventually you'll have to kill me. And even that can get you in trouble. Everybody knows you took me. If I end up dead, you'll have to account for it the next time you dock anywhere in human space.

'Why would you put yourself in that position?'

'I give up.' Nick flashed his smile around the bridge. 'Why?'

Without hesitation she replied, 'I can only think of two reasons. One is that you're a pirate. Whether you admit it or not, that means you do business with forbidden space. And *that* means I'm valuable to you. You can make quite a deal for me. If you can hand over a cop with her brain intact, you'll end up so rich you'll never have to do anything illegal again.

'If that's true, you've obviously got no intention of returning me to Com-Mine. Getting me here was the whole point of framing him.

'But there's a problem with that explanation. If you were planning to hand me over to forbidden space, you wouldn't be traveling this slow, no matter what I wanted. You wouldn't give Security time to reconsider your deal – you wouldn't take the risk that they might change their minds and come after you. You would be using every kilo of thrust this ship has. You might even be willing to gamble on tach.

'That leaves only one other possibility.'

'Are you sure you want to go on?' Nick asked conversationally. 'You've probably said enough. I like your first explanation fine. After all, I must want to protect my "connection" in Security. Assuming I really have one. The more I look like I'm running, the worse things look for him. Or her.'

Morn didn't stop. If he was warning her, she ignored it. 'If you're the kind of man who sells human beings to forbidden space,' she retorted, 'you probably don't care what happens to your connection. I'm worth losing a traitor or two for.

'I like my second explanation better.

'Maybe,' she said, 'you're a pirate – and maybe you aren't. Maybe your reputation is fake, and piracy is just cover. Maybe you rescued me because you're under orders.

'It's common knowledge that Data Acquisition is a euphemism for sabotage and trickery. I'm Enforcement Division – I don't know anything about DA. But that's Hashi Lebwohl's department. I've heard rumors about him.' In fact, in the Academy she'd heard any number of rumors about Hashi Lebwohl. 'He likes spies. He likes operatives who have access to bootleg smelters and shipyards and maybe access to forbidden space.

'Maybe you work for him.'

A low voice said contemptuously, 'Shit.' No one else interrupted her.

'That would explain how you were able to get what you wanted from Security – why they trusted you with Station supplies, why they let you go, why they let you have me.

'In which case, maybe you took me so you can turn me over to DA – so they can find out what happened to *Starmaster*, or what I know about *Bright Beauty*.' She'd accused Com-Mine Station of sabotaging *Starmaster*. If that report reached UMCPHQ, Min Donner – or possibly Hashi Lebwohl – might not trust Security enough to leave Morn at Com-Mine. 'But you had to do it in a way that didn't blow your cover – and wouldn't ruin the case against him. If anyone ever found out he was arrested for a crime fabricated by the UMCP, he would be released, and the UMCP would lose credibility, authority.'

Morn herself was dismayed by the concept. Almost from birth, her idea of the UMCP had included incorruptible honesty; integrity instead of treachery. But when she engaged *Starmaster*'s self-destruct, she'd blown herself into a completely different set of presuppositions and exigencies.

Grimly she concluded, 'Your connection in Security is a UMCP agent. You aren't going to send me back to Com-Mine because you don't want me to tell anybody there the truth.'

By the time she stopped, Nick was no longer looking at her. He'd fallen into a reverie, gazing at the blank screens as if he didn't see them. The muscles of his face relaxed; they were almost slack, almost vulnerable, as they'd been when he slept. Nobody said anything, and Morn didn't glance around. She kept her attention on Nick.

Then Vector Shaheed broke the silence. 'She's got you, Nick,' he said calmly. 'If you send her back now, she'll be convinced you aren't either a pirate *or* a cop. Your reputation will be ruined. You'll probably cease to exist. Hell, we'll all probably cease to exist.'

Somebody above Morn muttered, 'What the fuck's *that* supposed to mean?' She ignored him.

Darkness flushed into Nick's scars as he glared at the engineer, but he didn't retort. Instead he held Vector's gaze until it became obvious that Vector wasn't going to look down. Then Nick faced Morn again.

He wasn't smiling now. His expression was intense and congested, as if she'd thwarted or exposed him in some way. His threats were plain in his voice as he said, 'Give me your id tag. I can tell them you aren't coming back, but if I don't give them your codes they'll chase us for sure.'

Involuntarily Morn winced a little. Nick's manner scared her – and she didn't want to give up her tag. Even Angus had let her keep that much of her identity. Without it, she would never be able to use a UMCP – or Security – computer or communications network again. Even ED might not believe that she was Morn Hyland, Captain Davies Hyland's daughter.

'Wouldn't it be better if I did that?' she offered, trying not to sound frightened. 'I know verification codes they can't argue with. And if they run a scan on my voice, they'll have proof I'm doing my own talking.'

Fortunately Nick didn't have to think long about her suggestion. After a couple of moments he nodded once, stiffly.

'In that case,' she went on, in a hurry to finish before she ran out of adrenaline and began to shake again, 'I need to know what they want, what they think I've got – why they want me back.'

Behind his threats Nick's tone was sulky. 'Lind, give us playback.'

Lind knew his Captain well enough to obey quickly. He danced fingertips across his console, and a flat voice slightly frayed by distance came over the bridge speakers.

Although she had reason to think she was safe, Morn listened in dread, irrationally afraid to hear words that would doom her.

The voice identified itself by name, position, and authorization code: apparently it belonged to Milos Taverner, Deputy Chief of Com-Mine Station Security. It specified *Captain's Fancy* by name and registration. Then it said:

'Captain Succorso, you have a woman aboard, UMCP Ensign Morn Hyland, active assignment UMCP destroyer *Starmaster*. She has evidence material to our case against Angus Thermopyle, Captain and owner, *Bright Beauty*.'

For completeness, the voice cited *Bright Beauty*'s registration.

'*Bright Beauty*'s datacore may have been altered. Datacore evidence against Captain Thermopyle is inadequate. We suspect a memory chip was removed. We suspect Morn Hyland has it in her possession.

'Return Ensign Hyland to Station for questioning.

'Acknowledge.

'Repeat.'

The voice began again at the beginning. Lind silenced it.

'Is that true?' Nick demanded before Morn had a chance to gauge the scale of her reprieve. 'Are you *still* working for him? Is he using you to smuggle the evidence away, so he can't be convicted?'

Morn could hardly think. A reprieve. A gift. Security didn't know about the zone-implant control. Nobody knew. Her secret was safe.

'No,' she replied, forcing herself to talk in order to conceal her relief. 'He never let me near his datacore. He didn't give me anything. If he pulled a chip,' which ought to be inconceivable – not physically difficult, of course, but effectively useless – since it was impossible to know which chip contained what data, in addition to which the removal of a chip could always be detected, and removing a chip was enough of a crime to cost Angus his license to own and operate *Bright Beauty*, 'he must have disposed of it himself.'

'They can prove that themselves,' Vector observed unnecessarily. 'They don't need Morn's testimony.' After a pause he added, 'There's no other way to tamper with a datacore. That's the whole point of having them. If what they record could be changed, they wouldn't be good for anything.'

'So they're lying.' Carmel had a penchant for assertive statements. 'They have some other reason for wanting her back.'

Unexpectedly Mikka put in, 'No. That's too risky. She's UMCP. They can't silence her. If we took her back, and she found out they were lying, they would be in shit up to their eyebrows. The tampering must be real. They just don't know how it was done yet. They think maybe she can tell them.'

'Or maybe,' Morn said to Nick, so giddy with relief that she was willing to take risks, 'this is a smoke screen. Your connection knows you won't take me back. He can say anything he wants. He's trying to cover his ass.'

Nick aimed a black glance at her, then looked away. After a moment, he started to laugh harshly. 'That fucking bastard,' he said in grudging admiration. 'If I knew how to tamper with my datacore, we would all be safe forever. And rich. We could make enough credit selling that secret to buy our own Station.'

Before anyone else ventured an opinion, he pointed Morn toward communications and commanded Lind, 'Record her. If we like what she says, we'll send it.'

Still obeying promptly, Lind got his console ready.

Sustained by her reprieve, Morn walked the curve of the bridge to Lind's post. He ignored her, kept his eyes on his hands, as she lifted her id tag over her head and plugged it into his board. There, just for a second, she hesitated. She was taking a dangerous step: as soon as she said her verification code, Nick would have it; he could use it and her tag however he wished. She would be that much more isolated, that much more exposed to him and his crew.

Nevertheless she'd created this situation: she couldn't afford to falter now. When the board had copied what it needed, she put the tag back around her neck inside her shipsuit. Then she spoke as if she were saying a final good-bye to herself and all her old life.

'This is Morn Hyland, Ensign, UMCP.' Distinctly she articulated the verification code. 'I have authorized business aboard *Captain's Fancy*, which does not fall under your jurisdiction. If you need acknowledgment, query Min Donner, Enforcement Division, UMCPHQ.'

That was safe to say, since Com-Mine was certain to query Min Donner in any case.

'I have no evidence in Com-Mine Station's case against the Captain of *Bright Beauty*.' Her inability to utter Angus' name eroded her stability, but she kept going. 'To my knowledge, datacore tampering is impossible. I did not witness the removal of any chips. If they were removed, they were not given to me. My grievances against the Captain of *Bright Beauty* are personal, and I do not choose to prosecute them publicly.'

In that way, she kept faith with Angus Thermopyle. She may have betrayed everyone else, but she was true to him.

'Captain Nick Succorso of *Captain's Fancy* has my support and co-operation. Refer all further inquiries to UMCPHQ, Enforcement Division.'

To her own surprise, she added, 'Farewell, Com-Mine Station.'

After that her throat closed, and she couldn't say anything else.

'That'll do,' Nick told Lind. 'Send it. No repeats. If they miss part of it, let them sweat.

'Vector, I want you in the drive space. We're going to give Station about ten minutes, so they'll decide we aren't running. Then we're going to burn.'

Without warning Morn's stomach turned over. Again she felt the brisance of panic, compressing her heart and lungs against her rib cage. 'Burn' meant heavy g. The hardest acceleration *Captain's Fancy*'s thrusters could produce.

If Nick feared her gap-sickness, he didn't show it. Instead he snapped out orders. 'Mikka, take her back to her cabin. Lock her in. Be sure she can't get out while we burn. I want her secure until we're out of g – and she can convince us she's sane.' Pivoting his seat, he faced Morn with a feral grin. 'Staying alive is *her* problem.'

Before Morn could think or react, Mikka grabbed her arm and pulled her through the aperture, off the bridge. A few minutes later she was back in her cabin. Outside, Mikka locked the door.

Nick's second left her alone with the gap-sickness which had killed her father and most of the people she'd ever loved.

ANCILLARY DOCUMENTATION
Datacores

For convenience, history is often viewed as a conflict between the instinct for order and the impulse toward chaos. Both are necessary: both are manifeStations of the need to survive. Without order, nothing exists: without chaos, nothing grows. And yet the struggle between them sheds more blood than any other war.

The instinct for order is an expression of humankind's devout desire for safety (which permits nurture), for stability (which permits education), for predictability (which permits one thing to be built on another) – for equations of cause and effect simple enough to be relied upon. Indeed, without resistance to change, growth itself would be impossible: resistance to change creates safe, stable, predictable environments in which change can accumulate productively.

The instinct for order is therefore aggressive. It actively opposes any alteration of circumstance, any variation of perspective, any hostility of environment or intention. It fights to create and defend the conditions it seeks.

The impulse toward chaos is a manifeStation of humankind's inbred knowledge that the best way to survive any danger is to run away from it. This instinct focuses on the resources of individual imagination and cunning, rather than on the potentialities of concerted action. Its most common overt expression involves an insistence upon self-determination (freedom from restriction), individual liberty (freedom from requirement), and nonconformity (freedom from cause and effect). However, such insistence is primarily a rationalization of the desire to flee – to survive by escape.

Therefore the impulse toward chaos is also aggressive. The very act of escape breaks down systems of order: it contradicts safety, avoids stability, defies cause and effect. Like the instinct for order, it fights to create and defend the conditions it seeks.

Nevertheless stability and predictability themselves would be impossible without chaos. Chaos exerts the pressure which requires order to shape itself accurately. Without accuracy, order would self-destruct as soon as it came into being.

For these reasons, the struggle between order and chaos is eternal, necessary – and extremely expensive. By nature, human beings are at their most violent and belligerent in self-defense. The cost of their survival would be prohibitive in any less fecund universe.

In this context, the importance of datacores is easily understood.

Both metaphorically and actually, they were powerful tools for order. They gave the governments of Earth – and their effective enforcement arm, the United Mining Companies Police – the ability to *find out what happened* to any ship anywhere in human space. Ultimately anything that could be known could be controlled – or at least punished.

Of course, this was not the rationalization when they were first introduced. Then the rationalization was simply that space was vast; the gap, mysterious; accidents, common. If the future wanted to learn from the past – in order to make space travel safer – it needed to know what the past was. Therefore a record was required of what every ship knew, did, and experienced, so that its past would be available for analysis and understanding. And, naturally, this record had to exist in some unalterable form, so that it couldn't be falsified by damage or self-interest, by stupidity or malice. Surely it stood to reason that every ship should carry the technology to make such recordings – for the sake of all future spacefarers.

However, the possibilities for control were so obvious that enforcement of these records was not left to reason. It became an absolute requirement: no ship could be built and registered unless it carried, in effect, an automatic and permanent log which would keep track of everything that ship did or encountered: every decision, every action, every risk, every malfunction, every crisis.

The codes which unlocked these logs belonged to the UMCP.

The datacores designated for use as permanent and automatic logs were a development of CMOS (complementary metal oxide semiconductor) technology. The great advantage of CMOS chips was that they drew power only when they changed state: that is, when information was written to them. Because of this, they could store data in a physically permanent form, without a sustained energy supply. Like any other chip, however, they were accessible to electronic emendation: once power was applied to the source and drain, the chip's state could be altered; its data could be changed.

The invention of SOS (silicon on sapphire) CMOS chips was a step in the direction of real permanence. However, true datacores were not possible until the development of silicon on diamond semiconductors. SODCMOS chips were too intractable for ordinary computer use; but they were ideal for storing data in an unalterable form. Crudely put, SOD semiconductors never changed state at all: they added state. Instead of storing data in the normal on-or-off binary form, they stored it in an accumulation of on-then-off sequences. Therefore the 'on' which preceded the 'off' remained transparent when the data was accessed.

Not only were the data unalterable, but any attempt to alter them was unalterably recorded. In effect, this provided a kind of Write Only Memory: with the proper UMCP codes, it could be read; but it could never be rewritten.

Inevitably the impulse toward chaos took exception to the whole idea of the datacore.

At this period, however, the instinct for order was ascendant. The threat of forbidden space gave it an unprecedented legitimacy. For that reason, the requirements of the UMCP – backed by the imponderable commercial muscle of the United Mining Companies – were usually granted. No economically vulnerable government of a genophobic species could refuse – especially when the requirement sounded so reasonable. By law, every human ship carried a datacore. If it did not, it was denied registration; which in turn meant that it would be denied dock anywhere in human space.

Vehement proteStation founded on arguments for self-determination and individual liberties gained only two compromises in the final legislation. First, since the police were given sovereignty over all datacores, they were prohibited from seizing access to any datacore unless they possessed evidence that some crime had been committed. Second, to protect the privacy of ordinary citizens, any non-UMCP – or non-Security – ship was permitted to keep its sickbay log separate from its datacore; in effect, to operate its sickbay systems hermetically. Ordinary citizens might not be able to travel without id tags from which their files could be read by any UMCP or Security computer; they might not be able to control the contents of those files; but at least aboard ship they could sedate their insomnia or treat their warts without making that information available to the police.

The impulse toward chaos feared – loudly – that it was only a matter of time before the instinct for order began to supply ships with datacores which contained programming designed to override anything the ship or its Captain might decide to do – programming intended to limit the ship's choices, control the ship's actions. In most circles, however, this fear was considered implausible. For the UMCP to prejudge the exigencies which a ship might encounter a thousand light-years from Earth would involve carrying the instinct for order to suicidal extremes.

Even the most frightened nonconformists, the most paranoid libertarians, had no cause to think that either the United Mining Companies or the United Mining Companies Police were suicidal.

CHAPTER 4

She had so little time – and no idea what to do. Nick had said ten minutes, heavy g in ten minutes. And she knew almost nothing about her gapsickness; she didn't know how to control it.

She'd already disabled her zone-implant's capacity to simply shut her off, render her catatonic.

Fool.

Something else. She had to do something else, and do it fast. Nick wasn't going to wait for her to master her panic. He was punishing her for her small triumph on the bridge, that was one reason he'd decided to go into full acceleration so quickly, even though he risked burning her brain away—

He had a gift for revenge.

At most only a minute or two remained. A minute or two before heavy g drove her completely insane.

The zone-implant control was her only hope. She'd retrieved it from its hiding place; she had it in her hand. But which function should she use? She couldn't guess what part of her brain had been damaged, where her vulnerability lay; which complex of neurons was responsible for the utter clarity with which the universe spoke to her, commanding ruin.

She couldn't think.

Goddamn it, she swore at Angus, where are you when I need you?

Without warning *Captain's Fancy* reduced spin; internal g drained out of the cabin. Standard procedure: it saved wear on the equipment and spared the crew the distress of being pulled in more than one direction at once; it also freed the thrust drive from fighting the inertia of spin.

She had no more time. Frantically she reached her bunk, rolled herself into it, pulled up and sealed the blanket so that she wouldn't fall out when shifting g reoriented the furniture. That way the berth would serve her as a kind of g-couch, absorbing as much of her body's stress as it could.

Almost at once a low rumble came through the hull – the muffled, sudden thunder of the thrusters.

In desperation she jerked up the control and hit the button which would flood her with rest, wash her away into sleep and oblivion. Then she jammed the black box under her mattress.

Right or wrong, that solved all her problems – at least for the time being. Panic and consciousness left her as if they were squeezed away by the sudden pressure which made her as massive as death. She filled up with relaxation as she filled up with weight; g itself felt like irrefusable slumber.

Nevertheless she went on cursing while her mind lasted,

Fool.

Nobody could stand the strain of full thrust for long: nobody aboard would survive unless Nick reduced g at regular intervals. If she'd asked somebody on the bridge how long burn would last, she could have set the control's timer to let her go when acceleration eased.

But she hadn't done that, not her, *fool, fool,* and now it was too late. She was lost. She wasn't going to wake up until somebody found the control and switched it off. Until somebody found the control—

— and switched it off—

The next thing she knew, the walls were moving on either side of her. Which didn't make sense – and in any case her cabin didn't have walls like that. But apparently it was true.

Other details also didn't make sense. What was she doing upright? Why did she feel like she was hanging by her arms? She couldn't account for those things. Yet they appeared as true as the walls.

But of course the walls weren't moving: she was. Her boots dragged the deck. She was being carried forward; she could feel hard shoulders braced under her arms.

That pressure brought back her panic.

By the time she reached the lift, she was awake enough to struggle.

She was too weak. Immeasurable sleep still clung to her, sapping her strength; her muscles were clogged with transition. Nevertheless she continued to fight, feebly but stubbornly, until a voice nearby said, 'Let her go. Let's see if she can stand.'

The shoulders removed themselves.

She nearly fell on her face.

More by luck than anything else, she managed to catch herself against the door of the lift.

'Hang on,' the voice said. 'You'll be all right. We're taking you to sickbay.'

It was starting to sound familiar.

Holding her breath for stability, she turned around and forced her eyes to focus on the two men who stood an arm's length away, watching her.

One of them was Vector Shaheed.

The other may have been the same man who'd sat at the data console while she was on the bridge. She couldn't be sure. He was large enough. And not very well put together—

Neither of them had the zone-implant control. At least not out in their hands where she could see it.

Vector's voice was the one that sounded familiar.

'Morn, say something,' he urged gently. 'Convince us you aren't crazy.'

She blinked at him and tried to think, but she couldn't understand his question. She had too many of her own, too much fear: her brain was full of hubbub, like the sound of a mob coming closer. Her whole body ached; she felt like she'd spent hours in a slag pulverizer. G did that – g and helpless sleep.

With an effort, she croaked, 'Why—'

Why am I here?

Why am I awake?

'We need to know if you're still gap-sick,' Vector explained. 'If you are, we're going to take you to sickbay and run some tests. See if we can find a way to bring you out of it.' His smile was stretched too thin: he looked exhausted. 'This is Orn Vorbuld.' He indicated his companion. 'We don't have a medtech aboard, but he has a lot of experience with sickbays.'

Still Morn missed the point; her brain was running too far behind her circumstances. She couldn't get past the dilemma of being taken to sickbay.

Any routine examination performed by any decent sickbay's cybernetic systems would reveal her zone-implant. And *Captain's Fancy* surely had a decent sickbay. If Vector took her there, he would learn the truth.

He already knew the truth. Didn't he? Why else was she awake? He must have found the control and switched it off.

Helpless, weak, as good as beaten, she groaned on the verge of tears. 'No sickbay. Please.'

'Why not?' He studied her closely, but without impatience.

In contrast, his companion stared at her as if he feared she were about to burst into flames.

Abruptly the strain of her conflicting panics – she was already caught, she was about to be caught – seemed to create a clear space between them like the eye of a coriolis; a place where she could think.

Maybe Vector hadn't found the control. He didn't act like he knew about it. Maybe she was awake because he'd taken her out of its range.

Maybe she wasn't lost.

Sick with relief, she almost let herself sink to the floor. But she didn't; she couldn't afford to look that weak. Instead she cleared her throat and lifted her head to face her escorts.

'I don't like sickbays. I'm not crazy. I just took too much cat. I didn't know how long' – she could feel pain in all her muscles – 'how long we were going to burn.'

Orn Vorbuld continued staring at her dumbly.

'Who gave you cat?' inquired Vector. His manner concealed the danger of the question. Nick hadn't ordered drugs for her.

'I had it with me. From *Bright Beauty*'s stores. When I found out I had gap-sickness, I stole some.' Unnecessarily she added, 'I didn't trust him.'

Vector could probably guess that she meant Angus Thermopyle.

The engineer still scrutinized her. 'You said heavy g brings it on. How do you know when it's over?'

To protect herself, she managed a wan smile. 'Do I look like I'm trying to engage self-destruct?'

Vector's smile was habitual, almost inflectionless; she couldn't tell whether he believed her or not.

Apparently he did. After a moment he stepped past her to the intercom beside the lift.

'I think she's all right,' he reported. 'I'll take her to the galley and get some food into her.'

Without waiting for an acknowledgment, he turned to his companion. 'You're due for sleep, Orn. If you don't get some soon, you're going to fall down.'

Orn Vorbuld didn't seem to realize he'd been dismissed. He squinted at Morn as if she were growing brighter in some way; soon she would be too bright to be looked at directly. With the air of a man reaching a difficult decision, he said to her, 'You're too much for Nick.' His tone was timid; it made the words sound like a question.

One of his thick hands reached out and stroked her hair.

Then he walked away.

Morn ignored him. As soon as Vector said the words 'galley' and 'food,' she realized that she hadn't had anything to eat since she'd left *Bright Beauty*. Her sleepiness was nearly gone, but her weakness remained. She needed food.

Vector took her arm gently and keyed the lift. As the door opened and he steered her inside, he remarked casually, 'Orn is a genius of an odd sort. He's a good data first, primarily because he can make computers walk on water. And you can tell just by looking at him that he knows too much about sickbays.

'Unfortunately he has the glands of an ape.'

Was the engineer trying to warn her? Morn dismissed the question. Her brain could only handle one thing at a time. Vector hadn't found the control. He wasn't taking her to sickbay. That was enough. Now she wanted food.

When they reached the galley, it was empty. *Captain's Fancy* must have stopped burning some time ago, and the rest of the crew had already had a chance to eat. Vector seated her at the table, tapped his orders into the console of the foodvend, then went to begin making coffee.

Peripherally she noted how stiffly he moved. The rest of her concentrated on the thought of food and the smell of coffee. One thing at a time.

As soon as he placed a steaming tray in front of her, she ate without caring how good the meal was. At the moment she didn't even care what it was.

He ate across the table from her. He must have been hungry himself, but he didn't hurry. She finished well before he did.

Seeing she was done, he got up, filled two mugs with coffee, set them on the table, and sat down again. But he continued to eat in silence, giving her time to collect herself. Maybe he was trying to calm her for reasons of his own. Or maybe he was naturally courteous; or even kind. Whatever his motives, she took advantage of the opportunity he provided.

By the time he pushed his tray aside, she was ready.

She couldn't match his mildness, but she tried to sound relaxed as she asked, 'How long did we burn?'

'Four hours.'

Morn raised her eyebrows. 'That's a lot of g.'

Vector took a sip of his coffee, then agreed, 'It's about as much as some of us can stand – even with drugs. Too much, really. But we don't want to get caught. We shut down thrust an hour ago. Right now, we're scanning like mad. If anybody comes after us, we'll have to burn again, whether we can stand it or not. So far –' He spread his hands.

'When we reduced g, Mikka tried to rouse you over the intercom. You didn't answer. She knew you were still alive, she said, because' – his smile broadened slightly – 'she could hear you snoring. But she couldn't make you wake up. Nick wanted her to take the bridge so he could get some rest himself. Orn and I volunteered to see what we could do for you.'

Morn didn't respond. She was busy thinking. Four hours at full acceleration was a *hell* of a lot of g. People died under that kind of pressure. Nick wasn't just in a hurry: he was urgent; perhaps desperate.

And yet she'd survived the crisis. She'd slept through her madness; discovered a way to cope with it. That was hope – more hope than she'd expected. For a moment, it was enough.

To fill the silence, or to give her time to think, Vector continued talking.

'We've reached roughly two-thirds of our theoretical maximum speed. If we burn for another two hours, we'll zero out thrust. For a ship this size, our drive is pretty powerful, but any engine can only produce so much push. After that, we'll coast. Unless,' he added, 'they chase us. In that case, we'll all learn more than we ever wanted to know about heavy g. Without a reliable gap drive, our options are limited.

'Even if they don't chase us, we're still going to wish we had a reliable gap drive. No matter how much speed we generate, it won't be enough. We'll be coasting for a *very* long time.'

That comment pulled Morn out of herself. It sounded remarkably like an offer of information. Scrambling inside, she moved to take advantage of it.

'How long? Weeks?'

Vector studied his coffee. 'More like months.'

She mouthed the word, *Months*?

'We have to go the long way around. If anybody follows us – Com-Mine Security or the UMCP – we're in big trouble. Actually, we're still heading away from where we want to go. But if you knew the ship better – or if you had a particularly good inner ear – you could tell we're running a course correction right now. It's *very* gradual. We aren't going to take the risk of encountering any other ships – or of getting caught – while we curve.'

The course correction was certainly gradual. Her sense of balance was normally sensitive enough to tell her when she was experiencing g along more than one vector. She had to wonder if he was telling her the truth – and, if so, why.

'For a ship with no gap drive,' she commented, 'we're trying to cross a lot of space. Where are we going?'

'Repairs,' the engineer answered succinctly. 'We need to reach a shipyard where we can get the gap drive fixed.'

Morn faced him in surprise. Discounting Com-Mine Station itself, she couldn't think of any shipyard in human space that *Captain's Fancy* could reach using only thrust. The ship's speed might well go as high as 150,000 kilometers per second; but even that much velocity was trivial compared to the light-years between the stars.

Forgetting caution, she asked, 'What shipyard? Where is it?'

Vector's eyes were as clear as clean sky. 'You know I can't tell you that.'

'No, I don't,' she retorted. 'As far as I can see, you shouldn't be talking to me at all. As long as you're doing something I don't understand, you can't expect me to guess where your limits are.'

He smiled, unperturbed. 'As I say, we're going to be coasting for a long time. That means we're going to see so much of each other we're likely to turn homicidal. We'll all have an easier time if we try to be friendly.'

She didn't smile back. Vector Shaheed, she told herself, was male. Like Nick Succorso and Angus Thermopyle. If he was 'friendly,' he wanted something from her.

She was prepared to give Nick what he wanted. For her own survival. That's what the zone-implant control was for.

But nobody else. Nobody. Ever.

Deliberately cold, she said, 'And we're doing all this on UMCP orders. We're doing it to keep Hashi Lebwohl's nose clean for planting Station supplies on *Bright Beauty*. Loyalty is a good thing, but this is ridiculous.'

Just for a moment, Vector appeared perplexed. Then his expression cleared. 'Ah. Your theory that Nick is a DA operative. Now I understand. 'Listen to me.' He leaned forward to emphasize his words, and his round face gave up its smile. 'I wouldn't count on that assumption if I were you. I wouldn't even repeat it. It's too dangerous. You took enough of a chance when you mentioned it the first time.'

She scowled at him. 'Why? I'm a cop myself.' She had no reason to trust him – and no reason to let him think she did. 'Why else did Nick decide to keep me, if he didn't have UMCP orders?'

Abruptly Vector stood up; he went to the coffee maker and refilled his mug. All his movements were wooden, as if his joints had frozen while he sat.

Not facing her, he said, 'Nick kept you for his own reasons. He'll tell you what they are – if he ever feels like it.

'As for the rest of us—

'There isn't anybody aboard this ship who doesn't hate the UMCP.' An undercurrent of vehemence ran through his mild tone. 'And we've got cause. We can just barely tolerate you as it is. If you try to taint Nick with your own crimes, we'll use your guts for thruster fuel.'

'"Crimes"?' His anger stopped hers; but it didn't stop her questions. 'What are you talking about? I didn't ask you to frame *Bright Beauty*. I never got the chance. That was your crime, not mine.'

'The crime of being a cop,' Vector returned without hesitation. However, his vehemence was gone: it vanished as suddenly as it came. 'The UMCP is the most corrupt organization there is. It makes piracy look like philanthropy.'

While Morn stared at him, he returned stiffly to his seat. With his mug in front of him, he faced her, smiling and mild, like a man who knew nothing about anger. 'Let me tell you a story.'

Reeling inwardly, she nodded. She'd been shocked by the bare concept of UMCP complicity in Angus' false arrest; but the step from betraying a pirate to being 'the most corrupt organization there is' was a large one. If it were true, it made lies out of her own reasons for becoming a cop. It stained her father, whom she considered the most incorruptible man she'd ever known; it transformed her mother's death into something foolish, pitiful. If it were true—

She listened to Vector Shaheed as if – for the time being, at least – every other question or consideration had ceased to exist.

'You may not realize,' he said evenly, 'that piracy is an unusual vocation for a man like me. I'm not violent. I'm not rebellious – or even larcenous. The truth is, I'm not even a particularly good engineer. If you'd had time to think about such things, you might have wondered what I'm doing here.

'I'll tell you.

'By training, anyway, I'm a geneticist, not an engineer. Engineering is something I picked up later, after I decided to change careers. Before that, I worked for Intertech. In genetics.

'Actually, that's where I met Orn. He was the computer expert for our section. He was prone to accidents even then, and some of his surgical reconstructions were more successful than others, but he was in better shape then than he is now. At first I didn't care for him. He was too – too unscrupulous for my taste. We used to say he'd fuck a snake if it just opened its mouth wide enough. But he was a wizard with computers, and we all depended on him.

'Anyway, I was a geneticist, and as soon as I proved I was good enough I got assigned to some top-priority research. The kind of research where they check the gaps between your teeth and the slush in your bowels to make sure you don't take anything classified home with you when you leave work. Intertech was always twitchy about security – you've probably read about the trouble they were in years ago, the riots and so on – and they were getting worse all the time.'

He paused to drink some of his coffee. Morn may have done the same: she was concentrating too hard to notice.

'From our point of view, that was understandable. Intertech's charter forbids genetic tampering. You probably know that.' Morn nodded. 'It's a universal prohibition. Even the United Mining Companies charter says the same thing. Intertech could have been dismantled if the things our section did were looked at the wrong way.

'We were working,' he said as if the statement had no special significance, 'on a defense against genetic warfare. An immunization for RNA mutation.'

Morn's throat closed in shock; she almost stopped breathing. *An immunization for RNA mutation.* She may have been only a UMCP ensign, but no space-going man or woman could have failed to recognize the implications. *A defense against genetic warfare.* If that were achieved, it would be the most important single discovery since Juanita Estevez stumbled on the gap drive. It would transform human space. It would defuse – and conceivably resolve – the peril of forbidden space. It might even end the problem of piracy, if the pirates were deprived of what was by far their largest market.

No wonder Intertech was 'twitchy about security.' The patents alone on such a discovery might make the company rich enough to buy out the UMC.

But Vector was still talking. While she struggled to catch up with him, he went on, 'As you can imagine, we had to be pretty good at tampering ourselves before we could find a way to protect genetic coding against alteration. And we were good. The truth is, we were close. We were so close I used to dream about it at night. It was like climbing a ladder where you can't see the top because it disappears into a cloud. I couldn't see the end, exactly, but I could see every rung along the way. All I needed was a handlight, and I could have guessed my way past the rest of the rungs to the answer.

'What I dreamed, you see,' he said half apologetically, 'was that I was going to be the savior of humankind. We were all part of it, of course, our whole section – and we wouldn't have been able to do that kind of work without Orn – but *I* was the one who could see the rungs. *I* was the one who knew how close we were to the end of the ladder.'

Then his smile twisted ruefully, as if he were amused by his own regret. 'That's as far as I got.'

'What happened?' asked Morn. A few short weeks ago, she'd been a young officer on her first mission, with ideals she'd adopted from her family, and enough experience of loss to know that such ideals were important. The idea of an achievement as vital, as *tremendous*, as a mutagen immunization – the idea of being able to do that many people that much good – still touched her, despite Angus and gap-sickness.

Vector shrugged stiffly. 'One day, when I went in to work, I found I couldn't call my research up on the screen. We didn't do that kind of research in a bio lab. It was too complex and time-consuming to be run physically. We did it all with computer models and simulations. And my research was just gone. The whole project was gone, everything the whole section was doing. No matter whose authorization we used, or what priority it had, our screens came up blank.

'It was Orn who figured out what happened. He rigged his way into the system and found it was full of embedded codes none of us knew anything about. When those codes were activated, they closed down the project. Sealed it off. None of us could get the smallest fraction of our data back. The system wouldn't even recognize our names.

'Those codes were UMCP.' As he spoke, his voice resumed its under-tone of vehemence, harsh and bleak. 'Not UMC. This wasn't just a situation where the United Mining Companies wanted to protect itself in case Intertech became too powerful. Orn knew that because the codes included source- and copy-routes. They came from a dedicated UMCP computer over in Administration, and they copied everything we did to the same place.'

She listened as if she were transfixed. What he was saying made her skin crawl.

'That computer was DA. It wasn't supposed to have the capability to do anything except scan Intertech research, looking for developments the cops might find useful. But when Orn got into the system, he learned that computer had the power – and the *authority* – to blank the entire company.

'You're young,' he said to Morn abruptly. 'You haven't been out of the Academy, or away from Earth, very long. Have you ever heard *one* rumor about an immunization against RNA mutation? Has anyone *ever* given you a reason to believe we don't need to spend the rest of our lives in terror of forbidden space? Have the cops – or the UMC – ever released our data?'

Stunned, she shook her head.

'We had the raw materials for a defense, we had all the rungs. And they took it, they *suppressed* it.' Vector's eyes were so blue they seemed incandescent. 'They don't want us to know that the way we live now isn't necessary – and it sure as hell isn't inevitable. Forbidden space is their excuse for power, their justification. If we had an immunity drug, we wouldn't *need* the United Mining Companies fucking Police.'

He made an effort to control himself, but it didn't work. 'Think about it for a while,' he broke out. 'At least a dozen billion human beings, all condemned to the terror and probably the fact of genetic imperialism, and for what? For *nothing*. Except to consolidate and extend the power of the cops. And the UMC. In the end the whole of human space is going to be one vast gulag, owned and operated by the UMC for its own benefit, with the cops for muscle.

'I'm one of the lucky ones.' Now at last Vector's anger began to recede; but his smile didn't come back. 'I got out. Intertech shut down our section and transferred all of us, but I kept in touch with Orn. Mostly because he has so few scruples, he tends to meet people with none at all. I quit Intertech and apprenticed engineering on one of the orbital smelters. Then Orn got me a job on a small, independent orehauler, along with a few other' – at last he permitted himself a mildly sarcastic grin – 'disaffected souls. We took over the ship and went into business for ourselves. Eventually we met Nick. Orn understands illegals, and I understand brilliance, so we joined him. We've been here ever since.'

There he stopped. Maybe he could see how profoundly he'd disturbed her. Or maybe he was just exhausted himself, worn out by too much mass and too little rest. He stood up as if he had to fight resistance in every joint, apparently intending to leave her alone with the implications of what he'd said.

But he wasn't done after all. Halfway out of the galley, he paused to ask, 'Do you know why I move like this?'

Morn shook her head dumbly.

'Arthritis,' he told her. 'Once I made the mistake of interfering with one of Orn's less scrupulous pleasures. He beat me up. Rather severely. Quite a few of my joints were bruised or damaged. That's where arthritis starts. It gets a toehold on old wounds or scar tissue. Then it spreads. Heavy g is – agony.

'G is agony, agony g,' he said as if he were quoting, 'that is all ye know in space, and all ye need to know.'

As he left, he concluded, 'I prefer it that way. As far as I'm concerned, the pirates are the good guys.'

She stayed in the galley alone for a long time. She'd just survived a bout of gap-sickness: for the first time since *Starmaster* sighted *Bright Beauty*, she'd discovered a reason for hope. Nevertheless she felt none: she felt abandoned and desolate. She'd become a cop because she'd wanted to dedicate herself to the causes and ideals of the UMCP; perhaps, covertly, because she'd wanted to avenge her mother. But if Vector was right – if he was telling the truth—

In that case, the UMCP had perpetrated an atrocity so colossal that it beggared her imagination; so profound that it altered the meaning of everything she'd ever valued or believed; so vile that it transformed the moral order of human space from civilization and ethics to butchery and rape, from Captain Davies Hyland to Angus Thermopyle.

Now what was she supposed to hope for? That Vector was lying? If so, she would never be able to prove it. And she would never be able to eradicate what he'd told her from her brain: it would always be there, tainting her thoughts, corrupting her as surely as forbidden space. No matter how much personal integrity her father – or she herself – had possessed, he and she may have been nothing more than tools in malign hands.

Alone in *Captain's Fancy*'s galley, with a mug of cold coffee in front of her and nowhere to go, Morn Hyland spent an hour or two grieving for her father – and for everything he represented in her life. She'd only killed his body; and only because of an illness she hadn't known about. Vector Shaheed had damaged his image, his memory.

That grief was necessary. Until it was done, she couldn't summon enough anger to return to her cabin and the zone-implant control.

CHAPTER 5

When she tried to return to her cabin, however, she discovered that she had a problem she hadn't anticipated. Her black box was still on, transmitting sleep to the centers of the brain. As soon as she reentered the control's range, she began to grow drowsy.

And her door lock was set to a five-second delay. Her zone-implant had that much more time in which to overwhelm her.

Fool! she swore at herself. *Fool*. Her lack of foresight was going to ruin her. If she fell asleep before she could reach the box and switch it off, she would be unconscious until somebody rescued her again. Nick or his people would inevitably grow suspicious. And she couldn't simply avoid her cabin. Nick would insist on taking her there for more sex.

In any case, she needed the control.

Too angry and desperate to hesitate, she retreated down the corridor until she reached the point where her zone-implant let go of her. Then she headed for her cabin at a run.

Angus had taught her to do such things.

Key the lock.

Wait: five interminable seconds. Her urgency frayed away, and her self-command sank toward the bottom of a quagmire of helpless rest. By the time the door slid open, she was staggering, barely able to hold up her head, keep her eyes open.

Plunging forward, she hit the edge of the berth, thrust her hands under the mattress.

The control wasn't there.

Yes, it was. She'd misjudged its position. When she hunted, her fingers touched it; grabbed it.

As she toppled to the floor, her thumb caught the button which canceled her implant's emissions.

For several minutes she lay still, breathing hard while she drifted up out of panic and sleep. Then she resumed her quest for survival.

When Nick brought his hunger back to her cabin, she was busy experimenting with the zone-implant control: training her fingers to reach the buttons she wanted; testing the effect of the control's various functions.

Her door barely gave her enough warning. She was engrossed in trying to tune the zone-implant subtly and accurately enough to speed up her brain, her ability to think, without making herself obviously hyperactive. Nevertheless a part of her mind was listening for the lock's chime. Just in time she snapped off the control and thrust it deep in her pocket.

Nerves jangling from the stress of too many transitions, she turned to face the door.

Nick came in grinning, jaunty and relaxed. Nothing in his eyes, or in the suffused hue of his scars, suggested anger. Apparently he'd satisfied his desire for revenge and was willing to forget about it now.

That eased one of her many fears.

'Scan's still clear,' he remarked as he relocked the door. 'I'm pretty sure we aren't being chased. If anybody wanted to catch us, they wouldn't be this casual about it. We can afford to wait a while before we burn again.'

Morn did her best to smile at him. That was hard without the zone-implant's help. If anything, the nausea she tasted when she thought about his hunger was growing worse. Vector's attack on the UMCP made everything worse. And the strain of jumping through synaptic hoops left her as ragged and drained as a long, bad hallucination.

Fortunately her hand was still in her pocket. Moving cautiously, her fingers found the buttons she needed.

'Maybe I was too tired to think straight last time,' he went on, grinning satyrically, 'or maybe I've had so much on my mind since then that I don't trust my own memory. But I could have sworn you're the best woman I ever had.' His scars were so dark that they seemed to stand out from his face – three black welts angling under his right eye, two under his left. 'I want to see if you can do that again.'

Morn swallowed hard because her throat was full of bile, and said in a husky whisper, 'Try me.'

She engaged the zone-implant control, took her hand out of her pocket. Then she unsealed her shipsuit and let it fall.

When he saw her naked, he breathed once, softly, 'Morn.' Sweeping her into his arms, he bore her backward to the bunk.

This occasion was a reprise of the last one. He was the fooled artist, exalted by her unquenchable and misleading response: she was the false instrument, pretending it was his manhood which drove her wild. What they did together didn't diverge from the template she'd established earlier until he'd expended his hunger in a climax so poignant that it brought tears to his eyes.

This time, however, he didn't fall asleep afterward. Instead he lay beside her and held her tightly in his arms while his breathing slowed and his tears dried on his scars. At last he murmured at her ear, 'I was right.' His tone was almost tender. 'There's nobody like you. No woman has ever wanted me enough to give herself up like that.'

'Nick,' she replied, 'Nick,' rubbing her breasts against him and caressing his penis because the control was still on and he'd left her short of the neural apotheosis which would have cauterized her brain, brought her true desire and rage to an end.

His tone was almost tender: his smile was almost fond. 'If I didn't know better,' he told her, 'you might make me believe there really is such a thing as love.'

She began to grow frantic. Until he was ready to let her get dressed, she couldn't reach the zone-implant control. It was still in the pocket of her shipsuit. So she took the risk of pushing him too far: even though he was sated, she ran her mouth down his belly and began to lick him between his legs.

Her ploy worked. Grinning again, he said, 'Later,' and rolled off the bunk.

She was afraid he wouldn't leave. If he didn't – if he lingered for any reason – she might expose herself. She couldn't suppress the passion which the zone-implant imposed on her.

Fortunately he didn't linger. Perhaps he didn't yet trust her enough to want her for anything more than sex. As he slipped back into his shipsuit, he said, 'We're going to burn for two more hours. That'll be about as fast as we can go and still have thrust left if we need to maneuver. Then we'll be done with heavy g. We'll all have time to relax.' At the door, he added, 'Don't let yourself get sick. You and I are going to do a lot of relaxing together.'

The moment he left, she flipped off the bunk, found the control, and canceled it.

This transition wasn't as damaging as the last one. Just recently she'd learned how to vary the intensity of the zone-implant's functions. Now she engaged rest at a low level to soften her neural distress.

A short time later the bridge crew gave her an acceleration alert. When *Captain's Fancy* stopped internal g, she sealed herself in her blankets and set the control's timer for two hours and ten minutes. As soon as she felt thrust ignite through the hull, she put herself to sleep.

She passed that crisis as well.

She might conceivably have passed it without the zone-implant. She had no way of knowing exactly how much g was required to trigger her gap-sickness. Any thrust drive was ruled by the law of diminishing returns: the faster *Captain's Fancy* went, the smaller became the difference between her velocity and the pressure of her thrusters; therefore the same amount of thrust produced steadily less acceleration, until velocity and pressure achieved a state of balance. After that the drive was just a waste of fuel: *Captain's Fancy* could coast as fast without it. In consequence the second period of burn was inherently less stressful than the first.

If Morn had stayed awake, she might have learned what her own limits were.

When the control timer clicked off, however, and she drifted back to consciousness, she was glad she hadn't risked the experiment. Her body ached as if she suffered the same arthritis which stiffened Vector Shaheed, and her head felt sodden and sore, like the aftermath of being drunk. She didn't believe she could have stayed sane without her zone-implant's protection.

The rest of *Captain's Fancy*'s people experienced a completely different kind of relief.

They'd escaped Com-Mine Station without additional damage. They were done with the ordeal of heavy g for the foreseeable future. And they were almost certainly not going to encounter any other ships out here, not traveling at space-normal speeds this far from Station – a distance too small for gap drives, but rapidly becoming too great for any ordinary traffic that relied on thrust.

To all appearances, they were safe.

Of course, there was always the danger that a pursuit ship would attempt a blink crossing. Nick's people had performed that maneuver themselves: they knew it was possible. But any pursuer who went into tach to close the distance was in for a surprise. *Captain's Fancy* had already veered far off any trajectory Station could have plotted for her; she was veering farther all the time. Directional thrust sank its teeth into the vacuum steadily, bringing the ship by slow degrees around to her eventual heading.

Nick Succorso left only a skeleton crew on the bridge: command, scan, data. For the rest of the ship, he threw a party.

To celebrate the rescue of the lovely and astonishing Morn Hyland, he said. From the vile clutches of Captain Angus sheepfucker Thermopile, he explained. And to commemorate the start of the first vacation this ship and her crew had ever had, he added. *Captain's Fancy*'s stores offered a large array of recreational drinks and drugs. Before long nearly everybody aboard was either drunk or stoned.

That kept some of Morn's problems at bay for a while.

Carousal was only a stopgap, however; a way for men and women without zone-implants to effect transition. When it was done, and its aftereffects had been endured, Nick's people had to face a new difficulty.

They had to think of some way to pass the time.

They weren't accustomed to long voyages. *Captain's Fancy* was a gap ship, not an in-system hauler. In all probability, she'd never spent more than a month out of port since Nick first acquired her. Her crew had to think of some way to occupy themselves.

And most of them had volatile temperaments. They were illegals – better trained to fight for their lives than to fend off boredom. For them, a 'vacation' without expensive sex or bars or intrigue or any of the other resources a Station offered soon lost its attractions. A week of mood-altering substances, sleep, and mutual harassment was all right. After that trouble and tempers began to fester.

Once in a while, Morn heard sounds like blows in the halls. At awkward moments obscenities were piped throughout the ship, filling *Captain's Fancy* with manic humor or fury. The people she encountered when Nick took her to the galley or the mess seemed to grow more slovenly, truculent, and damaged every day.

Toward the end of the second week, Vector Shaheed made an occasion to remark to Nick, 'I think we're about ready.'

Nick grinned confidently and shook his head. 'Soon.'

Vector shrugged and went away.

A few days later Mikka Vasaczk took the risk of coming to the door while Nick was in Morn's cabin. Nick left Morn naked and panting on the bunk to let his second in.

Mikka entered with a glare, but it wasn't aimed at Morn. She had a dramatic bruise over one eye; the knuckles of both hands bled. Before Nick could speak, she snapped, 'This has gone on long enough. That damn libidinous null-wave transmitter you installed as data third clubbed me with a spanner. She said I was keeping men away from her. *Me*. If half these people weren't your abandoned lovers, we wouldn't be having this problem.'

She scowled at Nick balefully.

He flashed a smile back at Morn, then said to Mikka, 'All right. I guess they're ready for a little discipline.

'Round them up. Use a gun if you have to. I don't care if they're asleep or dead drunk. I'll talk to them in an hour. We'll put them to work.'

His second didn't salute or reply. Wheeling her hips, she turned and left.

When his people were assembled, Nick talked to them about their behavior and attitudes as if he found the whole subject secretly hilarious. Then he ordered a complete overhaul of every part of the frigate which could be worked on outside a shipyard.

'It's going to take you at least a couple of months,' he concluded, 'so you'd better get started.'

That solved the ship's problems for a while. Not everyone accepted the order graciously, but even the angriest and most discontented crew-members didn't want to cross Nick Succorso. And soon they were too busy to cause any more trouble.

Unfortunately Morn's difficulties were only made worse.

For one thing, Nick now had even more time to spend with her. The work could be left to Mikka's supervision: he personally had nothing to do except test the limits of Morn's responsiveness. There were days when he hardly left her cabin.

At first, he stayed with her only for sex and sleep: that was bad enough. But gradually, as he grew accustomed to her response – as he began to trust it – deeper hungers rose toward the surface in him. He started talking to her; as days passed into weeks, he talked to her more and more. She had to keep her black box concealed under the mattress and hope he didn't find it: he left her so few opportunities to turn herself on and off that she was forced to perform most of her functions while he slept.

At times she sensed a need in him so deep that it was virtually bottomless – a need for his own efficacy or virility which could only be temporarily assuaged, never truly relieved. It showed not only in the way he went about sex, but in the way he talked. Apparently what he enjoyed most was repeating stories other people (so he said) told about him – stories of escapes and rescues, victories and acts of piracy; buccaneering stories, dramatic and brave. He never confirmed whether these stories were true, but his relish for them remained constant. He needed them – and his need drove him to her. In fact, the more she fed his hunger, the more compulsory it became: the more she listened to him and responded to him, the more he desired her.

She hated that: she hated him and everything he did. Sometimes her revulsion grew so acute that she lay awake while he slept, gritting her teeth and imagining how good it would feel to cut his guts open and pull his testicles out through his abdomen.

Nevertheless she suffered his presence; she burned with passion at his touch; she encouraged him to talk. She could see what the things he did meant.

She was becoming valuable to him.

Despite her increasing nausea, she protected her own survival by giving him what he wanted.

And his attachment did have one apparent benefit: as long as he was pleased with her, she had the freedom of the ship. As long as she was always available for him, she could go where she wished, look where she wished. Nobody stood in her way. Even Mikka Vasaczk left her strictly alone.

When she took advantage of her freedom, she found Vector immured in his engines, or Carmel and Lind up to their elbows in wiring; video showed her people in EVA suits crawling across *Captain's Fancy*'s shell; lifts were regularly out of service while they were taken apart and put back together again by the second engineer, a gangling youth with unruly hair and bad skin whom everybody called Pup, even though he obviously hated it.

Familiarity with her surroundings wasn't enough to ease her distress, however. She wanted something more.

She wanted access to the ship's computers – to the logs; even to the datacore. From them she might be able to learn where she was, where she was going. She couldn't test Vector's story one way or the other, but she might find evidence of UMCP complicity in Angus' arrest. She might be able to learn who Nick Succorso really was.

That knowledge might conceivably have helped her; but she didn't get it. Because of the overhaul, the computers were always attended. Even the auxiliary bridge was never deserted, although it was tucked out of the way in the drive space, next to the console room where Vector monitored his engines.

In fact, her freedom of the ship was really a disadvantage. It didn't provide her with what she wanted. On the other hand, it subjected her to a nerve-wracking series of encounters with Orn Vorbuld.

Vector's badly repaired friend must have been watching her all the time: that was the only explanation she could think of for his ability to locate her whenever she was alone. He was the ship's computer expert: he was probably capable of rigging the maintenance computer's sensors to keep track of her. Eventually she began to hesitate when she had an opportunity to leave her cabin because she knew that, sooner or later, she would have to fend him off.

He seldom spoke to her; but he never let her pass without touching her. On the first occasion, he only repeated the caress he'd once given her hair. But on the second, he managed to rub a hand across her breasts before she moved out of his reach. On the third, he squeezed her breasts so hard that they ached for an hour afterward.

Later he caught hold of her and kissed her like a lamprey. She wasn't able to break loose until she contrived to slam the heel of her boot against the back of his knee.

She hurt him enough to make him let go but not enough to make him stop stalking her.

This was a crisis of another kind. She could have isolated herself in her cabin, of course. Or she could have told Nick what was happening: she knew him well enough now to believe that he wouldn't tolerate Orn's actions. But both those options stank of defeat – and she'd already suffered more defeats than she could bear.

She didn't tell Nick. And she didn't hide in her cabin.

Instead she went to talk to Vector Shaheed.

She found him, as usual, in the drive space. She couldn't see him, but she heard him working inside the heavy shell of the gap field generator, still trying to repair the drive himself. To attract his attention, she pounded on the shell with her palm and shouted, 'Vector!'

A variety of clunking noises answered her. Then the engineer emerged painfully from the service hatch, a circuit probe in one hand.

'Morn.' His round face was pink with exertion, but his manner was as mild as ever. 'What can I do for you?'

She felt no need to pretend she wasn't angry. She required anger. Without it, she would be at the mercy of her fear and revulsion.

'What's the matter with that so-called friend of yours?' she demanded harshly. 'I think he's going to rape me.'

Vector blinked at her for a moment, apparently unable to guess whom she meant. Then his eyes cleared. 'Oh, Orn.

'I told you,' he commented. 'He has the glands of an ape – and no scruples. If you convinced him you had syphilis, I don't think even that would slow him down. As far as I can tell, he has no physical fears. Sickbay can fix anything.

'Of course, Nick won't like it.' He paused, considering the situation, then added, 'You don't really have a problem.'

Morn tried to replicate the lash she'd sometimes heard in her father's voice. 'I don't?'

Vector smiled as if his thoughts were already back in the shell with the gap drive.

'You're a big girl now. All you have to do is stop him.'

All those hours with Nick had left her primed for an explosion. 'I'll stop him, all right.' Fuming, she turned and strode away.

But she had no idea how to do it.

She'd been trained in the Academy: she knew how to defend herself. On the other hand, Orn Vorbuld was bigger, much stronger. And she couldn't risk using the enhanced resources of her zone-implant: quickness, concentration, numbness to pain. To do that, she needed to carry the control with her – and she could too easily imagine that it might be discovered.

She wanted a gun. A good impact pistol would be nice. Even a laser-cutter would suffice. But nobody aboard *Captain's Fancy* was likely to give her a weapon without Nick's permission; and that would necessitate an explanation.

Fulminating like a vial of acid, she went to the galley for a mug of coffee and a chance to think.

As a precaution, she sat at the table with her back to the foodvend, facing the outer corridor so that Orn wouldn't be able to take her by surprise.

He arrived so promptly that she almost believed Vector had told him where to find her. But of course the engineer hadn't known where she was headed when she left the drive space—

Orn came into the galley, a flush of anticipation on his face. Not for the first time, she noticed how big his hands were; they looked like slabs of meat.

She stood up sharply.

He stopped. For a moment they confronted each other over the table.

Like his voice, his eyes were incongruously timid; he stared at her in apprehension, as if she were hot enough to scald him. But she already knew there wasn't anything timid about him. She wasn't misled when he said like a frightened boy, 'I want you.'

'Too bad,' she retorted. 'I don't want you.'

If he had any ear at all for disgust, he would know she was telling the truth.

Obviously he wasn't worried about her disgust. 'Yes, you do,' he said with as much certainty as his voice could convey. 'Women are like that. They don't care who they get it from. They think they do, but they don't. They just want it.

'Nick's too soft on you. I'll show you what it's really like.'

Remembering Angus, Morn wanted to spit in Orn's face. 'You're wrong about that,' she snapped. 'I already know. I promised myself the next man who tries it is going to end up dead.

'Does Nick,' she countered before he could move, 'know you're like this?'

Orn's grin bore no resemblance to his voice, or his eyes: it was blood-thirsty and unconcerned. 'Nick knows something more important than that,' he returned, still sounding afraid. 'He knows he needs me. He just doesn't know why. He doesn't know I put a virus in the computers – the same day I came aboard. I'm the only one who knows how to work around it. Usually I put it on hold. But it isn't on hold now. Anybody who tries to get into the systems without me will trigger a complete wipe. Everything will disappear.

'Unless you keep your mouth shut and give me what I want, one of us is going to have to tell him about that.'

Despite her anger, he shocked her. A complete wipe! That was as good as suicide: it would kill *Captain's Fancy* and everybody aboard. Despair surged up in her; despair and loathing. He was like Angus. He had more weapons than she could face, more ways to control her—

When he stepped forward and reached across the table to take hold of her, she flung her coffee into his eyes.

Take that and be damned, you sonofabitch!

Rounding the table while he yowled, she hammered him across the bridge of his nose with her mug. Blood spattered down his cheeks. As fast as she could, she followed that blow with a spear-hand jab for the base of his throat.

Although he was blinded by coffee and blood, he somehow managed to catch hold of her wrist.

That was all he needed.

She tried a whirling turn. If she could spin hard enough, catch him on the temple with her elbow, she might stun him, make him let go.

But he turned with her. Using her own momentum, he slammed her headfirst into the wall.

When she hit, her brain went to jelly, and all her muscles failed.

She kept on flailing randomly, but to no purpose. Gripping her wrist, he hit her again and again; she thought he was going to hit her until she broke. Then, abruptly, he stopped. He didn't want her dead. He wanted her alive; he wanted her in pain. Like Angus. Releasing his hold, he snatched at her shipsuit with both hands and ripped it off her shoulders.

Voices came from somewhere, but they meant nothing; they didn't make a difference. She fought for control of her limbs. The sleeves of her shipsuit were down around her elbows, binding her arms so that she couldn't use them. And Orn was too strong for her. He drove her out of the galley, shoved her against the opposite wall. She was headed for the floor.

'Get her, Orn,' someone said happily. 'Show her you won't take no for an answer. Show her you don't care what Nick thinks.'

'Fuck her!' another voice demanded. 'Fuck her hard! Make her bleed!'

When he closed his fists on her breasts and tried to clamp his mouth over hers, she dropped into a crouch.

Despite her blank brain and her weakness, she coiled herself under him and brought her knee up into his groin.

With a gasp, he recoiled.

'Again!' a voice called like a cheer. 'Hit him again!'

Staggering along the wall, she turned and tried to run.

He tackled her before she went three steps. His weight landed on top of her as she struck the floor. The impact paralyzed her. She couldn't resist as he rolled her over and began to tear her shipsuit the rest of the way open.

'Clear the mess.' Nick spoke in a conversational tone, but his voice cut through Morn's hurt. 'We're going to need some room.'

Orn froze.

Morn heard boots running. Then Nick said casually, 'Orn, I think you've just made a serious mistake. In fact, I think it's the last mistake you're ever going to make.'

Morn caught a ragged breath as Orn scrambled off her and jumped to his feet.

'She damaged you,' Nick commented. 'That's good. Let's go to the mess. You can wash the blood out of your eyes. Then we'll see if there's any way you can survive this.'

'Nick—' Orn began. His voice was full of incongruous panic and threats.

'Come on, Orn,' Vector said. When Morn sat up, closed her shipsuit, and raised her head, she saw the engineer standing beside his friend. 'You must have known this was going to happen. At least he's giving you time to think. Maybe you can think of something to save you.'

Drawing Orn along by the arm, Vector moved in the direction of the mess.

Belatedly someone offered to help Morn. She threw the hands off and levered herself stiffly to her feet.

Nick glanced at her. 'How bad is it?' he asked as if he had no particular interest in her answer.

She shook her head. 'Let me have a gun.' Her legs were frail, and her head reeled; she had to lean on the wall to keep her balance. 'I'll kill him myself.'

Nick chuckled harshly and followed Orn.

In moments virtually the entire crew was assembled in the mess. If anyone was left on the bridge, it had to be somebody Morn didn't know. The tables and chairs had been moved out of the center of the mess; men and women stood among them around the walls. While Vector cleaned Orn's face, Nick walked out into the middle of the floor alone and stood waiting. He was surrounded by grins and frowns, excitement and fear, but nobody said anything. Morn's strained breathing was the only sound in the room.

Abruptly Nick remarked, 'Orn, you've given me a problem.'

Orn turned to face his Captain. 'No, I haven't.' His voice was more timid than ever. Nevertheless the way he turned, the way he moved, reminded Morn that Vector had said of him, *He has no physical fears.* 'If you want her for yourself, all you have to do is keep her locked up. I told you – I warned you she would cause trouble. Since you decided to let her run around loose, I figured you didn't mind sharing her.'

'You don't understand.' In contrast to Orn, Nick sounded smooth and easy, as if he ran on frictionless bearings. 'I'm not talking about her, I'm talking about you. You're good with computers – maybe the best I've seen. Now I'm going to have to replace you.'

There was fright in Orn's eyes, if not in his stance. 'You don't have to replace me.'

'You know better than that,' Nick replied. 'You've been with me a long time. You know the rules.'

'But you never brought a woman like her aboard!' Orn protested. 'Not a woman who looks like her. You should have kept her locked up. I'm only human, Nick. I'm just a man – like you. What do you want from me?'

Nick's grin was as feral as a predator's. 'I want you to say good-bye, Orn.'

At last some of the fearlessness Vector had ascribed to Orn showed in his voice. 'Nick, don't do this,' he said almost firmly. 'If you touch me, you're a dead man. I won't have anything left to lose.'

As soon as he said that, Morn knew she would have to intervene. The virus: *a complete wipe*. Somebody had to tell Nick—

Somebody had to tell him he couldn't afford to kill Orn.

Hugging her sore ribs, she glared at Orn Vorbuld and said nothing.

'You're going to end up dead,' Orn concluded. 'Even if you beat me. Which I don't think you can do.'

In response, Nick threw back his head and laughed.

He was still laughing as he kicked Orn in the temple.

Orn saw the blow coming in time to slip the worst of it past his ear. Despite his ungainly appearance, he was fast. The ease with which he'd mastered Morn was no accident. And he was bigger than Nick by at least twenty kilograms; he had heavier muscles. The punch that countered Nick's kick looked powerful enough to topple a gantry.

Nick caught the punch with a rising block, snapped a short blow into Orn's belly, then danced away before the bigger man could grapple with him.

Orn shrugged off the pain as if it were trivial. 'You fucker,' he panted. 'You've got a death wish.'

Unsealing his shipsuit, he reached inside it and pulled out a knife with a long, black blade. Steady in one fist, he held it poised for Nick's vitals. With his other hand, he wiped fresh blood off his face.

'Now, aren't you ashamed of yourself?' asked Nick sardonically. 'Knives are against the rules. Do you think a little gut-sticker like that is going to scare me?'

Fast and deadly, he kicked again.

This time Orn was ready – and this time the kick was a feint. When Orn tried to slash Nick's leg, Nick hooked his kick around and ripped the knife out of Orn's hand with the heel of his boot.

The knife skittered away.

Stolidly Mikka Vasaczk stepped forward and picked it up.

Orn spat at her, '*Bitch*!' and flung himself at Nick.

For a moment Orn's attack was so hard and furious that he seemed to have Nick on the defensive. Nick blocked with his fists and elbows, ducked and bobbed to avoid blows. One punch clipped his jaw with enough force to jam his teeth together loudly; another rocked his head back; a third made him stagger. He appeared to be going down—

Two or three people shouted warnings or encouragement – but not to Orn. Vector stood with his arms folded across his chest, shaking his head for his friend.

Morn watched the fight helplessly, so sick with anger that she could hardly stand. She was doomed either way. If Orn won, he would kill her – she was sure of that. Unless she found some way to give him what he wanted without being killed for it. And if Nick won, the whole ship was finished.

A complete wipe.

So why didn't she do something? Why didn't she try to stop the fight? Wasn't it better to risk being raped a few times than to die? She'd saved Angus, hadn't she? Why did she care how many other men who wanted to brutalize her she kept alive?

No, not again; not after Angus.

Let them die, she thought coldly. Let them all die.

Panting in hoarse, raw spasms, Orn drove Nick back against one of the tables. Nick was still on the defensive; he couldn't retreat farther. He blocked hard and fast, misdirecting most of Orn's force; but he didn't land any blows of his own. No matter how well he protected himself, Orn was able to hurt him. One clear, solid hit would break his skull, or his neck—

'Stop playing with him!' Mikka barked suddenly. 'He might get lucky!'

As if that were his cue, Nick lashed out with one foot; the side of his boot struck Orn's shin.

The kick was hardly more than a slap: it was too short for power, had too little weight behind it. Nevertheless it made Orn shift his balance backward.

During that small instant, Nick hit him with three sharp uppercuts to the belly, three blows that had all the strength of his legs and all the torque of his shoulders behind them.

Orn stumbled – and Nick slammed the heel of his palm straight into Orn's throat.

Gagging, Orn fell.

He tried to roll and rise. Nick promptly kicked him once in the stomach, once in the ribs, once in the forehead. The last kick was surgically precise: it lifted him up onto his knees and left him there with his head lolling as if he'd been positioned for execution.

Nick paused to evaluate his handiwork.

Orn couldn't move. He could hardly breathe: he had broken ribs, and his larynx may have been damaged. His eyes were glazed; his mouth hung open, drooling blood. Blood made most of his face look like pulp.

With an air of formality, Mikka Vasaczk stepped away from the wall and handed Nick Orn's knife.

Orn didn't move as Nick Succorso slashed his face, three times under one eye, twice under the other. More blood streamed from his jaw and splashed onto his knees.

'Morn,' he gasped as if he were drowning. 'Morn, please.'

Orn's appeal made Nick turn to look at her.

She came close to saying, Give me the knife. Let me finish him. Her wish to see Orn dead was so intense that it nearly swept all other considerations away. She wanted him dead, wanted to kill him herself. Seeing him beaten now didn't satisfy her; not at all. Instead his help-lessness seemed to stoke a dark fire inside her, feeding her hunger for his blood.

Let me finish him.

But then a strange dislocation of consciousness came to her rescue. She could feel Angus Thermopyle in her, thinking her thoughts, saying what she wanted to say. Give me the knife. Let me finish him.

That stopped her.

As if she were recoiling from a precipice, she panted, 'He told me you can't kill him. You can't afford to.'

Nick's bruises made his face look congested with fury; he might have been planning to hit her himself. Like his eyes, his grin was sharp and murderous.

'He says he planted a virus in the computers,' she explained. 'And he's the only one who can work around it. He put it in the first day he came aboard. You've been at his mercy ever since. If you try to do anything without him, you'll trigger a complete wipe.'

Her words stung everyone around her like a stun-prod. Mikka and

Pup went pale; Vector closed his eyes as if he were ill; men and women Morn didn't know stared horror and dismay at Orn.

Blazing, Nick wheeled back to the data first. As if he didn't understand, he demanded, 'You did *what*?'

With his remaining strength, Orn nodded once. The cuts Nick had given him ran like tears.

'If that happens,' Morn finished, 'we're lost. We'll never arrive any-where. We won't be able to find our way. We'll coast out here until we go mad. Or starve.'

Poised in front of Orn, Nick asked Vector dangerously, 'Is he capable of that?'

The engineer shrugged without opening his eyes. 'Sure.' As always, he spoke mildly. Nevertheless he looked old and bleak, almost haggard despite the roundness of his face. 'From his point of view, it was a reasonable thing to do. Like buying life insurance.'

Abruptly Nick started laughing again – a rough sound with death in it. 'There's no question about it, Orn, you motherfucker. I don't get mad easily, but you have definitely found a way to piss me off.'

'Nick —' Mikka said. She may have been trying to warn him. Or stop him.

He ignored her. Whirling suddenly, he kicked Orn's head so hard that everybody in the mess heard Orn's neck break.

'Nick.' This time Mikka said his name like a moan. But he still ignored her.

Grimly he left the room. As he passed her, he said to Morn as if he held her accountable, 'I hope they taught you something about computers in the Academy.'

Morn hugged herself and tried to believe that she wasn't going to be the next person Nick killed.

CHAPTER 6

In the aftermath of the fight, Morn Hyland felt weary and sore, drained to the bone.

She couldn't seem to take her eyes off Orn's corpse. Like everyone else in the mess, she studied him as if she were praying to see him move, hoping for some sign that he wasn't dead. But he lay with his face in a small puddle of the blood from his smashed nose and the cuts Nick had given him. Everyone had heard his neck snap.

They were all going to die because of him.

Unlike the crew, however, she didn't regret his death. Such men didn't deserve to live, no matter how expensive it was to get rid of them.

And Nick had said, *I hope they taught you something about computers in the Academy.* At last she was going to get access to the ship's systems – which meant that she might learn the answers to some of her questions.

The idea failed to lift her spirits.

How could she help save *Captain's Fancy*? She was no computer wizard. And it wasn't worth the effort. If the ship survived, so would she – and then she would have to go on dealing with men like Orn Vorbuld and Nick Succorso; fighting them off or surrendering to them until her black revulsion cracked its containers and devoured her mind. She should have thought of some way to save herself from Orn. She should have – but she hadn't. It was beyond her.

'All right, boys and girls,' Mikka Vasaczk said harshly, 'the party's over. We've all got work to do. You know what the stakes are, so pay attention.'

Around the mess, people raised their heads. Some of them plainly wanted orders; they wanted to be told what to do, as a defense against their fear. Others were already too scared.

'What work?' The woman who spoke was an artificial blonde with sullen features. 'I don't know how to cure a computer virus. None of us does. We just use the systems, we don't design them. Orn was the only one who could do that.'

Mikka replied with a smile as humorless as the blade of Orn's knife. 'Fine. If you think Nick's beaten, you go tell him. All I want is a chance to watch. He'll make you think Vorbuld got off easy.'

Without warning her voice cracked into a shout like a cry from her dour and unyielding heart.

'*Have any of you EVER seen Nick beaten?*'

Now she had them: every eye in the mess was fixed on her. There were no more protests.

Mikka took a deep breath to steady herself, then repeated, 'We've all got work to do. I want the firsts on the bridge. Mackern, you're promoted to data first.'

Mackern was a pale, nervous man with a nearly invisible mustache. His only apparent reaction to his promotion was a desire to disappear into the bulkheads.

'That makes you second, Parmute,' Vasaczk continued to the artificial blonde.

'The rest of you, get back to the overhaul. Shut it down – secure everything. I want us tight and ready for maneuvers in an hour. Anybody who isn't done by then can trade jobs with Pup.'

The boy they called Pup met her threat with a flash of hope. For him, any trade would be an improvement.

'Do it now,' Mikka finished grimly. 'The timer is running.'

Still looking ashen and old, Vector Shaheed pushed his swollen joints away from the wall. At once the whole crew started to move as if he'd broken them out of a stasis-field.

In ten seconds Morn and Mikka were alone with Orn Vorbuld's body.

With an air of grim restraint, Mikka turned to Morn. Her eyes held a fierce gleam, fanatical and deadly. 'This is your fault,' she rasped. 'Don't think I'm going to forget that. Don't ever think I'm going to forget.'

Morn held Mikka's glare without flinching. Everything was beyond her; for the moment, she didn't care whether she survived.

'Goddamn it,' Mikka chewed out, 'what do you use for brains? Do you do all your thinking with your crotch? Any imbecile could have told you not to tackle Orn alone. Hell, *Pup* could have told you. You should have talked to Nick before things got this bad. If you'd warned him in time, we might have been able to avoid this mess.'

Morn shrugged. She had no reason to justify herself to Nick's second. And yet she found that she couldn't refuse. The nature of Mikka's anger touched her. She could imagine her mother being angry in just that way, if someone had threatened Morn.

Stiffly she asked, 'How many times have you been raped?'

Mikka dismissed the question with an ungiving scowl. 'We aren't talking about rape. We're talking about *brains*.'

Morn wasn't deflected. 'After a while,' she said, 'you hurt so bad that you don't want to be rescued anymore. You want to *eviscerate* that sonofabitch for yourself. Eventually you don't even care that you haven't got a prayer. You need to try.

'If you don't try, you end up killing yourself because you're too ashamed to live.'

Nick's second opened her mouth to retort, then closed it again. For a moment she continued to frown as if nothing could reach her. When she spoke, however, her tone had softened.

'Go to sickbay. Don't come to the bridge until you've done something about those bruises.' Unexpectedly she dropped her gaze. 'If you feel better, you'll think better. Maybe you can think of some way to limit the damage.'

Turning on her heel, Mikka left the mess.

Limit the damage.

Morn remained with Orn for a minute or two. She wanted to see if it was possible to feel any grief or regret for him.

No. For him her only regret was that she hadn't been able to beat him herself.

Think better.

Because she saw no danger in it, she obeyed Mikka. After all, she was alone. Under the circumstances, no one was likely to intrude on her. She could easily erase the results of her examination from the sickbay log before she went to the bridge. And she needed the stim sickbay would probably give her: she needed artificial help to counteract her accumulating despair. Since she still didn't feel reckless enough to carry her zone-implant control with her, she would have to rely on stim.

Dully she went to sickbay and stretched out on the table to let the cybernetic systems supply whatever treatment they decided she required.

She got stim, as well as an analgesic which softened her hurts. In addition, one of the drugs stilled the nausea which had become a constant part of her life, so familiar that she was hardly aware of it. Distracted by that simple relief, she almost forgot to take the elementary precaution of checking the results of the examination before expunging them.

At the last moment, however, she remembered.

What she learned hit her as hard as Orn; revolted her as much as Nick; threatened her as acutely as Angus.

The records informed her that she was pregnant.

Her child was a boy.

The computer told her exactly how old he was.

Too old to be any son of Nick Succorso's.

In her womb like a malignancy, dark and inoperable, she bore the child of Angus Thermopyle.

Well, she thought on a rising note of hysteria, that explained the nausea.

It was insane. What was she doing pregnant? Most spacefaring women made sure they were infertile, whether they wanted children or not. Life in space was too fragile: any risk to themselves was a risk to the entire ship. In any case, no ship – except, perhaps, the most luxurious passenger liners – had the facilities for rearing infants. Most women found the whole prospect too horrible to contemplate. If they wanted children, they had them on Station.

But for Morn the problem was infinitely worse. Like *Captain's Fancy*, her baby was doomed. The end would almost certainly not be quick, however: it would be protracted and appalling. Once the computers wiped, the ship would lose astrogation, navigation. The vessel itself might coast the black void until the end of time – a sailing coffin because everyone aboard had died of thirst or hunger. But that wouldn't happen for many long months. In the meantime Morn's plight would deteriorate steadily.

As her pregnancy progressed, she would become less attractive to Nick – less worth preserving. She would become physically more vulnerable. And the closer Nick and his people came to death, the more they would blame her for it. In all likelihood, she and her baby would be the first to die.

And this was Angus' son, Angus Thermopyle's child. The fetus was already as brutal as his father, damaging her survival in the same way that Angus had damaged her spirit.

How could she be pregnant? What had happened to the long-term birth control injections she'd accepted routinely back in the Academy? They were supposed to be good for up to a year, and she'd had her last one only – only—

Only a year ago.

Without warning she began to weep.

Oh, shit!

She'd forgotten all about getting another injection. Her periods had never been particularly difficult. And from the Academy she'd been assigned to *Starmaster*, her father's command, a ship on which most of the people she'd lived and worked with were family. She hadn't wanted sex with anybody aboard. Engrossed in the excitements and responsibilities of her first post, she hadn't given much thought to sex at all.

An immediate abortion was the only sane solution. The sickbay systems could do it in a matter of minutes.

But she couldn't force her hands to key in the necessary commands. She couldn't force herself to lie back down on the surgical table.

As suddenly as it flared up, her weeping subsided.

Instead of fear or dismay or outrage, she was filled with a strange numbness – a loss of sensation as inexorable as the effects of her zone-implant. She was in shock. Orn's attack; the fight; the danger to *Captain's Fancy*: her emotional resources were exhausted. The decision to have an abortion was beyond her.

Fortunately it could be postponed. Nothing had to be decided right this minute. The sickbay could rid her of the fetus whenever she wanted.

Angus' son.

Numb or not, she was too ashamed – and too afraid – of what she carried to risk letting anyone else find out about it. However, Angus had taught her more than she realized. She didn't expunge the sickbay log. That was too risky: it might attract suspicion. Instead she edited the records so that whoever chanced to check them would see she'd come here as ordered, but wouldn't find any evidence of her zone-implant, or her baby.

Like Angus, Nick had disconnected his sickbay from *Captain's Fancy's* datacore. The sickbay log had no copies. Soon nothing incriminating remained to threaten her.

Temporarily safe, she left sickbay.

Maybe she should have gone by her cabin to pick up her black box. Nick would expect her to help tackle the problem of Orn's virus, and she was too numb to think: she needed help. But she needed her numbness as well. If she used the zone-implant to sharpen her brain, she would have to face the dilemma of her pregnancy.

Cradling the sense of shock as if it were an infant in her womb, she went to the bridge.

Nick was there, sitting in his command seat, drumming his fingers on his board while he waited for his people to check their systems. When Morn crossed the aperture to stand beside him, he gave her a quick, fierce grin like a promise that he didn't regret killing Orn for her; that he was too excited by the challenge of saving his ship to fear failure. For once, his scars throbbed with a lust which had nothing to do with her. Instead of marring him, his bruises seemed to accentuate his vitality.

Then he shifted his attention back to his crew.

Morn looked at the display screens for information. But they were blank, probably because the ship's speed made them effectively useless. So she scanned the bridge.

Only the engineering Station was vacant: Vector and his second were probably in the console room. All the other firsts were at their posts.

'Status,' Nick commanded in a tone of veiled eagerness, as if he were having a wonderful time.

His mood ruled the bridge. The dread Morn had observed in the mess had no place here. Even Mackern, occupying Orn Vorbuld's seat for the first time, worked his board with a degree of concentration which approximated confidence.

Almost immediately Carmel answered. 'Scan checks out fine. At this velocity, we might as well be blind ahead. We're outrunning our effective scan time. And the starfield is dopplering noticeably. But the computer compensates for that. We can fix our position well enough.'

'Communications the same,' reported Lind. 'There's nothing out there to hear except particle noise' – the residual crackle and spatter of deep space – 'but if there was, we could pick it up.'

'Targeting and weapons the same,' put in a woman named Malda

Verone. She sounded vaguely disinterested; under the circumstances her systems were the least vital ones aboard.

Nick nodded and waited.

Hunching over his board, Mackern said, 'I'm running diagnostics. We've got all the usual debug programs.' He pulled at his mustache while he worked. 'So far, they don't show anything.'

Nick shook his head. 'Orn knew what our resources are. He wouldn't leave us a virus we could cure that easy.'

As if in confirmation, Mackern scowled at his readouts, then sat up straight. 'Done. Diagnostics say we're in good shape.'

Carmel snorted scornfully. No one else bothered to comment.

After a moment a man with a husky voice and no chin said a bit apprehensively, 'Sorry for the delay. I wanted to dummy helm to the auxiliary bridge before I ran any tests. That way, if anything shuts down on me, we can hold our course correction. We won't drift.'

Casually Nick replied, 'Good.'

'Helm checks out,' the man continued. 'We're green on all systems. Except the gap drive, of course.'

Nick nodded again. Morn glanced at his board and saw that all the command status indicators were green as well.

Orn's virus was still dormant.

Grinning more sharply, Nick swung his seat around to face Morn. 'Any suggestions?'

She was supposed to help save the ship; she knew that. But she was profoundly numb, almost unreactive, as if beneath the surface her priorities were undergoing their own course correction. For the time being, she had no real attention to spare for *Captain's Fancy*'s problems.

'In the Academy,' she said from a distance, responding only so that Nick wouldn't probe her, 'they taught me to do two things for a computer virus. Isolate the systems – unplug them from each other so the virus can't spread. And call Maintenance.'

Nick chuckled sardonically. 'Good idea.' To all appearances, he didn't actually want her help. He was at his best here, matching his wits and his ship against his enemies. What he wanted was an audience, not advice. Over his shoulder, he asked, 'You got that, Lind?'

'They don't answer,' Lind retorted with a sneer. 'Must be on their lunch break.'

Gratified, Nick spread his hands and swung back toward the bridge screens.

'You heard the lady. Isolate the systems.'

Around the bridge, his people hurried to obey.

Left alone, Morn made a vague effort to think about the situation. At a guess, *Captain's Fancy* had seven main computers protected deep in her core: one to run the ship herself (lifts, air processing, internal g, waste disposal, intercoms, heat, water, things like that); five for each of the bridge functions (scan, targ and weapons, communications, helm, and data and damage control); and one, the command unit, to synergize the others. That design was inherently safer than trusting to one megaCPU – and in any case few ships had any need for the raw computing power a megaCPU could provide. So the immediate problem was to determine where Orn's virus resided. Without risking the spread of the infection.

Of course, he could have planted his virus in more than one computer. Or in all of them.

If she hadn't felt so far away, she might have been dismayed at the sheer scale of the problem. No one aboard knew how to cure a virus once it was located. If they had to track it through all seven systems—

Nick ran a few commands on his board, presumably to set the maintenance computer on automatic. Then, unexpectedly, he turned to Morn again. As they swelled, his bruises seemed to sharpen the focus of his eyes.

As if he were resuming a conversation which had been interrupted just moments ago, he remarked, 'There's only one problem with your theory that I'm a UMCPDA operative.'

That remark cut through her numbness. All at once, the protection wrapped around her womb was gone; she felt like she'd been kicked in the belly. Why bring *that* up? Why bring it up *now*? What was going on here? What had she missed?

What new danger was she in?

What, she thought before she realized it, would happen to her baby?

Grinning at her incomprehension, he said, 'I'm out of money,' as if that explained everything.

Lind, Carmel, and the helm first all laughed, not in disbelief, but in recognition of a difficulty so constant that it had become a joke.

Morn stared at Nick and tried to recover her numbness; tried to conceal herself behind veils of shock.

He enjoyed her stunned expression for a moment. Then he relented.

'Where we're going, they don't do work on spec. The fucker who runs the place calls himself "the Bill" because he gets paid before anything else happens. And I'm broke. *Captain's Fancy* is broke. We can pay the docking fee, that's all. We can't afford to get the gap drive repaired. And we sure as hell can't afford to get a virus flushed out of our computers. Assuming we're able to get there at all – which at the moment looks problematical.

'As long as we don't lose thrust, life support, and scan, we've got a chance. For one thing, I can do algorithms in my head. That makes me a pretty fair blind reckoning navigator. And for another, there are ships patrolling to make sure people like us don't miss our destination.' This, too, was a joke which the bridge crew understood, but which was lost on Morn. 'But none of that is going to do us any good without credits.'

'I still don't see —' Morn murmured dimly. 'What does this have to do with me?'

'If I'm some insidious UMCPDA operative,' Nick said with a flourish, 'what the fuck am I doing in this mess? Why haven't I got money? Why is the almighty Hashi Lebwohl willing to risk losing me like this, when all he had to do was have us met off Com-Mine by a courier drone programmed to tight-beam credits?

'There's something you may not understand about me, Morn.' His grin was full of relish – and other obscure perils. 'I won't work for a man who doesn't *pay*.'

This time, everyone on the bridge chuckled appreciatively.

Yet Morn continued to flounder. 'I don't get it.' She'd lost her defenses. Angus' child seemed to use up her mind: she couldn't understand any other danger unless it was spelled out for her. 'What's the point? Why are we doing this, if we can't afford repairs in any case?'

Nick looked positively delighted – as happy as he did when he was having sex with her, driving her to transports she couldn't resist. 'I'm out of money,' he repeated. 'But I've got something I can sell.'

She held her breath, afraid to guess what was coming.

'I can sell you.'

There it was at last, the truth; the reason he'd taken her, the reason he kept her. To buy the kind of repairs he couldn't get anywhere legally.

'You're UMCP,' he added unnecessarily. 'You've got a head full of valuable data. As long as you're alive and conscious and at least marginally sane, you're probably valuable enough to buy me a whole new ship.'

Just a few hours ago, she might have lashed out at him. He was planning to sell her like a piece of cargo. Everything she'd forced herself to endure in order to procure safety had been wasted. Driven by accumulating revulsion and stifled rage, she might not have been able to contain herself.

After a while, she'd told Mikka, *you hurt so bad that you don't want to be rescued anymore.*

But the knowledge that she was pregnant changed her. A baby. Angus' son. Her father's grandson. And in the whole of vast space she had no other family: she'd killed them all.

She would kill this infant, too, as soon as she got the chance. He was malignant inside her, male and murderous: she would flush him down the sickbay disposal and be damned for it. Why should she give him any better treatment than she'd given her father – or than his father had given her?

In the meantime, however, the baby was hers; he was all she had left. If she didn't defend him, he was going to die. Or he would be used against her. Either way, his life or death would be out of her hands. But he was *hers:* whether he lived or died was *hers* to decide. If she gave that up – if she surrendered her right to make this one choice for herself – she might as well lie down and die.

Caught by surprise and unexpectedly vulnerable, she gave her child the only protection she had available. For the second time, but deliberately now, she let herself burst into tears.

It was easier than she would have believed possible.

She heard more laughter, but she ignored it. She didn't care how many people sneered at her. All she cared about was Nick's reaction.

He ignored the laughter as well. His mouth went on smiling crookedly, but his gaze lost its relish. Suddenly his eyes looked haunted and lost, as if he, too, were helpless in a way that unnerved him.

'I didn't mean you.' He was barely able to keep his voice steady. 'I meant your information. Your id tag. All those access and security codes. That's what I need to sell – that's my price for saving your life.'

Abruptly he was angry, almost shouting. 'I don't work for Hashi Lebwohl or any other fucking cop, and neither do you. Not anymore. You're *mine* – and, by hell! you're going to prove it by giving me something I can sell.'

Then his tone softened again. 'So I can get my ship fixed.'

In an effort to stop crying, Morn raised a hand to her mouth and bit her knuckle. Crying made her ugly; she knew that. And she couldn't afford to be ugly in front of Nick Succorso. Not now; maybe not ever. But her whole heart was full of tears.

She was pregnant. Carrying a baby.

For a moment her grief was so intense that she couldn't fight it down.

Then, however, she tasted blood on her tongue. Swallowing a sob, she regained her self-control.

'Just get us there,' she said in a gulp. 'I'll do my part.'

That promise was the most sincere response she'd ever given Nick.

As if he couldn't face her expression, he swung away. His fists closed and unclosed in his lap, working for calm.

As soon as he could produce his familiar nonchalance, he scanned the bridge and commented, 'The next time you spaceshits feel like laughing at her, try to remember you're laughing at me, too.'

Lind flinched visibly. The woman at the targ board, Malda Verone, ducked her head, hiding her face behind her hair.

Poised and dangerous, Nick held his people until they were all still, almost frozen. Then he moved. Keying his intercom, he said, 'Mikka, I want you. If you can spare the time.'

The intercom didn't work. He'd already disengaged the controls.

That small mistake seemed to restore his equilibrium. The grin came back into his eyes. 'Morn, stop snuffling,' he ordered casually. 'You're ruining my concentration.'

When he chuckled, some of the tension around him dissipated.

Morn felt him watching her with his peripheral vision, but she didn't look at him.

A minute later Mikka Vasaczk came onto the bridge of her own accord. Clipped to her belt, she wore a handcom, as well as a coiled lifeline with a small magnetic clamp on one end – emergency equipment in case internal g failed.

Scowling impartially, she paused beside Morn. At the sight of Morn's swollen eyes and damp face, she asked in a neutral tone, 'Feeling better?'

Morn rubbed the blood off her mouth and nodded.

'It shows,' Mikka remarked.

Then she dismissed the question of Morn's condition and went to stand on the other side of Nick's seat.

'We're ready,' she reported. 'The rest of the seconds are down in the core with the computers. They've all got handcoms. They aren't wizards, but they can do resets. If you want, they can unplug everything, isolate the systems physically.'

Nick accepted the information with a nod. Leaning forward, he said to the bridge, 'All right, let's get started. The sooner we locate our virus, the more time we'll have to work on it.

'We aren't going to lose function. All the equipment is hardwired.' Everybody aboard already knew this: he was speaking to clarify his own thoughts. 'The worst that can happen is that we'll have to reset everything. But if we get wiped, we'll lose anything soft. Including all our data. That means we'll lose the last of our credits.' He grinned fiercely. 'Maintenance will work, but the system won't know how many of us there are. It won't be able to balance out heat and air comfortably. We'll lose our logs. We won't know how much food we've got left.

'Targ will lose ship id,' he continued. 'That's not minor. We won't be able to program weapons accurately if we're attacked. Communications will lose all our codes. Which will make it hard for us to talk to anybody. But scan and data are the most vulnerable. Scan will still bring in information, but the computers won't be able to interpret it. And we'll lose everything we need for astrogation – star id, charts, galactic rotation, Station vectors, shipping lanes. Hell, we won't even be able to tell where forbidden space is.'

Nick's second snorted harshly. The other crewmembers kept their reactions to themselves.

'We can't hardcopy the data. We haven't got that much paper. They probably don't have that much paper back on Com-Mine. And we would need months to reenter everything – which might not solve our problem anyway. If the virus is still resident, it would just rewipe the data as soon as we restored it.

'So here's what we're going to do. I'll run some commands. If my board goes down by itself, it's an easy fix. We can dummy it back from the auxiliary bridge. In fact, we might be able to erase the virus that way.

'If my board stays up, we'll reconnect the other systems one at a time and try them until we hit trouble.

'Questions?' he asked. 'Comments? Objections?'

Scan and helm shook their heads. Everybody else sat and waited.

Morn's mouth had gone dry, and she seemed to have difficulty breathing, as if life support were already out of balance. Any spacefaring vessel was computer-dependent. Her visceral dread of *a complete wipe* was even greater than her fear of puncture or detonation, her fear of vacuum. On that point, she knew, everybody aboard agreed with her.

But she didn't expect the command board to crash. As Nick had said, that might be an easy fix – and she felt sure Orn hadn't left *Captain's Fancy* anything easy. No, the virus probably resided in the data computer itself, where it could do the most damage; the computer to which Orn had had the most regular access.

So she wasn't surprised when Nick's board stayed up and green. In simulation, he reversed thrust, slammed *Captain's Fancy* to the side, opened hailing channels, shut down internal g, fired matter cannon, ran spectrographic analyses of nearby stars: everything worked.

'That damn motherfucker,' he swore amiably. 'Why did he have to turn out to be such an insidious bastard?' But he wasn't discouraged. 'All right. Helm is relatively secure at the moment. We'll leave it alone. I'm going to take maintenance off automatic.' His eyes glinted with combative amusement. 'Let's see how they like it when I turn off the heat in the core.'

Malda giggled nervously.

'They won't notice any difference for a while,' Mackern said. 'The whole ship insulates them.'

Carmel rolled her eyes. In exasperation, Mikka retorted, 'That's why it's a safe experiment.'

'Mackern,' Nick drawled, 'you have no sense of humor.' He was already at work, keying the functions of his board, running programs to bring the internal systems back under his control. In a minute or two he was ready.

Morn couldn't taste any improvement in the air. It still felt tight in her lungs, congested with CO_2. Not for the first time, she thought about the black box back in her cabin. It could help her tone down her anxiety.

Anxiety wasn't good for babies—

'Belts,' Nick said crisply.

His people checked their belts. Mirroring each other unconsciously, Morn and Mikka gripped the arms of Nick's g-seat.

He glanced around the bridge. Then he announced, 'Core heat off,' and tapped a couple of his buttons.

The faint click of the keys was clearly audible.

With a distant groan of servos, *Captain's Fancy* lost internal spin.

At the same instant every spacefarer's worst nightmare came true.

All power to the bridge failed.

Readouts, boards, illumination: everything went black. The whole ship plunged into a darkness as deep as the blind gap between the stars.

Mute in the void of her own mind, Morn wailed as if *Starmaster* had just gone down again; as if she'd killed her ship again, and everyone she loved.

Intertech, a strong research and exploration company based on Outreach Station orbiting Earth, was both the precipitating cause and the primary victim of one of the definitive events in humankind's history: the Humanity Riots.

In one sense, Intertech's two functions – research and exploration – were an odd combination: in another, they fit naturally. Of course, the company was originally chartered for pure research. However, its use of the conditions and technologies available in space was highly successful. Focusing on matters of biology and genetics, the company first established itself by developing a germ which fed on plastics, effectively reducing a wide range of polymers to compost. This proved a lucrative contribution to waste- and pollution-management on Earth. Later research provided a variety of medicines, including one with benefits for people suffering from a well-publicized form of smog-linked leukemia. Another project developed rejuvenation and longevity drugs. Intertech's most profitable discovery, however, was the catecholamine inhibitor – popularly considered a 'cataleptic,' therefore called 'cat' – which soon replaced most tranquilizers, l-tryptophan derivatives, sedatives, and lithium compounds in the treatment of stress disorders, insomnia, adrenaline poisoning, and depression.

Cat alone brought in enough money to enable Intertech to expand its function into exploration.

The relevance of exploration to research was unpredictable, but clear. Thanks to the development of the gap drive, vast numbers of star systems were now within reach, each evolved out of its own particular nuclear soup, each with its own special isotopes and chemicals and materials, each composed of new resources and opportunities. In fact, one of

Intertech's first probe ships, *High Hope*, brought back a new radioactive isotope (subsequently named Harbingium for the nuclear chemist aboard *High Hope* who first identified it, Malcolm Harbinger) which proved astonishingly useful in recombinant DNA: Harbingium's emissions were so specific to the polymerase which bound nucleotides together in RNA that they made possible genetic research which had until then remained stubbornly theoretical.

Intertech's stock – like Intertech itself – was booming. Until the onset of the Humanity Riots.

The Humanity Riots themselves were an interesting demonstration of genophobia. That humankind distrusted anything different than itself had always been common knowledge. As a species – as a biological product of its own planet – humankind apparently considered itself sacred.

In this, Earth's dominant religions were only more vocal than other groups. No other fundamental distinction prevailed. Life had evolved on Earth as it was supposed to evolve: the forms of life provided by this developmental process were right and good; any alteration was morally repugnant and personally offensive. On this point, conservationists and environmentalists and animal rights activists were at one with Moslems and Hindus and Christians. Prosthetic surgery in all its guises, to correct physical problems or limitations, was acceptable: genetic alteration to solve the same problems was not.

As one crude example, humankind had no objection to soldiers with laser-cutters built into their fingers or infrared scanners embedded in their skulls. On the other hand, humankind objected strenuously to soldiers genetically engineered for faster reflexes, greater strength, or improved loyalty. After all, infrared scanners and laser-cutters were mere artifacts, tools; but faster reflexes, greater strength, and improved loyalty were crimes against nature.

For this reason, genetic research was routinely conducted in secret: in part to cloak it from commercial espionage; but primarily to protect the researchers from public vilification.

However, humankind's reaction went far beyond public vilification when Intertech's 'crime against nature' became known. That crime precipitated the Humanity Riots.

This happened because the Intertech probe ship *Far Rover* brought humankind its first knowledge of the Amnion.

The knowledge itself was contained in a cryogenic vessel, in a mutagenic material which – so the theorists finally decided – represented an Amnion effort to establish contact. At the time, it was considered fortuitous that the vessel had been discovered by an Intertech ship. After all, Intertech was uniquely qualified at the time to unlock the code of the mutagen, learn its meaning. Eventually, however, the discovery proved disastrous.

By definition, the material sent out by the Amnion was mutagenic. That meant its code could only be broken by geneticists. But it also meant that the code was contained in the mutagen's ability to produce change, to effect fundamental genetic alterations – alterations so profound that they restructured nucleotides, rebuilt RNA, transformed DNA; so profound, in fact, that any Earth-born life-form became essentially Amnioni.

Unfortunately – from Intertech's point of view – contact with alien life could hardly be kept secret. The company was forced to study the mutagen under intense scrutiny. And that study naturally involved applying the mutagen to rats, monkeys, dogs, and other test animals, all of which quickly grew to be as alien as the mutagen itself. This generated genophobia of seismic proportions. Humankind was already in a state of bedrock outrage when the decision was made within Intertech to test the mutagen on a human being.

When the results of that experiment became known – when the woman who volunteered for the job was transformed like the animals and died horribly in a state of spiritual shock – the Humanity Riots began.

Death to genetics and geneticists.

Death to Intertech.

Death to anything which threatened pure, sacrosanct, Earth-born life.

By the time the riots ended, Intertech was a corporate wreck.

Yet the company's problems remained. The Amnion still existed. The need to understand the mutagen still existed. By default, Intertech had become a crucial player in a galactic drama – the contest between humankind and the Amnion. Without capital or credit, the company was expected to deal with the challenge *Far Rover* had brought to Earth.

Under the circumstances, Intertech had no choice but to seek acquisition by some more viable corporate entity. Reluctantly, a bid was accepted from Space Mines, Inc. (later the United Mining Companies).

Aside from the necessary cash, the only obvious price SMI had to pay was an amendment to its charter, requiring SMI as a whole to forswear genetic engineering and to protect humankind from genetic corruption by the Amnion.

If Intertech had been able to preserve its integrity, much of the history of human space might have been different.

ANGUS

When the order came to have Angus Thermopyle frozen, it arrived by gap courier drone straight from UMCPHQ, tight-beamed to Com-Mine Station Security as soon as the drone resumed tard.

The order was signed by Hashi Lebwohl, Director, Data Acquisition, United Mining Companies Police.

Angus had suddenly become a very special prisoner.

Even Milos Taverner could only speculate why that had happened after all this time. Any number of people discussed the subject with him: his Chief; most of his fellow officers in Security; several members of Station Center; two or three people who, like his Chief, sat on Station Council.

They all asked the same questions.

Did you know this was coming?

No, Milos hadn't known this was coming. He could say that honestly. During the months since Angus' arrest and conviction, UMCPHQ had paid only the most routine attention to his case. Copies of his files had been reqqed: that was all. Even the information that a UMC Police Ensign, Morn Hyland, had arrived with Angus and left with Nick Succorso had prompted no particular response – not even from Min Donner, who had a reputation for almost fanatical loyalty to her people in Enforcement Division. No action had been taken on Morn Hyland's accusation that the UMCP destroyer *Starmaster* had been sabotaged by Com-Mine Station. Security's requests for instructions concerning Ensign Hyland had been ignored.

Well, then, what makes him so special?

Milos had no new answer. Angus Thermopyle was exactly what he'd always been. He was valuable for his purported knowledge of piracy and smuggling, of bootleg shipyards, of merchants who could handle stolen ore and supplies in vast bulk, even of forbidden space. He was no more and no less special than ever.

So what *did* change? Is this what UMCPHQ wanted all along? Were they just waiting for the authority?

That's my best guess, the Deputy Chief replied candidly. Unquestionably it was a change that the authority for such a demand now existed. The recent passage of the Preempt Act had granted jurisdiction over all human space, including the separate Security entities of each individual Station or company, to the United Mining Companies Police. Prior to the act, Com-Mine Security had been required to supply the UMCP with nothing except cooperation. Now Hashi Lebwohl – or any UMCP Director – could demand the cryogenic encapsulation of as many convicts as he liked.

Unfortunately the passage of the Preempt Act shed no light on the reasons for UMCPHQ's interest in this individual convict.

All right. So they must have wanted him all along. They just didn't have the authority to take him. Why do we have to *freeze* him? Why go to all the expense of cryogenic encapsulation? Why can't we just armcuff him and turn him over to the next ship that happens to be heading for Earth?

Those questions made Milos' stomach hurt: they came too close to things he shouldn't have known. He rubbed his scalp helplessly and reached for his packet of nic.

To preserve him? he ventured.

What for? Who in hell would want to preserve the likes of Angus Thermopyle?

Milos had no safe answer. He tried again.

To transport him?

Why bother? With an armcuff and a few precautions, he could be carted like cargo anywhere in human space. That would be as safe as some damn freezer.

Most of the men and women Milos had conversations with concentrated on that issue. Com-Mine Station's Chief of Security simply had more right to demand an explanation.

'Why? Why *freeze* him?'

Because he felt he had no choice, Milos risked a degree of honesty.

Squirming inside, he replied, 'To silence him? Keep him from talking to us? UMCPHQ is delighted we haven't been able to break him. They don't trust us. They don't want us to know the things he might tell us.'

To Milos' relief, his superior had come to essentially the same conclusion. Fuming, the Chief said, 'By hell, I won't have it. That bastard has been making life miserable around here ever since I can remember. He's committed so many crimes, and gotten away with them so completely, it makes me sick. If anybody takes him apart, it's going to be us.'

That wasn't exactly what Milos wanted to hear. He wanted to be rid of Angus, and the sooner the better. Stifling a twinge of nausea, he asked, 'What will you do?'

'Talk to Center,' said the Chief. His personality was as harsh and simple as his loyalties. 'Talk to Council. They'll back me up – at least for a while. They don't like this kind of treatment any more than I do.

'That damn Preempt Act is new. We can pretend we don't understand it. We can claim we don't know the right procedures. We can even demand confirmation. UMCPHQ might not let us get away with it for long, but we can buy a little time.

'Goddamn it, Milos, *break* that bastard.'

'I'll try,' Milos promised, groaning inside.

He relayed this decision to people who were interested in it. Then he and his subordinates redoubled their efforts to crack Angus' silence.

Of course, no one mentioned any of this to Angus himself. He experienced a sudden upsurge in beatings of all kinds; in the use of drugs which reduced his skull to a hive of skinworms; in the application of sleep deprivation and sensory distortion. But he was given no explanations. He was left to draw whatever conclusions he could from the change in his treatment.

Nevertheless through abuse and deprivation, damage and pain – and despite his visceral horror of incarceration – he persisted in his intransigence by the simple heroism of cowardice. He believed that as soon as his tormentors got what they wanted from him they would kill him. Therefore the only way he could keep himself alive was by keeping his mouth shut.

And he'd made a pact with Morn Hyland. It was tacit, but he stood by it. She hadn't betrayed him. Instead she'd escaped Com-Mine with Nick.

He knew this because no one had accused him of imposing a zone-implant on her. And no one had accused him of the crime which had caused the Hyland ship, *Starmaster*, to go after him in the first place. If she'd remained on Station, he would be dead by now – and not necessarily because she testified against him. The simplest routine physical would have revealed the presence of the implant. Therefore he knew she'd kept her part of the bargain. So he didn't betray her.

In this stubborn refusal to speak, he had certain advantages which no one could take away from him.

One of them was the life he'd lived, the long years which had taught him more than even his roughest guards would ever know about the uses of brutality. The beatings which stressed his bones and the stun which made him puke were, for the most part, no worse than the abuse he'd received throughout his childhood and adolescence, or during extended periods of time since then. Indeed, his present mistreatment was no worse than some of the things he'd done to himself, in order to stay alive when the odds were large against him. The years may have weakened his body, but they hadn't diminished his understanding of pain – or his dedication to survival.

Man for man, he was tougher than anybody who hurt him. And he was accustomed to being ganged up on. He was at his best when he was most afraid. His dread of his own helplessness made him almost superhuman.

Another of his advantages was that he knew how to make his interrogator break into a sweat. The same degraded and costly intelligence which grasped what the sudden increase in his tortures meant – Com-Mine Security had run into an unexpected time limit, and if they didn't break him soon they would lose their chance – also guessed a great deal about Milos Taverner's role in this protracted questioning.

The primary charge against Angus was a fabrication. Prior to his arrest, he'd learned that Nick Succorso had dealings with Security. And of course Nick couldn't have used Station supplies to frame him without Station connivance – without the help of a double agent in Security. Taverner's behavior during the months of interrogation made Angus sure he knew who the double agent was. He had a coward's intuitive hearing: he could tell when the man asking him questions didn't really want answers.

So he clung to his silence, despite the new ferocity of his treatment, and waited for the Deputy Chief to run out of time.

The pose he took in the meantime was that of a beaten man ready for death. His guards naturally distrusted this pose; and they had reason. But he didn't care. Now all he cared about was conserving his strength until something shifted.

Earlier he'd used the pose for other reasons.

At first, immediately after his arrest – during the preliminary interrogations, as well as his trial and conviction – he'd had no need for a pose. Ordinary truculence had sufficed to defeat every challenge, every demand. If he felt anything beyond his normal black hate, it was relief. He'd managed to avoid a sentence of execution. And hidden inside his relief was a helpless, visceral gratitude toward Morn Hyland for keeping her part of the bargain.

But that was before they'd told him *Bright Beauty* would be dismantled for spare parts. When he'd heard that his ship, *his ship*, would be destroyed, that it would cease to exist, the logic of his emotions was altered. Anything resembling relief or gratitude vanished in a hot seethe of horror and outrage; a distress so intense that he howled like an animal and went berserk until he was sedated.

After he recovered from the initial shock, he adopted the pose that he'd lost the will to live.

He continued to glare unremitting malice at Taverner during their sessions together: he didn't want to let his questioner off the hook. When he was alone, however, he became listless, unresponsive. From time to time he neglected his food. Sitting slumped on his bunk, he stared at the strict, almost colorless walls of his cell, at the floor, at the ceiling – they were indistinguishable from each other. Occasionally he stared at the lighting as if he hoped it would make him blind. He didn't so much as flinch when the guards came after him with stun. They had to manhandle him into the san to keep him clean.

They were suspicious of him. That was inevitable. But they were also human – susceptible to boredom. And he had a coward's patience, a coward's stubborn will to endure. Despite the incessant, acid seethe of his emotions, he could wait when he had to. On this occasion, he waited for a month without showing anything except doomed resignation to anyone except Milos Taverner.

Finally the idea that he was slowly dying took hold. By degrees, his guards became careless around him.

At last he took his chance.

In the small hours of Station night – although how he knew that it was night was a mystery, since the lighting in his cell never varied – he tore a strip off his sheet and tied it around his neck so tightly that his eyes bulged and he could scarcely breathe. Then he collapsed on the bunk.

He was monitored, of course; but the guard who came to check on him was in no hurry. Suicide by self-strangulation was difficult, if not impossible. Only Angus' general weakness gave him any chance of success.

He was retching with anoxia and practically insane when the door opened and a guard came in to untie him.

Lulled by weeks of boredom, the guard left the cell open.

He had a handgun holstered on his hip, a stun-prod in his fist. Such things didn't deter Angus. He took the stun-prod and blazed the guard in the face with it. By the time the observers at the monitor realized what was happening, he'd freed his neck, helped himself to the handgun, and jumped through the doorway.

The gun was an impact pistol, a relatively low-powered weapon primarily intended to shoot down prisoners at close range; but it sufficed to deal with the only people Angus encountered in the corridors outside his cell, a patrolling guard and a minor functionary, probably a data clerk. He was still monitored, of course. However, Security knew he couldn't escape. He had nowhere to go – they thought. So they were quicker to check on the people he'd stunned and shot than to give chase.

As a result, he almost reached his goal. He came *that* close—

For months while he stared at the walls and ceiling and floor as if he were dying, he'd been busy studying Com-Mine in his mind, collating what he knew about the Station's infrastructure with what he'd observed about the layout of the Security section. With an accuracy that made him seem almost prescient, he'd deduced the general location of the nearest service shaft which led to the waste processing plant.

If he could get down into that shaft, he had a chance. By its very nature, the plant itself was a labyrinth of shafts and pipes, crawlways and equipment. He might be able to elude pursuit for days – or kill anybody who came after him. In fact, the only sure way to deal with him would be to gas the entire plant; and something like that would take days to set up. Which would leave him time to do the Station itself as much damage as he wished. It might even leave him time to escape into DelSec or the docks. And from there he could hope to stow away on some departing ship.

If he could just get down into the service shaft—

The guards caught him while he was trying to force the shaft cover.

They shot at him: he returned fire. For a moment he achieved a standoff.

Unfortunately one of their shots hit the shaft cover and bent it, jammed it. Without an avenue of escape, he was lost. When his gun ran out of charge, he was recaptured.

Predictably enough, the abuse he received became much worse after that. He'd humiliated his guards, and they required him to pay for it. And his pain was made all the more excruciating by the knowledge that he would never get another chance. Even terminally bored guards wouldn't fall for the same ruse twice.

On the other hand, his first session with the Deputy Chief after his escape confirmed his suspicions about Milos Taverner. The fact that he wasn't prosecuted for killing one of his guards demonstrated that he still had a lever he could use. If he needed to, he could trade Taverner for his life.

Despite everything Com-Mine Security had done to him, he still wasn't broken.

Eventually the beatings and deprivation and drugs eased back to their former levels. When they increased again later, he knew how to interpret the change. So he resumed his listlessness, his pose of self-abandonment. He let himself grow thinner and weaker as if he'd lost the capacity to care – and to hell with whether anybody believed him or not. That no longer mattered. He was simply conserving his strength.

Pain was something which was done to his body; but its power was a function of his mind. He couldn't stop his guards from hurting him, but he could defuse the effect of the beatings and drugs. By an act of will, he withdrew into himself until his brain existed in a different place than his distress. If he lost weight or muscle, that meant nothing. Let his physical self suffer: he'd never counted the cost of the things he did to survive. Precisely because he was determined to live, he risked growing so weak that he might die.

The truth was that Angus Thermopyle had never tried suicide, not once in his whole life. He'd done horrible things to himself, things which could easily have resulted in his death; but he'd always done them in order to survive. During all the time he was held prisoner on Com-Mine Station, he never thought about killing himself.

Later he wished he had.

Nobody told him what was in store for him. Increased abuse was his only hint of his doom until the day when Milos Taverner visited him in his cell.

That in itself was a surprise. Angus had always seen Taverner in the interrogation room: the Deputy Chief was too fastidious to have much taste for the state in which the guards kept Angus – or the state in which Angus kept himself. Except for his nic-stained fingers, Taverner was so clean that Angus wanted to puke on him, just for laughs.

Nevertheless Taverner's unexpected visit wasn't as surprising as the fact that the Deputy Chief wasn't alone.

He had a woman with him.

She was tall, handsome, and lean, with streaks of gray in her jet hair, an uncompromising mouth, and hot eyes. The way she moved left no doubt in Angus' mind that she was a match for him: even the small flexing of her fingers was at once smooth and tense, poised between relaxation and violence – a balance she'd acquired through years of training. On her hip, she carried a handgun, a sleeker and far more powerful version of the impact pistol Angus had used in his escape. Her gaze gave the impression that she could see everything without shifting her eyes. Although she had an air of authority, she wore nothing more elaborate than a plain blue shipsuit. It was unmarked by any ornament or insignia except an oval patch on each shoulder: the generic starfield emblem of the UMCP.

Before she entered the cell, she turned to the guard who'd accompanied her and Taverner.

'Switch off your monitors,' she said crisply. 'I don't want any record of this.'

Milos nodded in confirmation, but his support was probably unnecessary. Her tone was that of a woman who knew she would be obeyed. And the nervous alacrity of the guard's salute guaranteed compliance.

When the guard left to relay her order, she came into the cell and closed the door.

Her nose wrinkled in disgust as she surveyed Angus and his quarters. 'You don't waste care on your prisoners, do you, Milos?'

Taverner's shrug looked vaguely helpless. He wasn't happy. As if involuntarily, he pulled a packet of nic out of his pocket. Then he caught himself. Scowling, he shoved the packet back.

'He does this deliberately,' he replied with an effort. 'The psy-profile indicates he's suicidal, but he's faking it. The only time we believed him, he nearly got away from us.'

The woman nodded dismissively. 'I know. I've read the file. Assuming the data you sent us wasn't doctored.' Her sarcasm had a light touch: that was all she needed. 'Which, of course, I assume it wasn't.'

Milos winced. 'Do you want to talk about this here – in front of him? I've got a private office.' The blotches on his scalp were curiously distinct. 'He remembers everything. Don't think he doesn't. He's already trying to figure out how he can use you.'

Angus watched with his yellow eyes hooded and kept his malice to himself.

'That's the point.' The woman's anger was complex. 'He's got the right. After what you've put him through, he's got the right. You already have enough advantages. I'm not going to give you another one.'

But then the sight of the Deputy Chief's discomfiture seemed to soften her ire. As if to be fair, she added, 'We've trusted you this far. You haven't let us down.'

Milos' retort had a curious dignity. 'I don't care whether you trust me or not. Just take him – shut him up, get him off Station. Before we both take damage.'

The woman cocked an eyebrow. 'If you're in such a hurry, why didn't you comply with Hashi's order?'

Hashi's order. A stun-prod of panic touched Angus' guts. Hashi Lebwohl, DA Director, UMCP. Every illegal who ever worked the belt knew Hashi Lebwohl by rumor and reputation. They said he was a madman.

You already have enough advantages. I'm not going to give you another one. What the hell was *that* supposed to mean?

But Taverner didn't react to the name. He kept his unfamiliar dignity as he explained, 'Security was offended. Even Center was offended. If they weren't trying to return the insult, you wouldn't be escorted here by a mere Deputy Chief. You would have an entire retinue. But they'll still give you what you want. All you have to do is tell them in person.'

'Thanks to you.'

The woman spoke facing Angus. Angus couldn't determine whether or not she was talking to him.

'How so?' Milos asked. His moment of dignity had passed. Now he just looked uneasy. He may not have trusted his subordinates to turn off the monitor.

'The Preempt Act,' she answered. 'How do you suppose we got that passed? Why do you suppose we asked you to help Captain Succorso frame him?' Her tone made no distinction between *asked* and *ordered*. 'That was the lever we needed – a traitor in Com-Mine Security, somebody who was willing to help a pirate like Captain Succorso steal Station supplies. Morn Hyland's accusation that *Starmaster* was sabotaged here helped, but we needed more. We needed corroboration. When we were able to demonstrate that Security on Com-Mine Station – the Station closest to forbidden space – couldn't be trusted, most of our opposition crumbled.'

The Deputy Chief nodded. His features showed depression rather than surprise. In a morose voice, he said, 'As long as you're determined to crucify me—'

'I'm not going to crucify you,' the woman put in. 'You don't care what he hears. He isn't going to tell anybody. He won't get the chance.'

'Then answer a question,' Milos continued. 'Did you ever care whether *Starmaster* was really sabotaged? Did you do all that just so you could get your hands on him?'

'Of course not.' The woman was angry again. 'But it's the only reason that concerns you.' After a moment she added, '*I* care about *Starmaster*. But we're pretty sure Hyland's accusation was a lie.'

Taverner searched for his packet of nic, stopped himself again. 'How do you know that? Why would she lie? Why would she do that for him? What's going on here?' His voice betrayed a tremor. 'What kind of hold did he have on her?'

Angus could hardly breathe. How did they know Morn lied about *Starmaster*? Had they caught her? Caught her and discovered the zone-implant?

Was that the time limit Security was up against? Were they in a hurry to break him before he was fried for giving Morn Hyland a zone-implant?

This time, however, the woman ignored Milos' questions – and Angus'.

Under his hooded gaze, he saw her move so that she stood directly in front of him. Maybe she wanted a better look at him. Or maybe she wanted him to be sure she was talking to him.

'I'm Min Donner,' she said, 'Director, Enforcement Division, United Mining Companies Police.

'From now on, you're going to work for us.'

When she said her name, Angus' heart froze. Min Donner. Involuntarily he raised his eyes to her face, and his mouth hung open. Min Donner herself. The woman who sent out *Starmaster* – the woman they called Warden Dios' 'executioner.' He believed her instantly – there were no lies hidden anywhere in her strict face – and the conviction appalled him.

Things were bad enough if he was in danger of the death penalty for what he'd done to Morn Hyland. He still had a defense against that. But if the likes of Hashi Lebwohl and Min Donner had taken an interest in him – if he was going to be turned over to them—

'Don't touch me,' he rasped. Fear gave him strength; he faced her with his hate blazing in his eyes. 'Leave me here. If you try to take me, I'll talk. I'll tell everybody I was framed. I'll tell them how. When that gets out, you and your precious Preempt Act won't be worth shit.'

Min Donner didn't reply. Apparently she was done with Angus. For a moment she held his gaze, just to show him she could. Then she turned back to Milos.

Now she sounded distantly amused as she said, 'Get packed. You're coming with us.'

That hit the Deputy Chief hard. At least Angus wasn't the only one being threatened. Milos was suddenly terrified. All the color dropped out of his face. His mouth shaped words, protests, appeals, but he couldn't make a sound.

'I'll keep it simple,' she said. 'You've been reqqed. Under the Preempt Act. Officially, we want your knowledge of him – to help us deal with him. But the real reason is for your own protection. You're too vulnerable here. If somebody stumbled onto your' – she sneered – 'extracurricular activities, you would take real damage.

'So would we.

'Come on.' Abruptly she strode to the door and slapped it once with her palm. 'You probably have a lot of getting ready to do.'

Weapons poised, expecting trouble, a guard opened the door. When he saw Donner, however, he stood out of the way and snapped to attention.

Ignoring the guard, she walked away.

Milos remained in the cell; he struggled for breath as if he'd been jabbed in the stomach. His face was so pale, and his expression so apoplectic, that he might have been on the verge of an infarction.

He and Angus stared at and through each other, as horrified together as if they'd just learned that they were brothers.

Without warning, the Deputy Chief lurched forward as if he were about to swing his fist at his prisoner.

Angus didn't know what Milos intended: he didn't care. He was too scared. He caught Milos' arm, jerked him off balance, and hit him in the lower abdomen hard enough to fold him in half.

Before the guard could reach him, Angus grabbed Milos by the ears and raged straight into his face, '*You sonofabitch! What have you done to me?*'

Then a stun-prod caught the back of Angus' skull, and he fell backward, convulsing like an epileptic.

By the time he'd regained control over his limbs and stopped retching, he was armcuffed between two angry guards and being forced along a corridor into an unfamiliar part of the Security section. He thought he glimpsed a sign that said MEDICAL, but he couldn't be sure because of the sickening way the walls yawed on either side of him. Hopeless and vicious, he tried to break free; but of course the cuffs and the guards held him, and stun left his muscles so elastic that he couldn't control them; there was nothing he could do to save himself.

'Listen,' he gasped, 'listen to me, you don't know what's going on, you've got a traitor, they—'

The guards stopped long enough to slap a strip of gag tape over his mouth. Then they dragged him into motion again.

Because of the tape, he almost strangled on his own yells when the guards pushed him into a large, sterile room and he realized that it was full of the equipment for cryogenic encapsulation.

The nightmares he'd spent his life fleeing had caught up with him.

CHAPTER 7

Darkness.

Darkness as complete as black space; separated from black space by a fragile hull which had vanished as though it never existed. The void was inside, vacuum and the utter cold of death.

Darkness and gasping; atavistic panic.

Morn clung to the arm of Nick's g-seat, clung so hard that her own force lifted her legs from the deck, sent her body drifting. She was supposed to be tougher than this. She was UMCP: the Academy had trained her for such emergencies. But when the dark came upon her it was a thing of such absolute certitude that she had no defense against it. It was like gap-sickness. She'd killed all of them, her whole family; she had no one left except the child. There could be no defense against the fathomless abysm between the stars.

None of the people around her had any defense. Except that she could still feel g.

Not the centrifugal g of spin; nothing that definite. This was linear, soft but persistent, g along a vector that opposed the pull of her arms.

The course correction – Helm had been dummied to the auxiliary bridge. The steady and delicate lateral thrust which curved *Captain's Fancy* toward her eventual heading was still at work.

The ship was still alive.

Abruptly Mikka's voice barked across the bridge. 'Liete! Liete Corregio! Reset maintenance! We need light up here. We need air!'

Liete Corregio was command third. Mikka must have left her in the core to take charge.

Words that sounded like gibberish to Morn crackled back from Mikka's handcom. Nick's second retorted, 'What the fuck do you *think* happened? I said *reset*!'

Light flickered into a nearly instantaneous blaze across the bridge. With a palpable whine, *Captain's Fancy* resumed internal spin.

Caught by her own weight, Morn hit the deck sharply; the soles of her feet stung, and she came close to hyper-extending her left knee. Only her grip on Nick's seat kept her upright.

The gasping around her changed to relief.

'That sonofabitch!' Carmel growled. 'What a place to put a virus.'

Nick shook his head. A small grin still drew at his mouth, but he was frowning hard. He didn't appear to be aware of what his hands did as he disengaged the maintenance computer from his command board.

Mikka snapped into her handcom, 'Thanks,' then clipped the unit to her belt. Facing Nick, she asked, 'You don't think so? Then what the hell caused us to power down like that?'

'Oh, it was the virus, all right,' he said thoughtfully. 'But it's too easy. We can run the internals on automatic indefinitely, if we have to. Orn knew that. It isn't enough of a threat. The real problem is somewhere else.'

Morn had to agree. Her visceral dread of the void left her convinced that she couldn't get enough air into her lungs, even though the scrubbers had gone down for less than a minute; yet she felt sure Nick was right. A virus that couldn't paralyze the ship more effectively than this wouldn't have contented Orn.

Irrationally concerned, she tried to feel the baby inside her, estimate his condition. But of course he was too young to make himself tangible.

Grimly she determined to have him aborted at her earliest opportunity. She couldn't afford to be confused by fear for a baby she hadn't chosen and didn't want. The idea that he might have been damaged by the sudden loss and return of g – or by her own trepidation – brought her nausea back.

'My God, it's a bloody plague!' Lind cackled on the verge of hysteria. Opening channels across his board, he shouted into the dark void, 'Antibiotics! We need an-ti-bi-otics!'

At once Mikka strode up the arc of the bridge to cock her hips ominously in front of Lind's Station. 'You want a demotion?' she demanded. 'Scorz would love your job.'

Lind bit down his distress, jerked his head from side to side.

'Then shut up. The rest of us are trying to think.'

'What's next?' Malda Verone asked carefully. 'Do you want to try to isolate this virus, or should we test something else?'

Nick gave her a dangerous smile. 'Let's test targ.'

'Reactivate your board. Charge one of the cannon. Put targeting up on the screen.'

Malda started to obey, then paused to comment, 'I'm blind without scan.'

'Reactivate, Carmel,' Nick commanded without hesitation. 'Link with targ.'

'Link goes through your board,' Carmel observed. 'We might lose scan data as well as targ. We might lose command.'

'Just do it.' Nick's tone left no room for argument. 'You want to try shooting blind at this velocity?' A moment later he added, 'We've already tested my board.'

'Nick' – Mikka faced him with her unflinching scowl – 'maybe it would be better to take this more slowly. We've got time.'

Nick didn't raise his voice. 'I want to find that virus.'

His second shut her mouth.

No one else spoke. Carmel and Malda worked in silence, concentrating fiercely.

Now that she'd made up her mind about her baby, Morn felt curiously eased, relieved of difficulties; almost light-headed. The decision was like abandoning herself to her zone-implant: it freed her from her fears and limits, her deep and corrosive revulsion. She was no longer afraid of what might happen next.

Weak from prolonged strain, she left Nick's side and moved to the vacant engineer's Station; she fitted her back to the contours of the g-seat and belted herself down. Mikka glared at her distrustfully, and Nick gave her a quick glance, covertly uncertain; but nobody protested.

'Ready,' Carmel announced.

'Here.' Malda tapped keys, and a targ-grid sprang to life on one of the big screens. Green phosphors outlined a simulated attacker, a ship on a parallel course. Readouts across the screen showed distance, velocity, ship id, weapons status: Morn stared at them. Malda had chosen a target configuration with a distinct resemblance to *Starmaster*.

Starmaster had been designed to look more like an orehauler than a fighting ship. The simulated target was a freighter of some kind.

Morn couldn't shake the odd, dislocated sense that she was about to watch her family die again.

'Fire,' Nick ordered.

Malda hit her keys.

Morn thought she heard an impalpable electronic sigh as the screen went dead.

From where she sat, she could see the targ board past Malda's lowered head and swinging hair. All the status indicators had gone out; the readouts were blank.

'Shit!' snarled Carmel. 'We've lost scan!'

Lind emitted a crackle of alarm.

Shouting into her handcom, Mikka Vasaczk instructed the seconds in the core to reset targ and scan.

Nick brandished a grin full of fight and desperation. The light in his eyes was hot; feverish past his bruises. 'Status,' he demanded harshly. 'Give me status.'

Hardwired systems resumed function. Malda's board came back up almost instantly; Carmel's did the same. The scan first began typing as fast as scattershot, testing equipment and information. More slowly, less sure of herself, Verone went to work as well.

Nick couldn't contain himself. 'Goddamn it!' he barked. 'Give me status!'

Carmel punched the side of her console with one fist and swung her seat to face him. 'I'm wiped,' she said in a hard voice. 'We can see, but we can't identify any of it.'

She didn't need to explain that scan was useless without spectrographic star id; without the ability to compensate for doppler shifts; without filtering for interstellar ghosts and shadows; without the vast data base which identified the differing reflections of ships and planets, asteroid belts and solar winds.

'Same here,' Malda added in a strained tone. 'I can't even call up simulations.'

'Mackern' – Nick wasn't asking a question – 'you've got backup on that data.'

Concentration drew sweat from the new data first's forehead. His voice sounded like it might crack under the stress. 'I've got backup.'

'Restore,' Nick commanded. 'Scan first, then targ.'

Morn shook her head. Not good enough. Her head was so light that she could shake it easily. Even if the restore worked, it would solve nothing, reveal nothing.

Unless the virus had wiped itself.

She didn't believe that.

What Nick was doing could only make the problem worse.

Nobody asked her opinion, however.

But Mikka may have been thinking the same thing. She repeated Carmel's earlier objection. 'That goes through your board. We might lose data itself this time.'

Nick's eyes blazed fever at her. Dangerously calm, he asked, 'Have you got any better ideas? Or do you just like running blind and defenseless?'

'No.' Mikka didn't back down. 'I just don't think we need to be in a hurry about this. We've already lost scan and targ. If we lose data, too, we're finished.'

Morn shook her head again.

For a moment Nick looked poised to erupt at Mikka. His scars pulsed hotly, and his teeth flashed. His bruises were growing livid. *Captain's Fancy* was being attacked; Orn had attacked him. He was driven to defend his ship.

But his ship needed the people who worked for her; he needed his crew. Instead of raging, he put on casualness like a cloak.

'She,' he commented, nodding at Morn, 'doesn't think we're finished.' His tone was amiable and ominous.

Then he turned to Mackern.

'What are you waiting for?'

Sweat streaked Mackern's face; it dripped from his jaw onto his hands and console. With the sleeve of his shoulder, he tried to wipe his eyes. 'It takes a minute to set up.' His fingers trembled over the board. 'I've got to identify the data and route it.' In a weak voice, he added, 'I've never done this before.'

Rhetorically Carmel asked, 'How in hell did you get to be data first on a ship like this?'

Nick grinned like his scars. 'On-the-job training. It's good for you.'

Mackern didn't respond.

Detached from the tension around her, Morn considered her situation. She wasn't concerned about the danger to *Captain's Fancy*'s data, not in any immediate sense. For some reason, she hadn't realized earlier that she could solve this problem. Perhaps she'd been confused by Orn and violence; or by the fact that she was pregnant. But she knew now that she held the solution.

She was UMCP. She still had her id tag – and her codes.

She didn't need to think about that. The ship's problems had lost interest for her. Instead she considered the implications of her decision to abort her son.

Externally there were no implications. No one knew she was pregnant: her child's demise would change nothing. All the implications were internal.

Like any woman, she'd often thought about having children. The excitement of life growing within her – the necessary pain and release of birth. From time to time, she'd imagined wanting a son. She'd imagined naming him after her father.

But not like this. This baby was Angus Thermopyle's last crime against her. He'd been conceived in cruelty and rage: a simple command to the sickbay systems would destroy him. That was just.

And yet she'd lost her initial sense of shock and betrayal. Instead her determination to be rid of her baby left her feeling light-headed and detached, like a woman who'd decided on suicide.

A minute later Mackern said tightly, 'Ready. I think.'

'Then do it,' Nick replied.

Mackern took a deep breath and entered the command.

Both scan and data went down simultaneously.

Unable to stop himself, Mackern groaned and covered his head with his arms.

Malda looked like she was hyperventilating.

'We're finished,' Lind said, wide-eyed and appalled. 'We're lost. We're lost.'

Helplessly the man at the helm echoed, 'Lost.'

'Oh, shut up.' Mikka's shoulders slumped; she sounded beaten. 'Reset,' she said into her handcom. 'Scan and data.'

As soon as her board came back up, Carmel tested it and reported that she was still wiped.

With an effort, Mackern pulled his arms down. But then he hung fire; he couldn't seem to decide which keys to hit. Staring through his sweat, he gaped at his board and didn't move. His lips trembled as he asked, 'Did I do that? Is it my fault?'

Muttering obscenities, Mikka Vasaczk started around the bridge toward the data Station. She may have intended to slap him. Or maybe she knew enough about data to relieve him.

Nick stopped her with a small slash of one hand – a gesture so self-contained that Morn nearly missed it. Mikka confronted Nick from almost directly over his head. Offering the handcom, she asked, 'Should I call Parmute?'

Nick shook his head slightly, dismissed her intervention. He was fighting for *Captain's Fancy*'s life. That meant he had to take care of his people.

'Mackern.'

The data first sat up straight, as if Nick had run a lash along his spine. 'I'm sorry, Nick,' he said without looking at his Captain. 'I'm not Orn – I'm not good enough. I don't know anything about viruses.'

'Mackern,' Nick repeated, as distinct as a filleting knife. 'I want a report.'

'Yes,' Mackern winced out. 'I'm sorry. Yes.'

Tremors ran through his shoulders as he jabbed his fingers at the keys in front of him.

When his equipment resumed function, he began testing *Captain's Fancy*'s data. Hardwired systems running at microprocessor speeds reported back to him almost instantly.

'It's gone.' His voice sounded hollow in the silence; haunted. 'All our data – everything.' He may have wanted to cry out, but he was too scared. 'It's all been wiped.'

'We're lost.'

'Goddamn it, Nick!' Mikka rasped. 'I warned you.'

Surrounded by swelling, Nick's scars were as bright as an ooze of blood under his gaze.

For the third time, Morn shook her head.

The danger was real; she knew that. She understood the nightmare of a blind voyage down the endless gullet of the galaxy. But it didn't touch her. As long as the ship's position could be fixed – as long as the ongoing course correction could be measured against *Captain's Fancy*'s destination – she wasn't doomed. None of them were.

Someone must have spoken to her. If so, she wasn't aware of it: her true attention was focused elsewhere. After a moment, however, she realized that everybody was looking at her.

Mackern's lips trembled with dismay. Mikka and Carmel glared their distrust. Lind's eyes bulged, and his larynx worked like a piston. Malda Verone held her hair back with both hands, as if that enabled her to restrain her fear. The way the helm first stared made him look like he'd swallowed his chin.

'I said, *why?*' Nick repeated. He had no patience for her preoccupation. 'Mackern and Lind keep saying we're lost. You keep shaking your head.' Threats were plain in his voice. 'I want to know *why.*'

Morn made an effort to bring herself back from the calm, unconcerned place where her decision of death resided. 'I'm sorry.' Her voice was like her head, light and separate. 'I thought you understood. You talk about the fact that I'm UMCP. I didn't realize I needed to explain.'

Nick contained his exasperation with difficulty. 'Explain what?'

'I don't know anything about viruses. I can't cure what Vorbuld did. But you don't need to worry about a wipe like this. You haven't lost anything. The problem isn't data, it's function. You can look at anything you want. The virus doesn't prevent you from looking. You just can't take action without crashing your systems.'

You may not even be able to stop this course correction without wiping helm.

'Morn —' Nick began; he was close to fury.

'Have you lost your mind?' Mikka cut in, fuming at her. 'Function is hardwired! The data is already gone!'

Morn still shook her head. 'No, it's not.'

For one heartbeat, everybody stared at her; two; three.

Then a light like a burst of joy shot across Nick's face. 'Because you're UMCP!'

She faced him squarely. 'I can access your datacore.' It was a temporary fix, but it would work. 'Every scrap of data you ever had is copied there. Automatically. Constantly. And that's hard memory. It can't be wiped. It can't be tampered with.

'I can access it for you. I've got my id tag. I know the codes. I can copy everything back into your systems. It may take a day or two' – the sheer volume of information in the datacore probably ran to thousands of gigabytes – 'but you'll have everything back where it was a few minutes ago.'

'Amazing!' the helm first breathed as if he were in awe.

Nick's eyes shone at her with plain delight.

'Wait a minute,' Mikka said. 'Wait a minute.' She sounded stunned, as if she'd been hit in the sternum. 'What about the virus?'

Morn shrugged without dropping Nick's gaze. 'I presume it's recorded in the datacore.' She was hardly aware of her own certainty. 'It'll come back with everything else.'

'So we'll still have the same problem.'

'But you can navigate,' answered Morn. 'You can tell where you are.' What more do you want from me?

Abruptly Nick rubbed his hands together, then slapped his console. He'd recovered his relish. 'By hell, we're going to beat this thing. I don't give a fuck about viruses. Let the Bill flush the damn thing for us. While we've got it, we'll work around it. We can leave the internal systems on automatic. We may not be comfortable, but we'll be alive.

'We'll use the computers to run our calculations, plan what we need to do. Then we'll cut them out of the loop and enter commands manually. It'll be sloppy as shit, and we won't be able to fight our way past a signal buoy, but at least we might get where we're going.

'All right?' he asked. 'Is everybody happy?' But he obviously didn't expect an answer. 'Let's get started.

'Mackern, let her at your board. She can set it up. Then you and Parmute can run it.'

With an expansive sweep of his arm, he gestured Morn toward the data Station.

Light-headed and certain, guided by new priorities, she unbelted herself from the engineer's seat and walked past Mikka, Carmel, and Lind toward the data first.

Lind grinned at her like a puppy; Carmel frowned noncommittally. Mikka scrutinized her hard as she passed, then asked Nick, 'Do you trust her?'

'What harm do you think she can do?' he countered. 'We're already wiped. Without that data, she's as lost as we are.'

That was true. On this point, Morn had no treachery in her. Angus himself might have been honest now.

But he wouldn't have lifted a finger to save his son. If she were still under his control, he might have used some of the more esoteric functions of her zone-implant to give her the most painful abortion possible.

As she moved, she pulled the chain of her id tag up over her head.

Mackern stared at her. His skin had a gray, strained tinge, and his gaze was rimmed with sweat.

Because he seemed to have nothing whatever in common with men like Orn Vorbuld and Nick Succorso and Angus Thermopyle, she smiled at him as she jacked her tag into his board.

He didn't smile back. He couldn't: he was afraid to hope.

With her tag and her access codes, she tapped into *Captain's Fancy*'s datacore; she set it to provide the same kind of playback Com-Mine Security would have used to search for evidence which might convict Angus of something worse than stealing supplies. Then she told Mackern, 'Before you initiate, you'll have to route the data and set the computers to copy it. You know how to do that.'

He nodded once, carefully, as if he didn't trust the muscles in his neck.

'When playback ends,' she continued, 'all you have to do is unplug my id tag. That resets the datacore. And it'll release your board. Then you can get back to work.'

He mumbled something which may have been 'Thanks.'

Still smiling for his benefit, she turned away.

Nick watched her across the bridge with passion in his eyes and blood in his scars.

Riding the moment, as well as the nameless change within her, she said without premeditation or anxiety, 'Nick, I'm tired of being a passenger. I want to work. Let me be data third. I've got some of the right training – and I can learn the rest.'

Let me into the systems. Let me find out what we're doing, where we're going. Give me a chance to learn the truth.

Trust me.

Mikka started to protest; but when she saw the expression on Nick's face, she stopped herself, clamped her mouth shut.

His grin intensified. As if he were playing an elaborate game, he said, 'I'm like a genie in a bottle.' His tone was a mixture of insolence and

269

lust. 'Rub me the right way, and I grant wishes.' Abruptly he waved his arms in a flourish around his head. 'Poof! You're data third.'

Tight with strain and uncertainty, Lind, Malda, and the helm first laughed nervously. Mikka and Carmel frowned their suspicions. Mackern let out a small sigh, a thin gust of relief.

Morn gave Nick a crisp salute like the ones she'd so often given her father. Playing the game back at him, she kept the echoes of death and loss off her face.

'Captain Succorso, permission to leave the bridge.'

'Permission granted,' he replied as if she'd just made a suggestion lascivious enough to quicken his pulse.

Still riding the moment, Morn Hyland crossed the aperture and left the command module.

Without her id tag; almost without any identity she knew or recognized. She'd given that up to purchase something she was in no position to evaluate.

But she didn't go to sickbay. Filled by a strange, thorough calm, she felt no urgency to act on her decision.

CHAPTER 8

She didn't go to sickbay. She also didn't go down to the ship's core in search of Parmute, the data second, who would be responsible for making sure she knew her duties.

Instead she went to her cabin to prepare herself for Nick.

She felt sure he would come as soon as he had the chance: as soon as he confirmed that the datacore playback was proceeding normally; as soon as he and Mikka Vasaczk had made their plans to 'work around' the virus. She'd seen the lust in his eyes and scars. The more she proved herself worth having, the more he would want her; would want to prove his power over her.

She was ready for that. The zone-implant made her ready.

But when she was alone in her cabin, lying naked on her bunk with her black box poised under the mattress, she found herself thinking strange thoughts.

What would it be like to have a baby?

She studied her belly to see if the life within her was noticeable. She probed her breasts to learn if they'd begun to swell and grow tender. What sort of pressure would she feel, that would make the pain of childbirth desirable? On an intellectual level, she knew such questions were months premature. Yet they interested her because she was anxious, curious – and lonely. She would never have chosen to be pregnant. But now that pregnancy had been imposed on her, it began to surprise her more and more.

What effect would the zone-implant have on her baby?

Would it drive him mad? Could all those inappropriate hormones and neurotransmitters damage him? Would her feigned and limitless lubricity make him more like his father, or less?

Oh, shit.

Without warning, her detachment melted away; her calm streamed out of her, deliquescing like wax. Frightened by the direction of her thoughts, she shook herself, tried to recover her sense of sanity. What the hell did she care what the zone-implant did to her unwanted fetus? No matter what happened, she was going to have an abortion. Wasn't she? Sooner or later – when she had time and privacy to visit sickbay again. Wasn't she? The clot of chemicals and malice in her womb was just one more consequence of being raped. Like rape, it violated her right to make her own choices. The sooner she rid herself of it, the better.

That was true. It was *true*, dammit.

But if it were true, what did she make of the fact that she'd already chosen a name for her baby?

Without noticing it, as if while her back was turned, she'd decided to call him Davies Hyland. After her father.

Shit!

She wanted to weep again, in frustration and grief. Abruptly she sat up, swung her legs off the bunk to meet her distress standing. At once she began to pace as if she'd been caught and caged. Was she truly so reduced, so damaged, so lost, that she could consider *keeping* the offspring of Angus Thermopyle's hate? Did she place her own value so low that she was willing to give Angus' corrupt seed room in her own body, to grow and thrive?

No! Of course not. *Of course not*. She would go get an abortion as soon as Nick expended himself and fell asleep.

And when she did that, she would be alone: as alone as she'd been after she'd killed her family; as alone as she'd been with Angus at his worst. That small worm of protoplasm gnawing its way toward parturition within her was all she had left. When she killed it, too, her bereavement would be complete.

The child was a boy, a human being. Her father's grandchild. And he was a reason to live. A reason that didn't have anything to do with rage or hate – or with whether the UMCP was as malign as Vector said. A reason which contradicted the lesson Angus had worked so hard to teach her: that she deserved to be utterly alone and helpless forever, sustained only by the neural chicanery of the zone-implant, and by her own stubbornness.

If she kept Davies, she would no longer be alone. She would have a family again; someone who belonged to her—

Someone who deserved better than to be blown up because she couldn't tell the difference between sanity and self-destruct. Or to be flushed down the sickbay disposal because she couldn't face the danger of keeping him alive. No matter who his father was; no matter what dark legacy his progenitors left him.

She'd believed things like that once, back in the days when she was truly a cop, and the UMCP was honest. Maybe some part of her still did.

Keeping the child would be like surrendering to Angus Thermopyle.

Which was exactly what she'd done by trading his life for the zone-implant control. She'd chosen to let his crimes against her go unpunished rather than to face the consequences of those crimes without the aid of the black box. The question of how reduced or damaged or lost she was had been answered long ago. The only issue that remained was at once simpler and less ponderable.

This fetus threatened her survival aboard *Captain's Fancy*, her value to Nick. How much was survival worth to her?

Was it worth more killing?

How much loneliness could she endure?

Caught and caged by her past, abandoned by calm, she paced back and forth as if she didn't know which way to turn, clenching her fists together and knotting her shoulders as if to strangle someone. Despite her fiercest efforts, however, she couldn't recapture the suicide's light-headed certainty which had taken her over when she'd decided to abort her son.

She was still pacing when her door chimed. True to prediction, Nick had come for her. She barely had time to dive onto the bunk and key her zone-implant control before the delay programmed into the lock let the door open. As a result, she was flushed and panting as he entered, apparently avid.

At once she saw that he'd changed since she'd left the bridge. His scars continued to throb under his eyes, but his grin was gone; his elation had faded. His bruises made him look battered and uncertain. He'd discovered a doubt of some kind.

Not a doubt of *Captain's Fancy*'s safety or survival: that would only have sharpened his focus, made him fight harder. It must have been a doubt of himself.

Because he was here, she assumed the doubt had something to do with her.

When the door closed behind him, he paused. In a distant voice, he asked, 'Why do you do that?'

A compulsory ache rose in her: she could hardly think. Already the change in him was no longer clear to her. 'Do what?'

'Why do you make me wait five seconds before your door opens?'

She'd prepared herself for that question long ago. Husky with need, she replied, 'I don't want you to catch me doing anything' – she flicked a glance toward the san – 'ungraceful.'

Apparently that answer was good enough: the subject didn't really interest him. Dismissing it, he moved closer. At his sides, his fingers worked, curling involuntarily into claws and then straining straight.

If the zone-implant's control over her had been less perfect, she would have been afraid.

Abruptly he surged forward, caught her by the wrists, jerked her half upright on the bunk. His eyes burned at her.

'Do you know how I got these scars? Have you heard that story?'

She shook her head. The realization that she'd engaged the control too soon, that she'd made herself helpless at the wrong moment, brought a moan up from her throat.

'A woman did it. She was a pirate – and I was just a kid. Normally she would have merely sneered at me and walked away. But I had information she wanted, so she didn't sneer. Instead she seduced me to help her catch a ship. And I believed her. I didn't know anything about contempt – or about women. I thought she took me seriously.

'But after she got that ship, she didn't need me anymore. That was when she started laughing at me. She butchered all the crew, everybody she found aboard, but she left me alive. First she cut my face. Then she abandoned me, left me alone on that ship to die slowly, so that I would understand just how much contempt she had for me. Maybe she thought I would kill myself or go crazy before I died of thirst.

'Are you laughing at me?'

Morn stared back at him. She should have at least tried to look frightened or indignant, but she was stupid with inappropriate desire.

'Why did you stay with Captain fucking Thermo-pile?' His hands twisted pain through her wrists, and his eyes blazed. 'Why did you come to me? What kind of plot is this? How are you going to betray me?'

At last she understood. He feared that he was growing dependent on her. Women were things he used and then discarded when he'd had enough of them. If they had useful abilities, he made them part of his crew. But he didn't invest himself in them; he didn't need them.

Until now.

Now he'd begun to realize how much power she had with him. And he was scared.

'Answer me,' he demanded through his teeth, 'or I'll break your goddamn arms.'

'Try me,' she whispered from the depths of her false and illimitable passion. 'Find out if I'm laughing. You know what that feels like. You'll be able to tell the difference.'

A sound like a throttled cry came out of him. Releasing one of her wrists, he drew back his arm and hit her so hard that she slammed to the mattress, and the walls grew dark around her.

Then he flung off his boots, ripped his shipsuit away, and landed on her like a hammer.

Artificially responsive, she accepted the way she was hurt and answered it with ecstasy.

Take that and be damned, you bastard!

She hated him far too much to laugh at him.

When he was exhausted and asleep, she took out her control and changed its functions to soften her wounds, numb her revulsion; ease the horrors of transition. After that she climbed past him out of the bunk, put on her shipsuit, hid the black box in her pocket, and went to sickbay.

She didn't encounter anyone along the way. That was probably a good thing; but she didn't care who saw her like this.

Reaching her destination, she locked herself in. Then she instructed the medical systems to treat her black eye and swollen face, her bleeding lips, her bruised arms and ribs, her torn labia. She didn't turn off her zone-implant until sickbay had done its best to take her hurts away.

But she didn't get an abortion. And she didn't try to hide her pregnancy. The only information she deleted from the log pertained to the exact age of her fetus – and to the electrode buried in her brain.

That done, she returned to her cabin. Shivering with transition and disgust, she stripped off her shipsuit, scrubbed herself in the san until her skin was raw, then got back into the bunk.

She hadn't decided to keep little Davies. She simply wanted to preserve the evidence that Nick Succorso had beat up a woman with a baby.

In case she needed it.

Apparently she didn't need it. As soon as he woke up, she saw that his doubt was at rest. His eyes were clear, his scars were as pale as whole skin, and he'd recovered his grin. The bruises Orn gave him had started to fade.

He was mildly surprised at her condition: she should have looked much worse. He approved of her explanation, however. At peace with himself, entirely unchagrined, he instructed her to go to the auxiliary bridge so that Alba Parmute could begin teaching her her duties. Then he headed for the bridge to learn how the datacore playback proceeded.

Morn was ready to get to work: she was full of readiness and murder. She had decisions to make, and decisions required information. She left her cabin immediately.

At Nick's orders, Parmute was waiting for Morn when she reached the auxiliary bridge.

It was up in the drive space beside the engineering console room where Vector Shaheed or his second monitored *Captain's Fancy*'s relatively gentle navigational thrust. The auxiliary bridge itself was narrower and less vertiginously curved than its counterpart, since it was formed around the bulkheads of the ship's core; but it contained all the same g-seats, consoles, and screens. Past its arc, the walls of one end were visible from the other. Sitting in front of the data board, Morn could see all the other Stations without craning her neck.

The habitual sullenness of Alba Parmute's face and manner reinforced the impression that she was another of Nick's discarded lovers. Nevertheless her desire to find somebody else to share her bed showed in the artificiality of her hair and makeup, as well as in the blatant way she displayed her body: she wore her shipsuit only half sealed, and her breasts bulged ominously in the gap. Morn had no sympathy for her, however.

Disgusted at the thought of Nick and all things male, Morn found Alba's obvious hunger pathetic.

Unfortunately Alba's pouting mood – and her apparently perpetual state of libidinal impatience – failed to conceal the fact that she wasn't particularly bright. She was able to explain Morn's responsibilities in only the most concrete terms: how the duty-rotation worked; whom she took orders from; which buttons to push; which codes engaged the various data functions; what damage-control utilities *Captain's Fancy* had available. Any underlying *how* or *why* she ignored: she did all her work by rote herself, and expected Morn to do the same. By comparison, the self-doubting and ill-equipped data first, Mackern, was a wizard.

Nick and his ship had been more dependent on Orn Vorbuld than Morn had realized.

She was no wizard herself; but she soon found it easy to believe that she could be more valuable to *Captain's Fancy* than Alba Parmute was.

After enduring the general uselessness of Alba's instructions for half an hour, Morn grew frustrated enough to dare asking to be left alone on the auxiliary bridge. So that she could 'practice her duties.'

She was UMCP: she may have been untrustworthy. But Alba was bored – and anyway Morn wasn't male. The data second shrugged and went away.

That was Morn's chance, her first chance. She was determined not to waste it.

The compartments where she kept the black pieces of her hate were breaking down. Nick's violence – and the fact that she was pregnant – damaged her defenses. Bits of revulsion and self-loathing, outrage and dire need, leaked together inside her, fomenting bloodshed. Alone on the auxiliary bridge, in front of the data console as if its readouts could display her fate, she risked looking for answers.

But she didn't neglect the caution she'd learned from Angus. Careful and bitter, she keyed the intercom to the bridge and asked permission to activate the auxiliary data board so that she could study the equipment.

'Go ahead,' Nick answered. With his doubts at rest, he was in an indulgent mood. 'Study as much as you want. Just don't *do* anything. If you trigger another wipe, you're fired.'

Beating her knuckles against the console for self-control, she replied as cheerfully as she could, 'Thanks.' She had no intention of doing anything which might activate Orn's virus. She wasn't going to lay a finger on *Captain's Fancy*'s data: she was just going to look at it.

The system was unfamiliar, but not much different than the ones she'd used in the Academy, or aboard *Starmaster*. And Alba had given her the basic codes. As soon as the auxiliary board was ready, she checked on the progress of the datacore playback.

The information she needed had already been restored.

Navigational data. Astrogation and scan.

Like any new computer, this one had programming tics and quirks she didn't know about. For five or ten minutes, she floundered around in the system, flashing only gibberish across the displays. But then she found her way into a summary of the programming parameters, where she quickly learned the things Alba Parmute had neglected or been unable to tell her.

After that she began to obtain useful results.

Navigational data enabled her to plot *Captain's Fancy*'s trajectory away from Com-Mine Station. Astrogation and scan enabled her to fix the ship's present position and to call up a list of possible destinations – places which could be reached along this course.

The list was long. It included everything from points dead ahead around in a vast curve back to Com-Mine itself. But she restricted the field considerably by assuming that Nick intended to maintain lateral thrust for at least two more months and by discounting any goal that would take more than seven or eight more months to reach – in effect, by eliminating from consideration everything past the midpoint of the huge circle implied by *Captain's Fancy*'s arc.

When she was done, the list had become short.

So short that it made her blood run cold.

It included only a red giant with no significant satellites; the farthest tip, virtually uncharted, of the asteroid belt served by Com-Mine Station; one of the hostile outposts which guarded forbidden space; and a hunk of dead rock as big as a planetoid, hanging a few million kilometers inside the borders of forbidden space – far enough inside to be absolutely off limits for any human ship, and yet far enough away from the outpost to be accessible to any human ship willing to risk the consequences.

That rock had a name: Thanatos Minor.

Morn had heard of it. Its name made her shiver as though her heart were freezing.

She'd heard it in the Academy, whispered by people who were appalled by what it represented: a depth of betrayal so unfathomable as to work toward the destruction of the human species for mere gain.

Thanatos Minor. No wonder forbidden space sheltered it, condoned it, despite diplomatic protests, ambassadorial outrage – despite the fact that its very existence was prohibited by signed treaty. Forbidden space threatened every human being alive, even though the threat was genetic rather than military; even though no human ships were ever attacked, and no alien vessels ever crossed the border outward, and no accords were ever broken – except by such telling omissions as the refusal to extirpate Thanatos Minor. And Thanatos Minor served that threat more effectively than warships and matter cannon.

At least by reputation, the rock was a shipyard and clearinghouse for pirates. Ships were built there (ships like *Bright Beauty?*): ships went there for repairs. And pirates like Nick Succorso and Angus Thermopyle took their plunder there, to one of the few markets rich enough to buy ore and supplies on the scale they offered; a market fueled by forbidden space's unquenchable appetite for human resources, human technologies, and – if the rumors were true – human lives.

Morn ignored the red giant, the outpost, the asteroid belt. As surely as if Nick had given her the answer himself, she knew where *Captain's Fancy* was headed.

Thanatos Minor, where he would sell her secrets for money and repairs; where everything she knew about the UMCP would, in effect, be sold to forbidden space.

That wasn't just crime: it was treason. A betrayal of humankind.

She had no loyalty to the United Mining Companies Police. Vector had argued that her superiors and heroes to the highest levels were corrupt – and it was at least conceivable that he was right. He certainly believed his own evidence. Whether they were corrupt or not, however, she'd already turned her back on them: she'd accepted the zone-implant control from Angus and gone with Nick instead of giving herself up to Com-Mine Security. She was no longer a cop in any effective sense.

But none of that mattered here. She couldn't know whether the

UMCP had betrayed humankind. She had to consider whether she was prepared to betray humankind herself.

And if she answered, No! – what then? Then the question became: How could she prevent Nick from forcing that betrayal on her?

Automatically she calculated the remaining distance: nearly six months at half the speed of light along *Captain's Fancy*'s present course, including deceleration time – more heavy g.

What could she do?

What else, besides sabotage *Captain's Fancy*?

The best she could hope for was self-destruct, immediate death. Any other form of sabotage would leave her adrift in black space with a ship full of people who knew that she'd effectively killed them all. But the mere thought of self-destruct filled her with dark, cold terror. It meant murdering herself so absolutely that everyone connected to her died as well.

Or she could simply kill herself and let Nick go on without her.

She felt so trapped and cold that she was hardly able to continue breathing. Involuntarily her knuckles hit the edge of the data console until they cracked, and both her hands turned bloody. There was no way out of this mess that didn't involve self-murder; a surrender to the moral gap-sickness which had consumed her life ever since *Starmaster* had first sighted *Bright Beauty* and gone into heavy g.

No, she thought. No. It's too much. I can't bear it.

She hadn't come all this way just to kill herself. She hadn't suffered Nick's touch all this time, endured beating and revulsion, just to kill herself.

Trapped.

Finally the cold in her heart grew so intense that she had to clamp her arms across her chest and huddle over her stomach for warmth.

She was still in that position – hunched down as if to protect her baby – when Vector Shaheed found her.

He must have been passing outside on his way to his console room. From the doorway, he asked, 'Morn?'

She should have said something to make him go away. She should at least have concealed her hands. But she couldn't.

'Morn? Are you all right?' He came closer; he touched her shoulder.

Then his grip tightened. 'What the hell are you doing to yourself?'

Like a flare of cold fire, she rose to face his look of mild surprise, mild concern.

'You should have told me,' she rasped thickly. 'Back when I first asked you. You should have told me where we're going.'

Turning her back on him, she left the auxiliary bridge and went back to the artificial courage of her zone implant.

When a chime from the intercom informed her that it was time for her to take her turn on the bridge, she obeyed, even though her fingers were so stiff with crusted blood and pain that she could hardly move them. Reckless and uncaring, she carried her black box switched on low in her pocket, not to numb her physical hurt, but to muffle her emotional distress. The damage to her knuckles was useful: it helped keep her in the present. And her zone-implant prevented the present from over-whelming her.

Muted by subtle electronic emissions, she stepped onto the bridge to take her place as *Captain's Fancy*'s data third.

Liete Corregio was command third: this was her watch. Nevertheless Nick met Morn as she arrived. He gave her a sharp grin which she hardly knew how to answer, but he didn't say anything. Instead he dangled her id tag by its chain for a moment, then flipped it to her.

That told her the datacore playback was finished.

It might have told her other things as well, but she was in no condition to notice them.

Wincing involuntarily, she caught her id tag and closed it in her fist.

Then she did her best to keep her features blank against his reaction when he saw the state of her hands.

His eyes turned instantly hard; his grin locked into place. Without transition his body passed from movement to poised stillness. Casually – too casually – he asked, 'Morn, have you been fighting again?'

For a heartbeat or two, the effects of her zone implant almost broke. She'd been fighting, all right. And nothing was resolved. But the control held. A shade too late, she shook her head.

'I fell. Caught myself on my fists.'

As if that were the end of the matter, she pulled the chain over her head and dropped her id tag into her shipsuit.

He didn't appear to know whether to believe her or not. Non-committally he said, 'Go to sickbay. Liete can wait for you.'

Again Morn shook her head. 'If it hurts enough, it might teach me to be more careful next time.' Then she added, 'I want to do my job.'

Slowly the danger eased out of him. He may have decided to believe her. Or he may have believed that she hadn't lost whatever fight she'd been in. Her black box helped her look like she hadn't lost. With a shrug, he dismissed the subject.

To the command third, he said, 'You're on.' Then he left the bridge.

Morn looked at Liete Corregio, received a nod, and went to seat herself at the data station.

Every time she touched the keys in front of her, her knuckles hurt as if they were broken.

That was what she desired.

Liete was a small, dark woman with blunt features and a voice that barely carried across the bridge. In addition her manner conveyed so little obvious authority that at first Morn wondered whether Liete had obtained her position by being another of Nick's discarded lovers. But the command third looked too plain to suit Nick Succorso's romantic tastes. And before long Morn became convinced that Liete Corregio was nearly as competent as Mikka Vasaczk. She lacked Mikka's overt aggressiveness, but not her certainty or skill. Apparently Nick's tolerance for women like Alba Parmute didn't extend to the command positions aboard his ship.

Despite Liete's competence, however, *Captain's Fancy* was in serious trouble.

Part of the problem, of course, was that Liete's people were the weakest members of the crew. Regardless of Morn's opinion of Lind, for instance, she had to admit that he was orders of magnitude better than the communications third. The men who handled scan and targ were, respectively, an habitual drunk who understood demolition better than spectrography and a huge brawler so ham-fisted that he could scarcely hit one key at a time. And helm was managed by a malodorous weasel at once erratic and brilliant: he seemed capable of anything except following orders. Liete's ability to make such individuals function together grew increasingly impressive to Morn as time went on.

Unfortunately there was a larger difficulty. It involved Nick's decision to 'work around' Orn Vorbuld's virus.

None of Liete's watch had the least idea how to make their equipment operate manually. In fact, no one aboard could do it, except Vector, Pup, and Carmel; Mikka, Liete, and Morn; and Nick himself. Ships had been run cybernetically for so long that most spacefarers had no experience with anything else. Overrides existed, of course; and men and women who'd been trained in places like the UMCP Academy or Aleph Green understood them. But of necessity pirates attracted crew with motley histories and oblique skills, imprecisely relevant to the ship's needs. Nick's people simply didn't know how to do their jobs without exposing their computers to the virus.

Liete Corregio's assignment when Morn joined her watch – and for a number of weeks afterward – was to teach the thirds how to run *Captain's Fancy* without triggering wipe.

The process went badly from the beginning. Morn was on only her third watch when the drunk at the scan Station contrived to erase all his data. That cost the ship twenty hours while she ran another datacore playback.

A day or two later, Mikka Vasaczk's targ second, Karster, accidentally triggered a random matter cannon barrage which scorched a ten-meter-wide strip of *Captain's Fancy*'s skin and vaporized a doppler sensor before it was stopped. That cost the crew a week in EVA suits, working to replace the sensor.

And before anyone had a chance to recover, Alba Parmute, who considered EVA a personal affront, neglected to deactivate her board at precisely the same time that the scan second forgot to override while configuring the new sensor. That caused another complete wipe and more delays.

Mikka was in a fury. Since she hated stupidity more than she distrusted Morn, she demoted Alba to data third and promoted Morn to her own watch.

Liete accepted Alba with resignation. On *Captain's Fancy*, as on most ships, the true function of the command third was to endure problems which had defeated everyone else.

Nick watched all this with a smoldering glower which said as plainly as words that he was deciding whom to replace when – or if – he reached Thanatos Minor.

Every time Morn plugged her id tag back into the data board to run another playback, she asked herself why she was doing this. But she knew the answer: it was because she had no choice. Nick wouldn't have tolerated a refusal.

Caught by her bitterness at being helpless and her revulsion at sharing her bed, she tried to comfort herself by researching self-destruct. That solace failed her, however: *Captain's Fancy* had no built-in or pre-programmed way to blow up.

Nick was going to use her to betray all human space. She couldn't bear it – and she couldn't prevent it. Her belly had developed a small, tight bulge which would soon grow unmistakable; her nausea disappeared as her body learned to enjoy its new hormonal mix. And yet she was unable to achieve a decision. Her baby was becoming more and more real to her. The idea of keeping him made her want to weep: the idea of aborting him made her want to puke.

Gradually her two dilemmas became blurred: the need to kill herself or *Captain's Fancy*; the need to kill her son. They were separate, but they depended on each other. She couldn't make up her mind about one until she resolved the other.

Because she spent so much time under the influence of her zone-implant, emotionally muted so that she wouldn't try to disembowel Nick whenever he approached her, or to disable the entire data Station while Mikka Vasaczk watched, she was slow to recognize that there were changes at work in her.

Nick was predominantly gentle in her cabin, as if he'd been cured of doubt. Daunted by Orn's example, other men left her alone – even the targ third, who looked like he was accustomed to kill for sex. She had work to do, steady and demanding work which filled her time and deflected her distress. And Mikka's trenchant authority kept her concentration sharp.

Such things gave her time in which to pull herself together. On a level below her own awareness, inspired by hormones or old loyalty, or perhaps by some blind, intransigent unwillingness to let the Angus Thermopyles and the Nick Succorsos in her life break her, she began gathering up the ragged strands of herself and plaiting them into something new.

In retrospect, she wasn't quite sure when she'd stopped carrying her black box. One day she experimented with leaving it behind: after that she kept it hidden in her cabin. Soon six weeks had passed since Orn Vorbuld's death, and the time limit for a safe abortion was running out. *Captain's Fancy* was almost prepared to attempt minor manual course corrections.

And Morn was no longer the same woman.

The difference took effect one day when Nick came to the bridge during the changeover between Mikka's watch and Liete's. He nodded normally to Mikka as Liete relieved her; he gave Morn a grin that was only a little sharper, a bit more deeply tinged with blood, than usual. Yet his presence itself was unusual: ordinarily he waited for Morn in her cabin while Mikka's watch was relieved. As Morn followed the rest of the seconds off the bridge, he gestured the communications third away from his station and seated himself there.

She hardly had time to be sure she'd seen him accurately. She was already on her way to the auxiliary bridge.

She was in a hurry: she could be sure she didn't have much time. Nevertheless the distance to the auxiliary bridge gave her a few moments for consideration. She felt that she was thinking for the first time in weeks. Her original idea was to activate the auxiliary communications board and dummy it to its counterpart. That would enable her to observe what he did. Even if she missed his actual transmission, she might discover in which direction he'd beamed his message.

As soon as she analyzed the idea, however, she realized that Liete would know as soon as she activated the auxiliary communications board. Liete would tell Nick – and Nick wouldn't have any trouble guessing what Morn was up to.

But she had an alternative.

Nobody could edit a datacore. Every fact *Captain's Fancy* possessed, every action she took, was permanently stored. And that meant—

It meant that no matter how much information Nick purposely deleted from his transmission history, the datacore remained whole. Therefore playback restored the ship's information in an unedited condition.

If he hadn't thought of that – if he hadn't repeated *all* his deletions after each playback – she could look at whatever he'd tried to suppress.

From the auxiliary data Station, she could copy the message he was sending right now.

That she'd activated the auxiliary Station would show on Liete's command board. But what she was actually doing wouldn't. And she wouldn't have any trouble explaining away her desire to make use of the auxiliary data Station. She could think of an excuse that fit within her duties.

Under other circumstances, she would have kicked herself for not grasping all this earlier. Now she didn't have time.

The auxiliary bridge was fortuitously deserted. She had her id tag jacked into the console as soon as she hit the seat. To cover herself, she opened the intercom and asked Mikka's permission to do some research; but she didn't wait for an answer. Her fingers ran the keys. When Mikka asked her what kind of research she had in mind, she replied that she wanted to see if she could identify the defaults or protocols Orn's virus used to wipe the systems. By the time the command second said, 'Okay,' Morn had already begun restoring the transmission Nick had just erased.

What she learned struck her as hard as one of Nick's blows; but it didn't paralyze her; it didn't make her freeze, or stop.

The message itself was ciphered, of course. She couldn't read it – and had no time to try. But she recognized its destination and security codes, the codes which ensured it would be received by the right person, and no one else. In addition, the resources of the data board enabled her to plot its transmission vector. In moments she saw that the message had been tight-beamed to a set of coordinates she knew well.

The coordinates of a UMCP listening post.

One of the thousands of listening posts which had been set to help guard the border of forbidden space.

She was a cop: she knew how those listening posts worked. At intervals determined by UMCPHQ's priorities, a courier drone arrived at the post. The post dumped its accumulated data to the drone. The drone crossed the gap back toward Earth. It gave up its data to the UMCP transmission relay coasting outside Pluto's orbit; positioned there so that hundreds of drones serving thousands of listening posts – not to mention Stations and colonies – could avoid the planets, satellites, rocks, and ships which cluttered the solar system. The relay in turn beamed the data to UMCPHQ. Under the right conditions, the entire process could be astonishingly quick: significant delays occurred only when the courier drone had to carry its data at space normal speeds.

And Nick had left his dish aimed at the listening post. He was expecting an answer.

The implications chilled her. She felt that she was losing contact with reality, as if g had disappeared from under her – as if *Captain's Fancy* had lost internal spin, or gone awry in her trajectory across the void. Nick had sent a message to the UMCP. He was expecting an answer.

Oh, my God.

But she wasn't given a chance to sort her way through the morass. Before she could try to gauge the extent of Nick's treachery, she heard him ask sardonically, 'Any luck?'

Blanking her readouts, she swung her seat to face him.

He leaned in the doorway, grinning at her. After all this time, the sight of her still pulled his lips back from his teeth, darkened his scars. Maybe her disconcertion made her look frightened: maybe the idea that she was frightened excited him. Or maybe he was so caught up in the masque of her passion that he couldn't break free.

But she wasn't frightened; not now. She had gone past that without knowing it. And past trying to second-guess the consequences of her actions. She was thinking for the first time in weeks, and her questions were about to be answered. Deliberately she stared straight at him. Her tone was neutral with concentration.

'You sent a message to the UMCP.'

Instantly his whole body became still and ominous, poised like a bomb.

As if the subject were one of purely intellectual curiosity, she asked, 'Does your crew know you do things like that?'

His gaze was as steady as hers; his grin had no love in it. 'You're the only one who isn't in on the secret. And you still aren't – so don't push your luck.'

She ignored that. It was either true or false – and she doubted he would tell her which. Instead she said, 'I thought you were planning to sell me on Thanatos Minor. My information, anyway. Have you changed your mind?'

Only his mouth moved. Every other muscle held its poise; as far as she could tell, he didn't so much as blink.

'Who told you we're going to Thanatos Minor?'

'Nobody,' she said evenly. 'I figured it out.'

'How?'

She shrugged and indicated the auxiliary data console. 'I had to learn the equipment before I could do my job. Studying what astrogation says about our trajectory was good practice.'

His grin stretched a little tighter. 'And how did you find out I "sent a message to the UMCP"?' He made the name sound like an obscenity.

She told him.

He received the information without moving. When she was done, he demanded, 'How long have you been spying on me?'

She answered that question as well. On this subject, she no longer had any reason to lie.

'This is the first time. I didn't realize I could do it until a few minutes ago.' She let a hint of bitterness into her tone as she added, 'I've had a lot of other things on my mind.'

Then she returned to her own question. 'Why are you talking to the UMCP?'

As if she'd gained her point, he shifted his weight off the doorframe. Casually, like a lazy predator, he moved to the command Station and sat down. She turned to face him all the way, tracking him like targ.

For a moment his fingers massaged his scars as if he wanted to rub the blood out of them. Then he said, 'I can get more money for what you know if I hold an auction. But you can't hold an auction unless you've got at least two bidders. I'm giving your old buddies a chance to keep what you know secret by paying for the privilege.'

That was a lie: she recognized it immediately. It was plausible in itself; but it didn't explain how he knew the location of the listening post.

She didn't challenge his dishonesty, however. Let him think she was taken in: she had other issues to consider. Flatly she countered, 'They won't do it.'

'Why not?' he asked as if he weren't particularly interested in her answer.

'Because they can't be sure you won't take their money and still sell me when you get to Thanatos Minor.'

He shrugged. 'I already thought of that. I told them if I accept their bid I'll give you access to communications. You can report to them – tell them I'm keeping my end of the bargain. In fact, you can tell them anything you learn while we're getting our repairs done.'

She shook her head. 'Not good enough. An offer like that doesn't guarantee anything. They'll want a guarantee.'

Her argument didn't appear to bother him. 'It's worth a try. If they turn me down, we haven't lost anything.'

Oh, yes, you have, Nick Succorso, she thought. By God, you have.

But she didn't say that. As the change in her came into focus, she found herself thinking faster, more clearly.

Carefully, neutrally, she offered, 'I've got a better idea. Tell them if they pay enough you'll take me somewhere else. And you'll let me report to them that you really have changed course. Let me convince them you're keeping your part of the bargain.'

Between one heartbeat and the next, he lost his air of nonchalant disinterest. He stiffened in his seat; his gaze sharpened on her. In a harsh, slow drawl, he asked, 'Now, why would you want me to do a thing like that?'

If he thought he could make her falter, he was mistaken. Facing him as squarely as ever, she replied, 'Because I don't want to go to Thanatos Minor.'

'Why the hell not? Do you think you're still a cop? Do you think you've got a right to *care* who I sell your secrets to? You gave that up several billion kilometers ago. What makes you so fucking scrupulous all of a sudden?'

There her dilemmas came together. In his hot glare and her own danger, she saw how they depended on each other; and her intuitive indecisiveness vanished. Abruptly certain, she held his gaze as if he were the only one of them who had any experience with doubt.

'I'm pregnant,' she announced distinctly. 'I'm going to have a boy. He's due about the time you're planning to get your gap drive fixed – and I don't want to have him on Thanatos Minor. We'll both be too vulnerable. He could be used against me. Either one of us could be used against you.'

Praying that he would believe her – that he wouldn't demand an examination in sickbay to confirm what she said – she concluded, 'Nick, he's your son.'

CHAPTER 9

From the auxiliary command seat, Nick met her gaze. His tone was as deadly as the one he'd used with Orn Vorbuld.

'Abort it.'

Morn was glad that she'd never made the mistake of thinking he would welcome any child, even a son. And she was glad for a chance to defy him at last. In fact, she was delighted – so keenly pleased that her heart sang. Her greatest danger at the moment wasn't that she might back down: it was that she might let too much visceral joy show.

Softly she said, 'I don't want to.'

'I don't give a fuck in hard vacuum what you want,' he retorted. His grin looked bloody and threatening. 'I said, *abort* it.'

'Why?' Her reply was almost sarcastic in its sweetness. 'Don't you want a son? Reputation is only one kind of immortality. And it fades after a while. People forget what you've done. They forget the stories about you. You can have more than that. A son will preserve your genes.'

'Fine. Terrific. With my luck, the bastard will grow up to be a cop.' Nick had swung his seat toward hers: his hands gripped the contoured armrests. 'In any case, you can't raise a kid on a ship like this. You'll have to feed it, take care of it. You'll always be thinking about it – you won't be able to work. It'll get in the way. I'll be stuck with it for *years*.

'It'll be impossible. I'll have to leave you behind.'

'Listen to me, Morn. I'm only going to say this once. I want you to abort that little shit.'

There it was: *want*. His command word. *When you hear the word 'want,' you don't ask. It isn't up for discussion. You just do*. She was glad that she'd been able to drive him to this point so easily.

Without flinching, she answered, 'No.'

He snatched in a deep breath: he was about to explode. His pulse throbbed in his scars, making them as dark as the core of his passion. He'd killed people for defying him like this: she was sure of that.

But she was also sure he wouldn't kill her. Not yet; not while she was so valuable to him; not while he believed the masque. She sat still and waited for him to blast her. Or to restrain himself.

He let his breath out with a discernible tremor. 'Just this once,' he rasped between his teeth, 'I'm going to let you tell me what your reasons are.'

The time had come for lies. Because she was glad, they came readily.

'Nick, you know what they are. You don't need me to explain them. I'm a woman. And I love you. I want to have your baby.

'You aren't used to women who love you. You've been betrayed too often. But you've seen how I feel about you. I catch fire every time you touch me. Even when you hit me,' she added because she was gleeful enough to take any risk, 'I go wild.

'And I haven't got anybody else. I killed them all – *I killed them all*, Nick. I've got gap-sickness, remember? I *aborted* my whole ship. I'm not going to do that again.

'Right now, you're all I have. And I already know I won't have you for long.' This was part of the masque – the false instrument playing on the deluded artist. 'No man is ever satisfied with just one woman, and you're more of a man than anyone I've ever met. Sooner or later, I won't be enough for you. The same way Mikka wasn't enough, and Alba, and all the others. In the end, you'll replace me. But I'll never be able to replace you.

'When you're gone, I want to have something left. I want to have *your son*. I want to bear him and raise him, so that I'll always know you were real.' She emphasized her *want* in opposition to his. 'No matter how much time passes, or my memory fades, I'll know I didn't dream you. He'll remind me that at least once in my life I knew what passion was.'

Her lies touched him: she saw that. His hands flexed on the armrests; an oblique grief moistened the fire in his eyes. He believed the masque: he was accessible to this appeal.

At the same time he was too stubborn, too suspicious – and too intelligent – to lose his way so easily. He had to swallow twice before he could find his voice. Then he said, 'Crap.'

She wasn't daunted. Without hesitation, she responded, 'Try me.'

'I intend to,' he growled. 'What did you have in mind?'

Her defiance affected her like rapture; it almost made her laugh. After all this time, she finally had a use for her revulsion. But laughing would have had the wrong effect. Instead she leaned forward earnestly and braced her elbows on her knees, shifting her appeal that much closer to him.

'Nick,' she answered, nearly whispering, 'you need me. You want to sell me – or what I know – so you can pay for repairs. And you want me to have an abortion. We both know you can get what you want. You can hit me right now – you can knock me out and take me to sickbay. I couldn't stop you. You don't even need to worry about how I'll feel about it. You don't need my cooperation to sell me. You can just dope me with cat until we get to Thanatos Minor and then hand me over. I'm sure they've got drugs that will make me tell them everything I know.

'But you don't have to go that far. You can just ignore me. I say I want to keep your baby? I say I don't want to have him on Thanatos Minor? That's my tough luck. When we get there, you can dope me, baby and all, and sell me the way I am. If you're afraid I'll do something to *Captain's Fancy* in the meantime, you can take my id tag. That'll paralyze me pretty effectively.'

As she spoke, he watched her with growing steadiness, confidence. Deliberately she reminded him of his power over her. To set him up.

The things he could do to her no longer scared her.

When the fury had begun to fade from his scars, and his eyes were calmer, she sprang her trap.

'But if you do either of those things – if you force me to have an abortion, or if you force me to have my baby on Thanatos Minor – I'm going to tell whoever you try to sell me to that you've been bargaining with the UMCP.'

His sudden stillness told her that she'd hit him where he could be hurt.

'Then,' she continued, 'what I know won't be worth shit. There isn't anybody in space stupid enough to think that people like Min Donner and Hashi Lebwohl will just sit on their hands while you sell their secrets. The minute you tried to get the UMCP into the auction, you warned them of the danger they're in, and everything I know became obsolete.'

She went on leaning toward him as if she were begging rather than threatening: he leaned away from her as if he were appalled. Remorselessly, reveling in his distress, she explained, 'Every code, every route, every listening post will be changed. Every agent and ship will be warned. It doesn't matter what was really in that message of yours. It doesn't even matter that I can't prove anything. Just the doubt will be enough. That's something you can't take away from me – not unless you destroy my mind, and then I won't have any secrets left.

'All I have to do is tell whoever wants to buy me that you beamed a message to a UMCP listening post, and you won't be able to get enough for me to buy new scrubber pads.'

She had him. She *had* him. She was so sure of it that she nearly cheered.

And as soon as she had him, he got away.

Nick Succorso was a survivor – a man who always found a way to keep himself alive. But he was more than that, much more. According to his reputation, he was a pirate who never lost. Once Mikka Vasaczk had swayed the entire crew by shouting, *Have any of you EVER seen Nick beaten?*

He wasn't beaten now.

He absorbed the worst Morn could do to him; he was hurt by it. When she was done, he sat still and stared at her for a moment, holding himself as if he couldn't breathe; as if she'd hit him so hard that all the air was knocked out of him.

But then the fighting light came back into his eyes. A wild grin bared his teeth.

Abruptly he laughed – a harsh sound like an act of violence.

Frozen with sudden alarm, Morn returned his stare and couldn't move.

'You think you've got me, don't you?' he grated. 'You think you've given me a choice I can't refuse. I can let you keep your baby – I can stay away from Thanatos Minor. Then you'll go on loving me. My ship won't get fixed, but I'll have all the fucking sex I can stand. Or I can force you to abort. In which case you'll sabotage me so bad I'll have to sell my soul to the Bill just for supplies, and my ship still won't get fixed.

'I can't imagine why I don't fall all over myself to take you up on an offer like that.'

Now Morn was the one who held her breath. 'Maybe it's because I don't *want* a woman who thinks she can push me around.

'Or maybe,' he said in fierce, combative exultation, 'it's because I've got options you haven't considered.' For a moment her brain reeled; then it snapped back into clarity. She didn't try to speculate on what he meant. Instead she asked, 'Like what?'

With a surge as if he were moving to attack her, he shifted forward in his seat, thrusting his face toward hers, mimicking her posture. The inflexible skin of his scars pulled his grin into a grimace.

'Forbidden space has an outpost in this sector,' he said like a wash of mineral acid. 'You know that. You noticed it while you were figuring out where we're headed. We've still got a window on it – just barely. We can go there if we change course now.

'Do you know what they pay for live human beings? I can sell you outright, no matter how obsolete your information happens to be, and get enough cash to flush out that damn virus. While I'm at it, I can sell a loser like Alba Parmute and get enough more to repair my gap drive.'

That threat was worse than anything she'd expected, anything she'd imagined. *Sell her*? *To forbidden space*? Would he *do* that? She couldn't tell: she still didn't know him well enough to guess his limits. Fighting panic, she hurried to contradict him.

'And as soon as you start selling your crew, they'll never trust you again. Even illegals like yours are going to take exception. They may mutiny. You can't watch your back twenty-four hours a day. At the very least, they'll talk. They'll ruin your reputation. You won't be the Nick Succorso who never loses. You'll be the Nick Succorso who sells his own people to forbidden space.'

'That won't happen,' he replied like a knife, 'if I just sell *you*. You're UMCP – you're the enemy. Selling *you* will make me a goddamn hero.'

'But' – Morn felt that she was laboring against heavy g to keep up with him – 'you still won't have enough money. You'll be able to flush out the virus, or get your gap drive fixed, but not both. You won't have anything else to sell.'

Nick's eyes burned at her. He nodded once and dropped back in his seat. His scars had lost some of their color: they were pale and livid, like old bruises.

Yet his grin looked more ferocious than ever as he pronounced, 'Stalemate.'

He was right. They had each found the flaws in the other's position. Their threats canceled each other.

'Nick,' she said slowly, 'I want to keep my baby. And I *don't* want to be sold to forbidden space.' The idea was profoundly terrifying. She would have preferred to attempt EVA with a faulty suit. 'If you've got any suggestions, I'm listening.'

At that, he laughed again like a promise that she would never be safe. Then he leaned forward once more and pointed his index finger like the barrel of an impact pistol straight between her eyes.

Almost in a whisper, he said, 'You're damn fucking right I've got a "suggestion."

'This is *your* problem. *You* refused a direct order. So *you* get to solve it.'

Still aiming his finger at her, he left his seat to move toward her.

'Give me a cure for that virus.'

She gaped at him, unable to retort.

'If you do that,' he went on, right in front of her now, 'if you fix my ship so that she can maneuver and fight again, I'll let you keep your baby. I won't sell you to forbidden space. We'll go somewhere besides Thanatos Minor.

'If you *don't* —' He let the ultimatum hang for a moment. Then he breathed, 'You'll give yourself an abortion. And you'll keep your mouth shut about messages to the UMCP.'

'Nick —' Her throat knotted; she had trouble dredging up words. 'What makes you think I can cure a computer virus?'

Without warning, he moved his finger; he flicked her hard in the tender junction of nerves under her nose. While her eyes filled with involuntary tears, he said softly, 'What makes you think I care?'

Then he got up and walked off the auxiliary bridge; left her alone at the data Station with tears streaming down her cheeks as if she were beaten.

She had options, of course. It would be easy to activate the auxiliary data board and trigger another wipe. Then, if she were quick enough, she might be able to snatch an EVA suit and get off the ship before anyone caught her. That would give her a chance to ditch her id tag outside, where no one could ever find it. If she succeeded – and if she used the suit's maneuvering thrusters to put as much distance as possible between herself and *Captain's Fancy* – she might avoid the horrible things Nick and his crew would do to her before they died.

She would die herself when the suit's air ran out: she would suffocate alone in the vast dark. But at least her death would accomplish something.

It would put a stop to Nick Succorso.

As recently as two or three weeks ago, she might have tried that. She might have been desperate enough.

Now she dismissed it.

She'd changed too much to consider suicide.

Faced with Nick's ultimatum, she wanted to know what was at stake. Whatever his message to UMCPHQ contained, she was sure it had nothing to do with auctioning. His knowledge of the listening post's coordinates proved that he'd had dealings with the UMCP for some time – the kind of dealings which required them to remain in contact with each other.

Vector Shaheed had cause to believe the cops themselves were corrupt; treasonous to humankind. If he was right, it implied that Nick was engaged in something worse than simple piracy.

And if she killed herself little Davies Hyland would die with her.

Her desire to save him surprised her. On a conscious level, her claim that she wanted to keep him had been a smoke screen to disguise her real reasons for resisting being sold on Thanatos Minor. But now she saw that the claim was true. Maybe she wanted her son as a way of defying Nick; maybe she wanted him for himself; maybe she was overcome by the desire not to add Davies' name to the list of her victims; maybe she was under too much pressure to refuse the logic of her hormones: she didn't know. Whatever the explanation, however, the conclusion was clear: she had become prepared to fight for her baby's life.

Which meant she had to find a cure for Orn's virus. That was the decision she reached. Aware of what she was doing, and galvanized by it, she accepted Nick's terms, just as she'd once accepted Angus'.

The proposition was absurd on its face. She knew no more about such things than Nick himself did. Where could she start? What could she do that hadn't already been tried? How far could she push herself before she failed – before Nick forced her to accept defeat?

Nevertheless she put everything she had into the attempt.

Once again she took to carrying her zone-implant control with her, regardless of the danger.

She needed it to deal with Nick, of course. Caught up in his anger over her defiance, and perhaps intending to help her fail, he pursued sex with her as mastery rather than pleasure; he took her brutally in unexpected places, at unexpected times, when she needed to concentrate on other things. And yet as always her survival depended on her ability to preserve the illusion that she hungered for him whatever he did, that even rape only made her love him more. Without her black box, she would have been unable to maintain the masque for as much as five minutes – certainly not for all the long days which followed.

But she also needed the control to keep her attention sharp, to suppress her fatigue, to hold her fear at bay. She had to do her job on Mikka's watch – and she had to respond to Nick whenever he came at her. That left relatively few hours each day in which she could tackle the problem of the virus; too few. As much as possible, she elected to go without sleep.

Alive with artificial energy, she spent virtually all her spare time on the auxiliary bridge poring over *Captain's Fancy*'s programs: running every available diagnostic test on them; scrutinizing their logic; dividing them into their component parts and dummying each part separately to her board so that she could see how it functioned. When she slept, she did so not because she felt the need, but because she knew her body had limits which her zone-implant ignored. Her baby had limits. On some days, however, she forgot about limits and worked continuously. Frequently she neglected to eat. Her mind was like a thruster on full burn, consuming its resources in a white, pure fire that seemed to deny entropy and thermodynamics.

After several days of that, she looked as haggard and gap-eyed as a casualty of war; but she didn't know it.

A week passed, and part of another week, before she thought of an answer.

When it occurred to her, she spent no time at all wondering why she hadn't conceived of it earlier – or cursing herself for being so dense. She was too busy.

A datacore time-study.

More accurately, a study of *Captain's Fancy*'s basic programming as it was recorded over time in the datacore. That would enable her to compare the original programming with its present state. Then a simple comparison test would locate the changes Orn had written into the operating systems.

The job was horrendously complex to prepare, however. A plain one-to-one comparison between the present state of the ship's data and its state before Orn came aboard would have taken months to run and reported millions of discrepancies, the record of everything *Captain's Fancy* had seen and done since the starting date of the comparison. So Morn had to write a filter through which she could play back the data so that everything irrelevant to the condition and function of the programming itself would be excluded. Then she had to go over that body of information almost line by line in order to delete anything secondary, anything which would bog down the comparison to no purpose.

All that took most of four days. She could have done it in three if Nick hadn't insisted on using her so hard.

When she was finished – when she'd run her time-study and obtained its results – she finally felt an emotion so organic and spontaneous that it overwhelmed the zone-implant's emissions. Her artificial burn shut down, leaving her at the mercy of her mortality.

The comparison was conclusive. From the day before Orn came aboard to the present, no substantive changes, elisions, or amendments had been made to *Captain's Fancy*'s operational programming.

According to her study, there was no virus.

Several moments passed before Morn noticed that she was hunched over the auxiliary data board, sobbing like a bereft child. Caught between physical exhaustion, natural grief, and imposed energy, she couldn't seem to do anything except cry.

After a time, Vector Shaheed heard her and came to the auxiliary bridge. She had no idea what he was doing as he pulled her to her feet and dragged her out; no idea how much the strain hurt his joints, or where he was taking her. Weeping was all she had in her, and it wouldn't stop.

He took her to the galley, propped her in a chair at the table, and set a steaming mug of coffee in front of her.

'Don't worry about burning your mouth,' he instructed. 'Burns heal.'

The aroma rose into her face. Obedient to his order – or to an instinct she no longer knew she had – she swallowed her sobs long enough to pick up the mug and drink.

The coffee scalded her tongue and throat. For an instant pain broke through her helplessness.

Between one gulp for air and the next, she stopped crying. The zone-implant began to reassert control.

'That's better.' Vector's voice seemed to reach her through a veil, as if it were muffled by kindness. 'Any minute now you'll be able to think again. If you don't fall asleep first. Or just drop dead. You could kill yourself the way you're going.

'Do you play cards?'

She didn't react. All she cared about was the black heat of the coffee, the flaming hurt in her mouth.

'I know this seems like an inopportune moment for conversation,' he explained in his mild way, 'but I want to reach you while you're still – still accessible. You've been deaf and blind for weeks now. This may be my only chance.

'Do you play cards?'

The retreat of her grief left her exposed to exhaustion. Numbly she nodded. 'Poker. A little. In the Academy. I wasn't good at it.'

Apparently she'd given him some kind of permission. He seated himself, picked up a mug of coffee, and said casually, 'It's interesting how some games endure. Chess, for example. And poker – as a species, we've been playing poker practically forever. And then there's bridge. I've seen gaming encyclopedias that don't even mention whist – which is where bridge came from – but back when I worked for Intertech we used to play bridge for days. Orn was particularly good at it.

'Bridge and poker.' Vector let out a nostalgic sigh. 'The only time life is ever pure is when you're playing games like that. That's because they're closed systems. The cards, and the rules – and the ontological implications – are finite.

'But of course poker isn't really a *card* game. It's a game of people. The cards are just a tool for playing your opponents. That may be why you weren't good at it. Bridge comes much closer to direct problem solving – the extrapolation of discrete logical permutations. You can't ignore who your opponents are, naturally, but you win with your mind more than your guts.

'You're trying to win this one with your guts, Morn. You need to use your mind.'

Morn drank more coffee. She didn't say anything: she didn't have anything to say. Instead she concentrated on the pain in her throat.

'We have a maxim in bridge,' he continued. 'If you need a particular card to be in a certain place, *assume* it is. If you need a particular distribution of the cards, *assume* it exists. Plan the rest of your strategy as if you have a right to be sure of that one assumption.

'It doesn't always work, of course. In fact, you can play for days without it working once. But that's not the point. The point is, if your assumption is false you were going to fail anyway. That assumption represents the one thing you have to have in order to succeed, so you might as well count on it. Without it, there's nothing you can do except shrug and go on to the next hand.'

Morn was adrift in a void of exhaustion and overdriven synapses, anchored only by coffee and her burned tongue. Nothing Vector said made any sense. His little lecture sounded oddly purposeless, unmotivated. And yet he delivered it as if it were important somehow; as if he thought she needed it. With an effort, she resisted the impulse to switch off her black box and let herself collapse.

The electrical coercion in her brain seemed unable to master her fatigue. Nevertheless it reduced her numbness a bit. She cleared her throat and murmured thinly, 'Whose watch is this? I don't even know what day it is.'

Vector consulted a chronometer built into the food-vend. 'Liete's on for another hour. Then it's Nick's turn.' He hesitated momentarily before adding, 'You missed your last watch, but Nick told Mikka to let you stay with what you were doing. He may treat you like shit, but he's counting on you.'

Treat you like shit. That touched a sore place in her. A small sting of anger spread outward from the contact. The effect of the zone-implant grew stronger. Nick did indeed treat her like shit. She had every intention of making him pay blood for the privilege.

'So your advice' – she was too tired to speak distinctly, but she did her best to articulate every word – 'is to just *assume* I can cure this virus. *Assume* there's something I can do that doesn't depend on skills or knowledge I haven't got.'

In response Vector raised his mug like a salute. Smiling gently, he said, 'If you heard me say all that, there's hope for you yet.'

'In that case,' she replied, trying not to mumble, 'our entire approach has been wrong from the beginning. We have to assume that everything we've done so far is wrong.'

He nodded noncommittally. 'Do we? Is that the only assumption that gives us a chance?'

She ignored him. Maybe fatigue was what she needed to take the edge off the zone-implant's effect: maybe she'd been blinded by her own urgency, artificial and otherwise. Now she seemed to feel neurons which had been pushed to the point of shutdown come back on line. She was starting to think again.

'Where's Mackern?' she asked as if she had a right to expect Vector's help.

He studied her without adjusting his smile. 'He's on with Nick in an hour.'

So what? If Mikka could do without her, Nick could do without Mackern. 'I need him.'

Vector shrugged. Lifting himself stiffly to his feet, he moved to the intercom.

'With your permission, Nick,' he told the intercom, 'Morn wants to talk to Sib Mackern. She says she needs him.'

Obliquely Morn realized that she'd never heard Mackern's first name before.

Nick's voice came back: 'Where?'

'In the galley.'

'I'll send him.' The intercom clicked off.

The data first arrived only a minute or two after Vector sat down again. He must have been somewhere nearby when he received Nick's orders.

'You wanted to talk to me?' he asked Morn. The idea appeared to aggravate his uncertainty. Whatever he used instead of self-confidence to keep him going was as nearly invisible as his pale mustache.

She needed time to get her thoughts in order. For a moment she said nothing. Vector urged Sib Mackern to sit down. He offered the data first coffee. Sib preferred to remain standing; he refused the coffee.

Both men watched Morn as if they wanted to witness the exact moment when she fell asleep.

Sleep, she mused. Rest and death. She needed both – not necessarily in that order. But not yet.

'Sib.' She pulled up her attention with a jerk. 'What kind of name is that?'

'It's short for Sibal,' he replied, too nervous to give her anything except a straight answer. 'My mother wanted a girl.'

'Oh, well,' Vector sighed. 'If you were a girl, she would have wanted a boy. None of us ever win with our mothers.'

'Sib, I need you.' Morn had no energy to spare for Vector's sense of humor. 'Nobody trusts me. Nobody is going to do what I tell them. I haven't got access or authority. And I'm' – she could hardly hold up her head, despite the zone-implant's emissions – 'too tired to do anything myself. I need you.'

He didn't commit himself. 'Nick told me to help you.'

'Sib, you know more about computers than I do.' She brushed aside a demurral he didn't make. 'If you wanted to plant a virus aboard, how would you go about it?'

His gaze flicked to Vector, back to her. 'I don't understand.'

Unable to explain herself better, she repeated, 'How would you go about it?'

'If I knew how to plant a virus,' he objected, 'I might be able to cure this one.'

Morn stared her desperate and conflicted weariness up at him and refused to let him off the hook.

'But if I knew how —' He faltered; his mustache looked like a streak of dirt bleeding into his mouth at the corners. After a moment he began again more strongly. 'If I knew how, I could just sit down at the data board and write it in. But that would be the hard way.'

'Why?'

'It's an incredibly complicated job. I would have to study the entire system to find the right place for the virus. That takes time. A lot of time. And the coding for the virus has to be enormously complex – as well as enormously subtle. Otherwise it shows. Or it doesn't do what it's supposed to. Which takes more time. Somebody would almost certainly catch me.'

Rather helplessly, he added, 'You know that.'

She dismissed the issue of what she did or didn't know with a twitch of her hand. 'What would be the easy way?'

'Write it all ahead of time,' he said more promptly. 'Bring it aboard on tape – or in a chip. Then I could just copy it into the system whenever I had a minute to spare.'

'Fine,' Morn murmured as if she were dozing. 'You can write it all ahead of time. You can copy it in seconds. But you still need to study the system. You can't design your virus until you know the system.'

The data first nodded. 'Sure.'

'Vector, did Orn ever have a chance to study *Captain's Fancy*'s systems before you joined ship?'

The engineer's gaze was quizzical. 'Not that I know of. I can't be sure, but I don't think so.' Then he added, 'Nick would know.'

She also dismissed the issue of what Nick did or didn't know. 'Assume it. Assume he couldn't write the virus until he knew the system – and he couldn't get to know the system until he joined ship.'

A small frown creased Vector's round face. 'You're saying he must have written the virus after he and I came aboard.'

'No. Sib's right.' Fatigue made everything hard to explain. 'He was new. Nobody trusts new people. Nobody would let him spend five or ten uninterrupted hours at the computers without challenging him.' Not Mikka Vasaczk. And certainly not Nick, whose instinct for trouble was as searching as a particle sifter. 'He would have to do the work in little bits and pieces, while nobody was looking. It might take him weeks.

'But he said' – it was astonishing how clearly she remembered this – 'he said, "I put a virus in the computers – the same day I came aboard." The same day, not weeks later.'

'He may not have been telling the truth,' Vector observed.

'Assume he was. Now we have a virus that couldn't have been written earlier and wasn't written later.'

Vector studied his coffee as if it could cure his perplexity. 'So what are the alternatives?'

'Hardware,' Mackern breathed. He sounded like he was about to be sick.

Morn turned her tired gaze on him and waited.

'But that's impossible,' he protested to himself. 'I mean, it's not technically impossible. He could hardwire a virus into a chip or a card. Or a mother-board – that would be the most versatile. It would do the same thing as a program virus. He could order it dormant or activate it whenever he wanted.

'He could do the work before he came aboard. Then he would only need five minutes alone in the core to substitute his chip, or whatever.

'But it's still impossible.'

Vacillating between sleep and concentration, Morn asked, 'Why?'

'For the same reason he couldn't write the virus ahead of time,' Sib replied. 'There are too many different kinds of computers, as well as too many different kinds of programs to run them. He couldn't hardwire a *compatible* chip unless he already knew exactly what equipment we have. And we're assuming he couldn't know that before he joined ship.'

'Not to mention the expense,' Vector put in. 'Ordinary sods like us can just about afford a hard-memory chip or two for systems like these – if we've got steady jobs and we like to save. Mother-boards might as well be on the other side of the gap.'

'But not,' Morn murmured as if she'd decided on sleep, 'interface cards.'

The data first opened his mouth; closed it again. A wince in his eyes made him look like he was afraid of her.

'What do you mean,' Vector inquired tentatively, '"not interface cards"?' He gave the impression that he doubted she could answer the question.

'Not everything.' Without quite realizing it, she'd slipped her hands into her pockets; her fingers rested on the keys of the zone-implant control. She was so familiar with it that she could use it without looking at it. 'Not expensive.' Probably she should have felt brilliant, victorious: she should have felt that she'd achieved a breakthrough that would redeem her. But she lacked the energy for so much emotion. As soon as she finished what she was saying, she would turn off the control and let herself rest. 'And not impossible.'

'Morn' – Vector leaned forward, touched her arm – 'you're drifting. Try to stay with us a little longer.'

With an act of will which the zone-implant itself made possible, she took her fingers off the control.

'They aren't expensive,' she said dimly. 'If they were, "ordinary sods" couldn't afford to expand or upgrade their systems. And they can be hardwired like a chip, or a mother-board.' Especially in this case, when all that was needed was a relatively simple embedded wipe command with an on-off code. 'And there's no compatibility problem. Interface cards are standardized. That's why they can be cheap. They plug into standard slots – they run on standard operating systems. If you want to interface two computers, all you have to do is look at them, see what they are. Then you set a few dip-switches on your cards, plug them in, and connect the leads.'

As she spoke, Sib began to nod, ticking off points in his mind when she made them.

She forced herself to continue. 'All our computers seem to function fine independently. And they all wipe when we link them up. He could probably change out every interface card in the core in fifteen minutes.

'Has anybody searched his cabin?'

Vector's eyes were wide and round, as blue as surprise. 'Not that I know of. Why bother? He wasn't likely to leave a virus-owner's manual lying around.'

Waves of sleep rolled through her and receded again as the zone-implant fought them. She waited until one of them passed; then she said, 'You might find something interesting if you did.'

Mackern went on nodding as if he couldn't stop.

'It's worth a try.' Vector was back at the intercom before Morn noticed that he'd moved. She eased her fingers onto her black box again as he keyed the intercom and said, 'Mikka?'

The command second took a minute or two to answer. When she replied, she sounded grim and unreachable. 'I'm sleeping, goddamn it. Leave me alone.'

Unflappable as ever, Vector said, 'We're in the galley. I don't think you want to miss this, Mikka.'

By the time Mikka arrived, Morn was deep in dreams, cradling her head with her arms on the galley table.

When Vector nudged her awake, her brain was gone, lost in unnavigable weariness. She could focus her eyes on him – she was able to recognize Mikka and Sib standing behind him – but she had no idea what they wanted.

'Come on,' the engineer said gently. 'You don't want to miss this.'

Where had she heard that before? She couldn't remember.

There were other things she couldn't do as well. She couldn't protest. Or resist: all her resistance, every bit of her independent self, had fallen away into a black abysm of sleep. Numb and disconnected, she let Vector urge her up from her chair; she let him and Mikka take her out of the galley between them.

Out of the galley to the bridge.

Nick was there with his watch – Carmel and Lind, Malda Verone, the helm first. Sib Mackern's place at the data Station was empty, but he didn't move to take it; he stayed beside Mikka with Vector and Morn as if the four of them were joined in an obscure pact.

Nick faced them tightly. Morn couldn't read his expression, and didn't try. If Mikka and Vector had let go of her, she would have slumped to the deck.

'That took you long enough,' he said. She couldn't read his tone, either. 'What the hell's going on?'

'I'll spare you the details,' Mikka answered brusquely. 'Morn thinks she's figured out this virus. She convinced Vector and Mackern. They persuaded me to search Vorbuld's cabin.

'For some reason, he kept a box of interface cards in his locker. They look normal to me, but Mackern says he thinks they've been doctored. He thought we should replace all the interface cards in the core.' Morn felt the command second shrug. 'He's data first. I let him do it.

'He got a new set of cards from stores and changed out the old ones. Just to be on the safe side, I watched him do it. The old cards are all out. The new ones were sealed before he opened them, so they haven't been tampered with.

'If he's right – if Morn is right – the virus is gone.'

'If you don't mind' – now Morn could hear Nick's sarcasm – 'we'll test that a few times before I believe it.

'Mackern,' he ordered, 'the rest of you, get to work. I want to re-create the tests we ran the first time – I want to do exactly the same things that triggered those first wipes.'

Maybe he went on talking. Or maybe not. Morn couldn't tell: she was asleep again.

Vector and Mikka kept her on her feet; they held her approximately at attention while all the original tests were set up and repeated. But she didn't return to a state which resembled consciousness until Vector shook her and said into her ear, 'Everything works, Morn. You were right. You did it.'

Did it. Oh, good. She wasn't sure she knew what he was talking about.

But then the odd, constricted glare Nick fixed on her pulled up her head, made her take notice of him.

'You win.' He looked at her as if winning were the most dangerous thing she could have done. 'We had a bargain. You kept your end of it. I'll keep mine.

'You can have your damn baby.' The concession came out as a snarl. 'And you won't have to do it on Thanatos Minor. Vector says the gap drive will get us into tach and out again one more time. He doesn't want to stake his life on it, but he's willing to risk his *reputation*.' Nick rasped the word like a curse. 'I'm going to do both for you.'

His eyes blazed with murder or wild joy, she couldn't tell which.

'I'm going to take you to Enablement Station.'

As soon as Morn heard the name, she stopped breathing.

The entire bridge seemed to stop breathing.

'They'll help you have your baby, all right. And we won't have to put up with some squalling brat for the next decade or so. They'll give you a full-grown kid in about an hour.

'Maybe that way I won't have to leave you behind.'

His last words reached her, but she didn't absorb them. She was thinking, Enablement Station.

Forbidden space. The Amnion.

She may have heard Nick's vindictive laughter. He'd intended this from the moment he first made his bargain with her.

In spite of Vector's support, and Mikka's, she fainted as if she were dying.

ANCILLARY DOCUMENTATION
The Amnion

First Contact

Opinion is divided as to what should be formally considered 'first contact' with the Amnion. Some believe that humankind's relations with the only other (known) sentient – not to mention spacefaring – life-form in the galaxy cannot be considered to have begun until the first human met the first Amnioni. By some standards, this occurred aboard the Amnion ship *Solidarity*, when Sixten Vertigus, Captain of the Space Mines, Inc., probe ship *Deep Star*, on his own authority, and against strict SMI instructions, took the risk of an EVA transfer to *Solidarity*'s airlock and was assisted through the locks by a being which he later described as 'a humanoid sea anemone with too many arms.'

His instructions had been to establish proximity with any alien vessel or base, broadcast incessantly the tape which Intertech, a subsidiary of SMI, had prepared for the occasion, tape any returning broadcast his equipment could receive as long as possible without jeopardizing his mission, and then escape into the gap in a way that would confuse pursuit. SMI Chairman and CEO Holt Fasner professed himself unwilling to risk Earth for the sake of profit: he did not wish to reveal too much to beings whose intentions were unguessable.

Sixten Vertigus' disinclination to follow instructions assured him of his place in the history of human-Amnioni relations.

He was an idealist.

He had also been on this mission for a very long time – and Earth was so many light-years away that his decisions were in no danger of being countermanded.

However, the being which assisted him aboard *Solidarity* was a relatively minor functionary. Therefore analysts with a keener sense of protocol argue that 'first contact' took place when Vertigus met the 'Captain' of *Solidarity* (in this context, 'Captain' is an imprecise translation of an Amnion term which means, literally, 'decisive').

In a concrete sense, nothing much was accomplished during this meeting. Captain Vertigus' instruments established that the atmosphere aboard *Solidarity* was one he could breathe – if his life depended on it. This merely confirmed information which he had received much earlier from Intertech: specifically that the Amnion were oxygen-carbon-based, with metabolic processes at least analogous to humankind's. His attempts at speech with *Solidarity*'s 'Captain' gained only the preliminary tapes from which translations were eventually made.

However, Sixten Vertigus had no unrealistic expectations. His only goal – aside from his prohibited desire to lay eyes on at least one Amnioni – was to hand over to someone the tape which he had been instructed to broadcast, along with a player which would enable the Amnion to scrutinize the message at their leisure.

This tape contained a basis on which the Amnion could begin to translate human speech, mathematics, and data coding. Not incidentally, the tape included a message offering alliance and trade with SMI itself. Preferably exclusive.

The Amnion reacted with gestures and noises which meant nothing to Captain Vertigus. They were, however, not unprepared for his gift. And perhaps they understood the significance of the fact that he had come to them alone and unarmed. In exchange for the tape and player, they offered him a sealed canister which contained – research discovered this shortly after his safe return to *Deep Star* – mutagenic material nearly identical to the stuff that had brought him into this quadrant of space in the first place.

In their own way, the Amnion were attempting to communicate.

CHAPTER 10

When Morn finally awoke – in her cabin, sprawled facedown on her bunk – she had the sensation that a frightening amount of time had passed.

She'd dreamed of Amnion and horror; of rape worse than anything Angus Thermopyle had done to her. Her own screams would have awakened her long ago if she hadn't been clamped in sleep, bolted down by utter exhaustion. Screaming and nightmares made her slumber seem interminable.

In her dreams, Nick sold her to the Amnion.

That wasn't what he'd said he would do, but he did it anyway. And the Amnion pumped her full of mutagens until she grew transformed and monstrous; entirely nonhuman; alien, unrecognizable, and insane. People who were given Amnion mutagens always went mad – that's what she'd heard in the Academy. They forgot their humanity altogether: they *became* Amnion.

That was her punishment for winning her gamble with Nick Succorso. Nobody else was allowed to win when they played with him.

No wonder she screamed. She should have died. Merely dreaming such a thing should have stopped her heart. After the crazed and cruel overexertion of the past weeks, she should have been unable to sustain the shock of those visions.

Nick was taking her to Enablement Station. To the source of her horror.

Yet she was still alive. Time had passed, and she was waking up. The impersonal material of the pillow rubbed her cheek: the mattress supported her body's weight. She could feel her black box lumped under her hip; it was still in the pocket of her shipsuit.

If Nick meant to betray her, he hadn't done it yet.

He'd said, *They'll help you have your baby, all right. They'll give you a full-grown kid in about an hour.*

He'd said, *Maybe that way I won't have to leave you behind.*

She didn't understand. She had no idea what he was talking about. In the space of about thirty seconds on the bridge, he'd become as alien and fatal as the Amnion.

She seemed to wake up because she could no longer bear the terror of her dreams. But consciousness held other terrors. She didn't know how to face them.

'If you're coming around,' Mikka Vasaczk said stiffly, 'you might as well admit it. I can't keep Nick waiting forever.'

The sound of the command second's voice didn't surprise Morn. Her capacity for surprise was gone, exhausted by Nick and nightmares. Everything was a betrayal of one kind or another. There was nothing to be surprised about.

Nevertheless she rolled her head to look at her visitor.

Sitting in a chair near the door, Mikka appeared as ungiving as the bulkhead behind her. She held her arms folded under her breasts; her posture was rigid, as if she'd locked down all her joints. Yet an emotion which might have been hostility or need darkened her eyes.

Morn made an effort to swallow the dryness of long sleep. After a moment she mumbled, 'What's he waiting for?'

'He wants to be sure you're all right.' Mikka's tone was like her posture. 'We need to start deceleration, and he's worried about your gap-sickness. He's waiting for me to tell him you're awake and safe. And under control.'

Deceleration, Morn thought without surprise. Heavy g. *Clarity.* The idea made her want to turn away.

But Mikka's gaze held her. She swallowed again. 'Where are we?'

The command second didn't hesitate. 'A couple of days off Enablement. Which barely gives us time to slow down. If we go in too fast, the fucking Amnion are likely to vaporize us on general principles.'

Morn blinked at this information. A couple of days off Enablement. Already. While she slept all her choices had been taken away from her. She'd even missed the chance to hope that she and the whole ship might die in tach.

Dully she asked, 'The gap drive worked?'

'Just barely,' Mikka answered. 'Vector got us through. I didn't know he had it in him. The drive went critical and shut down when we hit the gap. He overrode the safeties – forced enough power into the field generator to bring us out again. And he was fast. We only missed our target reentry by a million kilometers.'

'That's still too close. We don't want to look like we're going to attack. Which is why we're in a hurry to decelerate.' She paused, then added, 'All that power slagged the drive. Too bad.' She may have been trying for sarcasm, but the words conveyed an ache of dismay. 'If Nick can't pull this off,' she concluded harshly, 'we'll never get out of forbidden space.'

'I don't understand.' Morn couldn't think about the gap drive; about getting out of forbidden space. 'Why would they let us approach at all?' *Captain's Fancy* was a human ship – an enemy by definition; in violation of treaty. 'Why aren't they going to vaporize us no matter what we do?'

'Oh, the Amnion don't care who goes into their space.' Mikka had a swelling outrage locked tight inside her. 'They might stop a warship, but nobody else. I'm not even sure they would do that. All they care about is who leaves.'

'I still don't—'

'They want human beings,' Mikka rasped. 'You never have to pay for the privilege of getting near them. But you better be damn ready to pay for the privilege of getting away.'

Morn seemed to hear screams echoing through her visitor's tension. Afraid of dreams, she swung her legs off the bunk and sat up. For a moment she rubbed her face, trying to remove the sensation of helplessness from her nerve endings. Then she put a hand into her pocket to feel the reassurance of the zone-implant control.

'How do you know so much about them?'

'Because,' Mikka growled, 'we've been here before.'

She didn't elaborate. That memory was locked inside her: it may have been the source of her outrage.

Morn tried a different approach. 'Well, if what you say is true,' she asked, 'why are we doing it? Why is Nick doing this?'

'He's perverse, that's why.' The muscles at the corners of Mikka's jaw clenched and unclenched. 'He's always been like this. He's fine as long as we're in enough danger. Then he's the best— But if things get too easy – or,' she added mordantly, 'if somebody solves too many of his problems for him – he goes off on wild tangents. Just when you think you're safe, he jerks g out from under you.

'I don't care what kind of deal he made with you. He didn't have to keep it.' Her tone hinted at a shout of protest. 'As soon as you figured out that virus, he could have changed his mind. There was nothing you could do about it. We had a nice, secure job set up for Thanatos Minor. The usual UMCP double dealing. He has a talent for giving them what they want and getting paid for it before they find out that it causes them more problems than it solves. We've had a lot of success that way, off and on. And we *like* letting the goddamn police pay us for screwing them.

'That's what we did when we got you off Com-Mine. We were just in too much of a hurry to make sure we got paid.'

Morn blinked at her dumbly, trying to absorb this information. But Mikka went on talking.

'All Nick had to do was ignore you – go to Billingate, do the job, get paid, have *Captain's Fancy* repaired, and leave before you cops realized you were in worse trouble than ever. But that would have been too easy. Instead we're stuck on the ragged edge of survival, hoping he can work enough miracles to keep us all alive one more time.'

Her bitterness was plain. However, her manner gave Morn the impression that she was bitter about something else entirely.

It made no difference. *That's what we did*. Morn didn't care why Mikka was bitter. She only cared that no one had ever talked to her this openly about Nick's dealings with the UMCP before. *When we got you off Com-Mine*. There was more going on here than she knew. She wasn't the only one being betrayed. And she could still make choices. If she keyed all the functions of the zone-implant simultaneously at full intensity, she could probably burn out her brain in an instant: she had that one last defense against being sold. She could afford to see how far the command second would go.

Her eyes drifted around the cabin for a moment; she considered the walls and door and intercom with a frown of puzzlement, as if she didn't quite recognize them. Then she brought her gaze back to Mikka's.

'Nick is waiting for you.' Morn's tone was carefully neutral, unchallenging. 'You're supposed to make sure I'm all right – and under control – so he can start deceleration. There isn't much time left. Why are you telling me all this?'

Mikka didn't hesitate. Her hostility and her need came to the same thing. Stiffly she replied, 'I want you to trust me.'

Morn raised her eyebrows. *Trust* you? Nick's second? She stared mutely at the woman and waited.

After a moment Mikka explained as if she were taking a personal risk, 'I want you to tell me how you do it.'

The dryness had come back into Morn's throat. Her voice caught as she asked, 'Do what?'

'All of it,' Mikka retorted. She seemed to hold herself rigid so that she wouldn't pace violently or pound the walls. Perhaps it was her fear of the Amnion that made her so vulnerable. 'The whole thing. How you survived Angus Thermopyle. How you got away from him. How you're able to go for weeks without rest, and carry a workload that would kill a cyborg on permanent stim until you look like an animated null-wave transmitter, and still solve a problem that the best of us have been beating our brains out over. How you make Nick – ' For an instant she faltered. Her jaws clenched. But then she tightened her self-command. 'How you make him need you.

'He's never done anything like this before. He's perverse, all right – but not for women. He doesn't fuck women he trusts. If he starts to trust one, he stops fucking her and finds somebody else. Or if he starts fucking one, he stops trusting her. Or he just gets bored.

'You've done something to him. None of us recognize him. Half of us are in shock. The rest are so scared we're shitting in our suits. I would have staked my life that he would never risk himself like this – or his ship – for any woman. He as sure as hell didn't do it for *me*, the last time we were here. But you've got him doing it. Just so you can have a baby.

'I want to know how.'

The bile in Mikka's voice was as thick as nausea. Facing her, Morn answered softly, 'What makes you think I've got a choice? If I did anything else, I would be dead by now.'

A scowl like a spasm twisted Mikka's features. 'Listen to me, Morn.' By an act of will, she kept herself still. 'Until you came along, I was the most competent woman I've ever met. If you don't count Nick and one or two other men, I was the most competent *person* I know. I can run every Station on this ship. If I have to, I can run them for days. If *Captain's Fancy* fell apart, I could weld her back together from core to skin. I know to the hour how long our scrubber pads will last, or our food. I can handle anybody aboard except Nick in a fair fight. I'm good with guns.' Grimly refusing to falter again, she said, 'In bed I've got the stamina of a sex addict. My hips are too big, but I've got good breasts and great muscle tone. Nick dropped me when he started trusting me – but at least I know he *trusts* me.

'And you make me look like a gap-eyed starlet in a bad video.'

Deliberately setting aside her defenses, Mikka said, 'I need to understand you. Otherwise I'm finished.'

Morn could have responded, *As soon as I explain it*, I'm *finished*. But instinctively she knew that wasn't true: not at this moment, when Mikka had chosen to expose so much of herself. And Morn had been alone for too long: she had told too many lies, suffered too many losses. Like her visitor, she needed to set aside her defenses – if only for a minute with an honest enemy.

Without trying to second-guess the consequences, she said, 'There's nothing wonderful about it. There's nothing wonderful about me. When he found out I had gap-sickness, he' – once again, her throat refused Angus' name – 'the Captain of *Bright Beauty* gave me a zone implant. That's how he made me stay with him – how he made me do what he wanted. But he knew that if Com-Mine Security found the control on him, they would execute him. So at the last minute he offered it to me.

'I took it. I traded his life for it.'

Mikka was stunned. She dropped her arms, and her mouth fell open; her eyes went out of focus as if she were staring at the implications of Morn's revelation. Shock registered on her face, along with what looked like a flare of dismayed compassion. She stood up as if she were suddenly in a hurry to leave the cabin. Just as suddenly she sat down again and refolded her arms.

For a moment the only response she could muster was an inarticulate grunt, as if she'd been poked in the stomach.

Then, slowly, her gaze came back to Morn. She took a deep breath, let out a sigh, and lowered her arms to her sides.

'Well, that's a comfort,' she murmured. 'It's good to know you aren't really four times better than I am.'

Almost casually, Morn asked, 'Are you going to tell Nick?'

'Hell, no!' Mikka said at once. 'If he can't tell the difference between real passion and – and what you give him – that's his problem.'

Abruptly she stood again. 'I've been here too long. He's going to ask awkward questions. I've got to lock you in so we can decelerate. Is there anything you want first?'

One piece of honesty led to another. Morn didn't gauge the risk: she simply answered, 'I want to talk to Nick.'

The command second's eyes narrowed. 'He isn't going to like that. He's under a lot of pressure.'

Morn shrugged. 'So am I.' Apparently he'd made a deal with the UMCP to rescue her from Angus. Apparently, also, the UMCP were corrupt. It was therefore conceivable that the UMCP wished him to take her to Enablement Station – that they intended him to sell her. She wanted an explanation from him. She was no longer afraid of his anger. Her only fear now was that he would give her to the Amnion.

She got to her feet, facing Mikka expectantly.

Mikka frowned. 'If you tell him about your zone implant,' she said sternly, 'he'll feel betrayed. He may kill you.'

'I know,' Morn replied. 'But there are other things that scare me worse right now.'

Mikka grunted again. But she stood and gestured toward the door. 'After you.'

Morn wrapped her fingers around her black box and gripped it hard. It was her last resort – and her last hope. As long as she had it, she could still kill herself: she could still escape whatever Nick might try to do to her.

With Mikka she went to the bridge.

When they entered, Nick wheeled his seat to face them as if he were about to fling curses. His face was tight with tension; his eyes hinted at urgency. As soon as he saw Morn, however, he halted. 'What're you doing here?' he demanded. Abruptly he turned on Mikka. 'What did you bring her here for?'

His second cocked her hips and raised her palms, disavowing responsibility. 'She wants to talk to you.' Her tone was no more trenchant than usual. 'Since she's the reason we're here, I thought you might give her a few minutes.'

Around the bridge, everyone stopped working. Carmel kept her head bent over her board, but Lind, Sib Mackern, and Malda Verone craned their necks to watch, and the helm first pivoted his seat for a better view.

Nick aimed a look like pure hate at Mikka; but his scars were as pale as old bone. He faced Morn again.

'We haven't got time for this.'

With his strained features and murderous eyes, he seemed as dangerous as a charged matter cannon. Nevertheless Morn was no longer afraid of him.

'It's my life,' she said, answering a question he hadn't asked. 'And my baby's. I've got a right to know.

'You burned out the gap drive to get us here. Unless you've got resources you haven't mentioned, you'll never get back to Thanatos Minor. It's too far away. And you don't have anywhere else to go. Even if the Amnion let you leave Enablement Station, you'll never see human space again.

'This is an unholy mess, Nick. I want to know why you're doing it.'

I want to know what's at stake.

Like Mikka, he looked like he'd been driven to honesty. 'Don't you understand?' he snarled. He seemed cornered and frantic, trapped by his own foolhardiness; yet he wasn't beaten. Being trapped fired a deep, combative rage inside him. 'I want to keep you. This is the only way I can do it.

'This is the choice you gave me. If I don't let you keep your fucking baby, you're going to sabotage me. You made that perfectly clear. But if I do let you keep it—'

With his fist, he made a gesture of fierce negation. 'That's impossible. We're *illegal*! We run and fight, and half the time we take damage. We can't spend the next ten or fifteen years nursemaiding your *brat* – or covering for you while you do it. If you have a baby, I'll have to ditch you.

'This is the only answer I've got left. The Amnion.'

Mackern's face ran sweat. Malda looked like she wanted to throw up. Lind made obscure clinking noises with his teeth.

Nick ignored them all to concentrate his fury on Morn.

'They can force-grow babies. Maybe you didn't know that. The cops want you to be a nice little genophobe – they wouldn't want you to understand what real genetic engineering is good for. The Amnion can take that piece of garbage out of you and give you back a physically mature kid while *you* take a fucking *nap*.

'*All I* have to do is make a bargain that'll stick. The Amnion keep their bargains. They never cheat when it comes to money. Or DNA. All I have to do is offer them something they want badly enough.

'Have I made myself clear?' he concluded savagely. 'Now get off the goddamn bridge. We need to decelerate. Go back to your cabin. If you don't, I'll have Mikka pump you so full of cat you'll think you're never going to wake up.'

Morn hardly heard the command. She hadn't known the Amnion could force-grow babies; but the information didn't surprise her. She couldn't think about such things. If she felt any surprise, it was of an entirely different order.

Could it be that everything she'd done to herself with her black box, all her efforts to stifle her nausea and abhorrence, were going to pay off?

'I still don't understand,' she murmured. 'You've had hundreds of women. Why do you want to keep me?'

Nick bared his teeth as if he were about to howl. 'Are you really this stupid? Do I have to draw you a goddamn *map*?

'*I'm Nick Succorso*. People talk about me for parsecs in all directions. I'm *the* pirate, the one they tell stories about, the only man who does what he wants in the whole galaxy. I'm the man who makes his own laws, the man who sneers at Station Security, the man who makes idiots out of the UMCP, the man who dances with the Amnion and gets away with it. Hell, I even beat Captain Angus sheepfucker Thermo-pile. I beat everybody.' As he spoke, the lust came back into his scars, pulsing darkly; his rage was transported. 'I can go anywhere in human space because nobody's ever been able to prove anything against me, and when I walk into a bar they whisper my name into all the corners. Total strangers pass my reputation along. Total strangers want to give me whatever they have, just so that they can hope to be included in one of the stories.

'I *like* that. I *deserve* it.'

The helm first bobbed his head. Carmel chuckled appreciatively. Mikka watched with a congested expression, all her conflicts hidden.

Nick didn't notice them. He stabbed a finger at Morn. 'You're already included. A cop who gave up the whole UMCP to be with me – you're already part of one of the best stories. But this one's going to be even better. People are going to be talking about *Nick Succorso*, who risked his life and his ship and everything against the Amnion so that Morn Hyland could have his son. They're going to tell that story long after the United Mining Companies spaceshit Police have become as extinct as the humpback whale.'

He stopped, breathing hard, his scars black, as if he'd identified a personal apotheosis.

Morn couldn't face him. Down in the bottom of her heart, a small hope had begun to sing. She believed him at last. He wasn't going to sell her. Or her baby. A man who lived for the kind of stories that were told about Nick wouldn't betray her or anyone who belonged to him to the Amnion.

She had won: more than he knew; more than she would have thought possible.

Because of her small hope, she failed to hear that there was more than exaltation in Nick's voice. There was also an undertone of acid, a gnawing doubt. A man who lived for the stories told about him shouldn't have to tell them himself. He was the artist, dependent on his absolute mastery of his tools. For him, it would be intolerable if he'd been fooled; if his tools were false; if the story became that of *Nick Succorso, who risked his life and his ship and everything so that a woman who didn't love him could have her baby.*

It would be intolerable if anyone – even total strangers – ever had reason to laugh at him.

Morn missed that. In a faint voice, as if to test him, she replied, 'But I still don't understand. Why me? Why do all this for me?'

Without meaning to, she hit the sore place in him. Sudden rage and violence boiled up in him, seething from an old core of betrayal.

'I'll show you,' he grated. 'Take off your shipsuit.'

Abruptly Carmel raised her head, slapped keys on her board. 'Nick, we've got traffic. Amnion ships – warships, by their configuration.'

Mikka Vasaczk wheeled to the scan first. 'Course?'

Carmel hit more keys. 'Not toward us. They're converging on Enablement.'

'Hailing?' Mikka demanded of Lind.

Lind tightened the receiver in his ear, ran commands on his board. 'Nothing. If they're talking, it isn't beamed out here.'

Mikka spun back to Nick and Morn. 'Nick, we've got to decelerate. Enablement serves all the outposts. Warships go in and out all the time. The ones we've spotted could be routine. But we can't risk coming up on them at this velocity. They won't believe anything we say until we slow down.'

Nick ignored her: he ignored the bridge. His gaze held Morn's, as unwavering as death; his scars throbbed as if they might ooze blood.

'I said, take off your shipsuit.'

Here. In front of the whole bridge. He wanted to prove himself against her here.

Only minutes ago she would have refused him almost calmly. Inspired by a transcendent fear of the Amnion, she would have risked defying him. She would have had nothing left to lose. While she lived, she loathed him. His every touch revolted her. He was a pirate and a traitor; he was male. That he wanted to humiliate her by fucking her in front of his watch would have been more than she was willing to bear.

And her zone-implant enabled her to escape him—

But he'd given her reason to hope that she might not die; that she might still be able to save herself and Davies; that the Morn Hyland who had once cared about such things as treason and children wasn't altogether doomed. Long before she'd decided to keep her baby, she'd named him after her father because she'd wanted to recover the things her father represented – the conviction and commitment. On an intuitive level, she'd wanted to care about and believe in herself. That, she now realized, was why her decisions about her baby's fate and her own had depended on each other.

In a sense, Nick had given her back her life.

Now everything was different.

When she didn't obey, he came out of his seat at her, launched by fury and doubt.

She faced him without flinching.

But he didn't touch her, didn't hit her, didn't tear the fabric from her shoulders. Blazing like a laser, he stopped inches away from her; his face twisted savagely.

Between his teeth, so softly that no one else could hear him, he breathed, 'Morn, please' – begging her to let his people see that his power over her was complete.

Then she knew that she was safe. He'd swallowed the lie: he was addicted to the masque. As long as she helped him keep his doubts at bay, he would never give her up.

For the sake of her safety, and Davies' – for the sake of the Morn Hyland who had been broken and nearly killed by Angus Thermopyle – she reached into her pocket and brought up a surge of artificial lust from her zone-implant control. Then she unsealed her shipsuit and stepped out of it.

A delicate pink hue flushed her skin, but it wasn't shame.

With everyone on the bridge watching, she gave herself to Nick like a woman who would have bartered her soul for his caress.

He took her on the deck; hard and fast and desperate. From that position, she couldn't see anyone else's face except his – and Mikka Vasaczk's.

Mikka's eyes bled tears, grieving involuntarily: perhaps for herself; perhaps for Morn, or for Nick; perhaps for them all.

CHAPTER 11

Captain's Fancy had to decelerate hard. Nevertheless she didn't undergo as much g as she did when she left Com-Mine. Nick felt he had more time to work with. He believed that as long as Enablement could see *Captain's Fancy* braking, the Station would probably listen to what she had to say before deciding whether or not to destroy her.

So he fired reverse thrust at less than full burn for two hours at a time; then he let his ship coast for two hours before decelerating again, so that his people could at least try to recover from the strain. For the same reason, his crew rotated watches on a four-hour cycle.

In that way, alternately braking and coasting, he took Morn Hyland toward her first meeting with the Amnion.

Because of her gap-sickness, she was virtually useless most of the time. While the ship slowed, she had to remain in her cabin, blanked out by her zone-implant.

That made the hours hard to bear.

If she could have worked, she might have been less vulnerable to her growing apprehension. But as she drew closer to Enablement Station, her dread increased – a dread so visceral that it was almost cellular; her genes themselves might have been crying out in fear. Despite Nick's assurances, she was terrified of the Amnion. They were a threat to the integrity of her membership in the human species. They had the power to change the most fundamental thing she knew about herself.

The idea of submitting herself to them – of letting them take Davies from her and 'force-grow' him in one of their labs – filled her with horror.

Of course, she could have eased her dread by putting herself to sleep for the entire approach. Appeased by her submission on the bridge, Nick had given her exact information about his plans for g. She could have set the timer on her black box and slept for eighteen or twenty-four hours without fear that anyone would need her in the meantime.

For some reason, she was acutely reluctant to escape in that way.

She told herself this was because she wanted to know what was going on. She wanted to know how Nick would protect his ship. And she wanted to know what he and the Amnion said to each other, what kind of bargain he would strike with them. All the details on which her survival depended might be worked out during those rests between decelerations. If she weren't present when Nick talked, she wouldn't hear anything.

So each time the thrusters fired she set her timer for slightly more than two hours; and each time when she woke up she headed for the bridge. As an excuse for being there, she took along coffee or food for the watch; then she lingered unobtrusively, hoping that Nick or Mikka or Liete wouldn't send her away. Whenever possible, she provided Sib Mackern or Alba Parmute with an hour or two of relief.

Yet gradually she became aware her reluctance grew from another source.

She was beginning to distrust the effects of her zone-implant.

At the moment of her greatest triumph over Nick Succorso, some of her revulsion for him had perversely transferred itself to the means by which she'd bested him. She'd become ashamed of the way in which she'd won. He'd never intended to sell her to the Amnion: therefore he deserved better.

Her zone-implant control gave her power over herself. It made her valuable to Nick. It enabled her to survive. But it did nothing to heal her lacerated opinion of herself. Precisely because its resources were artificial, it eroded her self-esteem.

If she wanted to believe in herself, she needed the things her father represented in her life. She needed honesty and integrity; courage; the willingness to die for her convictions.

She needed her son.

Which meant that she needed the Amnion.

This realization scared her so profoundly that she began thinking more and more about leaving her black box switched off during deceleration. The idea of spending two hours locked up alone and conscious with her gap-sickness came increasingly to seem like the lesser evil. If she did that, she might learn something about the severity or duration of her illness. She might discover the limits of the destructive clarity with which the universe spoke to her. She might even find out how cunning she could be when she was sick—

Putting herself to sleep felt like a surrender to genetic terror. Each time she went back to her cabin, she had to exert a greater force of will to overcome her impulse to leave her zone-implant control alone.

Nevertheless she coerced herself. If she wanted her son – if she wanted conviction and commitment – she had to face her fear.

Morn switched herself off while *Captain's Fancy* decelerated. She haunted the bridge while *Captain's Fancy* coasted.

With nothing to stop it, her dread multiplied, replicating itself from cell to cell inside her like a malignant neoplasm.

When Nick had cut two thirds of his ship's velocity, he started talking to Enablement Station.

By this time, two of the Amnion warships had reacted to his arrival. One altered course to a trajectory that would intersect *Captain's Fancy*'s just outside her attack range: the other assumed a defensive attitude between her and Enablement. But still no demands for identification or explanation had been beamed at her. Lind had begun to receive the kind of traffic data – control space coordinates, ship vectors, docking approach lanes – any Station might transmit for the sake of vessels arriving out of tach. Nothing else had come in.

'They're waiting to hear from us,' Nick said, settling himself more firmly in his command seat. 'We're the aliens here – I guess they figure it's up to us to go first.'

He looked strong and sure of himself, eager for the chance to measure himself against whatever happened. A stranger would have said that he was rested and well, ready for anything. Morn knew him better, however. She could see that fatigue and the aftereffects of doubt affected him like a low-grade infection. Strain made his grin inflexible, like a rictus; his hands did everything too quickly; his eyes hinted at emergencies. He didn't object to Morn's presence, but he glanced at her sidelong at unexpected moments, as if he feared what she might do.

Mikka Vasaczk was on the bridge as well, looking as angry as ever – and competent to the bone. And Vector Shaheed occupied the engineer's

Station. He smiled at Morn with impersonal geniality from time to time, but he didn't say anything. Everyone else belonged to Nick's watch: Carmel, Lind, the helm first, Sib Mackern, Malda Verone. The rest of Mikka's people were presumably resting. Liete's watch had been ordered to battle Stations around the ship.

'Send them standard id,' Nick told Lind. 'Ship, captain, registry, last port. Don't beam it too tight. We want those warships to hear everything.'

Lind jerked a nod. Like Nick's, his nervousness showed in the speed of his hands; but his fingers didn't fumble. After a moment he reported, 'Done.'

Enablement would presumably take some time to decide on a response. Morn knew better than to hold her breath. Nevertheless she had to force herself to breathe: dread and uncertainty seemed to close her lungs. She'd never heard of force-growing babies, had no idea how it was done or what its dangers were. And she couldn't imagine why Nick thought he could trust the Amnion to deal honorably.

Targ and helm had nothing to do but wait. Carmel kept herself busy pulling data out of the vacuum and passing it to Mackern for analysis. Mackern ran studies of the scan data, comparing it to *Captain's Fancy*'s stored knowledge, refining his picture of the Station and its control space. But neither of them paid any attention to the results.

Abruptly Lind croaked, 'Here it comes.'

'On audio,' Nick snapped.

Lind complied with a touch to his board. At once a voice made mechanical by static and distance came from the speakers.

'Enablement Station to encroaching human ship. You are in violation of treaty and presumed hostile. Identification transgresses acceptable norms. Restate and explain.'

Presumed hostile. Mikka didn't react; but Mackern groaned involuntarily, wiped sweat out of his eyes. Malda hunched over the targ board and began keying status checks.

'Interesting,' Vector murmured. 'Do they mean we've identified ourselves in the wrong form, or *as* the wrong form?'

Lind looked to Nick for instructions.

Nick didn't hesitate. If he was worried, he kept it to himself. 'Repeat id. Tell them we've been here before – give them the date for confirmation. Tell them we need help for a medical difficulty, and we're prepared to pay for it.'

Swallowing convulsively, Lind obeyed.

Morn thought that she would suffocate before the Amnion replied again. She knew Nick wouldn't welcome questions at a time like this; but she felt that if she didn't do something to counter her dread she would founder in it.

'Why did you do it?' she asked stiffly. 'Why did you come here before?'

Mikka flicked a glance at Nick, then looked hard at Morn, warning her. 'We had essentially the same problem. We needed repairs we couldn't afford. That time we got paid well.'

Her scowl darkened as if she were on dangerous ground. 'This time it may not be so easy.'

'The circumstances were a little different that time,' Nick commented laconically. 'What made the deal so attractive was that we got paid by both sides. That was almost as much fun as beating Captain fucking Thermopile.'

'Which is why,' Mikka put in grimly, 'it may not be so easy this time.' Like Nick, she spoke to Morn; but her words seemed to be addressed to him. 'The Amnion may think we cheated them.'

The fever in Nick's eyes flared, but his scars stayed pale. 'Which is precisely why,' he countered, 'they won't be able to turn me down now.'

'Nick,' Lind gulped.

Enablement's answer came in.

'Enablement Station to encroaching human ship. You are in violation of treaty and presumed hostile. Identification transgresses acceptable norms. Previous arrival and departure of the ship *Captain's Fancy* is confirmed. The name "Nick Succorso" is contrary to established reality and presumed false. Amnion defensive *Tranquil Hegemony* has orders to repel approach. Transmit acceptable identification.'

'"Contrary to established reality,"' muttered Malda anxiously. 'What the hell is that supposed to mean?'

Morn found that she was holding her breath again.

'You weren't with us last time,' Nick answered with apparent ease. 'These bastards don't recognize people by name – and they sure as hell don't recognize them by what they look like. As far as they're concerned, appearance has nothing to do with identity. The only thing they recognize is genetic code. I think the slimy sods can actually smell each other's DNA.'

He grinned fiercely. 'They've got reason to think I can't be here. If I'm not dead, I must be' – his teeth gleamed – 'somebody else.'

'Mackern,' he ordered, 'you've got my gene data. It's in my id file. Here's access.' He tapped codes into his board. 'Copy it to Lind.'

Sib went to work with his hands shaking.

'Lind,' Nick continued, 'repeat the previous message. All of it. Add my DNA structure. Request instructions for approach deceleration and trajectory.'

'Right.' Lind tightened the receiver in his ear. After a moment he nodded to Mackern. 'Got it.' Tensely he began transmission.

The bridge was so quiet that Morn could hear the click of every key; she could hear the almost subliminal hum of the air-scrubbers.

Mikka moved closer to Nick's console and pointed at the intercom. 'With your permission?'

Nick nodded.

She thumbed the toggle. 'Liete?'

Liete Corregio's voice replied, 'Here.'

'Reassure me,' Mikka demanded brusquely.

'We're all on Station.' The intercom muffled whatever emotion Liete's voice carried. 'Alba feels sorry for herself. The rest of us are as ready as we're likely to get.'

'Stay that way.' Mikka shut off the intercom.

'I don't understand,' Morn said, breathing deliberately so that she wouldn't stop again. 'What kind of deal did you make with them? Why do they believe you would die – or turn into somebody else?'

She could think of an explanation herself, but it was so sickening that she didn't want to consider it. She certainly didn't want to say it aloud. Nevertheless she needed to know—

With an abrupt motion, Nick swung his seat to face her. A hint of color came into his scars, underlining his eyes with risks. 'Take a guess.' His casualness sounded slightly ragged, frayed by strain. 'If you think this is a good time to ask questions, you can help figure out the answers.'

Dread closed around Morn's heart. She opened her mouth, but no words came out.

'Nick,' Vector interrupted mildly, 'none of us like this, but she's got more at stake than anyone else. She has two lives to lose. Even you've only got one. Naturally she wants to know what we're up against.'

Nick wheeled toward the engineer. 'What're you doing here?' he snapped. 'Aren't you supposed to be in the drive space?'

Vector shrugged delicately. 'What for? The thrusters are fine. And Pup can read an alert blip as well as I can. He'll let us know if anything goes red.'

'Did I hear you right?' Nick said through his teeth. 'Are you refusing an order?'

At once Vector unbuckled himself from his seat and pushed his sore joints erect. 'Of course not. I'll go wherever you tell me.'

His gaze held Nick's calmly.

After a moment Nick relented. 'Oh, sit down,' he growled. 'Watching you move around makes my knees hurt.' Then he turned back to Morn.

'Why is it that whenever you come to the bridge I feel like I'm being interrogated? This is my ship. I'm the goddamn *Captain* here. If I wanted to be questioned every time I do something, I would trade jobs with Pup.'

'Nick, I – ' Morn tried to swallow the taste of dread in her mouth. But it wasn't Nick she feared. Because she'd been false with him so often, she was honest this time. 'I'm just scared. I ask questions so I won't panic.'

Slowly the muscles around his eyes sagged as his irritation eased. He looked weary; almost scared himself. When he'd studied her for a while, he nodded. 'There's nothing secret about it – not here. We're all in this together. You might as well know.

'Besides, you're a cop,' he said in a dull rasp. His gaze drifted away from her as he started to talk. 'You'll like this.

'The Amnion want resources. Everybody knows that. They're desperate for ores and metals, any kind of raw materials, as well as the hard technologies we're so good at. Not because they aren't capable of finding and processing their own materials, or building their own equipment. We wouldn't have to deal with them if they couldn't do things like that. But their techniques have drawbacks. They don't have our' – he sneered the words – 'mechanistic ingenuity. I've heard they make steel by feeding iron ore to a viral acid that digests it and then shits it refined. Compared to ordinary smelting, that's wildly inefficient. They want everything they can get or learn from us.

'But the resource they want most is human beings.' His tone sharpened. 'Living, conscious, viable human protoplasm. They do things to it – they can transform it in ways that would make your skin crawl.

'They can make it Amnion, if they want to. That's how they propose to conquer us.'

Morn listened so hard that her pulse throbbed in her temples and the bones of her skull ached.

'If you liked the work,' he drawled, 'you could become as rich as the stars selling human beings to the Amnion. Hijack any ship you want, run it to one of the outposts. They'll buy as many people as you can sell at prices you can't imagine. And they always play fair – they always keep their bargains – because they don't want to frighten off the people who supply them. *Trade* is so important to them it's practically a religion.

'The last time we were here' – his face tightened with satisfaction at the memory, restoring the relish of his grin – 'I traded them me. I let them give me one of their damn mutagens in exchange for enough credit to get *Captain's Fancy* repaired. They thought it was going to be a hell of a deal for them. In the end, they would get my ship as well as me.

'But it didn't work out that way.'

That was the answer Morn feared. She nearly asked him not to go on, not to say it: if he didn't say it, she might not have to believe it.

Before he could explain, however – and before she could protest – Lind interrupted them.

'Here it comes, Nick.'

Nick spun his seat away from Morn.

The voice crackled in the speakers as if it were alien to *Captain's Fancy*'s electronics.

'Enablement Station to encroaching human ship. You are in violation of treaty and presumed at hazard. Ship's identification is confirmed. Captain's identification is nonconforming to known reality, but is presumed accurate. Approach is acceptable. Instructions follow.'

A burst of numbers and codes filled the air like static; Lind routed the information to helm and data. Then the voice continued.

'Known reality and presumed identification must be brought into conformity. An account of the discrepancy is required. "Help for a medical difficulty" will be offered in trade. Trade will be discussed when encroaching human ship *Captain's Fancy* has complied with approach instructions.'

The voice stopped. For a moment the speakers relayed the empty, stippling noise of the vacuum. Then Lind switched them off.

Nick tapped his right fist once, twice, on his console, absorbing the implications of Enablement's message. Quickly he reached his decision. He turned his seat again.

'Analysis,' he demanded from helm. 'What do they want?'

The helm first raised his head from his readouts. 'One more deceleration. It's long for us, but not hard. Commencing in' – he tapped keys, read the answer – 'four point one eight minutes. The instructions are exact. Braking intensity, duration, trajectory. When we cut thrust, we'll be' – he hit more keys – 'four hours off Station at normal approach speeds.'

'In other words,' Malda put in, 'we'll be a sitting target if they decide to blast us. We might get in a hit or two, but we won't stand a chance of saving ourselves.'

'Nick,' Mackern murmured without looking away from his readouts, 'that trajectory lines us up straight for one of the docking bays.'

'The same docks where those two warships are headed now,' commented Carmel.

'Are there other ships docked?' Mikka asked.

Carmel reported, 'Half a dozen.'

The command second nodded sharply. 'Then they aren't going to blast us,' she asserted. 'If they were, they wouldn't give us a chance to hit that kind of target before we die.'

'They aren't going to blast us,' Nick snapped, 'because they want to make a deal.'

'Set it up,' he told the helm first. 'We're going in by the numbers, exactly the way they want it.

'Mikka, secure for deceleration. Have your people ready to move as soon as we stop braking. I'll take us in – you'll have command after that.'

Without hesitation, Mikka keyed Nick's intercom and started issuing orders.

Over his shoulder, Nick harked, 'Morn, get back to your cabin. You've got about three minutes. If you go into Enablement gap-sick, this whole thing might fall apart.'

Morn needed answers; she needed to hear the truth, despite her dread. But she had no time. Stifling a groan of frustration and urgency, she asked, 'How long are we braking?'

The helm first consulted his readouts. 'Three hours eighteen minutes.'

She left the bridge at a run.

She cut it as fine as she dared: three and a half hours by the timer on her black box. Then she struggled off her bunk into *Captain's Fancy*'s comfortable internal g and headed for the bridge.

Maybe she'd cut it too fine: her brain felt leaden in her skull, stunned by artificial sleep and lingering, destructive clarity. But she couldn't afford stupidity now; or ignorance. And Nick was already fed up with her questions. To appease him, she detoured to the galley and prepared a pot of coffee and a tray of sandwiches. Then she made her way forward, carrying the coffee, the tray, and several mugs.

If she missed what Nick and the Amnion said to each other – if she missed their deal, or misunderstood it—

She stepped through the aperture just as Mikka Vasaczk called the seconds to relieve Nick's watch.

The effects of strain and g filled the bridge.

Vector Shaheed was in worse shape than anyone else. His face was swollen and gray, the color of cold ashes: he looked like he'd come through a small but ominous cardiac incident. But he wasn't the only one who appeared worn out, close to collapse.

Malda sprawled in her seat with her head back, sucking air raggedly through her nose. Lind stared at the screens without seeing them: he wasn't aware that his eyes were crossed. The helm first kept massaging his face as if he were trying to bring back his chin; his palms made a raw sound against the stubble of his beard. Carmel's gaze remained definite, uncompromised, but her posture slumped as if the pressure of braking had shortened her bones. Mackern rested his forehead weakly on the data console, dripping sweat over the keys.

Mikka moved with her usual dour certainty; her voice betrayed only fatigue, not exhaustion. Nevertheless the cost of her endurance showed in the lines of her face: her scowl looked deep and ineradicable, as if it had been etched into her skull with mineral acid.

As for Nick, the tense energy had gone out of his movements; every shift of his shoulders and arms was slow, heavy, freighted with stress. His eyes were dull, and the skin of his cheeks under his beard looked pale and stiff, as old as his scars.

Despite his weariness, he was busy calling reports from the other bridge Stations to his readouts. At intervals he asked questions in a tone that made his people answer promptly.

After a moment he noticed Morn. With a grunt of acknowledgment, he took a mug and a sandwich, held the mug for her to fill it; then he nodded her toward the rest of his watch.

Mikka picked up a mug and a couple of sandwiches. So did Carmel. Vector accepted coffee with a wan, grateful smile, but declined food. Lind mumbled, 'I don't drink coffee,' as if that fact – or the fact of being served – embarrassed him; however, he snagged a sandwich with a hand like a grapple. Too tired to think about eating, the helm first and Malda ignored Morn. When she nudged Sib Mackern to get his attention, she found that he was already asleep.

Abruptly Lind clapped a hand to his receiver. Discarding his sandwich, he punched on audio.

'Enablement Station to presumed human Captain Nick Succorso.'

Now the transmission source was close enough to be clear. Without static, the voice sounded sharper and, paradoxically, more alien. It jerked Sib awake, pulled Malda and the helm first out of their respective stupors. Morn's hands shook on the edges of the tray; she put it down so that she wouldn't drop it.

Nick closed his eyes and waited for the message to continue.

'You are in violation of treaty and presumed at hazard. You require "help for a medical difficulty." Sanctuary is offered. Unification with the Amnion is offered. Thus known reality and presumed identification can be brought into conformity. Hazards and difficulties will be resolved.

'Reply.'

Sanctuary. Unification. Brought into conformity. Morn shoved her hands into her pockets to steady them; she tightened her fingers around the reassuring shape of her black box. *Captain's Fancy* was being offered mutagens that would put an end to her crew's humanity.

Nick didn't open his eyes. He also didn't sound worried. 'Copy this, Lind. "Captain Nick Succorso to Enablement Station. Deceleration stresses human tissue. We need rest. Reply to your proposal follows in thirty minutes."

'Send it.'

While Lind obeyed, Nick stood up from his seat and tried to stretch some of the pain out of his muscles.

Mikka's watch began arriving on the bridge. Malda Verone immediately turned over the targ board to her replacement and left. Scorz, a fleshy man with perennial acne, took Lind's place. At a word from Nick, Sib gave the data Station to Morn: *Captain's Fancy* was done with heavy g, so Morn was safe.

Vector Shaheed stayed where he was.

The helm first surrendered his seat to the helm second, a twitchy woman named Ransum who tended to execute jerky maneuvers because her hands were too abrupt. Carmel also got out of her replacement's way. But neither she nor the helm first moved to leave the bridge.

'Nick,' Carmel said bluntly, 'I want to know what you're going to do.'

Nick cocked an eyebrow at this demand as if he couldn't decide whether to take offense or not.

'I know I need sleep, but I don't want to miss anything,' she explained.

He gave her a piece of his familiar, malicious grin. 'Too bad. Morn and I get to have all the fun.

'I'll make a deal, and Mikka and Vector and I will set up some insurance. After we dock, Morn and I are going on Station. When we come back, we'll have a kid with us – and enough credit to get the gap drive fixed. Unless somebody screws up. In which case, you'll be back on watch because we'll be running for our lives.'

Carmel nodded, satisfied. 'Come on,' she said to the helm first. 'You're even worse off than I am.' Taking him by the arm, she drew him off the bridge.

Nick swallowed the last of his coffee and gestured Mikka into the command seat.

'Routine approach,' she told her people as she took over Nick's board. 'There's nothing special about this. The Amnion gave us instructions. We'll follow them.

'Karster' – Karster was targ second, a taciturn man with the size and unformed features of a boy – 'rumor has it the Amnion can detect weapons – even weapon status – at incredible distances. Shut everything down. Then set your board to power up on one key. I want to be able to go combat-ready as fast as possible.'

Without a word, Karster began to work.

Trying to distract herself from her apprehension, Morn tapped keys across the data board, pulling everything from scan, helm, and communications together. But she was in no condition to concentrate on it. She couldn't keep her mind away from Nick and dread.

He'd begun to walk the bridge like a man who needed exercise to focus his mind. Again and again he passed in front of Morn; he passed in front of all the Stations. But he didn't glance at her or anyone else: his attention was fixed inward. Nevertheless on each circuit Morn saw the vitality slowly come back into his eyes, the energy return to his movements.

'Vector,' he said without looking at the engineer, 'we need insurance. I want you to rig a self-destruct. Key the thrust drive to explode – tie in the fuel cells, torpedoes, matter cannon, anything that can generate brisance. Give me enough force to take out a big chunk of the Station. If something goes wrong, I want to be able to hold Enablement hostage.

'The Amnion,' he commented sardonically, 'don't like destruction.'

'If you need help, ask Morn. She's got access to the way we arranged it the last time.

'Set it up to Mikka's board.'

'That'll take a while,' Vector replied evenly. 'The engineer I apprenticed with didn't teach suicide.' His smile widened. 'I've never wanted to kill myself. I would rather be dead.'

'You've got until we dock,' Nick snapped.

'Then I'd better get started.' Lifting himself upright with his arms, Vector limped through the aperture.

Around the bridge, scan, helm, and communications handled the ordinary business of approach. They passed information and adjustments back and forth. Scorz murmured into his pickup in a voice like machine oil.

Ignoring them, Nick continued with his instructions.

'Mikka, you've done this before. It's your job to make them believe the threat. If you hear me call for help – or if you just think we've been gone too long – tell them what Vector did. Send them diagrams, tell them what to scan for, anything that will convince them we can self-destruct on a prohibitive scale. Demand us back in one piece. And a safe departure.

'Make them *believe* it. The whole point of a gamble like this is to make it so real that we don't have to use it.'

Mikka nodded once, roughly. 'I'm not like Vector,' she grated. 'I've studied suicide.'

Grinning, Nick asked Morn how much time he had left.

She checked her log and told him, 'Five minutes.'

'Scorz.' Nick stopped beside the communications console. 'I want you to tight-beam this to the precise source of their last transmission. No leakage, no eavesdropping. Let me know when you're ready.'

Morn could hardly read her board. Pressure mounted inside her; in spite of coffee and adrenaline, her brain felt swollen, almost tumorous, in her head. She wished she could get Enablement Station on video. She wanted to know what the place she dreaded looked like. Scan told her only that it was shaped like a huge globe, instead of the torus preferred by human designers. But there were no stars near enough to illuminate the Station, and its own lights were still out of range.

The ship was being nudged slightly off trajectory by Enablement's gravitation. The helm second made a jerky correction.

Scorz reported, 'Ready.'

Unable to do anything else, Morn watched as Nick keyed communications himself and said, 'Captain Nick Succorso to Enablement Station. I have a reply to your proposal.'

Then he stopped and waited.

The fighting gleam was back in his eyes; the lines of his face had regained their eagerness.

He was answered almost immediately.

'Enablement Station to presumed human Captain Nick Succorso. Reply is required. Conformity of purpose must be achieved. You will be repelled otherwise.'

As if he were reciting a formula which he found privately ludicrous, Nick replied, 'Conformity of purpose is mutually desirable. Sanctuary is not. Hazard to us will disappear if we can achieve conformity of purpose.' His tone made a sneer out of the alien cadences. 'You require an account of the discrepancy between known reality and presumed identification. We require medical assistance. We also require credit.' He named a sum large enough to pay for an entirely new gap drive. 'I propose that we achieve conformity of purpose through the mutual satisfaction of requirements.'

A pause hummed gently in the speakers. Then the voice returned.

'The sum you require is large.'

Nick shrugged. 'The knowledge I offer is precious. It has relevance to all Amnion dealings with human space.'

Another pause.

'What is the nature of your medical difficulty?'

Nick turned his grin on Morn. 'We have a pregnant human female. Her fetus is unacceptable among us. We require a fully mature human child.'

This time there was no pause. 'Presumed human Captain Nick Succorso, all your requirements are large. Specificity is necessary. How do you offer to account for the discrepancy between known reality and presumed identification?'

'Blood sample,' Nick replied succinctly.

'In sufficient quantity?' demanded the voice.

'One deciliter.'

After a moment of rumination, the voice said, 'The quantity is sufficient.'

'My requirements are indeed large,' Nick continued at once. 'What I offer is also large. You require specificity. This is my proposal. The human female and I will enter Enablement Station. We will be taken to the place where the child may be matured. I will concede one deciliter of my blood. Then the child will be matured, and I will be given an acknowledgment of credit. When these matters have been accomplished, the human female with her child and I will return to our ship. *Captain's Fancy* will depart Enablement Station immediately. We will depart Amnion space at our best speed.

'In this way, conformity of purpose will be achieved.'

Without delay, the voice commanded, 'Await decisive reply. Continued approach is acceptable,' and stopped transmitting.

Nick didn't switch off the pickup or bridge audio. He stood with his head cocked to one side, grinning as if he expected an answer right away.

Morn forced herself to turn her head, scan the bridge. Like her, Karster on targ and the scan second wanted to ask questions; Mikka scowled her concern; Ransum twitched nervously: Scorz shifted his weight as if the seat under him were slick. Nevertheless Nick's expectant stance kept them all quiet.

Seconds passed, measured out by the ship's chronometers. *Known reality and presumed identification must be brought into conformity.* What did that mean? What *could* it mean, except the thing she feared?

Ransum, the helm second, couldn't endure the silence; she was too tense. 'Nick – ' she began.

Instantly livid, Nick fired a glare at her that withered her in her seat. Like the crack of a whip, he barked, 'Shut up!'

Just as instantly, he resumed his attitude of calm poise.

Morn felt that the bridge was collapsing around her, sinking into Nick as if he were a black hole.

Then the speakers came to life; they seemed to blare as if Scorz had inadvertently turned up the gain. Nick snapped alert, balancing on the balls of his feet with his hands ready.

'Enablement Station to presumed human Captain Nick Succorso,' the Amnioni voice said without preamble, 'your proposal is acceptable. Conformity of purpose will be achieved through the mutual satisfaction of requirements. Immediate acknowledgment is required.'

Nick jabbed a punch at the empty air; his teeth flashed like a predator's. Distinctly he recited the formula.

'It is acceptable. Conformity of purpose will be achieved through the mutual satisfaction of requirements.'

Then he reached across the communications board to switch off the pickup.

Brandishing his fists, he shouted triumphantly, 'Got you, you son-ofabitch!'

Only the reassuring shape of the zone-implant control in Morn's pocket kept her from whimpering.

Enablement Station loomed into video range, but now she had no time to study it. For the better part of two hours, she channeled information to Vector, who wasn't inclined to suicide, and suggestions to Karster, who didn't know enough about his board to set up an adequate batch command. And then *Captain's Fancy* began to receive docking instructions from Station. Data research was required to determine the degree of compatibility between the ship's equipment and Enablement's.

She was too busy to panic – or to ask any more questions.

Dock was less than half an hour away when Nick ordered Alba Parmute to the bridge and told Morn to leave the data board.

As she got out of her seat, she hid her hands in her pockets so that he wouldn't see them shaking.

'Give Mikka your id tag,' he ordered. 'I don't want Enablement to know they've got a chance at a UMC cop. They don't normally cheat – but that might tempt them to make an exception.'

Morn hated to surrender her tag. But she also couldn't deny that he was right. And the time when she could have opposed his intentions was long past: it was on the other side of the gap.

She pulled the chain over her head and handed her id tag to the command second.

Nick gestured her to accompany him off the bridge.

Clenching her teeth in an effort to hold her voice steady, she asked, 'What now?'

'Meet me at the suit lockers,' he replied briskly. 'Amnion air is breathable – sort of – but we're going to treat this like EVA. That gives us some extra protection. They can't trick or force mutagens into us while we're wearing those suits. And suit communications can reach Mikka from anywhere on Enablement.'

Before she could reply, he strode away.

She almost went after him; she didn't want to be alone, not now, with a crisis she dreaded ahead of her, and no idea how far she could trust anyone. The thought of an EVA suit gave her an odd comfort, however. She was grateful for a chance to carry her own atmosphere with her; grateful to wear a layer of impermeable mylar and plexulose between her skin and anything Amnion.

The only problem was where to put her black box. She considered that difficulty as she hurried toward the lockers. EVA suits had plenty of pouches and pockets; if she put her control in one of them, she could reach it at need.

But what if the Amnion required her to take off her EVA suit in order to force-grow little Davies?

The idea chilled her like ice down her back.

It was plausible – even predictable. How could she reach the control then, in front of witnesses? Probably in front of Nick?

And how could she bear all her fears without the help of her black box?

Trembling from the core of her bones to the tips of her fingers, she decided to keep the control in her shipsuit.

In fact, she needed its help now. When she reached the lockers – before Nick could catch up with her and see her change – she combined functions and intensities to cast a haze over her emotions; a haze which numbed her dread, but still allowed her to think. Then, while false neural relief eased her tremors, she selected an EVA suit in her size, checked its status indicators to be sure it was ready, and began putting it on.

Nick was only a minute behind her. He approached the lockers grinning, his eyes alight with risks. As he pulled open his personal locker and took out his suit, he remarked in a tone of grim pleasure, 'You're going to have a hell of a story to tell your kid. He'll be the only brat in the galaxy whose parents thought he was worth taking chances like this for. I don't even *want* the little bastard, and yet here I am.'

'Nick – ' Her zone-implant could only calm her incrementally: tight layers of fear had to be peeled away before they could be numbed. And he hadn't yet answered the most important question gnawing at her. Carefully she asked, 'What do they mean, "Known reality and presumed identification must be brought into conformity"? I don't understand.'

He didn't look at her; he was busy with his suit. But his grin sharpened. Away from the bridge and other people, he was willing to explain.

'I told you I let them give me one of their mutagens, but it didn't take. "Known reality" is that when human beings get that mutagen, they turn Amnion. *Pure* Amnion – RNA, loyalty, intelligence, everything. "Presumed identification" is that I'm apparently the same man I was before they treated me. What I've offered them is a chance "to account for the discrepancy" – to find out why their mutagen didn't take.'

Only the emissions of her black box enabled Morn to pursue her question.

'Why didn't it?'

His laugh was harsh enough to draw blood.

'I've got an immunity drug. Your precious Hashi Lebwohl gave it to me. Data Acquisition at its finest. The real reason I came here before was to test it for him.'

That was the reply she'd dreaded. UMCP corruption. And a betrayal of humankind so profound that its implications shocked her out of her calm. Her zone-implant might as well have been switched off. Abysms of treachery seemed to gape around her like the gaps between the stars.

Not Hashi Lebwohl's treason: not the UMCP's.

Nick's.

'And you're going to let them have it?' she demanded. 'You're going to let them take it out of your blood and study it, so they can learn to counteract it?'

His laugh sounded like a snarl. His tongue twisted inside his cheek: between his teeth, a gray capsule appeared.

'I haven't taken it yet.'

He shifted the capsule back against his gum.

'It's not an organic immunity. It's more like a poison – or a binder. It ties up mutagens until they're inert. Then they get flushed out – along with the drug. The immunity is effective for about four hours.

'I'm not going to take it until after they sample my blood. That way they won't learn anything. The drug won't be in my system yet. And if we're lucky we'll be long gone before they finish their tests.'

He was planning to cheat the Amnion.

Abruptly his gaze slid away from hers. 'I can't give it to you. They'll need your blood, too, or else they won't know enough about you to force-grow your brat. I can't take the chance that they'll find the drug.'

Before Morn could react, the intercom chimed, and Mikka's voice said, 'Five minutes to dock, Nick. Secure for zero g.'

The zone-implant seemed to take forever to gain control over Morn's wailing nerves.

CHAPTER 12

For a while she drifted as *Captain s Fancy* cut internal spin; she and Nick clung to the zero-g grips and floated together. Like him, she'd left her faceplate open. But she couldn't meet his gaze. He was focused on her acutely. Congested blood darkened his scars, and his gaze burned. Her eyes stared past his as if she were stunned.

She should have set her zone-implant higher. Its effects weren't enough. She was about to meet the Amnion for the first time. It was possible that she was about to lose her humanity altogether, that the genetic core of her identity would be taken from her. She should have set her implant's emissions high enough to make her completely blank. Then at least she might have been spared this visceral, human dread.

But the control was in the pocket of her shipsuit, inside her EVA suit. She couldn't reach it now.

She and Nick had lost the floor as if they were in freefall, but that was an illusion. The Station's mass plucked at them, urging them to let go of the grips; the bulkhead past her boots began to feel like the floor. Still she and Nick held on. The floor would shift again when *Captain's Fancy* docked – when the ship surrendered herself to Enablement's internal g.

'One minute,' Mikka Vasaczk's voice announced from the intercom. 'No problems.'

Morn's identity was already under attack. Even without mutation, her understanding of her self and her life was being altered; force-grown to a different shape.

Nick had an immunity drug for the Amnion mutagens.

It had been given to him by Hashi Lebwohl – it belonged to the UMCP.

And the UMCP had withheld it from humankind. The cops, *her people*, had left all human space naked to alien absorption, when they had the means to effectively end the threat.

What kind of people did such things? What kind of men and women had she and her father committed themselves to?

Vector Shaheed was right. *The UMCP is the most corrupt organization there is.*

How could she have been so wrong? How could her father and her whole family have been so wrong?

A jolt shuddered through the hull: impact and metal stress. The contact relayed the hum of servomechanisms, the clampdown of grapples and transmission cables, the limpet attachment of Enablement's sensors. On a human Station, Morn would also have heard the insertion of airlines, the brief hiss of equalizing pressure. Not here: human and Amnioni only breathed each other's air when they had no other choice.

She and Nick dropped to the new floor.

Mikka said, 'Dock secure, Nick. Vector confirms drive on standby. We're keeping power up on all systems. They won't like that, but without it we can't destruct.'

Nick nodded as if he were replying, but he didn't key the intercom. To Morn, he muttered, 'Don't look so terrified. Nothing is going to happen to you unless it happens to me first.' Then he grinned sourly. 'If you don't count having a baby.'

'Message from Station,' Mikka reported.

Nick turned away to toggle the intercom. 'I'm listening.'

At once a mechanical voice said, 'Enablement Station to presumed human Captain Nick Succorso. Drive shutdown required. System power threatens dock integrity.'

Nick didn't hesitate. 'Tell them, "Storage cell damage prevents adequate power accumulation. Drive standby necessary to sustain support systems."'

After a moment Mikka said dryly, 'Done.'

The reply was prompt. 'Drive shutdown required. Enablement Station will supply power.'

'Tell them,' Nick snarled, '"Conversion parameters too complex. We desire prompt departure. We resist delay."'

'Ain't that the truth,' Mikka muttered as she complied.

She relayed the answer when it came.

342

'Enablement Station to presumed human Captain Nick Succorso.' Nick mimicked the words with a sneer as the voice spoke. 'Amnion defensives *Tranquil Hegemony* and *Calm Horizons* are ordered to exact compensatory damage for any breach of dock integrity.'

'Acknowledge that,' Nick instructed Mikka. 'Remind them we have a deal. "Conformity of purpose will be achieved through the mutual satisfaction of requirements." Point out we have every reason to protect their interests as long as they protect ours.'

That response took a little longer. Then Mikka said again, 'Done.'

Nick flashed a grin like a glare at Morn. '"Compensatory damage", my ass. Those bastards haven't seen a "breach of dock integrity" until they see us self-destruct. There won't be anything left of those fucking warships except particle noise.'

Or of us, Morn thought. But she didn't speak. Bit by bit, the zone-implant reduced her to a state of dissociated calm, in which numbness and panic coexisted side by side.

In addition to the usual tools and maneuvering jets for EVA work, Nick had an impact pistol clipped to his belt. While he waited for what the Amnion would say next, he detached them all and stowed them in his locker. Morn's suit carried no weapons, but she automatically did the same with her tools and jets. She would have liked to take at least a welding laser in self-defense; however, she knew the Amnion wouldn't react favorably.

Abruptly Mikka said, 'Here it is, Nick,' and switched Enablement's transmission to the intercom.

'Enablement Station to presumed human Captain Nick Succorso,' the alien voice articulated. 'Two humans will be permitted to disembark *Captain's Fancy*, yourself and the pregnant female. You will be escorted to a suitable birthing environment. There you will concede one deciliter of your blood. When you have complied, you will be given confirmation of credit, and the female's fetus will be brought to physiological maturity. Then you will be returned to *Captain's Fancy*.

'Acknowledgment is required.'

'Do it,' Nick told Mikka tightly.

'Your airlock will be opened now,' said Enablement. Nick looked over at Morn. 'You ready?'

Instead of screaming, she nodded dully.

'Mikka,' he said into the intercom, 'I'm switching to suit communications. Make sure Scorz knows what he's doing.'

He snapped down his faceplate, secured it, and powered up his EVA systems. By the time Morn had followed his example, he was talking to the communications second.

'How am I coming in, Scorz?'

'Clear and easy, Nick.'

'Mikka, do you hear me?'

'You're on broadcast,' Mikka answered. 'Everybody can hear you.'

'Morn?' Nick asked.

'I hear you.' Morn's voice sounded both loud and muffled in her own ears, simultaneously constricted by the helmet and masked by the hiss of air.

'Good. If you miss one word, Scorz, I'll have your balls. And watch for jamming. Mikka, if they try that, get us out.'

'Right,' Mikka said.

'We're going now.' Nick hesitated fractionally, then added, 'Keep us safe.'

As if the admonition were an insult, Mikka growled, 'Trust me.'

'If I have to,' he retorted.

'Come on, Morn.' He was already at the door which opened from the suit locker into the access passage of the airlock. 'Let's get this over with.'

The note of strain in his voice compelled her. So numb that she was no longer sure what she did, she followed him.

With her suit sealed, she felt a moment of dizziness, a crawling in the pit of her stomach. The polarized plexulose of her faceplate seemed to bend her vision, twisting Nick out of shape, causing the walls to lean in. She knew from experience, however, that the effect would quickly become unnoticeable.

It wouldn't protect her from what she was about to see.

At the control panel, Nick verified that the airlock was tight, then tapped in a sequence to open the doors. Taking Morn by the arm, he pulled her into the lock.

The space was large enough to hold half *Captain's Fancy*'s crew. Nick went to the inner panel and shut the doors. At once a warning light came on, indicating that Mikka had sealed the ship.

He hit more buttons, and the outer door slid aside. Beyond the Station-side access passage, Enablement's airlock was already open.

Two Amnion stood just outside it, waiting.

Stumbling between fear and calm, as if she were going mutely insane, Morn let Nick lead her forward.

In the Station airlock, they crossed a scanning grid that looked more like a tangle of vines than a technological apparatus. She and Nick were tested for weapons and contaminants, then let pass.

She moved as if she were wading through mire. Every step took her closer to the Amnion and horror.

She wished she could blame her faceplate for the way they looked to her; but she knew she couldn't. Polarization and plexulose weren't responsible for the terror which her heart pumped instead of blood – a terror thickened to sludge by her zone-implant.

The guards were hominoid in the sense that they had arms and legs, fingers and toes, heads and torsos, eyes and mouths; but there all resemblance to *Homo sapiens* ended. Their racial identity was a function of RNA and DNA, not of species-specific genetic codes. They played with their shapes the way humans played with fashion, sometimes for utility, sometimes for adornment.

They wore no clothing: they had developed a protective crust, as rough as rust, which made garments irrelevant. Keen teeth like a lamprey's lined their mouths. Their viscid eyes – four of them spaced around their heads for omnidirectional vision – didn't need to blink. Both Amnion were bipedal: however, one of them had four arms, two sprouting from each side; the other had three, one at each shoulder, one in the center of its torso. Their strangeness made them loom like giants, although they were only a little larger than Nick or Morn.

Draped from their shoulders were bandoliers supporting unfamiliar weapons.

Both of them wore what appeared to be headsets. That made sense. Translation was a complex process, and probably wouldn't be entrusted to guards in any case; so all communication would be patched between the authorities on Enablement and *Captain's Fancy*. This was confirmed when the alien voice came over Morn's earphones, although neither guard had spoken.

'Presumed human Captain Nick Succorso, you are accepted on Enablement Station. You will be escorted to the birthing environment.'

One Amnioni gestured toward a transport sled parked out in the dock. 'Let's go,' Nick said.

The way the guards moved their heads suggested that they could hear him.

Morn felt another piece of her reality detach itself and slip away. In this place, nothing was fixed; all nightmares became possible.

Light fell like sulfur from hot pools in the ceiling. She stared around her as if she were fascinated; but all she wanted was to avoid focusing her eyes on her guards.

The dock itself was generically similar to the dock of any human Station: a huge space crisscrossed with gantry tracks and cables; full of cranes and hoists and lifts. Nevertheless all the details were different. The straight lines and rigid shapes of human equipment were nowhere in evidence. Instead each crane and sled looked like it had been individually grown rather than constructed; born in vats rather than built. The same biotechnologies which made steel by digesting iron ore produced gantries which resembled trees, vehicles which might have been gross beetles. She'd been taught in the Academy that Amnion scan and detection systems were considerably more accurate than anything available to humankind; their computers ran faster; their guns were more powerful. The Amnion had no lack of technical sophistication: what handicapped them was the inefficiency of their manufacturing methods.

Like her black box, thinking about such things did nothing to heal Morn's dread. Inside her, hysteria beat against the walls erected by her zone-implant.

What was about to happen to her son violated the most fundamental tenets of her flesh. A baby not carried to term in a woman's womb was deprived of the basis of its personality, the core experience on which human perception rested: tests with fetuses gestated in artificial wombs had proven this over and over again. A baby who went incomplete from his mother's body to physical maturity in the space of an hour might be deprived of human personality and perception altogether.

And Nick had an immunity drug for Amnion mutagens. The UMCP was corrupt—

The zone-implant had lost its effect on her mind. Yet it controlled her body. Lassitude filled her limbs like peace: she was no more capable of opposing Nick or fighting for her life than she was of fending off the mounting pressure of lunacy.

Still holding her arm, he led her between the guards toward the transport sled.

The sled appeared to be made of the same rusty material which formed the skin of the Amnion. One guard stepped into the splayed beetle and sat at the incomprehensible controls; the other waited behind Nick and Morn. He, too, stepped over the side, then turned to help her join him. Almost forcing her down beside him, he seated himself in one of the crooked seats.

The other guard climbed into the rear.

With a liquid gurgle and spatter, as if it were powered by acid, the sled began to move.

'Nick,' Morn said, 'I want to name him after my father.'

'What?' Nick's head jerked toward her; through his faceplate, his eyes glared angry astonishment.

'I want to name him after my father.' She'd never said this to him before. 'Davies Hyland. I want to name him Davies Hyland.'

'Are you out of your mind?' Confined by the helmet, his voice hit her ears loudly. 'This is no time to discuss it.

'It's important to me.' She knew this was no time to discuss it: not now; not here. Everybody aboard *Captain's Fancy* could hear her; so could the authorities of Enablement Station. But she couldn't stop. Her fear was making her wild. And her memory of her father was the only thing left that she could still trust; the part of her that valued him was all she could fight for. 'I didn't mean to kill him. I loved him. I want to name my baby after him.'

'Goddamn you, Morn.' Nick sounded suddenly distant, as if he were receding from her. Wet, sulfuric light reflecting down his faceplate hid his expression. 'I don't give a flying fuck at a black hole what you name the little shit. Just keep your fucking mouth shut.'

For the first time in what seemed like hours, she caught a glimpse of relief.

Davies.

Davies Hyland.

At least she would be able to recognize that much of herself in him, no matter what else happened. Maybe his name would make him human.

As if it ran on oil, the sled glided across the dock into a hall as wide as a road. Black strips in the floor took hold of the sled and guided it like rails. Other strips could have handled other traffic; yet the hall was empty. The fluid noise of the sled's drive was the only sound from either direction. The Station kept everything except its walls secret from alien eyes. The hall curved steadily, and she thought it declined as it curved, as if Enablement were designed in spirals, helixes, instead of concentric circles – down and around in a tightening circuit, like the descent into hell.

The damp yellow light was more intense here. It played and gleamed across Morn's EVA suit like a decontamination beam, burning away undetectable microorganisms; burning away reality; at last burning away fear. Somewhere deep within her, she surrendered slowly to the zone-implant.

Nick's voice was abrupt in her ears. 'Where are you taking us? I don't like being this far from my ship.'

Both guards looked at him. From the earphones, Enablement's mechanical voice said, 'Conformity of purpose will be achieved through the mutual satisfaction of requirements. Your requirements necessitate a suitable birthing environment.'

He growled a curse under his breath, then insisted harshly, 'Delay doesn't conform to your purpose or mine.'

'Time,' came the reply, 'is not accessible to manipulation.'

As if out of nowhere, Vector Shaheed asked amiably, 'Is that philosophy or physics?'

Morn began to relax more completely.

'Goddamn it – ' Nick began.

'Vector!' snapped Mikka, 'I told you to be quiet.' A moment later she added, 'Sorry about that, Nick.'

'Oh, hell,' Nick retorted, 'let's all talk at once. If we're going to turn this into a farce, we might as well go all the way.'

For a moment the earphones went silent. Then the alien voice inquired, 'Presumed human Captain Nick Succorso, what is "farce"? Translation is lacking.'

Nick's fingers dug into Morn's arm. 'Ask me later,' he rasped. 'If I like the way you conduct this trade, I'll give you "farce" as a gift.'

'Presumed human Captain Nick Succorso,' countered the voice immediately, 'you claim humanity. Thereby you claim enmity to the Amnion. Also your identity does not conform to known reality. That also constitutes enmity to the Amnion. Understanding is necessary for trade. What is "farce"?'

Before Nick could reply, Vector spoke again. '"Farce" is a form of play in which humans make themselves ridiculous for the amusement of other humans. Its purpose is to reduce tension and provide community of feeling.'

Clenching his free fist and Morn's arm, Nick waited. The sled ran fifty meters down the hall before the voice answered, 'Translation is acceptable.'

After a long pause, he said, 'All right, Vector. I'll call us even this time. But don't try me again.'

No one from *Captain's Fancy* responded.

As smooth as a frictionless bearing, the sled eased to a stop in front of a wide door.

The door was marked with a black strip. To Morn it was indistinguishable from the strips on the floor. But it must have been coded in some way only the Amnion could read: perhaps by pheromones; perhaps by spectrum variation which the sulfuric light made visible to Amnion optic nerves.

The guard in the rear stepped out of the sled, spoke into its headset. At once the door slid aside.

Inside was a large room, unmistakably a lab. At a glance, Morn saw computers and surgical lasers, hypos and retractors, retorts, banks of chemicals, gurneys that looked like they'd been grown from Amnion skin, and at least two enclosed beds similar to crèches. This must be the 'suitable birthing environment' – the place where she and little Davies would live or die.

Almost calm, she looked at the Amnioni waiting for her and Nick.

It resembled the guards to the extent that it had the same red-brown crust for skin and the same cutting teeth; also it wore a headset. But its eyes were large and trinocular. The arm reaching from the center of its chest was the primary one, both longer and stronger than the several limbs around it. The Amnioni's three-legged stance made it as solid as a pedestal.

One secondary hand – how many fingers did it have? six? seven? –

349

gripped a hypo fitted to a clear vial. Another held what may have been a breathing mask of some kind.

The Amnioni spoke. 'This is the birthing environment,' Morn heard through her helmet. 'Here conformity of purpose will be achieved. Enter.'

'Who are you?' Nick demanded as if he were having second thoughts.

The Amnioni tilted its head, perhaps as an expression of curiosity. 'The question lacks precision. Do you request genetic or pheromonic identification? Humans are not known to be capable of processing such information. Or does your question pertain to function? Translation suggests the nearest human analogue is "doctor."

'You have expressed a desire for haste. Why do you not enter?'

Nick looked at Morn.

From her angle, a wash of sulfur across his helmet erased his face. Dumbly she nodded. Her circumstances and her own actions gave her no choice. And her brain was sinking steadily under the influence of her zone implant. There was nothing left for her to do except follow the dictates of instinct and biology: focus what remained of her will on the well-being of her baby, and let everything else go.

Holding her arm as if he feared to let her go, Nick moved her through the doorway into the lab.

The guards followed.

When the doors closed behind them, they positioned themselves on either side of Morn and Nick.

The doctor scrutinized each of them in turn: it may have been trying to guess which one of them was 'presumed human Captain Nick Succorso.' Then, with a decisive movement, it transferred the hypo to its central hand.

'It has been agreed,' said the voice in Morn's earphones, 'that you will concede one deciliter of your blood.' The doctor presented the hypo. 'When you have complied, you will be given confirmation of credit.' One of its secondary hands opened to reveal a credit-jack, similar in size and shape to Morn's id tag – the form of financial transfer specified by the United Mining Companies' treaties with the Amnion. 'Then the female's fetus will be brought to physiological maturity.' Another arm gestured toward one of the crèches. 'As a courtesy, the offspring will be supplied with garments.'

Steady as a pillar, the doctor waited for a response.

For a long moment Nick seemed to hesitate.

'Has it not been agreed?' asked the Amnioni.

Roughly Nick stuck out his hand. 'Permit me to inspect your hypo.'

The doctor spoke into its headset. This time no sound reached Morn. In silence the Amnioni handed Nick the hypo.

He held it up to the light, studied it from several angles. When he was sure that the vial was empty – innocent of mutagens – he returned the hypo.

Still roughly, as if each movement cost him an effort, he unsealed his left glove and pulled it off, then peeled the sleeve of his suit back from his forearm.

'I have always believed that the Amnion trade honestly,' he announced. 'Should that belief prove false, however, I have arranged to spread the knowledge throughout human space.'

In a dim way, Morn hoped that the Amnion weren't equipped by culture or experience to recognize the bluff of a frightened man.

'Conversely,' replied the mechanical voice, 'human falseness is established reality. The risk of trade is accepted because what you offer has value. Nevertheless the satisfaction of requirements must be begun by you.'

'Oh, hell,' Nick muttered to no one in particular. 'It'll make a good story even if I lose.'

With a jerk, he offered his forearm to the hypo.

At once two of the doctor's secondary hands gripped Nick's wrist and elbow. Efficient and precise, the Amnioni pressed the hypo over the large veins in his forearm; rich blood welled into the vial.

In a moment the vial was full. The doctor withdrew the hypo.

Snarling at the way his hands shook, Nick tugged down his sleeve; he shoved his fingers into his glove and resealed it. Morn imagined him biting into the capsule of the immunity drug and swallowing it. But the idea no longer disturbed her. A mad, clean calm that seemed to border on gap-sickness filled her head. She felt that she was floating a few inches off the floor as she watched the Amnioni give Nick the credit-jack, watched Nick shove it into one of his suit's pouches.

Like a mantra, she repeated her son's name to herself.

Davies. Davies Hyland.

If any part of her was worth saving, this was it.

'Now,' Nick rasped, 'the baby.'

The doctor was speaking again. 'The efficacy and safety of the procedure is established. All Amnion offspring are matured in this fashion. Certainly the human female is not Amnion. Yet even with a human the efficacy of the procedure has been established. Her blood will provide the computers with information for the necessary adjustments. The genetic identity of her offspring will not be altered.

'What are your wishes concerning her body? Will you trade for it? Suitable recompense will be offered. Or do you wish to dispose of it in your own fashion?'

Morn heard the words as if they were in a code she couldn't decipher. At her side, Nick went rigid.

'What do you mean,' he demanded dangerously, '"dispose of it"? What are you talking about? I want to take her with me as alive and healthy as she is right now.'

'That is impossible,' replied the doctor without discernible inflection. 'You were aware of this. It is presumed that your requirement contains the knowledge of its outcome. Among Amnion, the efficacy and safety of the procedure is established. Among humans, only the efficacy is established.

'The difficulty involves' – the Amnioni cocked its head, listening – 'translation suggests the words "human psychology." The procedure necessitates' – the doctor listened again – '"a transfer of mind." Of what use is a physically mature offspring with the knowledge and perceptions of a fetus? Therefore the offspring is given the mind of its parent. Among Amnion, this procedure is without difficulty. Among humans, it produces' – another cock of the head – '"insanity." A total and irreparable loss of reason and function. Speculation suggests that in humans the procedure instills an intense fear which overwhelms the mind. The female will be of no further use to you. Therefore the offer is made to trade for her.'

Total and irreparable loss – Morn did her best to concentrate on the danger, but her attention drifted sideways. Trade for her. No doubt the Amnion still wanted her because her sanity or madness was irrelevant to the mutagens. She should have been terrified.

But she was too far gone for that.

A transfer of mind. Little Davies would have her mind. He would be truly and wholly her son. There would be nothing of Angus Thermopyle in him.

Her struggle to find a better answer than rape and zone-implants and treason wouldn't end here. The things her father represented to her might still survive.

She was only aware of Nick peripherally, as if he existed at the edges of a reality which contracted around her moment by moment, making everything clear.

He was close to violence. Releasing her arm, he clenched his fists in an unconscious throttling gesture. Sulfur glared from his faceplate. Through his teeth, he gritted, 'That is unacceptable.'

After a momentary pause the voice said, 'Presumed human Captain Nick Succorso, it is acceptable. You have accepted it.'

'No, I didn't!' he shouted back. 'Goddamn it, I didn't know! I wasn't *aware* that I was asking you to destroy her mind!'

'Presumed human Captain Nick Succorso,' countered the voice implacably, 'that is of no concern. An agreement has been reached. That agreement will be acted upon.

'The agreement involves the human female, not you. Her acceptance is indicated by her presence. And your enmity to the Amnion is established. You are suspected of falseness in trade. It is presumed that you will return to human space and report that the Amnion have failed to act upon an agreement. Trust in the Amnion will be damaged. Necessary trade will be diminished. That is unacceptable. Without trade, the goals of the Amnion are unobtainable.'

'Right!' Nick retorted. 'And your precious trade will be *diminished* when human space hears that you destroyed one of my people against my expressed wishes! I don't care what you think she does or doesn't accept. I'm not going to let you do it. I didn't *know* what the consequences are!'

'On the contrary' – the voice was remorseless – 'records of this event will demonstrate Amnion honesty. They will demonstrate that the female accepts the agreement. You are betrayed by your ignorance, not by the Amnion. Human caution will increase, but human trade will not diminish.'

Nick wheeled to verify the positions of the guards as if he were measuring his chances of escape. Then he barked, 'Mikka—'

Morn stopped him.

'Nick, it's all right.' If he ordered Mikka to begin self-destruct, the command second would obey; and then everything would be wasted. 'I'm not afraid.'

He turned on her as if he were appalled. 'You're *what*?'

'We've come too far to back out now.'

It must have been her black box talking, not her. She was still sane, she *was*, and 'a transfer of mind' dismayed her to the core; the consequences for little Davies shocked her spirit. He would be born thinking he was *her*, his brain would be full of rape and treason when nature intended only rest and food and love. The whole idea was intolerable, abhorrent; she knew that because she wasn't crazy.

And yet she wanted it. If her mind was transferred to her baby, it would be transferred without the corrosive support, the destructive resources, of her zone-implant.

'You need to get *Captain's Fancy* repaired, and I need my son. I don't care what it costs. I'm not afraid. I don't mind taking the chance.'

'It'll finish you,' he hissed through her earphones, bringing his head closer until his faceplate touched hers. "Total and irreparable loss of reason and function." I'll lose you.'

Vector Shaheed said her name, then broke off.

'Morn,' Mikka Vasaczk breathed softly, 'you don't have to do this.'

'I don't mind taking the chance,' she repeated, listening to the sound of ruin like an echo in her helmet.

Before Nick could interfere, she turned to the Amnioni and said, 'The agreement is acceptable.'

The doctor replied, 'It will be done.'

Nick let out a short, frayed howl like a cry of grief.

She walked away from him, leaving him to the guards.

At the nearest crèche, she stopped and began to unlock her faceplate.

The doctor offered her the breathing mask it held. She shook her head and murmured, 'Not yet.'

When she opened the faceplate and took off her helmet, acrid Amnion air bit into her lungs, as raw as the stink of charred corpses; but she endured it. She had one more thing to do to complete her surrender.

Stripping off the EVA suit, she stood, effectively naked, beside the crèche. Then she reached into the pocket of her shipsuit and grasped her black box; she adjusted the intensity of its emissions until they brought her right to the edge of a serene and unreachable unconsciousness.

Nearly fainting, she accepted the breathing mask.

As she pressed it to her mouth, oxygen and anesthesia enveloped her in the attar of funerals and old sleep.

'*Morn!*' Nick cried again. But now she could no longer hear him.

Unnecessarily gentle, since she was in no condition to know what anyone did, the Amnioni kept her asleep while it worked. It stretched her out in the crèche; with its deft secondary arms, it removed her shipsuit and set it beside her.

Blood was drawn. Electrodes were attached to her skull, to the major muscle groups in her arms and legs.

Then an alien serum was injected into her veins, and a biological cataclysm came over her.

In minutes her belly swelled hugely. A short time later, water burst between her legs; her cervix dilated; contractions writhed through her.

As careful as any human physician, the Amnioni accepted Davies Hyland from her body. The doctor bound and cut the umbilical cord, cleaned the struggling little boy – struggling for human air – with monstrous tenderness, then set the child in the second crèche, attached electrodes corresponding exactly to the ones which held Morn, inserted IVs, and closed the creche.

At once a normal O/CO_2 mix surrounded the baby, and new respiration turned him a healthy pink.

At the same time more chemicals were injected into Morn to smooth her recovery. Plasma replaced lost blood; coagulants and neural soothers enriched her body's responses to damage.

In the second crèche, a form of biological time-compression began. A potent amino soup, full of recombinant endocrine secretions and hormones, fed every cell in Davies' small form, triggering in seconds DNA-programmed developments which should have taken months to complete; sustaining a massive demand for nutrients and calories; enabling his tissues to process growth and waste with an efficiency at once ineffable and grotesque – as wondrously vital and consuming as cancer.

Under the subtle distortions of the crêche's cover, his body elongated itself, took on weight and muscle; his features reshaped themselves as baby fat spread across them and then melted away, and their underlying bones solidified; his hair and nails grew impossibly long, until the doctor trimmed them. At the same time, the electrodes copied Morn's life and replicated it in him: the neural learning which provided muscle tone, control, skill; the experience which gave language and reason reality; the mix of endocrine stimulation and memory which formed personality, made decision possible.

As Nick had promised, the process was finished in an hour.

In effect, Morn Hyland gave birth to a sixteen-year-old son.

First Contact (continued)

The contrary argument – that 'first contact' had taken place years previously – is based on the fact that Captain Vertigus learned nothing new (aside from the matter of appearance) or vital about the Amnion. That they were technologically sophisticated, especially in matters of biochemistry; that they were oxygen-carbon based; that they were profoundly alien: all could be deduced from the contents of the satellite which an Intertech ship, *Far Rover*, had discovered in orbit around the largest planet in the star system she had been sent to probe.

This occurred prior to the Humanity Riots – and to Intertech's absorption by SMI. *Far Rover* had been studying that system for nearly a standard year when the satellite was discovered. She continued her studies for several months afterward – but now with a radically altered mission. At first, of course, she had been looking for anything and everything: primarily resources, habitability, and signs of life. But since until now no one had ever found signs of life, her attention had been fixed on more mundane matters. However, after the discovery of the satellite, she forgot the mundane. She stayed in the system long enough to be certain that the satellite was not of local origin. Then she crossed the gap back to Earth.

Her arrival surely had enough scientific, economic, and cultural impact to qualify as 'first contact.'

Far Rover made no attempt to open or examine the satellite: she lacked the facilities. The alien object, untouched, was transported to Earth in a sealed hold, where it remained until the Intertech installation on Outreach Station was able to activate a sterile lab for it. Then, as carefully as anyone knew how, the satellite was opened.

It proved to contain a small cryogenic vessel, which in turn contained a kilo of the mutagenic material that comprised – although no one knew it at the time – the Amnion attempt to reach out to other life-forms in the galaxy.

Study of the mutagen went on for three years at a frenetic pace before Captain Vertigus and *Deep Star* were commissioned.

That the substance in the vessel was a mutagen was discovered almost routinely. In the normal course of events, scientists of every description ran tests of every kind on minute samples of the substance. Naturally most of the tests failed to produce any results which the scientists could understand. Earth science being what it was, however, the tests eventually included feeding a bit of the substance to a rat.

In less than a day, the rat changed form: it became something that resembled a mobile clump of seaweed.

Subsequently any number of rats were fed the substance. Some of them were killed and dissected. Pathology revealed that they had undergone an essential transformation: their basic life processes remained intact, but everything about them – from their RNA and the nature of their proteins and enzymes outward – had been altered. Other altered rats were successfully bred, which showed that the change was both stable and self-compatible. Still others were put through the normal behavioral tests of rats; the results demonstrated conclusively, disturbingly, that the mutation produced a significant gain in intelligence.

Experiments were attempted with higher animals: cats, dogs, chimpanzees. All changed so dramatically that they became unrecognizable. All were biologically stable, able to reproduce. All were built of fundamental enzymes and RNA native to each other, but wholly distinct from anything which had ever evolved on Earth.

All showed some degree of enhanced intelligence.

By this time, Intertech as a corporate entity was positively drooling. The potential for discovery and profit was immeasurable, if the mutagen could be traced to its source. Theorists within the company and out agreed that the satellite must have been designed to accomplish one of two things: communication or propagation. The propagationist theory, however, suffered from one apparent flaw: the mutated rats, cats, dogs, and chimps simply were not intelligent enough. They retained the limitations of their species. In other words, the mutagen was clearly inadequate to replicate its makers on lower life-forms.

Nevertheless by either theory a source existed – somewhere – not just for mutated Earth-forms with higher intelligence, but for entirely new sciences, resources, and possibilities.

But how could the satellite be traced to its source? As 'first contact' with alien life, the object was exceptionally frustrating in this regard. Hence the emphasis placed on Sixten Vertigus and his experiences. Except for its cryogenic workings, the satellite contained nothing which could be analyzed: no drive, no tape, no control systems; certainly nothing as convenient as a star chart.

If the satellite were intended as a means of communication, its message had to lie in the mutagen itself.

It did.

The course of Earth's history was changed when the decision was made within Intertech to risk the mutagen on a human being.

The woman who volunteered for the assignment probably hoped for some kind of immortality, personal as well as scientific. After all, the experimental animals which had been permitted to live were viable, hardy, and intelligent. They were also benign: they could reproduce with their own kind, but could not spread the mutagen. If her intelligence increased similarly, she might become the most important individual humankind had yet produced. And she might open the door to discoveries, opportunities, and riches which would earn her enduring reverence.

Unfortunately she only survived for a day and a half.

During that time, she changed as the animals had changed: she became, according to observers, 'a bipedal tree with luxuriant foliage and several limbs.' But the only sign of advanced intelligence was that, an hour or so before she died, she wailed for paper. As soon as she got it, she spent several minutes scribbling furiously.

When she collapsed, heroic efforts were made to resuscitate her. They failed utterly. The medical technology was all wrong: it had little relevance to her new structure.

An autopsy showed that she had become genetically and biochemically kin to the mutated rats and chimps – a product of the same world. She had been transformed from her RNA outward. Nevertheless she was the only mutated life-form to die quickly of 'natural causes.' In the opinion of the pathologists who studied her corpse from scalp to toenails, she died of 'fright.'

Conceivably the mutation had produced an uncontrollable adrenaline reaction.

Equally conceivably the knowledge of what she had become – the knowledge she gleaned from the mutagen – terrified her beyond bearing.

Whatever the explanation, her 'immortality' could be gauged by the fact that few texts on the subject mention her by name.

Or it could be gauged by this, that her final scribbles eventually led humankind into a fatal relation with the Amnion.

Mostly she had written numbers, strings of figures which had no meaning to anyone – or to any of Intertech's computers – until a young astronomer as crucial, and as forgotten, as the volunteer herself thought to analyze them as galactic coordinates.

Those coordinates enabled Captain Sixten Vertigus and *Deep Star* to establish contact with the Amnion for the first time.

CHAPTER 13

Morn began drifting toward consciousness when the Amnioni eliminated anesthetic from the mix of air she took in through the breathing mask.

The process seemed to require a long time. Controlled by her zone-implant as well as by alien drugs, she was helpless to bring herself back. Gradually she became aware of the numb ache in her loins – the stress of parturition muffled by some powerful analgesic. She felt the distension of her belly: the elasticity of her muscles had been strained away. But those things weren't enough to focus her attention; she couldn't concentrate on them.

Yet her body continued to throw off the effects of the anesthetic. Eventually she realized that she could hear Nick's voice.

'Morn,' he demanded, 'wake up! You said you weren't afraid. Prove it. Come back!'

Some part of her heard his fury, recognized that he was in a killing rage. She could feel his hands shaking her shoulders, shaking her heart. She remembered that she hated him.

'Those bastards cheated us! They did something to him!'

He broke into a fit of coughing.

Another piece of her, a separate compartment, understood that she shouldn't have been able to hear him. He was wearing an EVA suit, and she had no earphones. Nevertheless it wasn't his voice or his coughing that snagged her attention.

They did something to him.

Him? Who?

Like a momentary gap in dense smoke, a glimpse of light, the answer came to her.

Davies. Her son.

The Amnion had done something to her son.

She lay still, as if she were deaf; as if she were lost. Nothing external showed that she was fighting urgently for the strength to open her eyes.

She had the impression that Nick pulled away from her. His voice went in a different direction as he snarled, 'You *cheated*, you fucking sonofabitch. You did something to him.'

Davies Hyland. Her son. The reason she was here – the reason she'd surrendered herself.

Nick was answered by another voice she shouldn't have been able to hear. It was full of pointed teeth and sulfuric light.

'Presumed human Captain Nick Succorso, that is a false statement. The Amnion do not accept false statements. You charge a betrayal of trade. It is established that the Amnion do not betray trade. Your own tests will demonstrate that the offspring is human. The genetic identity is exactly what it was in the female's womb. Your statements are false.'

Another fit of coughing tore at Nick's lungs. When he could talk again, he rasped, 'Then why does he look like *that*?'

The alien voice conveyed a shrug. 'Your question cannot be answered. Is there a flaw in the offspring's maturation? It is not apparent. Tests indicate no genetic defect. However, if you wish the offspring altered, that can be done.'

'You bastard,' Nick spat, nearly retching. 'He doesn't look like *me*.'

'Presumed human Captain Nick Succorso,' the voice explained with what may have been Amnion patience, 'your genetic identity has no point of congruence with that of this offspring. He is not your – translation suggests the word "son." Therefore resemblance would be improbable.'

Nick's silence was as loud as a shout.

With an effort that seemed to drain the marrow from her bones, leaving her as weak as paper, Morn opened her eyes.

For a moment a flood of sulfur from the ceiling blinded her. But once her eyes opened they blinked on their own. Tears streaked the sides of her face, leaving damp, delicate trails that were more distinct to her nerves than any of the consequences of giving birth. She felt naked from her scalp to her toes; yet something kept her warm. By increments she moved closer to true consciousness.

Soon she was able to see.

A shape in an EVA suit with the faceplate open stood several paces away, near the other crèche. Sour yellow light gleamed up and down the mylar surface.

Nick.

He confronted a rusty and monstrous shape which must have been the Amnion doctor.

Towering over the crèche, the Amnioni said into its headset and the acrid air, 'The offspring resumes consciousness. In humans a period of adjustment is required. The transfer of mind produces – translation suggests the word "disorientation." For a time the mind will be unable to distinguish itself from its source.

'Data is inadequate to predict the course of this disorientation. Speculation suggests that adjustment can be rapid with proper stimulation.'

The doctor moved one of its arms along the side of the crèche, and its protective cover opened.

Morn saw bare limbs twist, heard a wet cough. The sound was weak; it seemed to come from a baby who couldn't get enough air.

Her baby.

She tried to move.

Some weight held her down. It wasn't heavy, but it was too great for her. She couldn't understand it. Had the Amnioni put her under restraint?

With an effort, she shifted her gaze to her own form.

There were no restraints. The weight was only the light fabric of her shipsuit. Presumably the doctor had stripped her so that her baby could be born. Then it must have dressed her again.

She was too weak to carry the burden of a mere shipsuit. Like an infant, she needed to come naked back to herself.

Somehow she turned her head so that she could look at the other crèche again.

The doctor put a breathing mask to the mouth of the body in the crèche; secured the mask with a strap. The coughing stopped, but the frail, uncertain movement of the limbs continued.

With three of its secondary arms, the Amnioni lifted her son into a sitting position. For a moment he remained there, breathing strenuously; then the doctor helped him move his legs off the crèche so that he could stand.

Except for the mask over his mouth and the relative slightness of his build, he might as well have been Angus Thermopyle.

The sight would have shocked her, if she'd been capable of shock. But her zone-implant held her so close to blankness that she couldn't react to the image of the man who'd ravaged her flesh, shattered her spirit.

He was only an hour old, and already he appeared like a bloated toad, dark and brutal. His arms and chest were built for violence; he stood with his legs splayed as if to withstand the abuse of the universe. His penis dangled from his crotch, as ugly as an instrument of rape.

Only his eyes betrayed the heritage of his mother. They were Morn's color – and full of her dread.

His fear made him look as helpless as a child.

Davies Hyland. Her son.

Her mind in Angus' body.

He needed her. For him this moment was worse than it could ever be for her. He suffered everything that had ever terrorized her – but he had no zone-implant.

His extremity gave her the strength to slide one hand into the pocket of her shipsuit.

'Again,' said the Amnioni, 'the offer is made to accept the female. A suitable recompense will be negotiated. Her usefulness to you is gone. The only means by which her reason can be restored requires alteration of her genetic identity.'

'In other words,' Nick snarled, 'you want to make her Amnion.' His voice was raw with coughing. Through his open faceplate, Morn saw that his face was slick with sweat or tears, the result of the bitter air he breathed so that she would be able to hear him.

Too weak and still too close to unconsciousness for subtlety, she didn't try to adjust her black box; she simply switched it off.

Then she rolled over the edge of the crèche.

While the jolt of impact and transition slammed through her, she heard the doctor intone, 'The procedure produces a total and irreparable loss of reason and function.'

At the edge of her vision, she saw Nick's boots stamp toward her. He stopped at her side; his knees flexed.

'Get up,' he gasped.

She tried, but it was beyond her. Like a stretched elastic cord when it was released, her mind seemed to snap away – out of the void where it had been held; toward the need of her son. In her thoughts, she surged upright, hurried to his aid. For him an incomprehensible awakening would be made more terrible when he saw her and believed that she was himself. He would need help to absorb the truth; help to counter his fear; help to understand who and what he was, and not go mad.

Yet her body only lay on the floor, trembling. She braced her arms, but couldn't lever her chest up. The pressure on her swollen breasts made them ache impersonally, like distant fire.

Coughing until his voice nearly failed, Nick croaked, '*Get up*, you bitch!'

She couldn't.

As if she were weightless, he caught her by the fabric of her shipsuit and hauled her off the floor; he flung her against the edge of the crèche, then spun her to face him. From inside his helmet, his eyes glared: black; beyond appeal. His scars were flagrant with blood and rage.

'Goddamn it! You put me through all this, and he isn't even mine! That's Thermopyle! *He isn't even mine!*'

Then he went down because Davies had come off the other crèche and punched him in the back with all Angus' harsh force.

Unable to catch herself, Morn flopped on top of Nick.

Gasping, he arched his back and tried to squirm away from the pain as if his ribs were broken.

When she rolled off him, she found Davies stooping over her. As soon as she stopped moving, he bent closer, dropped to his knees. His eyes searched her face as if he were transfixed with horror.

More Amnion were there – the guards. Between them, they picked Nick up and held him so that he couldn't attack. He struggled like a man whose ribs weren't seriously damaged. Nevertheless the raw air ripped at his lungs, and every exertion made him cough harder, draining his strength.

'Restore the integrity of your suit,' the doctor told him, 'so that breathing will be easy. Your words will be broadcast to each other.'

'He was going to hurt you,' Davies breathed. His vocal cords were sixteen years old, but his voice had the innocent inflections of a child; he sounded like a young, lost version of his father. Dismay as deep as the dimensional gap stared out of his eyes. 'I couldn't let him do that.

'You're me.'

She wanted to wrap her arms around his neck and hug him against her sore breasts, but she was too weak. And other things were more important. 'No,' she said through her mask and her frailty and the stress of transition. 'That's not true. You've got to trust me.'

His instinctive crisis showed on his face, the conflict between the impulse to believe in her because she was him and the need to reject her because she shouldn't have been separate from him. It was the fundamental crisis of maturation made grotesquely, extravagantly worse by the way it came upon him – all in minutes, instead of slowly over sixteen years.

Reaching up to him, she gripped his arms – arms like his father's; arms so strong that they'd once beaten Nick. 'None of this makes sense to you,' she said as if she were pleading. 'I know that. Everything feels wrong. If you think hard you may be able to remember what happened. I'll explain it all – I'll help you every way I can. But not now. Not here. You've got to trust me. You think you're Morn Hyland, but you're not. *I'm* Morn Hyland. You know what she looks like. She looks like me. You don't.

'Your name is Davies Hyland. I'm your mother. You're my son.'

Nick's voice boomed as if it were playing over speakers large enough to fill an auditorium. 'And Angus goddamn Thermo-pile is your fucking father!'

While he raged, the doctor – or the Enablement authorities – turned down the volume of their broadcast. He seemed to fade as he cursed.

Davies' eyes flicked toward Nick. Morn saw them narrow with inherited revulsion. Then he looked back down at her. At once his disgust returned to panic.

'I don't understand,' he whispered past his mask. 'You're me. You're what I see in my head when I see myself. I can't remember— Who is Angus Thermo-pile?'

'I'll help you,' she insisted urgently. 'I'll explain everything. I'll help you remember. We'll remember it all together.' Her own mask seemed to hamper her voice; she couldn't make it reach him. 'But not now. Not here. It's too dangerous.

'Just trust me. Please.'

'This does not conform to established reality,' said the doctor. Morn heard strange Amnion cadences with one ear, language she knew with the other. 'The procedure produces total and irreparable loss of reason and function. Analysis is required.' As if speaking to one of the computers, the Amnioni instructed, 'Complete physiological, metabolic, and genetic decoding, decisiveness high.'

Abruptly Davies took her in his arms and lifted her. He set her on her feet and started to let go of her; but when her knees buckled, he caught and supported her by her elbows. Like his father, he was an inch or two shorter than she.

Almost strangling on his distress, he murmured, 'I'm Morn Hyland. You're Morn Hyland. This is wrong.'

'I know,' she replied from the bottom of her heart. 'I know. It's wrong.' Desperately she tried to confirm his grasp on reality, so that he wouldn't go mad. 'But I didn't have any other way to save your life.' Or my soul.

He continued to stare at her with his eyes full of bleak, unremitting fear.

'You better believe her,' Nick snarled viciously. 'She's never told *me* the truth, but she's telling it to you. She damn near got us all dispersed to infinity in the gap so she could save your shit-miserable life.'

Morn ignored him. Her son needed her, *her son*; her mind in Angus' body. His dread was as palpable to her as her own. She had no attention to spare for Nick's outrage – or his grief.

The doctor came to stand beside her and Davies. 'You wish to be clothed,' it said. 'It is understood that humans require garments.' One of its arms offered a shipsuit and boots made of a strange material that appeared to absorb light. 'The frailty of human skin is conducive to fear. This is a racial defect, correctable by Amnion.'

With a small shock, Morn realized that the doctor may have been trying to comfort Davies.

'Do it,' she urged him softly. 'Get dressed. We'll go back to *Captain's Fancy*. We can talk there.'

Then she stepped back to show him that she could stand without his support.

He complied, not because he believed her, not because he set his fear aside in order to trust her – she knew this in the same way that she knew herself – but because his nakedness made him feel vulnerable to harm and manipulation. Awkwardly, as if his brain weren't entirely in control of his movements, he accepted the shipsuit and put it on;

he shoved his feet into the boots. The fit was approximate, but adequate.

The sulfuric light didn't appear to touch him anywhere except on his face and hands; his clothes shed it like water. But it gave his face a jaundiced hue, and the contrast made him look at once more and less like his father: more malign, and less certain of it.

'Are you done?' Nick rasped. 'I want to get out of here.'

'The return to your ship is acceptable,' said the Amnioni. 'You will be escorted.' An instant later it added, 'Further violence is not acceptable.'

The guards let go of Nick's arms.

'Tell him to leave me alone.' Davies' appeal sounded like that of a scared child – of the scared child inside Morn.

'I'm not going to touch you, asshole,' retorted Nick. 'Not here. You're coming back to my ship. Once you're aboard, I'll do anything I fucking *want* to you.'

Davies' eyes turned to Morn in alarm and supplication.

'I can't tell you not to be afraid,' she said unsteadily. 'I'm scared of him, too. But we can't stay here. You know that. Somewhere inside, you know that.' She was frantic for strength, for the ability to make her words reach him and be believed. 'Somewhere inside, you know how to defend yourself. And I'm on your side. Completely.' She spoke to her son, but she wanted Nick to hear her and understand that she was threatening him. 'I'll do everything I can to help you.'

Davies held her gaze for a long moment as if without her he would drown in his dread. Then, slowly, he nodded.

One of the guards opened the door to the outer hall and the transport sled.

'Come on.' Nick turned and strode out of the lab.

The doctor picked up Morn's EVA suit, gave it to her. She bundled it under one arm so that her other hand was free to reach into her pocket. Still wavering, she followed Nick.

The entire center of her being, from her crotch to her heart, ached dully, as if something essential had been torn away. She concentrated on that so she wouldn't be overwhelmed by her concern for her son.

Ahead of her, Nick stepped into the sled. She did the same.

So did Davies.

Staring straight past the shoulders of the Amnioni driver as if he could no longer bear to look at her, he rode with her back through Enablement Station to *Captain's Fancy.*

By the time they reached the high emptiness of the dock, he couldn't conceal the fact that he was trembling. Already, she guessed, his grasp on what little he knew about himself had begun to fail, eroded not only by the shock of seeing himself in someone else and hearing his identity denied, but also by his father's physical legacy – by testosterone and male endocrine balances. And then there were the unguessable aftereffects of his mother's use of a zone-implant while he was in her womb. In a short time, Morn realized, he would cease to think in ways she could predict or even understand.

She had to resist an impulse to put her arms around him as if he really were a child.

Instead she eased her hand into the pocket of her shipsuit.

She needed to be ready for whatever Nick might do when they boarded *Captain's Fancy.* Yet she couldn't risk betraying her zone-implant by regaining strength too easily. When her fingers felt sure on her black box, she tapped the functions which would supply her with energy; but she set them at a low level.

The effect wasn't a relief. The same neural stimulation which sharpened her mind and quickened her reflexes also counteracted the drugs she'd been given to numb her pain. But she accepted that. Pain, too, was a resource: like her apprehension for Davies and her fear of Nick, it helped bring her into focus.

The sled eased to a halt near *Captain's Fancy's* outer lock. The lock still stood open, waiting.

Both Amnion got out.

Nick and Morn did the same. After a moment's hesitation, Davies swung his legs over the side of the sled.

One of the guards spoke into its headset. To Morn's surprise, Enablement continued broadcasting voices so that she and Davies could hear them and their translation.

'You may reenter your ship,' the speakers announced. 'Departure will not be permitted.'

Nick wheeled on the guards. '*What?*'

The Amnioni voice spoke again. 'You may reenter your ship. Departure will not be permitted.'

369

'You sonofabitch, that violates our agreement. *Departure* is part of the trade.'

Neither of the guards answered.

'Presumed human Captain Nick Succorso,' replied the alien voice, 'departure has been agreed. It will be permitted. Delay is necessary. Established reality is in flux. Events do not conform. Consideration is required. Departure will be postponed.'

'No!' Nick shouted back. 'I don't agree! I want *out* of here!'

There was no response. The air was as empty as the dock.

Both guards pointed toward *Captain's Fancy*'s locks.

Neither of them touched their weapons.

They didn't need to.

'Goddamn it!' snarled Nick. '"Trade" with the Amnion is like swimming in the fucking sewer of the universe.'

Nearly running, he headed for his ship.

'Come on.' Morn took Davies' arm and urged him forward. 'Whatever he does to us, it'll be better than being abandoned here.'

Deliberately, as if he were making a point, Davies disengaged his arm. But then he accompanied Morn through the Station's scan- and decontamination-lock.

Doom haunted his eyes. Yet with every passing moment his movements grew more secure as his brain and body adjusted to each other.

In the ship's airlock, Nick pounded impatiently on the control panel, muttering, 'Do it, Mikka. Seal the ship. Let me in.'

Almost on Morn's and Davies' backs, the door swept shut. Panel lights indicated that the Amnion air was being pumped out, replaced by the ship's human atmosphere. Another light showed that the inner doors were being unlocked.

Nick couldn't wait for the air to clear. Roughly he knocked loose the seals of his helmet, pulled it off his head, then jabbed open the intercom and hissed, 'Let me *in*.'

Morn understood. Suit communications might still be patched through Enablement. However, the intercom was safe.

'Nick,' Mikka demanded as the control panel went green and the inner doors opened, 'what the hell's going on?'

Ripping open his EVA suit, he strode into his ship. 'How in shit should I know?' he retorted; but he was too far from the lock intercom pickup to be heard. When he'd kicked off his suit, he toggled the nearest intercom.

'Don't ask stupid questions. You heard everything I heard. Those bastards! If they make us stay long enough, they'll have time to test my blood. They'll know I cheated.

'Keep self-destruct ready. Start nudging drive off standby. Ease some charge into the matter cannon. And disconnect communications. Don't let Station hear anything unless I'm talking to them.

'We're coming up.'

Leaving Morn to close and seal the inner doors, he headed for the bridge.

Quickly Morn pulled the breathing mask off her head; dropped it and her EVA suit beside Nick's. Then she keyed in the close-and-lock sequence for the doors and started after him.

But she stopped as soon as she realized that Davies wasn't with her.

He sat hunched with his back to the doors and his knees hugged against his chest. His forehead rested on his knees.

In that posture, he was so unlike Angus Thermopyle that she nearly wept for him. He urgently needed his father's obsessive and brutal instinct for survival.

She went back to him. After she said his name, however, her throat closed, and she couldn't go on.

'I don't understand this.' His thighs and the mask muffled his voice. 'I can't remember anything.

'He's going to do something terrible to me.'

Harsh because of her own grief and desperation, she snapped, 'That's probably true. He's not a nice man. But we've got to face it. We don't have any choice. He can leave us here – he can leave us to the Amnion. Then we'll lose everything. We won't be human anymore. They'll pump mutagens into us, and we'll become like them. If we're lucky, we won't even notice that we've joined a race that wants to get rid of the entire human species.

'Davies, listen to me. As far as I'm concerned, you're the second most important thing in the galaxy. You're my *son*.' You're the part of me I need to believe in. 'But the *first*, the *most* important thing is to not betray my humanity. As long as I've got life or breath to fight with, I won't let that happen to me. Or anybody else.'

She knew how to reach him: she knew the motivational strings that pulled his will. They were still the same as hers; he hadn't had time to change. And now she had the strength to convey conviction. Her zone-implant provided that.

Slowly his head came up. The look in his eyes reminded her of something she'd once loathed and feared.

'If he tries to hurt you,' Davies said, 'I'm going to tear his arms off.'

She gave a sigh of relief and dread. 'It doesn't work that way. He doesn't care about you, so he won't try to hurt me. He's more likely to hurt you as a way of getting even with me.'

Despite his expression, he still sounded like a child, singsong and uncomprehending. 'What did I do to him? I mean, what did you do to him when I was you?'

As firmly as she could, she renewed her promise. 'I'll tell you. I'll tell you everything. And you're going to remember a lot of this, when you get the chance. But not now. We need to go to the bridge. If we're going to defend ourselves, we need to know what's happening.

'Can you do it?'

Just for a moment, past his dark, distended features and threatening gaze, she caught a glimpse of her own father in him, the man he was named for.

'I can do it.'

Then the glimpse was gone. He looked like no one except Angus Thermopyle as he threw off his mask and rose to his feet.

Her heart shivered with love and abhorrence as she led him away.

When they reached the bridge, it seemed crowded. Mikka's watch was still in place, and Vector Shaheed occupied the engineer's Station. But Nick had taken the command seat from Mikka, which left her nowhere to sit. And she wasn't the only one on her feet. Liete Corregio stood nearby, along with the huge, clumsy brawler, Simper, who served as targ third, and Pastille, the rank, weaselly helm third.

Heads swiveled as soon as Morn and Davies stepped through the aperture. Vector's mouth dropped open, perhaps in surprise at Davies' resemblance to Angus; Alba Parmute gave the boy a quick glance of sexual appraisal. But Morn's attention was instantly on Nick. At first she missed the way the other people looked at her: the hard glare in Mikka's eyes; Liete's shielded gaze; the targ third's hunger; Pastille's frank sneer.

Until she felt the force of their stares, she failed to notice the fact that all four of them wore guns.

'Are you sure this is necessary?' Mikka asked Nick. 'They aren't going anywhere. Hell, they aren't *trying* to go anywhere.'

'Do it,' Nick snapped without turning his head. 'Lock them up. Separately. I haven't got time to worry about them right now. And disable their intercoms. I don't want them talking to each other.'

'Nick—!' Shock snatched a cry of protest out of Morn before she could stop herself.

In unison, Mikka, Liete, and the two men drew their impact pistols. Simper leered like he'd been given permission for some deliciously nasty self-indulgence.

'Nick' – Morn tried again, more carefully – 'don't do this. He can't be alone right now. Let me at least talk to him. We need to talk. He still thinks he's me. If he has to be alone with that, he'll lose his mind.'

'Let him,' snarled Nick. 'I don't care how many minds he loses. You aren't going to talk to him until I find out why you've been lying to me. In fact, you aren't going to talk to him until I find a way to make sure you never lie to me again.

'If you don't *shut up* and go, you'll pay for it.'

The targ third grinned harder.

'Nick,' Scorz said unsteadily, 'message from Enablement.'

Everyone froze.

'Audio,' Nick ordered through his teeth.

Scorz keyed his board. At once the mechanical voice said, 'Enablement Station to presumed human Captain Nick Succorso, prepare to receive emissary.'

Nick sat up straighter.

'Trade is necessary. Speculation suggests negotiation will be' – a momentary pause – 'delicate. Emissary will speak for the Amnion. To encourage negotiation, he will board your ship alone. Conformity of purpose will be achieved through the mutual satisfaction of requirements.'

Nick leaned forward. 'Scorz, copy this. "Further explanation is necessary. No Amnioni will board *Captain's Fancy* if I am kept in ignorance. What are your requirements?" Send it.'

Hands quivering slightly, the communications second obeyed.

Enablement's reply was almost instantaneous. 'The Amnion require possession of the new human offspring aboard your ship.'

In that moment, Morn felt the bottom drop out of her heart.

Wheeling his seat, Nick swung around to face her. His eyes burned with malice and triumph. 'Tell them,' he told Scorz, '"Your emissary is acceptable."'

Then he flung a burst of laughter straight into her panic.

Clenching his fists, Davies took a step forward.

At once Mikka aimed her gun at his head; Liete pointed hers into his belly.

'Oh, hell,' Nick chuckled to Mikka, 'let them stay. I want them to hear what this "emissary" says. That should be the most fun I've had all day.'

Liete kept her thoughts to herself; but a mixture of relief and anguish twisted Mikka's features as she lowered her weapon.

As hot as a welding laser, Nick's gaze held Morn's.

'I don't really care that much about making you tell the truth,' he said softly, almost sweetly. His mouth stretched tight over his teeth. 'I prefer revenge. Something tells me you're about to find out what it costs when you lie to me.'

The only thing that kept her from jumping at Nick and trying to claw his eyes out was the look of dumb, desperate terror on Davies' face.

CHAPTER 14

The Amnion require—

The targ third was disappointed: he liked rape as much as demolition, and he wanted Morn to himself. But Pastille was smart enough to see broader possibilities of distress. He laughed soundlessly, like a mute echo of Nick, showing his unclean teeth.

No one else except Nick looked at Morn.

— require possession—

Liete's voice held a barely audible rub of tension as she dismissed Pastille and Simper from the bridge. They obeyed, handing their guns to Mikka on the way. Liete walked off around the curve, dissociating herself from Morn and Davies – or perhaps from Nick and Mikka.

Mikka stowed two of the impact pistols in a gun locker. Like Liete, she kept her own weapon.

Scorz concentrated on the communications board. Alba studied Davies some more; deliberately she pulled the seal of her shipsuit an inch lower. Ransum, the helm second, made a show of testing her Station, her hands fluttering like scraps of paper in a breeze. The man on targ, Karster, stared at the back of Nick's head. With nothing to do, the scan second sat in a meditative pose – hands folded in his lap, eyes closed.

Vector, too, had his eyes shut; the muscles of his face were slack. Without his phlegmatic smile, his face seemed to lose some of its roundness, sagging over its bleak, underlying bones.

— possession of the new human offspring—

Ignoring Nick, Morn said to her son, 'Hang on.' Her throat worked convulsively, jerking out words. 'We're in this together. He's just making threats to scare you. He wants to punish you for not being his.'

'Try me,' Nick put in harshly.

Morn stepped between him and Davies; she turned her back on Nick to aim all her artificial conviction at Davies. 'He can't hurt you without hurting me. And he can't hurt me without hurting himself.'

'If you believe that' – anger throbbed in Nick's voice – 'you're sicker than I thought.'

'I'm his lover,' she continued to Davies, 'the best lover he's ever had. He'll have to give me up if he hurts you. He'll lose me completely. He can always kill me, but he'll never be able to make me do what he wants again.'

'You *lied* to me!' Nick shouted.

Morn nearly turned on him; nearly retorted, You bastard, I've never told you the truth about anything. —*require possession*— She was frantic to deflect Nick's malice from her son; frantic enough to take any risk—

But the sight of Davies held her.

As she watched, his resemblance to Angus increased. Catalyzed by fear and incomprehension, he seemed to take on the inheritance of his father by an act of will. The color of his eyes was wrong, but their porcine squint became pure Angus; and the darkness behind them, the fathomless dread, mimicked exactly the old, acid seethe of fear which drove Angus' brutality.

She'd sold her soul to the zone-implant in an effort to survive the consequences of that brutality. Simply seeing Angus' image in front of her cramped her heart, as if she no longer had enough room inside her for her own pulse, her own blood.

But he wasn't Angus Thermopyle, he *wasn't*, he was Davies Hyland, her son. He may have had Angus' genes and body; his perceptions may have been flavored by Angus' particular endocrine stew; his knowledge of himself may have been tainted by her memories of Angus. Yet he'd received his mind from *her*. All his starting points were different than his father's. She had to believe that he would also reach different conclusions.

'Nick.' Scorz's voice reached Morn through her turmoil. 'Enablement's talking again.'

Morn heard a slight susurrus of bearings and servos as Nick pivoted his seat. Instinctively she turned as well. Again he commanded, 'Audio.'

'Enablement Station to presumed human Captain Nick Succorso,' reported the bridge speakers, 'the Amnion emissary awaits acceptance aboard your ship.'

'Tell them' – despite his fury, Nick had resumed his nonchalant, dangerous poise – '"The Amnion emissary will be accepted as soon as an escort has been arranged." Send it.

'Mikka,' he went on immediately, 'you're the escort. Don't let that thing aboard until you're sure there's only one of it. Keep it covered the whole time – we don't have to pretend to be nice about this.

'Liete, it's your job to make sure Morn and the asshole here don't do or say anything to get in my way.'

A small spasm like a clench of protest tightened Mikka's scowl. Nevertheless she grunted an acknowledgment and left the bridge. Liete responded by coming down the curve to stand behind Morn and Davies with her hand on her impact pistol.

Davies was still too naïve to keep his thoughts to himself. And his mind had been formed from Morn's: his thoughts grew from her need and revulsion. 'Someday,' he muttered, 'I'm going to give him a new asshole to remember me by.'

Nick snorted another laugh.

The Amnion require possession—

Morn put her hand in her pocket and increased the intensity of her zone-implant's emissions.

With Davies at her shoulder, and Liete Corregio's gun at her back, she waited for the emissary.

Abruptly Nick said to the bridge, 'All right, listen. We've got things to think about before Mikka gets back.' He'd set his fury aside for the moment. 'The Amnion want to make a deal. I would hate,' he drawled, 'to miss an opportunity like this. But we've already got everything we asked for. Including' – he held up the credit-jack -'enough money to repair the gap drive. Hell, we've got enough money to *replace* that fucker. So what're we going to bargain *for*?'

Liete didn't hesitate. 'A chance to get out of here.'

'Why?' he demanded. 'They've already told us we can go. Why should we ask for something they've already promised?'

Vector opened his eyes. 'No, Nick. Liete's right.' His gaze was dull, and he didn't smile; if anything, the flesh of his face seemed to droop more heavily from its underpinnings. 'It's not that simple. You said yourself, if they keep us long enough, they'll have time to finish testing your blood. But the situation is worse than that. If we leave slowly enough, they'll still have time. And then they'll come after us.

'They'll catch us.' His voice sounded as arthritic as his joints. 'Right now, we couldn't outrun a lifeboat – if it had a gap drive. And we're' – his hands opened and closed on his board – 'half a *light-year* from Thanatos Minor. A full year for us at our best speed. They'll have that long to hunt us down, while we're trying to survive on six or nine months' worth of food.'

'Get to the point,' Nick said with the same insouciant, ominous drawl.

'The point,' Vector sighed as if he were hardening himself against Morn's urgent stare, 'is that if you don't give them Davies just to recompense them for being cheated, we're all finished. We haven't got a prayer.'

'Who is *he*?' Davies asked Morn, none too quietly, as if he were making up a list of enemies and wanted to include Vector.

— possession of the new human offspring—

'Not now,' she hissed to him. 'Please.'

Nick ignored her and Davies. Instead he countered Vector, 'What if we trade them for repairs on the gap drive?'

'I thought of that.' Despite his slumped posture and slack features, Vector didn't flinch from facing Nick. 'But it won't work. It'll take too long. From what I've heard, their equipment has all the same pieces ours does, but the designs are incompatible. We'll have to let them tinker with our drive until they can rig a fix. We could be here for days. And that gives us another problem. We'll have to let them aboard. We'll have Amnion on the ship the whole time. We'll be too vulnerable. They could sabotage us – or just take over – whenever they want.'

The engineer made *Captain's Fancy*'s ruin seem inevitable; but Nick dismissed that. Still more casually, as if he were arriving at a point he'd foreseen all along – as if he were springing a personal trap – he asked, 'What if we trade them for parts, and you do the repairs?'

Vector continued to hold Nick's gaze; but his mouth slumped open. After a moment he murmured, 'Nick, I'm not that good.'

'You'd better be,' Nick replied almost cheerfully, 'because that's the only shot we've got. I'll give you three hours.'

At the edges of her vision, Morn saw sweat suddenly beading on Vector's face, reflecting small, wet bits of light from his round visage. But she wasn't thinking about him now, or about what he said. He was right, of course: without a usable gap drive, *Captain's Fancy* was as good as dead; too far from human space to escape when Nick's cheat was discovered. But that dilemma had nothing to do with her now. Her problem was entirely different.

Nick was going to do it; he was serious. He had every intention of giving Davies back to the Amnion.

Only her zone-implant enabled her to swallow a wail. For a moment she hung right on the edge of attacking Nick – of performing some mad act which would get her killed right away, while she was still human and safe; which might get Davies killed as well when he tried to defend her. Better to die in a fight on the bridge of Nick's ship than to become Amnion—

But her implant's artificial clarity held her. Instead of crying out or attacking, she went further.

The influence of her black box was a form of insanity; and from its neural stimulation, its coerced impulses, she began to weave a fabric of recourse so extreme that it made wails and violence look sane by comparison.

She could do it. If she was careful, she could do it.

And if she failed—

If she failed, nothing on *Captain's Fancy* or Enablement Station would prevent her from exacting retribution. She would let nothing prevent her.

Liete stood too close: Morn couldn't speak to Davies without being overheard. She had to trust that he would be able to retain his own sanity when Nick gave him back to the Amnion.

Despite the extremity of her intentions, she still had the capacity – her zone-implant gave her that – to be shocked when Mikka Vasaczk brought Enablement's emissary to the bridge.

Either the creature at Mikka's side had once been human and had been given a mutagen which wasn't entirely successful, or it had begun as Amnion and its people had failed in their attempts to make it appear human. Morn guessed the former, if only because the human parts of the creature were so convincing.

In general, as well as in some details, it – or he – was recognizably a man. He had one human arm, and most of his chest was unflawed. Above his boots, the skin of his shins was pale and ordinary. Half his face looked and moved like any other man's. And he breathed the ship's atmosphere with only a modicum of respiratory difficulty.

But his shipsuit – like Davies', made from an alien material which shed light – had been cut away to accommodate the thick knobs of Amnion skin that had taken over his knees. His other arm was also bare: Amnion tissues needed no covering. And the inhuman half of his face was made for the sulfuric light and acrid air of Enablement Station. An Amnion eye stared unblinking from that side; some of the teeth under it, revealed by a partially lipless maw, were pointed like the guards'.

'Nick' – Mikka spoke tonelessly, all her emotions clamped down – 'this is the Amnion emissary.

'That,' she said, pointing Nick out to the creature at her side, 'is Captain Nick Succorso.'

Still holding her gun, she stepped back to stand watch beside the aperture.

'I wish to sit,' said the creature in a voice like flakes of rust.

Everyone stared at him. Davies scowled like the smoke from an oil fire, disturbed for reasons he might not have been able to name. A look of nausea twisted Alba's face. Vector's sweat and pallor gave him the appearance of an invalid. Ransum drummed her fingernails on her board as if their staccato beat kept her tension in check. Karster and the scan second were plainly appalled; maybe they'd never seen anything Amnion before. Gripping the arms of his seat, Scorz muttered dumb obscenities to himself.

The scars under Nick's eyes appeared to curve like little grins. 'Too bad,' he replied. 'We don't have any extra seats.'

The human half of the emissary's face twitched at this announcement; the Amnion side didn't. With exactly the same inflection, he repeated, 'I wish to sit.'

Nick leaned forward as if his hostility made him eager. 'Are you deaf? Is that why they gave you this job? Because you can't hear? That'll make you a tough sonofabitch to negotiate with. I said we don't have any extra seats.'

The creature turned his head. He seemed to take note of Liete's gun as well as Mikka's. His discrepant eyes followed the curve of the bridge around in a circle. If he had any particular interest in Davies, or Morn, he didn't show it.

As if he were unalterable – as if the Amnion had made him incapable of change – he said, 'I wish to sit.'

'In that case,' Nick snapped, letting his anger show, 'you might as well leave. If you're going to waste our time demanding courtesies we haven't got, we don't have anything to talk about.'

The emissary's nod suggested complete incomprehension. Again he said, 'I wish to sit.'

A glare of bloody mirth filled Nick's eyes. 'All right, Mikka. Shoot off its legs. Then it can sit on the fucking deck.'

Mikka raised her pistol and took aim.

The Amnioni must have understood what he was hearing. He turned to regard Mikka. His human eye blinked rapidly, signaling agitation; his inhuman eye stared blankly. Then he returned his gaze to Nick.

'I wish to sit.'

Nick confronted the emissary as if he were perfectly willing to have the Amnioni dismembered. But the creature didn't flinch or betray any other reaction – except by the semaphore of his human eye – and after a moment Nick flung up his hands. 'Shit Almighty!' he groaned. 'If this is the way you do business, we're all going to die of boredom before we get anywhere.

'Sit *there*.' He stabbed a gesture at the helm Station. 'Ransum, out. Deactivate your board and let our guest fucking *sit*.'

Ransum jumped up; her fingers skittered across her console. As soon as all the indicators were dead, she backed out of the emissary's way.

Expressionlessly the creature moved to the helm station and sat down. As if he were composing himself, he folded his mismatched hands together on the console.

'For your purposes,' he said like oxide being rubbed off old iron, 'my name is Marc Vestabule. As you can see, I'm something of an experiment. I was once – one of you. The Amnion wished to see if we could alter my genetic identity without changing my form. The attempt was imperfectly successful.

'However, my original identity gives me certain advantages in dealing with humans. I can' – he paused – 'understand them.

'A few concepts fade, and at intervals I lose blocks of language. It appears that certain forms of knowledge and perception are genetically rather than neurologically encrypted. I mention this to account for myself in case my responses occasionally lack precision. Nevertheless I am normally proof against the denotative confusion which hampers our efforts to interpret human speech and thought. Therefore I have been invested with decisiveness. I am empowered to make commitments in this situation.

'What are your requirements?'

In his own way, Nick had been 'invested with decisiveness.' Unwilling to appear hesitant, he said promptly, 'As it happens, I've got several. Here's the first one.

'I want an explanation.'

The emissary blinked and stared. 'It is likely that I am able to understand you. However, it is clearly preferable that you do not rely on my ability to guess your meaning. Please be specific.'

'I want to know why this so-called "human offspring" is suddenly so important. You weren't interested in him earlier. Now you act like he's something special. I want to know why.'

Vestabule remained momentarily silent, perhaps to suggest that he was considering the question. Then he replied, 'Surely this is of no concern to you. For your purposes, our reasons can have no relevance. Your interest here has to do with the scale of our motivation, not its content. You want to know how much we are willing to pay.'

'Not necessarily,' Nick retorted. 'I'm not sure I care how much you're willing to pay. This deal is your idea, not mine. I've already got what I came for. And that includes the "human offspring." But I don't like surprises. I don't like mysteries. I want to know why you're here. What makes this particular human valuable to you?'

'Very well,' the emissary conceded. Nick's insistence didn't cause him any discernible discomfort. 'I will tell you that he represents an anomaly. He does not conform to established reality.

'Of course, the source of the anomaly is the human female.'

When she heard that, a fire as consuming as an ore-laser seared through Morn. The source— The Amnion knew her secret. The doctor had discovered it while she was helpless in the crèche.

'The source does not interest us, however,' Vestabule continued. 'We are interested in the ontology of the anomaly – its development and consequences.'

'Why not?' demanded Nick. 'That sounds backward. Why aren't you interested in the source?'

The answer was simple. 'Because we understand it.'

'Be specific.'

No, Morn pleaded, don't say it, *don't say it*.

'We know why her condition does not conform to established reality. In your terms, we know why she did not go crazy when her mind was copied.'

Nick pursued his question unrelentingly. 'Why?'

The emissary may have shrugged. If he did, his shipsuit disguised the movement. 'Her mind was protected.'

'How?'

As if he were announcing Morn's doom, Vestabule replied, 'If her defenses were organic, they would interest us. But they are not. Her brain contains a radio electrode. Its emissions served to inhibit the particular neurochemical transmitters which relay fear.' Doom and rust. 'Crudely put, she was unable to experience her own terror. We have some knowledge of these devices, but we were unfamiliar with this application.

'Surely you were aware of this. We speculate that your reason for coming here was to test her immunity. Otherwise you would not have risked her among us – unless you have some overriding purpose which concerns the human offspring.'

Nick was already out of his seat, surging at Morn. Even her artificial reflexes weren't quick enough to dodge him – or to prevent Davies from trying to save her.

Jumping in front of her, Davies lashed a fist at Nick's head.

Nick slipped the blow aside and charged past Davies as if he meant nothing.

At almost the same instant, Liete came up behind Davies, clubbed him to the floor with her handgun.

Nick plowed into Morn; he drove her back against the bulkhead. In a howl of rage and loss, he cried, 'A zone-implant! You've got a fucking *zone-implant*! It was all a *lie, all* of it!'

Davies struggled to reach his feet, but his limbs were jelly; he collapsed to the floor again. Making sure of him, Liete knelt on his spine and pressed her gun against the base of his skull.

Energy and panic flamed in Morn; she burned to use it, ached to hit Nick in the face until his features were pulp and his own blood blinded him. But she forced herself to stand still. Her intentions were too extreme for simple violence. While he cocked his fist to hammer her head at the wall, she braced herself to duck; but she didn't struggle.

'*Nick!*' Mikka's yell cracked through the air. Her pistol jabbed between Morn's face and Nick's: its muzzle jammed into his scars. '*Not now! Not here!*'

Nick recoiled as if the command second had set a stun-prod to his heart.

In an instant he regained his self-control. Slowly he raised one hand until his index finger pointed between Morn's eyes.

'Kiss him good-bye. This is going to cost you everything. Starting with your son.'

His look was a blaze of murder, as bright and fatal as the scalpel Angus had once forced her to hold against her breast; deep blood made his scars seem new, as if she'd just caused them.

Lithe and feral, he returned to the command Station and took his seat. Facing the emissary, he growled, 'So you aren't interested in the source. That's good, because you can't have her. What do you want to do with her brat?'

Vestabule appeared baffled, as if he didn't know the word 'brat.' Then his gaze clarified, and he answered, 'Analyze him.

'We wish to determine what effect her immunity has on him, on the integrity of his knowledge, his memories, his reason. If humans – if I could have been spared my fear of the Amnion, my own mutation might have been more successful.'

Nick jerked a nod as if he understood – or didn't care.

Davies made small whimpering noises, but Liete didn't let him up.

Without inflection, the Amnioni asked again, 'What are your requirements?'

Nick was in control of his movements, but his emotions were another matter. Ire crawled across his features. 'What do you think?'

The emissary waited as if he considered the question rhetorical. Nick didn't answer it, however; so Vestabule said, 'A scan probe was sent to the point at which your ship emerged from the gap. Analysis of your particle trail suggests that you have suffered what might be called a tachyon accident. Certain emissions far surpass established norms. We speculate that your gap drive has failed. We speculate that you cannot depart Amnion space.'

'And since we're stuck here,' Nick snarled, 'no doubt you want to make us feel welcome. In fact, you probably want to make us all think we belong here.'

Vestabule's human eye blinked like the shutter of a signaling lamp.

With an effort, Nick smoothed out his expression until only a taut grin remained. Almost casually, he asked, 'Vector, what're our requirements?'

The engineer had said that he wasn't good enough. In addition, his manner earlier had suggested that he was distressed by the idea of trading Davies to the Amnion. Nevertheless he was one of Nick's people: he didn't let his doubts show in front of Marc Vestabule. Crisply he announced, 'We need a hysteresis transducer and a modulation control for our gap field generator.' Then his tone sharpened. 'And we need customized adapters to interface human and Amnion equipment.'

The emissary nodded. He'd come prepared for this deal. 'It is acceptable. Conformity of purpose will be achieved through the mutual satisfaction of requirements.'

Nick didn't echo the ritual. Instead he demanded, 'When?'

Again Vestabule may have shrugged. 'The equipment itself can be delivered immediately. And suitable adapters are nearly ready. We have an interest in the ability to conform human and Amnion technologies. Efforts have already been made in design and preparation. If your engineer will provide mounting, contact, and load specifications, the growing of the adapters will be completed promptly.'

Keeping his face from Morn so that she couldn't see his expression, Nick accepted the offer. 'All right,' he muttered. 'Conformity of purpose will be achieved through the mutual satisfaction of requirements.'

From the deck, Davies tried to snarl a curse. But Liete's gun seemed to nail him down; he was helpless to move or protest.

More distinctly, Nick went on, 'My engineer will transmit the specs in ten minutes. When the equipment and adapters are ready, the exchange will take place in our airlock. One Amnioni will bring what we need to the lock. The human offspring will be waiting there with one guard. We'll trade. Then we're going to seal the ship. As soon as our repairs are done, we'll leave. Is that clear? No delays, no obstacles. You'll assign us a departure trajectory, and we'll get the hell out of here.'

'It is acceptable,' repeated Vestabule.

'Then what're you waiting for?' Nick snapped harshly. 'Go away. Just looking at you makes me feel like I've got hives.'

Without hesitation or haste, the emissary pushed himself out of the helm seat.

'Morn,' Davies groaned. He may have been asking her for help. Or he may have been lost in her memories, trying through the pain in his head and the pressure on his spine to figure out who he really was.

Closing her heart, Morn turned to Mikka.

The command second had resumed her post beside the aperture. Before anyone could interfere, Morn approached her. In a voice loud enough to carry, she told Mikka, 'I'm going to my cabin. I presume you're going to lock me in. You can do that from here.'

Mikka's eyes were dark, almost bruised, but they didn't waver.

More softly, Morn continued, 'Let me know when the trade happens. Please. I can't save him – and I know Nick isn't going to let me talk to him. But even if he can't hear me, I want to be able to say good-bye at the right time. I need that.'

Mikka held Morn's gaze; the corner of her upper lip twitched toward a sneer or a snarl. After a moment she nodded stiffly.

Several strides ahead of the Amnion emissary and the command second, Morn left the bridge.

Nick knew about her zone-implant. Her son had been traded away.

There was nothing left to restrain her.

CHAPTER 15

Hurrying, she chose a route to her cabin that took her past one of *Captain's Fancy*'s tool lockers.

As she opened the locker, she began to tremble. If someone caught her doing this, she was finished. But she couldn't afford to hesitate: she had too little time. Despite the risk, she helped herself to a circuit probe, a coil of fine wire, a simple screwdriver, and a wiring laser; she hid them in her pockets. Then she moved on toward her cabin, nearly running.

She wasn't worried about what Nick might do to her in the next few hours. He was being challenged on too many sides at once. He had the Amnion to deal with, and the danger that his ship might never get out of forbidden space. In addition he had to consider the reactions of his people to the fact that he was willing to sell human beings. When he traded Davies away, he gave the entire crew reason to distrust him. If he didn't do something to restore confidence in himself – and do it soon – *Captain's Fancy* might be crippled by doubt.

At the same time, he'd just received his first true glimpse of the masque Morn had played against him. Now he had to recognize that everything he'd felt for her and every decision he'd made regarding her was founded on a lie.

Under the circumstances, he would leave her alone until after *Captain's Fancy* escaped Enablement; until he was far enough from the Station to feel safe. And that time might be days away; it might never come. She would face it when or if it happened.

No, her main worry where he was concerned had to do with her black box. Had he realized yet that her zone-implant was meaningless unless she also had a zone-implant control? Was he too busy to bother taking it away from her?

As long as he let her keep it, she retained her advantage.

When she reached her cabin and keyed the panel, the door swept open.

She felt certain Nick wouldn't neglect to lock her in as soon as the computer told him she'd entered her cabin. Nevertheless she went in and let the door close.

At once a small amber light on the interior panel indicated that she was a prisoner.

Now she didn't need to hurry. The Amnion could deliver the equipment immediately, but not the adapters. And even in his worst fury, Nick wouldn't hand over Davies until the Amnion fulfilled their part of the bargain. She might have an hour – or she might have five. Plenty of time.

She hurried anyway. Desperation and the effects of her zone-implant made her manic.

With the screwdriver, she pried open the door's control panel.

She was as careful as her internal frenzy permitted. Any mistake would alert the computer; would alert Nick. But she'd gone beyond restraint, and the electrical pressure in her brain left no room for uncertainty. Driven by cold, visceral horror and absolute rage, she felt immune to error.

With the probe, she tested the circuits until she understood them. Then she positioned pieces of wire – as crooked and yet legible as handwriting – to bypass both the locking mechanism and its sensor, so that the computer would always report that the door was shut and locked. When she'd welded her wires into the circuits, she burned out the bypassed controls.

Now the door couldn't be opened or closed electronically; but she could shove it aside with the friction of her palms.

She was ready.

The time had come for her to wait.

That should have been impossible. Her son was being traded to the Amnion. They would run tests on him until his psyche tore and his spirit snapped. Then they would make him one of them. They might very well turn him into an improved version of Marc Vestabule. Waiting should have been inconceivable.

It wasn't. Her zone-implant made her capable of anything.

On some level, she knew that its emissions were as addictive as any drug, and as destructive. But that didn't matter: they were also effective. With them, she could have put herself to sleep. Or she could have tuned her body to the pitch of orgasm until her brain went into noradrenaline overload, and everything she would ever think or feel boiled away.

However, she had a more complex form of suicide in mind.

After a few adjustments to her black box, she sank into a trance of concentration in which her mind was charged simultaneously with vitality and peace: a trance that allowed her to remember everything she'd ever learned about *Captain's Fancy* – every code, every command sequence, every logic tree – as well as every precaution Nick had taken for Enablement Station.

Instead of going hysterical with apprehension and helplessness, she spent her time preparing to fight the entire ship.

Try to stop me now. Just try.

There was nothing left to restrain her. At last she could be utterly what Angus Thermopyle had made her.

The zone-implant left no room for doubt. In her concentrated trance, she saw only one thing which might go wrong.

What if Mikka didn't tell her when the trade took place?

Then she and Davies were both lost. He would be abandoned to the Amnion, and she would be at Nick's mercy until she died.

The fear that Mikka might fail or betray her should have been enough to tip her over the edge.

But it wasn't. Dread was human: hysteria and revulsion belonged to flesh and blood. She'd left such emotions behind.

The only one she retained was her long, unappeased rage.

And Mikka didn't let her down. Nearly two and a half hours after Morn had entered her cabin, the intercom chimed.

'Morn?' the command second asked softly, as if she were whispering. 'Morn?'

Nearly two and a half hours. Was that enough time for the Amnion to run their tests on Nick's blood? Morn didn't know. How they cultured and examined their specimens was a mystery to her.

'Morn?' Mikka repeated. The intercom's tiny speaker conveyed only a hint of anguish. 'He's gone.'

Nearly two and a half hours. That may or may not have been all the time the Amnion needed, but it was enough for Morn. Keying herself out of her trance, she brought up energy and strength that made her feel like a charged matter cannon.

'We've got the equipment and adapters,' Mikka continued uncertainly. 'Vector was impressed. He says they look perfect. He's already in the drive space. He says if they're as perfect as they look he can have us ready for thrust in half an hour' – *Captain's Fancy* couldn't use either of her drives while he was inside the engines – 'and tach in an hour.'

She may have been trying to comfort Morn. You didn't lose your son for nothing. At least now we'll have a chance.

Morn didn't answer. She owed Mikka that: as long as she didn't answer, Mikka was protected. No one could prove that the command second had spoken to her.

Bracing her hands on the door, she pressed it aside and stepped past it. Then she closed it to disguise her absence.

If someone saw her now, she would have to silence whoever it was. She was ready for that. But the passage was empty. By this time, Liete's watch should have relieved Mikka's; Nick's should be on emergency Stations around the ship. However, Morn was artificially sure those things hadn't happened. Nick's best people would be with him on the bridge. And while *Captain's Fancy* was docked no one was needed on emergency Stations. The rest of the crew would be in the galley or the mess, listening to the intercom for anything Nick let them hear.

If they weren't, they were dead.

Or she was.

Morn went down to the auxiliary bridge.

Liete Corregio was there.

In a sense, it was fortuitous that Morn's certainty had only misled her to that extent.

And Liete was alone; she sat in the command seat with her back to the doorway; she'd activated her board so that she could keep track of what was happening to the ship: more good fortune.

But she still wore her handgun.

Morn would have to deal with the command third somehow.

She didn't hesitate. Her zone-implant inspired her. Deep within herself, she'd reached a place of madness and focus where there was no doubt.

Silent as oil, she eased across the deck and punched Liete once, hard, behind the right ear.

Liete snapped forward; her forehead cracked against the console. When she slumped to the side, she left a smear of blood on the board.

Quickly Morn checked her pulse, her eyes: she didn't want to kill the command third. But Liete was barely unconscious. Good. Hurrying because she couldn't predict what the Amnion would do to Davies, or when, Morn took Liete's handgun. Then she unsealed the command third's shipsuit, pulled her arms out of the sleeves, and resealed the suit with her arms pinned inside. Not as good as a straitjacket, but good enough so that Liete couldn't do anything sudden to surprise Morn.

Morn dragged Liete to the wall near the door, propped her there. She closed the door and locked it. After that she seated herself at the command Station and repositioned it to face the door – a precaution in case Nick tried to force his way in while she worked.

A small groan trailed between Liete's lips. Blood from her forehead dripped past her nose and around her mouth.

Morn ignored her.

Now.

She felt that she'd arrived at a moment of apotheosis. She'd been alone on the auxiliary bridge of *Starmaster* when she'd killed her father, killed most of her family.

Now.

Self-destruct.

Perhaps this was what gap-sickness felt like. Perhaps circumstances and her black box had re-created that particular abrogation of sanity.

No matter. This time she was going to save somebody who depended on her. If it could be done, she was going to save her son.

Clear and confident, she set her fingers to the keys of the auxiliary command board.

First she opened her intercom so that she would hear anything Nick chose to share with the rest of the ship. Then she went to work.

Her instructions to the command computer had to be both subtle and compulsory, so that they wouldn't attract attention while they took precedence over other operations. She needed to dummy Vector's jury-rigged destruct sequence to her board: that required her to tap into targ, engineering, and maintenance, as well as into Nick's console. Then she had to issue codes which would deactivate those functions from the bridge, reroute them to her. Along the way, she also needed to commandeer control over the auxiliary bridge doors and life-support – not to mention the airlock which connected *Captain's Fancy* to Enablement Station. In addition, she required communications: she would be useless if she couldn't talk. And she had to achieve all this in a way that couldn't be countermanded.

The destruct sequence was easy: it wasn't integral to the ship's systems, had no built-in overrides. Nick had obviously intended to dismantle it as soon as he escaped Enablement. Besides, she'd helped Vector design it; she remembered it exactly. But the rest demanded an almost eidetic recall of everything she'd learned from the ordeal of her attempt to cure Vorbuld's virus.

The state which her zone-implant imposed on her mind gave her the necessary recall.

The most crucial thing, the real trick, was to disable Nick's priority codes. This was *his* ship, programmed to let him supersede all other instructions no matter who issued them. As matters stood, he could shut her down the instant he realized what she was doing.

And yet she'd already conceived a simple solution to the problem – a solution so simple that he might never figure it out.

She wrote an intervening batch command to his board, a command which his priority codes would activate before they took effect; a command which altered his codes by transposing a few digits so that none of the computers would recognize them.

He would be unable to countermand her until he erased the batch command. And that wouldn't happen until he realized what she'd done.

Now. When she keyed in his priority codes herself, all the control she needed would switch to her board. It would belong to her until she gave it up.

Liete groaned again, twitched, opened her eyes. Like the trickle of blood from her forehead, she breathed, 'What the hell are you doing?'

As if he were answering, Nick's voice came over the intercom. 'Liete, check on Vector. He can't hear me in there. I want a status report. Find out when we can get out of here.'

'Nick,' Liete moaned, so weakly that he couldn't hear her, 'Morn's here. She's taken over the auxiliary bridge.'

It didn't matter if Nick heard Liete. Morn was ready.

No, she wasn't. There was one more precaution—

Nick waited for Liete's answer. The intercom stayed open: it picked up Lind's voice in the background.

'Nick, something's happening to my board.'

Morn was out of time. Precautions would have to wait.

With a few keys, a few codes, she risked everything.

Indicators articulated her board: instructions and confirmations sped across her readouts. A subliminal shift in the ambient power-hum of the auxiliary bridge seemed to promise that the systems she needed belonged to her now.

She had communications.

She had life-support.

She had doors and airlocks.

She had self-destruct.

She could make herself feel like singing; but that wasn't necessary.

'Liete!' Nick demanded. 'What the fuck are you doing down there?'

Morn silenced the intercom. 'Shut up and sit still,' she told Liete. 'I've got your gun.' She raised the impact pistol. 'I don't want to kill you, but I won't let you interfere.'

Liete licked her lips and tried to swallow, but her mouth was too dry. After a moment she nodded.

Now.

Morn snapped the intercom back on.

'Nick, this is Morn. I'm on the auxiliary bridge.'

'*Morn, you*—' he began.

She cut him off. 'I've got the self-destruct. It's primed and ready. And I've canceled your priority codes. You can't override me.

'If you leave me alone, there's a chance we may all survive. I'm even going to protect your credibility with the Amnion. But you sold my son, and I won't stand for that. If you get in my way, this ship and most of Enablement will end up as atomic powder.'

Her zone-implant enabled her to concentrate on as many different things as necessary. While she talked, she wrote in her last precaution – another batch command.

This one would work off her board. When it was ready, she could press down on the toggle which displayed the ship's chronometer on her readouts, and if anything happened to her – if anything made her take her finger off the toggle – the self-destruct would be engaged. *Captain's Fancy* would blow in milliseconds.

'Cut her off!' Nick shouted to somebody else. 'Cut power to the auxiliary bridge! Override her – get your boards back!' He hit his keys so hard that the sound carried over the intercom, punctuating his rage.

Nothing wavered on her board. Her control held.

'Nick,' she asked conversationally from the depths of her own fury, 'don't you want to know what I'm going to do?'

'Mikka, get down there!' he yelled. 'Cut through the door – cut her to pieces, if you have to!' But a second later he changed his mind. 'No, I'll do it. You take the bridge. *I want my ship back*! I'm going to tear her fucking guts out with my *hands*!'

'Mikka,' said Morn, grinning back at Liete's horrified stare, 'he isn't listening. Maybe you will. I've got the self-destruct on a batch command.' This was now true. 'It's set to the chronometer toggle. My finger is on the toggle.' Her finger pressed the key firmly to the surface of the board. 'If I'm attacked, or threatened – or even surprised – and my finger comes off the toggle, the ship will blow.

'You can't stop it. There aren't any overrides. And I really have canceled his priority codes.' One lie more or less made no difference to her. Let everyone wonder whether her programming skills were that good. 'You'd better make him understand that. He sounds like he's gone off the deep end.'

'Morn!' The command second's shout cracked over the intercom. 'What in God's name are you trying to do?'

Save us all. Believe it or not. Even sweet, desirable presumed human Captain Nick fucking Succorso.

'Just listen,' she replied. 'You can't cut off my communications output, but you can hear it. In about a minute, you'll understand everything.'

Including why you need to keep Nick from messing with me.

She left the intercom open. Part of her brain continued to process the gabble of voices from the bridge – Malda Verone's distress and Carmel's anger, Sib Mackern's inchoate protests, Lind's near hysteria. From the engineer's Station, Pup kept whimpering, 'Get out of there, Vector, please, get out of there,' as if proximity to the thrusters were Shaheed's only peril. But none of that deflected Morn.

How long would it take Nick to grab a cutting laser and a gun, and reach the auxiliary bridge?

That didn't deflect her, either.

With a few quick taps on the command console—

pressing the chronometer toggle flat to the board

— she opened communications with the Amnion.

'Enablement Station, this is Morn Hyland. I'm the human female who gave birth to the offspring you just took from *Captain's Fancy*. I want my son back.'

There was no answer.

It was possible that Enablement couldn't hear her – that she'd committed an error of some kind, or that the Station had simply cut reception. She didn't believe either of those things; she didn't worry about them. Extremity and artificial strength made her certain.

'Enablement Station, I've taken control of this ship. I've rigged a self-destruct – it ties both drives and all our fuel into the weapons systems. You know enough about us to guess how much damage that can do. An explosion like that will probably take out twenty-five to forty percent of the Station.

'I'm going to blow us all up unless I get my son back.'

Still no answer.

Morn chuckled as if she were delirious. 'Enablement Station, if you don't reply, I'm going to assume your answer is negative – and then I won't have anything left to live for. Captain Succorso will kill me, if you don't. You have five seconds. Starting' – she kept time with the toe of one boot – 'now.

'Five.

'Four.

'Three.'

'Enablement Station to presumed human Captain Nick Succorso,' said the mechanical voice of Amnion authority. 'What occurs aboard your ship? Answer immediately. There is falseness here. Do you seek to annul the mutual satisfaction of requirements?'

Oh, there's falseness here, all right. Humans are like that. You can't begin to guess just how much falseness there is.

'Enablement,' Mikka snapped rapidly, 'this is command second Mikka

Vasaczk. Captain Succorso is unavailable. He's trying to find a way to stop this Morn Hyland.

'What she says is true. She's sabotaged bridge function – she has control from the auxiliary bridge. Our instruments indicate she's created a self-destruct.' Apparently Mikka also was willing to lie. 'She's turned the whole ship into a bomb, and she's got her finger on the detonator.

'We urgently request you reply to her. Don't give her an excuse to blow us up. She's that offspring's mother. Losing him has driven her insane. She's going to kill us all if you don't at least talk to her.'

Well, good for you, Mikka, Morn thought. Nick may have gone into meltdown, but you're still using your head.

'Morn.' Over the intercom, Vector sounded tense, almost frightened. 'Christ on a crutch, woman! What do you think you're *doing*?'

Good. Vector was safe. He couldn't have heard what was going on unless he'd finished hooking up the Amnion replacements and come out of the engine space to begin testing them.

'Vector,' she answered, 'we're hanging by a thread here. Maybe we'll make it, maybe we won't. At the moment I'm not sure I care which. But I think you'd better get that gap drive functional as quick as you can. If the thread holds, we'll need to get out of here *fast*.' Just to make everybody nervous, she asked, 'How good are you at going into tach cold?'

If he replied, she didn't hear it. Instead she heard hammering on the door of the auxiliary bridge—

—and Nick's voice over the intercom, shouting, 'Goddamn you, Morn! This is my ship! *My ship*!'

—and an Amnioni saying, 'Enablement Station to Morn Hyland. What is the purpose of this threat? The Amnion emissary Marc Vestabule reports that trade for the new human offspring was negotiated directly with presumed human Captain Nick Succorso. His requirements have been satisfied. It has been stated repeatedly that the ship *Captain's Fancy* may depart Enablement Station freely. This is – translation suggests the word "honorable" trade. Why do you seek to dishonor your dealings with the Amnion?'

'Listen to me!' Morn spat back at Enablement. Sudden fury fired through her, and she flung every gram of it into the communications pickup. 'I'm only going to say this once.

'Captain Succorso may have traded directly with *you*, but he didn't do the same with *me*! That "offspring" is *my son*. Do you hear me? *My son*. Captain Succorso didn't have the right to give him away, and *I* refuse to give him up!'

As she watched, a hot, red spot like a flower bloomed near the lock of the door. Almost at once, a trickle of slag started down the surface. A smell of ozone charged the air.

Liete Corregio began struggling inside her shipsuit, writhing to get her arms free.

'Maybe I'm insane,' Morn raged at the Station. 'Maybe that "force-growing" process just cost me reason, not function.' That idea might give her threat credibility. 'I don't know, and I don't care. *I want my son back*! I want him back *now*. If I don't get him, I'm going to blow myself up, and this ship, and as much of your goddamn Station as I can take with me, because I just don't *give a shit*!'

With her free fist, she pounded off the communications pickup. Into the intercom, she shouted, 'Mikka! Stop Nick! Do you hear me? Stop him!'

When the command second replied, she sounded worn out and beaten. 'Have you ever actually *tried* that? I'm not sure it can be done.'

'Enablement Station to Morn Hyland. Your behavior is a violation of trade. For this, you have earned the unending enmity of the Amnion. As soon as you depart Enablement Station, the defensives *Tranquil Hegemony* and *Calm Horizons* will hunt you until you have been destroyed.'

Furiously Morn punched the pickup back on. '"Unending," my ass,' she snarled. 'It's going to end in about five minutes if you don't give me my son back.'

At the same time Mikka protested from the bridge, 'Enablement Station, that's not fair! *We* didn't do this! She's threatening all of us, not just you. You can't punish us for what she does. If you start doing business like that, no human is ever going to trade with the Amnion again.'

The command second was still thinking, still fighting for *Captain's Fancy*'s survival – and, incidentally, for Davies'.

The Amnion authorities ignored her. 'Enablement Station to Morn Hyland,' said the flat, alien voice. 'Proof of your self-destruct is required.'

Morn was ready for that, too. 'Here it comes,' she rasped; ozone filled her throat. 'Don't miss it.'

Stabbing a few keys, she dumped a literal copy of every instruction and sequence in the auxiliary command board along Enablement's transmission line. Everything. Including Nick's priority codes. She was in no mood to be selective. Even with that information, the Amnion wouldn't be able to stop her: they had no link to *Captain's Fancy*'s internal systems.

Liete forced the seal of her shipsuit apart a few centimeters. Jamming her fingers into the gap, she began tearing the suit open.

Morn dropped her free hand to the impact pistol.

Abruptly the lock failed. A beam of red, coherent light flicked, then vanished. The door swept out of Nick's way.

He blazed into the room like a solar flare. The cutting laser was his only weapon – the only weapon he needed. His scars were dark acid eating at his face; his eyes were black holes. He came one step past the doorway, two. As steady as steel, he aimed the laser at Morn's chest and switched it on.

He missed because Liete threw herself across the barrel of the laser.

Red ruin hit the screen beyond Morn's shoulder. The display melted blank before the beam was cut off.

With her weight on the laser and Nick's arm, Liete pulled him to the floor. He tried to drive her aside with the butt, but she squirmed out of the way, twisted herself on top of him.

'Nick, listen to me!' she shouted into his face. Small drops of her blood splashed onto his features. 'I'll tackle her myself, if you tell me to! I'll walk over there and jump at her. But hear me first. Listen!

'She's keyed self-destruct to the chronometer toggle – and she's got her finger on the toggle!'

When her warning reached him, Nick froze.

'If you touch her,' Liete continued, 'if anybody touches her, she'll lift her finger. She doesn't have to be alive to do it. And we can't stop her. She won't let us get that close.'

'Besides,' Morn commented in a tone of murderous satisfaction, 'I've got a gun.' She held up the impact pistol. 'I'm not going to miss. Not at this range. Not when I've got a chance to kill the man who sold my son.'

'*Then kill me!*'

Nick swung the laser across his body, hammering Liete off him. Gasping as if he'd broken her ribs, she rolled away.

'*Kill me now!*'

He surged to his feet. Facing straight down the muzzle of Morn's gun, he pointed the laser between her eyes.

'*I'm not going to let you have my ship!*'

But he didn't fire.

She didn't, either.

She would have loved killing him. She relished the bare idea of tightening her finger on the trigger. She wanted to see his face crumple and spatter from an impact-blast – wanted it so intensely that the desire made her giddy.

Nevertheless she restrained herself.

'You bastard,' she sighed as if she no longer cared what he did. With a negligent flick, she tossed her gun at his feet. 'Stop thinking with your gonads and use your brain. We're all going to live or die in the next few minutes, and the only thing you can do about it is make us die faster.' She nodded at her finger on the toggle. 'But if you'll leave me alone, I might just get us out of here in one piece. If Vector does his job right.'

Awkward with pain, Liete climbed to her feet. New blood seeped from a gash on her cheek, joining the ooze from her forehead. Her eyes were glazed, barely conscious. She was able to stand, however.

Nick's gaze widened as Morn discarded her gun; but his grip on the laser didn't waver. Almost without transition, however, his scars had gone as pale as his face. He looked like all the blood was draining out of his heart.

Through his teeth, he breathed, 'You're bluffing.'

'That's what Enablement thinks,' she retorted. 'That's why we might end up dead. But you don't have to believe it. Talk to Mikka. She's still got most of her command functions. She can look at what I've done. She just can't change it without your priority codes – and I've made them useless.'

Nick's cheeks and forehead had turned ashen, the color of old bone. His eyes grew bleak, haunted by memories of despair and contempt. 'Morn,' he said to her softly, 'I don't lose. I don't *lose*. If you beat me here, I swear to you I'll make you and fucking Thermo-pile's son pay so much for it that you'll wish you'd sold *yourselves* to the Amnion.'

She wanted to spit at him. She wanted to sneer, Don't underestimate yourself – I've been in hell and agony ever since you first touched me. Yet she resisted those desires, just as she'd refrained from shooting him.

Instead she made a sacrifice which seemed more expensive, and infinitely harder, than killing herself. She offered him a way out of his dilemma; a way to salvage his ego.

She said, 'I'm not trying to beat you. I'm trying to beat the Amnion.'

He muttered, 'The shit you are.' But his scorn-ridden gaze betrayed an appeal, as if despite his outrage he were begging her to make what she said true.

'Enablement Station to Morn Hyland.'

Morn turned away from Nick. Keying communications, she answered harshly, 'I hear you.'

'False trade is unacceptable,' said the mechanical voice. 'You have been dealt with honorably. Therefore the human offspring belongs to the Amnion. This is unalterable. He must belong to the Amnion.'

She started to retort; Nick surprised her by holding up his hand, demanding silence. Still clutching his laser, he walked toward her.

She pressed the chronometer toggle hard enough to whiten her knuckles. But when he reached her Station, he dropped the laser. Instead of attacking, he leaned so close to her that she could smell the fury on his breath, as acrid as Amnion air.

'Enablement,' he rasped to the communications pickup, 'this is Captain Succorso. You'll get your damn offspring. I'll make sure of that.'

While he spoke, his gaze held Morn's, daring her to contradict him. 'You're right – you traded for him honorably. But Morn's calling the shots at the moment. She can blow us up, and there's nothing I can do about it.

'But she's only human,' he snarled. 'She's got to rest sometime. And she can't do that unless she releases self-destruct.

'I'll get my ship back,' he promised. 'And when I do, you can have the offspring.'

'Presumed human Captain Nick Succorso,' said Enablement promptly, 'you have made a commitment which you will be required to fulfill.'

As if his words had freed the Amnion from an impasse, the Station announced, 'Morn Hyland, your offspring waits outside your airlock. You will be permitted to take him aboard.'

Permitted—

Nick, you shit.

— *to take him aboard.*

Without her zone-implant, she might have sagged in relief, might have lost control of herself or the situation. Fortunately the charge in her brain held. Silencing the pickup, she told Nick, 'Go back to the bridge. Get us out of here. When I feel secure, I'll tell you how to restore your priority codes.

'Liete,' she continued as if she were still certain, 'take your gun and get Davies. Make sure he comes alone – and they haven't planted anything on him.' For instance a tracking device to help them find him again. 'Tell Nick when it's safe to go.'

Liete nodded dumbly. Half stumbling, she retrieved her impact pistol and left.

Nick had recovered his grin. Still leaning close to Morn as if he wanted to smother her, he said, 'You're finished. I hope you know that – I hope it breaks your heart. You aren't human, not with that fucking electrode in your head, and for all I know you can go for years without rest. But you're still finished. Gap-sickness will get you.

'We're going to head for human space. As soon as Vector says we're ready, we'll start accelerating. That's how much time you've got left. You mentioned going into tach cold, but you know we can't do that. Stationary objects in gap fields tend to reappear near where they started. Slow-moving objects tend not to go where they're aimed. We need a certain amount of speed – and that means hard g. Unless you want to spend weeks picking up velocity.'

And hard g triggered her gap-sickness.

'You can't get around it. You didn't go through all this just so you could blow us up an hour from now. Before we hit the gap, you'll have to give my ship back.

'Then you won't have any way to make me do it. You won't be able to prevent me if I decide to stop and give them that asshole. We're just marking time here – just going through the motions. As soon as you come up against your gap-sickness, you're *mine*.'

Morn laughed in his face.

What he said was true, of course. But she meant to overcome that obstacle as well. She was already as close to gap-sickness as she intended to get.

In the meantime, she had the satisfaction of seeing doubt run like lightning across the dark background of his gaze.

He pulled back in dismay. 'You're crazy,' he rasped; but the words carried no conviction. Once again her zone-implant made her more than he was; enabled her to outdo him.

Wheeling away to hide his chagrin, he strode off the auxiliary bridge.

Left to herself, Morn Hyland cackled like a madwoman.

She knew that in the end she couldn't win this contest. She probably wouldn't survive it. He would regain control of his ship: her gap-sickness made that inevitable. But she and her son would be safe from the Amnion. When they died, their deaths would be as brutal as Nick could make them – and they would be human.

And there was still a chance that she could change Nick's mind. His doubt was a tectonic fault running through the core of his personality. If she could find the keystone, she might be able to shift it—

For some reason, tears streamed down her cheeks as if she were weeping.

Later. She would worry about things like that later. Right now, she had other problems.

'Nick,' Liete reported over the intercom, 'he's aboard. He says they didn't have time to do anything to him. As far as I can tell, he's clean.'

'Lock him up somewhere,' Nick ordered immediately. 'I don't want him wandering around the ship.'

'Davies,' Morn inserted, nearly choking on a grief she couldn't name, 'are you all right?'

Sounding preternaturally like his father, he replied, 'If you call being this helpless "all right."'

Just for a moment, her relief was strong enough to overwhelm the zone-implant's emissions.

She considered demanding that he be allowed to join her, then dismissed the idea. She couldn't credibly insist that she was willing to blow up *Captain's Fancy* and Enablement Station simply to spare Davies incarceration.

'Take care of yourself,' she told her son, even though she wasn't sure he could still hear her.

With her free hand, she called up the self-destruct batch command to one of her readouts and began editing it.

'Enablement Station, this is command second Mikka Vasaczk. Prepare to disengage.'

First things first. Carefully she removed the sequence which keyed self-destruct from the chronometer toggle. When she'd replaced the old batch command with this new version, she was able to lift her finger.

More relief. Her imposed capability seemed to be failing. She wanted to put her head down on the console.

With an audible thunk and jolt, *Captain's Fancy* separated from dock.

At once g changed. Suddenly insecure in her seat, she paused to belt herself down. Then she went back to work.

Mikka's intercom remained open. Morn heard her ask, 'Drive status?'

'Thrust is green.' Pup's voice had a note of fright which made him sound even younger than he was. 'Vector says you can have it whenever you want. He's still working on the gap drive. The new equipment functions fine, but the control parameters need adjustment. And some of the tests don't seem to run right.'

'Take us out of here,' Mikka instructed the helm first. 'Follow their protocols exactly. They already have too many reasons not to trust us. Don't give them another one.'

'Are you getting this, Morn?' Nick put in. 'You're running out of time.'

He'd left the intercom open, hoping to torment her.

The first small touch of thrust nudged her against the side of her seat. They were leaving Enablement Station; escaping the Amnion. She and her son. No matter what Nick did to her later, she was winning now.

With an effort of will, she continued her preparations for the crisis of g.

She'd learned this trick from Angus. No, 'learned' wasn't the right word for it. She'd seen him do it; she'd experienced its results; she'd even looked at it, in the files he'd let her see. But to remember it now, remember it well enough to reproduce it after so many months, so much intervening pain—

She had to make the effort.

While her artificial clarity gradually frayed and faded, she wrote a new batch command. Not for the self-destruct this time: for her black box itself.

As Angus had once done, she created a parallel zone-implant control, using the circuits of the auxiliary communications Station. Through the command board, she switched the functions of her black box to those circuits, then shoved the box itself into her pocket for what may have been the last time. After that, she programmed the parallel control to put her to sleep the moment *Captain's Fancy* experienced g higher than 1.5 – and to wake her up again when it dropped below that.

Even 1.5 was a risk; but she had to assume that her flawed mind could stand at least a little strain. If she set her sleep threshold any lower, she would be unconscious while g was still soft enough to let Nick's people move against her.

If this worked – if she remembered it right, did it right – she could avoid her gap-sickness without being forced to relinquish the self-destruct. Nick had never been in her cabin with her during acceleration or deceleration: he didn't know how she took care of herself. Before he could risk challenging her, he would have to discover – or guess – what her defenses were. And that might take time.

It might take long enough for *Captain's Fancy* to cross the gap.

Once he reached human space, he might reconsider the commitment he'd made to the Amnion.

Morn's arrangements took a long time to set up. They were complex – and she was losing recall. Emotional exhaustion drained her despite the pressure of the electrode in her brain.

At the fringes of her awareness, she noticed the steady increase of g as *Captain's Fancy* took on thrust.

From the bridge, Carmel's report reached her: *Tranquil Hegemony* and *Calm Horizons* were following *Captain's Fancy* outward.

Abruptly Mikka entered the room. Without hesitation, she sat down at the auxiliary scan Station. Scowling impersonally, she announced, 'Nick sent me to keep an eye on you. Don't worry, I won't get in your way.'

A new threat. Mikka would see her helplessness under g. To protect herself, Morn slid her finger back onto the chronometer toggle. But her attention was contracting: her window of clarity shrank. She struggled with her preparations. If she made a mistake, g would drive her mad—

Then, over the intercom, she heard Vector say, 'I don't know about this, Nick.'

'I'm in no mood to guess,' Nick snapped back. 'Say what you mean.'

'The new equipment checks out fine, as far as I can tell,' Vector answered. 'I've got it powered up, and it looks stable. But, Nick' – the engineer faltered momentarily – 'some of the tests don't run. They come up blank. The rest are absolutely green, dead-center tolerances. But these ones— There must be fifty possible explanations. I'll need a month to try them all.'

'Chance it,' Morn croaked into the intercom.

'No!' Nick shot back, 'I won't do it. Morn, you're out of time. You can't stay awake on that toggle for another month. And I'm not going to risk tach. We need too much g – you'll blow us up. And if the drive fails, we'll fry in the gap.

'Face facts, Morn! There's no way out of this one.'

A visceral dread, cold and familiar, closed her throat. She had to force herself to reply. 'And if we run tests for a month, Enablement will have plenty of time to find out you cheated them. Then those warships are going to start shooting.'

He would listen to that: he had to.

Grimly she continued, 'I'll give you ten minutes to pick up velocity. I'm setting the timer now.' Her fingers keyed commands. 'After that, I'm finished with you. I'll self-destruct.'

'Morn!' Vector protested. 'What about your gap-sickness?'

As hard as she could, she kicked Nick in the keystone of his doubt. 'Goddamn it!' she shouted because she was terrified. 'What the hell do you think I've got a zone-implant *for*?'

Let him believe she wasn't helpless. Let him believe she didn't need unconsciousness to protect her. Please let him believe that.

She could tell by the way Nick cursed that he did.

'Secure for burn!' he yelled at his ship. He didn't want to wait ten minutes. 'You've got thirty seconds!' At once he began barking instructions for Vector and the helm first.

Thirty seconds. Time for one last bluff – one last, desperate attempt to keep herself and Davies alive. Fear mounted like a storm in her as she turned to Mikka.

'You know what's at stake for me,' she said as firmly as she could. 'You know I'm out of choices. I'm going to turn my seat so you can't see how I take care of myself.' So Mikka wouldn't see her go to sleep; wouldn't see her release the chronometer toggle. 'That's for your protection as well as mine.'

Please don't try to jump me. I beg you.

Mikka shrugged distantly. 'It's your neck. I'm not the one who has to face him when this is over.' A moment later she added, 'I'm reasonably sure you're not going to blow us up now. And I want out of Amnion space myself.'

As time ran out, Morn swung the command Station so that the back of her seat concealed her from Mikka.

Then the tactile howl of full thrust fired through *Captain's Fancy*'s hull, and Morn's mind went away.

Progress in science is often a matter of discovering what works first and discovering why it works afterward. Dr Juanita Estevez of SpaceLab Station developed a functioning gap drive five years before she had any idea what it was.

By some standards, her greatest achievement was her demonstration that it was possible to design and build a gap drive without ever having been aware that the gap existed. Her ignorance was indicated by the fact that, when she finally learned what her invention did, she referred to the effect as 'going into tach' and 'resuming tard,' as though tachyon/tardyon principles were somehow involved. Plainly they were not – and yet her terminology persisted. A century after the first gap ship returned successfully from its first mission, people still talked about 'going into tach' when the gap drive was engaged and 'resuming tard' when the gap crossing was complete.

Of course, Dr Juanita Estevez was a genius – or, as some of her colleagues insisted, 'a major loon.'

The device which eventually proved to be a gap drive prototype she built believing it to be a 'matter disassembler': objects of various kinds were placed within the field of the device; power was applied; the objects disappeared, 'disassembled' into their component particles and, presumably, dispersed into the atmosphere. Because she was a private individual with a strongly developed instinct for self-protection, Dr Estevez was in no hurry to attract attention for her work. Instead she concentrated her research in two primary areas: she attempted to measure the emission of 'disassembled' particles into the atmosphere; and she strove to discover the limits of the 'disassembling' process by experimenting with objects of various weights and structures.

The former produced no results. The latter – eventually – opened the frontiers of the galaxy.

Until coincidence intervened, however, she had no way of knowing that her test objects did indeed go somewhere, not 'disassembled' but whole; or that where the objects went involved a complex interaction between the strength of the field, the potential strength of the field, the mass of the object, and the direction and velocity in which the object was moving when the field was energized (in this case, SpaceLab Station spin provided both direction and speed). She knew only that the objects were in fact gone, and that they left no measurable emissions.

But one day she energized her field to 'disassemble' a block of solid titanium. At virtually the same instant, an explosion occurred in one of SpaceLab Station's bulkheads – fortuitously, a redundant cargo hold bulkhead intended to protect the occupied regions of the Station if, through accident or terrorism, the cargo should detonate and the hold decompress. The cause of the explosion became apparent when the block of titanium was found in the hole of the bulkhead: the block had come through the gap into a physical space already occupied by the bulkhead; and since the block was solider, harder, the bulkhead tore itself loose.

Of course, no one realized the event's significance until Dr Estevez rather sheepishly admitted that the block was hers.

From that moment, it was only a matter of time before human beings began to venture beyond their own solar system.

The initial research was, inevitably, confused and cautious. Dr Estevez was chagrined by her misunderstanding of her own experiments; and embarrassment made her even more protective and territorial than she might have been otherwise. SpaceLab Station's Administrator of Research was torn between his desire to pursue Dr Estevez's experiments and his wish to wrest control of the invention away from her. And the administrator of Facilities was opposed to the entire project on the grounds that SpaceLab's ecology was too fragile to absorb the risk that more bulkheads or perhaps even the Station's skin might be damaged.

Nevertheless Dr Estevez's research had become too dramatic to be thwarted; and eventually its potential benefits became too obvious to be denied. New versions of the 'disassembler' (now called the 'Juanita Estevez Mass Transmission Field Generator') were built; more objects were passed through the gap and relocated; vast computer analyses of the experiments and the results were run. Then predictions were made, and more tests were run to verify the predictions.

The gap drive worked before any but the most abstruse thinkers had conceived of the gap itself. Interdimensional travel became a reality as soon as the interactions of the gap field (primarily mass, velocity, and hysteresis) were adequately quantified – long before any theoretical understanding of the gap itself achieved broad acceptance within the scientific communities of Earth.

As usual, humankind took action first and considered the consequences later.

Dr Estevez should have expected – but did not – that as soon as a theory of the gap became current scientific coin, her name for her own invention would fall out of use. The JEMTFG became, first, 'the interdimensional drive,' and finally, 'the gap drive.' In a sense, she was only remembered for her mistakes: references to 'tach' and 'tard' endured; and the term 'an Estevez' referred to 'a major blunder with beneficial results.'

She died an extremely bitter, as well as an extremely wealthy, woman.

Angus Thermopyle woke up many times and remembered none of them. The nightmare he'd spent his life fleeing had hold of him. There was nothing he could do to make it let go.

He didn't wake up while he was frozen, of course. He'd been frozen for a number of reasons, and that was one of them: so that he wouldn't wake up. While he slept, he couldn't talk.

However, there were other reasons as well. Cryogenic transportation was safer than numbing him with sedatives or doping him with cat. It offered less risk of neurological damage – and Hashi Lebwohl didn't want one synapse or ganglion harmed. The UMCP Director of Data Acquisition had complex intentions for Angus, all of which depended on preserving the integrity of what Angus knew, remembered, and could do.

So he was kept frozen while Min Donner completed her business on Com-Mine Station: the meetings demanded by protocol; the elucidation of policy; the discussions concerning piracy, forbidden space, and the Preempt Act. Then he and Milos Taverner were taken back across the gap to UMCPHQ.

Soon after that, Angus began waking up – and forgetting it. Before they could do anything else, UMCPDA's surgeons had to unfreeze him. Until they did so, his body and brain were as intractable as permafrost. So he was shifted from the cold tomb of his cryogenic capsule to the warmer helplessness of cat and anesthetics and surgical restraints. On brief occasions, he was allowed to rise toward consciousness so that the surgeons could test their work. But those occasions were too brief to cling to – and the pain he felt until the drugs took him back down into the dark was too acute. In self-defense, he edited them out of his mental datacore.

As a result, he had no understanding at all of what the surgeons did to him; what form his nightmare had taken.

He wasn't aware that they peeled back his flesh like the skin of a fruit in order to install utility lasers as keen as stilettos along the bones of his forearms and hands. When the operation was done, there was a strange gap between the third and fourth fingers of each hand, a gap over which his fingers couldn't close. Connected to their power supply, those weapons would be able to cut open locks and thoraxes with equal facility.

He wasn't aware that his hips and knees and shoulders were taken apart and reinforced to double or even triple the effective strength of his muscles; or that struts to support and shield his spine were installed in his back; or that another shield was molded over his ribs; or that a thin, hard plate was set under his shoulder blades to anchor and reinforce his arms, protect his heart and lungs – and to hold the power supply and computer which would eventually become part of his identity.

He wasn't aware that his eyes were removed and fitted with prostheses which were then wired into his optic nerves, thus enabling him to see electromagnetic spectra that no organic vision could perceive – spectra relevant to such diverse applications as alarm systems and computer circuitry.

He wasn't aware that zone-implants were installed in his brain: not one electrode but several. When they were activated, they would control him with a subtlety that made the things he'd done to Morn Hyland look like hatchet-work.

And he certainly wasn't aware that weeks went by while all these operations were performed. In fact, only advanced surgical procedures and potent curative drugs enabled the doctors to do such things to him in weeks instead of months or years. Making cyborgs wasn't easy; and the difficulties were increased in his case because his designers had to assume that he would be unalterably opposed to his own technological enhancement.

Not because he had moral or visceral objections: nothing in the UMCP files suggested that Angus Thermopyle would reject being made a cyborg for its own sake. No, he would fight forever against his own enhancement because he would never be allowed to command it. The same technology which made him superior to his former self would also rule him; deprive him of volition completely. When the surgeons were done, Angus would be nothing more than a tool, a biological extension of the UMCP's will.

With luck, he would be the perfect tool. He would retain his mind, memory, and appearance – retain everything which made him dangerous to the UMC and human space. He could go everywhere he used to go, do everything he used to do. But now his every action would serve his new masters.

In their own way, the surgeons worked to transform him as profoundly as an Amnion mutagen.

If all the operations were successful.

That was the crucial question. Neural probes and metabolic modeling could only provide so much information. They couldn't prove whether or not the surgeons' efforts succeeded. And the computer which would control him could only be calibrated in reference to his specific electro-chemical 'signature,' his unique endocrine/neurotransmitter balances.

Eventually the doctors needed him awake.

So they began withdrawing their drugs from his veins; began sending delicate stimulations into his brain. By careful degrees, they urged him out of the sleep which gave him his only protection against horror and pain.

When he regained enough consciousness to thrash against his restraints and scream, they began teaching him who he was.

You have been changed.

You are Joshua.

That is your name.

It is also your access code.

All the answers you will ever need are available to you. Your name gives you access to them. Find the new place in your mind, the place that feels like a window, the place that feels like a gap between who you are and what you remember. Go to that place and say your name. Joshua. Say it to yourself. Joshua. The window will open. The gap will open. All the answers you need will come to you.

Joshua.

Say it.

Joshua.

Angus screamed once more. If weeks of surgery hadn't left him so weak, he might have been able to burst his restraints. But he couldn't, so he curled into a fetal ball and did his best to turn himself into a null-wave transmitter. The link between his brain and his temporary computer remained inactive. If he thought anything, if he ever let himself think again, he would remember his nightmare – remember that they'd dismantled his ship; remember the large, sterile room full of equipment for cryogenic encapsulation; *remember the crib* – and then the abyss from which he'd fled all his life would open under his feet.

Nevertheless he was already cooperating with his doctors. Every internally generated whimper and twitch provided them with exactly the data they required – the neural feedback which allowed them to verify their assumptions and calibrate their instruments.

When they were satisfied with what they'd gained this time, they let him sleep again.

The next time, they pushed him harder toward consciousness.

You have been changed.

You are Joshua.

That is your name.

It is also your access code.

All the answers you will ever need are available to you. All you have to do is say your name. Think it to yourself. Accept it.

Joshua.

Say it.

Joshua.

No.

Say it.

I won't.

Say it!

With a savage twist, Angus pulled his right arm out of its restraints. Punching wildly, he knocked away one of the doctors, smashed a monitor, ripped down all his IVs. He might have succeeded at injuring himself if someone hadn't hit the buttons on his zone-implant control, switched him off.

The link between his brain and the computer remained inactive.

Goddamn it, a doctor muttered. How can he fight? He isn't awake enough. He ought to be as suggestible as a kid.

But Angus didn't need to be awake to fear his nightmare. In the end, all the various and violent fears of his life were one fear, one great rift of terror which reached from his perceptual surface to his metaphysical core. He'd never hesitated to fight anything, destroy anything, which threatened to open that abyss—

sprawled in his crib

— anything except Morn Hyland. But that was because, by the insidious logic of rape and abuse, she'd come to belong to him, in the same way that *Bright Beauty* belonged to him. Like *Bright Beauty*, she'd become necessary, even though that necessity made her infinitely more threatening—

with his scrawny wrists and ankles tied to the slats

— but they'd dismantled his ship. With Morn it was different. They'd taken her away. Now, like his horror, she was somewhere where he couldn't control her, she might be anywhere—

while his mother filled him with pain

— she was everywhere, hunting him with his doom in her hands, stalking him to open under his feet—

jamming hard things up his anus, down his throat, prying open his penis with needles

— so that he would begin the long plunge into terror and never be able to climb out again, never be able to escape the complete, helpless agony which lurked for him at the center of his being—

and laughing

and afterward she used to comfort him as if it were him she loved, and not the sight of his red and swollen anguish or the strangled sound of his cries.

Because he had nowhere else to go, Angus Thermopyle fled into himself to escape himself.

The doctors didn't let him get away, however. With sleep, they confused his escape; and as soon as he lost his way, they prodded him toward consciousness again, using new drugs, new stimulations.

You have been changed, they said.

You are Joshua.

That is your name.

It is also your access code.

All the answers you will ever need are available to you. All you have to do is say your name.

This time, his fear of what he remembered, or might remember, was greater than his fear of their coercion. In the end, every fear was the same; but until that end was reached, he could still make choices. And the right choice might postpone the abyss.

'My name,' he croaked, retching against the dry disuse of his vocal cords, 'is Angus.'

At the same time, another name formed in his mind, as clear as a key. *Joshua.*

A choice. To preserve the possibility that he might someday be able to make other choices.

The link was activated.

'That's it,' said a distant voice. 'He's welded. Now we can start to work.'

'Work,' in this case, meant intensive physical therapy and long hours of tests, as well as more interrogation. And Angus had no choice about any of it.

His zone-implants gave the doctors complete mastery over his body. They could twitch any of his muscles at will; they could make him run or fight or accept abuse or lift weights; they could certainly require him to endure their tests. This appalled and enraged him, of course. Nevertheless, when he understood how totally they could control him, he started obeying their instructions before they could resort to compulsion. For him, the distress of coercion was worse than the humiliation of compliance. Obedience only made him wail with rage, with desire for revenge: helplessness restored his nightmare.

His doctors had no idea that he was wailing. On their readouts, they could see the intensity of his neural activity, but they couldn't interpret it. So they amended the programming of his computer to watch for that activity as a danger sign. If his electrochemical spikes and oscillations became too intense along certain parameters, the computer would use his zone-implants to damp them. As long as he remained cooperative, however, they left the inside of his head alone.

Interrogation was another matter.

It bore no resemblance to the treatment he'd received from Milos Taverner and Com-Mine Security. This questioning was entirely internal. In fact, while his computer ran its inquiries, no human ques-

415

tioner needed to be present. The computer simply elicited answers and recorded them.

It did this by the plain yet sophisticated application of pain and pleasure. While the interrogation programs ran, the gap in his head seemed to open, and a set of restrictions and possibilities entered his mind. He thought of them as a rat-runner's maze, although the walls and alleys weren't physical, or even visual. If he violated the restrictions, his pain centers received stimulation: if he satisfied the possibilities, he was flooded with pleasure.

Naturally the restrictions had to do not with the content of his answers but with their physiological honesty. If he could have lied without betraying any symptoms of dishonesty, his answers would have been accepted. But his computer and zone-implants scrutinized his symptoms profoundly. They could measure every hormonal fluctuation; they could distinguish between noradrenaline and catecholamine in the function of his synapses. In practice, lies were always detected.

Angus struggled against his interrogation for what felt like a long time – a day or two, possibly three. The computer couldn't control his mind as it did his body; it could only exert pressure, not coercion. And he'd always been able to resist pressure. Milos Taverner certainly hadn't broken him. Grinding his teeth, swearing pitilessly, and sweating like a pig, Angus tried to endure the interrogations as if they were psychotic episodes brought on by too much combined stim and cat; as if their horrors were familiar and therefore bearable.

Unfortunately his flesh betrayed him.

In contrast to his physical therapy sessions, which induced a mental surrender, his interrogations brought on a bodily yielding. His brain was a physical organ: it hated the pain and loved the pleasure on an organic level, entirely independent of his volition. His autonomic being responded only to sensation. Instinctively it rebelled against being subjected to so much pain when so much pleasure was available.

Using zone-implants and the computer-link, his interrogators broke Angus Thermopyle. They made it look easy.

The only thing he was able to do in his own defense was to break selectively – to answer questions in ways that allowed him to skip some of the facts.

What happened to *Starmaster*?

Self-destruct.

Who did it?

Morn Hyland.

Why?

Gap-sickness. Heavy g makes her crazy.

So you were lying when you accused Com-Mine of sabotage?

Yes.

Why?

I wanted to keep her with me.

Why was *Starmaster* under heavy g?

Chasing me.

Why?

Because I ran. I knew they were cops. As soon as I saw them, I ran. They came after me.

That was true. Like *Bright Beauty*'s datacore, it contained only a few elisions. He was a known illegal: his impulse to run from cops didn't require explanation.

How did you know they were cops?

Field mining probe. I looked at their hull. Nobody but the cops could afford a hull like that.

Then how did you end up with Morn Hyland?

I needed supplies. My air-scrubbers were shot. Water was bad. When *Starmaster* blew, I went back for salvage. Found her alive.

She was a cop. Why did you keep her alive?

I needed crew.

How did you make her work for you?

How did you make her stay with you?

Why did you want to keep her with you?

Angus didn't fear that question. He wasn't worried about being executed for his crimes; not anymore. After all the expense and trouble of making him a cyborg, the cops weren't likely to kill him. They wanted to use him: from their point of view, his crimes made him valuable. The information he needed to protect, the question he needed to avoid, was a different one.

I gave her a zone-implant. That was the only way I could trust her as crew. And it was the only way I could make her let me fuck her.

He reported this with so much satisfaction that none of his doctors ever doubted him.

What did you do with the control?

Got rid of it. So Com-Mine wouldn't execute me. They didn't find it. I don't know where it is now.

His body reported the accuracy of this statement to the computer. No one doubted him.

Perhaps it was his satisfaction more than his elisions that misled the people who designed and studied his interrogations. He was questioned long and often. His crimes were probed and analyzed. His treatment of Morn was studied. He was required to account for her escape with Nick Succorso. His suspicions of Milos Taverner were recorded. Everything he said was factual – physiologically honest.

And yet he contrived to protect himself. Time and again, he led the interrogation programs away from the questions he feared. As a result, he never said – was never required to say – anything which didn't conform to the evidence which *Bright Beauty*'s datacore had supplied against him.

No one learned from him that *Bright Beauty*'s datacore had been edited; that he was capable of editing his ship's datacore.

Conceivably none of the people involved in designing and training and interrogating him ever understood how dangerous he was. Their equipment had him under control; that control couldn't be broken; therefore he was safe.

Because he was safe, the traffic through his quarters increased as more and more people came to take a look at him: technicians in related fields, motivated by professional curiosity; doctors and other experts who wanted to observe him for themselves; random personnel interested in nothing more than a glance at Hashi Lebwohl's pet illegal. To all appearances, Angus ignored them. The old malice of his gaze was turned inward. As much as possible, he dismissed everything that wasn't an instruction or a question with coercion or pressure behind it.

Nevertheless he noticed immediately when Hashi Lebwohl himself, DA Director, UMCP, began visiting him.

Of course, he'd never seen Lebwohl before. And the rumors he'd heard didn't discuss Lebwohl's appearance; they didn't go beyond the insistence that the DA Director was crazy – and lethal. Yet he found this visitor instantly recognizable.

In contrast to the clean doctors and immaculate technicians, Lebwohl wore a disreputable lab coat and mismatched clothes over his scrawny frame like a signature. His old-fashioned shoes refused to stay tied. Glasses with scratched and smeared lenses sagged down his thin nose; above them, his eyes were the theoretical blue of unpolluted skies. His eyebrows twisted in all directions as if they were charged with static. And yet, despite his air of having wandered in from a classroom where he hectored Earth's slum kids, everyone else deferred to him. When people passed by him, they gave him a wide berth, as if the charge in him were strong enough to repel them.

Angus knew intuitively that this man was responsible for what had been done to him – and for worse to come.

Hashi Lebwohl visited several times without speaking to him. He conversed with the doctors and techs in an asthmatic wheeze, sometimes asking questions, sometimes making suggestions, which revealed his intimacy with their work. But he didn't say a word to Angus until the evening after the physical therapists had declared him fit for whatever UMCPDA had in mind.

The time was Station night. Angus knew that because his computer had begun to answer simple, functional questions when it wasn't otherwise occupied; also because the techs had just told him to take off his daysuit, put on lab pajamas, and get into bed. Two of them were still in the room, apparently running a last check on his equipment before putting him to sleep. When Hashi Lebwohl entered, however, one of the techs immediately handed him the remote which served as a zone-implant control. Then both men left.

At the same time the status lights on all the monitors winked off.

Hashi peered at Angus over his glasses. Smiling benignly, he tapped buttons on the remote with his long fingers.

Involuntarily Angus got off the bed and stood in front of Lebwohl with his arms extended on either side as if he were being crucified.

Lebwohl tapped more buttons: Angus urinated into his pajamas.

As warm salt spread down Angus' legs, Hashi sighed happily.

'Ah, Joshua,' he wheezed, 'I think I am in love.'

Angus wanted to take off his pajamas and ram them down the DA

Director's throat. However, he wasn't given that option. He was simply required to stand still with his arms outstretched, hoping that his reinforced body could bear the strain.

Someone knocked on the door. Without glancing away from Angus' legs, Lebwohl said, 'Come.'

Two more people came in, closing the door behind them.

Angus had no difficulty identifying Min Donner: the Enforcement Division Director hadn't changed since he'd last seen her. The lines of her face and the fire in her eyes were as strict as ever. Even here, she wore a handgun: without it, she might have considered herself naked.

But he'd never seen the man with her before. Donner's companion had a flourish of white hair atop his leonine head, and a smile which Angus instinctively loathed – the smile of a pederast who found himself in charge of a boys' reform school. Fleshy and sure of himself, he joined Donner and Lebwohl as if he were the first among equals.

A name patch over his left breast indicated that he was Godsen Frik, Director of Protocol, UMCP.

Sweet shit! Protocol, Data Acquisition, Enforcement Division. Who was left? Was every important fucker in the entire UMCP going to come watch Angus piss on himself?

After a glance at Angus, Frik commented, 'You've been playing, Hashi.' His voice was a confident rumble. 'He isn't a toy, you know.'

'Is he not?' Lebwohl took Frik's remark as a form of flattery. 'If you are wrong, then he exists to be played with. If, on the other hand, you are right, then I am bound by duty to ensure that you and the estimable Donner are safe in his presence. How better to verify his tractability than to – *play* with him?'

'And you're sure he *is* safe?' asked Frik.

'My dear Godsen,' wheezed Lebwohl, showing the remote, 'he will stand that way until he dies, unless I instruct otherwise.'

Min Donner made no effort to conceal her distaste. A sneer twisted her mouth as if Angus weren't the only man in the room who smelled bad. Impatiently she said, 'Your report claims he's ready.'

'Physically ready,' amended the DA Director equably. 'His interface with the computer is well developed, but must be refined. And his programming has not yet been written to his datacore. When those things are ready, he will be also.'

'He will be tested, of course, but no difficulty will be encountered. I state that categorically. *We* have been ready to do such work for some time.'

'Good,' rumbled Godsen.

But Hashi wasn't done. 'Are you?' he asked the PR Director.

'Are I what?' Frik countered humorously.

'Are you ready for that unfortunate but inevitable day when what we do here becomes known?'

'Hell, Hashi,' Godsen chuckled, 'I've been ready forever. This ain't recombinant DNA. We all hate the Amnion with a pure and simple passion, but nobody gets the collywobbles when they think about technological enhancement. Human beings are used to it – we've been doing things like this ever since crutches and splints. And he's *illegal*. The slime of the universe. Hell, just the smell of him would take the starch out of a virgin. I'm prepared to argue' – his voice took on an orotund cadence – 'that the technological reclamation of men like Angus Thermopyle is the best alternative imaginable. He has spent his life opposing the UMC and all it stands for. That he should now be used to help preserve humankind from the gravest threat it has ever known is only just.' He chuckled again. 'Or words to that effect.'

Hashi wheezed a hum of approval. 'My dear Godsen, I have always said that you are good at your job.'

'When?' the ED Director demanded. Apparently she had no tolerance for the game Lebwohl and Frik were playing. 'When is he going to be ready?'

'What's your hurry?' asked Godsen promptly. 'We've been waiting a long time for this. We can wait a little longer.'

'As I recall,' she retorted with plain bitterness, 'you said the same thing about Intertech's immunity drug – and we're still waiting.' Her rebuff appeared to silence Frik, so she turned to Hashi. 'This little meeting was your idea. If you aren't going to tell us he's ready, why are we here?'

Lebwohl offered a small shrug. 'I wish to explain how he works, so that you can provide your own input for his final programming. Any requirements or restrictions which occur to you, any difficulties that you foresee – these can still be taken into account.'

'And you couldn't do this through normal channels?'

'My dear Min, I can hardly wish *everyone* in UMCPHQ to understand the details of our work.'

'On the contrary,' Min snapped, 'I think you *do* wish everyone to understand. You didn't call us here to tell us how he works. You just want to show him off.'

'So what?' put in Godsen. 'It's reassuring. Nobody's going to trust the "slime of the universe" unless *we* say he's safe – and you, for one, won't be able to say that unless you believe it. This is our chance to *see* how safe he is.'

However, the DA Director took Min Donner's attitude more seriously. Angus stood there crucified as Hashi murmured, 'My, my, you *are* in a hurry.'

'You bet your ass I am.' Except for the sneer around her nose, her features remained blank, controlled. Yet her whole face seemed to take fire from her eyes. 'Have you *read* his interrogations?'

'Oh, please,' Godsen responded as if he didn't want to be left out. 'We've all read them. Eventually we're going to go blind reading them.'

Min ignored Frik. 'Do you,' she continued, '*understand* what he's done to her?'

'Her?' Lebwohl's blue eyes shone with knowledge, but he waited for Min to continue.

'He gave her a zone-implant so he could rape and use her. And that's *after* she came down with gap-sickness and destroyed her own ship, killed her whole family. He *broke* her. None of us could stand up under that kind of abuse. Nobody could.

'And then he gave her the zone-implant control.'

Locked in his own mind, Angus snarled obscenities that his computer couldn't hear. Morn was like *Bright Beauty*: he'd used and tormented her horribly; but he'd also been faithful to her. The failure of his promise to her raised his rage to a new level.

'Wait a minute,' Godsen objected. 'How do you know that?'

'He broke her,' Donner burned into Hashi's gaze, 'and he gave her a case of zone-implant addiction, which is another kind of rape entirely, and then he handed her the control.'

The PR Director raised his voice. 'I said, how do you know that?'

'But she doesn't have it now,' Min went on as if Protocol didn't exist; as if only ED and DA mattered. 'She probably kept it just long enough to complete her addiction. Craziness and zone-implant addiction – those kinds of problems *show*. Succorso must have noticed them almost immediately. And when he did, he took the control away from her.

'*Now* what kind of trouble is she in? She's got gap-sickness, she's been broken, she's a raving addict, and she's *owned* by a man who's only slightly more charming than Thermopyle here.' She slapped the back of her hand in Angus' direction. 'I want her back, Hashi. She's one of my people, and I want her *back*.'

'Listen to me!' Godsen roared like a klaxon. 'How do you know he gave her the control?'

Together Hashi and Min turned on Frik. 'Because, my dear Godsen,' Hashi said placidly, 'Com-Mine Security did not find it.'

Gritting her teeth, Donner explained, 'If they did, they would have executed him before we could stop them. Taverner wouldn't have been able to stop them. They hate him too much.'

'But that's terrible!' Godsen protested.

'So I've been saying,' drawled Min sardonically.

'If word gets out, if people hear about this –' Frik sounded genuinely distressed. 'One of our people, with gap-sickness and a zone-implant, wandering around loose – under the control of a known pirate. People are going to ask why we let that happen. We've got to get her back.'

'I agree,' Donner rasped. 'We've got to get her back.' She turned on Lebwohl again. 'That's why I'm in a hurry. I don't like any of this – and I'm liking it less by the minute.' The passion in her voice blazed higher as she spoke. 'I want him *ready* and on his way. He's my only chance to rescue her. If she isn't past hope already.'

This time Hashi looked a little nonplussed. 'My dear Min,' he said as if he were breathing sand, 'I am not certain that his programming can accommodate your wishes.'

She poised herself as if she were about to draw her gun. 'What do you mean?'

'Forgive me. I spoke imprecisely. I mean, I am not certain that his programming will be allowed to accommodate your wishes.'

'That's outrageous,' snorted Godsen. 'Of course he's got to rescue her. You aren't listening. I tell you, we've got a disaster on our hands. The only way we can salvage the situation is by rescuing her.'

'I understand your concern,' Hashi replied placatingly. 'However, you must realize that our position is not so simple. I mean, the position of those of us in this room. Let me explain with a question. When our Joshua was arrested by Com-Mine Security, your Morn Hyland fled with Captain Succorso. Why did we permit that to occur?'

'We weren't there,' Frik said. 'We couldn't stop it.'

But Min had a different answer. 'Orders,' she snapped.

'Naturally,' said Lebwohl. 'Of course. But that is not an answer. Why were those orders given? What reasoning lies behind them?'

The ED Director grew more bitter by the moment. 'I don't know. He's keeping it to himself.'

Hashi agreed with a nod. 'So we must speculate.

'Consider the hypothesis that Morn Hyland was a condition for Captain Succorso's cooperation. He wanted her, and we want him. Therefore we had no choice but to let him have her.

'This is plausible, but unsatisfactory.

'It is certain that Com-Mine Station could not be allowed to keep her. If they did, they would inevitably have learned the truth – that our Joshua was innocent of the charge against him. Indeed, that the charge was invented by Captain Succorso and our valued ally, Deputy Chief of Security Milos Taverner. Then we would have been exposed. The Preempt Act would have failed, and our Director of Protocol would have been faced with a disaster of' – his eyes gleamed – 'astronomical proportions.

'However, to relieve the dilemma by allowing Captain Succorso to take her is altogether questionable. Personally I would have preferred to terminate her. She is a random element – and Captain Succorso himself is a rogue. Together they will cause more difficulties than they resolve.

'I cannot persuade myself that we have placed ourselves in this position merely to satisfy Captain Succorso's wishes.'

'In other words,' Donner said angrily, 'you think there's something else going on here. You think Joshua won't be programmed to rescue her for the same reason we let her get away with Succorso – and we won't be told what that reason is.'

'In essence,' Hashi said, 'yes.'

Angus' arms had begun to burn with strain, but he didn't have the choice of letting them drop.

'We'll see about that,' Godsen proclaimed. 'Protocol isn't going to take this lying down. Sure, I'm all in favor of Joshua here. I hope he nukes Thanatos Minor to slag. And Captain Succorso with it. You're right – Succorso's a rogue. Having an agent like him isn't worth the risk.

'Some risks I'm willing to take. You know that. Using illegals like Succorso and traitors like Taverner to help us pass the Preempt Act and give us Joshua – that was worth the danger. In fact, it was my idea. If word got out, we were all cooked. But I don't think we could have passed the Act any other way.

'This is another matter. We have nothing to gain by taking the chance that Succorso and Hyland might go critical on us. We should have blasted them to powder as soon as they left Com-Mine. But we didn't, so now we've got to accept the consequences.

'I'm going to fight this one.' He faced Donner as if he expected applause – or at least gratitude. 'You can count on my support. If we don't at least try to rescue your Morn Hyland, we're too vulnerable.'

Min wasn't grateful. She snorted, 'What makes you think he'll listen?'

He? Angus thought. He? Were they talking about Warden Dios? The UMCP Director?

Who else could give these three people orders?

Did the most powerful man in human space force them to let Morn go with Succorso?

Godsen Frik's voice had a petulant, almost defensive tone as he retorted, 'I can go over his head.'

Both Hashi Lebwohl and Min Donner looked away from the PR Director as if they were shocked or shamed. Studying the floor, Min said softly, 'The way you did about the immunity drug.'

Dangerous red flushed across Godsen's face; but he didn't respond.

Still addressing the floor, Donner muttered, 'I don't like playing this dirty.'

Now Frik spoke back. 'Oh, don't go all virtuous on us. You've got as much blood on your conscience as anyone else. Probably more. Why else do they call you his executioner?

'You brought Joshua here, didn't you?'

'I obey orders,' she replied as if to herself. 'I trust him. I have to. But we're supposed to be cops. What good are we if we aren't honest?'

Hashi shrugged delicately. 'What is honest? We define a goal. Then we devise a means to achieve it. Is this not honest?'

Some of the blood on Min's conscience showed in her eyes as she glared at Lebwohl. 'I'm getting nauseous,' she growled. 'You said you're going to tell us how he works. Do that, so I can leave.'

A smile quirked the corners of Hashi's mouth. 'I will.

'But I must warn you,' he said to both his fellow Directors. 'If you disapprove of the possibility that our Joshua will not be programmed to rescue Morn Hyland, you will certainly not be comforted by what I tell you now.'

'What's that supposed to mean?' demanded Godsen.

'I will spare you the technical details,' Lebwohl replied. 'A general outline is sufficient.

'When Joshua's programming has been designed, and all its priorities and variables have been approved, it will be written to the datacore of his computer. In effect, it will become an integral part of him. The interface between his mind and his computer will allow him to act on the basis of his experience and knowledge – as long as he attempts nothing which in any way violates his programming. He will have the moral equivalent of two minds. One, ours, will impose our instructions on him. The other, his, will act on those instructions.

'Within its limits, the system is reliable. Because of the control supplied by his zone-implants, he will be entirely unable to perform any action which does not conform to his programming.

'Unfortunately the system *is* limited. Simply put, the difficulty is that we can never envision every situation or exigency which Joshua will confront. And if his circumstances become such that they are not adequately covered by his programming, he will be able to take independent action – action which might conceivably damage us or our interests. This you already know.'

'Of course we know it,' Frik rumbled. 'We aren't stupid.'

Hashi's blue gaze appeared to reserve judgment on that point, but his tone conveyed no insult. 'The solution we have devised is that Joshua will not work alone. He will be accompanied by a "partner." This partner will appear to be his subordinate, but will have the capacity to amend his programming as needed. Joshua's computer will recognize his partner's voice, and when his partner speaks the proper codes his new instructions will be written directly to his datacore.

'Naturally, if we see reason to adjust Joshua's programming ourselves, we need only contact his partner. Changes can be made in a few moments.'

Both Min and Godsen waited as Hashi studied them. After a moment, the DA Director said, 'Joshua's partner has already been selected and is now being trained. As you may imagine, he cannot be controlled as Joshua himself is controlled. If he were, his own programming limitations might well hamper Joshua's effectiveness. But we have selected a man whom we consider peculiarly well suited for the task. And I can assure you that his training has been intensive.'

Donner gritted her teeth and went on waiting.

Angus didn't have the capacity to clench his jaws; nevertheless he, too, waited.

'Don't drag it out, Hashi,' said Godsen. 'Who is he?'

Hashi Lebwohl beamed.

'Why, none other than our trusted ally and colleague, Milos Taverner.'

Somewhere in the back of Angus' mind, a small hope flickered to life.

'*Taverner*?' Frik spat. 'Are you out of your mind? You're going to trust this entire operation to a man like *Taverner*? He has the scruples of a trash recycler. He's already sold out Com-Mine Security. All we had to do was *pay* him enough. He's probably selling *us*, too. If he isn't, he'll do it as soon as he's offered enough credit.'

'I think not.' Lebwohl was unruffled. 'We have several safeguards.

'First, of course, a datacore is unalterable. Our Milos cannot effectively issue instructions which run directly counter to Joshua's programming. And every instruction he gives – indeed, every word he utters in Joshua's presence – will be permanently recorded. Our Milos will be unable to conceal what he has done.

'In addition, his unreliability is known. We have all the evidence we require. If our Milos seeks to betray us, he will be destroyed. We have left him no doubt of this.'

Hashi smiled benevolently, then continued.

'In any case, whatever your objections, you must consider the question of credibility. Joshua's partner must appear to be Angus Thermopyle's subordinate. The Captain Thermopyle who is known upon Thanatos Minor would never serve under another – and would never accept as a subordinate any man who was not demonstrably illegal. His programming will allow him to expose his partner's treacheries, to explain – and thereby protect – him. That will leave Milos helpless to do anything other than serve us.'

Frik wasn't satisfied, but Min didn't give him another chance to protest.

'No, Hashi.' She sounded almost calm. 'It's untenable. You can't do it. I wondered why we took Taverner away from Com-Mine, but I assumed it was to cover all of us if he got caught. I never thought you wanted him for something like this.'

'He's an impossible choice. You can't give a known traitor control over a weapon like Thermopyle. One of *my* people is at stake here. I'm going to fight you on this.'

And delay the operation? Angus argued in his paralyzed silence. No, don't do it, you don't want that.

Hashi faced Donner squarely. 'It has been decided,' he asserted. 'The Director approved the order weeks ago.' He paused, then added happily, 'I am proud to say that the suggestion was mine. I consider our Milos the perfect choice.'

Min bunched her fists, raised them in front of her. But she didn't have anyone to strike. Through her teeth, she snarled, 'Lebwohl, you're a shit.'

Hashi's eyes narrowed. In a prim wheeze, he retorted, 'It will not surprise you, I think, to hear that I hold you in similar esteem.'

'Come on, Min.' An apoplectic flush covered Godsen's face. 'I'm going to talk to the Director. I want you with me.'

Min flashed a scathing glare at him, turned away roughly, and strode out of the room.

'And when the Director refuses to alter his decision,' Lebwohl said to Godsen, 'you will again attempt to "go over his head." This time, you will not succeed. The game is deeper than you understand, and you will drown in it.'

Sputtering, the PR Director hurried after Min.

When Donner and Frik were gone, Hashi spent some time playing with Angus before putting him back to bed. But Angus did his best to ignore the humiliation. He had no choice, of course – but now he suffered the way his arms and penis burned with less rage and old terror. He had been given something to hope for, something which helped him dissociate himself from his nightmare.

He concentrated on that because he was physically powerless to castrate the DA Director.

CHAPTER 16

When *Captain's Fancy* hit the gap, she began to come apart.

According to her chronometers, the emergency was brief, so brief that its extremity became almost incomprehensible. As soon as she gained the velocity he wanted, Nick engaged her gap drive, and she went into tach. And as soon as she went into tach, dimensional physics started undoing her atom by atom, pulling her to nothingness like smoke in a slow wind.

For a few seconds she drifted along the rim of nonexistence.

The gap field generator had failed at exactly the wrong instant.

The crisis was too quick for logic. Only imagination and intuition were fast enough to save Nick's people.

Specifically Vector Shaheed saved them: not because he was a wizard at his job, but because he panicked. Inspired by imagination or intuition, he panicked in the right way.

He was already afraid. The new Amnion equipment had passed most of his tests perfectly – and had come up blank on others. Those few tests had simply refused to run. And that scared him.

Alone in the drive space, with *Captain's Fancy*'s survival riding on him – with Morn Hyland's finger pressed to the ship's self-destruct, and equipment he couldn't trust in his gap field generator – calm, phlegmatic Vector Shaheed lost his nerve.

When Nick ordered tach, Vector's hands leaped like intuitions at his control board. Milliseconds after the gap field was engaged, he hit his overrides, trying to cancel the ship's translation from Amnion to human space.

In theory, that was the wrong thing to do. It had never been done before: no one who survived the gap had ever tried it. *Captain's Fancy* should have winked away; should have become a phantom, a ghost ship sailing unchartable dimensional seas.

However, in this case the theory itself was wrong. The gap field generated by the Amnion equipment was anomalous: open-ended in a way no sane gap field was ever intended to be. Instead of hastening *Captain's Fancy's* extinction, Vector's overrides snatched her back into normal space.

They also burned out all the control circuits and several components of the drive. *Captain's Fancy* resumed tard with her gap drive slagged.

She came out of the gap like a blast from a matter cannon; hit normal space with a dopplering howl, as if all the stars around her wailed. Instantly scan and navigation went crazy. Her velocity was so great, so far beyond anything her thrusters could have produced, that her computers weren't programmed for it. Time-dilation effects distorted everything; sensors broke into electronic gibberish. The computers took long minutes to recalibrate themselves – to deduce the ship's condition and begin compensating for it.

When at last they were able to make sense of the new data, they reported that *Captain's Fancy* was traveling at .9C: roughly 270,000 kilometers per second.

That should have been impossible. No human ship was built to attain such speed. On the other hand, there was no g involved, no stress. Internally the ship might as well have been drifting. The dilemma was all external; and for the present it involved no immediate hazards. The computers were simply ill prepared to interpret the information *Captain's Fancy's* probes and sensors received from the starfield and the deep dark.

Nearly an hour passed before astrogation could tell Nick where he was.

Morn Hyland had a similar problem. Long before she actually recovered consciousness, she had a nagging sense that something was amiss. Something physical: her body was in the wrong place, or the wrong posture. Anxious as delirium, her dreams made her thrash from side to side, whimper in her sleep, strain to reach controls which weren't there.

Self-destruct. If something had gone wrong, she needed to push the button. Her threats were wasted unless she could carry them out, no one would ever believe her again, the little power she'd gathered for herself would fray through her fingers like smoke.

If she pushed the button, Davies would die. Her son would die. While he was still half insane with dislocated identity and flawed memories. He would never have a chance to become himself; the part of her she considered worth redeeming.

That was better than letting Nick give him to the Amnion.

She stabbed at the self-destruct until her whole hand hurt, and the strain made her arm quiver; but nothing happened.

The button was gone.

The auxiliary command console was gone.

Her hands were empty. Powerless and doomed. Oh, God.

Forcing her eyes open, she saw the familiar walls of her cabin.

She lay on her berth with her hands clenched over her sternum. They fought each other as if her right struggled to prevent her left from ruin.

Nick knew about her zone-implant.

He'd promised Davies to the Amnion.

All her power was gone.

'Are you awake?' a voice asked. She should have been able to recognize it. 'I've been worried about you. Mikka must have hit you pretty hard. I would have taken you to sickbay, in case you've got a concussion, but Nick said no. Can you hear me? If you can, try to say something.'

If she couldn't recognize his voice, she should have at least been able to look at him and see who he was. But when she made the attempt, pain like impact rifle fire punched the back of her head, and the cabin dissolved in a blur of tears.

Mikka must have hit her hard, all right. In the end, the command second had declared her loyalties. But how could she have done it? *Captain's Fancy* must have been under heavy g: otherwise Morn wouldn't have been asleep. Then how had Mikka been able to leave her seat?

There must have been a delay of some kind. Morn must have been too profoundly exhausted to wake up quickly when thrust cut out and her zone-implant released her. And during that delay, Mikka had come up behind her—

'Come on, Morn,' the voice said. 'Try. You need to wake up. Don't make me shake you. I might damage you – and you're hurt enough already.'

As if she'd known who he was all along, she identified the speaker. Vector Shaheed.

Try. All right. She could do that. It was necessary.

Swallowing pain and tears, she struggled to ask, 'Where—'

'You're in your cabin,' he answered. 'We're all alive – at least for the time being. I'll probably never understand how, but we survived.'

Despite a blinding series of detonations from her occipital lobe, she shook her head. That wasn't what she needed to know.

'Where—'

Had they escaped forbidden space? Were they safe from the Amnion?

'Where is your son?' Vector inquired. 'Is that what you're asking? Nick has him locked up. The last I heard, he's all right. He looks as murderous as his father, but nobody's done anything to him. Nobody's had time.'

Morn knotted her fists to keep herself from moaning. Past the detonations, she croaked, 'Where are we?'

'Ah, shit,' sighed Vector. 'I was afraid that's what you wanted to know.

'Oh, well. You've got a right to an answer.

'We didn't make it, I'm sorry to say. The new components failed. We came out of the gap so fast that we exceeded our operational parameters. For a while we couldn't get astrogation working. The computers couldn't make sense out of the scan data. But I just talked to the bridge a little while ago. Nick—'

He faltered, then said, 'Nick wanted me to report on your condition. When I called the bridge, he told me they've finally been able to fix our position.

'We're still in Amnion space. That's the bad news. The good news is that we've covered most of the distance to Thanatos Minor. In fact, we're so close that we'll have to start decelerating in a day or two. Somehow we managed to turn a disaster into a blink crossing.

'But I guess that isn't good news from your point of view.'

Morn shook her head again. Now she was crying because she needed to. Still in Amnion space. Still in reach of Amnion warships. Nick had made a deal for her son. The warships would demand that he keep his end of the bargain.

Her only hope had been that the Amnion wouldn't follow if *Captain's Fancy* crossed far enough into human space.

Like her power, her hope was gone.

'If I were you,' Vector said softly, 'I wouldn't give up.'

That surprised her. She hadn't expected him – or any of Nick's people – to know or care how many hopes she lost. In fact, she didn't understand why he was here at all: keeping her company, answering her questions; comforting her.

In a small voice, like a damaged child, she asked, 'What do you mean?'

What can I do to save him? What's left?

The engineer shrugged distantly. 'Nick is – well, in the absence of full psychoanalysis, let's just say he's relatively heartless. Under normal circumstances, trading away your son wouldn't cause him any sleepless nights. But under *any* circumstances, trading away your son and getting cheated would make him livid. And the Amnion cheated us. That's pretty obvious.'

Cheated? Obvious?

Morn stared at Vector and waited for him to go on.

'Nick probably hates you right to the bone. If he weren't so busy, he'd be hunting for ways to hurt you. Your son is his best chance. But no matter how much he hates you, he isn't going to keep his end of that bargain when he knows he's been cheated.'

Still Morn waited.

'Actually,' Vector mused as if he were digressing, 'he should have seen this coming. I guess he hates you too much to think straight. Nobody who was thinking straight would have talked the way he did in front of that "emissary." He made it too obvious that he wanted to get rid of your son. So why didn't Vestabule try to dicker? Why did he accept Nick's terms?

'I think it's because they don't really want your son. He was just an excuse for another deal. What they really wanted was to give us those gap components.

'Those components weren't flawed. They weren't imperfectly compatible. They were *designed* to fail when we went into tach. The Amnion sold them to us to get rid of us – to *erase* us.'

Ignoring the twisting of her vision and the pain as keen as splinters of bone inside her skull, Morn propped herself on her elbow in an effort to face Vector more directly.

'Are you telling me you think they believe we're already dead, so they won't come after us?'

Vector nodded.

The idea was too seductive to accept. 'But why?' she demanded. 'Why did they try to kill us?'

'Presumably because they know Nick cheated *them*.'

'But he didn't, did he?' she protested. 'Not really. I mean, he offered them a chance to test his blood when he knew the results would be useless, but he never promised they would be anything else. He can always claim he kept his end of the bargain exactly.'

'That's their dilemma,' Vector agreed. 'He kept the bargain and cheated them at the same time. They don't want to get a reputation for acting in bad faith themselves, and yet they don't want to let him get away with cheating them.

'And *how* he cheated has got to be of overwhelming importance to them. How can he be immune to their mutagens? If they can't answer that question, all their dealings with human space are suspect.

'What they wanted most, probably, was to capture us, so they could learn the truth – and get a fresh supply of human beings at the same time. But they couldn't do that. They could never be sure we didn't have a gap courier drone ready to take word of what happened to us back to human space.

'So erasing us in the gap was by far their safest choice. That way, no one would ever know we were killed or cheated. And the secret of Nick's immunity might die with us.

'By the time they learn we're still alive, we should be safe on Thanatos Minor – if you call that safe. It's public, at any rate. We'll have illegals from all over the galaxy as witnesses. The Amnion won't be able to attack or even capture us without ruining their own reputation.'

Morn didn't want to trust Vector. She didn't want to leave herself that open, that vulnerable. But she couldn't quench the flicker of hope which he fanned to life. If the Amnion were not an immediate problem, then she only had Nick to deal with—

Oh, please. Let it be true. Let it be true.

She had never feared Nick as much as she feared the Amnion.

She still couldn't see the engineer accurately. Tears kept smearing her vision. But now they weren't simply tears of pain and despair.

'Vector, why?' Her voice was thick with frailty. 'Why are you doing this? I threatened your life. For a while, I was willing to kill you all. Why are you doing this for me?'

She should have been listening more closely to the undercurrents in his voice. She should have found some way to blink her sight clear so that she could read his expression. Then she might have been prepared for his answer.

When he replied, he sounded bleak and arthritic; speaking damaged him like heavy g. 'I'm keeping you sane. So he can hurt you more.'

Vector.

Stiffly he climbed to his feet. 'I've fixed your door,' he said in the same tone. 'You won't be able to rig it again.

'I'll go tell him you're awake.'

The door hissed open for him, swept shut. The status lights on the control panel told her it was locked.

By the time it opened again, and Nick Succorso stalked into her cabin, her vision had improved. The back of her head still felt like the site of a thermonuclear accident, but her tears had stopped, and she was able to concentrate. Her vulnerability had gone to ice; at the core, she'd become hard and untouchable, like supercooled rage.

She needed to be hard. Otherwise the sight of his strained features and flagrant scars would have cracked her courage.

He had reason to look like that, she reminded herself. He was the fooled artist, betrayed by a tool he'd thought belonged to him body and soul. She'd given him something which touched him at the heart of his dark and complex needs – and now he knew that the gift was false.

And he was perfectly capable of murdering people for less cause.

He paused briefly just inside the door, letting her see what she was up against; giving her a chance to gauge her danger by the intensity of his expression. Then he came at her like the slam of a piston and struck her so hard across the cheek that she crumpled to her bunk.

Fires like novas blazed through her head. Incandescent pain paralyzed her: white conflagration blinded her. She couldn't defend herself as he rummaged through her shipsuit until he found her black box; she couldn't do anything to stop him as he took control of her life away from her.

Gripping the box, he stepped back. Holding it up so that he could watch her while he studied it, he read the function labels.

Ablaze with pain, she was helpless to react when he pressed one of the buttons.

It did nothing to her.

'There,' he rasped as he buried her zone-implant control in his own pocket. 'Now it's off.

'Get up.'

She couldn't. She heard the command in his voice; she understood her peril. But she was too weak to obey, too badly hurt. Without artificial help, she was only human – a woman who was already exhausted, already beaten.

'I said, *get up.*'

Somehow she levered her arms under her, pried herself into a sitting position. Confused and drained by the clangor of suns, that was as far as she could rise.

'You're mine now, you bitch,' he snarled. 'You've diddled me and lied to me for the last time.

'For a while there, I thought you'd turned Vector against me. I even had doubts about Mikka. But you couldn't manage that. You have limits, don't you? I'm going to make sure you keep them.' He slapped his pocket. 'I'm going to make you suffer – I'm going to make you bleed and die like an ordinary human being, instead of some goddamn superwoman.

'This is your last chance. Get *up*!'

'Why?' Despite the pain, her core of ice held solid. 'So you can hit me again? I'm done with that. I'm done acting like one of your toys. If you want to make me "bleed and die", you'll have to come get me. I won't help you.

'And I'll make you pay for it. I swear I'll make you pay for it.'

Somehow.

Like the lash of a solar flare, he caught hold of her, snatched her to him. Almost spitting into her face, he demanded, 'How do you think you're going to do that?'

She glared back at him, ice against his fire.

'You can't dismantle that self-destruct. Your priority codes are still useless.' That was a guess, but a safe one: he hadn't had time to solve the problems she'd left him. 'Your ship is a bomb waiting to explode. And

437

you don't know how I've programmed it. Maybe I've set it up to blow if I don't input to it every couple of hours.

'You can probably figure out what I did to your codes. Or you can use my control to make me tell you. But you might not be able to do it in time. Thanatos Minor works for the Amnion. You illegals always think you work for yourselves, but you serve them. As soon as we're in scan range, that shipyard will tell them we're still alive. Then you'll have warships after you.

'If you aren't quick enough, you'll have to face them with a live self-destruct and no priority codes.'

She could see that he heard her. His rage didn't diminish, but it changed character. His instinct to fight for his ship and his own survival took precedence over his need to hurt her.

'That's temporary,' she went on. 'You can solve all those problems without me. But until they're taken care of, you'll have to keep me alive – you'll have to keep my brain intact. Maybe that'll give you time to realize there's a better reason why you don't want to hurt me. Or Davies.'

He heard her. He couldn't help himself. She was talking about issues he couldn't ignore. And she still had one advantage over him, even without her zone-implant: she knew him better than he knew her. He was the one who'd been blinded by their masque of passion. It had revealed him – and concealed her.

Rage turned his skin the color of his scars; the cords of his neck knotted. But he didn't hit her. Through his teeth, he grated, 'What reason?'

'Because,' she articulated distinctly, as if she didn't care that he was angry enough to extinguish her, 'you're Captain Nick Succorso, and you never lose.'

He glowered at her like the muzzle of a gun. His fists didn't release her.

'You want people to believe that. You want every illegal or cop who's ever heard of you to believe it. But it's bigger than that. You *need* your crew to believe it. They don't love you for your charm. Even your women don't. They love you for your reputation. They love the Nick Succorso who never loses.

'So how do you think you look right now? How do you think your reputation looks? For the sake of a woman who was "diddling" you, a woman you couldn't figure out because she had a zone-implant, you risked your life and your ship in forbidden space – and the result was a disaster. You got yourself in so much trouble that you had to let the Amnion cheat you. In fact, you got yourself in so much trouble that you had to sell them a *human being* just so they would have the chance to cheat you. And then the mother of that human being took over your ship. She put her finger on the self-destruct and forced you *and* the Amnion to do what she wanted.

'For a man who never loses, that was a real triumph.'

As she spoke, Nick's face set like concrete, hardened to blankness. His scars faded; the fury in his eyes receded. In that way, she knew her threat was potent. She'd driven him to regain his self-mastery.

His rage had been something she understood. But now she couldn't read him. He was dangerous in a new way, as if the peril in him had become absolute.

She was absolute herself, on the edge of her resources – and her doom. She didn't falter.

'What do you think you'll accomplish by torturing or killing me – or my son? Is that going to restore your reputation? You know better. You'll still be the Nick Succorso who lost, but now everybody will know that when you lose you punish helpless women and children for it.

'*That* story will spread, just like all the others. People aren't going to talk about you as the hero in a war against corrupt cops.' Her voice rose, hinting at bloodshed. 'They're going to talk about you as if you're Angus Thermopyle.'

That was the first time she'd said Angus' name aboard this ship. It was only the second time she'd ever said it aloud.

'Or what?' Nick countered with an impersonal snarl, leaving his rage in the background. 'You wouldn't have brought this up if you weren't going to offer me an alternative.'

Like *Captain's Fancy* in the gap, Morn rode the rim of nonexistence and fought to save herself.

'Or,' she told Nick, 'you can change the story.'

'How?' His face was concrete; but his quickness betrayed the intensity of his attention.

'You can accept me,' she replied without hesitation, 'welcome me, put me back on duty. You can smile and look like a hero. You can even act like we've been fucking each other's brains out for hours.'

He started to sneer a retort; but she overrode him.

'You can give your people a chance to think that we did it together – that we planned this to get Davies and *Captain's Fancy* away from the Amnion without ruining your credibility, and without being blasted. How could you have done it otherwise? You didn't have anything except my son to sell for those gap drive components. But if you sold him, you couldn't get him back without breaking your bargain. Your only hope was to run a scam – to use me against the Amnion.

'They won't believe it at first. But they'll start to wonder. They can't be sure you would have killed me if Liete hadn't stopped you. And I'll back you up. Eventually they'll have to believe it. As long as you treat me like we did it together. And you don't hurt Davies. You don't have to pretend you like him – or want him around. He isn't your son. Just leave him alone.

'Think about *that* story for a minute,' she urged, steaming like dry ice. 'Is there anyone in human space who's *ever* had the nerve to run a scam like that on the Amnion?'

As far as she was concerned, all the glamorous tales about Nick Succorso were lies anyway. Why should this one be any different?

Abruptly he let go of her and pushed her away. Her legs failed; she fell back on the berth. Standing over her, he breathed so heavily that he seemed to be shuddering. The lines of his face were remorseless.

After a moment he whispered, 'I'll kill you for this.'

She met him squarely. 'I know.'

'But I'll pick a better time. Unless you don't back me up. Then I won't have any reason to wait.' He took another hard breath, let it out slowly. 'Tell me how to restore my codes.'

Morn held his glare. 'I want to see Davies. He needs me.'

'No chance,' Nick growled at once. 'He's the only hold I've got on you. I don't trust this.' He slapped his pocket again. 'For all I know, it's a dummy, and you've got half a dozen others hidden around the ship.'

She shook her head. She didn't care what he believed about her black box: she was suddenly afraid for her son.

'Nick, listen,' she said as steadily as she could. 'He'll go crazy by himself. Maybe he's crazy already. He's got my mind – he thinks he's me.' For the second time, she pleaded, 'At least let me talk to him.'

'No,' Nick retorted harshly. 'You've been lying to me. You've been lying from the moment I first saw you with Captain fucking Thermopile. And I believed you. I thought you really gave yourself. But you were just using me. Like all the others.' He'd become as cold as she was – and as unreachable. 'Tell me how to restore my codes.'

In hope and despair, she told him.

He nodded once, acknowledging the effectiveness of her gambit. Then he turned to the door.

When it opened, he faced her as if for the last time. There was a look of farewell in his eyes. Nevertheless his tone was raw and malign.

'You're back on Mikka's watch. But when you're not on duty, I want you *here*. I'm going to keep you out of trouble. As soon as I can afford the time' – he indicated his pocket and bared his teeth – 'we'll find out how you like being on the other side of this thing.'

After he left, the door locked behind him.

Nursing the pain in her head, Morn stretched out on her bunk and tried to keep herself from wailing at the thought of her son's plight.

CHAPTER 17

Half an hour later, the intercom chimed, summoning Mikka Vasaczk's watch to the bridge.

After a moment the door control status indicators in Morn's cabin winked green. Nick had unlocked her.

She hurried out into the passageway before he could change his mind.

She should have gone to sickbay. The pain in her head abated too slowly: each beat of her heart knifed through her as if she were in the grip of a cerebral hemorrhage. At alarming intervals her vision slid double; and the effort required to bring her eyes back to single focus made her sweat and tremble with old, familiar nausea. Stress or numbness caused her fingers to tingle. Maybe one of her occipital bones was cracked. Or maybe the top of her spine – or her brain itself – was bruised. If she developed a hematoma inside her skull, or along her spinal cord, she might drift into paralysis as the swelling grew.

Nevertheless she headed for the bridge, not sickbay.

She was urgent to get her hands on the data board.

Without the support of her zone-implant, she was so weak that she felt invalid, hardly able to walk. From time to time she blundered against the walls. In one of the surviving compartments of her mind, she wondered how deep her addiction to her black box had become; wondered whether she would have to go through withdrawal on top of her other problems. The weight of her limits threatened to overwhelm her. But she kept going.

She had too few chances left. She couldn't afford to miss any of them.

When she crossed the aperture to the bridge, Nick met her with a grin that might have looked lascivious if it hadn't been so bloodthirsty – or if his scars hadn't been the pale gray color of cold ashes.

She was the last of Mikka's watch to arrive. Except for Sib Mackern and Nick himself, the firsts had already left – no doubt desperate for rest. But everyone on the bridge turned to stare at Morn.

Obviously Nick hadn't told them that she was about to resume her duties.

Mikka's glower was unreadable, effectively blank. Maybe she could guess what Morn's arrival meant – or maybe she didn't care. The knuckles of her right hand were swollen and discolored, but she gave no sign that they hurt.

Scorz stared with his mouth open, as if he'd forgotten to breathe. The scan second's eyes flicked between Morn and Nick; he seemed to wish he had a doppler sensor to gauge the meaning of Morn's presence. The twisting of Karster's features made him look like a boy with a math problem he couldn't solve.

Involuntarily, caught by shock, Mackern murmured, 'I don't believe it.' A crisis of doubt stretched his features. 'Morn, are you all right? He said – but I assumed –' Abruptly the data first shut his mouth as if he were appalled by his own thoughts.

'Are you serious, Nick?' demanded the twitchy helm second, Ransum. She was too tight with anxiety to keep quiet. 'Do we have to work with her? She just about got us all killed.'

'You're going to work with her,' Nick replied with a grin, 'and you're going to like it. If you think anything else, you don't know me very well.'

'But what about the self-destruct?' put in Scorz. 'If you let her touch the computers, she can still blow us up.'

'I told my watch,' Nick retorted flatly. 'Now I'll tell you. I've got my priority codes back. Vector has already dismantled the self-destruct.' Only the knotted muscles in his neck betrayed the strain of self-coercion. 'It served its purpose. We don't need it anymore.'

'Holy shit!' Karster breathed as if he'd been struck by a revelation. 'You did it deliberately.'

Then he realized what he'd said. Turning back to his board, he began working studiously, pretending he was busy.

The implications in the air were too dangerous to be faced directly. The rest of Mikka's watch followed Karster's example. Suddenly only Nick and Mikka were left looking at Morn.

Nick, Mikka – and Sib Mackern.

Uncertainty tangled around the data first: he couldn't find his way out of it. He seemed more distressed by Morn's presence on the bridge than by anything else she'd done. As if the words were being forced out of him, he asked her, 'Were you *bluffing*?'

The question sounded like an accusation. Apparently he preferred to think of her as an enemy.

Her head throbbed horribly, and she was tired of lies. For Davies' sake, however, she faced Mackern squarely. 'We needed those gap drive components. And I need my son. How else could we do it?'

Mikka might have challenged the lie. She'd been with Morn on the auxiliary bridge: she'd seen the truth for herself. Nevertheless she said nothing. Instead she folded her arms across her chest and went on glowering impartially. Earlier she'd supported Nick with her fist: now she supported him with her silence.

For a moment Mackern's mouth opened in protest; sweat or tears filled his eyes. But then, looking suddenly frightened, he mastered himself. In a fumble of movements, as if he'd lost the habit of his limbs, he left the data Station and made his way off the bridge.

Nick's nod hinted at satisfaction as he turned to Mikka.

'You're on,' he said, standing up from the command console. 'If I'd known we could go this fast, I would have tried it long ago. Just hold us steady. Monitor *everything*. And work up a status report we can trust. I don't want any surprises at this velocity. We'll start thinking about deceleration tomorrow.

'Morn,' he continued almost casually, 'try to analyze what happened. You've got our science data – Vector can give you whatever engineering has. If we understand this, we *might* be able to control it. We might even be able to do it on purpose. Knowing how to hit speeds like this would be worth a fortune.'

Morn accepted the order; but she didn't move toward the data Station. With the best approximation of nonchalance she could manage, she asked, 'Nick, how is Davies?'

She was pushing her luck. A grimace twisted Nick's face, and he growled, 'How the hell should I know? I haven't exactly had time to hold his hand.'

A tremor started up in her, threatening her self-command. She fought it down. Needles of pain probed her vision: she ignored them. Carefully she said, 'That's what I mean. You've been too busy to worry about him. Did you tell anybody else to take care of him? How's he doing?'

Nick flashed a savage glare at her. He didn't break the pact, however. Snarling under his breath, he slapped the command Station intercom. 'Liete!'

The command third answered a moment later, 'Nick?'

'Morn is concerned about our guest,' he sneered. On this subject, he didn't need to hide his anger. 'He's your problem. He probably wants food. He can have that. And he probably wants companionship. He can't have that. If he gets loose, I'll take it out of your hide. I've got enough problems without having to play foster parent for somebody else's bastard.'

Quietly, so that her voice wouldn't shake, Morn said, 'Thanks.' Then she went quickly to the data Station, sat down, and belted her fear to the seat.

She was in trouble.

Her head throbbed unconscionably. She couldn't produce enough saliva to keep her mouth and throat working. Her fingers were numb and imprecise, resisting the data board. Under pressure, her eyes slid out of focus; and when that happened, her stomach twisted queasily. Her duties alone threatened to be too much for her – and yet she also had other problems to tackle.

She needed help; needed her zone-implant. Every difficult thing she'd accomplished aboard *Captain's Fancy* had been done with artificial strength and concentration. But now those benefits were denied her: she was left with only their cost.

Addiction. Limits. And the knowledge that without her black box she might never prove equal to the challenge of saving herself, or her son.

Sometimes her vision failed because she'd been hit so hard. Sometimes it failed because she was weeping. The board in front of her blurred, and the display screens dissolved in streaks.

Nick would call it a betrayal if she let anyone see her weep. But she couldn't tell whether any of the people around her noticed her condition.

She had to do better.

She had to try. That necessity held: it was the cold, hard core of what kept her going. Davies was even more helpless than she was. Unless she found some way to reach him, he was lost.

She had to try.

At first the effort was beyond her. By themselves, the tests and data Mikka required would have been enough to use up her resources; but in addition she had to work on the analysis Nick wanted. She had no time to get anything else done; no concentration to spare; no strength at all.

But then, as unexpectedly as if he'd just come out of the gap, Pup appeared at her Station with a mug of coffee and a plate of sandwiches.

'Vector said,' the boy mumbled, 'you haven't had time to eat anything. He sent this for you.' Self-consciousness affected him like chagrin. When she didn't move to accept Vector's offering, he added awkwardly, 'He asked Mikka. She says it's okay.'

'Hell,' Scorz drawled, 'if I'd known I could get my meals delivered just by threatening to blow up the ship, I would have done it long ago.'

Ransum giggled nervously.

Morn took the coffee and food. Hiding behind her hair, she murmured, 'Thank you,' and waited for Pup to leave.

When he was gone, she ate and drank, and became a little stronger. Some of the life returned to her fingers.

After a few minutes she started working on her personal problems.

She put the tests and information Mikka wanted up on one of the big screens and kept them moving to show that she was busy. On another display, she ran a search-and-compare program to look through *Captain's Fancy*'s data for analogues to what had happened in the gap.

But her console readouts she used for research which had nothing to do with her duties.

Simplest problems first. Without much difficulty, she discovered where Davies was being held.

His cell was one of the passenger cabins. In fact, his room was only two doors from hers. That didn't make him physically accessible: he would be monitored – and Nick would make certain that she had no chance to sneak out of her cabin. But just knowing where her son was eased her distress. And his circumstances could have been worse: Nick could have decided to secure him by sealing him in one of the ejection pods *Captain's Fancy* used as lifeboats. In a cabin Davies could at least move around; keep himself clean; be comfortable.

She still didn't know how to reach him. But trying to think about that problem stunned her sore brain. To distract herself, she went to work on the ship's communications log.

That research was harder. She had to study the log without letting Scorz – or Mikka – catch what she was doing. And her duties still demanded her attention. The command second wanted to test alloy fatigue hypotheses, to learn what effect time dilation and particle stress might have on *Captain's Fancy*'s hull. Some theorists had argued that as a physical object approached the speed of light it would bleed substance until it was reduced to light. If *Captain's Fancy* was bleeding, Mikka wanted to know about it. And Morn's search-and-compare programs repeatedly came up empty, requiring her to redefine their parameters. For an hour, she was unable to nudge the information she desired out of the communications computer.

Then she got it.

Nick had sent only one message since resuming tard.

It hadn't been aimed at Thanatos Minor. Instead it had been beamed at the nearest UMCP listening post.

It was a demand for help.

Nick reported his position, direction, and velocity, and claimed – without explanation – that he was being pursued by Amnion warships. He reminded the UMCP that they couldn't afford to let him be captured. He urged them to send a destroyer into forbidden space to save him.

No chance, Morn said to herself as she read the message. If you think you're worth that, you'd better think again. The UMCP may have been willing to conceal an Amnion mutagen immunity drug from the rest of humankind; but for that very reason no one at UMCPHQ would have approved the risks Nick had just taken. He'd proven himself too foolish to live. Any ship the UMCP sent out would come as a threat, not as help.

After that, however, she couldn't go on. Nick's dealings with UMCPHQ didn't give her any leverage with him, any way to make him let her talk to Davies. And she couldn't imagine how to reach Davies on her own. Her watch wore to an end without the answer she needed most.

When Mikka signaled for Liete's people, Nick arrived to escort Morn back to her cabin.

The fever in his eyes and the strain in his grin told her what his intentions were: she didn't need to interpret the leer he forced toward her, or the significant way he tapped the pocket of his shipsuit. Without warning, her eyes filled with tears again, and the last energy seemed to run out of her muscles. Only her zone-implant had enabled her to bear his touch; and now that control would be used against her.

'I hope she's worth it,' Scorz muttered – not to Nick, but for Nick to overhear.

'You'll never know,' Nick retorted a little too harshly.

Just for a moment Morn recovered her anger. She couldn't smile for Nick, or act pleased, so she kept her part of the pact by making an obscene gesture in Scorz's direction.

Karster and Ransum laughed tightly as she left the bridge.

As soon as she and Nick were through the aperture, he stopped grinning.

He held her arm as if he thought she would try to get away. Because she couldn't, she tried to tell herself that she would be able to endure whatever he did to her; that for her son's sake she could face being under Nick's power the same way she'd been under Angus'. But she knew she was lying.

When they reached her cabin, he rasped, 'This is where the fun starts,' and thrust her through the doorway.

Somehow, against the edge of her bunk, she turned to face him.

The door slid shut. He held her black box like a grenade, gripped it so hard that the cords on the back of his hand stood out.

He may have wanted her to plead with him. Fall on her knees and beg. That may have been what he needed.

If it was, he didn't get it. Without control over her zone-implant, she couldn't do anything else for herself; but she could refuse to beg.

His fist started to shake. His scars were the color of dried bone, all the passion desiccated out of them.

Morn faced him, waiting for him to explode; waiting for her ordeal aboard *Bright Beauty* to begin again.

Abruptly he said, 'I told you about the woman who cut me.'

His voice quivered like his hand.

She waited without blinking; almost without breathing.

'What you did was worse.'

She held his aggrieved gaze. Maybe she should have said something, but nothing came to her. Her refusal to plead was all she had left.

His hand tightened and shook until she thought her black box might break. But he didn't touch any of the buttons. His skin stretched across his features, as pale as his scars. His lips looked like the edges of an old wound.

'The thing is,' he panted, still quivering, 'now that I've got you, I don't want you. I never wanted you. What I wanted was to *be* wanted.'

While she stared at him, refusing him, he put her control back in his pocket. 'You can be pretty sure I'll take care of your brat. I need him. Just turning him over to the Amnion wouldn't be good enough. I want to be able to make you watch while they change him.

'After that, I'll probably let them have you, too.'

He turned on his heel and left.

As soon as the door closed, its lights indicated that it was locked.

Davies. Oh, Davies, she prayed. Help me.

She needed rest desperately. Whenever she fell asleep, however, she plunged directly into nightmares that made her sweat like Angus and scream like the damned.

They were all the same. In them, the universe suddenly opened around her, giving her clarity, filling her with perfection. When it spoke, its message was absolute truth – and absolutely necessary. Her obedience was so clear and perfect that it felt like joy.

Her father or her son stood in front of her. They were also her mother, and her father's sisters; they were Min Donner and several of her instructors at the Academy; they were herself, raped and desolate. But that confusion only made them clearer, more perfectly comprehensible. They were all saying

Morn, save us

like utter anguish

so she took small, perfect explosives, and attached them to her father's heart, or her son's, or her own, and watched with clear, vindicated joy as the detonations tore everyone she'd ever loved to bloody bits.

Then her cries woke her up in a welter of sweat, as if her bones were being squeezed dry.

After Liete's watch, and Nick's, she took another turn on the bridge.

449

This time Vector didn't send her food or coffee; but when her watch was over, Nick escorted her to the galley and let her fix herself a meal before he led her back to her cabin and locked her in.

Perhaps because food made her stronger – or perhaps because more time had passed since she'd lost the protection of her zone-implant – her nightmares got worse.

I'm going crazy, she thought while hoarse terror echoed in her memory. I'm finished.

But this time she had an idea.

Craziness had its uses. It was unpredictable: no one would expect it. And since she was already finished, she had nothing else to lose.

She was almost calm as she took her place among Mikka's watch. Her nightmares had left her haggard, but drained; her fears had been temporarily appeased. Hiding behind the work Nick and Mikka wanted done, she tapped into *Captain's Fancy*'s maintenance computer.

She didn't tamper with the lock on her door – or on Davies'. That would be too obvious: Nick or Mikka would surely catch her. But they might not be so careful about the intercoms—

Concealed by stress reports and gap studies, she routed a channel between her cabin and Davies', and fixed it open. That was risky. If Nick entered her cabin, Davies would hear everything he said: if Davies made a sound, Nick would hear it.

She accepted the danger because she had no alternative.

She might be crazy and doomed, but at least she would get a chance to speak to her son.

Unless Davies was beyond reach—

That could easily be true. He was locked up, alone with his fundamental confusion of identity. But that confusion was more than just psychological turmoil: it was a state of complete hormonal chaos. Driven by his imponderable transition from fetus to young manhood – and from his mother's artificially intense sexual stew to his own maleness – his physical state must be wildly out of balance.

Human beings weren't made to survive that kind of stress. In the Amnion sense, they weren't designed for it. They could never replace the years of love and nurturance which nature required. Without those years, Davies was as lost as his father.

The urgency of her desire to help him rose in Morn's throat like a scream. But she had to wait until she reached her cabin.

Nick continued to escort her; continued to grip her arm as if he thought she would run away. She dreaded him doubly now: he might hear that her intercom was open. However, he'd become calmer during the past day. He didn't look like a man who suffered from nightmares. And the approach to Thanatos Minor gave him things to think about which must have engaged or satisfied him more than Morn did. He didn't say anything as he took her to her cabin. He simply steered her to her door and locked her in.

When she was alone, she began to tremble.

She couldn't imagine how much stress Davies was under. Her mind hadn't exactly been in its natural state when it was copied. The effects of her zone-implant must have altered the electrochemical data imprinted on his neurons. So he had to be different than she was, even though every learned component of his identity came from her. But would that make him weaker or stronger? The little contact she'd had with him suggested that there were blind patches among his memories. Were they temporary? Would those absent places help or harm him in his isolation and confusion?

For several minutes she was too afraid to speak.

But he needed her. If she didn't help him, no one else would.

She went into the san for a drink of water to clear her throat. Then she braced herself against the wall beside the intercom and said softly, as if she feared eavesdroppers, 'Davies? Can you hear me?'

At once she heard a grunt of surprise, the sound of boots.

'Don't touch the intercom,' she told him quickly. 'I fixed this channel open. If you key anything, you'll switch me off.' And Nick or Liete will realize what you're doing.

'Morn?' he asked. 'Is that you?'

Her son's voice. He sounded exactly like his father – if his father had been younger, and less violently defended against his own fear.

'Where are you? What's going on? Why is he doing this to me? Why does he hate me?

'Morn, what have I done? What am I?'

Her son.

'Davies, listen.' She tried to reach him through his distress. 'I want to answer your questions. I want to tell you everything. But I don't know how much time we have. If nobody notices what I did to the intercom, we'll be able to talk for a long time. But anybody who checks might catch us. We need to make this count.

'Are you having trouble remembering things?'

She heard his breathing as if he had his mouth pressed to the intercom. After a long pause he said like a small boy, 'Yes.' Then, more fiercely, he added, 'I don't even know who I am. How can I remember anything?'

Be patient, she ordered herself. Don't rush him. 'What kind of trouble?'

'It just stops.' The pickup flattened his voice: he might have been feeling grief or fury. 'I'm a girl. *I remember* that, Morn. My home is on Earth. I've got a mother and a father, just like everybody else. Her name is Bryony, *his* is Davies, that's my father, not me. They're both cops – but she died ten years ago, their ship was crippled and almost destroyed in a fight with an illegal, he was lucky to survive. I'm a cop *myself*, I went to the Academy, I was assigned to my father's ship. None of this makes any *sense.*'

'I know.' Morn throttled her own sense of urgency in an effort to comfort him. 'I can explain it all, but I need to know where it stops. What's the last thing you remember?'

Maybe he couldn't hear her. As if the gap between them were light-years long, he croaked, 'Whenever I think about you – I mean, about you separate from me – I feel like I'm being raped.'

'*Please.*' Sudden weeping filled her throat. She had to swallow hard before she could force up words. 'I want to help you, but I can't until I know where your memories stop.'

Davies was silent for a long time – so long that waiting for him nearly broke her heart. But at last he spoke. From across the gap, he said, 'The ship was *Starmaster*. She was a UMCP destroyer, but we were covert, pretending to be an orehauler. We'd just left Com-Mine Station for the belt, and we spotted a ship called *Bright Beauty*. We'd been warned about her. Her Captain was Angus Thermopyle' – he stumbled over the name as if he didn't know why it was familiar – 'and we were told he was one of the worst, but nobody could prove it. We saw him' – Davies' tone conveyed a shudder – 'burn out a defenseless mining camp, so we went after him.

'I was at my combat Station on the auxiliary bridge. We started after *Bright Beauty*. That's the last thing I remember.'

Listening to him, Morn didn't know whether to feel relief or regret. His memories cut out at the moment when she'd first been hit by gap-sickness. At least for the time being, he'd been spared all the horrors she'd experienced. That was probably why he was still sane enough to talk.

If she could help him before those memories returned, he might be able to deal with them.

Nevertheless she was left with an appalling burden of explanation.

'All right,' she said, ignoring her own dismay because his need was so much greater. 'Now I know where to begin.

'This is the most important thing. Nothing that you remember – or ever will remember – about being Morn Hyland happened to you. You know that's true because you're obviously not a girl. You don't resemble your own memories. They aren't yours. That's *my* past. *I'm* Morn Hyland. *You* are Davies Hyland, my son.

'When I found out I was pregnant, I decided not to abort you. But I couldn't have you aboard this ship. She's an illegal's ship, Davies. Her name is *Captain's Fancy*, and she belongs to that man who acts like he hates you, Nick Succorso. We were on the run. Our gap drive was damaged – we couldn't reach any safe port.' She edited her account drastically, not to falsify it – he would never be able to trust her if she lied now – but to make it bearable. 'So Nick took us into forbidden space. To Enablement Station – to the Amnion.'

Davies' silence sounded worse than swearing or protests. He had enough of her memories to understand her.

'They have a "force-growing" technique, a way to make fetuses physiologically mature fast. I agreed to that because I couldn't think of any other way to keep you. But a fetus has no experience, no learning, no mind. The Amnion can grow a body, but they can't create an intelligence, a personality. So they copy it from the mother.

'That's why you think you're me. When you were born, you were given my past – my memories, my training – to make up for the fact that you didn't have your own.

'The man you remember is my father, Captain Davies Hyland of *Starmaster*. He's your grandfather. I named you after him because I loved and admired him – and because I want to keep some part of him alive.'

I killed all the rest.

But she couldn't say that: she couldn't risk triggering the memories he'd been spared. Not until she'd given him a context for them; until she'd convinced him that they belonged to her, not to him.

'Nobody hates you,' she continued, urging him to believe her. 'Not you personally. I told you that. Nick treats you like this because he hates me.

'That's why he traded you to the Amnion. You didn't do anything. You aren't to blame. He's just trying to find ways to hurt me.'

As if from an immeasurable distance, Davies asked, 'Why?'

Still editing, Morn replied, 'Because he's an illegal, and I'm a cop. That's one reason. There are others – better ones – but I don't want to talk about them until you're ready.'

Davies, what're you thinking? What're you feeling? What do you need?

The wall was too hard, too impersonal. She needed to see her son's face, wanted to hold him in her arms; ached to place herself between him and his crisis.

She expected him to ask what those other reasons were. When it came, his question surprised her.

'Morn, why do my memories stop? Your life didn't. You got pregnant. You left *Starmaster* and ended up here. You got yourself in so much trouble that you had to go to the Amnion for help. Why don't I remember any of that?'

'I'm not sure,' she replied slowly, feeling her way. 'I'm not an expert on force-growing.' Or psychic trauma. 'But I think it's because the memories are so bad. I won't lie to you. What happened was – hideous.' And to save her mind from her terror of the Amnion, she'd used her zone-implant to blank her fear. Maybe that had inhibited the transference of the memories which scared or hurt her most. 'What you remember,' she said as bravely as she could, 'stops right at the point where I first came down with gap-sickness.

'That's my problem, not yours,' she added, hurrying to reassure him. 'You don't have it. For one thing, it's not an inherited trait. For another, you've already been through the gap. If you were susceptible, it probably would have shown up by now. I'm a rare case – my gap-sickness stays dormant most of the time. It only becomes active when it's triggered by heavy g.

'When *Starmaster* started chasing *Bright Beauty*, we had heavy g for the first time. After that, terrible things started happening. If you're lucky, you'll never remember them.'

The intercom made Davies' voice sound like it came from the far side of the galaxy. 'They're the reason Nick Succorso hates you.'

'Yes,' she answered thinly, as if his assertion left her faint. 'Some of them.'

'Morn, I need to know what they are.' He was suddenly urgent. 'Maybe you're the one he hates, but I'm the one he's taking it out on. He gave me back to the Amnion. Now he's got me locked up – he's just waiting for his chance to do something worse to me.

'I need to know why. Or I won't be able to stand it.'

His demand hurt more than she would have believed possible. He was her son; the surviving remnant of her father's beliefs and commitments. He would judge her by standards to which she'd dedicated her life – until gap-sickness and Angus Thermopyle had degraded her. To tell him the truth would shame her utterly.

So what? she asked herself. What does it matter now? If you were stuck where he is, you would feel the way he does.

Baring her soul, she answered, 'Because I lied to him.'

'That's all?' Davies rasped like his father. 'He hates you because you lied to him?'

'Yes. Because I lied to him where it hurt the most.' Every word set claws of chagrin and remorse into her heart, but she forced herself to go on. 'He's a tormented man, and I used that against him.

'He never wanted me to have you. He wanted me for sex, that's all. So he ordered me to abort you. He could have forced me – he could have done anything to me. I told him every lie I could think of that might change his mind.

'I told him you're his son.'

'But I'm not,' Davies said across the gap. 'My father is Angus Thermopile. He said so. Angus Thermopyle. The man who slaughtered those miners.'

The intercom muffled his implicit accusation, yet Morn heard it like a shout. You're a cop, and you got pregnant with a man like Angus Thermopyle! You gave me *him* for a father!

But her son was too frightened to accuse her. Nothing in her background prepared him for his plight. 'Is that really why he hates you?' he asked as if he were pleading. 'They're both illegals. I thought they might be partners. I thought my father was somewhere aboard.

'I thought he might come see me' – Davies' voice broke like a kid's – 'might come help me.'

'No,' Morn answered miserably. 'He isn't here. He's in lockup back on Com-Mine. They didn't get him for what he did to those miners, but they found a charge they could make stick.

'He's the only man in human space that Nick hates worse than the cops. If Nick had known before you were born that' – she said the name again – 'Angus Thermopyle was your father, he would have aborted you with his bare hands.'

Without any warning at all, the door slid open, and Nick strode into her cabin.

Dark blood filled his scars, underlining his gaze with fury. A snarl uncovered his teeth. Both his hands clenched into fists.

'Morn?' Davies asked anxiously. 'What was that?'

His voice over the intercom didn't surprise Nick.

'You like to live dangerously,' he sneered at Morn. 'Doesn't it ever occur to you that you can't afford to mess with me? I don't have to put up with you' – abruptly he faced the intercom – 'or with you, either, you fucking bastard.' His anger flashed like a cutting laser. 'I can have you both *shot*, and nobody here or back at UMCPHQ will even bother to wince.'

'Try it,' Davies retorted, instantly belligerent – like his father – and too inexperienced to restrain himself. 'Try letting one of your illegals get that close to me.'

Nick toggled the intercom with a blow of his fist.

'Liete,' he snapped, 'disable Davies' intercom. From now on, he's *deaf*, understand? I don't want him to hear *anything*.'

'I understand,' replied Liete calmly.

Nick punched the intercom off and swung back toward Morn.

He was going to hit her: she knew that. She could read the particular tightness in his shoulders, the knotted lines of his stance. He had no other outlet. He was going to wait and stare at her until her own fear paralyzed her. Then he was going to hit her hard enough to break bones.

He might shatter her ribs, or her jaw. If she were lucky, he might burst her skull.

She almost said, Oh, get it over with. I'm tired of waiting for you to go out of control.

The intercom stopped her.

'Nick.' Tension had replaced Liete's usual stoicism. 'You're wanted on the bridge.'

That got Nick's attention. He spun to the intercom again, keyed it with his thumb. 'What's going on?'

'We've got company,' the command third reported. 'An Amnion warship. She just resumed tard right on the edge of our scan.

'She's between us and Thanatos Minor.'

Nick slapped off the intercom and hit the door at a run.

Morn followed before he had a chance to lock her in.

CHAPTER 18

As soon as Nick noticed her, he wheeled on her. 'Goddamn it—'

'Nick,' Morn urged, breathless with intensity, 'you need me.' The passage was empty: no one was likely to overhear what she said. As fast as she could find words, she argued, 'Maybe you can survive the Amnion. You can't survive a crew that doesn't believe in you. You need me with you. To keep alive the idea that we're in this together. As long as you can make them think we're on the same side, they'll believe you're still the Nick Succorso who never loses.'

'In other words,' he fired back at her, 'you want me to trust you. You just disobeyed my direct orders, and now you want me to risk everything I've got left that you'll back me up.'

'That was private,' she retorted. His interruption of her efforts to help Davies had left her terrified and furious; careless of consequences. 'This is public. Even *you* can understand the difference.'

With an inarticulate snarl, he swung at her.

But he didn't hit her; he snatched hold of her arm. Nearly flinging her off her feet, he impelled her toward the lift.

'Make it good,' he rasped as he rushed her along. 'The harder you push me, the less I have to gain by keeping you alive.'

Make it good. She no longer had any idea what that meant. Minute by minute, she knew less and less about her own decisions; about the implications of her own actions. She'd lost control in more ways than one. The gap between what she thought or planned and what she did was growing wider. Everything about her had a tight, feverish quality, as if she were going into withdrawal.

Nevertheless she answered his demand as if he could count on her – as if she were sure of herself.

Together they hurried through *Captain's Fancy* to the bridge.

Relief showed through Liete Corregio's blunt competence at their arrival. Unlike Morn, she'd been to sickbay: her injuries had been treated. In addition, she'd had a certain amount of rest. And she'd never lacked confidence in her fundamental abilities. Yet she plainly didn't want command of the ship in this situation. Her relief indicated that she no longer knew how to regard her captain. She didn't want to face an Amnion warship without him because she couldn't count on his approval.

Nick ignored her reaction, however. Scanning the displays, he snapped, 'Status.'

Liete nodded at one of the screens. 'She showed up five minutes ago. Popped out of tach just inside our range. Scan data on her isn't very good yet. For one thing, we're still fumbling with real-time distortion across our sensors. For another, we simply aren't programmed for this much doppler. We're having to oversample eight and ten times just to filter out the noise. At the moment, I can't even tell you which direction she's going.

'But she's Amnion. We're sure of that. And the emission signature resembles one of those warships we left back at Enablement. *Calm Horizons*.

'By some monumental coincidence, she's between us and Thanatos Minor. I mean, *right* between. Unless one of us shifts, we're going to hit her.'

Frowning at the screens, Nick asked, 'How is that possible?'

Liete nodded at the smelly and carnivorous helm third.

'Easy,' Pastille answered, twitching his whiskers. He was glad for a chance to show off his expertise. 'Alba and I could do it.' His grin implied that the computational problem was simple, not that he thought highly of Alba Parmute. 'Give them our velocity, acceleration, and vector, an accurate mass reading, reliable hysteresis parameters, and a good estimate of how much power our gap field generator can handle, and they can plot our theoretical crossings from Enablement to infinity.

'If they had to guess at our hysteresis parameters and power capacity, they couldn't do it. But they supplied the components, so they had exact information. If they're pessimistic enough to think we might survive their brand of sabotage, they wouldn't have any trouble knowing where to look for us – as long as we resumed tard on their side of the border.'

Morn knew all this. She was sure Nick did, too. But hearing it gave him time to think – and gave the bridge crew time to absorb her presence with him.

Abruptly he turned to communications. 'Are they sending?'

The communications third, improficient at the best of times, looked badly flustered now. 'I – I don't know,' he stuttered, 'I'm not sure. There's so much static.'

'Live dangerously,' Nick drawled ominously. 'Take a guess.'

The targ third, Simper, sniggered behind his heavy fist.

The flustered man turned pale. Looking at Liete as if for protection, he said in a small voice, 'I don't think so. If they are, the computer can't make sense out of it.'

'It's still early,' Liete put in. 'As I say, we don't know yet which direction they're heading. We can't measure the distance accurately enough. Even if they started sending as soon as they hit tard, we might not get it yet.'

'Does it work both ways?' Morn asked quickly. 'Are they having the same trouble tracking us?'

Liete considered the question. 'I don't see why not. At any rate, I think we can be sure they aren't expecting to see us like this. They're probably surprised to see us at all. They should be astonished to see us moving so fast.'

'Right!' Now Nick was ready. He began to issue orders. 'You' – he stabbed a finger at Morn – 'take the data board.' Grinning harshly, he added, 'No offense, Alba, but I want someone there who doesn't think with her crotch.'

Alba Parmute pouted like her swelling breasts, but she obeyed.

Nick hit the command Station intercom. 'Lind. Malda. I want you on the bridge.' He seemed to be turning up an internal rheostat, intensifying himself to meet the challenge. Moment by moment, he looked more like the Nick Succorso who never lost. 'Right away would be good. Right now would be better.'

On her way to the data Station, Morn passed Alba. The data third tried to sneer, but she couldn't conceal her speculative sexual awe at Morn's hold on Nick.

Morn grinned back – and was shocked when she realized that her grin was the same as Nick's. She was becoming more like him all the time.

Like him. And like Angus.

For a moment, the recognition stunned her. Automatically she sat down at the data board, belted herself in. But the readouts and lights in front of her meant nothing. Without the defense of her zone-implant, her identity was being transformed by stress; deformed beyond recognition.

Then Nick's voice reached her.

'Morn, let's assume we've identified that fucker right. Pull up everything we have on *Calm Horizons*. Let's start calculating what we're up against.'

As if he'd hit a switch in her, her ability to function clicked back on. She began tapping keys, executing commands, pouring data across the displays.

Shortly Malda Verone arrived to replace Simper. Muttering to himself, Lind assumed the communications Station, screwed a pickup into his ear, and began applying filters to the blurred noise of the vacuum.

'Don't miss anything,' Nick told him. 'We need to make decisions fast. At this velocity, lateral thrust is going to be like cracking eggs with a sledgehammer. We need to keep our course corrections as small as possible. But until we know what they want, we can't decide what to do about it.'

'I'm on it,' Lind reported without shifting his concentration. 'If they fart, I'll make music out of it.'

'Just be sure it still stinks,' gibed Pastille.

Nick ignored the riposte. 'Malda, I want everything ready. Matter cannon won't do us much good – unless we get a chance to shoot broadside – but I want them charged anyway. The same for the lasers.' *Captain's Fancy* was well equipped with industrial lasers: they were invaluable for unsealing pirated ships. Like the matter cannon, however, they were light-constant – too slow relative to *Captain's Fancy*'s present velocity. From that point of view, her speed was a disadvantage. It would reduce the effectiveness of her weapons. 'And prime the static mines.'

Malda Verone didn't acknowledge the order: she was already working on it.

'Allum,' Nick continued to the scan third, 'I want more information. I want to know whether that fucker's coming or going, and how fast.'

'So do I,' Allum responded in a discouraged tone. 'But the readings just aren't clear. If my board works any harder, it's going to smoke.'

But a moment later he said excitedly, 'Wait a minute. The computer's catching up.' Staring at his readouts, he reported, 'She's going the same way we are. Exactly the same heading. Speed' – he hit a key or two – 'approximately .4C.'

Which meant that *Captain's Fancy* was overtaking the Amnion warship at half the speed of light.

Eagerness focused Nick's attention. 'Morn, what do we know about that ship? What can she do?'

Morn sorted data. 'That class of warship uses a slow brisance thrust. They can go as fast as we can – I mean under normal circumstances – but they can't generate as much g. So they aren't very agile. That fits with our readings on *Calm Horizons*. That's the good news.'

Abruptly her mouth went dry.

'The bad news is that she's big enough to carry super-light proton cannon. That's one of the advantages of slow brisance thrust – it allows spare power capacity.' Morn's mother had been killed by a super-light proton beam. 'We can't survive a hit. If we have to fight, agility is about the only thing we've got going for us.'

Her feverish sensation began to feel more like chills. Adrenaline out of control. Withdrawal—

If Nick did any heavy g evasive maneuvers, she was in serious trouble. He had her black box.

Her mother had been killed.

Lind's voice cracked as he announced, 'They're sending!'

Nick sat forward tensely. 'Let's hear it.'

Lind keyed the speakers. With a burst of black static, they came to life.

'Amnion defensive *Calm Horizons* to human ship *Captain's Fancy*.' The flat voice came through particle noise as loud as a rattle of nails in a drum. 'You are required to decelerate. Conformity of purpose has not been achieved. Amnion requirements have not been satisfied. If they are not satisfied, you will be presumed hostile. *Calm Horizons* will destroy you.

'To survive, you must decelerate.'

A sting of panic went through Morn. *Requirements have not been satisfied.* Phosphene bursts made it impossible for her to focus on the displays. Her mouth was so dry that she couldn't swallow. The Amnion still wanted Davies.

Or they were after the secret of Nick's immunity.

Nick chewed his knuckle for a moment. 'What's the lag?' he demanded. 'How far away are they?'

'Five minutes,' Lind reported promptly. 'That's an estimate, but it should be about right. The computers are getting a better picture all the time.'

'Five minutes,' Allum verified from scan. 'That checks.'

Ninety million kilometers. And closing at a relative velocity of 150,000 kilometers per second. Space enough to maneuver in. Time enough for desperation.

The ship's scan wasn't that good. Of course not. The Amnion warship could function because her equipment was superior to anything human: no human scan had that kind of range. *Captain's Fancy* was reading old information – particle traces dispersing across the vacuum – and extrapolating from it. Ironically the velocity she'd been given by sabotage was what enabled her to interpret scan data over such distances; gave her a chance to defend herself. A Station like Com-Mine would have been blind to *Calm Horizons'* presence.

'Nick,' Morn said, forcing up words from her desiccated throat, 'tell them we've got damage. Tell them when the gap drive blew it burned out the thrust control systems. We can't decelerate.'

He shook his head. 'They'll know that isn't true.' His concentration was so pure that he didn't react to the message underlying her suggestion. 'They designed those components. They know exactly how our gap drive failed.

'Lind, copy this. "Captain Nick Succorso to Amnion warship *Calm Horizons*. I have regained command of my ship. I regret that the satisfaction of your requirements was prevented by mutinous action among my subordinates. However, I am unwilling to decelerate. My own requirements were not satisfied. Gap drive damage necessitates urgent arrival at Thanatos Minor. Because of the nature of our damage, the satisfaction of your requirements is no longer compelling."' Carefully he refrained from accusing the Amnion of cheating. '"We will alter course to avoid collision." Send it.

'Pastille, this is your chance to prove you've got a right to be such a smartass. I want a one degree correction. And I want it *soft*. Less than one g. At this speed, that vector will miss them by a wide enough margin.'

'What good will that do?' asked the helm third. 'They'll shift to compensate.'

Calmly Nick returned, 'Did I ask your opinion?'

'No.'

'Then just do it. If you can't calculate your own algorithms, get the computer to figure them for you.

'Tell me as soon as they start to alter course,' he instructed the scan third.

To conceal his irritation or chagrin, Pastille turned to his board.

Instinctively Morn clenched her hands on the edges of the data console and waited for g – for the burst of clarity which would destroy her.

But Pastille was good at his job, when he chose to be. She felt a sudden pressure as her weight tried to sink across the centrifuge of *Captain's Fancy*'s spin; however, it only seemed heavy because it rotated in and out of phase with the ship's internal g. And it was over in a moment. It left her giddy and feverish; but that was relief, not gap-sickness.

'Done,' Pastille reported petulantly.

'You all right, Morn?' asked Nick.

The intent of his question was complex, but its import was simple. She nodded.

Five minutes lag. Ten for a message to go and an answer to come back. No, not that long. *Captain's Fancy* was closing the gap at half the speed of light, not counting the minute decrease in relative speed caused by the course correction. The lag was shrinking fast.

Morn didn't have much time.

'Nick,' she offered tensely, 'what about a bluff?' As her sensation of fever mounted, she began to think that clarity would have been an improvement. She couldn't trust Nick – and the symptoms of withdrawal would only get worse. 'We can tell them we've already beamed a report to Thanatos Minor and human space. If anything else happens to us, the word of how we were betrayed will spread. The only way they can save their reputation for honest trade is by leaving us alone.'

'That might work,' Liete commented thoughtfully.

'Or it might convince them they don't have anything to lose by killing us,' Nick countered. 'If their reputation is already damaged, why not give themselves the satisfaction of blasting us?

'I've got a better idea.'

Again he toggled the intercom. 'Mikka, how do you feel about going EVA at two hundred seventy thousand kps?'

Mikka took a moment to respond; when she did, her tone was non-committal. 'I would rather break my kneecaps. What have you got in mind?'

'Static mines,' he said crisply. 'I want a cloak of them around us – twenty or thirty at least. But if we launch them from targ, Amnion scan might be good enough to read the power-flash. I can't risk that. We need a manual launch.'

'What good will that do?' asked Pastille for the second time. 'If we surround ourselves with static, we'll be blind. We won't see it coming when they hit us.'

Nick shot the helm third a curdling look. Pastille closed his mouth.

If the same question troubled Mikka, she kept it to herself. 'I won't have to go outside,' she answered. 'I can do it from one of the locks. How much dispersion do you want?'

'I don't care about the distance – not at this range. I just want it *slow*. And thin. I don't want to cast a shadow on their scan.'

'When?' the command second asked.

Nick glanced at Malda; when she nodded, he told Mikka, 'They've been primed. Get them ready fast. But don't launch until I tell you.' With a fierce grin, he added, 'Make sure you're secure. I don't want to lose you when we maneuver.'

Snapping off the intercom, he turned back to Pastille.

'If you think I don't know what I'm doing,' he said distinctly, 'you'd better put on a suit and jump ship. We won't miss you.'

Pastille ducked his head. Biting his lips, he murmured bitterly, 'Sorry, Nick. It won't happen again.'

'Just for the record,' Nick continued in a snarl, 'how do you suppose that fucker's targ is going to handle our velocity? They're too far away for real-time tracking. If they want to hit us, they'll have to hypothesize our position. I intend to make that difficult.'

Morn wasn't listening. Her throat kept getting drier, and she had more and more trouble breathing. All she cared about was how the Amnion would respond to his message.

Which one of their requirements were they determined to satisfy?

'Nick, they've shifted,' Allum reported from scan.

Morn reached for the data from scan so that she could plot it; but Pastille was faster – probably trying to redeem himself. Quicker than she could work, with her eyes dazzled by random neural blasts and her fingers going numb, he processed the information. Then he barked, 'Intercept course. If we stay on this heading, they'll cross our line just in time for impact.' He hesitated, then asserted, 'We've gained about two minutes.'

Lind's voice caught as he said, 'Message coming in.'

'Audio,' Nick instructed.

'Amnion defensive *Calm Horizons* to human Captain Nick Succorso.' Decreasing distance had marginally improved reception from the warship. 'You are required to decelerate. This is mandatory. If you do not comply, you will be destroyed.

'Your speed makes communication difficult. Therefore negotiation is not feasible. You state that gap drive damage causes the satisfaction of Amnion requirements to be "no longer compelling." This statement is unclear. You transgress Amnion space. Therefore all Amnion requirements are "compelling." Speculation suggests that you consider the Amnion culpable for gap drive damage. Very well. You are considered culpable for the failure of Amnion efforts to resolve uncertainty concerning your identity. If you accuse the Amnion, you will be accused in turn. The Amnion accusation predates yours.

'If you wish to effect repairs and depart Amnion space safely, you must deliver the human offspring, Davies Hyland, as agreed.'

In recognition and horror, Morn hissed, 'Nick, you can't!'

He silenced her with a slash of his hand.

Deaf to her protest, the impersonal voice went on, 'The "mutinous action" of your subordinates has postponed this requirement, not canceled it. You will concede him as recompense for safe conduct from Amnion space – and for Amnion credit which you have obtained by culpable means. To accomplish this, you must decelerate.

'You are instructed to match velocity with Amnion defensive *Calm Horizons*. When you have done so, you will transfer the human offspring, Davies Hyland. Then you will be escorted to Thanatos Minor – or to the borders of human space, if you prefer.'

Nick, no.

The alien voice continued implacably, 'Unless Amnion requirements are satisfied, you will be destroyed. No reply or protest will be heeded. Only deceleration is acceptable.'

'Lag!' Nick demanded as soon as the transmission stopped. 'What's the lag?'

Lind was prompt. 'Nine minutes there and back, give or take. They heard us in five. We got their answer in four.'

'So they've been committed to their new course for at least four minutes?'

'Right,' Allum and Pastille said in unison.

'Lind, copy this.' Nick grinned savagely. '"Captain Nick Succorso to Amnion warship *Calm Horizons*. Get a horse." Send it.'

Morn sat staring at him, as light-headed as if she were about to pass out.

He hit the intercom. 'Mikka, you ready?'

'Standing by,' she answered.

'Don't launch yet. Secure for maneuvers.'

At once he faced Pastille again. 'All right, ace. Do it again. *Gentle* course correction, no more than one g. Put us back on a straight line for Thanatos Minor.'

'But they'll just –' the helm third began. Morn could see him sweating in his whiskers.

'"Slow brisance thrust,"' snorted Malda. 'Get it through your head.' She may have been trying to spare Pastille Nick's ire. 'Even if they can accelerate forever, they do it slowly.'

'We're using their first course correction against them.' Nick's tone was casual, but the look in his eyes suggested that Pastille wouldn't live much longer. 'Their own inertia will prevent them from being able to intercept us.

'Are you *satisfied*' – he made the word sound Amnion – 'or do you want to be relieved?'

In other words, Morn thought dumbly as Pastille worked, the only way *Calm Horizons* could stop *Captain's Fancy* was with a long-range broadside.

Nick had set that up. He'd forced the Amnion into a position where their only choice was to fire. And their target was moving at an unprecedented speed.

He had no intention of surrendering Davies.

For some reason, she couldn't breathe. When the course correction hit, she nearly flopped out of her seat, not because the g was hard, but because her head was already reeling.

'Done,' Pastille said for the second time, sounding scared.

Through the intercom, Nick told Mikka, 'Now!'

Almost immediately she replied, 'They're launched. Give me twenty seconds to seal the lock.'

'Do it,' he said, and clicked her off.

Then he addressed the bridge. 'Now we're committed. It's too late to back down. If anybody screws up, we're all fried. Morn, figure out how much time that fucker needs to get in firing position. Once they see us shift, they'll know they can't catch us. I want you to calculate their best shot at us.

'Allum, tell me the exact instant you see them start shifting themselves.

'Pastille, when I give the word, I want straight one-g braking thrust. No more than that. I want it for exactly ten seconds. Then cut it.

'Malda, the instant those ten seconds are up, fire the static mines.

'Morn?'

Morn had difficulty pushing herself upright. She tried to say, 'I'm all right,' but the words didn't make any sound. Adrenaline seemed to go off in her head like small suns, distorting her vision, cramping her lungs. Withdrawal— Dependent on artificial control, her synapses had apparently forgotten how to manage themselves. She couldn't tell the difference between her readouts and her nightmares

her father or her son begging

Morn, save us.

Oh, sure. How could she do that? She couldn't even save herself. She was being torn down to her subatomic particles, dispersed by betrayal into the immedicable gap between her addiction and her mortality.

'*Morn!*' Nick yelled in sudden alarm. '*Don't touch that board!*'

She wasn't gap-sick; but he reached her before she had a chance to say so. He caught hold of her wrists, jerked them away from the console, shoved her back in her seat.

At the same time Liete Corregio said stolidly, 'It's up to you, Pastille. Show us you're worth having around. Calculate what that warship has to do to get their best shot at us. If you can pull it off, I'll ask Nick to forgive you.'

'I'm all right,' Morn whispered into Nick's strained face.

'No, you're not,' he retorted.

Too light-headed and wracked to lie, she murmured, 'It's not gap-sickness. It's withdrawal.'

You think I've played dirty with you. What do you think I've done with myself?

'I can do my job,' she croaked past her thick tongue.

'The hell you can.'

All she could see was the pale blur of Nick's face.

'Four minutes.' She snagged the number out of her whirling head. 'They need four minutes.'

Pastille was talking in the background. 'Here's a guess. They'll see our shift three and a half minutes after we did it. They'll need five minutes to haul that tub around into position.'

'Four,' Morn insisted, 'if their computers are better than ours.'

'They're better,' Nick said out of the blur.

'All right, four,' Pastille put in. 'A broadside will take only another minute to hit us. We'll be that close. Say eight and a half minutes from our course correction. That's all approximate. I can do a first-order hypothetical countdown to improve the guess.'

'I can do it.' Morn fought to focus her eyes. 'Let me do my job.'

Nick held her hard, as if he were trying to estimate her condition by the tension in her arms. Then, abruptly, he leaned close to her, put his cheek to hers. 'You bitch,' he breathed against her ear. 'It's nice to see *you* suffering for a change.'

Dropping her wrists, he walked back around the bridge to stand beside Liete at the command Station.

Morn braced herself on the sides of the console and tried to find the still place in the center of her spinning mind.

A first-order hypothetical countdown. An estimate of the moment when *Calm Horizons* would fire – an estimate in which the only allowed variable was time-dilation. *Captain's Fancy*'s computers had been working for at least a day now to gauge that variable. She ought to be able to run a countdown that was reasonably accurate.

If she could think.

But 'reasonably accurate' wouldn't be good enough. She had to do better than that.

469

She couldn't think. Whenever she tried, anxiety slammed through her, and her vision jolted out of focus.

She didn't need to think. Somewhere in her computer were programs that could think for her. All she had to do was use them.

Morn, save us.

Utter anguish.

Hoping to counteract the phosphene dance, she rubbed her eyes roughly. Then she began calling data to her board.

Start the countdown from the moment of course correction: anchor everything on that instant. How much time was left? Seven minutes? Six? She could check, but she didn't bother. Watching her life slip away would only increase her panic.

The speed of light: that was constant. Take as constant everything *Captain's Fancy* knew about Amnion warships in general; about *Calm Horizons* in particular. Take as constant the decision to destroy *Captain's Fancy* – and the need for the best obtainable angle of fire. And time-dilation itself was constant: the two ships' respective abilities to cope with it were the only true variables. Treat them as one.

Muster the data. Initiate the calculations.

Hit all the right keys.

Please.

'Got it,' she said, although she wasn't sure she spoke loud enough for anyone to hear her. 'It's on the screen. It might not run steadily. I've put in an automatic self-test and correction. The computer will estimate the accuracy of its own time-dilation compensations. Then it'll adjust the countdown.'

All her joints had begun to ache. The sensation of fever was growing stronger, and her head throbbed. She needed water, but didn't have the strength to ask for it. She closed her eyes to give herself a moment's rest.

Like a voice in a dream, she heard Liete say, 'Better check it, Pastille.'

Almost immediately the helm third responded, 'It looks right. I don't know how she does it. The last time I went through withdrawal, I couldn't find my head with both hands. That "self-test and correction" is a great idea.'

Involuntarily Morn went to sleep—

— and thrashed awake again as if someone had set a stun-prod to her chest. When she squeezed her sight clear enough to see the screens, she found that the moment she'd predicted for *Calm Horizons* to fire had almost come. If she were right, the broadside would be on its way in ninety seconds.

One hundred fifty seconds to destruction.

Super-light proton fire was light-constant; as fast as scan. *Captain's Fancy* would get no warning before the barrage arrived.

Pastille and Malda hunched over their boards; Allum scrutinized his scan readouts. Everyone else studied the screens. But nobody had anything to do. Except wait.

As they watched, the computer's self-correction program took the countdown ahead by fifteen seconds.

Without shifting his gaze, Nick said, 'Pastille, I hope you're ready.'

'If I get any readier,' the helm third muttered thinly, 'I'll pass out.'

'Malda?' Nick asked.

The targ first jerked a nod.

'Isn't this fun?' Nick sounded suddenly happy. 'If we aren't going to survive, we won't know it until we're already dead.'

One minute forty seconds.

Nick, Morn said. Let me talk to Davies. Let me say good-bye. But her dry throat locked the words inside her.

The countdown kicked ahead another eight seconds.

'On my word, Pastille,' Nick warned. '*Exactly* on my word.

'Malda, you're on your own.

'Have you noticed,' he remarked conversationally, 'that every time the countdown shifts, it gets shorter? Never longer. Makes you wonder, doesn't it? Maybe our figures are too generous. Maybe we're closer to dying than we think.'

One minute ten.

Morn had the impression that she'd given up breathing. It didn't seem worth the effort. For one clear moment she could say honestly that it made no difference to her whether she lived or died. The Amnion were welcome to whatever remained after the broadside hit.

There were still twenty seconds left on the screen when Nick said like the crack of a whip, '*Now.*'

Pastille hit braking thrust so fast that Morn sprawled onto her console.

The static mines swept ahead, taking *Captain's Fancy*'s place in the warship's projections.

Ten.

Nine.

The new g wasn't much; Morn knew that. It felt strong because it pulled her at right angles to the ship's gravity; but it wasn't heavy. Surely it wasn't heavy enough to make her sick. And yet she couldn't lift her head off the board.

Eight.

Seven.

Six.

Complex g and zone-implant addiction withdrawal. Together they were too much for her. She felt herself spreading out and away, ahead into the dark; riding a flight of primed static mines. When they went off, her brain would burst.

Her mother had died like this.

Five.

Four.

Three.

Nothing was clear now. She must have been breathing: otherwise she would have lost consciousness. But she couldn't remember doing it. Maybe gap-sickness was preferable after all. Her life was out of her hands. It would have been nice if she could have chosen her own death.

Two.

One.

Malda set off the mines.

At once discernible space disappeared in a blast of electronic chaos.

Only a heartbeat or two later – seven or eight seconds ahead of Morn's projection – a barrage ripped through the heart of the static. If *Captain's Fancy* had been hit, the blast would have stripped her down to her welds and blown her away along the winds of the vacuum. But it never touched her. In fact, blinded by her own mines, she never actually *saw* the Amnion fire. She only knew of its existence because its intensity transcended the static, drove her sensors white and then blank as their circuitry shut down to protect them. She never knew how narrowly she'd been missed.

As Nick had intended, all *Calm Horizons* saw was distortion.

By the time the Amnion sensors penetrated the static accurately enough to determine that *Captain's Fancy* hadn't been hit, his ship was beyond reach.

'Well,' he announced in a tone of grim satisfaction, 'now we know they're serious.'

Serious, Morn thought with her head resting on her board. Serious enough to destroy *Captain's Fancy* rather than let Davies get away. She probably ought to sit up, but she didn't really want to. Thanatos Minor was in Amnion space.

Apparently without transition, Nick stood in front of her. 'Come on.' He began unbelting her from her seat. 'You're useless here. I'll take you back to your cabin.'

She found herself clinging to his neck. For some reason, she couldn't tell which direction was up.

When they reached her cabin, he set her down on the bunk and took out her black box.

'I don't like doing this.' He was flushed with his success against *Calm Horizons*, and he wanted to take it out on her. 'I would rather watch you go through withdrawal for a while. But I can't risk it. You might go crazy. And my only alternative is to take you to sickbay for a dose of cat. That won't work because I don't know yet how long I'll want to keep you helpless. The sickbay computer won't accept a command to dope you indefinitely. So this is my only choice. Let's see how you like being null-wave for a while.'

As he reached for the buttons, a recognition of her own plight reached her through the static of withdrawal in her head. She croaked weakly, 'Wait.'

'Why?' he growled.

Survive. If she let him kill her – or drive her into gap-sickness – she would never be able to help Davies. The Amnion weren't likely to give up now. She fought to speak clearly.

'It's a short-range transmitter. You can't turn it on and take it with you. It'll lose effect.' Please understand. Please. You'll kill me. 'If you don't leave it here, it won't work.'

That made sense. Surely he could see that she was telling the truth?

'Tough shit,' he rasped as he keyed the function that was designed to render her catatonic.

Closing her eyes, she slumped inert.

When she was limp, he stretched her out on the bunk and sealed her into its g-sheath so that she wouldn't be battered to death when *Captain's Fancy* began braking. Although he probably couldn't spare the time, he stood over her for a moment, studying her. Then he breathed like a benediction, 'Fucking bitch.'

But he must have believed her. As he left the cabin, he put her zone-implant control away in one of the lockers.

Trembling, she forced herself out of the sheath and struggled to her feet.

This was her chance.

No, it wasn't.

She had to let him think that his control over her was complete. Whatever it cost her, she needed to preserve her last secret – needed to conceal the fact that she'd disabled this function. No matter how much she craved the power to possess herself again, she had to refuse it.

So she didn't try to hide the black box for herself. And she didn't try to sneak out of her cabin. There was heavy g ahead. She couldn't know when it would begin, or how long it would last. And she needed rest in the same way that her addiction needed a fix. Without much trouble, she found her zone-implant control. In despair, she tapped the buttons that would put her to sleep.

She didn't set the timer.

Replacing the box where Nick had left it, she dove back to her bunk and managed to reseal the g-sheath before her mind disappeared into the involuntary dark.

'The United Mining Companics Pre-Emptive Enabling Act for Security', known for convenience as 'The Preempt Act', was passed over the strenuous objections of libertarian politicians on Earth and against the opposition of the local administrations of most human Stations: Terminus; Sagittarius Unlimited; SpaceLab Annexe; New Outreach; Valdor Industrial; but, notably, *not* Com-Mine. Behind its legalisms and jargon, the thrust of the Act was plain: it gave the UMC Police jurisdiction and authority over local Security everywhere except on Earth itself.

Prior to the Act, local Security was required to give cooperation, information, and support to UMCP officers and agents whenever they were on Station; but UMCP 'turf' only began at the perimeters of Station control space – that is, at the effective limits of Station fire. The rationale for this restriction had to do with the UMCP Articles of Mission. According to the Articles, the UMCP existed to 'combat piracy and secure the defense of space.' Nothing more.

For some time, however, interpretation of the Articles had been predicated, not upon 'nothing more,' but upon 'nothing less.' In particular, no intelligent effort could be made to 'combat piracy' without confronting the problem of the Amnion. As the personnel, resources, and determination of the UMCP expanded, so did its mission, which soon came to include the defense of human space against any crime.

Once this interpretation of the Articles became current, its extension in the Preempt Act grew to seem more and more inevitable. In order to 'combat piracy and secure the defense of space,' the UMCP naturally needed to reach inward (toward human illegals, most of whom perforce based their operations on one Station or another) as well as outward (toward the Amnion). Within the hierarchy of the UMCP, passage of the Preempt Act was a major priority for a number of years.

Several factors conspired to make the Preempt Act seem necessary despite opposition to it. Increasing dread of the Amnion was one; the relative intransigence of the piracy problem was another. And to those was finally added doubt about the integrity of Security on particular Stations. The Thermopyle case on Com-Mine Station, in particular, while thankfully benign in its immediate consequences, was disturbing in its implications. There Security had apparently conspired with one suspected illegal to trap another – and had done so in a way which could have proved disastrous for Com-Mine itself. That the operation had not, in fact, proved disastrous was merely fortunate: that Com-Mine Security was actively involved with illegals, to the risk of its own Station, was irresponsible and dangerous.

Additionally, of course, Station Security was so far away, so completely cut off from any communication which was not relayed by ship – in short, so difficult to control – that it was easily distrusted.

Faced with a choice between the vigor and clarity of the UMCP on the one hand and the problematical reliability of Station Security on the other, a majority of the Governing Council for Earth and Space eventually accepted the United Mining Companies Directors' recommendation to pass the Preempt Act.

In some circles, the Preempt Act was considered minor legislation, just another part of the United Mining Companies' ongoing efforts to secure the safety of space on behalf of Earth and their own interests.

In others, it was viewed as the capstone of Warden Dios' and the UMCP's quest for power. The passage of the Preempt Act made the UMCP's hegemony complete.

CHAPTER 19

She awoke as if she were dying.

The transition moved her from oblivion to sickness and mortality; to terminal weakness and a sense of discomfort as profound as disease. In the dark nothing existed except her zone-implant and the long unconscionable seethe of her dreams. But as she was dredged toward consciousness, frailty and despair rose as if they were being created for the first time. She was urgently thirsty, wan from hunger – and too stunned, poleaxed by sleep, to know what those things meant. The transition itself was hurtful, a disruption of the imposed neural order of her brain and body. Her limbs and joints felt brutalized by strain. A clammy sensation clung to her skin, as if she were lying in blood. And she stank – a particular reek, nauseous and sweet, which reminded her of Angus and corpses.

She wanted to finish dying. She wanted to get it over with.

'Come on,' Nick urged as if he were anxious for her. 'I turned it off. The effects aren't supposed to be permanent. You didn't tell me this thing could paralyze you permanently. You can't get away from me like this.'

Of course. He thought she was blank with catatonia, not immersed in sleep. He expected to see a difference in her as soon as he switched off her black box.

Even now, while she was dying, she couldn't afford to let him guess the truth. She forced her eyes open. 'That's better,' he remarked.

Her eyes refused to focus. They were too sore, too dry. But blinking didn't help. Her eyelids rubbed up and down like sandpaper. The pain in her throat – or the smell – made her feel like gagging. Her mouth stretched wide, but she was too weak to retch; too empty.

'You stink,' Nick said like Angus. Exactly like Angus.

He had her zone-implant control.

A thin sigh that should have been a wail scraped past her tongue.

'You've been out too long. You're thirsty and hungry, but what you need first is a shower. You smell like you've got five kilos of shit in your suit.

'Here. I'll help you get up.'

She felt the g-sheath loosen and pull away as he unsealed it. Then he took hold of her arms and pried her upright.

The shock of transition would have been strong enough to unhinge her mind, if she'd been strong enough to feel its full force. Fortunately he was helping her in more ways than one. His support got her to her feet – and when he said 'shower,' she heard 'water.' Her need for water galvanized her, despite her weakness. Past the blur of his face and the blur of the walls, she fumbled toward the san.

Without touching her, he pulled open the seals of her shipsuit. Then he pushed her into the san and turned on the jets.

Water.

She gulped at it, swallowed as much as she could get into her mouth. The jets sprayed life at her. It filled her eyes, eased her throat; her body seemed to absorb it before it reached her stomach. After a moment so much of it had gone into her shipsuit that its weight pulled the suit off her shoulders. The stained, rank fabric clustered around her boots. Water ran inside her and out; it washed her flesh and her nerves. In a short time it restored her enough to realize that if she drank too much at once she might make herself sick.

Nick had come back. He'd switched off her zone-implant control, thinking he was bringing her out of catatonia.

Captain's Fancy must be done decelerating. She wouldn't have been asleep long enough to get this thirsty and hungry, to foul herself this badly, if the ship hadn't finished braking.

Or something else had happened.

She needed to be awake. She needed food and strength.

Nick's voice reached her through the spray. 'Don't go to sleep in there. I'm in no mood to wait around.'

He didn't sound impatient.

Leaning against the wall, she bent down and removed her boots, shoved her shipsuit off her ankles. Transitional shivers ran through her like a chill: she raised the temperature of the water to warm them away.

An automatic buzzer warned her that the san's suction drain was blocked. To clear it, she pushed her sodden shipsuit out of the way. She would have liked to wash her hair, scrub herself thoroughly; but Nick was waiting for her, and she had no idea why. Although she was barely able to stand, she turned off the water and stepped out of the cubicle.

There was a clean shipsuit ready. Nick must have gotten it out of the locker for her.

Why was he doing all this?

She dried herself weakly, put on the shipsuit, and went back into the main room of her cabin to face him.

She found him in a state of demented calm.

His eyes met hers unsteadily and flicked away; roved the cabin; returned to her body and the outlines of her face. Traces of passion licked and faded through his scars. At intervals, a muscle twitched in his cheek, pulling his lip back from his teeth. And yet his stance, the way he held his arms, even the angle of his neck suggested a deep repose, as if he were at peace with himself to an extent she'd never seen before.

As if he'd achieved a profound victory – or accepted a complete defeat.

'That's better,' he said while she stared at him, trying to guess where she stood with him. 'Now for some food.'

A tight, calm nod indicated a tray on a table beside him.

'Sit,' he continued. 'Eat. I'll tell you what's been happening.'

Why are you *doing* this?

She couldn't imagine what his intentions were. Nevertheless he was right: she needed food. The smell of coffee and *Captain's Fancy*'s version of hot oatmeal drew her. For the time being, at least, she'd been rescued from the ordeal of withdrawal; but that relief only left her more hungry. Like a convict taking her last meal in the presence of her executioner, she sat down to eat.

Nick stood over her while she tasted the oatmeal, sipped the coffee.

Abruptly he said, 'You can probably guess we're done decelerating. If you were the kind of woman who shits in her suit, you would have done it a long time ago.' His voice was like his demeanor: calm, at peace, but with flickers of passion running through it like distant lightning. 'The Bill likes ships to come into Thanatos Minor slowly, so we're doing that.

At this speed, we're roughly twenty-four hours out of dock.

'That much braking was hard on all of us. By the time we got past *Calm Horizons*, we'd missed our chance for a leisurely deceleration. I couldn't spare the time to take care of you until we'd achieved approach velocity – and established our "credentials" with the Bill. I mean identity, intentions, and credit. He's perfectly capable of calling in the Amnion, if he feels threatened enough, but he's got plenty of other ways to defend himself when he needs them.'

Morn couldn't meet the strange unsteadiness of his gaze. She concentrated on her food while he talked. The oatmeal had been liberally sweetened. Despite her need for calories, she ate slowly so that she wouldn't overburden her abused digestion.

'For one thing, he's got a real arsenal on that bloody rock. And there are other ships in. I mean, aside from the Bill's. Anybody who does business with him will fight for him. He insists on that – but those ships would do it anyway. Illegals like that need him too much not to defend him.

'You've never been to Thanatos Minor. You're in for a surprise. It's practically civilized. The Bill must have five thousand people there, all working for him.'

Into her coffee, Morn murmured, 'All working for the Amnion.'

'No.' Nick sounded amused rather than offended. 'They're just taking advantage of what the Amnion are willing to pay. "War profiteering" is an old and honorable profession. It isn't their fault it only works one way. It isn't their fault the Amnion don't have any illegals who want to do the same kind of business with human space.'

Without transition, as if he were still on the same subject, he said, 'Morn, I want you to make love to me. No zone-implants, no lies. I want you to show me what you can do when you aren't cheating.'

Alarm jolted through her so hard that she dropped her spoon. It clattered on the floor, as loud as if it were breaking.

'If you can make me believe you want me enough,' he finished, 'I'll let you go.'

Oh, shit. So *that* was it. For an instant she shivered on the verge of weeping.

Then her dismay turned to fury.

Raising her head so that he could see the darkness in her eyes, she

480

said, 'In that case, you'd better switch me off right now. You'd better kill me. The idea of touching you makes me want to puke.'

For some reason, her vehemence didn't disturb his calm. His gaze met hers and skittered away; returned; fled again. His cheek twitched, and brief hints of blood stained his pale scars. Yet his physical repose remained complete. His smile was soft, almost forgiving. Triumph or defeat had carried him past his doubts.

'Then I'll offer you something else,' he said peacefully. 'If you'll make love to me with your whole heart – just once, so I can find out what it's like – I'll let you talk to your brat. Hell, I'll let you *see* him. You can spend the rest of the day just holding his hand.'

Davies! she thought in a storm of suppressed dismay and grief. A chance to talk to him, see him – a chance to do what she could to keep him from going mad – a chance to defend the legacy of her father.

Straight at Nick, she said, 'I guess I underestimated you. You're starting to make Angus Thermopyle' – suddenly that name was easy to say – 'look pretty good.'

For an instant the small spasm in his cheek turned his smile into a snarl. His tranquillity held, however.

'I guess you did,' he remarked as if that were the friendliest thing he'd ever said to her. With a slow, relaxed movement, he took her black box out of his pocket. 'Oh, don't worry,' he reassured her involuntary chagrin, 'I'm not going to use this. I don't want to take the chance of turning you into a null-wave transmitter. And I'm not going to force you to have sex with me. I've never needed a woman that badly. This' – he gestured with the control – 'is just a precaution. Now that I know how you feel about me – how much you *hate* me' – his smile was easy, unthreatening – 'I want to be sure I can protect myself.'

Without shifting his feet, he stretched out his arm and toggled her intercom. 'Mikka?'

Mikka's voice came from the speaker. 'Here.'

No hint of malice showed in his tone as he said, 'Give Morn a closed channel to our other guest. They need a chance to talk privately. She's worried about him. And that poor sonofabitch is probably worried about himself.'

'Right,' Mikka answered.

When he left the intercom, its status lights indicated that it was still on.

Strolling casually, he went to the bunk. With the pillow propped to support his back, he sat down, rested his legs in front of him. He looked comfortable enough to take a nap. Smiling at Morn's astonishment, he pointed her toward the intercom with his free hand.

She had trouble clearing her throat. Coffee, food, and water weren't enough: she wasn't ready for this. Swallowing convulsively, she asked, 'What's the catch?'

'If you weren't so busy underestimating me,' he replied, at peace with himself, 'I would say, you are. But, under the circumstances, you can't afford to worry about things like that.'

Urging her, he pointed at the intercom again.

'Morn?' Davies asked anxiously. 'Are you there? What's going on? Is he going to let you talk to me?'

Paralyzed by fear, Morn sat and stared horror at Nick. She couldn't speak – couldn't think. She wanted to fling herself at him, try to kill him; not because she believed she could succeed, but because when he defended himself her despair and dread would come to an end.

Nick raised his voice. 'Davies, this is Nick. Morn is with me – we're in her cabin. I've given her permission to talk to you. It's a private channel. Nobody can hear you, except me. But I guess she doesn't trust me.

'Maybe you can reason with her.'

Davies—

'Morn,' Davies said immediately, 'don't trust him. He's up to something.' That was his father talking. 'Maybe there's something he needs to know, something he thinks you might tell me. Don't say anything unless you're sure it's safe.'

He sounded certain, as sure of his judgments as a kid. But he was also lost and lonely, as only a kid could be. As if he couldn't help himself, he asked, 'Morn, are you all right? You're all I've got. Don't let anything happen to you.'

Oh, my son. It's already happened. Can't you tell that? I just don't know what it is.

Nick went on smiling. 'Did you have any trouble during deceleration?

I don't know if Liete remembered to warn you. You could have been banged up pretty badly.'

'Nobody warned me,' Davies snapped back. 'You probably told her not to. If I slammed up against a bulk-head and broke my skull, that would solve a lot of problems for you. But I knew something was going to happen when you turned off internal g.'

Nothing disturbed Nick. 'Good for you.

'How's the state of your memory?' he continued pleasantly. His scars gave little glimpses of malice, which his tone denied. 'Have you been able to get past any of the blank spots? Are you starting to remember your father at all?'

'Nick Succorso' – Davies' intensity made the speaker crackle – 'you're garbage. You're illegal, and everything you do stinks. I don't have anything to say to you. If you want to ask me questions, come do it in person. Take your chances.' Precocious with an adult's mind in a teenager's body, he rasped, 'Take them like a man.'

'No,' Morn breathed, too softly for her son to hear her, 'don't provoke him. Don't give him an excuse. All he needs is an excuse.'

Nick's cheek twitched. 'You don't mean that, Davies. You think you do, but you don't. You're alone. You've got a mind you don't understand – and a body your mind doesn't fit. You need to know who you are. Where you come from. What you're made out of. That means you need to know about your father.

'You've probably got more of your mother in you than you can use, but you're your father's son, too. You need to know about Angus Thermo-pile. There's a lot I can tell you. I've learned a lot about him myself in the past few days.'

'Stop,' Morn hissed at Nick. 'Stop.'

'Did you know he's an illegal – one of the worst? Sure you did. You can probably remember that part. He's a pirate and a butcher and a petty thief. Right now, he's serving a life sentence in Com-Mine Station lockup for stealing supplies. They would have given him the death penalty, but they couldn't prove enough of his crimes.

'That may not make you think very highly of your mother. She's a cop. She's supposed to arrest men like Captain Thermo-pile, or kill them, not fuck them until she gets pregnant.

'But it wasn't like that. Your mother didn't start fucking illegals until she met me. Before that, she was actually quite innocent. You see, Captain Thermo-pile gave her a zone-implant. I'll bet you can remember what that is. After she demolished *Starmaster*, he rescued her from the wreckage. But she was a cop, so he couldn't trust her. He gave her a zone-implant to keep her under control. That's how he got her pregnant.

'It's a pathetic story. He turned her on until she would have been willing to suck her insides out with a vacuum hose, and then he fucked her senseless. For weeks, he made her do everything he'd ever dreamed a woman could do.

'That's your father, Davies. That's the kind of man you are.'

'Morn?' Davies said as if he were begging. 'Morn?'

Morn surged to her feet. 'I said, stop it!' Dismay filled her chest, crowded her throat: she could hardly breathe. 'That's enough!'

Nick studied her dispassionately while he went on talking to her son.

'But here's the interesting part of the story. Giving somebody a zone-implant – an "unauthorized" zone implant – is a capital crime. Why wasn't your father convicted? If she had a zone-implant, he must have had a zone-implant control. Why wasn't it found on him when he was arrested? How could he keep her from turning against him, if he didn't have her under control?'

'Nick!'

He overrode her. His smile was sweet with affection.

'The answer is, she'd learned to like it. He'd degraded her so much that she fell in love with it. She *wanted* it, Davies. Eventually she wanted it so much that he could trust her with her zone-implant control. It wasn't found on him because he'd already given it to her. She loved using it on herself.

'So what did she do with it when he was arrested? She didn't turn it over to Com-Mine Security like a good little cop. They would have removed her zone-implant – and your father would have been executed. She couldn't do that.

'Oh, I don't think she cared what happened to him. But she was a zone-implant junkie. She couldn't let them take it away from her. So she hid the control and escaped with me. Instead of doing *anything* a cop should have done, she kept what she loved most.' Still his tone held only peace, no malice. 'She used it to seduce me so that I would rescue her – not from Captain Thermo-pile, but from Com-Mine Security.'

'Morn?' Davies protested.

'All she's done since then,' said Nick, 'is perfect her addiction.'

'Morn?' The intercom gave out hints of anguish.

'Did she tell you she refused to abort you because she wanted to keep you? That isn't strictly true. The only real reason she insisted on keeping you is that she couldn't get an abortion without letting the sickbay test her. It would have recorded her zone-implant. If she'd had an abortion, I would have learned the truth about her.

'That's your mother, Davies. That's the kind of woman you came from.'

'Davies!' Morn cried. 'He's lying! He's got it wrong!'

She did her best to shout, *Of course I didn't want him to know about my zone-implant! That was the only way I could keep myself alive*. With all her strength, she struggled to tell her son, *But that's not why I refused an abortion! I refused because I **wanted** you!*

Unfortunately none of those words came out. As soon as she started to say them, Nick touched one of the buttons on her black box; and pain as hot as a welding laser seared through all her nerves simultaneously. The only sound she managed was a thin shriek as she fell writhing to the floor.

'Morn!' Davies bellowed. '*Morn!*'

Smiling, Nick scrutinized the zone-implant control. After a moment he found the function which allowed him to adjust the intensity of the emissions. Slowly he reduced her imposed agony to a simmer – hot enough to make her squirm and twist and whimper, not so hot that she couldn't hear Davies calling for her.

'All right,' Nick articulated. Through a haze of pain, Morn saw that his eyes were underlined with darkness. His tone made Davies go suddenly silent. 'I want you both to listen. When you hear what I have to say, I'm sure you'll agree it's important.

'There's one little detail about our situation that I neglected to mention. Must have slipped my mind.' His smile had become a predatory grin. 'As I told you, we're about a day out from Thanatos Minor. At this velocity, that's an easy distance for scan and communications. What I didn't tell you is that there's an Amnion warship almost exactly halfway between us and dock. *Tranquil Hegemony*. And they want the same thing *Calm Horizons* wanted. They want Davies.'

Morn gasped and groaned, but couldn't force words through her excruciation.

The sound of hoarse breathing, strained and hollow, came from the intercom.

'Superficially,' Nick explained as if he were chatting casually in the galley, 'it's a complex problem for all of us. On the one hand, they want Davies. On the other, they don't really want to fight for him. Not with the whole of Billingate watching. I'm sure they're sure they're in the right – but they know enough about ordinary human distrust to realize that none of their justifications will repair the damage to their credibility. And they can't be entirely sure they'll win in a fight. At these velocities, we can maneuver rings around a lumbering tub like that. We might cripple them. We might even destroy them.

'And if we couldn't do it alone, we might get help. It's one thing to do business with the Amnion. It's something else entirely to sit still and watch them blast a human ship. Some unexpected allies might turn up on our side.

'They don't want a fight if they can avoid it.'

Through her teeth, Morn gritted, 'You bastard. You fucking—'

Nick tapped buttons on the zone-implant control.

She didn't have time to flinch. Before she could expect more pain, a wave of cold washed through her. At once she began to shiver so hard that she lost her voice. Her temperature plummeted, plunging her into hypothermia. Her efforts to curse Nick came out as an unintelligible judder.

'As for us,' he said comfortably, 'well, I think I can beat them. And I *know* I can outmaneuver them. Are you listening, Davies? This is *your* life I'm talking about.'

A harsh rasp came from the speaker, but Davies didn't reply.

Nick shrugged. 'There's just one difficulty,' he continued. 'That fucker *Calm Horizons* is coming up behind us as hard as it can go – and I know I can't beat *two* Amnion warships. The best I can hope for is to get out of this part of space on the run. But if I do that – if we get away from here alive – what have I accomplished? We'll be an appalling distance from nowhere, with no gap drive, and no chance for repairs. We'll die slowly instead of quickly, that's all.'

Morn was nearly in shock; yet he didn't let her go. A further experiment with her black box brought her temperature back up. After a few unsuccessful attempts, he managed to take charge of her limbs. Pulling up her arm, he jabbed her fingers into her mouth, forcing her to gag herself.

'Do you think Hashi Lebwohl will send help?' he asked her amiably. '*You* believe that, if you can. *I* think he's cut me off. Before we ever went into forbidden space, he told me I was on my own. By now, he must have figured out that we made an "unauthorized" visit to Enablement. I think he's finally decided I'm more trouble than I'm worth. He hasn't answered any of my transmissions – and I've made them as urgent as I know how.

'As I say, it's a complex problem.

'Superficially.'

Grinning, he watched Morn choke.

'But when you think about it, it's really pretty simple. Because, you see, I don't *want* to keep Davies. I've been trying to get rid of him ever since he was born.

'So that's what I'm going to do.

'I've already thrashed out all the details with *Tranquil Hegemony.* Twelve hours from now, when we're alongside, I'll send Davies to them in an ejection pod. Then they'll let us dock in peace. In fact, they've agreed that both warships will go back to Enablement, just to demonstrate their good faith. We'll be able to get our repairs without having the Amnion breathing down our necks.

'It's the best solution all the way around.'

Through his calm, he sounded proud of himself.

Involuntarily Morn retched oatmeal and coffee past her fingers.

'What a shame,' he murmured happily. 'Just a minute ago you were clean. You almost looked good enough for some man to want – if he were desperate enough. But now' – he chuckled – 'I'm afraid all you look is bulimic.'

'What are you doing?' The flat tone of the speaker couldn't conceal Davies' distress. 'What are you doing to her?'

Abruptly Nick swung his legs off the bunk. He stood up and stepped over Morn to the intercom. His scars gleamed like black gashes across his cheeks as he snarled, 'You little shit, it's called revenge.'

Davies began to howl.

Then his voice vanished as Nick toggled the switch.

'Mikka,' Nick said.

Impartially grim, the command second answered, 'Here.'

'I'm afraid things have gotten out of hand. I had to tell her about Davies. She isn't taking it well. You'd better close the channel to his cabin. No, disconnect his intercom completely. If they talk, they'll just make each other worse.'

Davies' howl echoed in Morn's mind as if she could still hear it.

'Anything else?' Mikka asked.

Nick grinned. 'Just make damn sure she can't get out of here. I'll deal with her when I've got time.'

He clicked off the intercom.

Nearly strangling on her own vomit, Morn watched as he opened the door and closed it behind him without canceling the emissions from her black box.

She wasn't able to drag her fingers out of her mouth until he carried her zone-implant control beyond its transmission range.

CHAPTER 20

Gagging to clear her throat, Morn fought her way to her hands and knees. One of her hands braced itself in a puddle of oatmeal, but she ignored the sticky mess. She needed air, needed to breathe; yet every inhalation seemed to suck acid and vomit into her lungs. Transition wrenched through her. Anoxia dimmed her vision to a phosphene swirl. The cabin spun around her as if *Captain's Fancy* had lost internal g.

Breathe.

Acid cut into her esophagus, chewed on her vocal cords.

Breathe.

Straining her mouth wide, she began to draw air in small gasps.

Davies—

It wasn't bad enough that he was locked up, helpless, that he'd been sold to the Amnion. It wasn't bad enough that he had to face alone a crisis of identity so profound that it could have destroyed anyone. No. That didn't suffice for Nick. To satisfy his old, personal outrage, he'd undermined Davies to the core.

It's called revenge.

All her son had to work with, to use against the threat of madness, was what he could remember: his inherited self. Nick had made those memories, that self, look treacherous. He'd given Davies reason to believe that his worst enemies, the people who had hurt him most, were his mother and father; that his mind itself was a crime against him.

How could he hope to survive that kind of stress? How could she hope that for him? By the time the Amnion got him, they would be the only sanity he knew.

Morn reeled upright on her knees.

Another breath.

Another.

With her stained hand, she smeared vomit across her face, trying to wipe it away. She was insane herself, in the grip of a frantic and surreal clarity which understood everything and revealed nothing. She didn't know what she was going to do until it was already done.

Pulling as much air as possible into her lungs, she stumbled to her feet.

Nick had told Mikka to disconnect Davies' intercom; but he hadn't said anything about this one. And he wouldn't have reached the bridge yet. Surely Morn hadn't knelt in her vomit long enough for him to reach the bridge.

Unsteady and thickheaded, blind to herself, she lurched to the wall and snap-punched the intercom toggle as if she could make the equipment function by force.

Indicators lit: a channel opened.

A background murmur came from the speaker, a sense of depth or ambience too great for the constricted space of the bridge. Somehow she'd reached – or been given – a general channel to the rest of the ship.

Someone wanted her to be heard.

'Listen to me,' she croaked, hoarse with acid and need. 'He's going to give them my *son*.'

Why should they care? Most of them – maybe all of them – already knew what Nick was doing. And she was a cop: she was the enemy. What did she hope to gain? Who wanted to grant her this chance?

She took it without trying to understand. Frantic and clear, she put everything she had left into her voice.

'I know why you're here – some of you. I know why you do this. For some of you, it's just freedom, license. Being illegal gives you more choices, fewer hindrances. You've lost too much, missed too much. Now you can take what you want.'

She didn't know what to say. She was too weak – and had no eloquence. To steady herself, she imagined her voice reaching all the rooms and cabins of the ship, echoing inescapably in the corridors. She imagined herself being heeded.

'Is this what you want? Do you want to turn human beings over to the Amnion? Have you thought about what that means? It means you could be next. This time it's all right to give them my son. Next time it could be all right to give them *you*. Isn't that right, Alba? Pastille? Do you think Nick considers you worth keeping? Are you *sure*? What if he finds somebody on Thanatos Minor who can do your job better – or fucks better – or worships him more?

'Is that what you want?'

Spasms of coughing rose from her damaged throat and esophagus. But she couldn't afford to stop. She had no time: Nick would silence her as soon as he gained the bridge. In her mind, she could see him running to put an end to her appeal.

Weeping at the effort, she continued.

'But some of you have other reasons. You're here because the cops are corrupt – the whole damn UMC is corrupt – and this is the only way you can oppose them. Vector? Sib? Mikka? Can you hear me? The cops *are* corrupt. I didn't know that, but I know it now. I don't like it any more than you do. I became a cop because pirates killed my mother, and I wanted to *fight*. I wanted to fight anything that threatened human life and liberty and security. The things I've learned make me sick.

'But that's no reason to give my son to the Amnion! It doesn't hurt the cops, because they don't care anyway. It just betrays humanity, *all* humanity, you and me and every man or woman or child who's still alive.

'You've all got families. You all came from somewhere – you must have had mothers and fathers, brothers and sisters, relatives and friends. How about them? What would you sell them for? How would you look at yourself in the mirror afterward?

'Don't let him do this.' Until she'd said it, she didn't realize that she was urging mutiny. 'Find some other answer. There's got to be some other answer.'

She had no idea what that might be. In an important sense, Nick wasn't just the Captain of his ship: he was the ship itself. His codes ruled every function; he made all the decisions; his skills kept his people alive. Everyone who heard her was dependent on him.

Anyone who challenged him might end up where Davies was now.

Abruptly the intercom picked up her antagonist.

'I told you she wasn't taking it well,' Nick drawled. He sounded perfectly sure of himself; impervious to her threats. 'You've heard enough to know what I mean. You can cut her off now, Mikka.'

He'd been on the bridge the whole time. He'd been allowing Morn to speak; allowing the ship to hear her in order to prove himself. He was that secure.

She abandoned language and started screaming.

Raw with acid and strain, her visceral howl rang throughout *Captain's Fancy* until the indicators on her intercom went dead.

Because she wasn't done, she continued screaming. But now the walls of her cabin were all that heard her. She didn't stop until her throat gave out.

Then she collapsed in the chair and covered her face with her hands.

Patience.

The part of her that understood everything and revealed nothing didn't explain why. It simply told her: *patience*.

Wait.

Davies wouldn't be ejected to the Amnion for nearly twelve hours. A lot could happen in twelve hours. Entire lives might be won or lost. Hope and ruin could be as quick as gap-sickness.

First things first.

The first thing was to wait.

But not like this. From this position, she couldn't see her intercom.

Without knowing why, she moved the chair so that she had a clear view of the intercom's status indicators. Then, although she stank of hydrochloric acid and undigested oatmeal, and could probably have spared the time to go to the san and wash her face, she sat down again and waited.

Patience.

Every passing second brought the end nearer. The end of her son – and of herself. Nevertheless she was patient.

The sure, surreal part of her knew what it was doing. Nick was too curious about her, too interested in the progress of his revenge, to ignore her. When she'd been waiting, as motionless as catatonia, for an hour or so, the intercom status suddenly turned green.

He wanted to check on her by eavesdropping.

At once she began to whimper and mewl like a dying cat.

The strain of her earlier screams helped her sound broken and pathetic, demented beyond recognition. That was true, wasn't it? As far as she knew, she was telling him the truth.

She kept it up until he switched off the intercom. Then she got to her feet.

Unsteadily she went to the san and picked up every hard object she could find: brushes; the mending kit; dispensers for lotions, depilatories, hair treatments. Back in her chair, she piled her collection on her thighs and resumed waiting.

An hour?

More?

Less?

The advantage of her insane, uncomprehending clarity was that it didn't punish her for the passage of time. It told her to be patient – and it enabled her to obey.

Tranquil Hegemony and Thanatos Minor must have been looming on scan. By now, *Calm Horizons* was surely near enough to take part in whatever happened. She could think about such things, but she couldn't worry about them. Her capacity for worry was gone – buried or burned out. Davies' image was vivid to her, as if she could see every muscle of his face respond to the torment of his thoughts; but it didn't distress her.

Right now – waiting as if she'd been left null by a stun-prod – she was doing everything she could for her son.

Try me, she cackled in the silence of her skull. Try to beat me. I dare you.

What you keep forgetting is that Angus beat me long ago. There's nothing left for you.

He taught me everything I know.

When the intercom came on again, she burst into sobs and began flinging her pile of objects around the cabin, hailing the pickup with dispensers and brushes. Between sobs, she panted, 'Nick! Nick!' as if she'd ruptured her lungs. As soon she ran out of things to throw, she stood up, grabbed the chair, and used it to batter the walls.

'Nick!'

By the time the intercom switched off, she was sobbing with exertion, as well as with mad, unexplained cunning.

But now she was done waiting. It was time to take the next step.

Gasping for air, she staggered into the san.

No, first she needed shipsuits and bedding. She returned to her room, jerked open the lockers, hauled their contents to the floor. With her arms full, she went back to the san.

She jammed a pillow into the suction drain of the shower. She turned on the water and sealed the door.

Almost immediately she heard warning buzzers.

She wadded up a shipsuit and used it to plug the head. With a nail file, she wedged the flushing button so that it couldn't stop.

While a sterile wash full of recycling chemicals pumped into the head and began to overflow, she forced a pair of panties into the drain of the sink and turned on the water there.

The alarms became louder. Inarticulate and impersonal, *Captain's Fancy's* internal systems shouted at her to stop. If she put enough strain on them, the maintenance computer would cut off the supply of water to the entire ship.

Water was only water. A nuisance, nothing more; one small annoyance for Nick Succorso while he was busy with other things.

But he had to wonder what she would do next.

If she thought of water, would she think of fire? That would be another matter entirely. Every ship was vulnerable to fire in some way. Could he be sure that she had nothing in her cabin which would let her start a fire?

Walking through runnels of water from the sink and sterilizing chemicals from the head, she left the san and sat down in the middle of her mess on the floor.

Ignore me, Nick. Ignore me now.

Just try.

He couldn't do it. The part of her that understood knew he couldn't. He wasn't done with her yet. He couldn't take the chance that she would be able to surprise him with something so bizarre that it might kill her. And even if she didn't die, how much pleasure could he get out of torturing someone who'd gone irremediably crazy?

All she had to do was wait until the door swept open and he stood in front of her.

After a time she realized that she was sitting on the floor for a reason: so that he would think she wasn't going to attack him.

The door—

He—

She would have been afraid that she was imagining him, that he wasn't really there; but the expression on his face wasn't one she would have envisioned. It was a look of consternation, almost of shock. Whatever he'd anticipated would happen to her here alone, he hadn't expected this.

Therefore his presence was real. She was clear about that.

'I've been enjoying this,' he said tightly. 'I like listening to you lose your mind.' The dead pallor of his scars contradicted him. 'But it's gone on long enough. You're disturbing my concentration.'

In response, she picked up a depilatory dispenser and hurled it at his head.

He batted it away with one hand. The other plunged into his pocket and came out holding her zone-implant control.

'I didn't want to do this, but I guess I'll have to turn you off. Before you wreck the plumbing.'

Try me.

Deliberately Morn raised her hands and began clawing at the skin of her cheeks.

Try me, you sonofabitch.

In a hurry to prevent her from maiming herself, he pointed her black box at her and thumbed the buttons.

Off balance, she sprawled backward into the stream from the san.

For some reason, he kicked her bare foot. He may have wondered if she would react to the blow. But she didn't. Instead she lay as limp as a woman with a broken neck. Water trickled into the corner of her open mouth.

'I thought you were done hurting me,' he whispered because he knew she couldn't hear him. 'It looks like I was wrong.'

In disgust, he tossed her control into one of the lockers and strode out of the cabin.

The door closed after him.

He didn't neglect to lock it.

As if of their own accord, the streams from the san stopped. Someone on the bridge must have shut off her cabin's pumps and plumbing.

Only the water in Morn's mouth prevented her from laughing hysterically.

She jerked her head up, spat out the water, climbed to her feet as fast as she could. As if she feared that her black box would vanish into the gap of her nightmares, she rushed to pick it up. But it was real in her hands, tangible and true. Her fingers cupped its familiar outlines lovingly;

her respiration shuddered as she studied its transcendent possibilities.

Now.

Trembling, she tapped the buttons which sent a low wash of energy and strength along her nerves. Then she closed her eyes and spent a moment simply treasuring the artificial bliss of the sensation.

But it wasn't enough. She needed to soften her hurts. There. She needed better reflexes, better concentration. There. Soon she would need a lot more strength, but for now a slight increase was sufficient. There.

Fundamental hungers eased in her. The anguish of her limits sloughed off her shoulders. The ship's atmosphere became cleaner, sharper. She felt that she was restored to herself, that she was Morn Hyland again at last.

That, too, was a form of insanity. Nevertheless she embraced it like a lover.

She didn't realize that she'd actually damaged her cheeks until a drop of blood fell onto her hands.

Oops. She clenched her teeth to suppress a giggle.

Carefully quiet, because catatonics made no noise, she went to the san to look at herself in the mirror.

At the sight, she lost her impulse to laugh.

Her eyes were deeply sunken, bruised by abuse and withdrawal. New lines marked her face, as if she'd been scowling for months. Drying vomit stained one side of her mouth. Her skin was pallid, the color of illness, and the way it sagged against her bones seemed to indicate that she'd lost a lot of weight.

Against her paleness, the oozing welts on her cheeks resembled a grotesque parody of Nick's scars.

Her zone-implant didn't free her from her limitations. It merely gave her the capacity to push herself past the boundaries of her own survival.

That's enough, she thought in a tone of cold certitude. That's all I need.

She turned away from the mirror.

All right. No more maundering. She'd recovered her black box. Her next problem was to find a way out of her cabin.

But now she began to falter.

For some reason, her zone-implant eroded her sureness as it filled her with strength, with capability. It blocked her connection to the part of her that understood everything and revealed nothing. *How* could she get out of her cabin? At one point, she'd known the answer; she'd prepared herself for it. Now it eluded her.

Strength: that must be it. Her zone-implant made her strong – and gave her nothing else which could possibly be of any use here. No quickness of thought or action would free her from her prison. But if she applied enough strength—

The door had been designed to withstand pressure at right angles to its surface – decompression or battering – not in the direction of its own movement. The servomechanisms which opened and closed it would reverse themselves if they sensed an obstacle. So the problem was one of force and traction; of pushing hard enough in the right direction to engage the feedback circuits. Then the door would open itself.

And an obstruction alarm would tell the bridge exactly what was happening. Nick would come himself to stop her. Or he would send his people with guns—

No, she couldn't afford to be concerned about that. One thing at a time. First she had to get out of her cabin. Then she could worry about how to evade capture.

Standing at the door, she set her artificial strength as high as it would go – so high that the rush of endorphins and dopamine in her brain seemed to make a sound like a high wind, and her chest heaved because she couldn't take in enough air to support that much adrenaline. Then she planted her palms on the door, braced her body against the bulkhead, and shoved.

Shoved.

Pressure rose in her until her ears were full of wind and her eyes started to go blind. Her arms shuddered like cables with too much tension on them: she was probably strong enough to break her own bones. Small pains like vessels bursting mounted in her lungs.

Abruptly the skin of her palms tore. Slick with blood, her hands skidded across the door.

Helpless to catch herself, she lurched forward and cracked her head against the opposite bulkhead. From there, she fell to the floor.

The imposed neural storm was too intense: if she didn't diminish it, her synapses would fail like overburdened circuit breakers. Apparently locking the door deactivated its feedback sensors. Trembling on the verge of a seizure, she grasped her black box and reduced its emissions.

Her hands left blood on the keys.

So much for getting out of her cabin.

Hunched over her torn palms, she began to cry without realizing it. Possession of her zone-implant control wasn't enough: she needed something to hope for – and there was nothing. Some limits were absolute. No matter what she did to herself, she couldn't make her body pass through the solid door. Quickness, strength, concentration, freedom from pain – none of those advantages was of any use to her.

The part of her that understood hadn't planned for this.

Or it wasn't able to reach her through the effects of her zone implant.

Yet it kept her from crying loud enough to be heard over the intercom.

How much time did she have left? Blinking back her tears, she glanced at the cabin chronometer. Less than six hours. Was that all? She'd lost two or three hours somewhere. But it made no difference. Six hours or six hundred were the same.

She couldn't get out of her cabin.

She couldn't do anything to help Davies. He was lost. The next time she saw him – if she ever saw him again – he would be an Amnioni. He would remember nothing of their brief importance to each other. Unless he was given the same kind of mutagen which had transformed Marc Vestabule. Then he would be able to use his memories against her – and the UMCP – and all human space. By giving him birth, she'd betrayed him and her entire species; and there was nothing she could do about it.

She didn't know how to bear it.

But – the idea came with a jolt like an electric shock – she could kill Nick.

Eventually he would come to check on her; perhaps to turn off her supposed catatonia. He wouldn't expect to find her awake and charged with violence. If she hit him fast enough, hard enough, she might get past his defenses. All she needed was to land one blow—

All she needed was to drive the nail file through his throat.

She got up, went to the san, and unwedged the file from the head.

Her hands were sticky with blood, but they didn't hurt; her bruised head didn't hurt. Her zone-implant stifled those pains. Gripping the nail file, she returned to the door and tried to compose herself for more waiting.

To kill Nick. To exact at least that one little piece of retribution for her long anguish.

But she couldn't wait; not when she was primed with so much energy. Her muscles and her mind were incapable of stillness. She needed decisions, action; bloodshed.

Like her door, that was a conundrum she couldn't shove aside. She could wait: of course she could. All she had to do was reset the functions of her black box, put herself into a state of rest. Yet if she did that she wouldn't be able to react when Nick came. For him, she needed this harsh, compulsory keenness – and she didn't know when he would come. She meant to kill him: therefore she had to wait for him. But she couldn't wait without imposing an unnatural calm which would make killing him impossible.

There was no way out. The gap between what she needed and what she could do was impassable.

She was on the floor again, huddled among scattered shipsuits and sodden bedding. Unable to stop, she kept on crying uselessly.

But it didn't have to be this way. She'd lost herself somehow when she'd turned on her zone-implant. Before that, a lunatic and cunning part of herself had known what to do. She needed to recover that. She needed to restore her link to the part of her which revealed nothing.

There was only one way.

She had to face the remaining six or six hundred hours without artificial support.

No, she couldn't do it. It was too grievous to be borne. The bare idea set up a keening wail in her heart. Only her zone-implant kept her alive: nothing but its emissions protected her from the consequences of rape and gap-sickness, treason and bereavement. She couldn't give that up. If she turned off her black box, she would be left defenseless in the face of what she'd become.

But she had no choice. There was no other way across the gap.

In silent grief, as if she'd come to the end of herself, she began to cancel the functions of her black box, one at a time.

She did it slowly, to minimize the stress of transition. One function after another, she reduced their intensity by minor increments until their sensations were lost: one function after another, she switched them off only when she'd had time to accustom herself to the loss.

In that way, she surrendered herself to despair.

The cabin became dim around her, not because the light – or her vision – failed, but because it no longer mattered. It was simply the outward sign of an inward imprisonment; a tangible manifeStation of her irreducible mortality. Such limits were absolute. They couldn't be overcome or outflanked or avoided by hope – or by neural chicanery. In a plain test of power, Nick Succorso had beaten her, despite all the lies she'd told him, all the secrets she'd used against him. Her son, and her humanity, had been betrayed by her inability to ever be more than she was.

The part of her that understood everything refused to reveal its intentions. In the end, there was nothing left for her except the aggrieved and restless serenity of madness.

But be *quiet* about it. Go ahead, lose your mind. Just do it *quietly*.

Ignoring the blood that crusted her hands, she began to play slowly with locks of her hair. For a while she curled them around and around her fingers, wrapping them into delicate Möbius strips; endless metaphors. Later she separated them into finer and finer strands. When they were fine enough to take hold of one hair at a time, she started pulling them out.

In that way, she sank through the bottom of her despair into an autistic peace.

Like her cabin, which imprisoned her; and her body, which had brought her so much anguish; and all other external hindrances, which had demonstrated her futility: like those things, time itself lost its meaning. It passed her by, unregarded. Her hands and eventually her scalp hurt; but pain, too, was meaningless.

She had no idea what was happening when her door opened. Nothing was revealed to her.

Furtive and frightened, as if he sought to hide from a host of furies, Sib Mackern came into the room and closed the door.

CHAPTER 21

'*Morn.*' Mackern's whisper was as acute as a cry. '*Oh, God.*'

She regarded him dully, as if she had no idea who he was.

'*Morn.*' Sweat beaded on his pale face, darkened his thin mustache. 'Get up.' He panted unsteadily, not in exertion, but in fear. 'You haven't got much time.' The way his eyes flinched away from her and returned, around the cabin and back again, evoked the beating wings of his furies. 'Oh, God, what has he done to you?'

She felt a nameless agitation. The cabin was cluttered with disaster. When his gaze flinched, the whites of his eyes caught the light and gleamed sickly. She didn't shift her position; she hardly seemed to breathe. Her face was as haggard as madness. But the rhythm of her fingers in her hair accelerated. She pulled out the strands with a hint of vehemence.

'Listen.'

He dropped to his knees in front of her as if he were falling. Now his face was level with hers.

'You haven't got much time.'

She looked at him flatly, like a woman who'd gone blind.

Tentatively, nearly wincing, his hands moved toward her shoulders. He touched her – and jerked back as if she were hot enough to scald him. His gaze dropped to his knees; his mouth clenched crookedly. With an effort, he raised his eyes. Then he took hold of her arms.

'He doesn't know I'm here. It's not my watch. I waited until everyone was busy, so nobody would see me. But before I left the bridge, I deactivated his door control command circuits. The only thing his board shows is that you're still locked. He won't notice what I've done unless he tries to open your door.'

She blinked at the data first with blind, uncaring incomprehension. Everything he said sounded as familiar and indecipherable as the gap.

'You can get out.' Desperation mounted in him. 'Morn, you've got to hear me. I don't know what he did to you, but you've got to hear me. You can get out.'

That reached her. Something stirred in the dark core of her silence. *You can get out.* The lost or buried part of her that understood everything emitted a precise shiver of recognition. *Get out.*

Faster and faster, she curled hair around her fingers and pulled it out. 'Oh, Morn.'

The sweat on his face looked like tears. He wasn't a courageous man – or perhaps he simply didn't think he was – but he was frantic. Convulsively he snatched back one of his hands and slapped her face. Then he winced and bit his lips, terrified that he'd hurt her.

She let go of her hair, lifted the tips of her fingers to her stinging cheek. Soft as a dying breeze, she breathed, 'He can hear you. On the intercom.'

Mackern gasped. In panic he looked up at the intercom.

When he lowered his eyes again, they were haunted with strain. 'It's off,' he whispered. 'He isn't listening.'

She inhaled like a shudder.

Hints of his urgency glinted through her. What had he said? She'd already forgotten. Something— Had he said she could get out of her cabin?

Had he said she didn't have much time?

She couldn't remember his name.

Distress knotted in her guts. Her mouth stretched wide, as if she were about to wail.

'Morn, please,' Mackern begged. 'He'll kill me when he finds out. Don't waste it. Don't let it be for nothing.'

She heard him. By degrees, her alarm subsided. Intelligence rose to her in slow bubbles from the depths. She swallowed, and her eyes lost some of their blindness.

'"Time,"' she murmured. 'You said "time."'

'Yes!' he urged at once, encouraged and febrile at her response. 'We're almost alongside that warship, *Tranquil Hegemony* – twelve hours out of Billingate. He promised them an exact launch time. You've got' – he flung a glance at the cabin chronometer – 'twenty-six minutes.'

Once again his words slipped away from her. Billingate? *Tranquil Hegemony*? They were familiar, but she'd lost their meaning. Why was he talking about being killed? She still had twenty-six minutes left.

Deliberately she brought his name back from the place where she'd mislaid it. 'Sib Mackern. What're you doing here?' Pieces fit as she articulated them. 'He'll kill you for this.'

'I just can't stand it,' he replied as if he suddenly understood her, knew what she needed; as if his fear enabled him to follow her struggle out of despair. She needed words she could recognize, words that might restore her connection to sanity.

'When he sold your son the first time,' he explained, 'back on Enablement – I was ready to mutiny then. If I hadn't been alone. If I weren't such a coward.' His image of himself held no room for courage. 'Since I joined him, we've done things that made me sick. They gave me nightmares and made me wake up screaming. But nothing like that. Nothing like selling a human being to the Amnion.

'I've *seen* them, Morn,' he insisted as if he were the only witness. 'Those mutagens are evil. What they do is—' His whole body shivered with revulsion. No language sufficed for his abhorrence. 'You were right. Any one of us could be next.

'I thought then that I couldn't stand it. I had to do something about it, even if I *was* alone, and he killed me for it.

'But you saved me. You saved my life, Morn.' He was telling her the truth about himself: she could see that. The sweat on his face and the hunted fright in his eyes made his honesty unmistakable. 'You rescued Davies yourself.

'After that I was ready to do anything for you, anything at all, all you had to do was ask. But I didn't get a chance. He let you out. He acted – you both acted like you'd planned it together, like it was all just an elaborate trick, a ruse, to get away from Enablement. You confused me so badly, I didn't know whether to be grateful or appalled.'

Grimly he kept his voice at a whisper. 'I wanted to be grateful. You gave me a reason to keep working for him. You made me think he had limits, there were some crimes he wouldn't commit. But I was afraid that *this* was the real trick, that acting like you planned it together was the real ruse. That he didn't have limits. And if he didn't, you must be paying a terrible price to protect yourself and Davies.

'When we came in range of that warship, I learned the truth.

'I can't stand it. That's all. I just can't stand it.

'I want to help you,' he finished. 'This is the only thing I can do.'

It was working: as he spoke, he created links for her, spans across the vast space of her loss. More knowledge came up from the depths, new pieces of understanding. Nevertheless his presence in her cabin still refused to make sense.

'Why?' she asked again. 'What good will it do me when he kills you?'

'*Morn.*' Dismay twisted his face. 'Have you forgotten? Did he hurt you so badly that you can't remember?

'He's going to give them your son. He's going to launch Davies to them in an ejection pod in' – his eyes jerked to the chronometer and back again – 'twenty-one minutes.'

That was it: the keystone; the piece she needed. When it slotted into place, she was restored.

For the first time her eyes came fully into focus on her rescuer.

Stay calm, counseled the part of her that understood. Don't rush it. You've got enough time. Don't make any mistakes.

Intensely quiet in a way that left no doubt of what she meant, she asked, 'Where is he?'

Mackern wasn't calm. 'They took him to the pod, oh, twenty minutes ago.' She seemed to see the time draining from his face. 'I had to wait for that. Liete guarded this hall until they moved him. She said she didn't trust you to stay locked up. I couldn't risk coming here until she reported he was in the pod.

'She said – ' He swallowed hard to make his throat work. 'She said, "He didn't give us any trouble. He seems to be in some kind of shock. Like he knows what we're doing to him, but he's too demoralized to fight it."'

Nineteen minutes.

She didn't think about Davies. She didn't need to. He was already the reason for everything. Instead she focused one last question on Sib Mackern.

'Has he changed his priority codes?'

The data first shook his head. 'He hasn't had time.'

No, of course not. And why bother? The only person who might dare use those codes in his place was safely imprisoned, out of her mind.

That answer fit everything she'd planned and prepared without knowing it.

With an effort that made her joints ache, she climbed to her feet. 'Go back to your cabin,' she told Sib as she took out her zone-implant control. 'You're braver than you think.'

Blood and injury had stiffened her palms. Her fingertips were sore. But none of that mattered.

One function started to fill her limbs with strength.

'If either of us survives this, we'll owe it to you.'

Another steadied her nerves, restored her reflexes.

'I'll do whatever I can to protect you.'

Another enabled her to move her damaged hands as if they were supple.

'Be sure to relock this cabin.'

Sixteen minutes.

There was nothing she could do here to protect him. His life depended on his own precautions. Nodding her thanks, she keyed her door and moved into the corridor at a steady run.

'Good luck!' Sib hissed after her softly. 'Don't worry about me!'

She left him behind as if he'd ceased to exist.

The corridor was empty. Good. Already she felt full of force, charged like matter cannon. She would kill anybody who got in her way.

At any rate, she would try. But she didn't want that. She wanted no more blood on her hands. Her own was enough.

Silent on bare feet, she reached the lift and hit the call button.

Stay calm.

She was calm. Nevertheless she braced herself to attack anyone who might be using the lift.

No one was. The lift answered her almost immediately, as empty as the corridor.

She got in and ascended toward the ship's core – toward engineering and the auxiliary bridge.

If Nick were watching for her, he would have no trouble keeping track of where she was. The maintenance computer could tell him which doors opened and closed, which lifts were used; it could analyze the gradient drain on the air processing to tell him how many people occupied which corridors or rooms. But it wouldn't do any of those things unless he asked – and he wouldn't ask unless he were suspicious.

If Sib hadn't betrayed himself in some way—

If *Tranquil Hegemony* and the preparations for launch kept Nick occupied—

Fifteen minutes.

The lift stopped. The door opened.

Mikka Vasaczk stood there.

The command second stared at Morn in surprise.

No, not her, Morn couldn't attack *her*. She was the one who'd captured Morn for Nick. Yet Morn was in her debt, for courtesy and silence if not for active help. Someone else would have captured Morn eventually, if Mikka hadn't done it.

But Davies was helpless; he couldn't defend himself. If Morn didn't fight for him, he would go to the Amnion.

Coiled with the quickness of her zone-implant, she sprang at Mikka just as Mikka backed away and raised her hands, palms outward to show that she was unarmed.

Morn stopped herself in midstride.

Stay calm. You've got enough time.

Still holding up her hands, Mikka retreated to the wall. A scowl clamped her features, ungiving and austere.

'This is strange,' she articulated harshly. 'I could have sworn he said you were helpless. Things have gotten pretty bad when the Captain of a ship like this can't be trusted to turn on a radioelectrode.'

'Don't interfere,' Morn breathed through her teeth. 'I'm not your enemy.'

A sneer lifted Mikka's lip. The bleakness of her face was complete. In the same tone, she said, 'Did you know that Pup is my brother? When our parents died, he didn't have anywhere else to go. In any case, they were too poor to leave him any good choices. I got him this job so I could keep an eye on him.

'He can't be more than a couple of years older than Davies.

'You told me the truth once when I needed it. You took the chance that I might betray you. It's too bad I didn't see you down here. If I did, I could have tried to hit you again.'

Fourteen minutes.

Morn had no time to feel gratitude. Her heart labored too hard in her chest. The settings on her black box must have been too high: she could hardly get enough air to support them.

She turned and ran for the auxiliary bridge.

It wasn't far: partway down the length of the ship; partway around the core. The deck became an upward curve when she turned: she paid no attention to that. She only noticed the doors she passed – the ones which she knew were safe; the ones which might open on trouble.

The door to the engineering console room and the drive space stood wide. That was the one she needed. The primary circuits for the ejection pods were there. Another failsafe: if all other systems died, the lifeboats could still be launched from the engineering console.

She looked inside.

Vector Shaheed stood at one of his boards with his back to her.

Thirteen minutes.

Urgency and hyperventilation mounted in her. *Stay calm*. She had to go in there, had to get past Vector somehow. Yet she didn't want to hurt him. For his own reasons, he'd treated her decently. And he already had enough pain of his own. The thought of damaging him in order to help her son brought the taste of vomit back into her mouth.

Stay calm!

But there was something else she needed to do as well. She still had time. If she did it first, he might be gone – into the drive space, or out to the bridge – when she came back.

To save him – or to save what was left of herself – she flitted past him and entered the auxiliary bridge.

It shouldn't have been empty. This close to an Amnion warship, the entire crew should have been at combat Stations. But of course Nick had no intention of fighting. He'd already negotiated a peaceful 'satisfaction of requirements' with *Tranquil Hegemony*. That was his only practical hope: he couldn't defy both *Tranquil Hegemony* and *Calm Horizons*; not at these speeds; not in Amnion space. Why put more strain on his people, when they were already exhausted?

Morn went straight to the data Station.

Trusting her own skills and Alba Parmute's diffused attention on the bridge, she engaged the board and used it to reactivate bridge control over her cabin door. That was for Sib Mackern. Now nothing showed that he'd ever done anything to help her.

Eleven minutes.

Keying off the data console, she left the auxiliary bridge and returned to Vector's domain.

No luck: he was still there; still working. In fact, he stood at the primary pod board. The readouts she could see past his shoulders seemed to indicate that he was running status and diagnostic checks, verifying the operational condition of the pods; testing life-support; confirming programmed thrust for navigation and braking.

Making sure that the pod which would carry her son to his doom could be trusted.

Ten minutes.

If her inner countdown was accurate—

She couldn't wait. She would have to get past Vector somehow.

She stepped into the room and closed the door behind her.

At the sound, he turned.

She stopped to let him look at her – to let him see that she wouldn't attack him if she didn't have to.

He betrayed no surprise at the sight of her. His phlegmatic stoicism was equal to her unexpected arrival. More in greeting than in distress, he cocked an eyebrow. 'Ah, Morn.' If he felt anything unpleasant, it showed only in the faintly unhealthy flush which covered his round face. He looked like a man who'd been exerting himself against the advice of the sickbay computer. 'I suppose I should have guessed this would happen. Nick never seems to know the difference between what you can and can't do.'

He smiled as if he were mocking her; but she saw no mockery in him as he asked, 'Have you come to see Davies off?'

'Vector,' she said tightly, 'get away from that board.'

I don't want to hurt you. Don't make me hurt you.

Nine minutes.

He went on smiling. 'Oh, I don't think so. Nick specifically told me to make sure nothing goes wrong. On this ship, it doesn't pay to disobey orders – even implied ones. Since he never imagined that you could break free of your zone-implant, he didn't order me to stop you. Still his intent was clear enough. I can't afford to let you touch anything.

'In any case, you've got nothing to gain. If you stop the launch and pull Davies out, Nick will simply capture both of you and start the whole process over again. He'll apologize for the delay. Then he'll probably send both of you to that warship, just to demonstrate his "good faith." Everything you've done will be wasted.'

'Vector, I mean it.' Remaining still cost her an effort. 'Get away from that board.' She needed movement, action: her black box was set too high, and her son was running out of time. 'I've come too far to stop now. I'll sacrifice anything.'

She'd been prepared for days. Ever since Davies was born – and sold to the Amnion.

'I recognize that.' Nothing could have been less sarcastic than the mild scorn of Vector's smile. 'Unfortunately I don't have any choice. If I don't get out of your way, you'll probably kill me. At the moment, you look like you could do that with one hand. But if I do get out of your way, Nick will kill me.'

His stiffness as he folded his arms reminded Morn of the arthritis which threatened to cripple him; of his loyalty to his friend Orn, who had inflicted him with arthritis by beating him up.

Eight minutes.

'No doubt this was inevitable. I mean, the whole thing was doomed from the beginning. I don't belong here – I'm not the right kind of man for this life. I chose it because I couldn't live with the alternatives, but it never fit me. Or I never fit it. Outraged idealism seems like as good an excuse as any to turn illegal, but it doesn't work. The contradiction had to catch up with me eventually. You might say the only thing I've accomplished here is that I've given the moral high ground back to the people I hate.

'I'll be better off if I can end it now.'

'Vector, stop this! I haven't got time for it!' Her hands felt like they must surely give off sparks when she flexed them. She should have been gasping for air, but the ferocity of her need held her steady. ' "Outraged idealism" is a shitty excuse for giving human beings to the Amnion. You know that. But you don't want to face the logic of your own decisions, so you're trying to avoid it by despising yourself. You're trying to prove you *deserve* what the UMCP did to you. Who's going to question withholding an immunity drug from an illegal like you? Who's going to respect Orn Vorbuld's friends? But it's not that simple. Don't you see where that kind of reasoning leads?

'It leads to *genocide*, Vector. The destruction of the entire human species.

'Look at me. You think I'm here to save my son – and you're right. But I would do the same thing if *you* were in that pod. I would do the same thing for *Nick*.' That was the truth, regardless of her loathing for him. 'I've got more reason to hate the UMCP than you do. I've got more reason to be afraid of Nick. But I will see every one of us *dead* before I allow this kind of absolute *treason*.'

Seven minutes.

She took two steps forward, surging like a burst of flame.

'*Get out of my WAY!*'

Slowly he unfolded his arms. His gaze had gone inward: his face revealed nothing except its unhealthy flush. 'You're still a cop,' he murmured. 'No matter what you've done. At bottom, you're still a cop. One of the few. You say you would take the same risks if I were in the pod. I suppose I believe you. That's worth something.

'You're right, of course. I made the decisions that got me into this mess, and now I don't want to face the consequences. Those of us who truly and profoundly hate the cops really ought to do better than that.'

Shifting himself aside, he gestured Morn toward the ejection pod board.

She went for it so fast that she didn't see him plant his feet, settle his weight; she didn't see him draw back his arm. She barely caught a glimpse of his fist as he swung it at her head with all his mass behind it.

The blow slammed her against the wall, then dropped her to the floor as if she'd been nailed there.

Six minutes.

'Sorry about that.' Something muffled Vector's voice. He may have been sucking his cracked knuckles. 'You don't deserve it. I just had to be sure you didn't force me to do this.'

Apparently he glanced at the chronometer. 'You've got five minutes and forty-eight seconds.'

Her skull rang like a carillon. For a moment her zone-implant couldn't catch up with the pain. Through a racket of agony, she heard the door open and close.

Still a cop.

Force me to do this.

Five minutes—

Forget calm, a voice said to her, as distinct as a chime. You're out of time.

Clawing at the air, she flipped herself over, got her hands and knees under her.

Her zone-implant saved her: its emissions fought down the pain and weakness, cleared her head; did everything except give her adequate air. Gasping on the verge of unconsciousness, she struggled to her feet.

The board seemed to reel in front of her; her vision swam out of focus. Nevertheless she fumbled her way forward, found the controls to the door, and locked it. To delay anyone who might interfere.

Then an artificial stability took charge of her misfiring neurons. Her gaze sharpened on the readouts.

There.

The board told her which pod had been activated. It gave her a launch countdown, life-support status, departure trajectory, braking parameters. A plot from scan showed her *Captain's Fancy* and *Tranquil Hegemony;* showed her the pod's programmed course between them. The pod would decelerate straight into one of the warships' holds.

The scan plot was automatic. She wasn't on the auxiliary bridge: she didn't have access to scan itself, or to helm. She would have to rely on guesswork. But since the plot was automatic, it also showed Thanatos Minor looming in the background. And it gave her *Captain's Fancy's* velocity and heading – which in turn enabled her to estimate the distance and course to that lonely rock. She ought to be able to guess well enough.

The problem was time. Reprogramming the pod was complex. She only had four and a half minutes left, and she hadn't started yet. No time to paralyze Nick's command board. In any case, that could only be done from the auxiliary bridge. So anything she did might be countermanded – if Nick caught her at it.

She couldn't chance that.

Springing to the thrust board, she hit the overrides, cutting off drive control from the bridge; then she initiated the shutdown sequence. Now *Captain's Fancy* couldn't brake or maneuver. That in itself posed no threat to the ship, not this far from Thanatos Minor. But it would distract Nick—

In fact, he was already on the intercom, shouting, 'Vector? Vector! What the fuck are you doing?'

Three and a half minutes.

She slapped the intercom silent and returned to the pod board.

Now. No time for accidents or mistakes. If she could reprogram the pod before it launched, it would be out of reach as soon as it left the ship's ejection bay.

Her zone-implant made her unnaturally fast as she tapped in Nick's priority codes.

She had no intention of canceling the launch – of trying to save Davies aboard *Captain's Fancy*. Vector was right: that would achieve nothing. What she had in mind wasn't much better; but at least it would prolong her son's life for a while.

She didn't have anything else to strive for.

First she copied the pod's programming to one of her readouts. Carefully overriding the status indicators which would report a change to the bridge, she erased the programming from the pod. Then she began to write in new instructions.

Two minutes.

Accumulated stress frayed her breathing. Unable to pull in enough oxygen for its demands, her body seemed to burn itself as fuel. Spots swirled in front of her eyes, distorting the readouts, confusing her fingers. Her black box was set too high. At some point it would kill her.

She didn't falter.

Initially her orders were identical to the original ones. Launch unchanged. Trajectory unchanged. Those things gave her a starting point for her guesswork. Her instructions diverged at the moment of deceleration. Instead of braking, she told the pod to generate full burn and change course, away from *Tranquil Hegemony* toward Thanatos Minor. If no one warned the Amnion of what she'd done, they wouldn't have time to react: the pod would skip past them and away before they could try to reach it.

And they wouldn't shoot at it, no, definitely not, not after going to all this trouble to obtain Davies alive—

One minute.

But at that velocity it would crash fatally on the rock. Unless Billingate shot down the pod to protect itself. Either way, Davies would die in a helpless fireball. The pod had to decelerate enough to survive the impact; enough to show Billingate it posed no threat. And she had to estimate that: when to initiate deceleration, how much thrust to use.

She wasn't Nick: she couldn't do algorithms in her head.

Her son would die if she estimated badly.

No matter. Better to kill him by accident herself than to let him be subjected to Amnion mutagens.

Fifteen seconds before launch, she finished her programming and copied it to the pod.

That was the best she could do. She didn't expect to live long enough to find out whether it was good enough.

But just in case—

By the time the ejection pod nosed out of its bay and passed beyond recall, she'd already unlocked the door and left the engineering console room.

On the bridge, Nick stopped cursing Vector's silence long enough to watch the pod cross the distance to *Tranquil Hegemony*.

It wouldn't take long. The two ships were only five thousand kilometers apart – and the pod had slightly more than *Captain's Fancy*'s velocity, thanks to the short thrust of launch. Just a few more minutes. Then he could start to breathe again. The Amnion kept their bargains. They may have felt justified in giving him flawed gap drive components, but they wouldn't try any tricks or treachery here. Not this close to Billingate.

Nevertheless as he studied the displays he felt a premonition clutching at his scrotum. He knew in his balls that something was about to go wrong.

'Why would he do that?' Carmel asked with her usual blunt temerity. 'We're sitting targets without thrust. From this range, they can take us apart in tidy little pieces. Hell, they can knock off the command module and leave the rest of the ship intact.'

'I don't know,' Nick growled irritably. 'Figure it out for yourself. Or go find him and ask him. That'll be his last chance to say anything before I disembowel him.'

'We don't need thrust at the moment,' ventured the helm first on

Vector's behalf. 'And we've got plenty of time to restart the drive before we approach dock.'

In a neutral tone, Malda Verone said, 'I've got everything locked on them, Nick. If they fire, we should be able to hit them once or twice before we disintegrate.'

Nick ignored her. The pod was a quarter of the way to *Tranquil Hegemony*.

'He must be afraid they're going to fire,' Lind said abruptly. 'Maybe he thinks they'll hold off if we're helpless.'

Nick ignored that as well. He was viscerally certain that the warship wouldn't fire at him – so certain, in fact, that he hadn't bothered to get *Captain's Fancy* ready for a fight.

'But why?' protested Alba petulantly. 'Why wouldn't they kill us if we're helpless?'

Carmel shook her head. 'I've got a better question. Why does he think they're going to fire?'

That was it. Why would those fuckers fire? What excuse did they have?

What excuse were they about to get?

Suddenly Nick's premonition sprang into clarity. Swinging away from the screens, he barked, 'What has he done to the pod?'

Carmel and Malda stared in a shock of comprehension. Lind gaped as if he were about to drool.

As if answering a summons, Vector Shaheed came through the aperture onto the bridge.

His face had gone pale, as pallid as Nick's scars, as if his heart were about to fail him. Yet his smile remained characteristically mild; his composed manner revealed nothing.

'Vector,' Nick said, soft and deadly, 'I told you to watch the engineering console room.'

The engineer paused between one step and the next. His eyes widened slightly. 'What went wrong?'

Nick leaned over his board, aimed his fury straight at Vector. 'I *ordered* you to make sure nothing did.'

'I know. It didn't. I mean, it can't. It couldn't.' That was the closest Nick had ever heard Vector come to sounding flustered. 'There was nothing that *could* go wrong. I waited until I was sure of that.

'I know I shouldn't have left. But I had to get to sickbay – I had to get something for the pain, Nick. Otherwise I was going to be useless.

'You can check the computer. There were only five minutes left before launch. I was sure nothing could happen. So I locked the console room and went to sickbay.'

Carefully he repeated, 'What went wrong?'

Nick didn't answer. His premonition had moved from his crotch to his face. It felt like acid under his eyes.

He swung back to look at the screens.

The pod was close enough to *Tranquil Hegemony* to begin deceleration. It should begin right now.

Scan reported thrust.

Too much thrust.

The pod veered off its programmed heading and started to pick up speed. At full burn, it moved past the warship. In moments it was effectively beyond reach.

Crying out from the core of his doubt and need, Nick howled, '*MORN! You fucking BITCH!*'

'Nick,' Lind said in a strangled voice, '*Tranquil Hegemony* wants to talk to you. I think they're shouting.'

Instantly Nick swallowed his dismay. He would have time for it later. He would make Morn pay for it later. Right now he had about ten seconds in which to save himself and his ship.

Without transition, he shifted into his emergency mode – the state of whetted creative concentration on which his reputation rested. Relaxing in his seat despite the consternation around him, he resumed his air of nonchalant competence.

'Acknowledge that,' he told Lind. 'Tell them an immediate response follows. Then copy this.

'"Captain Nick Succorso to Amnion defensive *Tranquil Hegemony*. We have sabotage. Repeat, we have sabotage. We've lost thrust. Scan our power emissions for confirmation. We can't maneuver.

'"The ejection pod containing the human offspring Davies Hyland has also been sabotaged."' He checked the displays. '"It will impact Thanatos Minor –" Carmel, give Lind an ETA. "If the sabotage includes adequate deceleration programming, he may survive.

'"Sabotage was done by Morn Hyland."' For a second, his fury surged out of control. '*I'll tear her fucking guts out!*' Then he caught himself. Taking a deep breath, he instructed Lind, 'Don't copy that. Message continues. "She escaped imprisonment. I can't explain it. When I learn how it was done, I'll tell you.

'"Your requirements have not been satisfied. I regret this. I regret the appearance that I've dealt falsely with you. To dispel this appearance, I'll comply with any new requirements you wish to satisfy – if they don't threaten my own safety. Inform me what must be done to rectify Morn Hyland's treachery.

'"To demonstrate that my intentions are honest, I won't restart thrust until you grant permission."

'Send that. Put it on audio when they answer.'

Vector had recovered from his disconcertion. 'Will that work?' he asked quietly.

'You don't care,' Nick snarled over his shoulder. 'You aren't going to live long enough for it to make any difference.'

For the rest of his people, however, and to steady himself, he added, 'But they don't want to blast us, if they can help it. It'll make them look bad. Billingate can see we haven't got thrust. They can hear us trying to cooperate. And I'll bet we still have something those fuckers want' – he grinned murderously – 'something I would have given them for nothing.

'Malda,' he ordered sharply, 'put targ on standby. I want them to see us reduce our power emissions. The meeker we look, the better.'

Without waiting for a reply, he hit his intercom.

'Mikka. Liete. Organize a search. Make it fast – and thorough. Use everybody. I want you to find Morn. She got out of her cabin somehow. Don't ask me how. If somebody helped her, I'll castrate the sonofabitch.

'Start in engineering and the auxiliary bridge. Then try the drive space. Try the core – try the infrastructure. She might even be hiding in the hull, if she took an EVA suit.

'Find her, but don't let her kill herself. Don't let her arrange for you to kill her. We're going to need her. She won't do us any good dead.'

Snapping off the intercom, he rasped at the screen which displayed *Tranquil Hegemony*'s position, 'Come *on*, you bastards. Give me an answer. Tell me you're going to let us live. Tell me we're going to get out of this with a whole skin.'

'Who would help her?' asked the helm first. He was out of his depth and foundering. 'Who would dare?'

Because he couldn't keep himself still, Nick turned back to Vector. 'What did she offer you?' he demanded. 'Was it something perverse, like "immunity from prosecution"? Or was it just sex beyond your wildest dreams?'

The engineer met Nick's glare without any apparent difficulty. 'Check the sickbay computer,' he said steadily. The hostility around him didn't intimidate him. 'It'll tell you how bad my arthritis is. The truth is, there's nothing she *could* offer me. We're in no danger of "prosecution" out here. And' – his smile conveyed a suggestion of sadness – 'I'm in no condition for sex. I hurt too much.'

Swearing to himself, Nick swung away.

He couldn't wait. If the Amnion didn't answer soon, he would have to go find Morn himself. Or he would have to kill Vector right here on the bridge. The effort to remain in command of himself was too much. He needed violence.

He needed to make the woman who'd cut him *pay*.

'Here it comes, Nick,' Lind jerked out as the speakers crackled to life.

No one around the bridge breathed.

'Amnion defensive *Tranquil Hegemony* to human Captain Nick Succorso. You have dealt falsely. Amnion requirements have not been satisfied. However, your thrust drive status is confirmed. Speculation suggests that sabotage is plausible. Your failure to confine the saboteur Morn Hyland is culpable. Nevertheless your destruction will not advance Amnion interests.

'You will dock at the human installation called Billingate. If the human offspring Davies Hyland survives impact on Thanatos Minor, you will retrieve him and deliver him to the Amnion. In addition, you will deliver the saboteur Morn Hyland.

'During the interval, the Amnion will take steps to ensure your compliance.

'Indicate your acceptance of these requirements.'

Steps? What steps?

No, don't ask.

Nick cocked his fist above his board, threatening the air. Mordantly he asked his people, 'Any of you want to haggle? This is your last chance.'

Everyone watched him. No one spoke.

His fury rose like demonic glee as he said, 'Lind, tell them their requirements are accepted.' And with it came a burst of inspiration, a blind intuitive flash. 'Tell them I'll do everything in my power to make sure they get what they want.' He could hardly contain his excitement. 'Tell them we'll restart thrust as soon as they grant permission.'

What steps?

All his best decisions were made intuitively. That was what gave his reputation its air of romance, almost of enchantment. He never hesitated to act on his inspirations.

'When you're done with that,' he went on to the communications first, 'tight-beam a message to UMCPHQ. Use the coordinates and codes I gave you last time.

'Copy this.

'"I rescued her for you, goddamn it. Now get me out of this. If you don't, I can't keep her away from the Amnion."

'Send it.'

I'll teach you to cut me off, he told Hashi Lebwohl silently. And I'll give your fucking requirements more satisfaction than you can stand, he added to the nearby warship.

And *you* are going to foot the bill, he promised Morn.

What steps?

Vector's eyes glittered wetly, as if he were holding back tears. The helm first ducked his head. For reasons she probably didn't understand, Alba giggled tensely. Malda continued staring at Nick as if she were transfixed. Carmel's frown didn't express much approval.

'Mikka?' Nick snarled at the intercom. 'Liete? Have you got her yet? Do you need help?'

Neither Mikka nor Liete had found Morn.

If he'd told them to look in his cabin, they would have found her immediately. While he negotiated with the Amnion, and her son sped toward Thanatos Minor, she was there, searching with meticulous care for his store of the drug which rendered him immune to Amnion mutagens.

However, she wasn't recaptured until later, when she tried to conceal herself in one of the ejection pods.

Bitter and inarticulate, Mikka clamped Morn into an armcuff as Liete called the bridge to report.

'Take her to sickbay,' Nick snapped like a spatter of acid. 'Put her to sleep. I won't have time to deal with her until after we dock. And get that goddamn zone-implant control away from her!'

Morn shrugged as if she'd learned how to die. Expressionless and doomed, she put up no resistance as Mikka and Liete manhandled her to sickbay, stretched her out on the table, and filled her veins with cat.

ANGUS

Now that he knew where he was going, Angus Thermopyle found the waiting harder to bear. He wanted to get *away* from this place: away from the sterile rooms and corridors of UMCPDA's surgical wing; away from doctors and techs, therapists and programmers, who pretended that they had valid professional reasons for playing with him. The thought that he would be sent to Thanatos Minor affected him like a promise of escape. And the idea that he would be alone in deep space with no one except Milos Taverner to torment him felt like hope.

Get it over with, he snarled at Hashi Lebwohl's staff, even though they couldn't hear what he said in the silence of his mind. Let me out of here.

Ignoring him, they did their jobs with meticulous care. In theory, their control over him was perfect. The computer between his shoulder blades mastered him absolutely. Nevertheless they worked to ensure that he was as helpless in practice as in theory; that any hope he held out for himself was mere illusion.

So they spent hours putting him through simple feedback tests – for instance, measuring the differences in his reactions to the commands 'Run' and 'Run, Joshua.' If they said, 'Run,' he could choose whether or not to comply: if they said, 'Run, Joshua,' he ran, driven by his computer's control over his zone-implants. Then their neurosensors and computer-links measured his compliance or resistance in order to refine his programming.

Other tests were made, not by external instruction, but directly through his computer. The links were used to send him complex physical and mental tasks; and every detail of his response contributed to the perfection of his programming.

Still other tests involved giving him external, compulsory commands which violated his enforced internal exigencies. 'Joshua, break my arm.' Because he was outraged to the core of his being, Angus fought to obey: he would have loved to inflict a little pain. But his computer said, 'No,' and so his worst savagery came to nothing. He couldn't damage anyone known to his programming as a member of the UMCP.

Hope as a concept had no relevance under these conditions. He was a tool, nothing more: a sophisticated organic extension of an electronic device. As long as he lived, he would never make another important choice for himself.

If he'd been prone to despair, he would certainly have given way to it – and that self-abandonment would have accomplished nothing. Neither his programming nor his programmers cared about his emotional condition. Like escape and disobedience, suicide wasn't available to him. No matter how much he might feel like lying down and dying, his computer wouldn't allow it.

However, Angus wasn't prone to despair. An overriding passion kept him away from his personal abyss. Precisely because he had so much fear in him, he was able to endure it when a less damaged or malignant mind would have crumbled.

Since he had no choice, he concentrated on understanding and utilizing his new capabilities as fully as he could. On some level, his lasers and his increased strength, his computer and his augmented vision, all belonged to him. Within the narrow range allowed by his programming, they were his to use. As with *Bright Beauty* and Morn Hyland, he wanted to know what they were good for.

While Lebwohl's people tested him, he also tested himself.

Eventually he learned that his programming was in fact all that prevented him from getting away. In every other sense, he might as well have been designed and built to break out of UMCPHQ. The new dimension of his sight enabled him to identify and analyze alarms and locks. With his lasers, he could change circuitry or cut open doors – or kill guards. He was as strong as a great ape; as quick as a microprocessor. And his computer recorded everything for him. In fact, it was more useful than an eidetic memory, since it held a wide variety of independent databases which were gradually made accessible to him as his programmers trusted their control over him more and more.

If he'd been his own master, he could have dismantled his prison and fled.

But his zone-implants held him. He was required to wait.

In time, no doubt, the strain would have proved too great for him. However, his masters had exigencies of their own. Beyond the walls of Data Acquisition's surgical wing, events moved at a separate pace; out of reach; out of control.

One morning – his computer informed him that the time was 9:11:43.17 – a group of techs and doctors came into his room. One of them said, Sit on the edge of the bed, Joshua.

He obeyed because he couldn't do anything else. Another said, Stasis, Joshua.

Involuntarily he went into one of the null states they used when they wanted to deactivate his computer: a state in which his detached mind continued to work while his body became an inert lump, capable only of sustaining its own autonomic functions. As long as he was in that state, they could have torn off his fingernails, or cut his testicles, or driven spikes into his brain, and he would have been unable to do anything with his horror except perceive what they did – and remember.

But if they'd intended to harm him physically, they would have done so long ago. As they took off his lab pajamas and began to swab his back with antiseptics, he was appalled, not by their unexplained intentions, but by his own utter immobility.

With their customary efficiency, they made an incision between his shoulder blades to access his computer. When they unplugged his datacore, the gap in his mind which represented his computer-link turned as black and cold as the void between the stars. Now he was held in stasis by hardwired commands which were part of the computer itself.

Moments later, however, the doctors plugged in a new datacore. As soon as it came on-line, he felt the disturbing, insidious sensation of having been rebooted. A piece of his brain had just gone into a cyborg's equivalent of tach.

Then they disconnected all their links and leads and neurosensors. For the first time since his welding started, he was severed from all external equipment – from every compulsion or requirement which wasn't recorded in his datacore.

Finally they sealed their incision with tissue plasm and covered it with a bandage to protect it during the few hours it would take to heal.

End stasis, Joshua, one of them said.

Angus Thermopyle raised his head and looked around.

His observers were irrationally tense. A couple of the techs winced. The doctor closest to him turned a shade paler. He was perfectly under control: they knew that. Yet they were afraid of him. They couldn't forget who he was.

He hated them all. If he could have done anything to confirm their anxiety, he would have. Deliberately he took a deep breath, stretched his arms, cracked his knuckles as if he were free to do such things at last; as if for him the idea of freedom could ever be anything more than an illusion.

Softly he muttered, 'It's about time.'

The time, his computer informed him, was 9:21:22.01.

One of the doctors went to the intercom and reported, 'We're done. Tell the Director.'

'Here.' A tech tossed a shipsuit and a pair of boots onto the bed. 'Put these on.' The shipsuit was a dirty gray color, devoid of insignia – indistinguishable from the ones Angus had habitually worn aboard *Bright Beauty*. 'You've got about five minutes.'

In a clump, as if they wanted the safety of numbers, the doctors and technicians left him alone.

Every monitor in the room focused on him as if he might suddenly go berserk.

If he could have emitted electronic fields as well as perceiving them, he would have burned out the monitors – if his programming had allowed him that option.

No chance.

But that didn't matter. What mattered was that it had come. Whatever his masters wanted him for, it was about to start.

For the first time since he'd arrived here, his doctors couldn't tell how fast his heart was beating, how urgently his lungs called for air. So that the monitors wouldn't see any sign of his eagerness, he got up from the bed slowly; pushed his limbs into the shipsuit and his feet into the boots with an insolent lack of haste. Then he stretched back out on the bed, propped his head on the pillow, and folded his arms over his belly as if he were capable of waiting forever.

Fortunately nobody challenged his patience to see if he were bluffing. Less than a minute later, Min Donner strode into the room.

More than ever, she looked as ready as a hawk. Walking or still, her hand swung past her gun, instinctively poised. Her weight was always balanced; her muscles seemed permanently charged with relaxation, as if she were nanoseconds away from an explosion. As far as Angus knew – his new vision could supply him with hints – she had no technological augmentation. And yet she gave the impression that he was no match for her.

She made him feel that he'd better look away before she took offense at his scrutiny.

He would have resisted the impulse on general principles; but the fact that she wasn't alone caught his attention.

Milos Taverner was with her.

The former Deputy Chief of Com-Mine Security followed the ED Director into the room and met Angus' stare with a dull glower.

He didn't look well. Considering his fastidiousness, he seemed as unwell as if he'd been on a binge for weeks. His gaze was dissipated as well as dull; his cheeks – inadequately shaved or depilated – had the color of a corpse which had been left in water too long. The mottling on his scalp resembled the marks of an obscure disease. A nic hung from his lips, curling smoke into his eyes and dropping ash down his shipsuit. He kept his hands in his pockets as if to conceal the way they shook.

This was the man who held the keys – at least the external ones – to Joshua's future.

Angus grinned savagely. 'What's the matter?' he asked. 'You look like shit. Hell, you look like *me*. Didn't you enjoy the training? Learning to take orders from me must have been murder for a prissy cocksucker like you.'

Milos didn't shift his stance or move his hands. Around his nic, he said in a tone of sour hostility, 'Apologize, Joshua.'

Like a docile prisoner threatened by a stun-prod, Angus said at once, 'I'm sorry. Please forgive me.' Complex emissions from his electrodes compelled him.

Inside himself, however, he snarled, Enjoy it. Do as much of it as you can. I'll remember it all.

'Stop that, Milos,' Donner ordered. 'That's not what he's for.'

Milos ignored her. 'But since you ask,' he continued, 'no, I didn't enjoy the training. I didn't enjoy learning to look and act like a man who would crew for you. But there are compensations. I'm planning to get a certain' – he pursed his lips – 'satisfaction from the remainder of this assignment.'

'I'm sure you will,' Angus retorted. 'Traitors like you always do.'

The ED Director held up one finger like a command.

Taverner flicked a glance at her and shut up.

Grinning again, Angus did the same.

She nodded once, grimly.

In no doubt of her authority, she told Angus, 'Come with me.' Then she turned her back on him and strode out of the room.

Shoving his hands into his pockets to taunt Milos, Angus followed.

This was the first time he'd been out of his room without the attendance of guards and techs; without being attached to external computers and monitors. The experience increased his illusory sensation of freedom. Oh, there were guards in sight – and Min Donner herself served the same function. Yet the change behind the sensation was real. He was done with being tested – done with being cut and measured and coerced like an animal in a lab. For better or worse, his programming was complete. Now at last he would get out of this sterile, inhuman place. He would be given a chance to take action.

By its very nature, action involved movement into the unknown. Unknown to Angus himself, certainly; but also, in a more subtle and perhaps hopeful sense, unknown to his programmers.

The first thing he needed to do, in order to give that hope substance, was to get rid of Milos. That would have to wait, of course. Nevertheless he had every intention of tackling the problem as soon as possible.

In moments, Min had led him and Taverner out of DA's surgical wing into parts of UMCPHQ he'd never seen before. Impersonally helpful, his computer interpreted the wall-coding which enabled people to navigate the vast complex. If he'd known where he was going, he could have found the way himself. However, Donner didn't explain anything. And Milos – who probably knew the answer – kept his thoughts to himself. When his nic expired, he dropped the butt on the floor and lit another.

That and the way he hid his hands in his pockets were the only outward signs that he realized his safety was at an end.

Out of Data Acquisition. Across a section of Enforcement Division. Into Administration.

Angus' pulse increased. More and more, his eagerness resembled alarm.

Abruptly Donner stopped outside a door marked CONFERENCE 6.

Sardonically pleasant to mask his fear, Angus asked, 'Now what? I thought you were done torturing me.'

Again she held up one commanding finger. But she spoke to Milos rather than to Angus.

'Keep it simple,' she advised him. 'You'll live longer.'

Opening the door, she ushered the two men inside.

Angus found himself in a room like an interrogation chamber in an old video. Lit by a single light, a long table surrounded by hard chairs stood in the center of the space. The light was so bright, so narrowly focused, that the middle of the table gleamed as if it were hot; but its ends remained dim, shrouded, and the walls were barely visible. A quick glance told him that the corners were thick with monitors of all kinds. However, none of them was active. Apparently no one would eavesdrop on or record him this time.

That made his anxiety worse.

Min Donner pointed him into a chair within the circle of light. Milos she instructed to take a seat opposite him. Then she sat down at one end of the table. In the gloom, she looked as hard and unreachable as her reputation.

'This is fun,' Angus muttered. 'What do you want us to do now? Make friends?'

Min watched him from the dimness. Milos' dull gaze revealed nothing.

Impelled by mounting apprehension, Angus demanded, 'Did I tell you how he betrayed Com-Mine? How he and that glamorous fucker, Succorso, set me up? Hell, if more cops were like him, there wouldn't be anything left for *me* to do.'

The ED Director didn't move a muscle.

'Personally,' another voice remarked, 'I would be more interested in hearing how you acquired a name for such despicable crimes without accumulating evidence against yourself in your ship's datacore.'

Angus jerked his head to look at the other end of the table.

A man sat there.

Angus hadn't heard him come in. And he definitely hadn't been in that chair a moment earlier. Yet he was there now. Maybe he'd been hiding under the table. Or maybe the purpose of the contrasting dazzle and gloom was to let him come and go with as much stealth as he pleased.

He was hard to see, but Angus made out enough detail to perfect his fear.

The man had a chest as thick as a barrel, short, sturdy arms, strong fingers. Despite the dimness, the lines and angles of his face appeared as exact as if they'd been machine-tooled; his mouth, jaw, and forehead might have been cut from a block of steel. Gray hair uncompromisingly cut spread stiffly across his scalp. Only the crookedness of his nose moderated his features: it gave the impression that it had been broken several times.

Glints of light reflected piercingly from his single eye, the right one. Over the socket of the left he wore a synthetic patch glued to his skin.

Warden Dios.

UMCP Director.

In effect, he was the most powerful man in human space. Holt Fasner, UMC CEO, wielded the political influence, the economic muscle. But the fighting force intended to protect humankind from the Amnion took its orders from Warden Dios.

Oh, shit.

That patch was the clue which identified him. All the stories about Dios which circulated across space mentioned it. For reasons which varied according to the source of the story, Dios' left eye had been replaced by an infrared prosthesis which enabled him to read people as accurately as a vital stress monitor. He'd become a man to whom no one could lie.

Someone else, with different goals and priorities, would have had the prosthesis added like Angus' to his natural vision, so that it didn't show. Not Dios. He flaunted his augmented sight as if daring anyone to mislead him. According to some of the stories, he wore the patch as a courtesy to his subordinates, so that they wouldn't be disconcerted by having to look into a mechanical eye. Others said that he wore it because it made him appear more dangerous. Still others insisted that it concealed, not an eye, but a gun.

In any case, the patch would be no obstacle to the prosthesis. That material wouldn't stop either infrared wavelengths or impact fire.

Angus was on the verge of hysteria. Nevertheless his fear steadied him: he was at his best when he was terrified. 'Most of the time,' he answered as if he were calm, 'I did it by interrupting scan. My ship' – memories of *Bright Beauty* gave his voice a vibration of anger – 'didn't record what she couldn't see.'

Because his computer was no longer programmed to interrogate him, it let this statement pass.

'Then the interrupts should have been recorded.' Dios' tone was mild and firm. He didn't threaten anyone because he had no need of threats. 'I don't have your transcripts in front of me,' he said to Milos. 'What did you find in his datacore?'

Milos twisted as if he were squirming. Perhaps because he, too, feared the UMCP Director, he took the nic out of his mouth. 'There were glitches. We decided they were interrupts. We couldn't think of any other explanation.'

Dios smiled like a piece of steel. 'They were fortuitous, at any rate. I commend your foresight, Angus. Without those "glitches," Com-Mine Security would almost certainly have gathered enough evidence to execute you. Then neither of you would be available to us now.

'As it happens, we need you.' His eye glittered at Angus and Milos alternately. 'In fact, the need is so acute that you'll be leaving in about an hour. This will be your last briefing.'

Milos opened his mouth to speak, then changed his mind. Instead he put his nic back between his lips.

'From here,' the Director continued, 'you'll be taken to your ship. She's a Needle-class gap scout. Crew of two, space for eight. According to her official records, she has no armaments – just some rather sophisticated shielding and defenses. However, we've concealed a few refinements that will probably interest you.

'Actually' – he fixed his gaze on Angus – 'you know all about her. You could rebuild her from scrap, if you had to. But you haven't accessed the data yet, for the simple reason that we haven't told you her name. We call her *Trumpet*. You'll find a complete data base coded under that name.'

Deliberately Angus resisted the temptation to call up the information and look at it. He couldn't afford to be distracted.

Dios resumed. 'You'll depart on your mission as soon as you've familiarized yourself with *Trumpet*. You already know what your mission is. That is, *you* know, Milos. Angus, your programming will tell you what you need as you go along. But I'll say this.

'I intend you to destroy the shipyard called Billingate on Thanatos Minor. That's your destination.'

A new pang shot through Angus. He blinked to disguise his outrage. Destroy Billingate? The Director's arrogance offended him. He'd been dependent on places like Billingate more often than he cared to remember. Without them, he would have died long ago. Or been caught and convicted.

If you think I'm going to do that kind of bloody work for you—

On the other hand, it would be better to destroy Billingate than to be destroyed himself.

'Of course,' Dios added as if he were responding to Angus' emotion, 'it would be simpler to send a battlewagon and blast that rock to rubble. But our treaties with the Amnion prevent it. I don't want to precipitate an open war. In any case, it's likely that Thanatos Minor is fairly well defended. All in all, a covert approach is preferable.'

'Director.' Milos stiffened his resolve. 'I've said this before – often – but I'll say it again.' He kept his nic in his mouth as if it gave him courage. Light made the stains on his scalp vivid. 'I'm not the right man for this mission.'

Dios fixed Taverner with his single stare and waited for Milos to go on.

Exhaling smoke, Milos said, 'You've trained me for it. You probably don't have a substitute handy. But I'm still the wrong man. For one thing, I've had no experience with covert operations – or combat, either. A couple of months of training can't take the place of real experience. And for another' – he glanced at Min Donner as if he had an irrational desire to ask for her support – 'the experience I do have is all from the wrong side. Lying isn't my job.' Angus snorted at this, but Milos ignored him. 'Breaking down liars *is*. My experience – the training of my *life* – isn't just inadequate. It's wrong for this mission. It'll work against me. I'll make mistakes I won't even notice. I'll betray you – I won't be able to help myself.'

'In other words—' Angus began.

'You underestimate yourself, Milos,' put in Warden mildly. 'You aren't the wrong man.'

'— you're scared shitless,' Angus went on. 'The mere thought of being alone with me makes you crap your suit.'

'Nor are you the perfect man,' Dios continued as if he hadn't been interrupted. 'You're the only man.

'As I'm sure you've been told, we can't simply let Angus Thermopyle loose on an unsuspecting galaxy. Why is he free? How did he get his hands on a ship like *Trumpet*? We have to account for him somehow. He must be able to account for himself. He'll never be trusted otherwise.

'*You* are the answer. You're his cover, Milos. When you realized that Com-Mine Security was about to nail you for your – shall we say, indiscretions? – you broke him out of lockup. Precisely because you aren't trained for space, you needed him. Together you stole *Trumpet*.

'Without you, Milos – without you and no one else – I'm afraid he'll be totally ineffective.

'However,' the Director said to Angus, 'Milos makes an important point. If I were you, I wouldn't rely too heavily on his reflexes in emergency situations. His instincts haven't been' – Dios' eye gleamed – 'as well honed as yours.'

He sounded so clear and irrefutable – and so untouched by the dull panic glowering in Milos' eyes – that Angus couldn't resist challenging him.

Harshly he said, 'You probably think I'm grateful you're going to put me on a ship with a coward and a traitor who has bad reflexes as well as the power to shut me down whenever he panics. If I wanted to get away from you, he's the man I would choose to be in charge of me.'

For the first time, Min Donner spoke. 'Angus, nobody here makes the mistake of thinking you're grateful for anything.'

Angus ignored her. 'But that's beside the point, isn't it? You're throwing up static mines. You want me to be so keen on outmaneuvering this lump of shit that I won't think about what's really going on.'

'And what,' Dios asked steadily, 'do you imagine is "really going on"?'

'You tell me. We've both been here for months. Now all at once we're in a hurry. What makes your fucking "need" suddenly so fucking "acute"?'

In the dimness, Dios' mouth twisted; he may have been smiling. 'Events converge. Everything you need to know about them is already in your datacore. You'll be given access to it in due course. However' – he glanced down the table at Min, then returned his gaze to Angus – 'I'll just mention that people you know are involved. Nick Succorso and *Captain's Fancy* should be arriving at Billingate – oh, any time now.'

Calmly, as if the details had no special meaning, he added, 'He has Morn Hyland with him. We don't know where they've been, but an analysis of their transmission vectors suggests that they're approaching Thanatos Minor from the direction of Enablement Station.'

Morn.

'They've spent some time in forbidden space.'

Angus sagged in his chair. He didn't care about forbidden space. He cared about Morn Hyland. She was the only person alive who could betray his last secret; his last hope.

He was alive because he'd made a deal with her. Had she kept it? Would she keep it?

'Min,' the Director continued, 'what did Nick's last message say?'

'It was short,' Min answered as if she were restraining an impulse to snarl. 'It said, "I rescued her for you, goddamn it. Now get me out of this. If you don't, I can't keep her away from the Amnion."'

For Angus, the gravest danger wasn't that she might be given to the Amnion. It was that he might be programmed to rescue her, bring her back to the UMCP – and she wouldn't keep her promise.

And yet the thought of seeing her again seized his heart like a clutch of grief.

Behind his nic, Milos looked like he was about to vomit.

'I'm afraid,' Dios remarked, 'Nick Succorso isn't particularly trustworthy. But we really can't ignore the possibility that a UMCP ensign is about to fall into the hands of the Amnion.'

Without shifting his posture or his tone, he said to the ED Director, 'Take Milos to *Trumpet*. Make sure he remembers his instructions. Remind him of the consequences if he violates them. Don't worry about boring him – a little repetition won't do him any harm.

'I want to talk to Angus for a few minutes. I'll bring him to you when I'm done.'

Donner's gaze narrowed. 'Do you think that's safe?'

'Do you think it isn't?' Dios countered.

At once she got to her feet. Her face looked closed and hard in the gloom. 'Come on, Milos.'

Taverner's hands shook feverishly as he took the nic out of his mouth, dropped it on the floor, and stood up. He moved toward Min as if she would escort him to his execution.

They were at the door when Warden said softly, 'It isn't an insult, Min. Even I have to do without protection sometimes. If I'm not willing to take a few risks for my convictions, what good am I?'

'I ask myself that question,' she retorted in a rough voice, 'almost every day.'

As she and Milos left, the Director smiled after her.

It didn't make him look happy. It made him look like he was about to condemn someone. The glittering of his eye conveyed the impression that he hated doing that; loathed it with a passion too strong to be articulated.

Maybe, Angus thought, inspired by panic, Warden Dios was about to condemn himself. Maybe he was about to make a mistake that would improve his, Angus', chances.

That didn't seem very likely.

Alone with Warden Dios, he sat and sweated. The Director studied him, saying nothing. He could feel Dios' eyes on him, the hidden one probing for his secret. He wanted to duck his head – wanted to get out of the room. He wasn't the right man to face down the Director of the UMCP: he had too much panic bred in his bones. Let him go with Milos aboard *Trumpet*. Let him get back to people and places he understood. Then he would have a chance. Here he was lost.

Nevertheless his fear had taught him to hate – and hate gave him strength. He hated Warden Dios; hated everything the UMCP Director stood for. He hated cops and law-abiding citizens; hated romantics and idealists. He hated them because they had always hated him.

His hate enabled him to look Warden Dios in the eye.

'You're wasting time,' he rasped. 'The "need" is "acute", remember?'

'Tell me the truth, Angus,' Warden replied as if he weren't changing the subject. 'Those glitches aren't scan interrupts.' His gaze was fixed, not on Angus' face, but on his chest – on the IR emissions of his heart and lungs. 'They're elisions. You edited the evidence against you out of your datacore.'

Because he was already full to the teeth with fear and hate, Angus didn't flinch; he didn't so much as drop his eyes. Instead he gaped. 'You're crazy. If I could do a trick like that, I wouldn't be here at all. I would be sitting someplace like Billingate, making myself *rich* by doing that trick for every illegal ship in human space.'

'No, you wouldn't.' The Director was certain. 'You aren't that kind of man. You hate too much – you hate everybody. You wouldn't protect people like Nick Succorso, even if it made you rich.'

A moment later he sighed. 'But you can calm down. Believe it or not, your secret is safe with me. I won't ask you how you do it. I can't afford to know. That "trick", as you call it, is the most explosive piece of knowledge since Intertech's immunity drug. I was outplayed then. I don't propose to be outplayed again. It would be suicide for me to reveal what you know.'

Without transition, as if everything he did were part of a whole, unified by some principle Angus couldn't grasp, Warden said, 'Stasis, Joshua.'

A fire storm of panic had hold of Angus when his zone-implants shut him down. Still staring at the UMCP Director, he slumped forward until his head rested on the table, displayed like a sacrifice under the light.

'There are two ways to look at this,' Dios remarked as he rose to his feet. 'One is that I sent Min away for her own protection.' In one hand he carried a large black box. 'If she knew what I'm going to do, she might not be able to hide her relief.' He may have had it in his lap all along. 'Sooner or later, she would give herself away.'

Opening the box, he moved around the table. When he was behind Angus, he put the box down and began peeling Angus' shipsuit off his shoulders.

Although he couldn't focus his eyes, Angus recognized the box. It was a first aid kit.

'I could probably recover if she made Hashi suspicious enough to figure out what I'm doing. He's dangerous – not because he comes to the wrong conclusions, but because he gets to the right ones for the wrong reasons. That's what he did when he suggested using Milos to control you.'

As soon as he reached the sore place between Angus' shoulder blades, he stopped pulling down the shipsuit. With a jerk, he removed the bandage. His hands were as steady as stones as he took a scalpel from the first aid kit. Quickly he made a new incision. With a swab, he mopped blood away from Angus' computer.

Angus would have yelled if he'd been in control of his mouth – or his vocal cords.

'It's Godsen I'm really worried about,' Warden continued, talking to himself. 'If Min did anything to make *him* suspicious, she and I would both be finished. From that point of view, I really ought to keep this risk to myself.'

All at once, a strange cold void filled Angus' mind. The datacore had been unplugged from his computer.

'The other way to look at this is that I'm protecting myself.' Dios dropped the datacore unit on the table and lifted another out of his box. 'If Min knew *why* I'm doing this, she'd turn against me herself.' As soon as the new unit was plugged in, Angus felt his programming come back on-line. 'I probably wouldn't live long enough to worry about what happens when Godsen betrays me.'

No hesitation or insecurity slowed Warden's movements as he pinched the incision closed, sealed it with new tissue plasm. From his first aid kit, he selected a clean bandage and applied it carefully to Angus' back.

When he'd put the old datacore and bandage away, he pulled Angus' shipsuit back up and redid its seals. Then he moved.

A few steps took him into Angus' field of vision. Unable to see clearly, blinking autonomically, Angus watched as the Director rounded the end of the table and reentered the light, walking toward the chair where Milos had sat.

Angus lost sight of him for a moment. Then Warden reached across the table and shifted Angus' posture so that the UMCP Director and his newest tool could look at each other.

Dios sat down in Milos' chair – in the light – as if he wanted to be sure that Angus could see him as accurately as possible. Nevertheless Angus still slumped with his neck exposed like a man in an abattoir.

'Angus,' Warden said distinctly, facing Angus with his tooled jaw and his broken nose, his patch and his human eye, 'I've replaced your data-core. You know that your mind is still alert, even if you can't move. You won't be able to tell the difference. In any case, most of the changes are extremely subtle. But even if they weren't, you wouldn't recognize them because you can't compare the two programs. As far as you're concerned, the datacore you have now is the only one that exists.'

Angus blinked because his brain stem decided he should. His heart and lungs continued functioning. Something in Dios' manner told him that what he was about to hear was crucial, the crux of the whole situation.

'I wonder,' the Director continued, musing as if to himself, 'if you understand what we've done to you. We call the process "welding." When a man or woman is made a cyborg voluntarily, that's "wedding." "Welding" is involuntary.

'Technically, we've done you a favor. That's obvious. You're stronger now, faster, more capable, effectively more intelligent. Not to mention the fact that you're still alive, when you should have been executed years ago. And all you've had to give up is your freedom of choice.

'But I'm not talking about technical questions. In every other way, we've committed a crime against you.' As he spoke, his tone became more and more like his earlier smile – the tone of a man who couldn't begin to express how intensely he loathed his power, or perhaps his obligation, to inflict condemnation. 'In essence, you're no longer a human being. You're a *machina infernalis* – an infernal device. We've deprived you of choice – and responsibility.

'Angus, we've committed a crime against your soul. You may be "the slime of the universe," as Godsen says, but you don't deserve this.

'It's got to stop.' Dios folded his hands together on the table as if he were about to pray. 'Crimes like this one – or like withholding the immunity drug. They've got to stop.'

Angus went on breathing. His heart went on pumping blood. Occasionally he blinked. Those were the only responses available to him.

Eventually Warden Dios got back to his feet. When he'd picked up his black box and tucked it under his arm, he said, 'End stasis, Joshua.'

Then he took Angus out to the docks to join Milos Taverner and Min Donner aboard *Trumpet*.

This is the end of *Forbidden Knowledge*.
The story continues in
The Gap into Power
A Dark and Hungry God Arises.

ABOUT THE AUTHOR

Stephen Donaldson is a superb storyteller. He spent thirteen years in India, where his father was a medical missionary and orthopaedic surgeon; the idea for Thomas Covenant grew out of his father's works with lepers. The first trilogy, *Lord Foul's Bane, The Illearth War* and *The Power That Preserves*, won Donaldson the British Fantasy and John W. Campbell Awards and was followed by the second Covenant trilogy, *The Wounded Land, The One Tree*, and *White Gold Wielder*, the epic fantasy duology **Mordant's Need** – *The Mirror of her Dreams* and *a Man Rides Through* – availabe in an omnibus edition from Gollancz, and the World Fantasy Award-winning *Reave the Just and Other Tales*. He turned his hand to SF with the **Gap** novels: a five-novel high-action sequence rich in intrigue, corruption, and adventure, following the adventures of a fascinating cast of characters, both human and alien, published in four volumes by Gollancz. As Reed Stephens, Donaldson has also written a series of mystery novels. He lives with his family in New Mexico, where he is at work on the third novel of *The Last Chronicles of Thomas Covenant*.